ARCANUM & UNBOUNDED

THE COSMERE COLLECTION

BRANDON SANDERSON

First published in Great Britain in 2017 by Gollancz
an imprint of the Orion Publishing Group Ltd
Carmelite House, 50 Victoria Embankment
London EC4Y 0DZ

An Hachette UK Company

1 3 5 7 9 10 8 6 4 2

A CIP catalogue record for this book is
available from the British Library.

ISBN 978 1 473 21805 5

Printed in Great Britain by Clays Ltd, St Ives plc

www.brandonsanderson.com
www.orionbooks.co.uk
www.gollancz.co.uk

For Nathan Hatfield
Who helped the Cosmere come to be.

CONTENTS

ACKNOWLEDGMENTS

If I were to take the time to individually thank each and every person who helped with all the stories in here, this section might be as long as one of the stories themselves! Instead, I'm going to focus this note on the people who specifically helped put the collection together. (Along with the team that worked on *Edgedancer*, which is the story unique to this collection.)

But I do want to take a moment to give a hearty thanks to those who have worked with me on my short fiction over the years. Early in my career, I would never have dared consider myself a short-fiction writer—but ten years of practice has paid off, and the stories in this collection are the result. (Though do note, I use the word "short" loosely here. Most of these are very long for short fiction.)

A lot of wonderful people have helped me over the years; most of them are the names you'll commonly find at the start of my novels. I'm a lucky man to have had so much encouragement, feedback, and support during my career.

For *Arcanum Unbounded* specifically, Isaac Stewart (my longtime artistic collaborator) is responsible for the beautiful endpapers, the star charts, and most of the symbols you find inside the book. Ben McSweeney did the illustrations for the various stories, Dave Palumbo did the cover art, and Greg Collins was the designer.

Moshe Feder, editor for all of my epic fantasy novels, was the editor on this project—and though he wasn't officially the editor on many of the shorts when they were first published, he has a habit of stepping in and doing revisions for me, unpaid, on any short fiction I write. (Indeed, he gets mad if I don't send them to him, and refuses to invoice me if I try to pay him for them.) So he's done a ton of pro bono work over the years, helping me become a short-fiction writer. He deserves some extra praise for this.

And, as always, the Inciting Peter Ahlstrom was head of my in-house editorial efforts. (Literally in house. He works out of my home.) Peter is responsible for collecting all the comments from various people doing reads, adding his own detailed continuity and editorial notes, and then smoothing everything over once I've taken the hacksaw to stories.

The copyeditor was Terry McGarry. At Tor, thanks go to Tom Doherty, Marco Palmieri, Patti Garcia, Karl Gold, Rafal Gibek, and Robert Davis.

Joshua Bilmes was the agent on this in the United States, and John Berlyne was the agent in the UK. Heaps of thanks go to everyone at their respective agencies.

Our alpha and gamma readers on *Edgedancer* include Alice Arneson, Ben Oldsen, Bob Kluttz, Brandon Cole, Brian T. Hill, Darci Cole, David Behrens, Eric James Stone, Eric Lake, Gary Singer, Ian McNatt, Karen Ahlstrom, Kellyn Neumann, Kristina Kugler, Lyndsey Luther, Mark Lindberg, Matt Wiens, Megan Kanne, Nikki Ramsay, Paige Vest, Ross Newberry, and Trae Cooper.

And, as is traditional, I leave with a hearty thanks to my family: Joel, Dallin, Oliver, and Emily. You guys are awesome!

PREFACE

The Cosmere has always been full of secrets.

I can trace my grand plan now to several key moments. The first is the emergence of Hoid, who dates back to my teenage years, when I conceived of a man who connected worlds that didn't know about one another. A person in on the secret that nobody else understood. While reading books by other authors, in my mind I inserted this man into the backgrounds, imagining him as the random person described in a crowd—and dreaming of the story behind the story of which he was a part.

The second moment that helped all this come together was reading the later books in the Foundation series by Isaac Asimov. I was awed by how he managed to tie the Robot novels and the Foundation novels together in one grand story. I knew I wanted to create something like this, an epic bigger than an epic. A story that spanned worlds and eras.

The third moment, then, was the first appearance of Hoid in a novel. I inserted him nervously, worried about making everything work. I didn't have my grand plan for the Cosmere at that point, only an inkling of what I wanted to do.

That story was *Elantris*. The next book I wrote, *Dragonsteel*, was never published. (It's not very good.) But in it I devised Hoid's backstory, and the backstory of the entire universe I named the Cosmere. *Elantris* wasn't picked up by a publisher until years after that point—and when it was, I had the grand plan in place. Mistborn, Stormlight, and *Elantris* became the core of it. (And you'll find stories relating to all three in this collection.)

I would guess that most people who read my works don't know that the majority of the books are connected, with a hidden story behind the story. This pleases me. I have often said that I don't want a reader to feel that they need to have my entire body of work memorized in order to enjoy a story. For now, Mistborn is just Mistborn, and Stormlight is just Stormlight. The stories of these worlds are at the forefront.

That isn't to say there aren't hints. Lots of them. I originally intended these cameo hints between the worlds to be much smaller, particularly at first. Many readers, however, grew to love them—and I realized I didn't need to be quite as stingy with the hidden story as I was being.

I still walk a fine line. All of the stories you read are intended to be self-contained, at least within the context of their own world. However, if you do dig deeper, there is much more to learn. More secrets, as Kelsier would say.

This collection takes a step closer to the connected nature of the Cosmere. Each story is prefaced by an annotation from Khriss, the woman who has been writing the Ars Arcanum appendixes at the ends of the novels. You'll also find star maps for each solar system. With things like this, the collection goes further than I've gone before in connecting the worlds. It hints at what is to come eventually: full crossovers in the Cosmere.

The time for that hasn't arrived yet. If all this overwhelms you, know that most of the stories in here can be read independently. A few take place chronologically after published novels—and this is noted at the beginning of those stories, so you know how to avoid spoilers, if you want.

None of the stories in the collection require knowledge of the Cosmere as a whole. The truth is, most of what's going on in the Cosmere hasn't yet been revealed, so you couldn't be expected to be up to date on it all.

That said, I do promise that this collection will provide not just questions, but at long last, some answers.

ARCANUM UNBOUNDED

THE COSMERE COLLECTION

THE
SELISH
SYSTEM

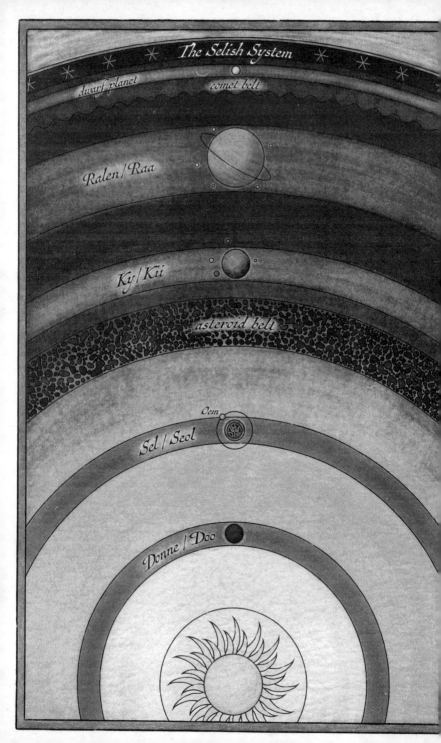

THE SELISH SYSTEM

ENTRAL to this system is the planet of Sel—home to multiple empires that, uniquely, have remained somewhat ignorant of one another. It is a willful kind of ignorance, with each of the three great domains pretending that the others are mere blips on the map, barely worth notice.

The planet itself facilitates this, as it is larger than most, with its size at around 1.5 cosmere standard, and gravity at 1.2 cosmere standard. Vast continents and sweeping oceans create a diverse landscape, with an extreme amount of variation on this one planet. Here you will find both snow-covered plains and expansive deserts, a fact I would have found remarkable upon my first visit, had I not by then discovered that this was a natural state of many planets in the cosmere.

Sel is notable for being dishardic, one of few planets in the cosmere to attract two separate Shards of Adonalsium: Dominion and Devotion. These Shards were extremely influential in the development of human societies on the planet, and most of their traditions and religions can be traced back to these two. Uniquely, the very languages and alphabets used today across the planet were directly influenced by the two Shards.

I believe that early on, the Shards took an unconcerned approach to humankind—and society was shaped by the slow, steady discovery of the powers that permeated the landscape. This is difficult to determine for certain now, however, as at some point in the distant past, both Devotion and Dominion were destroyed. Their Investiture—their power—was Splintered, their minds ripped away, their souls sent into the Beyond.

I am uncertain whether their power was left to ravage the world untamed for a time, or was immediately contained. This all happened during the days of human prehistory on Sel.

At this point, the bulk of the Investiture that made up the powers of Dominion and Devotion is trapped on the Cognitive Realm. Collectively, these powers—which have a polarized relationship—are called the Dor. Forced together as they are, trapped and bursting to escape, they power the various forms of magic on Sel, which are multitude.

Because the Cognitive Realm has distinct locations (unlike the Spiritual Realm, where most forms of Investiture reside), magic on Sel is very dependent upon physical position. In addition, the rules of perception and intent are greatly magnified on Sel, to the point that language—or similar functions—directly shapes the magic as it is pulled from the Cognitive Realm and put to use.

This overlap between language, location, and magic on the planet has become so integral to the system that subtle changes in one can have profound effects on how the Dor is accessed. Indeed, I believe that the very landscape itself has become Invested to the point that it has a growing self-awareness, in a way unseen on other planets in the cosmere. I do not know how this happened, or what the ramifications will be.

I've begun to wonder if something greater is happening on Sel than we, at the universities of Silverlight, have guessed. Something with origins lost in time. Perhaps the Ire know more, but they are not speaking on the topic, and have repeatedly denied my requests for collaboration.

Brief mention should be given to the entities known as the seons and the skaze, Splinters of self-aware Investiture who have developed humanlike mannerisms. I believe there is a link between them and the puzzle of Sel's nature.

The rest of the system is of little relevance. Though there are a number of other planets, only one exists in a habitable zone—if barely. It is barren, inhospitable, and prone to terrible dust storms. Its proximity to the sun, Mashe, makes it uncomfortably warm, even for one who has spent a good portion of her life on the Dayside of Taldain.

THE
EMPEROR'S
SOUL

PROLOGUE

GAOTONA ran his fingers across the thick canvas, inspecting one of the greatest works of art he had ever seen. Unfortunately, it was a lie.

"The woman is a danger." Hissed voices came from behind him. "What she does is an abomination."

Gaotona tipped the canvas toward the hearth's orange-red light, squinting. In his old age, his eyes weren't what they had once been. *Such precision,* he thought, inspecting the brushstrokes, feeling the layers of thick oils. Exactly like those in the original.

He would never have spotted the mistakes on his own. A blossom slightly out of position. A moon that was just a sliver too low in the sky. It had taken their experts days of detailed inspection to find the errors.

"She is one of the best Forgers alive." The voices belonged to Gaotona's fellow arbiters, the empire's most important bureaucrats. "She has a reputation as wide as the empire. We need to execute her as an example."

"No." Frava, leader of the arbiters, had a sharp, nasal voice. "She is a valuable tool. This woman can save us. We must use her."

Why? Gaotona thought again. *Why would someone capable of this artistry, this majesty, turn to forgery? Why not create original paintings? Why not be a true artist?*

I must understand.

"Yes," Frava continued, "the woman is a thief, and she practices a horrid art. But I can control her, and with her talents we can fix this mess we have found ourselves in."

The others murmured worried objections. The woman they spoke of, Wan ShaiLu, was more than a simple con artist. So much more. She could change the nature of reality itself. That raised another question. Why would she bother learning to paint? Wasn't ordinary art mundane compared to her mystical talents?

So many questions. Gaotona looked up from his seat beside the hearth. The others stood in a conspiratorial clump around Frava's desk, their long, colorful robes shimmering in the firelight. "I agree with Frava," Gaotona said.

The others glanced at him. Their scowls indicated they cared little for what he said, but their postures told a different tale. Their respect for him was buried deep, but it was remembered.

"Send for the Forger," Gaotona said, rising. "I would hear what she has to say. I suspect she will be more difficult to control than Frava claims, but we have no choice. We either use this woman's skill, or we give up control of the empire."

The murmurs ceased. How many years had it been since Frava and Gaotona had agreed on anything at all, let alone on something so divisive as making use of the Forger?

One by one, the other three arbiters nodded.

"Let it be done," Frava said softly.

DAY TWO

S HAI pressed her fingernail into one of the stone blocks of her prison cell. The rock gave way slightly. She rubbed the dust between her fingers. Limestone. An odd material for use in a prison wall, but the whole wall wasn't of limestone, merely that single vein within the block.

She smiled. Limestone. That little vein had been easy to miss, but if she was right about it, she had finally identified all forty-four types of rock in the wall of her circular pit of a prison cell. Shai knelt down beside her bunk, using a fork—she'd bent back all of the tines but one—to carve notes into the wood of one bed leg. Without her spectacles, she had to squint as she wrote.

To Forge something, you had to know its past, its nature. She was almost ready. Her pleasure quickly slipped away, however, as she noticed another set of markings on the bed leg, lit by her flickering candle. Those kept track of her days of imprisonment.

So little time, she thought. If her count was right, only a day remained before the date set for her public execution.

Deep inside, her nerves were drawn as tight as strings on an instrument. One day. One day remaining to create a soulstamp and escape.

But she had no soulstone, only a crude piece of wood, and her only tool for carving was a fork.

It would be incredibly difficult. That was the point. This cell was meant for one of her kind, built of stones with many different veins of rock in them to make them difficult to Forge. They would come from different quarries and would each have a unique history. Knowing as little as she did, Forging them would be nearly impossible. And even if she did transform the rock, there was probably some other failsafe to stop her.

Nights! What a mess she'd gotten herself into.

Notes finished, she found herself looking at her bent fork. She'd begun carving the wooden handle, after prying off the metal portion, as a crude soulstamp. *You're not going to get out this way, Shai,* she told herself. *You need another method.*

She'd waited six days, searching for another way out. Guards to exploit, someone to bribe, a hint about the nature of her cell. So far, nothing had—

Far above, the door to the dungeons opened.

Shai leaped to her feet, tucking the fork handle into her waistband at the small of her back. Had they moved up her execution?

Heavy boots sounded on the steps leading into the dungeon, and she squinted at the newcomers who appeared above her cell. Four were guards, accompanying a man with long features and fingers. A Grand, the race who led the empire. That robe of blue and green indicated a minor functionary who had passed the tests for government service, but not risen high in its ranks.

Shai waited, tense.

The Grand leaned down to look at her through the grate. He paused for just a moment, then waved for the guards to unlock it. "The arbiters wish to interrogate you, Forger."

Shai stood back as they opened her cell's ceiling, then lowered a ladder. She climbed, wary. If *she* were going to take someone to an early execution, she'd have let the prisoner think something else was happening, so she wouldn't resist. However, they didn't lock Shai in manacles as they marched her out of the dungeons.

Judging by their route, they did indeed seem to be taking her toward the arbiters' study. Shai composed herself. A new challenge, then. Dared she hope for an opportunity? She shouldn't have been caught, but she could do nothing about that now. She had been bested, betrayed by the Imperial Fool when she'd assumed she could trust him. He had taken her copy of the Moon Scepter and swapped it for the original, then run off.

Shai's uncle Won had taught her that being bested was a rule of life. No matter how good you were, someone was better. Live by that knowledge, and you would never grow so confident that you became sloppy.

Last time she had lost. This time she would win. She abandoned all sense of frustration at being captured and became the person who could deal with this new chance, whatever it was. She would seize it and thrive.

This time, she played not for riches, but for her life.

The guards were Strikers—or, well, that was the Grand name for them. They had once called themselves Mulla'dil, but their nation had been folded into the empire so long ago that few used the name. Strikers were a tall people with a lean musculature and pale skin. They had hair almost as dark as Shai's, though theirs curled while hers lay straight and long. She tried with some success not to feel dwarfed by them. Her people, the MaiPon, were not known for their stature.

"You," she said to the lead Striker as she walked at the front of the group. "I remember you." Judging by that styled hair, the youthful captain did not often wear a helmet. Strikers were well regarded by the Grands, and their Elevation was not unheard of. This one had a look of eagerness to him. That polished armor, that crisp air. Yes, he fancied himself bound for important things in the future.

"The horse," Shai said. "You threw me over the back of your horse after I was captured. Tall animal, Gurish descent, pure white. Good animal. You know your horseflesh."

The Striker kept his eyes forward, but whispered under his breath, "I'm going to enjoy killing you, woman."

Lovely, Shai thought as they entered the Imperial Wing of the palace. The stonework here was marvelous, after the ancient Lamio style, with tall pillars of marble inlaid with reliefs. Those large urns between the pillars had been created to mimic Lamio pottery from long ago.

Actually, she reminded herself, *the Heritage Faction still rules, so . . .*

The emperor would be from that faction, as would the council of five arbiters who did much of the actual ruling. Their faction lauded the glory and learning of past cultures, even going so far as to rebuild their wing of the palace as an imitation of an ancient building. Shai suspected that on the bottoms of those "ancient" urns would be soulstamps that had transformed them into perfect imitations of famous pieces.

Yes, the Grands called Shai's powers an abomination, but their only aspect that was technically illegal was creating a Forgery to change a person. Quiet Forgery of objects was allowed, even exploited, in the empire so long as the Forger was carefully controlled. If someone were to turn over one of those urns and remove the stamp on the bottom, the piece would become simple unornamented pottery.

The Strikers led her to a door with gold inlay. As it opened, she managed to catch a glimpse of the red soulstamp on the bottom inside edge, transforming the door into an imitation of some work from the past. The guards ushered her into a homey room with a crackling hearth, deep rugs, and stained wood furnishings. *Fifth-century hunting lodge,* she guessed.

All five arbiters of the Heritage Faction waited inside. Three—two women, one man—sat in tall-backed chairs at the hearth. One other woman occupied the desk just inside the doors: Frava, senior among the arbiters of the Heritage Faction, was probably the most powerful person in the empire other than Emperor Ashravan himself. Her greying hair was woven into a long braid with gold and red ribbons; it draped a robe of matching gold. Shai had long pondered how to rob this woman, as— among her duties—Frava oversaw the Imperial Gallery and had offices adjacent to it.

Frava had obviously been arguing with Gaotona, the elderly male Grand standing beside the desk. He stood up straight and clasped his hands behind his back in a thoughtful pose. Gaotona was eldest of the ruling arbiters. He was said to be the least influential among them, out of favor with the emperor.

Both fell silent as Shai entered. They eyed her as if she were a cat that had just knocked over a fine vase. Shai missed her spectacles, but took care not to squint as she stepped up to face these people; she needed to look as strong as possible.

"Wan ShaiLu," Frava said, reaching to pick up a sheet of paper from the desk. "You have quite the list of crimes credited to your name."

The way you say that . . . What game was this woman playing? *She wants something of me,* Shai decided. *That is the only reason to bring me in like this.*

The opportunity began to unfold.

"Impersonating a noblewoman of rank," Frava continued, "breaking into the palace's Imperial Gallery, reForging your soul, and of course the attempted theft of the Moon Scepter. Did you really assume that we would fail to recognize a simple forgery of such an important imperial possession?"

Apparently, Shai thought, *you have done just that, assuming that the Fool escaped with the original.* It gave Shai a little thrill of satisfaction to know that her forgery now occupied the Moon Scepter's position of honor in the Imperial Gallery.

"And what of this?" Frava said, waving long fingers for one of the Strikers to bring something from the side of the room. A painting, which the guard placed on the desk. Han ShuXen's masterpiece *Lily of the Spring Pond*.

"We found this in your room at the inn," Frava said, tapping her fingers on the painting. "It is a copy of a painting I myself own, one of the most famous in the empire. We gave it to our assessors, and they judge that your forgery was amateur at best."

Shai met the woman's eyes.

"Tell me why you have created this forgery," Frava said, leaning forward. "You were obviously planning to swap this for the painting in my office by the Imperial Gallery. And yet, you were striving for the *Moon Scepter* itself. Why plan to steal the painting too? Greed?"

"My uncle Won," Shai said, "told me to always have a backup plan. I couldn't be certain the scepter would even be on display."

"Ah . . ." Frava said. She adopted an almost maternal expression, though it was laden with loathing—hidden poorly—and condescension. "You requested arbiter intervention in your execution, as most prisoners do. I decided on a whim to agree to your request because I was curious why you had created this painting." She shook her head. "But child, you can't honestly believe we'd let you free. With sins like this? You are in a monumentally bad predicament, and our mercy can only be extended so far."

Shai glanced toward the other arbiters. The ones seated near the fireplace seemed to be paying no heed, but they did not speak to one another. They were listening. *Something is wrong*, Shai thought. *They're worried.*

Gaotona still stood just to the side. He inspected Shai with eyes that betrayed no emotion.

Frava's manner had the air of one scolding a small child. The lingering end of her comment was intended to make Shai hope for release. Together, that was meant to make her pliable, willing to agree to anything in the hope that she'd be freed.

An opportunity indeed . . .

It was time to take control of this conversation.

"You want something from me," Shai said. "I'm ready to discuss my payment."

"Your *payment*?" Frava asked. "Girl, you are to be executed on the morrow! If we did wish something of you, the payment would be your life."

"My life is my own," Shai said. "And it has been for days now."

"Please," Frava said. "You were locked in the Forger's cell, with thirty different kinds of stone in the wall."

"Forty-four kinds, actually."

Gaotona raised an appreciative eyebrow.

Nights! I'm glad I got that right. . . .

Shai glanced at Gaotona. "You thought I wouldn't recognize the grindstone, didn't you? Please. I'm a Forger. I learned stone classification during my first year of training. That block was obviously from the Laio quarry."

Frava opened her mouth to speak, a slight smile to her lips.

"Yes, I know about the plates of ralkalest, the unForgeable metal, hidden behind the rock wall of my cell," Shai guessed. "The wall was a puzzle, meant to distract me. You wouldn't *actually* make a cell out of rocks like limestone, just in case a prisoner gave up on Forgery and tried to chip their way free. You built the wall, but secured it with a plate of ralkalest at the back to cut off escape."

Frava snapped her mouth shut.

"The problem with ralkalest," Shai said, "is that it's not a very strong metal. Oh, the grate at the top of my cell was solid enough, and I couldn't have gotten through that. But a thin plate? Really. Have you heard of anthracite?"

Frava frowned.

"It is a rock that burns," Gaotona said.

"You gave me a candle," Shai said, reaching into the small of her back. She tossed her makeshift wooden soulstamp onto the desk. "All I had to do was Forge the wall and persuade the stones that they're anthracite— not a difficult task, once I knew the forty-four types of rock. I could burn them, and they'd melt that plate behind the wall."

Shai pulled over a chair, seating herself before the desk. She leaned back. Behind her, the captain of the Strikers growled softly, but Frava drew her lips to a line and said nothing. Shai let her muscles relax, and she breathed a quiet prayer to the Unknown God.

Nights! It looked like they'd actually bought it. She'd worried they'd know enough of Forgery to see through her lie.

"I was going to escape tonight," Shai said, "but whatever it is you want me to do must be important, as you're willing to involve a miscreant like myself. And so we come to my payment."

"I could still have you executed," Frava said. "Right now. Here."

"But you won't, will you?"

Frava set her jaw.

"I warned you that she would be difficult to manipulate," Gaotona said to Frava. Shai could tell she'd impressed him, but at the same time, his eyes seemed . . . sorrowful? Was that the right emotion? She found this aged man as difficult to read as a book in Svordish.

Frava raised a finger, then swiped it to the side. A servant approached with a small, cloth-wrapped box. Shai's heart leaped upon seeing it.

The man clicked the latches open on the front and raised the top. The case was lined with soft cloth and inset with five depressions made to hold soulstamps. Each cylindrical stone stamp was as long as a finger and as wide as a large man's thumb. The leatherbound notebook set in the case atop them was worn by long use; Shai breathed in a hint of its familiar scent.

They were called Essence Marks, the most powerful kind of soulstamp. Each Essence Mark had to be attuned to a specific individual, and was intended to rewrite their history, personality, and soul for a short time. These five were attuned to Shai.

"Five stamps to rewrite a soul," Frava said. "Each is an abomination, illegal to possess. These Essence Marks were to be destroyed this afternoon. Even if you had escaped, you'd have lost these. How long does it take to create one?"

"Years," Shai whispered.

There were no other copies. Notes and diagrams were too dangerous to leave, even in secret, as such things gave others too much insight to one's soul. She never let these Essence Marks out of her sight, except on the rare occasion they were taken from her.

"You will accept these as payment?" Frava asked, lips turned down, as if discussing a meal of slime and rotted meat.

"Yes."

Frava nodded, and the servant snapped the case closed. "Then let me show you what you are to do."

Shai had never met an emperor before, let alone poked one in the face.

Emperor Ashravan of the Eighty Suns—forty-ninth ruler of the Rose Empire—did not respond as Shai prodded him. He stared ahead blankly, his round cheeks rosy and hale, but his expression completely lifeless.

"What happened?" Shai asked, straightening from beside the emperor's bed. It was in the style of the ancient Lamio people, with a headboard shaped like a phoenix rising toward heaven. She'd seen a sketch of such a headboard in a book; likely the Forgery had been drawn from that source.

"Assassins," Arbiter Gaotona said. He stood on the other side of the bed, alongside two surgeons. Of the Strikers, only their captain—Zu—had been allowed to enter. "The murderers broke in two nights ago, attacking the emperor and his wife. She was slain. The emperor received a crossbow bolt to the head."

"That considered," Shai noted, "he's looking remarkable."

"You are familiar with resealing?" Gaotona asked.

"Vaguely," Shai said. Her people called it Flesh Forgery. Using it, a surgeon of great skill could Forge a body to remove its wounds and scars. It required great specialization. The Forger had to know each and every sinew, each vein and muscle, in order to accurately heal.

Resealing was one of the few branches of Forgery that Shai hadn't studied in depth. Get an ordinary forgery wrong, and you created a work of poor artistic merit. Get a Flesh Forgery wrong, and people died.

"Our resealers are the best in the world," Frava said, walking around the foot of the bed, hands behind her back. "The emperor was attended to quickly following the assassination attempt. The wound to his head was healed, but . . ."

"But his mind was not?" Shai asked, waving her hand in front of the man's face again. "It doesn't sound like they did a very good job at all."

One of the surgeons cleared his throat. The diminutive man had ears like window shutters that had been thrown open wide on a sunny day. "Resealing repairs a body and makes it anew. That, however, is much like rebinding a book with fresh paper following a fire. Yes, it may look exactly the same, and it may be whole all the way through. The words, though . . . the words are gone. We have given the emperor a new brain. It is merely empty."

"Huh," Shai said. "Did you find out who tried to kill him?"

The five arbiters exchanged glances. Yes, they knew.

"We are not certain," Gaotona said.

"Meaning," Shai added, "you know, but you couldn't prove it well enough to make an accusation. One of the other factions in court, then?"

Gaotona sighed. "The Glory Faction."

Shai whistled softly, but it *did* make sense. If the emperor died, there was a good chance that the Glory Faction would win a bid to Elevate his successor. At forty, Emperor Ashravan was young still, by Grand standards. He had been expected to rule another fifty years.

If he were replaced, the five arbiters in this room would lose their positions—which, by imperial politics, would be a huge blow to their status. They'd drop from being the most powerful people in the world to being among the lowest of the empire's eighty factions.

"The assassins did not survive their attack," Frava said. "The Glory Faction does not yet know whether their ploy succeeded. You are going to replace the emperor's soul with . . ." She took a deep breath. "With a Forgery."

They're crazy, Shai thought. Forging one's own soul was difficult enough, and you didn't have to rebuild it from the ground up.

The arbiters had no idea what they were asking. But of course they didn't. They hated Forgery, or so they claimed. They walked on imitation floor tiles past copies of ancient vases, they let their surgeons repair a body, but they didn't call any of these things "Forgery" in their own tongue.

The Forgery of the soul, that was what they considered an abomination. Which meant Shai really was their only choice. No one in their own government would be capable of this. She probably wasn't either.

"Can you do it?" Gaotona asked.

I have no idea, Shai thought. "Yes," she said.

"It will need to be an exact Forgery," Frava said sternly. "If the Glory Faction has any inkling of what we've done, they will pounce. The emperor must not act erratically."

"I said I could do it," Shai replied. "But it will be difficult. I will need information about Ashravan and his life, everything we can get. Official histories will be a start, but they'll be too sterile. I will need extensive interviews and writings about him from those who knew him best. Servants, friends, family members. Did he have a journal?"

"Yes," Gaotona said.

"Excellent."

"Those documents are sealed," said one of the other arbiters. "He wanted them destroyed . . ."

Everyone in the room looked toward the man. He swallowed, then looked down.

"You shall have everything you request," Frava said.

"I'll need a test subject as well," Shai said. "Someone to test my Forgeries on. A Grand, male, someone who was around the emperor a lot and who knew him. That will let me see if I have the personality right." Nights! Getting the personality right would be secondary. Getting a stamp that actually took . . . that would be the first step. She wasn't certain she could manage even that much. "And I'll need soulstone, of course."

Frava regarded Shai, arms folded.

"You can't possibly expect me to do this without soulstone," Shai said dryly. "I could carve a stamp out of wood, if I had to, but your goal will be difficult enough as it is. Soulstone. Lots of it."

"Fine," Frava said. "But you will be watched these three months. Closely."

"Three *months*?" Shai said. "I'm planning for this to take at least two years."

"You have a hundred days," Frava said. "Actually, ninety-eight, now."

Impossible.

"The official explanation for why the emperor hasn't been seen these last two days," said one of the other arbiters, "is that he's been in mourning for the death of his wife. The Glory Faction will assume we are scrambling to buy time following the emperor's death. Once the hundred days of isolation are finished, they will demand that Ashravan present himself to the court. If he does not, we are finished."

And so are you, the woman's tone implied.

"I will need gold for this," Shai said. "Take what you're thinking I'll demand and double it. I will walk out of this country rich."

"Done," Frava said.

Too easy, Shai thought. Delightful. They were planning to kill her once this was over.

Well, that gave her ninety-eight days to find a way out. "Get me those records," she said. "I'll need a place to work, plenty of supplies, and my things back." She held up a finger before they could complain. "Not my Essence Marks, but everything else. I'm not going to work for three months in the same clothing I've been wearing while in prison. And, as I consider it, have someone draw me a bath immediately."

DAY THREE

THE next day—bathed, well fed, and well rested for the first time since her capture—Shai received a knock at her door.

They'd given her a room. It was tiny, probably the most drab in the entire palace, and it smelled faintly of mildew. They had still posted guards to watch her all night, of course, and—from her memory of the layout of the vast palace—she was in one of the least frequented wings, one used mostly for storage.

Still, it was better than a cell. Barely.

At the knock, Shai looked up from her inspection of the room's old cedar table. It probably hadn't seen an oiling cloth in longer than Shai had been alive. One of her guards opened the door, letting in the elderly Arbiter Gaotona. He carried a box two handspans wide and a couple of inches deep.

Shai rushed over, drawing a glare from Captain Zu, who stood beside the arbiter. "Keep your distance from His Grace," Zu growled.

"Or what?" Shai asked, taking the box. "You'll stab me?"

"Someday, I will enjoy—"

"Yes, yes," Shai said, walking back to her table and flipping open the box's lid. Inside were eighteen soulstamps, their heads smooth and unetched. She felt a thrill and picked one up, holding it out and inspecting it.

She had her spectacles back now, so no more squinting. She also wore clothing far more fitting than that dingy dress. A flat, red, calf-length skirt and buttoned blouse. The Grands would consider it unfashionable, as among them, ancient-looking robes or wraps were the current style. Shai found those dreary. Under the blouse she wore a tight cotton shirt, and under the skirt she wore leggings. A lady never knew when she might need to ditch her outer layer of clothing to effect a disguise.

"This is good stone," Shai said of the stamp in her fingers. She took out one of her chisels, which had a tip almost as fine as a pinhead, and began to scrape at the rock. It *was* good soulstone. The rock came away easily and precisely. Soulstone was almost as soft as chalk, but did not chip when scraped. You could carve it with high precision, and then set it with a flame and a mark on the top, which would harden it to a strength closer to quartz. The only way to get a better stamp was to carve one from crystal itself, which was incredibly difficult.

For ink, they had provided bright red squid's ink, mixed with a small percentage of wax. Any fresh organic ink would work, though inks from animals were better than inks from plants.

"Did you . . . steal a vase from the hallway outside?" Gaotona asked, frowning toward an object sitting at the side of her small room. She'd snatched one of the vases on the way back from the bath. One of her guards had tried to interfere, but Shai had talked her way past the objection. That guard was now blushing.

"I was curious about the skills of your Forgers," Shai said, setting down her tools and hauling the vase up onto the table. She turned it on its side, showing the bottom and the red seal imprinted into the clay there.

A Forger's seal was easy to spot. It didn't just imprint onto the object's surface, it actually sank *into* the material, creating a depressed pattern of red troughs. The rim of the round seal was red as well, but raised, like an embossing.

You could tell a lot about a person from the way they designed their seals. This one, for example, had a sterile feel to it. No real art, which was a contrast to the minutely detailed and delicate beauty of the vase itself. Shai had heard that the Heritage Faction kept lines of half-trained Forgers working by rote, creating these pieces like rows of men making shoes in a factory.

"Our workers are *not* Forgers," Gaotona said. "We don't use that word. They are Rememberers."

"It's the same thing."

"They don't touch souls," Gaotona said sternly. "Beyond that, what we do is in appreciation of the past, rather than with the aim of fooling or scamming people. Our reminders bring people to a greater understanding of their heritage."

Shai raised an eyebrow. She took her mallet and chisel, then brought them down at an angle on the embossed rim of the vase's seal. The seal resisted—there was a *force* to it, trying to stay in place—but the blow broke through. The rest of the seal popped up, troughs vanishing, the seal becoming simple ink and losing its powers.

The colors of the vase faded immediately, bleeding to plain grey, and its shape warped. A soulstamp didn't just make visual changes, but rewrote an object's history. Without the stamp, the vase was a horrid piece. Whoever had thrown it hadn't cared about the end product. Perhaps they'd known it would be part of a Forgery. Shai shook her head and turned back to her work on the unfinished soulstamp. This wasn't for the emperor—she wasn't nearly ready for that yet—but carving helped her think.

Gaotona gestured for the guards to leave, all but Zu, who remained by his side. "You present a puzzle, Forger," Gaotona said once the other two guards were gone, the door closed. He settled down in one of the two rickety wooden chairs. They—along with the splintery bed, the ancient table, and the trunk with her things—made up the room's entire array of furniture. The single window had a warped frame that let in the breeze, and even the walls had cracks in them.

"A puzzle?" Shai asked, holding up the stamp before her, peering closely at her work. "What kind of puzzle?"

"You are a Forger. Therefore, you cannot be trusted without supervision. You will try to run the moment you think of a practicable escape."

"So leave guards with me," Shai said, carving some more.

"Pardon," Gaotona said, "but I doubt it would take you long to bully, bribe, or blackmail them."

Nearby, Zu stiffened.

"I meant no offense, Captain," Gaotona said. "I have great confidence in your people, but what we have before us is a master trickster, liar, and thief. Your best guards would eventually become clay in her hands."

"Thank you," Shai said.

"It was *not* a compliment. What your type touches, it corrupts. I worried about leaving you alone even for one day under the supervision of mortal eyes. From what I know of you, you could nearly charm the gods themselves."

She continued working.

"I cannot trust in manacles to hold you," Gaotona said softly, "as we are required to give you soulstone so that you can work on our . . . problem. You would turn your manacles to soap, then escape in the night laughing."

That statement, of course, betrayed a complete lack of understanding in how Forgery worked. A Forgery had to be likely—believable— otherwise it wouldn't take. Who would make a chain out of soap? It would be ridiculous.

What she *could* do, however, was discover the chain's origins and composition, then rewrite one or the other. She could Forge the chain's past so that one of the links had been cast incorrectly, which would give her a flaw to exploit. Even if she could not find the chain's exact history, she might be able to escape—an imperfect stamp would not take for long, but she'd only need a few moments to shatter the link with a mallet.

They could make a chain out of ralkalest, the unForgeable metal, but that would only delay her escape. With enough time, and soulstone, she would find a solution. Forging the wall to have a weak crack in it, so she could pull the chain free. Forging the ceiling to have a loose block, which she could let drop and shatter the weak ralkalest links.

She didn't want to do something so extreme if she didn't have to. "I don't see that you need to worry about me," Shai said, still working. "I am intrigued by what we are doing, and I've been promised wealth. That is enough to keep me here. Don't forget, I could have escaped my previous cell at any time."

"Ah yes," Gaotona said. "The cell in which you would have used Forgery to get through the wall. Tell me, out of curiosity, have you studied anthracite? That rock you said you'd turn the wall into? I seem to recall that it is very difficult to make burn."

This one is more clever than people give him credit for being.

A candle's flame would have trouble igniting anthracite—on paper, the rock burned at the correct temperature, but getting an entire sample hot enough was very difficult. "I was fully capable of creating a proper kindling environment with some wood from my bunk and a few rocks turned into coal."

"Without a kiln?" Gaotona said, sounding faintly amused. "With no bellows? But that is beside the point. Tell me, how were you planning to *survive* inside a cell where the wall was aflame at over two thousand degrees? Would not that kind of fire suck away all of the breathable air? Ah, but of course. You could have used your bed linens and transformed them into a poor conductor, perhaps glass, and made a shell for yourself to hide in."

Shai continued her carving, uncomfortable. The way he said that . . . Yes, he knew that she could not have done what he described. Most Grands were ignorant about the ways of Forgery, and this man certainly still was, but he *did* know enough to realize she couldn't have escaped as she said. No more than bed linens could become glass.

Beyond that, making the entire wall into another type of rock would have been difficult. She would have had to change too many things—rewritten history so that the quarries for each type of stone were near deposits of anthracite, and so that in each case, a block of the burnable rock was quarried by mistake. That was a huge stretch, an almost impossible one, particularly without specific knowledge of the quarries in question.

Plausibility was key to any forgery, magical or not. People whispered of Forgers turning lead into gold, never realizing that the reverse was far, far easier. Inventing a history for a bar of gold where somewhere along the line, someone had adulterated it with lead . . . well, that was a plausible lie. The reverse would be so unlikely that a stamp to make that transformation would not take for long.

"You impress me, Your Grace," Shai finally said. "You think like a Forger."

Gaotona's expression soured.

"That," she noted, "*was* meant as a compliment."

"I value truth, young woman. Not Forgery." He regarded her with the expression of a disappointed grandfather. "I have seen the work of your hands. That copied painting you did . . . it was *remarkable*. Yet it was accomplished in the name of lies. What great works could you create if you focused on industry and beauty instead of wealth and deception?"

"What I do *is* great art."

"No. You copy other people's great art. What you do is technically marvelous, yet completely lacking in spirit."

She almost slipped in her carving, hands growing tense. How *dare* he? Threatening to execute her was one thing, but insulting her art? He made her sound like . . . like one of those assembly-line Forgers, churning out vase after vase!

She calmed herself with difficulty, then plastered on a smile. Her aunt Sol had once told Shai to smile at the worst insults and snap at the minor ones. That way, no man would know your heart.

"So how *am* I to be kept in line?" she asked. "We have established that I am among the most vile wretches to slither through the halls of this palace. You cannot bind me and you cannot trust your own soldiers to guard me."

"Well," Gaotona said, "whenever possible, I personally will observe your work."

She would have preferred Frava—that one seemed as if she'd be easier to manipulate—but this was workable. "If you wish," Shai said. "Much of it will be boring to one who does not understand Forgery."

"I am not interested in being entertained," Gaotona said, waving one hand to Captain Zu. "Whenever I am here, Captain Zu will guard me. He is the only one of our Strikers to know the extent of the emperor's injury, and only he knows of our plan with you. Other guards will watch you during the rest of the day, and you are *not* to speak to them of your task. There will be no rumors of what we do."

"You don't need to worry about me talking," Shai said, truthfully for once. "The more people who know of a Forgery, the more likely it is to fail." *Besides,* she thought, *if I told the guards, you'd undoubtedly execute them to preserve your secrets.* She didn't like Strikers, but she liked the empire less, and the guards were really just another kind of slave. Shai wasn't in the business of getting people killed for no reason.

"Excellent," Gaotona said. "The second method of insuring your . . . attention to your project waits outside. If you would, good Captain?"

Zu opened the door. A cloaked figure stood with the guards. The figure stepped into the room; his walk was lithe, but somehow unnatural. After Zu closed the door, the figure removed his hood, revealing a face with milky white skin and red eyes.

Shai hissed softly through her teeth. "And you call what *I* do an abomination?"

Gaotona ignored her, standing up from his chair to regard the newcomer. "Tell her."

The newcomer rested long white fingers on her door, inspecting it. "I will place the rune here," he said in an accented voice. "If she leaves this room for any reason, or if she alters the rune or the door, I will know. My pets will come for her."

Shai shivered. She glared at Gaotona. "A Bloodsealer. You invited a *Bloodsealer* into your palace?"

"This one has proven himself an asset recently," Gaotona said. "He is loyal and he is discreet. He is also very effective. There are . . . times when one must accept the aid of darkness in order to contain a greater darkness."

Shai hissed softly again as the Bloodsealer removed something from within his robes. A crude soulstamp created from a bone. His "pets" would also be bone, Forgeries of human life crafted from the skeletons of the dead.

The Bloodsealer looked to her.

Shai backed away. "Surely you don't expect—"

Zu took her by the arms. Nights, but he was strong. She panicked.

Her Essence Marks! She needed her Essence Marks! With those, she could fight, escape, run . . .

Zu cut her along the back of her arm. She barely felt the shallow wound, but she struggled anyway. The Bloodsealer stepped up and inked his horrid tool in Shai's blood. He then turned and pressed the stamp against the center of her door.

When he withdrew his hand, he left a glowing red seal in the wood. It was shaped like an eye. The moment he marked the seal, Shai felt a sharp pain in her arm, where she'd been cut.

Shai gasped, eyes wide. Never had any person *dared* do such a thing to her. Almost better that she had been executed! Almost better that—

Control yourself, she told herself forcibly. *Become someone who can deal with this.*

She took a deep breath and let herself become someone else. An imitation of herself who was calm, even in a situation like this. It was a crude forgery, just a trick of the mind, but it worked.

She shook herself free from Zu, then accepted the kerchief Gaotona handed her. She glared at the Bloodsealer as the pain in her arm faded. He smiled at her with lips that were white and faintly translucent, like the skin of a maggot. He nodded to Gaotona before replacing his hood and stepping out of the room, closing the door after.

Shai forced herself to breathe evenly, calming herself. There was no subtlety to what the Bloodsealer did; they didn't traffic in subtlety. Instead of skill or artistry, they used tricks and blood. However, their craft was effective. The man would know if Shai left the room, and he had her fresh blood on his stamp, which was attuned to her. With that, his undead pets would be able to hunt her no matter where she ran.

Gaotona settled back down in his chair. "You know what will happen if you flee?"

Shai glared at Gaotona.

"You now realize how desperate we are," he said softly, lacing his fingers before him. "If you do run, we will give you to the Bloodsealer. Your bones will become his next pet. This promise was all he requested in payment. You may begin your work, Forger. Do it well, and you will escape this fate."

DAY FIVE

WORK she did.

Shai began digging through accounts of the emperor's life. Few people understood how much Forgery was about study and research. It was an art any man or woman could learn; it required only a steady hand and an eye for detail.

That and a willingness to spend weeks, months, even *years* preparing the ideal soulstamp.

Shai didn't have years. She felt rushed as she read biography after biography, often staying up well into the night taking notes. She did not believe that she could do what they asked of her. Creating a believable Forgery of another man's soul, particularly in such a short time, just wasn't possible. Unfortunately, she had to make a good show of it while she planned her escape.

They didn't let her leave the room. She used a chamber pot when nature called, and for baths she was allowed a tub of warm water and cloths. She was under supervision at all times, even when bathing.

That Bloodsealer came each morning to renew his mark on the door. Each time, the act required a little blood from Shai. Her arms were soon laced with shallow cuts.

All the while, Gaotona visited. The ancient arbiter studied her as she read, watching with those eyes that judged . . . but also did not hate.

As she formulated her plans, she decided one thing: Getting free would probably require manipulating this man in some way.

DAY TWELVE

S HAI pressed her stamp down on the tabletop.

As always, the stamp sank slightly into the material. A soulstamp left a seal you could feel, regardless of the material. She twisted the stamp a half turn—this did not blur the ink, though she did not know why. One of her mentors had taught that it was because by this point the seal was touching the object's soul and not its physical presence.

When she pulled the stamp back, it left a bright red seal in the wood as if carved there. Transformation spread from the seal in a wave. The table's dull grey splintery cedar became beautiful and well maintained, with a warm patina that reflected the light of the candles sitting across from her.

Shai rested her fingers on the new table; it was now smooth to the touch. The sides and legs were finely carved, inlaid here and there with silver.

Gaotona sat upright, lowering the book he'd been reading. Zu shuffled in discomfort at seeing the Forgery.

"What was that?" Gaotona demanded.

"I was tired of getting splinters," Shai said, settling back in her chair. It creaked. *You are next,* she thought.

Gaotona stood up and walked to the table. He touched it, as if expecting the transformation to be mere illusion. It was not. The fine table now looked horribly out of place in the dingy room. "This is what you've been doing?"

"Carving helps me think."

"You should be focused on your task!" Gaotona said. "This is frivolity. The empire itself is in danger!"

No, Shai thought. *Not the empire itself; just your rule of it.* Unfortunately, after eleven days, she still didn't have an angle on Gaotona, not one she could exploit.

"I *am* working on your problem, Gaotona," she said. "What you ask of me is hardly a simple task."

"And changing that table was?"

"Of course it was," Shai said. "All I had to do was rewrite its past so that it was maintained, rather than being allowed to sink into disrepair. That took hardly any work at all."

Gaotona hesitated, then knelt beside the table. "These carvings, this inlay . . . those were not part of the original."

"I might have added a little."

She wasn't certain if the Forgery would take or not. In a few minutes, that seal might evaporate and the table might revert to its previous state. Still, she was fairly certain she'd guessed the table's past well enough. Some of the histories she was reading mentioned what gifts had come from where. This table, she suspected, had come from far-off Svorden as a gift to Emperor Ashravan's predecessor. The strained relationship with Svorden had then led the emperor to lock it away and ignore it.

"I don't recognize this piece," Gaotona said, still looking at the table.

"Why should you?"

"I have studied ancient arts extensively," he said. "This is from the Vivare dynasty?"

"No."

"An imitation of the work of Chamrav?"

"No."

"What then?"

"Nothing," Shai said with exasperation. "It's not imitating anything;

it has become a better version of itself." That was a maxim of good Forgery: Improve slightly on an original, and people would often accept the fake because it *was* superior.

Gaotona stood up, looking troubled. *He's thinking again that my talent is wasted,* Shai thought with annoyance, moving aside a stack of accounts of the emperor's life. Collected at her request, these came from palace servants. She didn't want only the official histories. She needed authenticity, not sterilized recitations.

Gaotona stepped back to his chair. "I do not see how transforming this table could have taken hardly any work, although it clearly must be much simpler than what you have been asked to do. Both seem incredible to me."

"Changing a human soul is far more difficult."

"I can accept that conceptually, but I do not know the specifics. Why is it so?"

She glanced at him. *He wants to know more of what I'm doing,* she thought, *so that he can tell how I'm preparing to escape.* He knew she would be trying, of course. They both would pretend that neither knew that fact.

"All right," she said, standing and walking to the wall of her room. "Let's talk about Forgery. Your cage for me had a wall of forty-four types of stone, mostly as a trap to keep me distracted. I had to figure out the makeup and origin of each block if I wanted to try to escape. Why?"

"So you could create a Forgery of the wall, obviously."

"But why all of them?" she asked. "Why not just change one block or a few? Why not just make a hole big enough to slip into, creating a tunnel for myself?"

"I . . ." He frowned. "I have no idea."

Shai rested her hand against the outer wall of her room. It had been painted, though the paint was coming off in several sections. She could feel the separate stones. "All things exist in three Realms, Gaotona. Physical, Cognitive, Spiritual. The Physical is what we feel, what is before us. The Cognitive is how an object is viewed and how it views itself. The Spiritual Realm contains an object's soul—its essence—as well as the ways it is connected to the things and people around it."

"You must understand," Gaotona said, "I don't subscribe to your pagan superstitions."

"Yes, you worship the sun instead," Shai said, failing to keep the amusement out of her voice. "Or, rather, eighty suns—believing that even though each looks the same, a different sun actually rises each day. Well, you wanted to know how Forgery works, and why the emperor's soul will be so difficult to reproduce. The Realms are important to this."

"Very well."

"Here is the point. The longer an object exists as a whole, and the longer it is *seen* in that state, the stronger its sense of complete identity becomes. That table is made up of various pieces of wood fitted together, but do we think of it that way? No. We see the whole.

"To Forge the table, I must understand it as a whole. The same goes for a wall. That wall has existed long enough to view itself as a single entity. I could, perhaps, have attacked each block separately—they might still be distinct enough—but doing so would be difficult, as the wall wants to act as a whole."

"The wall," Gaotona said flatly, "*wants* to be treated as a whole."

"Yes."

"You imply that the wall has a soul."

"All things do," she said. "Each object sees itself as something. Connection and intent are vital. This is why, Master Arbiter, I can't simply write down a personality for your emperor, stamp him, and be done. Seven reports I've read say his favorite color was green. Do you know why?"

"No," Gaotona said. "Do you?"

"I'm not sure yet," Shai said. "I *think* it was because his brother, who died when Ashravan was six, had always been fond of it. The emperor latched on to it, as it reminds him of his dead sibling. There might be a touch of nationalism to it as well, as he was born in Ukurgi, where the provincial flag is predominantly green."

Gaotona seemed troubled. "You must know something that specific?"

"Nights, yes! And a thousand things just as detailed. I can get some wrong. I *will* get some wrong. Most of them, hopefully, won't matter—they will make his personality a little off, but each person changes day to day in any case. If I get too many wrong, though, the personality won't matter because the stamp won't take. At least, it won't last long enough to do any good. I assume that if your emperor has to be restamped every fifteen minutes, the charade will be impossible to maintain."

"You assume correctly."

Shai sat down with a sigh, looking over her notes.

"You said you could do this," Gaotona said.

"Yes."

"You've done it before, with your own soul."

"I know my own soul," she said. "I know my own history. I know what I can change to get the effect I need—and even getting my own Essence Marks right was difficult. Now I not only have to do this for another person, but the transformation must be far more extensive. And I have ninety days left to do it."

Gaotona nodded slowly.

"Now," she said, "you should tell me what you're doing to keep up the pretense that the emperor is still awake and well."

"We're doing all that needs to be done."

"I'm far from confident that you are. I think you'll find me a fair bit better at deception than most."

"I think that *you* will be surprised," Gaotona said. "We are, after all, politicians."

"All right, fine. But you are sending food, aren't you?"

"Of course," Gaotona said. "Three meals are sent to the emperor's quarters each day. They return to the palace kitchens eaten, though he is, of course, secretly being fed broth. He drinks it when prompted, but stares ahead, as if both deaf and mute."

"And the chamber pot?"

"He has no control over himself," Gaotona said, grimacing. "We keep him in cloth diapers."

"Nights, man! And no one changes a fake chamber pot? Don't you think that's suspicious? Maids will gossip, as will guards at the door. You need to consider these things!"

Gaotona had the decency to blush. "I will see that it happens, though

I don't like the idea of someone else entering his quarters. Too many have a chance to discover what has happened to him."

"Pick someone you trust, then," Shai said. "In fact, make a rule at the emperor's doors. No one enters unless they bear a card with your personal signet. And yes, I know why you are opening your mouth to object. I know exactly how well guarded the emperor's quarters are—that was part of what I studied to break into the gallery. Your security isn't tight enough, as the assassins proved. Do what I suggest. The more layers of security, the better. If what has happened to the emperor gets out, I have no doubt that I'll end up back in that cell waiting for execution."

Gaotona sighed, but nodded. "What else do you suggest?"

DAY SEVENTEEN

A COOL breeze laden with unfamiliar spices crept through the cracks around Shai's warped window. The low hum of cheers seeped through as well. Outside, the city celebrated. Delbahad, a holiday no one had known about until two years earlier. The Heritage Faction continued to dig up and revive ancient feasts in an effort to sway public opinion back toward them.

It wouldn't help. The empire was not a republic, and the only ones who would have a say in anointing a new emperor would be the arbiters of the various factions. Shai turned her attention away from the celebrations, and continued to read from the emperor's journal.

I have decided, at long last, to agree to the demands of my faction, the book read. *I will offer myself for the position of emperor, as Gaotona has so often encouraged. Emperor Yazad grows weak with his disease, and a new choice will be made soon.*

Shai made a notation. Gaotona had encouraged Ashravan to seek the throne. And yet, later in the journal, Ashravan spoke of Gaotona with contempt. Why the change? She finished the notation, then turned to another entry, years later.

Emperor Ashravan's personal journal fascinated her. He had written it with his own hand, and had included instructions for it to be destroyed upon his death. The arbiters had delivered the journal to her reluctantly, and with vociferous justification. He hadn't died. His body still lived. Therefore, it was just fine for them *not* to burn his writings.

They spoke with confidence, but she could see the uncertainty in their eyes. They were easy to read—all but Gaotona, whose inner thoughts continued to elude her. They didn't understand the purpose of this journal. Why write, they wondered, if not for posterity? Why put your thoughts to paper if not for the purpose of having others read them?

As easy, she thought, *to ask a Forger why she would get satisfaction from creating a fake and seeing it on display without a single person knowing it was her work—and not that of the original artist—they were revering.*

The journal told her far more about the emperor than the official histories had, and not just because of the contents. The pages of the book were worn and stained from constant turning. Ashravan *had* written this book to be read—by himself.

What memories had Ashravan sought so profoundly that he would read this book over and over and over again? Was he vain, enjoying the thrill of past conquests? Was he, instead, insecure? Did he spend hours searching these words because he wanted to justify his mistakes? Or was there another reason?

The door to her chambers opened. They had stopped knocking. Why would they? They already denied her any semblance of privacy. She was still a captive, just a more important one than before.

Arbiter Frava entered, graceful and long-faced, wearing robes of a soft violet. Her grey braid was spun with gold and violet this time. Captain Zu guarded her. Inwardly, Shai sighed, adjusting her spectacles. She had been anticipating a night of study and planning, uninterrupted now that Gaotona had gone to join the festivities.

"I am told," Frava said, "that you are progressing at an unremarkable pace."

Shai set down the book. "Actually, this is quick. I am nearly ready to begin crafting stamps. As I reminded Arbiter Gaotona earlier today, I do still need a test subject who knew the emperor. The connection between them will allow me to test stamps on him, and they will stick briefly—long enough for me to try out a few things."

"One will be provided," Frava replied, walking along the table with its glistening surface. She ran a finger across it, then stopped at the red seal mark. The arbiter prodded at it. "Such an eyesore. After going to such trouble to make the table more beautiful, why not put the seal on the bottom?"

"I'm proud of my work," Shai said. "Any Forger who sees this can inspect it and see what I've done."

Frava sniffed. "You should not be proud of something like this, little thief. Besides, isn't the point of what you do to *hide* the fact that you've done it?"

"Sometimes," Shai said. "When I imitate a signature or counterfeit a painting, the subterfuge is part of the act. But with Forgery, true Forgery, you cannot hide what you've done. The stamp will always be there, describing exactly what has happened. You might as well be proud of it."

It was the odd conundrum of her life. To be a Forger was not just about soulstamps—it was about the art of mimicry in its entirety. Writing, art, personal signets . . . an apprentice Forger—mentored half in secret by her people—learned all mundane forgery before being taught to use soulstamps.

The stamps were the highest order of their art, but they were the most difficult to hide. Yes, a seal could be placed in an out-of-the-way place on an object, then covered over. Shai had done that very thing on occasion. However, so long as the seal was somewhere to be found, a Forgery could not be perfect.

"Leave us," Frava said to Zu and the guards.

"But—" Zu said, stepping forward.

"I do not like to repeat myself, Captain," Frava said.

Zu growled softly, but bowed in obedience. He gave Shai a glare—that was practically a second occupation for him, these days—and retreated with his men. They shut the door with a click.

The Bloodsealer's stamp still hung there on the door, renewed this morning. The Bloodsealer came at the same time most days. Shai had kept specific notes. On days when he was a little late, his seal started to dim right before he arrived. He always got to her in time to renew it, but perhaps someday . . .

Frava inspected Shai, eyes calculating.

Shai met that gaze with a steady one of her own. "Zu assumes I'm going to do something horrible to you while we're alone."

"Zu is simpleminded," Frava said, "though he is very useful when someone needs to be killed. Hopefully you won't ever have to experience his efficiency firsthand."

"You're not worried?" Shai said. "You are alone in a room with a monster."

"I'm alone in a room with an opportunist," Frava said, strolling to the door and inspecting the seal burning there. "You won't harm me. You're too curious about why I sent the guards away."

Actually, Shai thought, *I know precisely why you sent them away. And why you came to me during a time when all of your associate arbiters were guaranteed to be busy at the festival.* She waited for Frava to make the offer.

"Has it occurred to you," Frava said, "how . . . useful to the empire it would be to have an emperor who listened to a voice of wisdom when it spoke to him?"

"Surely Emperor Ashravan already did that."

"On occasion," Frava said. "On other occasions, he could be . . . belligerently foolish. Wouldn't it be amazing if, upon his rebirth, he were found lacking that tendency?"

"I thought you wanted him to act exactly like he used to," Shai said. "As close to the real thing as possible."

"True, true. But you are renowned as one of the greatest Forgers ever to live, and I have it on good authority that you are specifically talented with stamping your own soul. Surely you can replicate dear Ashravan's soul with authenticity, yet also make him inclined to listen to reason . . . when that reason is spoken by specific individuals."

Nights afire, Shai thought. *You're willing to just come out and say it, aren't you? You want me to build a back door into the emperor's soul, and you don't even have the decency to feel ashamed about that.*

"I . . . might be able to do such a thing," Shai said, as if considering it for the first time. "It would be difficult. I'd need a reward worth the effort."

"A suitable reward *would* be appropriate," Frava said, turning to her. "I realize you were probably planning to leave the Imperial Seat following your release, but why? This city could be a place of great opportunity to you, with a sympathetic ruler on the throne."

"Be more blunt, Arbiter," Shai said. "I have a long night ahead of me studying while others celebrate. I don't have the mind for word games."

"The city has a thriving clandestine smuggling trade," Frava said. "Keeping track of it has been a hobby of mine. It would serve me to have someone proper running it. I will give it to you, should you do this task for me."

That was always their mistake—assuming they knew why Shai did what she did. Assuming she'd jump at a chance like this, assuming that a smuggler and a Forger were basically the same thing because they both disobeyed someone else's laws.

"That sounds pleasant," Shai said, smiling her most genuine smile— the one that had an edge of overt deceptiveness to it.

Frava smiled deeply in return. "I will leave you to consider," she said, pulling open the door and clapping for the guards to reenter.

Shai sank down into her chair, horrified. Not because of the offer— she'd been expecting one like it for days now—but because she had only now understood the implications. The offer of the smuggling trade was, of course, false. Frava might have been able to deliver such a thing, but she wouldn't. Even assuming that the woman hadn't already been planning to have Shai killed, this offer sealed that eventuality.

There was more to it, though. Far more. *So far as she knows, she just planted in my head the idea of building control into the emperor. She won't trust my Forgery. She'll be expecting me to put in back doors of my own, ones that give* me *and not her complete control over Ashravan.*

What did that mean?

It meant that Frava had another Forger standing by. One, likely, without the talent or the bravado to try Forging someone else's soul— but one who could look over Shai's work and find any back doors she put in. This Forger would be better trusted, and could rewrite Shai's work to put Frava in control.

They might even be able to finish Shai's work, if she got it far enough along first. Shai had intended to use the full hundred days to plan her escape, but now she realized that her sudden extermination could come at any time.

The closer she got to finishing the project, the more likely that grew.

DAY THIRTY

THIS is new," Gaotona said, inspecting the stained-glass window. That had been a particularly pleasing bit of inspiration on Shai's part. Attempts to Forge the window to a better version of itself had repeatedly failed; each time, after five minutes or so, the window had reverted to its cracked, gap-sided self.

Then Shai had found a bit of colored glass rammed into one side of the frame. The window, she realized, had once been a stained-glass piece, like many in the palace. It had been broken, and whatever had shattered the window had also bent the frame, producing those gaps that let in the frigid breeze.

Rather than repairing it as it had been meant to be, someone had put ordinary glass into the window and left it to crack. A stamp from Shai in the bottom right corner had restored the window, rewriting its history so that a caring master craftsman had discovered the fallen window and remade it. That seal had taken immediately. Even after all this time, the window had seen itself as something beautiful.

Or maybe she was just getting romantic again.

"You said you would bring me a test subject today," Shai said, blowing the dust off the end of a freshly carved soulstamp. She engraved a series of quick marks on the back—the side opposite the elaborately carved front. The setting mark finished every soulstamp, indicating no more carving was to come. Shai had always fancied it to look like the shape of MaiPon, her homeland.

Those marks finished, she held the stamp over a flame. This was a property of soulstone; fire hardened it, so it could not be chipped. She didn't need to take this step. The anchoring marks on the top were all it really needed, and she could carve a stamp out of anything, really, so long as the carving was precise. Soulstone was prized, however, because of this hardening process.

Once the entire thing was blackened from the candle's flame—first one end, then the other—she held it up and blew on it strongly. Flakes of char blew free with her breath, revealing the beautiful red and grey marbled stone beneath.

"Yes," Gaotona said. "A test subject. I brought one, as promised." Gaotona crossed the small room toward the door, where Zu stood guard.

Shai leaned back in her chair, which she'd Forged into something far more comfortable a couple of days back, and waited. She had made a bet with herself. Would the subject be one of the emperor's guards? Or would it be some lowly palace functionary, perhaps the man who took notes for Ashravan? Which person would the arbiters force to endure Shai's blasphemy in the name of a supposedly greater good?

Gaotona sat down in the chair by the door.

"Well?" Shai asked.

He raised his hands to the sides. "You may begin."

Shai dropped her feet to the ground, sitting up straight. "You?"

"Yes."

"You're one of the arbiters! One of the most powerful people in the empire!"

"Ah," he said. "I had not noticed. I fit your specifications. I am male, was born in Ashravan's own birthplace, and I knew him very well."

"But . . ." Shai trailed off.

Gaotona leaned forward, clasping his hands. "We debated this for weeks. Other options were offered, but it was determined that we could not in good conscience order one of our people to undergo this blasphemy. The only conclusion was to offer up one of ourselves."

Shai shook herself free of shock. *Frava would have had no trouble ordering someone else to do this,* she thought. *Nor would the others. You must have insisted upon this, Gaotona.*

They considered him a rival; they were probably happy to let him fall to Shai's supposedly horrible, twisted acts. What she planned was perfectly harmless, but there was no way she'd convince a Grand of that. Still, she found herself wishing she could put Gaotona at ease as she pulled her chair up beside him and opened the small box of stamps she had crafted over the past three weeks.

"These stamps will not take," she said, holding up one of them. "That is a Forger's term for a stamp that makes a change that is too unnatural to be stable. I doubt any of these will affect you for longer than a minute—and that's assuming I did them correctly."

Gaotona hesitated, then nodded.

"The human soul is different from that of an object," Shai continued. "A person is constantly growing, changing, shifting. That makes a soulstamp used on a person wear out in a way that doesn't happen with objects. Even in the best of cases, a soulstamp used on a person lasts only a day. My Essence Marks are an example. After about twenty-six hours, they fade away."

"So . . . the emperor?"

"If I do my job well," Shai said, "he will need to be stamped each morning, much as the Bloodsealer stamps my door. I will fashion into the seal, however, the capacity for him to remember, grow, and learn— he won't revert back to the same state each morning, and will be able to build upon the foundation I give him. However, much as a human body wears down and needs sleep, a soulstamp on one of us must be reset. Fortunately, anyone can do the stamping—Ashravan himself should be able to—once the stamp itself is prepared correctly."

She gave Gaotona the stamp she held, letting him inspect it.

"Each of the particular stamps I will use today," she continued, "will change something small about your past or your innate personality. As you are not Ashravan, the changes will not take. However, you two are similar enough in history that the seals should last for a short time, if I've done them well."

"You mean this is a . . . pattern for the emperor's soul?" Gaotona asked, looking over the stamp.

"No. Just a Forgery of a small part of it. I'm not even sure if the final product will work. So far as I know, no one has ever tried something exactly like this before. But there are accounts of people Forging someone else's soul for . . . nefarious purposes. I'm drawing on that knowledge to accomplish this. From what I know, if these seals last for at least a minute on you, they should last far longer on the emperor, as they are attuned to his specific past."

"A small piece of his soul," Gaotona said, handing back the seal. "So these tests . . . you will not use these seals in the final product?"

"No, but I'll take the patterns that work and incorporate them into a greater fabrication. Think of these seals as single characters in a large scroll; once I am done, I'll be able to put them together and tell a story. The story of a man's history and personality. Unfortunately, even if the Forgery takes, there will be small differences. I suggest that you begin spreading rumors that the emperor was wounded. Not terribly, mind you, but imply a good knock to the head. That will explain discrepancies."

"There are already rumors of his death," Gaotona said, "spread by the Glory Faction."

"Well, indicate he was wounded instead."

"But—"

Shai raised the stamp. "Even if I accomplish the impossible—which, mind you, I've done only on rare occasions—the Forgery will not have all of the emperor's memories. It can only contain things I have been able to read about or guess. Ashravan will have had many private conversations that the Forgery will *not* be able to recall. I can imbue him with a keen ability to fake—I have a particular understanding of that sort of thing—but fakery can only take a person so far. Eventually, someone will realize that he has large holes in his memory. Spread the rumors, Gaotona. You're going to need them."

He nodded, then pulled back his sleeve to expose his arm for her to stamp. She raised the stamp, and Gaotona sighed, then squeezed his eyes shut and nodded again.

She pressed it against his skin. As always, when the stamp touched the skin, it felt as if she were pressing it against something rigid—as if his arm had become stone. The stamp *sank in* slightly. That made for a disconcerting sensation when working on a person. She rotated the stamp, then pulled it back, leaving a red seal on Gaotona's arm. She took out her pocket watch, observing the ticking hand.

The seal gave off faint wisps of red smoke; that happened only when living things were stamped. The soul fought against the rewriting. The seal didn't puff away immediately, though. Shai released a held breath. That was a good sign.

She wondered . . . if she were to try something like this on the emperor, would his soul fight against the invasion? Or instead, would it accept the stamp, wishing to have righted what had gone wrong? Much as that window had wanted to be restored to its former beauty. She didn't know.

Gaotona opened his eyes. "Did it . . . work?"

"It took, for now," Shai said.

"I don't feel any different."

"That is the point. If the emperor could *feel* the stamp's effects, he would realize that something was wrong. Now, answer me without thought; speak by instinct only. What is your favorite color?"

"Green," he said immediately.

"Why?"

"Because . . ." He trailed off, cocking his head. "Because it is."

"And your brother?"

"I hardly remember him," Gaotona said with a shrug. "He died when I was very young."

"It is good he did," Shai said. "He would have made a terrible emperor, if he had been chosen in—"

Gaotona stood up. "Don't you dare speak ill of him! I will have you . . ." He stiffened, glancing at Zu, who had reached for his sword in alarm. "I . . . Brother . . . ?"

The seal faded away.

"A minute and five seconds," Shai said. "That one looks good."

Gaotona raised a hand to his head. "I can remember having a brother. But . . . I don't have one, and never have. I can remember idolizing him; I can remember pain when he died. Such *pain* . . ."

"That will fade," Shai said. "The impressions will wash away like the remnants of a bad dream. In an hour, you'll barely be able to recall what it was that upset you." She scribbled some notes. "I think you reacted too strongly to me insulting your brother's memory. Ashravan worshipped his brother, but kept his feelings buried deep out of guilt that perhaps his brother would have made a better emperor than he."

"What? Are you sure?"

"About this?" Shai said. "Yes. I'll have to revise that stamp a little bit, but I think it is mostly right."

Gaotona sat back down, regarding her with ancient eyes that seemed to be trying to pierce her, to dig deep inside. "You know a great deal about people."

"It's one of the early steps of our training," Shai said. "Before we're even allowed to *touch* soulstone."

"Such potential . . ." Gaotona whispered.

Shai forced down an immediate burst of annoyance. How dare he look at her like that, as if she were wasting her life? She loved Forgery. The thrill, a life spent getting ahead by her wits. That was what she *was*. Wasn't it?

She thought of one specific Essence Mark, locked away with the others. It was one Mark she had never used, yet was at the same time the most precious of the five.

"Let's try another," Shai said, ignoring those eyes of Gaotona's. She couldn't afford to grow offended. Aunt Sol had always said that pride would be Shai's greatest danger in life.

"Very well," Gaotona said, "but I am confused at one thing. From what little you've told me of this process, I cannot fathom why these seals even begin to work on me. Don't you need to know a thing's history exactly to make a seal work on it?"

"To make them stick, yes," Shai said. "As I've said, it's about plausibility."

"But this is completely implausible! I don't have a brother."

"Ah. Well, let me see if I can explain," she said, settling back. "I am rewriting your soul to match that of the emperor—just as I rewrote the history of that window to include new stained glass. In both cases, it works because of *familiarity*. The window frame knows what a stained-glass window should look like. It once had stained glass in it. Even though the new window is not the same as the one it once held, the seal works because the general concept of a stained-glass window has been fulfilled.

"You spent a great deal of time around the emperor. Your soul is familiar with his, much as the window frame is familiar with the stained glass. This is why I have to try out the seals on someone like you, and not on myself. When I stamp you, it's like . . . it's like I'm presenting to your soul a piece of something it should know. It only works if the piece is very small, but so long as it is—and so long as the soul considers the piece a familiar part of Ashravan, as I've indicated—the stamp will take for a brief time before being rejected."

Gaotona regarded her with bemusement.

"Sounds like superstitious nonsense to you, I assume?" Shai said.

"It is . . . rather mystical," Gaotona said, spreading his hands before him. "A window frame knowing the 'concept' of a stained-glass window? A soul understanding the concept of another soul?"

"These things exist beyond us," Shai said, preparing another seal. "We think about windows, we know about windows; what is and isn't a window takes on . . . meaning, in the Spiritual Realm. Takes on life, after a fashion. Believe the explanation or do not; I guess it doesn't matter. The fact is that I can try these seals on you, and if they stick for at least a minute, it's a very good indication that I've hit on something.

"Ideally, I'd try this on the emperor himself, but in his state, he would not be able to answer my questions. I need to not only get these to take, but I need to make them work together—and that will require your explanations of what you are feeling so I can nudge the design in the right directions. Now, your arm again, please?"

"Very well." Gaotona composed himself, and Shai pressed another seal against his arm. She locked it with a half turn, but as soon as she pulled the stamp away, the seal vanished in a puff of red.

"Blast," Shai said.

"What happened?" Gaotona said, reaching fingers to his arm. He smeared mundane ink; the seal had vanished so quickly, the ink hadn't even been incorporated into its workings. "What have you done to me this time?"

"Nothing, it appears," Shai said, inspecting the head of the stamp for flaws. She found none. "I had *that* one wrong. Very wrong."

"What was it?"

"The reason Ashravan agreed to become emperor," Shai said. "Nights afire. I was certain I had this one." She shook her head, setting the stamp aside. Ashravan, it appeared, had not stepped up to offer himself as emperor because of a deep-seated desire to prove himself to his family and to escape the distant—but long—shadow of his brother.

"I can tell you why he did it, Forger," Gaotona said.

She eyed him. *This man encouraged Ashravan to step toward the imperial throne,* she thought. Ashravan eventually hated him for it. *I think.*

"All right," she said. "Why?"

"He wanted to change things," Gaotona said. "In the empire."

"He doesn't speak of this in his journal."

"Ashravan was a humble man."

Shai raised an eyebrow. That didn't match the reports she'd been given.

"Oh, he had a temper," Gaotona said. "And if you got him arguing, he would sink his teeth in and hold fast to his point. But the man . . . the man he was . . . Deep down, that was a humble man. You will have to understand this about him."

"I see," she said. *You did it to him too, didn't you?* Shai thought. *That look of disappointment, that implication we should be better people than we are.* Shai wasn't the only one who felt that Gaotona regarded her as if he were a displeased grandfather.

That made her want to dismiss the man as irrelevant. Except . . . he had offered himself to her tests. He thought what she did was horrible, so he insisted on taking the punishment himself, instead of sending another.

You're genuine, aren't you, old man? Shai thought as Gaotona sat back, eyes distant as he considered the emperor. She found herself unsettled.

In her business, there were many who laughed at honest men, calling them easy pickings. That was a fallacy. Being honest did not make one naive. A dishonest fool and an honest fool were equally easy to scam; you just went about it in different ways.

However, a man who was honest and clever was always, *always* more difficult to scam than someone who was both dishonest and clever.

Sincerity. It was so difficult, by definition, to fake.

"What are you thinking behind those eyes of yours?" Gaotona asked, leaning forward.

"I was thinking that you must have treated the emperor as you did me, annoying him with constant nagging about what he should accomplish."

Gaotona snorted. "I probably did just that. It does not mean my points are, or were, incorrect. He could have . . . well, he could have become more than he did. Just as you *could* become a marvelous artist."

"I am one."

"A real one."

"I am one."

Gaotona shook his head. "Frava's painting . . . there is something we are missing about it, isn't there? She had the forgery inspected, and the assessors found a few tiny mistakes. I couldn't see them without help—but they are there. Upon reflection, they seem odd to me. The strokes are impeccable, masterly even. The style is a perfect match. If you could manage that, why would you have made such errors as putting the moon too low? It's a subtle mistake, but it occurs to me that you would never have made such an error—not unintentionally, at least."

Shai turned to get another seal.

"The painting they think is the original," Gaotona said, "the one hanging in Frava's office right now . . . It's a fake too, isn't it?"

"Yes," Shai admitted with a sigh. "I swapped the paintings a few days before trying for the scepter; I was investigating palace security.

I sneaked into the gallery, entered Frava's offices, and made the change as a test."

"So the one they assume is fake, *it* must be the original," Gaotona said, smiling. "You painted those mistakes *over* the original to make it seem like it was a replica!"

"Actually, no," Shai said. "Though I have used that trick in the past. They're both fakes. One is simply the obvious fake, planted to be discovered in case something went wrong."

"So the original is still hidden somewhere . . ." Gaotona said, sounding curious. "You sneaked into the palace to investigate security, then you replaced the original painting with a copy. You left a second, slightly worse copy in your room as a false trail. If you were found out while sneaking in—or if you were for some reason sold out by an ally—we would search your room and find the poor copy, and assume that you hadn't yet accomplished your swap. The officers would take the good copy and believe it to be authentic. That way, no one would keep looking for the original."

"More or less."

"That's very clever," Gaotona said. "Why, if you were captured sneaking into the palace trying to steal the scepter, you could confess that you were trying to steal only the painting. A search of your room would turn up the fake, and you'd be charged with attempted theft from an individual, in this case Frava, which is a much lesser crime than trying to steal an imperial relic. You would get ten years of labor instead of a death sentence."

"Unfortunately," Shai said, "I was betrayed at the wrong moment. The Fool arranged for me to be caught after I'd left the gallery with the scepter."

"But what of the original painting? Where did you hide it?" He hesitated. "It's still in the palace, isn't it?"

"After a fashion."

Gaotona looked at her, still smiling.

"I burned it," Shai said.

The smile vanished immediately. "You lie."

"Not this time, old man," Shai said. "The painting wasn't worth the risk to get it out of the gallery. I only pulled that swap to test security.

I got the fake in easily; people aren't searched going in, only coming out. The scepter was my true goal. Stealing the painting was secondary. After I replaced it, I tossed the original into one of the main gallery hearths."

"That's *horrible*," Gaotona said. "It was an original ShuXen, his greatest masterpiece! He's gone blind, and can no longer paint. Do you realize the cost . . ." He sputtered. "I don't understand. Why, *why* would you do something like that?"

"It doesn't matter. No one will know what I've done. They will keep looking at the fake and be satisfied, so there's no harm done."

"That painting was a priceless work of art!" Gaotona glared at her. "Your swap of it was about pride and nothing else. You didn't care about selling the original. You just wanted your copy hanging in the gallery instead. You destroyed something wonderful so that you could elevate yourself!"

She shrugged. There was more to the story, but the fact was, she *had* burned the painting. She had her reasons.

"We are done for the day," Gaotona said, red-faced. He waved a hand at her, dismissive as he stood up. "I had begun to think . . . Bah!"

He stalked out the door.

DAY FORTY-TWO

E ACH person was a puzzle.

That was how Tao, her first trainer in Forgery, had explained it. A Forger wasn't a simple scam artist or trickster. A Forger was an artist who painted with human perception.

Any grime-covered urchin on the street could scam someone. A Forger sought loftier heights. Common scammers worked by pulling a cloth over someone's eyes, then fleeing before realization hit. A Forger had to create something so perfect, so beautiful, so *real* that its witnesses never questioned.

A person was like a dense forest thicket, overgrown with a twisting mess of vines, weeds, shrubs, saplings, and flowers. No person was one single emotion; no person had only one desire. They had many, and usually those desires conflicted with one another like two rosebushes fighting for the same patch of ground.

Respect the people you lie to, Tao had taught her. Steal from them long enough, and you will begin to understand them.

Shai crafted a book as she worked, a true history of Emperor Ashravan's life. It would become a truer history than those his scribes had written to glorify him, a truer history even than the one written by his own hand. Shai slowly pieced together the puzzle, crawling into the thicket that had been Ashravan's mind.

He *had* been idealistic, as Gaotona said. She saw it now in the cautious worry of his early writings and in the way he had treated his servants. The empire was not a terrible thing. Neither was it a wonderful thing. The empire simply *was*. The people suffered its rule because they were comfortable with its little tyrannies. Corruption was inevitable. You lived with it. It was either that or accept the chaos of the unknown.

Grands were treated with extreme favoritism. Entering government service, the most lucrative and prestigious of occupations, was often more about bribes and connections than it was about skill or aptitude. In addition, some of those who best served the empire—merchants and laborers—were systematically robbed by a hundred hands in their pockets.

Everyone knew these things. Ashravan had wanted to change them. At first.

And then . . . Well, there hadn't been a specific *and then*. Poets would point to a single flaw in Ashravan's nature that had led him to failure, but a person was no more one flaw than they were one passion. If Shai based her Forgery on any single attribute, she would create a mockery, not a man.

But . . . was that the best she could hope for? Perhaps she should try for authenticity in one specific setting, making an emperor who could act properly in court, but could not fool those closest to him. Perhaps that would work well enough, like the stage props from a playhouse. Those served their purpose while the play was going, but failed serious inspection.

That was an achievable goal. Perhaps she should go to the arbiters, explain what was possible, and give them a lesser emperor—a puppet they could use at official functions, then whisk away with explanations that he was growing sickly.

She could do that.

She found that she didn't want to.

That wasn't the challenge. That was the street thief's version of a scam, intended for short-term gain. The Forger's way was to create something enduring.

Deep down, she was thrilled by the challenge. She found that she *wanted* to make Ashravan live. She wanted to try, at least.

Shai lay back on her bed, which by now she had Forged to something more comfortable, with posts and a deep comforter. She kept the curtains drawn. Her guards for the evening played a round of cards at her table.

Why do you care about making Ashravan live? Shai thought to herself. *The arbiters will kill you before you can even see if this works. Escape should be your only goal.*

And yet . . . the *emperor* himself. She had chosen to steal the Moon Scepter because it was the most famous piece in the empire. She had wanted one of her works to be on display in the grand Imperial Gallery.

This task she now worked on, however . . . this was something far greater. What Forger had accomplished such a feat? A Forgery, sitting on the Rose Throne *itself*?

No, she told herself, more forceful this time. *Don't be lured. Pride, Shai. Don't let the pride drive you.*

She opened her book to the back pages, where she'd hidden her escape plans in a cipher, disguised to look like a dictionary of terms and people.

That Bloodsealer had come in running the other day, as if frightened that he'd be late to reset his seal. His clothing had smelled of strong drink. He was enjoying the palace's hospitality. If she could make him come early one morning, then ensure that he got extra drunk that night . . .

The mountains of the Strikers bordered Dzhamar, where the swamps of the Bloodsealers were located. Their hatred of one another ran deep, perhaps deeper than their loyalty to the empire. Several of the Strikers in particular seemed revolted when the Bloodsealer came. Shai had begun befriending those guards. Jokes in passing. Mentions of a coincidental similarity in her background and theirs. The Strikers weren't supposed to talk to Shai, but weeks had passed without Shai doing anything more than poring through books and chatting with old arbiters. The guards were bored, and boredom made people easy to manipulate.

Shai had access to plenty of soulstone, and she would use it. However, often more elementary methods were of greater use. People always expected a Forger to use seals for everything. Grands told stories of dark witchcraft, of Forgers placing seals on a person's feet while they slept, changing their personalities. Invading them, raping their minds.

The truth was that a soulstamp was often a Forger's last resort. It was too easy to detect. *Not that I wouldn't give my right hand for my Essence Marks right now . . .*

Almost, she was tempted to try carving a new Mark to use in getting away. They'd be expecting that, however, and she would have real trouble performing the hundreds of tests she'd need to do to make one work. Testing on her own arm would be reported by the guards, and testing on Gaotona would never work.

And using an Essence Mark she hadn't tested . . . well, that could go very, very poorly. No, her plans for escape would use soulstamps, but their heart would involve more traditional methods of subterfuge.

DAY FIFTY-EIGHT

S HAI was ready when Frava next visited.

The woman paused in the doorway, the guards shuffling out without objection as Captain Zu took their place. "You've been busy," Frava noted.

Shai looked up from her research. Frava wasn't referring to her progress, but to the room. Most recently, Shai had improved the floor. It hadn't been difficult. The rock used to build the palace—the quarry, the dates, the stonemasons—all were matters of historic record.

"You like it?" Shai asked. "The marble works well with the hearth, I think."

Frava turned, then blinked. "A *hearth*? Where did you . . . Is this room bigger than it was?"

"The storage room next door wasn't being used," Shai mumbled, turning back to her book. "And the division between these two rooms was recent, constructed only a few years back. I rewrote the construction so that this room was made the larger of the two, and so that a hearth was installed."

Frava seemed stunned. "I wouldn't have thought . . ." The woman looked back to Shai, and her face adopted its usual severe mask. "I find it difficult to believe that you are taking your duty seriously, Forger. You are here to make an emperor, not remodel the palace."

"Carving soulstone relaxes me," Shai said. "As does having a workspace that doesn't remind me of a closet. You will have your emperor's soul in time, Frava."

The arbiter stalked through the room, inspecting the desk. "Then you have begun the emperor's soulstone?"

"I've begun many of them," Shai said. "It will be a complex process. I've tested well over a hundred stamps on Gaotona—"

"*Arbiter* Gaotona."

"—on the old man. Each is only a tiny slice of the puzzle. Once I have all of the pieces working, I'll recarve them in smaller, more delicate etchings. That will allow me to combine about a dozen test stamps into one final stamp."

"But you said you'd tested over a hundred," Frava said, frowning. "You'll only use twelve of those in the end?"

Shai laughed. "Twelve? To Forge an entire *soul*? Hardly. The final stamp, the one you will need to use on the emperor each morning, will be like . . . a linchpin, or the keystone of an arch. It will be the only one that will need to be placed on his skin, but it will connect a lattice of hundreds of other stamps."

Shai reached to the side, taking out her book of notes, including initial sketches of the final stamps. "I'll take these and stamp them onto a metal plate, then link that to the stamp you will place on Ashravan each day. He'll need to keep the plate close at all times."

"He'll need to carry a metal plate with him," Frava said dryly, "*and* he will need to be stamped each day? This will make it difficult for the man to live a normal life, don't you think?"

"Being emperor makes it difficult for any man to live a normal life, I suspect. You will make it work. It's customary for the plate to be designed as a piece of adornment. A large medallion, perhaps, or an upper-arm bracer with square sides. If you look at my own Essence Marks, you'll notice they were done in the same way, and that the box contains a plate for each one." Shai hesitated. "That said, I've never done this exact thing before; no one has. There is a chance . . . and I'd say a fair one . . . that over time, the emperor's brain will absorb the information. Like . . . like if you traced the exact same image on a stack of papers every day for a year, at the end the layers below will contain the image as well. Perhaps after a few years of being stamped, he won't need the treatment any longer."

"I still name it egregious."

"Worse than being dead?" Shai asked.

Frava rested her hand on Shai's book of notes and half-finished sketches. Then she picked it up. "I will have our scribes copy this."

Shai stood up. "I need it."

"I'm sure you do," Frava said. "That is precisely why it should be copied, just in case."

"Copying it will take too long."

"I will have it back to you in a day," Frava said lightly, stepping away. Shai reached for her, and Captain Zu stepped up, sword already half out of its sheath.

Frava turned to him. "Now, now, Captain. That won't be needed. The Forger is protective of her work. That is good. It shows that she is invested."

Shai and Zu locked gazes. *He wants me dead,* Shai thought. *Badly.* She'd figured him out by now. Guarding the palace was his duty, one that Shai had invaded by her theft. Zu hadn't captured her; the Imperial Fool had turned her in. Zu felt insecure because of his failure, and so he wanted to remove Shai in retribution.

Shai eventually broke his gaze. Though it galled her, she needed to take the submissive side of this interaction. "Be careful," she warned Frava. "Do not let them lose even a single page."

"I will protect this as if . . . as if the emperor's life depended on it." Frava found her joke amusing, and she gave Shai a rare smile. "You have considered the other matter we discussed?"

"Yes."

"And?"

"Yes."

Frava's smile deepened. "We will talk again soon."

Frava left with the book, nearly two months' worth of work. Shai knew exactly what the woman was up to. Frava wasn't going to have it copied—she was going to show it to her other Forger and see if it was far enough along for him to finish the job.

If he determined that it was, Shai would be executed, quietly, before the other arbiters could object. Zu would likely do it himself. It could all end here.

DAY FIFTY-NINE

S HAI slept poorly that night.

She was certain that her preparations had been thorough. And yet now, she had to wait as if with a noose around her neck. It made her anxious. What if she'd misread the situation?

She had made her notations in the book intentionally opaque, each of them a subtle indication of just how *enormous* this project was. The cramped writing, the numerous cross-references, the lists and lists of reminders to herself of things to do . . . Each of these would work together with the thick book as a whole to indicate that her work was mind-breakingly complex.

It was a forgery. One of the most difficult types—a forgery that did not imitate a specific person or object. This was a forgery of *tone*.

Stay away, the tone of that book said. *You don't want to try to finish this. You want to let Shai continue to do the hard parts, because the work required to do it yourself would be enormous. And . . . if you fail . . . it will be your head on the line.*

That book was one of the most subtle forgeries she'd ever created. Each word in it was true and yet a lie at the same time. Only a master

Forger might see through it, might notice how hard she was working to illustrate the danger and difficulty of the project.

How skilled was Frava's Forger?

Would Shai be dead before morning?

She didn't sleep. She wanted to and she should have. Waiting out the hours, minutes, and seconds was excruciating. The thought of lying in bed asleep when they came for her . . . that was worse.

Eventually, she got up and retrieved some accounts of Ashravan's life. The guards playing cards at her table gave her a glance. One even nodded with sympathy at her red eyes and tired posture. "Light too bright?" he asked, gesturing at the lamp.

"No," Shai said. "Just a thought in my brain that won't get out."

She spent the night in bed pouring herself into Ashravan's life. Frustrated to be lacking her notes, she got out a fresh sheet and began some new ones she'd add to her book when it returned. If it did.

She felt that she finally understood why Ashravan had abandoned his youthful optimism. At least, she knew the factors that had combined to lead him down that path. Corruption was part of it, but not the main part. Again, lack of self-confidence contributed, but hadn't been the decisive factor.

No, Ashravan's downfall had been life itself. Life in the palace, life as part of an empire that clicked along like a clock. Everything worked. Oh, it didn't work as well as it might. But it *did* work.

Challenging that took effort, and effort was sometimes hard to muster. He had lived a life of leisure. Ashravan hadn't been lazy, but it didn't require laziness to be swept up in the workings of imperial bureaucracy—to tell yourself that next month you'd go and demand that your changes be made. Over time, it had become easier and easier to float along the course of the great river that was the Rose Empire.

In the end, he'd grown indulgent. He'd focused more on the beauty of his palace than on the lives of his subjects. He had allowed the arbiters to handle more and more government functions.

Shai sighed. Even that description of him was too simplistic. It neglected to mention *who* the emperor had been, and who he had become. A chronology of events didn't speak of his temper, his fondness for debate, his eye for beauty, or his habit of writing terrible, *terrible* poetry and then expecting all who served him to tell him how wonderful it was.

It also didn't speak of his arrogance, or his secret wish that he could have been something else. That was why he had gone back over his book again and again. Perhaps he had been looking for that branching point in his life where he had stepped down the wrong path.

He hadn't understood. There was rarely an obvious branching point in a person's life. People changed slowly, over time. You didn't take one step, then find yourself in a completely new location. You first took a little step off a path to avoid some rocks. For a while, you walked alongside the path, but then you wandered out a little way to step on softer soil. Then you stopped paying attention as you drifted farther and farther away. Finally, you found yourself in the wrong city, wondering why the signs on the roadway hadn't led you better.

The door to her room opened.

Shai bolted upright in her bed, nearly dropping her notes. They'd come for her.

But . . . no, it was *morning* already. Light trickled through the stained-glass window, and the guards were standing up and stretching. The one who had opened the door was the Bloodsealer. He looked hungover again, and carried a stack of papers in his hand, as he often did.

He's early this morning, Shai thought, checking her pocket watch. *Why early today, when he's late so often?*

The Bloodsealer cut her and stamped the door without a word, causing the pain to burn in Shai's arm. He hurried out of the room, as if off to some appointment. Shai stared after him, then shook her head.

A moment later, the door opened again and Frava entered.

"Oh, you're up," the woman said as the Strikers saluted her. Frava set Shai's book down on the table with a thump. She seemed annoyed. "The scribes are done. Get back to work."

Frava left in a bustle. Shai leaned back in her bed, sighing in relief. Her ruse had worked. That should earn her a few more weeks.

DAY SEVENTY

So this symbol," Gaotona said, pointing at one of her sketches of the greater stamps she would soon carve, "is a time notation, indicating a moment specifically . . . seven years ago?"

"Yes," Shai said, dusting off the end of a freshly carved soulstamp. "You learn quickly."

"I am undergoing surgery each day, so to speak," Gaotona said. "It makes me more comfortable to know the kinds of knives being used."

"The changes aren't—"

"Aren't permanent," he said. "Yes, so you keep saying." He stretched out his arm for her to stamp. "However, it makes me wonder. One can cut the body, and it will heal—but do it over and over again in the same spot, and you *will* scar. The soul cannot be so different."

"Except, of course, that it's *completely* different," Shai said, stamping his arm.

He had never quite forgiven her for what she had done in burning ShuXen's masterpiece. She could see it in him, when they interacted. He was no longer just disappointed in her, he was angry at her.

Anger faded with time, and they had a functional working relationship again.

Gaotona cocked his head. "I . . . Now *that* is odd."

"Odd in what way?" Shai asked, watching the seconds pass on her pocket watch.

"I remember encouraging *myself* to become emperor. And . . . and I resent myself. For . . . mother of light, is that really how he regarded me?"

The seal remained in place for fifty-seven seconds. Good enough. "Yes," she said as the seal faded away. "I believe that is exactly how he regarded you." She felt a thrill. *Finally* that seal had worked!

She was getting close now. Close to understanding the emperor, close to having the puzzle come together. Whenever she neared the end of a project—a painting, a large-scale soul Forgery, a sculpture—there came a moment in the process where she could *see* the entire work, even if it was far from finished. When that moment came, in her mind's eye, the work was complete; actually finishing it was almost a formality.

She was nearly there with this project. The emperor's soul spread out before her, with only some few corners still shadowed. She wanted to see it through; she *longed* to find out if she could make him live again. After reading so much about him, after coming to feel as if she knew him so well, she needed to finish.

Surely her escape could wait until then.

"That was it, wasn't it?" Gaotona asked. "That was the stamp that you've tried a dozen times without success, the seal representing why he stood up to become emperor."

"Yes," Shai said.

"His relationship with me," Gaotona said. "You made his decision depend upon his relationship with me, and . . . and the sense of shame he felt when speaking with me."

"Yes."

"And it took."

"Yes."

Gaotona sat back. "Mother of lights . . ." he whispered again.

Shai took the seal and put it with those that she had confirmed as workable.

Over the last few weeks, each of the other arbiters had done as Frava had, coming to Shai and offering her fantastic promises in exchange for giving them ultimate control of the emperor. Only Gaotona had never tried to bribe her. A genuine man, and one in the highest levels of imperial government no less. Remarkable. Using him was going to be far more difficult than she would have liked.

"I must say again," she said, turning to him, "you've impressed me. I don't think many Grands would take the time to study soulstamps. They would eschew what they considered evil without ever trying to understand it. You've changed your mind?"

"No," Gaotona said. "I still think that what you do is, if not evil, then certainly unholy. And yet, who am I to speak? I am depending upon you to preserve us in power by means of this art we so freely call an abomination. Our hunger for power outweighs our conscience."

"True for the others," Shai said, "but that is not your personal motive."

He raised an eyebrow at her.

"You just want Ashravan back," Shai said. "You refuse to accept that you've lost him. You loved him as a son—the youth that you mentored, the emperor you always believed in, even when he didn't believe in himself."

Gaotona looked away, looking decidedly uncomfortable.

"It won't be him," Shai said. "Even if I succeed, it won't *truly* be him. You realize this, of course."

He nodded.

"But then . . . sometimes a clever Forgery is as good as the real thing," Shai said. "You are of the Heritage Faction. You surround yourself with relics that aren't truly relics, paintings that are imitations of ones long lost. I suppose having a fake relic for an emperor won't be so different. And you . . . you just want to know that you've done everything you could. For him."

"How do you do it?" Gaotona asked softly. "I've seen how you speak with the guards, how you learn even the names of the servants. You seem to know their family lives, their passions, what they do in the evenings . . . and yet you spend each day locked in this room. You haven't left it for months. How do you know these things?"

"People," Shai said, rising to fetch another seal, "by nature attempt to exercise power over what is around them. We build walls to shelter us from the wind, roofs to stop the rain. We tame the elements, bend nature to our wills. It makes us feel as if we're in control.

"Except in doing so, we merely replace one influence with another. Instead of the wind affecting us, it is a wall. A *man-made* wall. The fingers of man's influence are all about, touching everything. Man-made rugs, man-made food. Every single thing in the city that we touch, see, feel, *experience* comes as the result of some person's influence.

"We may feel in control, but we never truly are unless we understand people. Controlling our environment is no longer about blocking the wind, it's about knowing why the serving lady was crying last night, or why a particular guard always loses at cards. Or why your employer hired you in the first place."

Gaotona looked back at her as she sat, then held out a seal to him. He hesitantly proffered an arm. "It occurs to me," he said, "that even in our extreme care not to do so, we have underestimated you, woman."

"Good," she said. "You're paying attention." She stamped him. "Now tell me, why exactly do you hate fish?"

DAY SEVENTY-SIX

I *NEED to do it*, Shai thought as the Bloodsealer cut her arm. *Today. I could go today.*

Hidden in her other sleeve, she carried a slip of paper made to imitate the ones that the Bloodsealer often brought with him on the mornings that he came early.

She'd caught sight of a bit of wax on one of them two days back. They were letters. Realization had dawned. She'd been wrong about this man all along.

"Good news?" she asked him as he inked his stamp with her blood.

The white-lipped man gave her a sneering glance.

"From home," Shai said. "The woman you're writing, back in Dzhamar. She sent you a letter today? Post comes in the mornings here at the palace. They knock at your door, deliver a letter . . ." *And that wakes you up*, she added in her mind. *That's why you come on time those days.* "You must miss her a lot if you can't bear to leave her letter behind in your room."

The man lowered his arm and grabbed Shai by the front of her shirt. "Leave her alone, witch," he hissed. "You . . . you *leave her alone!* None of your trickery or magics!"

He was younger than she had assumed. That was a common mistake with Dzhamarians. Their white hair and skin made them seem ageless to outsiders. Shai should have known better. He was little more than a youth.

She drew her lips to a line. "You talk about *my* trickery and magics while holding in your hands a seal inked with my blood? You're the one threatening to send skeletals to hunt me, friend. All I can do is polish the odd table."

"Just . . . just . . . Ah!" The young man threw his hands up, then stamped the door.

The guards watched with nonchalant amusement and disapproval. Shai's words had been a calculated reminder that she was harmless while the Bloodsealer was the *truly* unnatural one. The guards had spent nearly three months watching her tinker about as a friendly scholar while this man drew her blood and used it for arcane horrors.

I need to drop the paper, she thought to herself, lowering her sleeve, meaning to let her forgery slip out as the guards turned away. That would put her plan into motion, her escape . . .

The real Forgery isn't finished yet. The emperor's soul.

She hesitated. Foolishly, she hesitated.

The door closed.

The opportunity passed.

Feeling numb, Shai walked to her bed and sat down on its edge, the forged letter still hidden in her sleeve. Why had she hesitated? Were her instincts for self-preservation so weak?

I can wait a little longer, she told herself. *Until Ashravan's Essence Mark is done.*

She'd been saying that for days now. Weeks, really. Each day she got closer to the deadline was another chance for Frava to strike. The woman came back with other excuses to take Shai's notes and have them inspected. They were quickly approaching the point where the other Forger wouldn't have to sort through much in order to finish Shai's work.

At least, so he would think. The further she progressed, the more impossible she realized this project was. And the more she longed to make it work anyway.

She got out her book on the emperor's life and soon found herself looking back through his youthful years. The thought of him not living again, of all of her work being merely a sham intended to distract while she planned to escape . . . those thoughts were physically *painful*.

Nights, Shai thought at herself. *You've grown fond of him. You're starting to see him like Gaotona does!* She shouldn't feel that way. She'd never met him. Besides, he was a despicable person.

But he hadn't always been. No, in truth, he hadn't ever *truly* become despicable. He had been more complex than that. Every person was. She could understand him, she could see—

"Nights!" she said, standing up and putting the book aside. She needed to clear her mind.

When Gaotona came to the room six hours later, Shai was just pressing a seal against the far wall. The elderly man opened the door and stepped in, then froze as the wall flooded with color.

Vine patterns spiraled out from Shai's stamp like sprays of paint. Green, scarlet, amber. The painting grew like something alive, leaves springing from branches, bunches of fruit exploding in succulent bursts. Thicker and thicker the pattern grew, golden trim breaking out of nothing and running like streams, rimming leaves, reflecting light.

The mural deepened, every inch imbued with an illusion of movement. Curling vines, unexpected thorns peeking from behind branches. Gaotona breathed out in awe and stepped up beside Shai. Behind, Zu stepped in, and the other two guards left and closed the door.

Gaotona reached out and felt the wall, but of course the paint was dry. So far as the wall knew, it had been painted like this years ago. Gaotona knelt down, looking at the two seals Shai had placed at the base of the painting. Only the third one, stamped above, had set off the transformation; the early seals were notes on how the image was to be created. Guidelines, a revision of history, instructions.

"How?" Gaotona asked.

"One of the Strikers guarded Atsuko of JinDo during his visit to the Rose Palace," Shai said. "Atsuko caught a sickness, and was stuck in his bedroom for three weeks. That was just one floor up."

"Your Forgery puts him in this room instead?"

"Yes. That was before the water damage that seeped through the ceiling last year, so it's plausible he'd have been placed here. The wall remembers Atsuko spending days too weak to leave, but having the strength for painting. A little each day, a growing pattern of vines, leaves, and berries. To pass the time."

"This shouldn't be taking," Gaotona said. "This Forgery is tenuous. You've changed too much."

"No," Shai said. "It's on the line . . . that line where the greatest beauty is found." She put the seal away. She barely remembered the last six hours. She had been caught up in the frenzy of creation.

"Still . . ." Gaotona said.

"It will take," Shai said. "If you were the wall, what would you rather be? Dreary and dull, or alive with paint?"

"Walls can't think!"

"That doesn't stop them from caring."

Gaotona shook his head, muttering about superstition. "How long?"

"To create this soulstamp? I've been etching it here and there for the last month or so. It was the last thing I wanted to do for the room."

"The artist was JinDo," he said. "Perhaps, because you are from the same people, it . . . But no! That's thinking like your superstition." Gaotona shook his head, trying to figure out why that painting would have taken, though it had always been obvious to Shai that this one would work.

"The JinDo and my people are *not* the same, by the way," Shai said testily. "We may have been related long ago, but we are completely different from them now." Grands. Just because people had similar features, Grands assumed they were practically identical.

Gaotona looked across her chamber and its fine furniture that had been carved and polished. Its marble floor with silver inlay, the crackling hearth and small chandelier. A fine rug—it had once been a bed quilt with holes in it—covered the floor. The stained-glass window sparkled on the right wall, lighting the beautiful mural.

The only thing that retained its original form was the door, thick but unremarkable. She couldn't Forge that, not with that Bloodseal set into it.

"You realize that you now have the finest chamber in the palace," Gaotona said.

"I doubt that," Shai said with a sniff. "Surely the emperor's are the nicest."

"The largest, yes. Not the nicest." He knelt beside the painting, looking at her seals at the bottom. "You included detailed explanations of how this was painted."

"To create a realistic Forgery," Shai said, "you must have the technical skill you are imitating, at least to an extent."

"So you could have painted this wall yourself."

"I don't have the paints."

"But you *could* have. You could have demanded paints. I'd have given them to you. Instead, you created a Forgery."

"It's what I am," Shai said, growing annoyed at him again.

"It's what you choose to be. If a wall can desire to be a mural, Wan ShaiLu, then *you* could desire to become a great painter."

She slapped her stamp down on the table, then took a few deep breaths.

"You have a temper," Gaotona said. "Like him. Actually, I know exactly how that feels now, because you have given it to me on several occasions. I wonder if this . . . thing you do could be a tool for helping to bring awareness to people. Inscribe your emotions onto a stamp, then let others *feel* what it is to be you . . ."

"Sounds great," Shai said. "If only Forging souls weren't a horrible offense to nature."

"If only."

"If you can read those stamps, you've grown very good indeed," Shai said, pointedly changing the topic. "Almost I think you've been cheating."

"Actually . . ."

Shai perked up, banishing her anger, now that it had passed the initial flare-up. What was this?

Gaotona sheepishly reached into the deep pocket of his robe and withdrew a wooden box. The one where she kept her treasures, the five

Essence Marks. Those revisions of her soul could change her, in times of need, into someone she *could* have been.

Shai took a step forward, but when Gaotona opened the box, he revealed that the stamps weren't inside. "I'm sorry," he said. "But I think giving you these now would be a little . . . foolish on my part. It seems that any one of them could have you free from your captivity in a moment."

"Really only two of them could manage that," Shai said sourly, fingers twitching. Those soulstamps represented over eight years of her life's work. She'd started the first on the day she ended her apprenticeship.

"Hm, yes," Gaotona said. Inside the small box lay sheets of metal inscribed with the separate smaller stamps that made up the blueprints of the revisions to her soul. "This one, I believe?" He held up one of the sheets. "Shaizan. Translated . . . Shai of the Fist? This would make a warrior out of you, if you stamped yourself?"

"Yes," Shai said. So he'd been studying her Essence Marks; that was how he'd grown so good at reading her stamps.

"I understand only one-tenth of what is inscribed here, if that," Gaotona said. "What I find is impressive. Truly, these must have taken years to craft."

"They are . . . precious to me," Shai said, forcing herself to sit down at her desk and not fixate on the plates. If she could escape with those, she could craft a new stamp with ease. It would still take weeks, but most of her work would not be lost. But if those plates were to be destroyed . . .

Gaotona sat down in his customary chair, nonchalantly looking through the plates. From someone else, she would have felt an implied threat. *Look what I hold in my hands; look what I could do to you.* From Gaotona, however, that was not it. He was genuinely curious.

Or was he? As ever, she could not suppress her instincts. As good as she was, someone else could be better. Just as Uncle Won had warned. Could Gaotona have been playing her for a fool all along? She felt strongly she should trust her assessment of Gaotona. But if she was wrong, it could be a disaster.

It might be anyway, she thought. *You should have run days ago.*

"Turning yourself into a soldier I understand," Gaotona said, setting aside the plate. "And this one as well. A woodsman and survivalist. That one looks extremely versatile. Impressive. And here we have a scholar. But why? You are already a scholar."

"No woman can know everything," Shai said. "There is only so much time for study. When I stamp myself with that Essence Mark, I can suddenly speak a dozen languages, from Fen to Mulla'dil—even a few from Sycla. I know dozens of different cultures and how to move in them. I know science, mathematics, and the major political factions of the world."

"Ah," Gaotona said.

Just give them to me, she thought.

"But what of this?" Gaotona said. "A beggar? Why would you want to be emaciated, and . . . is this showing that most of your hair would fall out, that your skin would become scarred?"

"It changes my appearance," Shai said. "Drastically. That's useful." She didn't mention that in that aspect, she knew the ways of the streets and survival in a city underworld. Her lock-picking skills weren't too shabby when not bearing that seal, but with it, she was incomparable.

With that stamp on her, she could probably manage to climb out the tiny window—that Mark rewrote her past to give her years of experience as a contortionist—and climb the five stories down to freedom.

"I should have realized," Gaotona said. He lifted the final plate. "That just leaves this one, most baffling of all."

Shai said nothing.

"Cooking," he said. "Farm work, sewing. Another alias, I assume. For imitating a simpler person?"

"Yes."

Gaotona nodded, putting the sheet down.

Honesty. He must see my honesty. It cannot be faked.

"No," Shai said, sighing.

He looked to her.

"It's . . . my way out," she said. "I'll never use it. It's just there, if I want to."

"Way out?"

"If I ever use that," Shai said, "it will write over my years as a Forger. Everything. I will forget how to make the simplest of stamps; I will forget that I was even apprenticed as a Forger. I will become something normal."

"And you want that?"

"No."

A pause.

"Yes. Maybe. A part of me does."

Honesty. It was so difficult. Sometimes it was the only way.

She dreamed about that simple life, on occasion. In that morbid way that someone standing at the edge of a cliff wonders what it would be like to just jump off. The temptation is there, even if it's ridiculous.

A normal life. No hiding, no lying. She loved what she did. She loved the thrill, the accomplishment, the wonder. But sometimes . . . trapped in a prison cell or running for her life . . . sometimes she dreamed of something else.

"Your aunt and uncle?" he asked. "Uncle Won, Aunt Sol, they are parts of this revision. I've read it in here."

"They're fake," Shai whispered.

"But you quote them all the time."

She squeezed her eyes shut.

"I suspect," Gaotona said, "that a life full of lying makes reality and falsehood intermix. But if you were to use this stamp, surely you would not forget everything. How would you keep the sham from yourself?"

"It would be the greatest Forgery of all," Shai said. "One intended to fool even me. Written into that is the belief that without that stamp, applied every morning, I'll die. It includes a history of illness, of visiting a . . . resealer, as you call them. A healer that works in soulstamps. From them, my false self received a remedy, one I must apply each morning. Aunt Sol and Uncle Won would send me letters; that is part of the charade to fool myself. I've written them already. Hundreds, which—before I use the Essence Mark on myself—I will pay a delivery service good money to send periodically."

"But what if you try to visit them?" Gaotona said. "To investigate your childhood . . ."

"It's all in the plate. I will be afraid of travel. There's truth to that, as I was indeed scared of leaving my village as a youth. Once that Mark is in place, I'll stay away from cities. I'll think the trip to visit my relatives is too dangerous. But it doesn't matter. I'll never use it."

That stamp would end her. She would forget the last twenty years, back to when she was eight and had first begun inquiring about becoming a Forger.

She'd become someone else entirely. None of the other Essence Marks did that; they rewrote some of her past, but left her with a knowledge of who she truly was. Not so with the last one. That one was to be final. It terrified her.

"This is a great deal of work for something you'll never use," Gaotona said.

"Sometimes, that is the way of life."

Gaotona shook his head.

"I was hired to destroy the painting," Shai blurted out.

She wasn't quite certain what drove her to say it. She needed to be honest with Gaotona—that was the only way her plan would work—but he didn't need this piece. Did he?

Gaotona looked up.

"ShuXen hired me to destroy Frava's painting," Shai said. "That's why I burned the masterpiece, rather than sneaking it out of the gallery."

"ShuXen? But . . . he's the original artist! Why would *he* hire you to destroy one of his works?"

"Because he hates the empire," Shai said. "He painted that piece for a woman he loved. Her children gave it to the empire as a gift. ShuXen is old now, blind, barely able to move. He did not want to go to his grave knowing that one of his works was serving to glorify the Rose Empire. He begged me to burn it."

Gaotona seemed dumbfounded. He looked at her, as if trying to pierce through to her soul. Shai didn't know why he needed to bother; this conversation had already stripped her thoroughly bare.

"A master of his caliber is hard to imitate," Shai said, "particularly without the original to work from. If you think about it, you'll realize I

needed his help to create those fakes. He gave me access to his studies
and concepts; he told me how he'd gone about painting it. He coached
me through the brushstrokes."

"Why not just have you return the original to him?" Gaotona asked.

"He's dying," Shai said. "Owning a thing is meaningless to him. That
painting was done for a lover. She is gone now, so he felt the painting
should be as well."

"A priceless treasure," Gaotona said. "Gone because of foolish pride."

"It was *his* work!"

"Not any longer," Gaotona said. "It belonged to everyone who saw it.
You should not have agreed to this. Destroying a work of art like that is
never right." He hesitated. "But still, I think I can understand. What
you did had a nobility to it. Your goal was the Moon Scepter. Exposing
yourself to destroy that painting was dangerous."

"ShuXen tutored me in painting as a youth," she said. "I could not
deny his request."

Gaotona did not seem to agree, but he did seem to understand.
Nights, but Shai felt exposed.

This is important to do, she told herself. *And maybe . . .*

But he did not give her the plates back. She hadn't expected him to,
not now. Not until their agreement was done—an agreement she was
certain she would not live to see the end of, unless she escaped.

They worked through the last group of new stamps. Each one took
for at least a minute, as she'd been almost certain they would. She had
the vision now, the idea of the final soul as it would be. Once she finished the sixth stamp for the day, Gaotona waited for the next.

"That's it," Shai said.

"All for today?"

"All forever," Shai said, tucking away the last of the stamps.

"You're done?" Gaotona asked, sitting up straight. "Almost a month
early! It's—"

"I'm *not* done," Shai said. "Now is the most difficult part. I have to
carve those several hundred stamps in tiny detail, melding them together, then create a linchpin stamp. What I've done so far is like getting

all of the paints ready, creating the color and figure studies. Now I have to put it all together. The last time I did this, it took the better part of five months."

"And you have only twenty-four days."

"And I have only twenty-four days," Shai said, but felt an immediate stab of guilt. She *had* to run. Soon. She couldn't wait to finish the project.

"Then I will leave you to it," Gaotona said, standing and rolling down his sleeve.

DAY EIGHTY-FIVE

YES, Shai thought, scrambling along the side of her bed and rifling through her stack of papers there. The table wasn't big enough. She'd pulled her sheets tight and turned the bed into a place to set all of her stacks. *Yes, his first love was from the storybook.* That was why . . . Kurshina's red hair . . . But this would be subconscious. He wouldn't know it. Embedded deeply, then.

How had she missed that? She wasn't nearly as close to being done as she'd thought. There wasn't time!

Shai added what she'd discovered to the seal she was working on, one that combined all of the various parts of Ashravan's romantic inclinations and experiences. She included it all: the embarrassing, the shameful, the glorious. Everything she'd been able to discover, and then a little bit more, calculated risks to fill out the soul. A flirtatious encounter with a woman whose name Ashravan could not recall. Idle fancies. A near affair with a woman now dead.

This was the most difficult part of the soul for Shai to imitate, for it was the most private. Little an emperor did was ever truly secret, but Ashravan had not always been emperor.

She had to extrapolate, lest she leave the soul bare, without passion.

So private, so *powerful*. She felt closest to Ashravan as she teased out these details. Not as a voyeur; by this point, she was a part of him.

She kept two books now. The formal notes of her process said she was horribly behind; that book left out details. The other book was her true one, disguised as useless piles of notes, random and haphazard.

She really was behind, but not so far as her official documentation showed. Hopefully, that subterfuge would earn her a few extra days before Frava struck.

As Shai searched for a specific note, she ran across one of her lists for escape plans. She hesitated. *First, deal with the seal on the door,* the note read in cipher. *Second, silence the guards. Third, recover your Essence Marks, if possible. Fourth, escape the palace. Fifth, escape the city.*

She'd written further notes for the execution of each step. She wasn't ignoring the escape, not completely. She had good plans.

Her frantic attempt to finish the soul, however, drew most of her attention. *One more week,* she told herself. *If I take one more week, I will finish five days before the deadline. Then I can run.*

DAY NINETY-SEVEN

H EY," Hurli said, bending down. "What's this?"

Hurli was a brawny Striker who acted dumber than he was. It let him win at cards. He had two children—girls, both under the age of five—but was seeing one of the women guards on the side. Hurli secretly wished he could have been a carpenter like his father. He also would have been horrified if he'd realized how much Shai knew about him.

He held up the sheet of paper he'd found on the ground. The Blood-sealer had just left. It was the morning of the ninety-sixth day of Shai's captivity in the room, and she'd decided to put the plan into motion. She *had* to get out.

The emperor's seal was not yet finished. *Almost.* One more night's work, and she'd have it. Her plan required one more night of waiting anyway.

"Weedfingers must have dropped it," Yil said, walking over. She was the other guard in the room this morning.

"What is it?" Shai asked from the desk.

"Letter," Hurli said with a grunt.

Both guards fell silent as they read. Palace Strikers were all literate. It was required of any imperial civil servant of at least the second reed.

Shai sat quietly, tense, sipping a cup of lemon tea and forcing herself to breathe calmly. She made herself relax even though relaxing was the last thing she wanted to do. Shai knew the letter's contents by heart. She'd written it, after all, then had dropped it covertly behind the Bloodsealer as he'd rushed out moments ago.

Brother, the letter read. *I have almost completed my task here, and the wealth I have earned will rival even that of Azalec after his work in the Southern Provinces. The captive I secure is hardly worth the effort, but who am I to question the reasoning of people paying me far too much money?*

I will return to you shortly. I am proud to say that my other mission here has been a success. I have identified several capable warriors, and have gathered sufficient samples from them. Hair, fingernails, and a few personal effects that will not be missed. I feel confident that we will have our personal guards very soon.

It went on, the writing covering both the front and the back, so that it didn't look suspicious. Shai had padded it with a lot of talk about the palace, including things that others would assume that Shai didn't know but that the Bloodsealer would.

Shai worried that the letter was too overt. Would the guards find it to be an obvious forgery?

"That KuNuKam," Yil whispered, using a native word of theirs. It roughly translated as a man who had an anus for a mouth. "That imperial KuNuKam!"

Apparently, they believed it really was from him. Subtlety could be lost on soldiers.

"Can I see it?" Shai asked.

Hurli held it out to her. "Is he saying what I think?" the guard asked. "He's been . . . *gathering* things from us?"

"It might not mean the Strikers," Shai said after reading the letter. "He doesn't say."

"Why would he want hair?" Yil asked. "And fingernails?"

"They can do things with pieces of you," Hurli said, then cursed again. "You see what he does each day on the door with Shai's blood."

"I don't know if he could do much with hair or fingernails," Shai said skeptically. "This is just bravado. Blood needs to be fresh, not more than a day old, for it to work in his stamps. He's bragging to his brother."

"He shouldn't be doing things like that," Hurli said.

"I wouldn't worry about it," Shai said.

The other two shared looks. In a few minutes, the guard change occurred. Hurli and Yil left, muttering to one another, the letter shoved in Hurli's pocket. They weren't likely to hurt the Bloodsealer badly. Threaten him, yes.

The Bloodsealer was known to frequent teahouses in the area each evening. Almost she felt sorry for the man. She had deduced that when he got news from home, he was quick and punctual to her door. He sometimes looked excited. When he didn't get news, he drank. This morning, he had looked sad. No news in a while, then.

What happened to him tonight would not make his day any better. Yes, Shai almost felt sorry for him, but then she remembered the seal on the door and the bandage she'd tied on her arm after he'd drawn blood today.

As soon as the guard change was accomplished, Shai took a deep breath, then dug back into her work.

Tonight. Tonight, she would finish.

DAY NINETY-EIGHT

SHAI knelt on the floor amid a pattern of scattered pages, each filled with cramped script or drawings of seals. Behind her, morning opened her eyes, and sunlight seeped through the stained-glass window, spraying the room with crimson, blue, violet.

A single soulstamp, carved from polished stone, rested facedown on a metal plate sitting before her. Soulstone, as a rock, looked not unlike soapstone or another fine-grained stone, but with bits of red mixed in. As if drops of blood had stained it.

Shai blinked tired eyes. Was she really going to try to escape? She'd had . . . what? Four hours of sleep in the last three days combined?

Surely escape could wait. Surely she could rest, just for today.

Rest, she thought numbly, *and I will not wake.*

She remained in place, kneeling. That stamp seemed the most beautiful thing she had ever seen.

Her ancestors had worshipped rocks that fell from the sky at night. The souls of broken gods, those chunks had been called. Master craftsmen would carve them to bring out the shape. Once, Shai had found that foolish. Why worship something you yourself created?

Kneeling before her masterpiece, she understood. She felt as if she'd bled everything into that stamp. She had pressed two years' worth of effort into three months, then had topped it off with a night of desperate, frantic carving. During that night, she'd made changes to her notes, to the soul itself. Drastic changes. She still didn't know if they had been provoked by her final, awesome vision of the project as a whole . . . or if those changes had instead been faulty ideas born of fatigue and delusion.

She wouldn't know until the stamp was used.

"Is it . . . is it done?" asked one of her guards. The two of them had moved to the far edge of the room, to sit beside the hearth and give her room on the floor. She vaguely remembered shoving aside the furniture. She'd spent part of the time pulling stacks of paper out from their place beneath the bed, then crawling under to fetch others.

Was it done?

Shai nodded.

"What is it?" the guard asked.

Nights, she thought. *That's right. They don't even know.* The common guards left each day during her conversations with Gaotona.

The poor Strikers would probably find themselves assigned to some remote outpost of the empire for the rest of their lives, guarding the passes leading down to the distant Teoish Peninsula or the like. They would be quietly brushed under the rug to keep them from revealing, even accidentally, anything of what had happened here.

"Ask Gaotona if you want to know," Shai said softly. "I am not allowed to say."

Shai reverently picked up the seal, then placed both it and its plate inside a box she had prepared. The stamp nestled in red velvet, the plate—shaped like a large, thin medallion—in an indentation underneath the lid. She closed the lid, then pulled over a second, slightly larger box. Inside lay five seals, carved and prepared for her upcoming escape. If she managed it. Two of them she'd already used.

If she could just sleep for a few hours. Just a few . . .

No. I can't use the bed anyway.

Curling up on the floor sounded wonderful, however.

The door began to open. Shai felt a sudden, striking moment of panic.

Was it the Bloodsealer? He was supposed to be stuck in bed, having drunk himself to a stupor after being roughed up by the Strikers!

For a moment, she felt a strange guilty sense of relief. If the Bloodsealer had come, she wouldn't have a chance to escape today. She could sleep. Had Hurli and Yil not thrashed him? Shai had been sure that she'd read them correctly, and . . .

. . . and, in her fatigue, she realized she'd been jumping to conclusions. The door opened all the way, and someone did enter, but it was not the Bloodsealer.

It was Captain Zu.

"Out," he barked at the two guards.

They jumped into motion.

"In fact," Zu said, "you're relieved for the day. I'll watch until the shift changes."

The two saluted and left. Shai felt like a wounded elk being abandoned by the herd. The door clicked closed, and Zu slowly, deliberately, turned to look at her.

"The stamp isn't ready yet," Shai lied. "So you can—"

"It doesn't need to be ready," Zu said, smiling a wide, thick-lipped smile. "I believe I promised you something three months ago, thief. We have an . . . unsettled debt."

The room was dim, her lamp having burned low and morning only just breaking. Shai backed away from him, quickly revising her plans. This *wasn't* how it was supposed to go. She couldn't fight Zu.

Her mouth kept moving, keeping him distracted but also playing a part she devised for herself on the fly. "When Frava finds out you came here," Shai said, "she will be furious."

Zu drew his sword.

"Nights!" Shai said, backing up to her bed. "Zu, you don't need to do this. You *can't* do this. I have work that needs to be done!"

"Another will complete your work," Zu said, leering. "Frava has another Forger. You think you're so clever. You probably have some wonderful escape planned for tomorrow. This time, we're striking first. You didn't anticipate *this*, did you, liar? I'm going to enjoy killing you. Enjoy it so much."

He lunged with the sword, its tip catching her blouse and ripping a line through it at her side. Shai jumped away, shouting for help. She was still playing the part, but it did not require acting. Her heart thumped, panic rising, as she rounded the bed in a scramble, putting it between herself and Zu.

He smiled broadly, then jumped for her, leaping onto the bed.

It promptly collapsed. During the night, while crawling under the bed to get her notes, she had Forged the wood of the frame to have deep flaws, attacked by insects, making it fragile. She'd cut the mattress underneath in wide slashes.

Zu barely had time to shout as the bed broke completely away, crashing into the pit she'd opened in the floor below. The water damage to her room—the mildew she'd smelled when first entering—had been key. By reports, the wooden beams above would have rotted and the ceiling would have fallen in if they hadn't located the leak as quickly as they had. A simple Forgery, very plausible, made it so that the floor *had* fallen in.

Zu crashed into the empty storage room one story down. Shai stood puffing, then peered into the hole. The man lay among the broken remnants of the bed. Some of that had been stuffing and cushioning. He would probably live—she'd been intending this trap for one of the regular guards, of whom she was fond.

Not exactly how I planned it, she thought, *but workable.*

Shai rushed to the table and gathered her things. The box of stamps, the emperor's soul, some extra soulstone and ink. And the two books explaining the stamps she had created in deep complexity—the official one, and the true one.

She tossed the official one into the hearth as she passed. Then she stopped in front of the door, counting heartbeats.

She agonized, watching the Bloodsealer's mark as it pulsed. Finally, after a few tormenting minutes, the seal on the door flashed one last time . . . then faded. The Bloodsealer had not returned in time to renew it.

Freedom.

Shai burst out into the hallway, abandoning her home of the last three months, a room now trimmed in gold and silver. The hallway outside had been so near, yet it felt like another country entirely. She pressed the third of her prepared stamps against her buttoned blouse, changing it to match that of the palace servants, with official insignia embroidered on the left breast.

She had little time to make her next move. Soon, either the Bloodsealer would make his way to her room, Zu would wake from his fall, or the guards would arrive for the shift change. Shai wanted to run down the hallway, breaking for the palace stables.

She did not. Running implied one of two things—guilt or an important task. Either would be memorable. Instead, she kept her gait to a swift walk and adopted the expression of one who knew what she was doing, and so should not be interrupted.

She soon entered the better-used sections of the enormous palace. No one stopped her. At a certain carpeted intersection, she stopped herself.

To the right, down a long hallway, lay the entrance to the emperor's chambers. The seal she carried in her right hand, boxed and cushioned, seemed to leap in her fingers. Why hadn't she left it in the room for Gaotona to discover? The arbiters would hunt her less assiduously if they had the seal.

She could just leave it here, in this hallway lined with portraits of ancient rulers and cluttered with Forged urns from ancient eras.

No. She had brought it with her for a reason. She'd prepared tools to get into the emperor's chambers. She'd known all along this was what she would do.

If she left now, she'd never *truly* know if the seal worked. That would be like building a house, then never stepping inside. Like forging a sword, and never giving it a swing. Like crafting a masterpiece of art, then locking it away to never be seen again.

Shai started down the long hallway.

As soon as no one was directly in sight, she turned over one of those horrid urns and broke the seal on the bottom. It transformed back into a blank clay version of itself.

She'd had plenty of time to find out exactly where these urns were crafted and by whom. The fourth of her prepared stamps transformed the urn into a replica of an ornate golden chamber pot. Shai strode down the hallway to the emperor's quarters, then nodded to the guards, chamber pot under her arm.

"I don't recognize you," one guard said. She didn't recognize him either, with that scarred face and squinty look. As she'd expected. The guards set to watching her had been kept separate from the others so they couldn't talk about their duties.

"Oh," Shai said, fumbling, looking abashed. "I am sorry, greater one. I was only assigned this task this morning." She blushed, fishing out of her pocket a small square of thick paper, marked with Gaotona's seal and signature. She had forged both the old-fashioned way. Very convenient, how he'd let her tell him how to maintain security on the emperor's rooms.

She got through without any further difficulty. The next three rooms of the emperor's expansive chambers were empty. Beyond them was a locked door. She had to Forge the wood of that door into some that had been damaged by insects—using the same stamp she'd used on her bed—to get through. It didn't take for long, but a few seconds was enough for her to kick the door open.

Inside, she found the emperor's bedroom. It was the same place she'd been led on that first day when she'd been offered this chance. The room was empty save for him, lying in that bed. He was awake, but stared sightlessly at the ceiling.

The room was still. Quiet. It smelled . . . too clean. Too white. Like a blank canvas.

Shai walked up to the side of the bed. Ashravan didn't look at her. His eyes didn't move. She rested fingers on his shoulder. He had a handsome face, though he was some fifteen years her senior. That was not much for a Grand; they lived longer than most.

His was a strong face, despite his long time abed. Golden hair, a firm chin, a nose that was prominent. So different in features from Shai's people.

"I know your soul," Shai said softly. "I know it better than you ever did."

No alarm yet. Shai continued to expect one any moment, but she knelt down beside the bed anyway. "I wish that I could know you. Not your soul, but *you*. I've read about you; I've seen into your heart. I've rebuilt your soul, as best I could. But that isn't the same. It isn't knowing someone, is it? That's knowing *about* someone."

Was that a cry outside, from a distant part of the palace?

"I don't ask much of you," she said softly. "Just that you live. Just that you *be*. I've done what I can. Let it be enough."

She took a deep breath, then opened the box and took out his Essence Mark. She inked it, then pulled up his shirt, exposing the upper arm.

Shai hesitated, then pressed the stamp down. It hit flesh, and stayed frozen for a moment, as stamps always did. The skin and muscle didn't give way until a second later, when the stamp *sank* a fraction of an inch.

She twisted the stamp, locking it in, and pulled it back. The bright red seal glowed faintly.

Ashravan blinked.

Shai rose and stepped back as he sat up and looked around. Silently, she counted.

"My rooms," Ashravan said. "What happened? There was an attack. I was . . . I was wounded. Oh, mother of lights. Kurshina. She's dead."

His face became a mask of grief, but he covered it a second later. He was emperor. He might have a temper, but so long as he was not enraged, he was good at covering what he felt. He turned to her, and living eyes—eyes that *saw*—focused on her. "Who are you?"

The question twisted her insides, for all the fact that she'd expected it.

"I'm a kind of surgeon," Shai said. "You were wounded badly. I have healed you. However, what I used to do so is considered . . . unsavory by some parts of your culture."

"You're a resealer," he said. "A . . . a Forger?"

"In a way," Shai said. He would believe that because he wanted to. "This was a difficult type of resealing. You will have to be stamped each day, and you must keep that metal plate—the one shaped like a disc in that box—with you at all times. Without these, you die, Ashravan."

"Give it to me," he said, holding his hand out for the stamp.

She hesitated. She wasn't certain why.

"Give it to me," he said, more forceful.

She placed the stamp in his hand.

"Don't tell anyone what has happened here," she said to him. "Neither guards nor servants. Only your arbiters know of what I have done."

The cries outside sounded louder. Ashravan looked toward them. "If no one is to know," he said, "you must go. Leave this place and do not return." He looked down at the seal. "I should probably have you killed for knowing my secret."

That was the selfishness he'd learned during his years in the palace. Yes, she'd gotten that right.

"But you won't," she said.

"I won't."

And there was the mercy, buried deeply.

"Go before I change my mind," he said.

She took one step toward the doorway, then checked her pocket watch—well over a minute. The stamp had taken, at least for the short term. She turned and looked at him.

"What are you waiting for?" he demanded.

"I just wanted one more glimpse," she said.

He frowned.

The shouts grew even louder.

"Go," he said. "Please." He seemed to know what those shouts were about, or at least he could guess.

"Do better this time," Shai said. "Please."

With that, she fled.

She had been tempted, for a time, to write into him a desire to protect her. There would have been no good reason for it, at least in his eyes, and it might have undermined the entire Forgery. Beyond that, she didn't believe that he *could* save her. Until his period of mourning was through, he could not leave his quarters or speak to anyone other than his arbiters. During that time, the arbiters ran the empire.

They practically ran it anyway. No, a hasty revision of Ashravan's soul to protect her would not have worked. Near the last door out, Shai picked up her fake chamber pot. She hefted it, then stumbled through the doors. She gasped audibly at the distant cries.

"Is that about *me*?" Shai cried. "Nights! I didn't mean it! I know I wasn't supposed to see him. I know he's in seclusion, but I opened the wrong door!"

The guards stared at her, then one relaxed. "It isn't you. Find your quarters and stay there."

Shai bobbed a bow and hastened away. Most of the guards didn't know her, and so—

She felt a sharp pain at her side. She gasped. That pain felt like it did each morning, when the Bloodsealer stamped the door.

Panicked, Shai felt at her side. The cut in her blouse—where Zu had slashed her with his sword—had gone all the way through her dark undershirt! When her fingers came back, they had a couple of drops of blood on them. Just a nick, nothing dangerous. In the scramble, she hadn't even noticed she'd been cut.

But the tip of Zu's sword . . . it had her blood on it. Fresh blood. The Bloodsealer had found that and had begun the hunt. That pain meant he was locating her, was attuning his pets to her.

Shai tossed the urn aside and started running.

Staying hidden was no longer a consideration. Remaining unremarkable was pointless. If the Bloodsealer's skeletals reached her, she'd die. That was it. She had to reach a horse soon, then stay ahead of the skeletals for twenty-four hours, until her blood grew stale.

Shai dashed through the hallways. Servants began pointing, others screamed. She almost bowled over a southern ambassador in red priest's armor.

Shai cursed, bolting around the man. The palace exits would be locked down by now. She *knew* that. She'd studied the security. Getting out would be nearly impossible.

Always have a backup, Uncle Won said.

She always did.

Shai stopped in the hallway, and determined—as she should have earlier—that running for the exits was pointless. She was in a near panic, with the Bloodsealer on her trail, but she *had* to think clearly.

Backup plan. Hers was a desperate one, but it was all she had. She started running again, skidding around a corner, doubling back the way she'd just come.

Nights, let me have guessed right about him, she thought. *If he's secretly a master charlatan beyond my skill, I am doomed. Oh, Unknown God, please. This time, let me be right.*

Heart racing, fatigue forgotten in the moment, she eventually skidded to a stop in the hallway leading to the emperor's rooms.

There she waited. The guards inspected her, frowning, but held their posts at the end of the hallway as they'd been trained. They called to her. It was hard to keep from moving. That Bloodsealer was getting closer and closer with his horrible pets . . .

"Why are you here?" a voice said.

Shai turned as Gaotona stepped into the hallway. He'd come for the emperor first. The others would search for Shai, but Gaotona would come for the emperor, to be certain he was safe.

Shai stepped up to him, anxious. *This,* she thought, *is probably my worst idea ever for a backup plan.*

"It worked," she said softly.

"You tried the stamp?" Gaotona said, taking her arm and glancing at the guards, then pulling her aside well out of earshot. "Of all the hasty, insane, foolish—"

"It *worked*, Gaotona," Shai said.

"Why did you come to him? Why not run while you had the chance?"

"I had to know. I *had* to."

He looked at her, meeting her eyes. Seeing through them, into her soul, as he always did. Nights, but he would have made a wonderful Forger.

"The Bloodsealer has your trail," Gaotona said. "He has summoned those . . . *things* to catch you."

"I know."

Gaotona hesitated for only a moment, then brought out a wooden box from his voluminous pockets. Shai's heart leaped.

He handed it toward her, and she took it with one hand, but he did not let go. "You knew I'd come here," Gaotona said. "You knew I'd have these, and that I'd give them to you. I've been played for a fool."

Shai said nothing.

"How did you do it?" he asked. "I thought I watched you carefully. I was *certain* I had not been manipulated. And yet I ran here, half knowing I'd find you. Knowing you'd need these. I *still* didn't realize until this very moment that you'd probably planned all of this."

"I did manipulate you, Gaotona," she admitted. "But I had to do it in the most difficult way possible."

"Which was?"

"By being genuine," she replied.

"You can't manipulate people by being genuine."

"You can't?" Shai asked. "Is that not how you've made your entire career? Speaking honestly, teaching people what to expect of you, then expecting them to be honest to you in return?"

"It's not the same thing."

"No," she said. "It's not. But it was the best I could manage. Everything I've said to you is true, Gaotona. The painting I destroyed, the secrets about my life and desires . . . Being genuine. It was the only way to get you on my side."

"I'm not on your side." He paused. "But I don't want you killed either, girl. Particularly not by those *things*. Take these. Days! Take them and go, before I change my mind."

"Thank you," she whispered, pulling the box to her breast. She fished in her skirt pocket and brought out a small, thick book. "Keep this safe," she said. "Show it to no one."

He took it hesitantly. "What is it?"

"The truth," she said, then leaned in and kissed him on the cheek. "If I escape, I will change my final Essence Mark. The one I never intend to use . . . I will add to it, and to my memories, a kindly grandfather who saved my life. A man of wisdom and compassion whom I respected very much."

"Go, fool girl," he said. He actually had a tear in his eye. If she hadn't been on the very edge of panic, she'd have felt proud of that. And ashamed of her pride. That was how she was.

"Ashravan lives," she said. "When you think of me, remember that. It *worked*. Nights, it *worked*!"

She left him, dashing down the corridor.

Gaotona listened to the girl go, but did not turn to watch her flee. He stared at that door to the emperor's chambers. Two confused guards, and a passage into . . . what?

The future of the Rose Empire.

We will be led by someone not truly alive, Gaotona thought. *The fruits of our foul labors.*

He took a deep breath, then walked past the guards and pushed open the doors to go and look upon the thing he had wrought.

Just . . . please, let it not be a monster.

Shai strode down the palace hallway, holding the box of seals. She ripped off her buttoned blouse—revealing the tight, black cotton shirt she wore underneath—and tucked it into her pocket. She left on her skirt and the leggings beneath. It wasn't so different from the clothing she'd trained in.

Servants scattered around her. They knew, just from her posture, to get out of the way. Suddenly, Shai felt more confident than she had in years.

She had her soul back. All of it.

She took out one of her Essence Marks as she walked. She inked it with bold strikes and returned the box of seals to her skirt pocket. Then, she slammed the seal against her right bicep and locked it into place, rewriting her history, her memories, her life experience.

In that fraction of a moment, she remembered both histories. She remembered two years spent locked away, planning, creating the Essence Mark. She remembered a lifetime of being a Forger.

At the same time, she remembered spending the last fifteen years among the Teullu people. They had adopted her and trained her in their martial arts.

Two places at once, two timelines at once.

Then the former faded, and she became Shaizan, the name the Teullu had given her. Her body became leaner, harder. The body of a warrior. She slipped off her spectacles. Her eyes had been healed long ago, and she didn't need those any longer.

Gaining access to the Teullu training had been difficult; they did not like outsiders. She'd nearly been killed by them a dozen different times during her year training. But she had succeeded.

She lost all knowledge of how to create stamps, all sense of scholarly inclination. She was still herself, and she remembered her immediate past—being captured, forced to sit in that cell. She retained knowledge—logically—of what she'd just done with the stamp to her arm, and knew that the life she now remembered was fake.

But she didn't *feel* that it was. As that seal burned on her arm, she became the version of herself that would have existed if she'd been adopted by a harsh warrior culture and lived among them for well over a decade.

She kicked off her shoes. Her hair shortened; a scar stretched from her nose down around her right cheek. She walked like a warrior, prowling instead of striding.

She reached the servants' section of the palace just before the stables, the Imperial Gallery to her left.

A door opened in front of her. Zu, tall and wide-lipped, pushed through. He had a gash on his forehead—blood seeped through the bandage there—and his clothing had been torn by his fall.

He had a tempest in his eyes. He sneered as he saw her. "You've done it now. The Bloodsealer led us right to you. I'm going to enjoy—"

He cut off as Shaizan stepped forward in a blur and smacked the heel of her hand against his wrist, breaking it, knocking the sword from his fingers. She snapped her hand upward, chopping him in the throat. Then she curled her fingers into a fist and placed a tight, short, full-knuckled punch into his chest. Six ribs shattered.

Zu stumbled backward, gasping, eyes wide with absolute shock. His sword clanged to the ground. Shaizan stepped past him, pulling his knife from his belt and whipping it up to cut the tie on his cloak.

Zu toppled to the floor, leaving the cloak in her fingers.

Shai might have said something to him. Shaizan didn't have the patience for witticisms or gibes. A warrior kept moving, like a river. She didn't break stride as she whipped the cloak around and entered the hallway behind Zu.

He gasped for breath. He'd live, but he wouldn't hold a sword again for months.

Movement came from the end of the hallway: white-limbed creatures, too thin to be alive. Shaizan prepared herself with a wide stance, body turned to the side, facing down the hallway, knees slightly bent. It did not matter how many monstrosities the Bloodsealer had; it did not matter if she won or lost.

The challenge mattered. That was all.

There were five, in the shape of men with swords. They scrambled down the hall, bones clattering, eyeless skulls regarding her without expression beyond that of their ever-grinning, pointed teeth. Some bits of the skeletals had been replaced by wooden carvings to fix bones that had broken in battle. Each creature bore a glowing red seal on its forehead; blood was required to give them life.

Even Shaizan had never fought monsters like this before. Stabbing them would be useless. But those bits that had been replaced . . . some were pieces of rib or other bones the skeletals shouldn't need to fight. So if bones were broken or removed, would the creature stop working?

It seemed her best chance. She did not consider further. Shaizan was a creature of instinct. As the things reached her, she whipped Zu's cloak around and tossed it over the head of the first one. It thrashed, striking at the cloak as she engaged the second creature.

She caught its attack on the blade of Zu's dagger, then stepped up so close she could smell its bones, and reached in just below the thing's rib cage. She grabbed the spine and yanked, pulling free a handful of vertebrae, the tip of the sternum cutting her forearm. All of the bones of each skeletal seemed to be sharpened.

It collapsed, bones clattering. She was right. With the pivotal bones removed, the thing could no longer animate. Shaizan tossed the handful of vertebrae aside.

That left four of them. From what little she knew, skeletals did not tire and were relentless. She had to be quick, or they would overwhelm her.

The three behind attacked her; Shaizan ducked away, getting around the first one as it pulled off the cloak. She grabbed its skull by the eye sockets, earning a deep cut in the arm from its sword as she did so. Her blood sprayed against the wall as she yanked the skull free; the rest of the creature's body dropped to the ground in a heap.

Keep moving. Don't slow.

If she slowed, she died.

She spun on the other three, using the skull to block one sword strike and the dagger to deflect another. She skirted around the third, and it scored her side.

She could not feel pain. She'd trained herself to ignore it in battle. That was good, because that one would have *hurt*.

She smashed the skull into the head of another skeletal, shattering both. It dropped, and Shaizan spun between the other two. Their backhand strikes clanged against one another. Shaizan's kick sent one of them stumbling back, and she rammed her body against the other, crushing it up against the wall. The bones pushed together, and she got hold of the spine, then yanked free some of the vertebrae.

The creature's bones fell with a racket. Shaizan wavered as she righted herself. Too much blood lost. She was slowing. When had she dropped the dagger? It must have slipped from her fingers as she slammed the creature against the wall.

Focus. One left.

It charged her, a sword in each hand. She heaved herself forward—getting inside its reach before it could swing—and grabbed its forearm bones. She couldn't pull them free, not from that angle. She grunted, keeping the swords at bay. Barely. She was weakening.

It pressed closer. Shaizan growled, blood flowing freely from her arm and side.

She head-butted the thing.

That worked worse in real life than it did in stories. Shaizan's vision dimmed and she slipped to her knees, gasping. The skeletal fell before her, cracked skull rolling free from the force of the blow. Blood dripped down the side of her face. She'd split her forehead, perhaps cracked her own skull.

She fell to her side and fought for consciousness.

Slowly, the darkness retreated.

Shaizan found herself amid scattered bones in an otherwise empty hallway of stone. The only color was that of her blood.

She had won. Another challenge met. She howled a chant of her adopted family, then retrieved her dagger and cut off pieces of her blouse. She used them to bind her wounds. The blood loss was bad. Even a woman with her training would not be meeting any further challenges today. Not if they required strength.

She managed to rise and retrieve Zu's cloak—still immobilized by pain, he watched her with amazed eyes. She gathered all five skulls of the Bloodsealer's pets and tied them in the cloak.

That done, she continued down the hallway, trying to project strength—not the fatigue, dizziness, and pain she actually felt.

He will be here somewhere. . . .

She yanked open a storage closet at the end of the hall and found the Bloodsealer on the floor inside, eyes glazed by the shock of having his pets destroyed in rapid succession.

Shaizan grabbed the front of his shirt and hauled him to his feet. The move almost made her pass out again. *Careful.*

The Bloodsealer whimpered.

"Go back to your swamp," Shaizan growled softly. "The one waiting for you doesn't care that you're in the capital, that you're making so much money, that you're doing it all for her. She wants you home. That's why her letters are worded as they are."

Shaizan said that part for Shai, who would feel guilty if she did not.

The man looked at her, confused. "How do you . . . *Ahhrgh!*"

He said the last part as Shaizan rammed her dagger into his leg. He collapsed as she released his shirt.

"That," Shaizan said to him softly, leaning down, "is so that I have some of your blood. Do not hunt me. You saw what I did to your pets.

I will do worse to you. I'm taking the skulls, so you cannot send them for me again. *Go. Back. Home.*"

He nodded weakly. She left him in a heap, cowering and holding his bleeding leg. The arrival of the skeletals had driven everyone else away, including guards. Shaizan stalked toward the stables, then stopped, thinking of something. It wasn't too far off . . .

You're nearly dead from these wounds, she told herself. *Don't be a fool.*

She decided to be a fool anyway.

A short time later, Shaizan entered the stables and found only a couple of frightened stable hands there. She chose the most distinctive mount in the stables. So it was that—wearing Zu's cloak and hunkered down on his horse—Shaizan was able to gallop out of the palace gates, and not a man or woman tried to stop her.

"Was she telling the truth, Gaotona?" Ashravan asked, regarding himself in the mirror.

Gaotona looked up from where he sat. *Was she?* he thought to himself. He could never tell with Shai.

Ashravan had insisted upon dressing himself, though he was obviously weak from his long stay in bed. Gaotona sat on a stool nearby, trying to sort through a deluge of emotions.

"Gaotona?" Ashravan asked, turning to him. "I was wounded, as that woman said? You went to a *Forger* to heal me, rather than our trained resealers?"

"Yes, Your Majesty."

The expressions, Gaotona thought. *How did she get those right? The way he frowns just before asking a question? The way he cocks his head when not answered immediately. The way he stands, the way he waves his fingers when he's saying something he thinks is particularly important . . .*

"A MaiPon Forger," the emperor said, pulling on his golden coat. "I hardly think *that* was necessary."

"Your wounds were beyond the skill of our resealers."

"I thought nothing was beyond them."

"We did as well."

The emperor regarded the red seal on his arm. His expression tightened. "This will be a manacle, Gaotona. A weight."

"You will suffer it."

Ashravan turned toward him. "I see that the near death of your liege has not made you any more respectful, old man."

"I have been tired lately, Your Majesty."

"You're judging me," Ashravan said, looking back at the mirror. "You always do. Days alight! One day I will rid myself of you. You realize that, don't you? It's only because of past service that I even consider keeping you around."

It was uncanny. This *was* Ashravan; a Forgery so keen, so perfect, that Gaotona would never have guessed the truth if he hadn't already known. He wanted to believe that the emperor's soul had still been there, in his body, and that the seal had simply . . . uncovered it.

That would be a convenient lie to tell himself. Perhaps Gaotona would start believing it eventually. Unfortunately, he had seen the emperor's eyes before, and he knew . . . he *knew* what Shai had done.

"I will go to the other arbiters, Your Majesty," Gaotona said, standing. "They will wish to see you."

"Very well. You are dismissed."

Gaotona walked toward the door.

"Gaotona."

He turned.

"Three months in bed," the emperor said, regarding himself in the mirror, "with no one allowed to see me. The resealers couldn't do anything. They can fix any normal wound. It was something to do with my mind, wasn't it?"

He wasn't supposed to figure that out, Gaotona thought. *She said she wasn't going to write it into him.*

But Ashravan had been a clever man. Beneath it all, he had *always* been clever. Shai had restored him, and she couldn't keep him from thinking.

"Yes, Your Majesty," Gaotona said.

Ashravan grunted. "You are fortunate your gambit worked. You could have ruined my ability to think—you could have sold my soul itself. I'm not sure if I should punish you or reward you for taking that risk."

"I assure you, Your Majesty," Gaotona said as he left, "I have given myself both great rewards and great punishments during these last few months."

He left then, letting the emperor stare at himself in the mirror and consider the implications of what had been done.

For better or worse, they had their emperor back.

Or, at least, a copy of him.

EPILOGUE:
DAY ONE HUNDRED
AND ONE

A ND so I hope," Ashravan said to the assembled arbiters of the eighty factions, "that I have laid to rest certain pernicious rumors. Exaggerations of my illness were, obviously, wishful fancy. We have yet to discover who sent the assassins, but the murder of the empress is *not* something that will go ignored." He looked over the arbiters. "Nor will it go unanswered."

Frava folded her arms, watching the copy with satisfaction, but also displeasure. *What back doors did you put into his mind, little thief?* Frava wondered. *We will find them.*

Nyen was already inspecting copies of the seals. The Forger claimed that he could retroactively decrypt them, though it would take time. Perhaps years. Still, Frava would eventually know how to control the emperor.

Destroying the notes had been clever on the girl's part. Had she guessed, somehow, that Frava wasn't really making copies? Frava shook her head and stepped up beside Gaotona, who sat in their box of the Theater of Address. She sat down beside him, speaking very softly. "They are accepting it."

Gaotona nodded, his eyes on the fake emperor. "There isn't even a whisper of suspicion. What we did . . . it was not only audacious, it would be presumed impossible."

"The girl could put a knife to our throats," Frava said. "The proof of what we did is burned into the emperor's own body. We will need to tread carefully in coming years."

Gaotona nodded, looking distracted. Days afire, how Frava wished she could get him removed from his station. He was the only one of the arbiters who ever took a stand against her. Just before his assassination, Ashravan had been ready to do it at her prompting.

Those meetings had been private. Shai wouldn't have known of them, so the fake would not either. Frava would have to begin the process again, unless she found a way to control this duplicate Ashravan. Both options frustrated her.

"A part of me can't believe that we actually did it," Gaotona said softly as the fake emperor moved on to the next section of his speech, a call for unity.

Frava sniffed. "The plan was sound all along."

"Shai escaped."

"She will be found."

"I doubt it," he said. "We were lucky to catch her that once. Fortunately, I do not believe we have much to worry about from her."

"She'll try to blackmail us," Frava said. *Or she'll try to find a way to control the throne.*

"No," Gaotona said. "No, she is satisfied."

"Satisfied with escaping alive?"

"Satisfied with having placed one of her creations on the throne. Once, she dared to try to fool thousands—but now she has a chance to fool millions. An entire empire. Exposing what she has done would ruin the majesty of it, in her eyes."

Did the old fool really believe that? His naiveness often presented Frava with opportunities; she'd considered letting him keep his station simply for that reason.

The fake emperor continued his speech. Ashravan *had* liked to hear himself speak. The Forger had gotten that right.

"He's using the assassination as a means of bolstering our faction," Gaotona said. "You hear? The implications that we need to unify, pull together, remember our heritage of strength . . . And the rumors, the ones the Glory Faction spread regarding him being killed . . . by mentioning them, he weakens their faction. They gambled on him not returning, and now that he has, they seem foolish."

"True," Frava said. "Did you put him up to that?"

"No," Gaotona said. "He refused to let me counsel him on his speech. This move, though, it feels like something the old Ashravan would have done, the Ashravan from a decade ago."

"The copy isn't perfect, then," Frava said. "We'll have to remember that."

"Yes," Gaotona said. He held something, a small, thick book that Frava didn't recognize.

A rustling came from the back of the box, and a servant of Frava's Symbol entered, passing Arbiters Stivient and Ushnaka. The youthful messenger came to Frava's side, then leaned down.

Frava gave the girl a displeased glance. "What can be so important that you interrupt me here?"

"I'm sorry, Your Grace," the woman whispered. "But you asked me to arrange your palace offices for your afternoon meetings."

"Well?" Frava asked.

"Did you enter the rooms yesterday, my lady?"

"No. With the business of that rogue Bloodsealer, and the emperor's demands, and . . ." Frava's frown deepened. "What is it?"

Shai turned and looked back at the Imperial Seat. The city rolled across a group of seven large hills; a major faction house topped each of the outer six, with the palace dominating the central hill.

The horse at her side looked little like the one she'd taken from the palace. It was missing teeth and walked with its head hanging low, back bowed. Its coat looked as if it hadn't been brushed in ages, and the creature was so underfed, its ribs poked out like the slats on the back of a chair.

Shai had spent the previous days lying low, using her beggar Essence Mark to hide in the Imperial Seat's underground. With that disguise in place, and with one on the horse, she'd escaped the city with ease. She'd removed her Mark once out, however. Thinking like the beggar was . . . uncomfortable.

Shai loosened the horse's saddle, then reached under it and placed a fingernail against the glowing seal there. She snapped the seal's rim with some effort, breaking the Forgery. The horse transformed immediately, back straightening, head rising, sides swelling. It danced uncertainly, head darting back and forth, tugging against the reins. Zu's warhorse was a fine animal, worth more than a small house in some parts of the empire.

Hidden among the supplies on his back was the painting that Shai had stolen, again, from Arbiter Frava's office. A forgery. Shai had never had cause to steal one of her own works before. It felt . . . amusing. She'd left the large frame cut open with a single Reo rune carved in the center on the wall behind. It did not have a very pleasant meaning.

She patted the horse on the neck. All things considered, this wasn't a bad haul. A fine horse and a painting that, though fake, was so realistic that even its owner had thought it was the original.

He's giving his speech right now, Shai thought. *I would like to have heard that.*

Her gem, her crowning work, wore the mantle of imperial power. That thrilled her, but the thrill had driven her onward. Even making him live again had not been the cause of her frantic work. No, in the end, she'd pushed herself so hard because she'd wanted to leave a few specific changes embedded within the soul. Perhaps those months of being genuine to Gaotona had changed her.

Copy an image over and over on a stack of paper, Shai thought, *and eventually the lower sheets will bear the same image, pressed down. Deep within.*

She turned, taking out the Essence Mark that would transform her into a survivalist and hunter. Frava would anticipate Shai using the roads, so she would instead make her way into the deep center of the nearby Sogdian Forest. Those depths would hide her well. In a few months, she would carefully proceed out of the province and continue on to her next task: tracking down the Imperial Fool, who had betrayed her.

For now, she wanted to be far away from walls, palaces, and courtly lies. Shai hoisted herself into the horse's saddle and bid farewell to both the Imperial Seat and the man who now ruled it.

Live well, Ashravan, she thought. *And make me proud.*

Late that night, following the emperor's speech, Gaotona sat by the familiar hearth in his personal study looking at the book that Shai had given him.

And marveling.

The book was a copy of the emperor's soulstamp, in detail, with notes. Everything that Shai had done lay bare to him here.

Frava would not find an exploit to control the emperor, because there wasn't one. The emperor's soul was complete, locked tight, and all his own. That wasn't to say that he was exactly the same as he had been.

I took some liberties, as you can see, Shai's notes explained. *I wanted to replicate his soul as precisely as possible. That was the task and the challenge. I did so.*

Then I took the soul a few steps farther, strengthening some memories, weakening others. I embedded deep within Ashravan triggers that will cause him to react in a specific way to the assassination and his recovery.

This isn't changing his soul. This isn't making him a different person. It is merely nudging him toward a certain path, much as a con man on the street will strongly nudge his mark to pick a certain card. It is him. The him that could have been.

Who knows? Perhaps it is the him that would have been.

Gaotona would never have figured it out on his own, of course. His skill was faint in this area. Even if he'd been a master, he suspected he wouldn't have spotted Shai's work here. She explained in the book that her intention had been to be so subtle, so careful, that no one would be able to decipher her changes. One would have to know the emperor with extreme depth to even suspect what had happened.

With the notes, Gaotona could see it. Ashravan's near death would send him into a period of deep introspection. He would seek his journal, reading again and again the accounts of his youthful self. He would see what he had been, and would finally, truly seek to recover it.

Shai indicated the transformation would be slow. Over a period of years, Ashravan would become the man that he'd once seemed destined to be. Tiny inclinations buried deep within the interactions of his seals would nudge him toward excellence instead of indulgence. He would start thinking of his legacy, as opposed to the next feast. He would remember his people, not his dinner appointments. He would finally push the factions for the changes that he, and many before him, had noticed needed to be made.

In short, he would become a fighter. He would take that single—but so hard—step across the line from dreamer to doer. Gaotona could see it, in these pages.

He found himself weeping.

Not for the future or for the emperor. These were the tears of a man who saw before himself a *masterpiece*. True art was more than beauty; it was more than technique. It was not just imitation.

It was boldness, it was contrast, it was subtlety. In this book, Gaotona found a rare work to rival that of the greatest painters, sculptors, and poets of any era.

It was the greatest work of art he had ever witnessed.

Gaotona held that book reverently for most of the night. It was the creation of months of fevered, intense artistic transcendence—forced by external pressure, but released like a breath held until the brink of collapse. Raw, yet polished. Reckless, but calculated.

Awesome, yet unseen.

So it had to remain. If anyone discovered what Shai had done, the emperor would fall. Indeed, the very empire might shake. No one could know that Ashravan's decision to finally become a great leader had been set in motion by words etched into his soul by a blasphemer.

As morning broke, Gaotona slowly—excruciatingly—stood up beside his hearth. He clutched the book, that matchless work of art, and held it out.

Then he dropped it into the flames.

POSTSCRIPT

In writing classes, I was frequently told, "Write what you know." It's an adage writers often hear, and it left me confused. Write what I know? How do I do that? I'm writing fantasy. I can't know what it's like to use magic—for that matter, I can't know what it's like to be female, but I want to write from a variety of viewpoints.

As I matured in skill, I began to see what this phrase meant. Though in this genre we write about the fantastic, the stories work best when there is solid grounding in our world. Magic works best for me when it aligns with scientific principles. Worldbuilding works best when it draws from sources in our world. Characters work best when they're grounded in solid human emotion and experience.

Being a writer, then, is as much about observation as it is imagination.

I try to let new experiences inspire me. I've been lucky enough in this field that I am able to travel frequently. When I visit a new country, I try to let the culture, people, and experiences there shape themselves into a story.

Once when I visited Taiwan, I was fortunate enough to visit the National Palace Museum, with my editor Sherry Wang and translator Lucie Tuan along to play tour guides. A person can't take in thousands of years of Chinese history in a matter of a few hours, but we did our best. Fortunately, I had some grounding in Asian history and lore already. (I lived for two years in Korea as an LDS missionary, and I then minored in Korean during my university days.)

Seeds of a story started to grow in my mind from this visit. What stood out most to me were the stamps. We sometimes call them "chops" in English, but I've always called them by their Korean name of *tojang*.

In Mandarin, they're called *yìnjiàn*. These intricately carved stone stamps are used as signatures in many different Asian cultures.

During my visit to the museum, I noticed many of the familiar red stamps. Some were, of course, the stamps of the artists—but there were others. One piece of calligraphy was covered in them. Lucie and Sherry explained: Ancient Chinese scholars and nobility, if they liked a work of art, would sometimes stamp it with their stamp too. One emperor in particular loved to do this, and would take beautiful sculptures or pieces of jade—centuries old—and have his stamp and perhaps some lines of his poetry carved into them.

What a fascinating mind-set. Imagine being a king, deciding that you particularly liked Michelangelo's *David*, and so having your signature carved across the chest. That's essentially what this was.

The concept was so striking, I began playing with a stamp magic in my head. Soulstamps, capable of rewriting the nature of an object's existence. I didn't want to stray too close to Soulcasting from the Stormlight world, and so instead I used the inspiration of the museum—of history—to devise a magic that allowed rewriting an object's past.

The story grew from that starting place. As the magic aligned a great deal with a system I'd been developing for Sel, the world where *Elantris* takes place, I set the story there. (I also had based several cultures there on our-world Asian cultures, so it fit wonderfully.)

You can't always write what you know—not exactly what you know. You can, however, write what you see.

THE
HOPE
OF
ELANTRIS

This story takes place after and contains major spoilers for *Elantris*.

M y lord," Ashe said, hovering in through the window. "Lady
Sarene begs your forgiveness. She's going to be a tad late for
dinner."

"A tad?" Raoden asked, amused as he sat at the table. "Dinner was
supposed to start an hour ago."

Ashe pulsed slightly. "I'm sorry, my lord. But . . . she made me promise to relay a message if you complained. 'Tell him,' she said, 'that I'm
pregnant and it's his fault, so that means he has to do what I want.'"

Raoden laughed.

Ashe pulsed again, looking as embarrassed as a seon could, considering he was simply a ball of light.

Raoden sighed, resting his arms on the table of his palace inside
Elantris. The walls around him glowed with a very faint light, and no
torches or lanterns were necessary. He'd always wondered about the lack
of lantern brackets in Elantris. Galladon had once explained that there
were plates made to glow when pressed—but they'd both forgotten just
how much light had come from the stones themselves.

He looked down at his empty plate. *We once struggled so hard for just a little bit of food,* he thought. *Now it's so commonplace that we can spend an hour dallying before we eat.*

Yet food was plentiful. Raoden himself could turn garbage into fine corn. Nobody in Arelon would ever go hungry again. Still, thinking about such things took his mind back to New Elantris, and the simple peace he'd forged inside the city.

"Ashe," Raoden said, a thought suddenly occurring to him. "I've been meaning to ask you something."

"Of course, Your Majesty."

"Where were you during those last hours before Elantris was restored? I don't remember anything of you for most of the night. In fact, the only time I remember seeing you is when you came to tell me that Sarene had been kidnapped and taken to Teod."

"That's true, Your Majesty," Ashe said.

"So, where were you?"

"It is a long story, Your Majesty," the seon said, floating down beside Raoden's chair. "It began when Lady Sarene sent me ahead to New Elantris, to warn Galladon and Karata that she was sending them a shipment of weapons. That was just before the monks attacked Kae, and I went to New Elantris, completely unaware of what was about to occur. . . ."

Matisse took care of the children.

That was her job, in New Elantris. Everyone had to have a job; that was Spirit's rule. She didn't mind her job—actually, she rather enjoyed it. She'd been doing it for longer than Spirit had been around. Ever since Dashe had found her and taken her back to Karata's palace, Matisse had been watching after the little ones. Spirit's rules just made it official.

Yes, she enjoyed the duty. Most of the time.

"Do we really have to go to bed, Matisse?" Teor asked, giving her his best wide-eyed look. "Can't we stay up, just this once?"

Matisse folded her arms, raising a hairless eyebrow at the little boy. "You had to go to bed yesterday at this time," she noted. "And the day before. And, actually, the day before that. I don't see why you think today should be any different."

"Something's going on," said Tiil, stepping up beside his friend. "The adults are all drawing Aons."

Matisse glanced out the window. The children—the fifty or so of them beneath her care—stayed in an open-windowed building dubbed the Roost because of the intricate carvings of birds on most of its walls. The Roost was located near the center of the city-within-a-city—close to Spirit's own home, the Korathi chapel where he held most of his important meetings. The adults wanted to keep a close watch on the children.

Unfortunately, that meant that the children could also keep a close watch on the adults. Outside the window, flashes of light sparked from hundreds of fingers drawing Aons in the air. It was late—far later than the children should have been up—but it had been particularly difficult to get them to bed this night.

Tiil is right, she thought. *Something* is *going on.* However, that was no reason to let him stay up—especially because the longer he stayed awake, the longer it would be before she'd be able to go out and investigate the commotion herself.

"It's nothing," Matisse said, looking back at the children. Though some of them had begun to bed down in their brightly colored sheets, many had perked up and were watching Matisse deal with the two troublemakers.

"Doesn't look like nothing to me," Teor said.

"Well," Matisse said, sighing. "They're writing Aons. If you're that interested, I suppose that we could make an exception and let you stay up . . . assuming you want to practice writing Aons. I'm sure we could fit in another school lesson tonight."

Teor and Tiil both paled. Drawing Aons was what one did in school—something that Spirit had forced them to begin attending again. Matisse smiled slyly to herself as the two boys backed away.

"Oh, come now," she said. "Go get your quills and paper. We could draw Aon Ashe a hundred or so times."

The boys got the hint and slipped back to their respective beds. On the other side of the room, several of the other workers were moving among the children, making certain that they were sleeping. Matisse did likewise.

"Matisse," a voice said. "I can't sleep."

Matisse turned toward where a young girl was sitting up in her bed-roll. "How do you know, Riika?" Matisse said, smiling slightly. "We just put you to bed—you haven't tried to sleep yet."

"I know I won't be able to," the little girl said pertly. "Mai always tells me a story before I sleep. If he doesn't, I can't sleep."

Matisse sighed. Riika rarely slept well—especially on nights when she asked for her seon. It had, of course, gone mad when Riika had been taken by the Shaod.

"Lie down, dear," Matisse said soothingly. "See if sleep comes."

"It won't," Riika said, but she did lie down.

Matisse made the rest of her rounds, then walked to the front of the room. She glanced over the huddled forms—many of whom were still shuffling and moving—and acknowledged that she felt their same apprehensiveness. Something was wrong with this night. Lord Spirit had disappeared, and while Galladon told them not to worry, Matisse found it a foreboding sign.

"What *are* they doing out there?" Idotris whispered quietly from beside her.

Matisse glanced outside, where many of the adults were standing around Galladon, drawing the Aons in the night.

"Aons don't work," Idotris said. The teenage boy was, perhaps, two years older than Matisse—not that such things really mattered in Elan-tris, where everyone's skin was the same blotchy grey, their hair limp or simply gone. The Shaod tended to make ages difficult to determine.

"That's no reason not to practice Aons," Matisse said. "There's a power to them. You can see it."

Indeed, there was a power behind the Aons. Matisse had always been able to feel it—raging behind the lines of light drawn in the air.

Idotris snorted. "Useless," he said, folding his arms.

Matisse smiled. She wasn't certain if Idotris was *always* so grumpy, or if he just tended to be that way when he worked at the Roost. He didn't seem to like the fact that he, as a young teenager, had been relegated to childcare instead of being allowed to join Dashe's soldiers.

"Stay here," she said, wandering out of the Roost toward the open courtyard where the adults were standing.

Idotris just grunted in his usual way, sitting down to make certain none of the children snuck out of the sleeping room, nodding to a few other teenage boys who had finished seeing to their charges.

Matisse wandered through the open streets of New Elantris. The night was crisp, but the cold didn't bother Matisse. That was one of the advantages of being an Elantrian.

She seemed to be one of the few who could see things that way. The others didn't consider being an Elantrian as advantageous, no matter what Lord Spirit said. To Matisse, however, his words made sense. But perhaps that had to do with her situation. On the outside, she'd been a beggar—she'd spent her life being ignored and feeling useless. Yet inside of Elantris she was needed. Important. The children looked up to her, and she didn't have to worry about begging or stealing food.

True, things had been fairly bad before Dashe had found her in a sludge-filled alley. And there were the wounds. Matisse had one on her cheek—a cut she'd gotten soon after entering Elantris. It still burned with the same pain it had the moment she'd gotten it. Yet that was a small price to pay. At Karata's palace, Matisse had found her first real taste of usefulness. That sense of belonging had only grown stronger when Matisse—along with the rest of Karata's band—had moved to New Elantris.

Of course, there was something else she'd gained by getting thrown into Elantris: a father.

Dashe turned, smiling in the lanternlight as he saw her approach. He wasn't her real father, of course. She'd been an orphan even before the Shaod had taken her. And, like Karata, Dashe was sort of a parent to all of the children they'd found and brought to the palace.

Yet Dashe seemed to have a special affection for Matisse. The stern warrior smiled more when Matisse was around, and she was the one he called on when he needed something important done. One day, she'd simply started calling him Father. He'd never objected.

He laid a hand on her shoulder as she joined him at the very edge of the courtyard. In front of them, a hundred or so people moved their arms in near unison. Their fingers left glowing lines in the air behind them—the trails of light that had once produced the magics of AonDor. Galladon stood at the front of the group, calling out instructions in his loose Duladen drawl.

"Never thought I'd see the day when that Dula taught people Aons," Dashe said quietly, his other hand resting on the pommel of his sword.

He's tense too, Matisse thought. She looked up. "Be nice, Father. Galladon is a good man."

"He's a good man, perhaps," Dashe said. "But he's no scholar. He messes up the lines more often than not."

Matisse didn't point out that Dashe himself was pretty terrible when it came to drawing Aons. She eyed Dashe, noting the frown on his lips. "You're mad that Spirit hasn't come back yet," she said.

Dashe nodded. "He should be here, with his people, not chasing that woman."

"There might be important things for him to learn outside," Matisse said quietly. "Things to do with other nations and armies."

"The outside doesn't concern us," Dashe said. He could be a stubborn one at times.

Well, most times, actually.

At the front of the crowd, Galladon spoke. "Good," he said. "That's Aon Daa—the Aon for power. Kolo? Now, we have to practice adding the Chasm line. We won't add it to Aon Daa. Don't want to blow holes in our pretty sidewalks now, do we? We'll practice it on Aon Rao instead—that one doesn't seem to do anything important."

Matisse frowned. "What's he talking about, Father?"

Dashe shrugged. "Seems that Spirit believes the Aons might work now, for some reason. We've been drawing them wrong all along, or something like that. I can't see how the scholars who designed them could have missed an entire line for every Aon, though."

Matisse doubted that scholars had ever "designed" the Aons. There was just something too . . . primal about them. They were things of nature. They hadn't been designed—any more than the wind had been designed.

Still, she said nothing. Dashe was a kind and determined man, but he didn't have much of a mind for scholarship. That was fine with Matisse—it had been Dashe's sword, in part, that had saved New Elantris from destruction at the hands of the wildmen. There was no finer warrior in all of New Elantris than her father.

Yet she did watch with curiosity as Galladon talked about the new line. It was a strange one, drawn across the bottom of the Aon.

And . . . this makes the Aons work? she thought. It seemed like such a simple fix. Could it be possible?

The sound of a cleared throat came from behind them and they turned, Dashe nearly pulling his sword.

A seon hung in the air there. Not one of the insane ones that floated madly about Elantris, but a sane one glowing with a full light.

"Ashe!" Matisse said happily.

"Lady Matisse." Ashe bobbed in the air.

"I'm no lady!" she said. "You know that."

"The title has always seemed appropriate to me, Lady Matisse," he said. "Lord Dashe. Is Lady Karata nearby?"

"She's in the library," Dashe said, taking his hand off the sword.

Library? Matisse thought. *What library?*

"Ah," Ashe said in his deep voice. "Perhaps I can deliver my message to you, then, as Lord Galladon appears to be busy."

"If you wish," Dashe said.

"There is a new shipment coming, my lord," Ashe said quietly. "Lady Sarene wished that you be made aware of it quickly, as it is of an . . . important nature."

"Food?" Matisse asked.

"No, my lady," Ashe said. "Weapons."

Dashe perked up. "Really?"

"Yes, Lord Dashe," the seon said.

"Why would she send those?" Matisse asked, frowning.

"My mistress is worried," Ashe said quietly. "It seems that tensions are growing on the outside. She said . . . well, she wants New Elantris to be prepared, just in case."

"I'll gather some men immediately," Dashe said, "and go collect the weapons."

Ashe bobbed, indicating that he thought this to be a good idea. As her father walked off, Matisse eyed the seon, a thought occurring to her. Maybe . . .

"Ashe, could I borrow you for a moment?" she asked.

"Of course, Lady Matisse," the seon said. "What do you need?"

"Something simple, really," Matisse said. "But it might just help. . . ."

Ashe finished his story, and Matisse smiled to herself, eyeing the sleeping form of the little girl Riika in her bedroll. The child seemed peaceful for the first time in weeks.

Bringing Ashe into the Roost had initially provoked quite a reaction from the children who weren't asleep. Yet as he'd begun to talk, Matisse's instincts had proven correct. The seon's deep, sonorous voice had quieted the children. Ashe had a rhythm about his speech that was wonderfully soothing. Hearing a story from a seon had not only coaxed little Riika to sleep, but the rest of the stragglers as well.

Matisse stood, stretching her legs, then nodded toward the doors outside. Ashe hovered behind her, passing the sullen Idotris at the front doors again. He was tossing pebbles toward a slug that had somehow found its way into New Elantris.

"I'm sorry to take so much of your time, Ashe," Matisse said quietly when they were far enough away not to wake the children.

"Nonsense, Lady Matisse," Ashe said. "Lady Sarene can spare me for a bit. Besides, it is good to tell stories again. It has been some time since my mistress was a child."

"You were Passed to Lady Sarene when she was that young?" Matisse asked, curious.

"At her birth, my lady," Ashe said.

Matisse smiled wistfully.

"You shall have your own seon someday, I should think, Lady Matisse," Ashe said.

Matisse cocked her head. "What makes you say that?"

"Well, there was a time when almost no Elantrian went without a seon. I'm beginning to think that Lord Spirit may just be able to fix this city—after all, he fixed AonDor. If he does, we shall find you a seon of your own. Perhaps one named Ati. That is your own Aon, is it not?"

"Yes," Matisse said. "It means hope."

"A fitting Aon for you, I believe," Ashe said. "Now, if my duties here are finished, perhaps I should—"

"Matisse!" a voice said.

Matisse winced, glancing at the Roost, filled with its sleeping occupants. A light was bobbing in the night, coming down a side street—the source of the yelling.

"Matisse?" the voice demanded again.

"Hush, Mareshe!" Matisse hissed, crossing the street quietly to where the man stood. "The children are sleeping!"

"Oh," Mareshe said, pausing. The haughty Elantrian wore standard New Elantris clothing—bright trousers and shirt—but he had modified his with a couple of sashes that he believed made the costume more "artistic."

"Where's that father of yours?" Mareshe asked.

"Training the people with swords," Matisse said quietly.

"What?" Mareshe asked. "It's the middle of the night!"

Matisse shrugged. "You know Dashe. Once he gets an idea in his head . . ."

"First Galladon wanders off," Mareshe grumbled, "and now Dashe is waving swords in the night. If only Lord Spirit would come back . . ."

"Galladon's gone?" Matisse asked, perking up.

Mareshe nodded. "He disappears like this sometimes. Karata too. They'll never tell me where they've gone. Always so secretive! 'You're in charge, Mareshe,' they say, then go off to have secret conferences without me. Honestly!" With that, the man wandered away, bearing his lantern with him.

Off somewhere secret, Matisse thought. *That library Dashe mentioned?* She eyed Ashe, who was still hovering beside her. Perhaps if she coaxed him enough, he'd tell her—

At that moment, the screaming began.

The shouts were so sudden, so unexpected, that Matisse jumped. She spun about, trying to determine the location of the sounds. They seemed to be coming from the front of New Elantris.

"Ashe!" she said.

"I'm already going, Lady Matisse," the seon said, zipping into the air, a glowing speck in the night.

The yells continued. Distant, echoing. Matisse shivered, backing up unconsciously. She heard other things. The ring of metal against metal.

She turned back toward the Roost. Taid, the adult who supervised the Roost, had walked out of the building in his nightgown. Even in the darkness, Matisse could see a look of concern on his face.

"Wait here," he said.

"Don't leave us!" Idotris said, looking around in fright.

"I'll be back." Taid rushed away.

Matisse shared a look with Idotris. The other teenagers who had been on duty watching the kids had already gone to their own homes for the night. Only Idotris and she remained.

"I'm going to go with him," Idotris said, stalking after Taid.

"Oh no you don't," Matisse said, grabbing his arm and pulling him back. In the distance, the yelling continued. She glanced toward the Roost. "Go wake the kids."

"What?" Idotris said indignantly. "After all the work we did to get them to sleep?"

"Do it," Matisse snapped. "Get them up, and have them put their shoes on."

Idotris resisted for a moment, then grumbled something and stalked inside the room. A moment later, she could hear him doing as she asked, rousing the children. Matisse rushed over to a building across the street—one of the supply buildings. Inside, she found two lanterns with oil in them, and some flint and steel.

She paused. *What am I doing?*

Just being prepared, she told herself, shivering as the screaming continued. It seemed to be getting closer. She rushed back across the street.

"My lady!" Ashe's voice said. She glanced up to see that the seon was flying back down toward her. His Aon was so dim that she could barely see him.

"My lady," Ashe said urgently. "Soldiers have attacked New Elantris!"

"What?" she asked, shocked.

"They wear red and have the height and dark hair of Fjordells, my lady," Ashe said. "There are hundreds of them. Some of your soldiers are fighting at the front of the city, but there are far too few of them. New Elantris is already overrun! My lady—the soldiers are coming this way, and they're searching through the buildings!"

Matisse stood, dumbfounded. *No. No, it can't happen. Not here. This place is peaceful. Perfect.*

I escaped the outside world. I found a place where I belonged. It can't come after me.

"My lady!" Ashe said, sounding terrified. "Those screams . . . the soldiers are attacking the people they find!"

And they're coming this way.

Matisse stood, lanterns clutched in numb fingers. This was the end, then. After all, what could she do? Nearly a child herself, a beggar, a girl without family or home. What could she do?

I take care of the children. It's my job.

It's the job Lord Spirit gave me.

"We have to get them out," Matisse said, sprinting toward the Roost. "They know where to look because we cleaned this section of Elantris. The city is huge—if we get the children out into the dirty part, we can hide them."

"Yes, my lady," Ashe said.

"You go find my father!" Matisse said. "Tell him what we're doing."

With that, she entered the Roost, Ashe hovering away into the night. Inside, Idotris had done as she asked, and the children were groggily putting on their shoes.

"Quickly, children," Matisse said.

"What's going on?" Tiil demanded.

"We've got to go," Matisse said to the young troublemaker. "Tiil, Teor, I'm going to need your help—you and all of the older children, all right? You have to try and help the young ones. Keep them moving, and keep them quiet. All right?"

"Why?" Tiil asked, frowning. "What's going on?"

"It's an emergency," Matisse said. "That's all you need to know."

"Why are *you* in charge?" Teor said, stepping up to his friend, folding his arms.

"You know my father?" Matisse said.

They nodded.

"You know he's a soldier?" Matisse asked.

Again, a nod.

"Well, that makes me a soldier too. It's hereditary. He's a captain, so I'm a captain. And that means I get to tell you what to do. You can be my subcaptains, though, if you promise to do what I say."

The two younger boys paused, then Tiil nodded. "Makes sense," he said.

"Good. Now *move!*"

The boys went to help the younger children. Matisse began to herd them out the front door, into the darkened streets. Many of them, however, had caught on to the terror of the night, and were too scared to budge.

"Matisse!" Idotris hissed, coming closer. "What is going on?"

"Ashe says New Elantris is under attack," Matisse said, kneeling beside her lanterns. "Soldiers are slaughtering everyone."

Idotris grew quiet.

She lit the lanterns, then stood. As she'd expected, the children—even the little ones—gravitated toward the light, and the sense of protection it offered. She handed one lantern to Idotris, and by its glow she could see his terrified face.

"What do we do?" he asked with a shaking voice.

"We run," Matisse said, rushing out of the room.

And the children followed. Rather than be left behind in the dark, they ran after the light, Tiil and Teor helping the smaller ones, Idotris trying to hush those who began to cry. Matisse was worried at bringing light, but it seemed the only way. Indeed, they barely kept the children moving as it was, herding them in the fastest way out of New Elantris—which was the way directly away from the screams, now frightfully close.

That also took them away from the populated sections of New Elantris. Matisse had hoped that they'd run into someone who could help as they moved. Unfortunately, those who weren't out practicing Aons were with her father, practicing with weapons. The only occupied buildings would have been the ones Ashe had indicated were being attacked. Their occupants . . .

Don't think about that, Matisse thought as their ragged band of fifty children reached the edges of New Elantris. They were almost free. They could—

A voice suddenly yelled behind them, speaking in a harsh tongue Matisse didn't understand. Matisse spun, looking over the heads of frightened children. The center of New Elantris was glowing faintly. From firelight.

It was burning.

There, framed by the flames of death, was a squad of three men in red uniforms. They carried swords.

Surely they wouldn't kill children, Matisse thought, her hand shaking as it held its lantern.

Then she saw the glint in the soldiers' eyes. A dangerous, grim look. They advanced on her group. Yes, they would kill children. Elantrian children, at least.

"Run," Matisse said, her voice quavering. Yet she knew the children could never move faster than these men. "Run! Go and—"

Suddenly, as if out of nowhere, a ball of light zipped from the sky. Ashe moved between the men, spinning around their heads, distracting them. The men cursed, waving their swords about in anger, looking up at the seon.

Which is why they completely missed seeing Dashe charge them.

He took them from the side, coming through a shadowed alleyway in New Elantris. He knocked down one soldier, sword flashing, then spun toward the other two as they cursed, turning away from the seon.

We need to go! "Move!" she cried again, urging Idotris and the others to keep going. The children backed away from the sword fight, heading out into the night, following Idotris's light. Matisse stayed near the back, turning with concern toward her father.

He wasn't doing well. He was an excellent warrior, but the soldiers had been joined by two other men, and Dashe's body was weakened by being Elantrian. Matisse stood, holding her lantern in trembling fingers, uncertain what to do. The children were sniffling in the dark behind her, their retreat painfully slow. Dashe fought bravely, his rusty sword replaced by one that Sarene must have sent. He knocked aside blade after blade, but he was getting surrounded.

I have to do something! Matisse thought, stepping forward. At that moment, Dashe turned, and she could see cuts on his face and body. The look of dread she saw in his eyes made her freeze up.

"Go," he whispered, his voice lost in the clamor, but his lips moving. "Run!"

One of the soldiers rammed his sword through Dashe's chest.

"No!" Matisse screamed. But that only drew their attention as Dashe collapsed, quivering on the ground. The pain had become too much for him.

The soldiers looked at her, then began to advance. Dashe had taken down more than one of them, but there were three left.

Matisse felt numb.

"Please, my lady!" Ashe floated down beside her, hovering urgently. "You must run!"

Father is dead. No, worse—he's Hoed. Matisse shook her head, forcing herself to stay alert. She'd seen tragedy as a beggar. She could keep going. She had to.

These men would find the children. The children were too slow. Unless . . . She looked up at the seon beside her, noting the glowing Aon at his center. It meant "light."

"Ashe," she said urgently as the soldiers approached. "Find Idotris ahead. Tell him to put out his lantern, then lead him and the others to someplace safe!"

"Someplace safe? I don't know if *any* place is safe."

"That library you spoke of," Matisse said, thinking quickly. "Where is it?"

"Straight north from here, my lady," Ashe said. "In a hidden chamber beneath a squat building. It is marked by Aon Rao."

"Galladon and Karata are there," Matisse said. "Take the children to them—Karata will know what to do."

"Yes," Ashe said. "Yes, that sounds good."

"Don't forget about the lantern," Matisse said as he flew away. She turned to face the advancing soldiers. Then, with a shaky finger, she raised a hand and began to draw.

Light burst from the air, following her finger. She forced herself to remain steady, completing the Aon despite her fear. The soldiers paused as they watched her, then one of them said something in a guttural language she assumed was Fjordell. They continued to advance on her.

Matisse finished the Aon—Aon Ashe, the same one inside of her seon friend. But of course the Aon didn't do anything. It just hung there, like they always did. The soldiers approached uncaringly, stepping right up to it.

This had better work, Matisse thought, then put her finger in the place that Galladon had demonstrated and drew the final line.

Immediately, the Aon—Aon Ashe—began to glow with a powerful light right in front of the soldiers' faces. They called out as the sudden flash of brilliance shone in their eyes, then cursed, stumbling back. Matisse reached down to grab her lantern and run.

The soldiers yelled after her, then began to follow. And, like the children earlier, they went toward the light—her light. Idotris and the others weren't that far away—she could see their shadows still moving in the night—but the soldiers had been blinded too much to notice the faint movements, and Idotris had put out his light. The only thing for the soldiers to focus on was her lantern.

Matisse led them away into the dark night, clutching her lantern in terrified fingers. She could hear them pursuing behind her as she entered Elantris proper. Sludge and darkness replaced the clean paving stones of New Elantris, and Matisse had to stop moving so quickly, lest she slide and stumble.

She hurried anyway, rounding corners, trying to stay ahead of her pursuers. She felt *so* weak. Running was hard as an Elantrian. She didn't have the strength to go very quickly. Already she was beginning to feel a powerful fatigue inside of her. She couldn't hear any more pursuit. Perhaps . . .

She turned a corner and ran afoul of a pair of soldiers standing in the night. She paused in shock, looking up at the men, recognizing them from before.

They're trained soldiers, she thought. *Of course they know how to surround an enemy and cut them off!* She spun to run, but one of the men grabbed her arm, laughing and saying something in Fjordell.

Matisse cried out, dropping the lantern. The soldier stumbled, but held her firm.

Think! Matisse told herself. *You only have a moment.* Her feet slipped in the sludge. She paused, then let herself fall, kicking at her captor's leg.

She was counting on one thing: She'd lived in Elantris. She knew how to move in the slime and sludge. These soldiers, however, didn't. Her kick landed true, and the soldier immediately slipped, stumbling into his companion and crashing back to the slimy street as he released Matisse.

She scrambled to her feet, her beautiful bright clothing now stained with Elantris sludge. Her leg flared with a new pain—she'd twisted her ankle. She'd been so careful in the past to keep free of major pains, but this one was stronger than anything she'd gotten before, far stronger than the cut on her cheek. Her leg burned with a pain she could barely believe, and it didn't abate—it remained strong. An Elantrian's wounds would never heal.

Still, she forced herself to limp away. She moved without thinking, only wishing to get away from the soldiers. She heard them cursing, stumbling to their feet. She kept going, hopping slightly. She didn't realize that she had moved in a circle until she saw the glow of New Elantris burning in front of her. She was back where she had begun.

She paused. There he was, Dashe, lying on the paving stones. She rushed to him, not caring anymore about pursuit. Her father lay with the sword still impaling him, and she could hear him whispering.

"Run, Matisse. Run to safety. . . ." The mantra of a Hoed.

Matisse stumbled to her knees. She'd gotten the children to safety. That was enough. There was a noise behind her, and she turned to see a soldier approaching. His companion must have gone a different direction. Yet this man was stained with slime, and she recognized him. He was the one she had kicked.

My leg hurts so much! she thought. She turned over, holding to Dashe's immobile body, too tired—and too pained—to move any further.

The soldier grabbed her by the shoulder and pulled her away from her father's corpse. He spun her around, the action bringing other pains to her arms.

"You tell me," he said in a thickly accented voice. "You tell me where other children went."

Matisse struggled in vain. "I don't know!" she said. But she did. Ashe had told her. *Why did I ask him where the library was?* she berated herself. *If I didn't know, I couldn't give them away!*

"You tell," the man said, holding her with one hand, reaching for his belt knife with the other. "You tell, or I hurt you. Bad."

Matisse struggled uselessly. If her Elantrian eyes could have formed tears, she would have been crying. As if to prove his point, the soldier held up his knife before her. Matisse had never felt such terror in her life.

And that was when the ground began to shake.

The eastern sky had begun to glow with the coming of dawn, but that light was overshadowed by a sudden burst of light from around the perimeter of the city. The soldier paused, looking up at the sky.

Suddenly Matisse felt warm.

She didn't realize how much she'd missed feeling warm, how much she'd grown used to the stale coolness of an Elantrian body. But the warmth seemed to flow through her, like someone had injected a hot liquid into her veins. She gasped at the beautiful, amazing feeling.

Something was *right*. Something was wonderfully right.

The soldier turned toward her. He cocked his head, then reached out and rubbed a rough finger across her cheek, where she had been wounded long ago.

"Healed?" he said, confused.

She felt wonderful. She felt . . . her heart!

The man, looking confused, raised his knife again. "You healed," he said, "but I can hurt you again."

Her body felt stronger. Yet she was still just a young girl, and he a trained soldier. She struggled, her mind barely beginning to comprehend that her skin was no longer blotched, but had turned a silvery color. It was happening! As Ashe had predicted! Elantris was returning!

And she was still going to die. It wasn't fair! She screamed in frustration, trying to wiggle free. The irony seemed perfect. The city was being healed, but that couldn't prevent this terrible man from—

"I think you missed something, friend," a voice suddenly said.

The soldier paused.

"If the light healed her," the voice said, "then it healed *me* too."

The soldier cried out in pain, then dropped Matisse, stumbling to the ground. She stepped back, and as the terrible man collapsed, she could finally see who was standing behind: her father, glowing with an inner light, the taint removed from his body. He seemed like a god, silvery and spectacular.

His clothing was ripped where he'd been wounded, but the skin was healed. In his hand he held the very sword that had been impaling him moments before.

She ran to him, crying—she could finally cry again!—and she grabbed him in an embrace.

"Where are the other children, Matisse?" he said urgently.

"I took care of them, Father," she whispered. "Everyone has a job, and that's mine. I take care of the children."

"And what did happen to the children?" Raoden asked.

"I led them to the library," Ashe said. "Galladon and Karata were gone by then—we must have missed them as they ran back to New Elantris. But I hid the children inside, and stayed with them to keep them calm. I was so worried about what was happening inside the city, but those poor things . . ."

"I understand," Raoden said. "And Matisse . . . Dashe's little daughter. I had no idea what she'd gone through." Raoden smiled. He'd given Dashe two seons—ones whose masters had died, and who had found themselves without anyone to serve once they recovered their wits when Elantris was restored—in thanks for his services to New Elantris. Dashe had given one to his daughter.

"Which seon did she end up with?" Raoden asked. "Ati?"

"Actually, no," Ashe said. "I believe it was Aeo."

"Equally appropriate," Raoden said, smiling and standing as the door opened. His wife, Queen Sarene, entered, pregnant belly first.

"I agree," Ashe said, hovering over to Sarene.

Aeo. It meant "bravery."

POSTSCRIPT

This short story has a rather interesting backstory.

If we flash back to January 2006, we find me having been dating Emily (who would eventually become my wife) for about two months. On one of our dates, Emily told me something amazing. One of her eighth-grade students—a girl named Matisse—had done a book report on *Elantris*. Now, Matisse didn't know that her teacher was dating me. She didn't even know that Emily knew me. It was just a bizarre coincidence.

This report she did was incredible. Instead of a simple write-up, she created a worldbook about Sel; it had sketches and bios of the characters, strips of Elantrian cloth stapled in as examples, and little pouches filled with materials from the book. Emily showed it to me, and it completely blew me away. Back then, I was still very new to being a published writer, and seeing the work that Matisse had put into her report was one of the most striking moments of my early career.

I wanted to do something special as a thank-you for Matisse, who still didn't know that her teacher was dating one of her favorite authors. I decided to write a little companion story to *Elantris*.

In any novel, there are events you decide to leave out for pacing reasons. I knew what was going on inside the city of Elantris when the attack by the Dakhor came. In the back of my mind, I also knew that the children were saved and protected by Dashe and Ashe the seon. I didn't want them to fall like the others; Karata had worked so hard to protect them, and letting the children not have to suffer through the slaughter at New Elantris was my gift to her.

I decided to write a little story to deal with all of this. And because Matisse had inspired me, I decided that I would name a character after her. The Matisse in the story doesn't act like the real Matisse. I didn't know the real Matisse; I'd never met her. Now, though, I've met her a number of times—she comes to my signings on occasion. She even gave us the original *Elantris* book-report book as a wedding gift.

Looking back at this story, I think it might be a tad on the sentimental side. I hope that it doesn't come off as too melodramatic. (Read outside the context of the *Elantris* novel, I think that it might.) But for what the story is, I'm quite pleased with it.

THE
SCADRIAN
SYSTEM

THE SCADRIAN SYSTEM

T HE inner system here is basically empty, save for the planet Scadrial, which is fortuitous—considering the vast changes the system has undergone because of the influence of its Shards.

The remarkable thing about Scadrial is how well humankind has flourished on it, despite these repeated cataclysms. Surely other planets in the cosmere have seen worse disasters, but on none of them will you find a thriving, technologically advanced society as exists on Scadrial.

Indeed, I am convinced that without the Lord Ruler's oppression of technology on the planet for a thousand years, Scadrial would have eclipsed all others in scientific learning and progress—all on its own, without the interaction between societies we enjoy in Silverlight.

Scadrial, another dishardic planet, is characterized by a host of unique features. It is one of only two places in the cosmere where humankind does not predate the arrival of Shards. Indeed, I am convinced from my studies that the planet itself *did not exist* before its Shards, Ruin and Preservation, arrived in the system. They picked a star with no relevant planets in orbit, specifically choosing this location because it was empty, so they could place there whatever they wished.

Yes, the Shards undoubtedly used humans from Yolen as a model (indeed, both of the Vessels for these Shards were human before their Ascensions) in creating life. Because of this, the flora and fauna on Scadrial are very similar to what you'll find on Yolen. (The non-fain parts, of course.) It is also very similar to Yolen in size and gravitation, both being exactly at 1.0 cosmere standard.

Though the Shards created this planet together, it quickly became the symbol of—and prize in—their conflict. To speak on the personal ties of the Vessels themselves is not my field of expertise; better to approach one of my colleagues who specializes in pre-Shattering biography and history, rather than an arcanist. I can say, however, that their conflict is manifested directly in the ways that Investiture is used on Scadrial.

This is a powerful magic, and one where humans themselves have often had access to grand bursts of strength. I would challenge one to identify another planet, save only Roshar, where one can find such strength of Investiture so commonly in the hands of mortals. Periodically throughout Scadrial's history, a man or woman gained access to vast amounts of power, with incredible effects. The most obvious evidence of this is the fact that the star charts Guyn has so kindly provided list *two* orbits for Scadrial. The planet was *literally moved* at various points by individuals wielding immense amounts of Investiture. (As an aside, this has wreaked havoc with trying to understand historical calendars on the planet.)

I have written much about the magics of this planet. Indeed, I could fill entire volumes with my thoughts on Allomancy, Feruchemy, and Hemalurgy. I maintain, however, that the one of these with the largest potential impact on the cosmere is Hemalurgy. Usable by anyone with the right knowledge, this dangerous creation has proven able to warp souls regardless of planet or Investiture, creating false Connections that no Shard designed or intended.

Though the planetary system is rather boring, Scadrial itself has proven intriguing time and time again. This is despite the fact that humans used to live on a relatively small portion of the planet. (A fact that began to change once the extreme environments of the Final Empire were removed.)

From the adaptations (both forced and unforced) of the humans living on her, to the vast transformations of landscape during her different eras, Scadrial remains my favorite planet for scholarly study in the cosmere. The interactions of her magics with natural physics are multitude, varied, and fascinating.

THE
ELEVENTH
METAL

This story may be read before the original Mistborn Trilogy.

K ELSIER held the small, fluttering piece of paper pinched between two fingers. The wind whipped and tore at the paper, but he held firm. The picture was wrong.

He'd tried at least two dozen times to draw it right, to reproduce the image that she'd always carried. The original had been destroyed, he was certain. He had nothing to remind him of her, nothing to remember her by. So he tried, poorly, to reconstruct the image that she had treasured.

A flower. That was what it had been called. A myth, a story. A dream.

"You need to stop doing that," his companion growled. "I should stop you from drawing those."

"Try," Kelsier said softly, folding the small piece of paper between two fingers, then tucking it into his shirt pocket. He would try again later. The petals needed to be more tear-shaped.

Kelsier regarded Gemmel with a calm gaze, then smiled. That smile felt forced. How could he smile in a world without her?

Kelsier kept smiling. He'd do so until it felt natural. Until that numbness, tied in a knot within him, started to unravel and he began to feel again. If that was possible.

It is. Please let it be.

"Drawing those pictures makes you think of the past," Gemmel snapped. The aging man had a ragged grey beard, and the hair on his head was so unkempt, it actually looked *better*-groomed when it was being whipped around by the wind.

"It does," Kelsier said. "I won't forget her."

"She betrayed you. Move on." Gemmel didn't wait to see if Kelsier continued arguing. He moved away; he often stopped in the middle of arguments.

Kelsier didn't squeeze his eyes shut as he wanted to. He didn't scream defiance to the dying day as he wanted to. He shoved aside thoughts of Mare's betrayal. He should never have spoken his concerns to Gemmel.

He had. That was that.

Kelsier broadened his smile. It took effort.

Gemmel glanced back at him. "You look creepy when you do that."

"That's because you've never had a real smile in your life, you old heap of ash," Kelsier said, joining Gemmel by the short wall at the edge of the roof. They looked down on the dreary city of Mantiz, nearly drowning in ash. The people here in the far north of the Western Dominance weren't as good at cleaning it up as people were back in Luthadel.

Kelsier had assumed there would be less ash out here—only one of the ashmounts was nearby, this far out. It *did* seem that the ash fell a little less frequently. But the fact that nobody organized to clean it up meant that it felt like there was far more.

Kelsier curled his hand around the coping of the wall. He'd never liked this part of the Western Dominance. The buildings out here felt . . . melted. No, that was the wrong term. They felt too rounded, with no corners, and they were rarely symmetrical—one side of the building would be higher, or more lumpy.

Still, the ash was familiar. It covered the building here just the same as everywhere, giving everything a uniform cast of black and grey. A layer of it coated streets, clung to the ridges of buildings, made heaps in alleys. Ashmount ash was sootlike, much darker than the ash from a common fire.

"Which one?" Kelsier asked, rotating his gaze among the four massive keeps that broke the city skyline. Mantiz was a large city for this dominance, though—of course—it was nothing like Luthadel. There weren't any other cities like Luthadel. Still, this one was respectable.

"Keep Shezler," Gemmel said, pointing toward a tall, slender building near the center of the city.

Kelsier nodded. "Shezler. I can get in the door easily. I'll need a costume—fine clothing, some jewelry. We need to find a place I can fence a bead of atium—and a tailor who can keep his mouth shut."

Gemmel snorted.

"I've got a Luthadel accent," Kelsier said. "From what I heard on the street earlier, Lord Shezler is absolutely *infatuated* with the Luthadel nobility. He'll fawn over someone who presents himself right; he wants connections to society closer to the capital. I—"

"You aren't thinking like an Allomancer," Gemmel cut him off, his voice gruff.

"I'll use emotional Allomancy," Kelsier said. "Turn him to my—"

Gemmel suddenly roared, spinning on Kelsier, moving too quickly. The ragged man snagged Kelsier by the front of his shirt and shoved him to the ground, looming over him, rattling the roof tiles. "You're Mistborn, not some street Soother working for clips! You want to be taken again? Snatched up by *his* minions, sent back to where you belong? Do you?"

Kelsier glared back at Gemmel as the mists began to grow in the air around them. Sometimes Gemmel seemed more beast than man. He began muttering to himself, speaking as if to a friend Kelsier couldn't see or hear.

Gemmel leaned closer, still muttering, his breath pungent and sharp, his eyes wide and frenzied. This man wasn't completely sane. No. That was a gross understatement. This man had only a fringe of sanity left to him, and even that fringe was beginning to fray.

But he was the only Mistborn who Kelsier knew, and dammit, Kelsier was going to learn from the man. It was either that or start taking lessons from some nobleman.

"Now you listen," Gemmel said, almost pleading. "*Listen* for once. I'm here to teach you how to fight. Not how to talk. You already do that.

We didn't come here so you could saunter in playing nobleman, like you did in the old days. I won't let you talk through this, I *won't*. You're Mistborn. You fight."

"I will use whatever tool I have to."

"You'll fight! Do you want to be weak again, let them take you again?"

Kelsier was silent.

"You want vengeance on them? Don't you?"

"Yes," Kelsier growled. Something massive and dark shifted within him, a beast awakened by Gemmel's prodding. It cut through even the numbness.

"You want to kill, don't you? For what they did to you and yours? For taking her from you? Well, boy?"

"Yes!" Kelsier barked, flaring his metals, shoving Gemmel back.

Memories. A dark hole lined by crystals sharp as razors. Her sobs as she died. His sobs as they broke him. Crumpled him. Ripped him apart.

His screams as he remade himself.

"Yes," he said, coming up onto his feet, pewter burning within him. He forced himself to smile. "Yes, I'll have vengeance, Gemmel. But I'll have it my way."

"And what way is that?"

Kelsier faltered.

It was an unfamiliar experience for him. He'd always had a plan, before. Plans upon plans. Now, without her, without anything . . . The spark was snuffed out, the spark that had always driven him to reach beyond what others thought possible. It had led him from plan to plan, heist to heist, riches to riches.

It was gone now, replaced by that knot of numbness. The only thing he could feel these days was rage, and that rage couldn't guide him.

He didn't know what to do. He hated that. He'd always known what to do. But now . . .

Gemmel snorted. "When I'm done with you, you'll be able to kill a hundred men with a single coin. You'll be able to Pull a man's own sword from his fingers and strike him down with it. You'll be able to crush men within their armor, and you'll be able to cut the air like the mists themselves. You will be a *god*. Waste your time with emotional Allomancy when I'm finished. For now, you kill."

The bearded man loped back to the wall and glared at the keep. Kelsier slowly reined in his anger, rubbing his chest where he'd been forced to the ground. And . . . something odd occurred to him. "How do you know what I was like in the old days, Gemmel?" Kelsier whispered. "Who are you?"

Lamps and limelights were lit in the night, their glow breaking out through windows into the curling mists. Gemmel hunkered beside his wall, whispering to himself again. If he heard Kelsier's question, he ignored it.

"You should still be burning your metals," Gemmel said as Kelsier approached. Kelsier bit off a comment about not wanting to waste them. He'd explained that as a skaa child, he had learned to be very careful with resources. Gemmel had just laughed at that. At the time, Kelsier had assumed the laughter was due to Gemmel's natural erratic nature.

But . . . was it because he knew the truth? That Kelsier *hadn't* grown up a poor skaa on the streets? That he and his brother had lived lives of privilege, their half-breed nature kept secret from society?

He hated the nobility, true. Their balls and parties, their prim self-satisfaction, their superiority. But he couldn't deny, not to himself, that he belonged among them. At least as much as he did among the skaa of the streets.

"Well?" Gemmel said.

Kelsier ignited some of the metals inside him, burning several of the eight metal reserves he had within. He'd heard Allomancers speak of those reserves on occasion, but had never expected to feel them himself. They were like wells of energy he could draw upon.

Burning metals inside of him. How strange it sounded—yet how natural it felt. As natural as breathing in air and drawing strength from it. Each of those eight reserves enhanced him in some way.

"All eight," Gemmel said. "*All* of them." He'd be burning bronze to sense what Kelsier was burning.

Kelsier had only burned the four physical metals. Reluctantly, he burned the others. Gemmel nodded; now that Kelsier was burning copper, all signs of his Allomancy would have vanished to the other man. Copper, what a useful metal—it hid you from other Allomancers, and made you immune to their emotional Allomancy.

Some spoke of copper derogatorily. You couldn't use it to fight; you couldn't change things with it. But Kelsier had always envied his friend Trap, who was a copper Misting. It was a powerful thing to know that your emotions were not the result of outside tampering.

Of course, with copper burning, that meant he had to admit that everything he felt—the pain, the anger, and even the numbness—belonged to him alone.

"Let's go," Gemmel said, leaping out into the night.

The mists were almost fully formed. They came every night, sometimes thick, sometimes light. But always there. The mists moved like hundreds of streams piled atop one another. They shifted and spun, thicker, more *alive* than an ordinary fog.

Kelsier had always loved the mists for reasons he couldn't describe. Marsh claimed it was because everyone else feared them, and Kelsier was too arrogant to do what everyone else did. Of course, Marsh had never seemed to fear them either. The two brothers felt something, an understanding, an awareness. The mists claimed some as their own.

Kelsier jumped down from the low roof, burning pewter to strengthen him so that the landing was solid. Then he followed Gemmel on the hard cobblestones, running on bare feet. Tin burned in his stomach; it made him more aware, made his senses stronger. The mists seemed wetter, their prickling dew cooler on his skin. He could hear rats scurrying in distant alleyways, hounds baying, a man snoring softly in a building nearby. A thousand sounds that would be inaudible to an ordinary person's ears. At times when burning tin, the world seemed a cacophony. He couldn't burn it too strongly, lest the noises grow distracting. Just enough to let him see better; tin made the mists appear more faint to his eyes, though why that should be he did not know.

He trailed Gemmel's shadowed form as they reached the wall around Keep Shezler and placed their backs to it. Atop that wall, guards called to one another in the night.

Gemmel nodded, then dropped a coin. The scrawny, bearded man lurched into the air a second later. He wore a mistcloak—a dark grey cloak that was formed of many tassels from the chest down. Kelsier had asked for one. Gemmel had laughed at him.

Kelsier walked up to the fallen coin. The mists nearby dipped and spun in a pattern like insects moving toward a flame—they always did that around Allomancers who were burning metals. He'd seen it happen to Marsh.

Kelsier knelt beside the coin. To his eyes, a faint blue line—almost like a spider's silk—led from his chest to the coin. In fact, hundreds of tiny lines pointed from his chest to each nearby source of metal. Iron and steel created these lines—one for Pushing, one for Pulling. Gemmel had told him to burn all his metals, but Gemmel often made no sense. There was no reason to burn both steel and iron; the two were opposites.

He extinguished his iron, leaving only the steel. With steel, he could *Push* on any source of metal that was connected to him. The Push was mental, but felt much like shoving against something with his arms.

Kelsier positioned himself above the coin and Pushed on it, as Gemmel had trained him. Since the coin couldn't go downward, Kelsier was instead thrown upward. He popped into the air some fifteen feet, then awkwardly grabbed the coping of the wall above. He grunted, hauling himself up over the edge.

A new group of blue lines sprang up at his chest, thickening. Sources of metal approaching him quickly.

Kelsier cursed, throwing out a hand and Pushing. The coins that had been flying toward him were Pushed back into the night, zipping through the mists. Gemmel walked forward, undoubtedly the source of the coins. He attacked Kelsier sometimes; their first night together, Gemmel had thrown him off a cliff.

Kelsier still couldn't completely decide if the attacks were tests, or if the lunatic was actually trying to murder him.

"No," Gemmel muttered. "No, I *like* him. He almost never complains. The other three complained all the time. This one is strong. No. Not strong enough. No. Not yet. He'll learn." Behind Gemmel was a pair of lumps on the wall top. Dead guards, leaking trails of blood along the stones. The blood was black in the night. The mists seemed . . . afraid of Gemmel, somehow. They didn't spin about him as they did other Allomancers.

That was nonsense. Just his mind playing tricks on him. Kelsier stood up, and didn't mention the attack. It wouldn't do any good. He just had to stay aware and learn as much as he could from this man. Preferably without getting killed in the process.

"You don't need to use your hand to Push," Gemmel grumbled at him. "Wastes time. And you need to learn to keep your pewter burning. You shouldn't have had such a hard time climbing up over the edge of the wall."

"I—"

"*Don't* give me an excuse about saving your metals," Gemmel said, inspecting the keep just ahead. "I've met children of the streets. They don't conserve. If you come at one of them, they'll use everything they have—every scrap of strength, every last trick—to take you down. They know how close to the edge they walk. Pray you never have to face one of those, pretty boy. They'll rip you apart, chew you up, and make new reserves for themselves out of what you leave behind."

"I was going to say," Kelsier said calmly, "that you haven't even told me what we're doing tonight."

"Infiltrating this keep," Gemmel said, eyes narrowing.

"Why?"

"Does it matter?"

"It sure as hell does."

"There's something important in there," Gemmel said. "Something we're going to find."

"Well, that explains everything. Thank you for being so forthcoming. Could you possibly enlighten me on the meaning of life, since you're so great at answering questions all of a sudden?"

"Don't know it," Gemmel said. "I think it's so we can die."

Kelsier suppressed a groan, leaning against the wall. *I said that*, he realized, *fully expecting to get some dry remark in return. Lord Ruler, I miss Dox and the crew.*

Gemmel didn't understand humor, even pathetic attempts at it. *I need to get back,* Kelsier thought. *Back to people who care about living. Back to my friends.*

That thought made him shiver. It had only been three months since the . . . events at the Pits of Hathsin. The cuts on his arms were mostly just scars now. He scratched at them anyway.

Kelsier knew his humor was forced, his smiles more dead than alive. He didn't know why he found it so important to hold off returning to Luthadel, but it was. He had exposed wounds, gaping holes in himself that had yet to heal over. He *had* to stay away. He didn't want them to see him like this. Insecure, a man who huddled in his sleep, reliving horrors still fresh. A man with no plan or vision.

Besides, he needed to learn the things Gemmel was teaching him. He couldn't return to Luthadel until . . . until he was himself again. Or at the very least a scarred version of himself, the wounds closed, the memories quieted.

"Let's be on with it then," Kelsier said.

Gemmel glared at him. The old lunatic didn't like it when Kelsier tried to take control. But . . . well, that was what Kelsier did. Somebody had to.

Keep Shezler was constructed in the unusual architectural style typical of any area of the Western Dominance far from Luthadel. Instead of blocks and peaks, it had an almost organic feel, with four tapering towers up front. He thought that buildings out here must be constructed of stone frames with a kind of hardened mud outside, sculpted and shaped to make all those curves and knobs. The keep, like the rest of the buildings, looked unfinished to Kelsier. "Where?" Kelsier said.

"Up," Gemmel said. "Then down." He jumped from the wall and threw a coin for himself. He Pushed against it, and his weight drove it downward. When it hit the ground, Gemmel launched higher toward the building.

Kelsier leaped and Pushed against his own coin. The two of them bounded across the space between the sculpted wall and the lit keep. Powerful limelights burned behind stained-glass windows; here in the Western Dominance, those windows were often odd shapes, and no two were alike. Had these people no understanding of proper aesthetics?

Closer to the building, Kelsier began to Pull instead of Push—he switched from burning steel to burning iron, then yanked on a blue line leading to a steel window frame. That meant he was Pulled upward, as if he were on a tether. It was tricky; the ground still tugged him downward, and he also still had momentum forward, so when he Pulled he had to be careful not to slam himself into things.

With Pulling, he gained more height. He needed it, as Keep Shezler was tall, as tall as any keep in Luthadel. The two Allomancers bounded up the front facade, grabbing or leaping from the knobs and bits of stonework. Kelsier landed on an outcropping, waved his arms for a moment, then snatched hold of a statue that had been placed there for no reason he could discern. It was covered in bits of glaze of different colors.

Gemmel flew past on the right; the other Mistborn moved with a deft grace. He threw a coin to the side, where it hit an outcropping. Then, by pushing on it, Gemmel nudged himself in just the right direction. He spun, mistcloak streaking the mists, then Pulled himself to a different stained-glass window. He hit and hung there like an insect, fingers grabbing bits of metal and stone.

Powerful limelight shone out through the window, which shattered the light into colors, spraying them across Gemmel as if he too were covered in bits of glaze. He looked up, a smile on his lips. In that light, with the mistcloak hanging beneath him, the mists dancing around him, Gemmel suddenly seemed more regal to Kelsier. Distant from the ragged madman. Something far more grand.

Gemmel leaped out into the mists, then Pulled himself upward. Kelsier watched him go, surprised to find himself envious. *I will learn*, he told himself. *I'll be that good.*

From the start, he'd been drawn to zinc and brass, Allomancy that let him play with people's emotions. It had seemed most similar to what he'd done unaided in the past. But he was a new man, reborn in those dreadful pits. Whatever he had been, it wasn't enough. He needed to become something more.

Kelsier threw himself upward, Pulling his way to the roof of the building. Gemmel kept going up past the roof, flying toward the tips of the four spires that adorned the front of the building. Kelsier dropped his entire bag of coins—the more metal you Pushed off, the faster and higher you could go—and flared his steel. He Pushed with everything he had, sending himself upward like an arrow.

Mists streamed around him. The colorful lights of the stained-glass windows withdrew below. A spire dwindled on either side of him, growing more and more narrow. He shoved off the tin cladding on one of them to nudge himself to the right.

With a final Push of strength he crested the very tip of the spire, which had a knob on top the size of man's head. Kelsier landed on it, flaring his pewter, which improved his physical abilities. That didn't just make him stronger; it made him more dexterous as well. Capable of standing on one foot atop a globe a handspan wide hundreds of feet off the ground. Having performed the maneuver, he stopped and stared at his foot.

"You're growing more confident," Gemmel said. The other man had stopped just shy of the tip of the spire, clinging to it below Kelsier. "That's good."

Then with a quick motion, Gemmel leaped up and swept Kelsier's leg from underneath him. Kelsier cried out, losing control and falling into the mists. Gemmel Pushed against the vials full of metal flakes that Kelsier—like most Allomancers—carried on his belt. That Push shoved Kelsier away from the building and out into the mists.

He plummeted, and lost rational thought for a moment. There was a primal terror to falling. Gemmel had spoken about controlling that, about learning not to fear heights or get disoriented while dropping.

Those lessons fled Kelsier's mind. But he was falling. Fast. Through churning mists, disoriented. It would take only seconds to hit the ground.

Desperate, he Pushed on those vials of metal, hoping he was pointed in the right direction. They ripped from his belt and smashed downward into something. The ground.

There wasn't much metal in them. Barely enough to slow Kelsier. He hit the ground a fraction of a second after Pushing, and the blow knocked the wind from him. His vision flashed.

He lay in a daze as something thumped to the ground beside him. Gemmel. The other man snorted in derision. "Fool."

Kelsier groaned and pushed himself up to his hands and knees. He was alive. And remarkably, nothing seemed broken—though his side and thigh smarted something wicked. He'd have awful bruises. Pewter had kept him alive. The fall, even with the Push at the end, would have broken another man's bones.

Kelsier stumbled to his feet and glared at Gemmel, but made no complaint. This probably *was* the best way to learn. At least it would be the fastest. Rationally, Kelsier would have chosen this—being thrown in, forced to learn as he went. That didn't stop him from hating Gemmel.

"I thought we were going up," Kelsier said.

"Then down."

"Then up again, I assume?" Kelsier asked with a sigh.

"No. Down some more." Gemmel strode across the grounds of the keep, passing ornamental shrubbery that had become dark, mist-shrouded silhouettes in the night. Kelsier hastened up beside Gemmel, wary of another attack.

"It's in the basement," Gemmel muttered. "Basement, of all things. Why a basement?"

"What's in the basement?" Kelsier asked.

"Our goal," Gemmel said. "We had to go up high, so I could look for an entrance. I think there's one out here in the gardens."

"Wait, that actually sounds reasonable," Kelsier said. "You must have hit your head on something."

Gemmel glared at him, then shoved his hand into his pocket and pulled out a handful of coins. Kelsier readied his metals, prepared to fight back. But Gemmel turned his hand to the side and sprayed them across a pair of guards who were jogging up the path to see who was walking through the grounds at night.

The men fell, one of them yelling. Gemmel didn't seem to care that it might reveal the two of them. He stalked on ahead.

Kelsier hesitated for a moment, glancing at the dying men. Employed by the enemy. He tried to feel something for them, but he couldn't. That part of him had been ripped out by the Pits of Hathsin, though a different part was disturbed at how little he felt.

He hurried on after Gemmel, who had found what appeared to be a groundskeeping shed. When he pulled open the door, however, there were no tools, just a dark set of steps leading downward.

"Steel burning?" Gemmel asked. Kelsier nodded.

"Watch for movement," Gemmel said, grabbing a handful of coins from his pouch. Kelsier raised a hand toward the fallen guards and Pulled on the coins Gemmel had used against them, flipping them up toward him. He'd seen Gemmel Pull on things lightly, so that they didn't streak toward him at full strength. Kelsier hadn't mastered that trick yet, and he had to crouch down and let the coins spray over his head into the wall of the shed. He gathered them up, then started down after an impatient Gemmel, who was watching him with displeasure.

"I was unarmed," Kelsier explained. "Left my pouch on top of the building."

"Mistakes like that will end with you dead."

Kelsier didn't reply. It *had* been a mistake. Of course, he'd planned to fetch the coin pouch—and would have, if Gemmel hadn't knocked him off the spire.

The light grew dim, then neared blackness as they continued down the steps. Gemmel didn't produce a torch or lantern, but instead waved at Kelsier to go first. Another test of some sort?

Steel burning within Kelsier let him identify sources of metal by their blue lines. He paused, then dropped the handful of coins to the ground, letting them bounce down the steps. In falling, they let him see where the stairs were, and when they came to a rest that gave him an even better picture.

The blue lines weren't really "seeing," and he still had to walk carefully. However, the coins helped a great deal, and he did see a door latch as it drew near. Behind, he heard Gemmel grunt, and for once it seemed appreciative. "Nice trick with the coins," the man murmured.

Kelsier smiled, approaching the door at the bottom. He felt out for it, grabbing the metal latch. He carefully eased it open.

There was light on the other side. Kelsier crouched—despite what Gemmel might think, he'd done his share of infiltrating and quiet nighttime thefts. He wasn't some new sprout. He had simply learned that survival for a half-breed like him meant either learning to talk or learning to sneak; fighting head-on in most situations would have been foolish.

Of course, not one of the three—fighting, talking, or sneaking—had worked that night. The night he'd been taken, a night when nobody could have betrayed him but her. But why had they taken her too? She couldn't have—

Stop, he told himself, padding into the room in a crouch. It was full of long tables crowded with various kinds of smelting apparatus. Not the bulky smithing kind, but the small burners and delicate instruments of a master metallurgist. Lamps burned on the walls, and a large red forge glowed in the corner. Kelsier felt fresh air blow through from somewhere; the other side of the room ended in several corridors.

The room appeared empty. Gemmel entered, and Kelsier reached back to Pull the coins to him again. Some were stained with the blood of the fallen guards. Still in his crouch, he passed a desk full of writing implements and small, cloth-bound books. He glanced at Gemmel, who strode through the room without any attempt at stealth. Gemmel put his hands on his hips, looking around. "So where is he?"

"Who?" Kelsier said.

Gemmel started muttering under his breath, moving through the room, sweeping some of the implements off the tables and sending them crashing to the floor. Kelsier slipped around the perimeter, intent on peeking into the side corridors to see if anyone was coming. He checked the first one, and found that it opened into a long, narrow room. It was occupied.

Kelsier froze, then slowly stood up. There were half a dozen people in the room, both men and women, bound by their arms to the walls. There were no cells, but the poor souls looked as if they'd been beaten within an inch of their lives. They wore only rags, and those were bloodied.

Kelsier shook himself out of his daze, then padded to the first woman in the line. He pulled off her gag. The floor was damp; probably someone had been here recently to toss buckets of water on the prisoners to keep the laboratory from stinking. A gust of wind from the distant end of the hallway that the room eventually opened into brought a breath of fresh air.

The woman grew stiff as soon as he touched her, eyes snapping open and growing wide with terror. "Please, please no . . ." she whispered.

"I won't hurt you," Kelsier said. That numbness inside of him seemed to be . . . changing. "Please. Who are you? What is going on here?"

The woman just stared at him. She winced when Kelsier reached up to untie her bonds, and he hesitated.

He heard a muffled sound. Glancing to the side, he saw a second woman, older and matronly. Her skin had been all but flayed from beatings. Her eyes, however, were not nearly as frantic as those of the younger woman. Kelsier moved over and removed her gag.

"Please," the woman said. "Free us. Or kill us."

"What *is* this place?" Kelsier hissed, working on her arm bonds.

"He's searching for half-breeds," she said. "To test his new metals on."

"New metals?"

"I don't know," the woman said, tears on her cheeks. "I'm just skaa, we all are. I don't know why he picks us. He talks about things. Metals, unknown metals. I don't think he's completely sane. The things he does . . . he says they are to bring out our Allomantic side . . . but my lord, I've no noble blood. I can't . . ."

"Hush," Kelsier said, freeing her. Something was burning through that deep knot of numbness inside of him. Something that was like the anger he felt, but somehow different. It was more. It made him want to weep, yet it was warm.

Freed, the woman stared at her hands, wrists scraped raw from the bindings. Kelsier turned to the other poor captives. Most were awake now. There wasn't hope in their eyes. They just stared ahead, dull.

Yes, he could feel it.

How can we stand a world like this? Kelsier thought, moving to help another captive. *Where things like this happen?* The most appalling tragedy was that he knew this sort of horror was common. Skaa were disposable. There was nobody to protect them. Nobody cared.

Not even him. He'd spent most of his life ignoring such acts of brutality. Oh, he'd pretended to fight back. But he'd really just been about enriching himself. All of those plans, all of those heists, all of his grand visions. All about him. Him alone.

He freed another of the captives, a young, dark-haired woman. She looked like Mare. After being freed, she just huddled down on the ground in a ball. Kelsier stood over her, feeling powerless.

Nobody fights, he thought. *Nobody thinks they can fight. But they're wrong. We can fight. . . . I can fight.*

Gemmel strode into the room. He looked over the skaa and barely seemed to notice them. He was still muttering to himself. He had taken just a few steps into the room when a voice yelled from the laboratory.

"What is going on here?"

Kelsier recognized that voice. Oh, he'd never heard it specifically before—but he recognized the arrogance in it, the self-assuredness. The contempt. He found himself rising, brushing past Gemmel, stepping back into the lab.

A man in a fine suit, white shirt buttoned to the neck, stood in the laboratory. His hair was short, after the most current trends, and his suit looked to have been shipped in from Luthadel—it certainly was tailored after the most fashionable styles.

He looked at Kelsier, imperious. And Kelsier found himself smiling. *Really* smiling, for the first time since the Pits. Since the betrayal.

The nobleman sniffed, then raised a hand and tossed a coin at Kelsier. After a brief moment of surprise, Kelsier Pushed on it right as Lord Shezler did. Both were thrown backward, and Shezler's eyes widened in shock.

Kelsier slammed back against the wall. Shezler was Mistborn. No matter. A new kind of anger rose within Kelsier even as he grinned. It burned like a metal, that emotion did. An unknown, glorious metal.

He could fight back. He *would* fight back.

The nobleman yanked on his belt, dropping it—and his metals—from his waist. He whipped a dueling cane from his side and jumped forward, moving too quickly. Kelsier flared his pewter, then his steel, and Pushed on the apparatus on one of the tables, flinging it at Shezler.

The man snarled, raising an arm and Pushing some of it away. Again, the two Pushes—one from Kelsier, one from his foe—struck one another, and they were both slammed backward. Shezler steadied himself against a table, which shook. Glass broke and metal tools clattered to the ground.

"Have you any idea what all of that is worth?" Shezler growled, lowering his arm and advancing.

"Your soul, apparently," Kelsier whispered.

Shezler prowled forward, coming close, then struck with the cane. Kelsier backed away. He felt his pocket jerk, and he Pushed, shoving the coins out of his coat as Shezler Pushed on them. A second later, and they would have cut through Kelsier's stomach—as it was, they ripped out of his pocket, then shot backward toward the wall of the room.

His coat's buttons started to shake, though they only had some metal leaf on them. He pulled off the coat, removing the last bit of metal he was carrying. *Gemmel should have warned me about that!* The leaf had barely registered to his senses, but still he felt a fool. The older man was right; Kelsier wasn't thinking like an Allomancer. He focused too much on appearance and not enough on what might kill him.

Kelsier continued to back away, watching his opponent, determined not to make another mistake. He'd been in street brawls before, but not many. He'd tried to avoid them—brawling had been an old habit of Dockson's. For once, he wished he'd been less refined in that particular area.

He edged along one of the tables, waiting for Gemmel to come in from the side. The man didn't enter. He probably didn't intend to.

This was all about finding Shezler, Kelsier realized. *So that I could fight another Mistborn.* There was something important in that. . . . It suddenly made sense.

Kelsier growled, and was surprised to hear the sound coming from him. That glowing anger inside of him wanted vengeance, but also something more. Something greater. Not just revenge against those who had hurt him, but against the entirety of noble society.

In that moment, Shezler—arrogantly striding forward, more concerned for his equipment than the lives of his skaa—became a focus for it all.

Kelsier attacked.

He didn't have a weapon. Gemmel had spoken of glass knives, but had never given one to Kelsier. So, he snatched up a shard of broken glass from the floor, heedless of the cuts on his fingers. Pewter let him ignore pain as he jumped toward Shezler, going for his throat.

He probably shouldn't have won. Shezler was the more accomplished and practiced Allomancer—but it was obvious he was unaccustomed to fighting someone as strong as he was. He battered at Kelsier with the dueling cane. But with pewter Kelsier could ignore that as well, and instead he punched his shard of glass into the man's neck—three times.

In seconds it was over. Kelsier stumbled back, aches beginning to register. Shezler might have broken some of his bones with his battering; the man had pewter too, after all. The nobleman lay in his own blood though, twitching. Pewter could save you from a lot of things, but not a slit throat.

The man choked on his own blood. "No," he hissed. "I can't . . . not me . . . I can't die. . . ."

"Anyone can die," Kelsier whispered, dropping the bloodied shard of glass. "Anyone."

And a thought, a seed of a plan, began to form in his mind.

"That was too quick," Gemmel said.

Kelsier looked up, blood dripping from the tips of his fingers. Shezler croaked a final attempt at breath, then fell still.

"You need to learn Pushes and Pulls," Gemmel said. "Dancing through the air, fighting as a real Mistborn does."

"He was a real Mistborn."

"He was a scholar," Gemmel said, walking forward. He kicked at the corpse. "I picked a weak one first. Won't be so easy next time."

Kelsier walked back into the room with the skaa. He freed them, one by one. He couldn't do much more for them, but he promised that he'd see them safely out of the keep's grounds. Maybe he could get them in touch with the local underground; he'd been in the city long enough to have a few contacts.

Once he had them all freed, he turned to find them looking toward him in a huddled group. Some of the life seemed to have rekindled in their eyes, and more than a few were peeking into the room where

Shezler's corpse lay on the floor. Gemmel was picking through a notebook on one of the tables.

"Who are you?" asked the matronly woman he'd spoken to earlier.

Kelsier shook his head, still looking toward Gemmel. "I'm a man who has lived through things he shouldn't have."

"Those scars . . ."

Kelsier looked down at his arms, sliced with hundreds of tiny scars from the Pits. Removing his coat had exposed them.

"Come on," Kelsier said to the people, resisting the urge to cover up his arms. "Let's get you to safety. Gemmel, what in the Lord Ruler's name are you doing?"

The older man grunted, leafing through a book. Kelsier trotted into the room and glanced at it.

Theories and suppositions regarding the existence of an Eleventh Metal, the scrawl on the page read. *Personal notes. Antillius Shezler.*

Gemmel shrugged and dropped the book to the table. Then he carefully and meticulously selected a fork from the fallen tools and other scattered laboratory remains. He smiled and chuckled to himself. "Now *that* is a fork." He shoved it into his pocket.

Kelsier took the book. In moments, he was ushering the wounded skaa away from the keep, where soldiers were prowling the yards, trying to figure out what was happening.

Once they were out into the streets again, Kelsier turned back to the glowing building, which was lit with bright colors and beautiful windows. He listened in the curling mists as the guards' shouting became frantic.

The numbness was gone. He'd found something to replace it. His focus had returned. The spark was back. He'd been thinking too small.

A plan began to bud, a plan he barely dared consider for its audacity. Vengeance. And more.

He turned into the night, into the waiting mists, and went to find someone to make him a mistcloak.

POSTSCRIPT

This short piece was originally published in the Mistborn Adventure Game pen and paper role-playing game by Crafty Games. When we signed on with Crafty, I promised them a short piece of fiction to go in the book, as a sweetener to fans.

I knew I wanted to do a Kelsier story, and it made sense to do a backstory piece digging into the time when he was training as a Mistborn. Showing Gemmel (whom Kelsier had mentioned in the main series) was important, as it is part of the story of how Ruin manipulated Kelsier into doing what he did in the first volume of the trilogy.

At the same time, I also knew that this story would potentially be read by people who hadn't read the series. Having played many RPGs myself, I know that often one or two people in the group get really excited by a setting and do a campaign there—towing along the rest of the group, who aren't as familiar with it.

One of my goals with this piece, then, was to have something that would act as a little showpiece for the setting—I wanted something the game master could give to his players who were unfamiliar with the books. Something that would get across the tone, explain the magic system quickly, and act as a short introduction.

Because of that, it's a little more expository than the other Mistborn pieces in this collection, which assume that you're already invested in the characters and setting.

ALLOMANCER JAK
AND THE
PITS OF ELTANIA

EPISODES TWENTY-EIGHT THROUGH THIRTY

SPECIAL BOUND COLLECTION
OF ALL THREE EPISODES!

EDITED AND ANNOTATED BY HANDERWYM,
JAK'S OWN FAITHFUL TERRIS STEWARD!

This story contains minor spoilers for *The Alloy of Law*.

I BEGIN this week's letter as I awake to a mighty headache.

Truly, dear readers, this pain was incredible—and the effect was a din inside my mind not unlike that of a hundred rifles firing. I groaned and rolled to my knees in the darkened chamber; my face had been resting upon cold rock. My vision shook and took time to recover.

What had happened to me? I remembered my contest with the koloss challenger—a brute sized like a steamrail engine, with strength to match. I had defeated him with a bullet through the eye, had I not? Had I not in so doing maintained the loyalty of the entire koloss clan?*

I climbed to my feet and felt gingerly at the back of my head. There, I found dried blood. Fear not, for the wound was not terrible. Surely I had weathered far worse. This was not nearly as bad as when I had found myself sinking in the ocean, my arms bound, my feet tied to a metal bust of the Survivor as I sank.†

---

* Indeed, this was the outcome of Jak's brave—perhaps foolhardy—plan. See episode twenty-six. At this point, Jak had been "king" of the koloss for three episodes, and had survived the latest of challenges to his authority, getting closer to the secrets they held regarding the Survivor's Treasure.
† See "Allomancer Jak and the Mask of Ages," episode fourteen. There, however, Jak writes that it

The arid air and whistling sound of the wind through broken rock indicated I was still in the Roughs, which was good. These lands of adventure and danger are my natural habitat, and I thrive upon the challenge they provide. If I were to spend too long in the safe and mundane environment of milky Elendel, I fear I would wilt away.

My enclosure was a natural cavern of some sort, with rough stone walls and drooping stalactites on the ceiling. The cavern was shallow, however, and I found that it ended only a few feet back from my initial position. I would not be escaping in that direction, then.*

Cautious of potential gunfire, I edged to the front of the cavern and looked out. As I had guessed from the slight chill to the air, I was elevated. My cavern was on the wall of a small canyon, and the mouth opened only to a steep drop onto a group of rounded rocks far below.

Across from me, atop the ridge on the other side of the canyon, a group of blue figures watched my cavern. The hulking koloss were older ones, their skin stretched and broken, their bodies tattooed and draped with leather created from the skin of the men they had slain and eaten.†

"Why have you stranded me here, dread beasts?" I shouted at them, my voice echoing in the canyon. "And what have you done with the fair Elizandra Dramali? If you have harmed one hair upon her ever-beauteous scalp, you shall know the fury of an Allomancer enraged!"

The savages offered me no reply. They sat around their smoldering fire, and did not even turn in my direction.

Perhaps my situation was not as ideal as I had decided upon my first assessment. The canyon wall outside my cavern was as slick as glass and was as steep as the price of whiskey at Marlie's waystop. I surely could not survive an attempt to climb down, not dizzy as I was from the wound.

---

was a bust of the Lord Mistborn. One wonders if Jak ever stops to read his accounts after their publication. Fortunately for me, he does not seem to.

* One might wonder why Jak felt he needed to escape, as he had not discovered if he was imprisoned, and had not yet tried walking out through the front of the cavern. If you have this concern, might I remind you of the last *eighteen times* Jak awoke with a headache at the beginning of an episode? Each time, he had been captured in some fashion.

† Jak is completely, blissfully unaware of modern scholarship regarding the koloss, which indicates that they rarely (if ever) use actual human skin for their trophies. Indeed, accounts of them eating humans are greatly exaggerated.

But neither could I simply wait. Miss Dramali, my dear Elizandra, might surely be in danger. Curse that woman and her headstrong ways; she should have remained at camp as instructed. I had no idea what might have happened to her, nor to faithful Handerwym.* The koloss would not dare harm him, because of their vow to the Terris people,† but surely he feared for my safety.

I gave little thought to how I had reached this dire location. I needed metal. My system was clean of it; I had burned the last to steady my hands and eyes as I took the perfect shot at the koloss challenger to my throne. Unfortunately, my captors had stolen Glint—brutes though they are, the koloss are wise enough to take the guns from a man, particularly after seeing my skill with my trusty sidearm. They had also taken my vials of metal. Perhaps they wanted to see if those contained whiskey. Some Roughs Allomancers do store their metals in such solutions, but I have always abstained from the process. The mind of a gentleman adventurer needs to retain clarity at all times.‡

Surely the hidden pouch of tin in the heel of my boot would serve me. By misfortune, however, the heel's hidden compartment seemed to have been knocked open during my initial scuffle with the koloss champion. I had lost the pouch! I made a note to myself to speak with Ranette about her heel contraption and its tendency to open unexpectedly.

Disaster! An Allomancer without metal. I was left with only my own wits as a tool. Those—though of no small measure—might not be enough. Who knew what kind of trouble the fair Elizandra might be in at this point?

Determined, I began to feel about the cavern. It was an unlikely chance, but we were in highlands prized precisely because of their keen mining opportunities. Indeed, the Survivor favored me this day, for I located a small glimmering strain of metal along the far wall. Almost

---

* I was actually asleep. It had been a very long day. I'm sure I'd have worried about him if it had crossed my mind to do so. The bed the koloss provided, however, was surprisingly comfortable.

† See episode twenty-five for our discovery of their vow not to harm the Terris, and their explanation for the respect they have paid me during our adventures. It is a matter which I have regarded with some interest.

‡ Didn't he just mention the whiskey he often drinks at the waystop? Perhaps the dens of thieves do not count as a place where a clear mind is required.

invisible, I discovered it only by touch.* In the dim cavern I could not judge the metal's full nature, but I had no other options.

Now, I have found from my infrequent trips to Elendel that I am regarded with a somewhat heroic reputation. I must assure you, good readers, that I am but a humble adventurer, not deserving of an unduly idolized status. That said, while I have never wished for glory,† I do value my reputation. Therefore, if I could remove from your memories the image of this next part of my narrative, I would do so.

However, it has ever been my goal to present to you a sincere and unexpurgated account of my travels in the Roughs. Honesty is my greatest virtue.‡ And so, I offer you the truth of what needed to happen next.

I knelt down and began to lick the wall.

I would not ever wish to look foolish before you, dear readers.§ But in order to survive in the Roughs, a man must be willing to seize opportunity. I did so. With my tongue.

This activity gave me very little tin to burn, but it was enough for a few moments of enhanced senses.¶ I used them to listen with care for some clue as to how I might escape this situation.

I heard two things with my tin-enhanced ears. The first was the tinkling of water. I peeked out of my cavern and saw that the rocks below hid a small stream I had not seen earlier. The other thing I heard was a strange scratching, like that of claws on a branch.

I looked up, hopeful, and there found a crow perched among a sprout of weeds growing from the rocky wall. Could it be?

"Well done!" the crow exclaimed to me in her inhuman voice. "You have found metal even in your prison, Jak. The Survivor is pleased by your ingenuity."

---

* Yes, according to the way he wrote that sentence, he turned invisible for one line. No, he won't let me change it.

† Uh . . .

‡ Technically, this is probably true.

§ Well, it was too late for that after volume one. . . .

¶ I will admit to a healthy skepticism about Jak's wall-licking episode. My research indicates that one is highly unlikely to find pure tin exposed in this way inside of a natural cave formation. Even cassiterite, a tin ore of some relevance, would be unlikely in this area—and that might be too Allomantically impure to produce an effect. But Jak *is* being truthful about having lost his pouch of tin. I found it on the ground of the camp following his second capture, full and unopened.

It *was* her. Lyndip, my spirit guide, sent by the Survivor to me during my most difficult times of trial.* I have long suspected her to be one of the Faceless Immortals,† as the legends speak of them being able to change forms and take the bodies of animals.

"Lyndip!" I exclaimed. "Is Miss Dramali well? The koloss have not harmed her?"

"They have not, bold adventurer," Lyndip said. "But she is captured by them and is being held. You must escape, and quickly, for a dire fate awaits her."

"But how am I to escape!"

"I cannot give you the method," Lyndip said. "I am a guide, but I cannot solve a hero's problems for him. It is not the way of the Survivor, who deems that all men must make their own way."‡

"Very well," I said. "But tell me, guide: Why was I taken captive again? Had I not earned the loyalty of the koloss clan; was I not their king? I defeated the challenger!"

I am certain my frustration shone through, and I hope you do not think less of me—dear reader—to see such harsh words spoken to my spirit guide. However, I was not only concerned for the safety of my dear Elizandra, but was also devastated to lose the loyalty of this tribe of koloss. Savages though they are, they had seemed close to revealing their secrets to me—secrets I was certain would lead me to the symbol of the spearhead, the bloody footprints, and the Survivor's Treasure.

"I do not know for certain," Lyndip said, "but I suspect it was because you used a gun to kill the challenger. Previously, in winning the loyalty of the clan, you did not shoot your rival but frightened him off with the placement of your bullet. Many koloss clans see killing at a distance with guns to be a sign of weakness, not strength."

---

* See episode seven of this narrative for Lyndip's most recent appearance. I will repeat what I said there: I did not see, nor have I ever seen, this supposed talking bird and cannot confirm her existence.

† Never mind that the Faceless Immortals are a mythological feature of the Path, not Survivorism. This theological mixup has never bothered Jak.

‡ I suspect Jak was hallucinating through this entire section, a result of the trauma to his head. Upon doing this edit, I wished several times to be similarly afflicted.

Ruthless beasts—savages indeed.* The gun is the most elegant of weapons, the weapon of a gentleman.

"I *must* escape and rescue the fair Elizandra," I said. "Guide, did you see how I reached this cavern prison? Do the koloss have a secret passage somewhere, and did they bring me up here by that method?"

"I saw, adventuresome one," Lyndip said. "But the truth is not what you will wish to hear. There was no secret passage—instead, you were *thrown* up here by some koloss below."†

"Rust and Ruin!" I exclaimed. Undoubtedly, the beasts—afraid of the powerful weapons I had used—had placed me here to die of starvation, rather than risking the anger of their gods by killing me with their own hands.

I needed a way out, and quickly. I looked out again, and noticed storm clouds in the near distance. This started me thinking. I glanced down at the trickle of water in the canyon floor below. As I had noticed, the sides of this canyon were particularly smooth. As if . . . weathered.

Yes! I spotted distinctive lines on the canyon walls—water lines, from when the river ran bold and deep. My avenue of escape was soon to come! Indeed, the rains dumped on the plains upstream, and water soon surged into the canyon and—propelled by the narrower confines here—the river began to swell.

I waited nervously for the right moment to enter the river, and in my waiting, found time despite my anxiety to pen this letter to you. I sealed it in the special, water-proof pocket of my rugged trousers with the hope that if I should meet my end, it would find its way to you somehow once my body was found.

As rain began to fall on the canyon itself, I could wait no longer. I hurled myself into the risen waters below.‡

---

* I once mentioned to Jak that my people, the Terris, were at one time considered savages—at least according to the records given us by Harmony. He put a hand on my shoulder and said, "It is all right. I am proud to count a savage as my friend." He was so sincere, I dared not explain just how insulting he was being.

† I find this strains plausibility, even for a Jak story. More likely, the koloss lowered him from above.

‡ This marks the conclusion of this episode and the beginning of the next—and no, I don't know how he wrote the last paragraph after sealing the letter in his trousers. Regardless, I doubt you think this is Jak's demise, considering this collected volume contains three episodes of which this is

My readers, I trust this message finds you well. As you may recall, last week's missive ended with a dangerous leap on my part toward a watery doom. I was certain that my time had come, but I am somewhat pleased to say that I have survived. Only "somewhat" because of the revelation that I must soon impart unto you. If you must read on, be warned: The contents of this letter are dreadful, and might produce discomfort— even sickness—in the more frail and youthful among you.

I did leap from my cavern prison into the rising waters of the river. I must severely advise my readers against this kind of activity unless presented with the most dire of circumstances. The waters of a Roughs-style flash flood are dangerous, full of eddies and deadly rocks. If I had been presented with any other option, I surely would have taken it.

The waters churned around me like a stampede. Fortunately, I had experience with surviving waters of this nature.*

The key to swimming in waters such as these is to not fight. One must travel with the current, as a ship allows the sea to pull it. Still, even keeping afloat in such a tempest requires practice, luck, and force of will.

With strength of arm, I managed to steer myself around the most deadly of rocks and survive as the waters of my small tributary merged with the greater waters of the Rancid, the greatest river of the area. Here, the larger amount of water caused slower currents, and I managed with some difficulty to swim to the shore and pull myself free.

Exhausted, still dizzy from my wound, I flopped to the bank of the river. No sooner was I free, however, than a set of strong arms hauled me into the air.

Koloss. I had been captured again.

The beasts hauled me, sopping wet, away from the roaring river. I left

---

only the first. However, many of the weekly broadsheet readers of his letters did indeed worry that this was the end of Jak. Just as they worried at the end of the other three hundred episodes. It often strikes me that I wish I could find these people and discover to whom they sold the contents of their skulls, and for how much. I personally much prefer the audience of the *bound* volumes, such as this one. Their keen regard for my personal annotations proves them to be of a superior taste and intellect.

* See "Allomancer Jak and the Waters of Dread" for several equally implausible instances of Jak swimming strong currents and whitewater rapids. I am left to wonder why these extreme events never happen in my presence.

a trail of water in the dust.* I did not fight against my captors. There were six of them, medium-sized koloss, their blue skin starting to pull tight across their bodies, ripping at the sides of the mouths and around the largest of muscles.

They did not speak to me in their brutal tongue, and I knew I could not defeat six at once. Not without my guns and without metal. I deemed it better to let them drag me where they wished. Perhaps I would be placed back in my cavern prison.

Instead, the koloss carted me toward an incongruous stand of trees, hidden within a small valley of rocks. I had never come to this location before—indeed, the koloss had always steered me away from this area, claiming that it was a wasteland. From whence, then, did come the trees?†

The trees hid a small oasis in the dusty ground, a place where water welled up in a natural spring. I found this curious, as prime watering holes are usually marked on my maps.

They drug me past the trees and around the watering hole, and I saw that it was very deep—so deep that the depths were blue, and I could not make out a bottom. The sides were all of stone. And, with a start, I realized that the pool was shaped vaguely like a spearhead.

Could this be it? The location of the Survivor's Treasure? Had I found it at long last?‡ I looked for the other sign, that of the bloody footprints spoken of in the legends. I did not see them until my wet form was dragged across the stones nearest to the pool.

If you travel long in the Roughs, you will find that water sometimes reveals the true color of stone. This is not so much the case in the city where many of you live, dear readers, as the stones are coated in grime and soot. But here, the land is clean and fresh. The water my body dripped on the stones revealed a pattern in the rock not unlike that of a set of footprints leading into the oasis pool.

---

* I am not sure what happened to the rain that was so instrumental in his escape last episode. He doesn't mention it again.

† An unnecessary "from" is the least of Jak's problems, so I left it. I did manage to snip sixteen superfluous commas from this page. Jak is also under the impression that *koloss* looks better with an exclamation point in the center, and I have yet to ascertain the reason. For my own sanity, I have removed these, though I worry it has come too late.

‡ Yup.

This was it! Though not true footprints, I could see how a weary traveler—reaching this location—might mistake them for such. The invented story of the Survivor himself—bleeding from his spear wound and stopping here to drink—made sense.

The place was accoutred with koloss tattoo designs traced on the rocks and had their leatherwork wrapping some of the tree trunks. This was obviously a holy place for them, which explained both the reason I had never heard of this oasis, and the reason men had vanished in this area. Any who stumbled across this spot were murdered for having witnessed what they should not.

What did it say for my future that they had brought me here?*

There were more koloss here, of course. Some were so ancient that they had burst their skin completely; these sat wrapped in leather to contain the slow seeping of blood from their flesh. If you have never seen a koloss ancient, consider yourself lucky. Their immensity of size is only matched by the strangeness of their features, lacking noses or lips, their eyes bulging from faces of red flesh. Most koloss die of heart attacks before reaching this state. These would continue to grow, even after losing their skin, until that fate claimed them.

In ancient times, ones such as these would be killed. In modern days, however, elderly koloss are revered—or so I had learned, but only through stories.† I suspect that the locations where all tribes keep their elders are as holy as this one.

My guards deposited me before the ancients. I climbed to my knees, wary.

"You have come," said one of the ancients.

"You are not human," another said.

"You have bested our leader and killed all challengers," said the third.

---

* As fanciful as Jak's description of this place sounds, I have seen it myself, and must second his description. The patterns do look like footprints, and the pool appears to have the shape of a spearhead. The koloss do not speak of it to anyone. Incredible as it seems, he actually found the location of the Survivor's Treasure. I take this as proof that Harmony watches over all of us, for only deity could have such a cruel sense of humor as to repeatedly allow a man like Jak to bumble into such remarkable success.

† For this revelation, see episode twenty-five of this narrative.

"What will you do with me?" I demanded, forcing myself to my feet. Sodden and dazed though I was, I would meet my fate head-on.*

"You will be killed," one said.

"It will be according to the will of the daughter of the one who challenged you," said another.

"You must join us," said another.

"Join you?" I demanded. "How?"

"All koloss were once human," said one of the ancients.

I had heard such statements before. And, dear readers, I realize that I disparaged them to you. I considered them silly and fanciful.

It is with a heavy heart that I must tell you that I was wrong. So very wrong. I have since learned the terrible truth. The ancients are right.

Koloss are people.

The process is terrible. To initiate a man into their ranks, they take him and pin him with small spikes of metal. This creates a mystical transformation, during which the man's mind and identity are savagely weakened. In the end, the person becomes as dull and simple as the koloss.

Koloss are not born. Koloss are made. Their barbarity exists inside of all of us. Perhaps this was what dear Handerwym was trying to tell me.†

They said that I had to join them. Was this to be my final end? To live my life as a brute in a distant village, my mind lost?‡

"You spoke of the daughter of the one who challenged me," I said. "Who is this?"

"Me," said a soft, familiar voice.

I turned and found Elizandra Dramali emerging from behind some trees nearby. She no longer wore her dress, and instead was wrapped in leathers that only *just* covered up her most intimate parts. Indeed, a full

---

* Or, in other words, "I couldn't escape immediately, but I wanted to be ready to run screaming like a child as soon as I had the opportunity. So I stood up."

† Well, no. But I'll accept it. Please note that what Jak is saying here is, unfortunately, true. I have seen the process with my own eyes, as have other scholars, and it is widely accepted that this description of the practice is true. I did try to explain this to Jak on several occasions.

‡ Not sure if this is possible. It would be much like dividing by a null set.

description of her figure would be too shocking for my more sensitive readers, and so I will forbear.*

She still wore her spectacles, and her golden hair was pulled back into its customary tail, but her skin . . . her skin was now a shade of blue, such as I had never before seen.

Elizandra, fair Elizandra, was *koloss-blooded.*†

"This can't be!" I exclaimed, staring at my beautiful Elizandra. The woman I had grown to love and cherish above all others. The woman who had somehow hidden her true nature from me all this time.

Elizandra was koloss-blooded.

I wish I did not have to write these words to you, my stalwart readers. But they are true, true as my poor heart bleeds. True as the ink on this page.

"Makeup," Elizandra said, demure eyes downcast. "As you can see, the blue cast to my skin is light, compared to some koloss-blooded. Clever use of powders and gloves have allowed me to hide what I am."

"But your mind!" I said, stepping toward her. "You think and have wit, unlike these beasts!"‡

I moved to reach toward her, but hesitated. Everything I knew about this woman was a lie. She was a monster. Not my fair, wonderful noblewoman, but a creature of the wilds, a murderer and a savage.

"Jak," she said. "I am still me. I was born to koloss, but have not accepted the transformation. My mind is as keen as that of any human. Please, my dear one, see past this skin and look into my heart."§

I could resist no longer. She might have lied, but she was still my

---

* This, of course, did not stop the newspaper editors from including a detailed sketch of this scene in their original printing of the episode.

† The original printing of this story ended the penultimate episode right here, which—I am told—nearly caused riots and prompted a special broadsheet the next day, containing the conclusion of the story. Fortunately, we had sent in all three of these episodes together, in a single pouch. It is a constant source of amazement to me that people are so interested in Jak's raw accounts, rather than waiting for my more sensible, annotated edition. This lack of taste upon the part of the general public is one of the very reasons I left Elendel to travel the Roughs in the first place. It was either that or shoot myself, and my oaths of a steward's pacifism forbid me from shedding blood.

‡ Studies have proven that koloss-blooded individuals are, on average, no less intelligent than ordinary humans—though obviously this is not true for full koloss who have accepted the transformation. Or for most adventurers.

§ I showed this scene to Elizandra, and her response was laughter. Take that as you wish. I would make note, however, that when *I* have spoken to her of this, she has not seemed nearly so ashamed of her heritage, though she did hide it from us all at first.

Elizandra. I stepped into her embrace, and felt her sweet warmth in this time of confusion.

"You are in grave danger, loved one," she whispered into my ear. "They will make you one of them."

"Why?"

"You frightened away their chief," Elizandra whispered. "And ruled the clan despite the challenges we provided. Finally, you killed their greatest champion. My mother."

"The champion was a *woman*?" I asked.

"Of course. Didn't you notice?"

I glanced at the gathered koloss, who wore loincloths, but generally no tops. If there was a way to distinguish the males from the females other than . . . ahem . . . peeking, I did not know it. In fact, I'd rather not have known that some of them were women. My crusty, wind-weathered cheeks did no longer often blush, for the things I've seen would rub your delicate minds raw. But if I'd been capable of a blush, I might have given one at that moment.

"I am sorry, then, for killing her," I said, looking back to Elizandra, who still held me.

"She chose her own course in life," Elizandra said. "And it was one of brutality and murder. I do not mourn her, but I will mourn you, should you be taken into their embrace, dear one. They speak of this being my will, but it is certainly not, though they will not listen to my protests."*

"Why did they lock me away to die in that cavern?" I asked.

"It was a test," Elizandra said. "A final challenge. They would have freed you after three days, if you had not escaped—but as you managed to, you have proven worthy to join their ranks and become their new chief in full. But to do so, you must undergo the transformation! You will lose most of your self, instead becoming one of them, a creature of instinct."†

---

* More laughter here. If you know Zandra, you'd probably realize that any statement that lacks three curses—and a comment about Jak's questionable parentage—cannot truly be attributed to her. But she *does* seem to be fond of him. For some reason.

† For those confused—which includes Jak—this really is the way that one becomes a full koloss. Their children are born with skin that ranges from blue to mottled grey, but not the deep blue of true koloss. These children are generally human, though they have some generous endowments of physical capability. Each child is offered the choice to make the final transformation when they reach

I had to escape, then. This fate would be worse than death—it would be a death of the mind. Though I have gained a great respect for the koloss savages,* I had no intention of ever joining them.

"You steered me here," I realized, looking toward Elizandra. "Ever since we found you in these Roughs, you have been guiding me toward this tribe. You knew of this pool."

"I suspected, from your descriptions of what you sought, this was the location of the treasure," said my fairest one. "But I did not know for certain. I had never been to the holy pool. Jak . . . once they transform you, they plan to do the same to me, against my will. I have resisted this all of my life. I would not let them take my mind as a youth—I will not allow it now!"

"Enough talk!" said one of the elders. "You will be transformed!"

The other koloss began to clap in unison. One of the ancients reached out a trembling, bloody hand, holding in his palm a handful of small spikes.

"No!" I exclaimed. "There is no need! For I am *already* one of you!"

Elizandra's hand tightened on my arm. "What?" she whispered.

"It is the only plan I can think of," I whispered back. Then, more loudly, I proclaimed. "I am koloss!"

"Not possible," said one of the ancients.

"You are not blue," said another.

"You have not the way," said the third.

"I slew your champion!" I declared. "What more proof do you need! Would an ordinary human be strong enough to do this?"

"Gun," said one of the ancients. "It takes not strength to use the gun."

Rust and Ruin! "Well then," I declared, "I will prove it in a final test. For I will bring you the treasure of the Survivor!"

The koloss grew silent. Their clapping stopped.

---

their twelfth year. Those who do not accept the transformation must leave and join human society. By my estimation, many do leave—but just as many ordinary humans, dissatisfied with their lives in the cities, make their way to the koloss tribes and join them, accepting the transformation. From there, no distinguishing is made between those who were originally humans or koloss-blooded.

* Not enough respect to refrain from calling them savages, of course.

"Not possible," said one of the ancients. "Even strongest koloss have failed."

"Then if I succeed, you will know I have told the truth," I said to the beasts.

I was setting myself up for certain death. I wish I could tell you that bravery steered my lips that day, but it was truly just desperation. I spoke of the only thing that occurred to me, the only thing that would let me delay.

If the legends were true, then the treasure was hidden "opposite the sky, raised only by life itself." Opposite the sky must mean at the bottom of the pool—so far down, I could not see it. I would have to dive in and recover the treasure.

"Not possible," said another ancient.

"I will prove it possible!" I declared.

"Jak!" Elizandra said, hand on my arm. "You're a fool!"

"A fool I might be," I said, "but I will not let them take me to be a koloss."

She pulled me to her, suddenly, and kissed me. Very little in life shocks me, dear readers, but that moment achieved the impossible. She had been so cold toward me at times that I was certain my affection would go unrequited.

But this kiss . . . this *kiss*! As deep as the pool beside us, as true as the Survivor's own teachings. As powerful as a bullet in flight, and as incredible as a bull's-eye at three hundred yards. The passion in it warmed me, casting off the chill of my sodden clothing and the fear of a trembling heart.

When she finished, metal flared to life inside of me. Though not an Allomancer, she'd poured some tin dust in her mouth, passing it to me in the kiss!

I pulled back, marveling. "You're amazing," I whispered.

"Well damn, Jak," she whispered back. "You've finally gone and said something smart, for once."*

---

* I believe that this is the only accurate quote from Elizandra in the entire story. She confided in me she threatened to shoot him in the . . . ahem . . . masculine identity if he didn't include it in the official narrative.

The koloss started to clap again. I picked the largest rock I could carry, then—taking a deep breath—leaped into the pool and allowed the rock to pull me downward.

It was deep. Unfathomably deep.*

The darkness soon swallowed me. Dear readers, you must imagine this complete darkness, for I do not believe I can do it justice. To be consumed by the blackness is itself a remarkable experience, but to be in the waters as light flees . . . there is something incredibly horrifying about such an experience. Even my steel nerves gave way to trembling as my descent continued.

A terrible pain struck my ears, though whether this was from my wound, I know not. I dropped for what seemed like forever, until my lungs were burning, my mind growing numb. I nearly let go of my rock.

I could not think. My wound threatened to overwhelm me, and though I could not see, I knew that my vision was growing cloudy. My body was failing me as I plummeted toward unconsciousness. I knew that I would die in these unseen depths.

At that moment, I thought of Elizandra being turned into a koloss, losing the beautiful wit that so charmed me. This thought gave me strength, and I flared my tin.

Flared tin brings clarity of mind, as I have said before. I have never welcomed it as much as I did then; those moments of lucidity forced away the shadow upon my mind.

I felt the coldness of the water, and the pain in my head seemed incredible, but I was *alive*.

I hit the bottom. Not daring to release my rock weight, I felt about me with one hand, frantic. My lungs burned like flared metals. Was it here?

Yes! It was. Something square and unnatural, a box of metal. A strongbox?

I tried to lift it, and managed to make it budge, but it was as heavy as my rock. With dismay, I realized that I could never carry this up to the

---

* And by that he means precisely 18.3 fathoms. I went back and measured.

surface. My body was too weak; swimming with such a weight was more than I could accomplish.

Was I to fail, then? If I reached the surface without the treasure, perhaps they would simply kill me, or perhaps they would make me like them—either way I would be finished.

I worked again to lift the box, but could swim only a few feet. I had no air, no strength. It was useless!

And then, I remembered the poem. Opposite the sky you shall find it, and it shall be raised only by life itself.*

Life itself. What was life down here?

Air.

I fumbled at the sides of the box and found a latch, which released some kind of object. It felt leathery, like a waterskin. I breathed into it, giving up all of the air in my lungs, air which no longer sustained me— but which might still serve me.† Then, I kicked off of the bottom, my metal spent, my air expended.

Eternity.

I burst from the surface of the pool as my vision clouded again. I saw only a moment of light before darkness snatched me back, but soft hands grabbed me and hauled me free of the water before I could sink to my doom. I smelled Elizandra's perfume, and recovered to the sight of her concerned face, cradling my head in her lap. The view of her leather costume from beneath was not particularly proper, but also not unappreciated.

"You fool," she whispered as I rolled over and coughed water from my lungs.

"He has failed!" exclaimed the koloss elders.

At that very moment, something bobbed to the surface of the pool— it appeared to be an inflated bladder of some sort, perhaps from a

---

* Yes, I am aware that he has quoted this poem six different times through the course of this narrative, and has said it a little differently each time. No, he will not allow me to change them and make them consistent.

† Those readers with a knowledge of buoyancy and pressure should probably stop here, as opposed to working out the mathematics of what a single lungful of air could manage under these circumstances.

sheep. I reached into the water and grabbed the strongbox that floated underneath.*

The koloss crowded around as I knelt beside the box and worked at the lock. Elizandra produced the key we had found in Maelstrom's mine, and it fitted† exactly. I turned it with a click, and opened the top.

Inside were spikes.

The koloss shouts first worried me, but they turned out to be shouts of joy. I looked to Elizandra, confused.

"New spikes," she said. "Many of them. With these, the tribe can grow. They were losing the wars with those nearby; my tribe has always been the smallest of those in the area. This will grow them by the dozens. It is a true treasure to them."

I sat back on my heels. I will express some regret to you, dear readers. I travel not for wealth, but for the joy of discovery and the opportunity to share the world with you—but still, this was not the treasure I had hoped to discover. A handful of small spikes? This was what I had searched for months upon months to find? This was the fabled wealth left by the Survivor himself?

"Do not look so morose, dear one," Elizandra said, dumping the spikes for the ancients to take. She pulled back with me as they gathered around. It appeared that the two of us had been forgotten in the excitement. "It seems we have our lives restored to us."

Indeed, the koloss did not stop us as we fled. We quickly left the small oasis valley, making toward the river and—hopefully—the rest of our caravan.‡

I still found myself disappointed. It was then that I noticed something. The box Elizandra carried hadn't tarnished much from what had undoubtedly been over three centuries spent under the waters. I gestured for her to hand it to me, and I buffed at the surface of the lid. Then, I blinked in surprise.

---

* If a bag of air was all that was needed to raise the treasure, one wonders why the grandest of all windbags himself needed the aforementioned sheep's bladder.

† Sigh.

‡ Yes, they forgot about me.

"What?" she asked, stopping in the path.

I grinned. "Pure aluminum, my dear—worth thousands. We have found our treasure after all."

She laughed and favored me with another kiss.

And it is here, my readers, that I must end the account of my travels in the Pits of Eltania. The treasure found, our lives lost—and then recovered—I had fulfilled the dying wish of dear, fallen Mikaff.

It was my grandest adventure yet, and I believe I will rest for a short time before striking out again. I have been hearing of strange lights in the southern skies that can only hide another mystery.

Until then, adventure on!*

---

* And so, we come to the end of another annotated volume. I'm certain that discerning readers of elegance and respectability will appreciate my long-suffering efforts in keeping Jak alive, if only because I suspect these edited accounts provide them with an individual blend of amusement on long winter evenings. I bid you farewell, then. Jak promises further adventure and mystery, but I make a more humble promise. I'm going to try to get him to use proper punctuation in his letters for once in his life. I believe my task to be the more difficult of the two, by far.

Handerwym of Inner Terris
The 17th of Hammondar, 341

POSTSCRIPT

This is the second of the stories I wrote for Crafty Games, this one to be published in their *Alloy of Law* supplement.

I took a different direction on this story. Since I'd done the first one as more of a showpiece to new readers, I wanted this one to be something deep and interesting for established readers. Revealing how the koloss are made and exist in the second era of Scadrial's sequence seemed the kind of secret that would be intriguing to people.

Many years ago, my brother Jordan came to me wanting to do a radio drama as a podcast. He wanted it to be scripted, written by me—but I just didn't have time. (Writing Excuses was born out of this, though I believe he eventually went to Dan Wells to do some episodes of something more scripted.) He pitched it as the story of an old-time adventurer/explorer. Though I couldn't do the piece, I did spend years thinking about what I might have done, had I had the time.

Allomancer Jak is a direct response to this. The gentleman adventurer, over the top, based off old pulp stories. Writing only that, however, seemed like it wouldn't work. In the Wax and Wayne books, I was already telling stories that were a more authentic evolution of pulp stories, with more solid characterization and less melodrama.

Jak, then, had to be about contrast—a way to highlight the old against the new. Whether he is actually the blowhard that his "faithful steward" implies he is, or whether he's more of a quixotic adventurer with boundless optimism, he is supposed to present a certain level of inauthenticity. A contrast to Wax, in the way that you might contrast the newer incarnations of Batman with the old Adam West Batman. (Note that I love both.)

As an aside, writing Handerwym's annotations was one of the most amusing things I've ever done as a writer.

MISTBORN:
SECRET
HISTORY

This novella contains major spoilers for the original
Mistborn Trilogy and minor spoilers for *The Bands of Mourning*.

PART ONE
EMPIRE

1

KELSIER burned the Eleventh Metal.

Nothing changed. He still stood in that Luthadel square, facing down the Lord Ruler. A hushed audience, both skaa and noble, watched at the perimeter. A squeaking wheel turned lazily in the wind, hanging from the side of the overturned prison wagon nearby. An Inquisitor's head had been nailed to the wood of the wagon's bottom, held in place by its own spikes.

Nothing changed, while everything changed. For to Kelsier's eyes, two men now stood before him.

One was the immortal emperor who had dominated for a thousand years: an imposing figure with jet-black hair and a chest stuck through with two spears that he didn't even seem to notice. Next to him stood a man with the same features—but a completely different demeanor. A figure cloaked in thick furs, nose and cheeks flush as if cold. His hair was tangled and windswept, his attitude jovial, smiling.

It was the same man.

Can I use this? Kelsier thought, frantic.

Black ash fell lightly between them. The Lord Ruler glanced toward the Inquisitor that Kelsier had killed. "Those are very hard to replace," he said, his voice imperious.

That tone seemed a direct contrast to the man beside him: a vagabond, a mountain man wearing the Lord Ruler's face. *This is what you really are,* Kelsier thought. But that didn't help. It was only further proof that the Eleventh Metal wasn't what Kelsier had once hoped. The metal was no magical solution for ending the Lord Ruler. He would have to rely instead upon his other plan.

And so, Kelsier smiled.

"I killed you once," the Lord Ruler said.

"You tried," Kelsier replied, his heart racing. The other plan, the secret plan. "But you can't kill me, Lord Tyrant. I represent that thing you've never been able to kill, no matter how hard you try. I am hope."

The Lord Ruler snorted. He raised a casual arm.

Kelsier braced himself. He could not fight against someone who was immortal.

Not alive, at least.

Stand tall. Give them something to remember.

The Lord Ruler backhanded him. Agony hit Kelsier like a stroke of lightning. In that moment, Kelsier flared the Eleventh Metal, and caught a glimpse of something new.

The Lord Ruler standing in a room—no, a cavern! The Lord Ruler stepped into a glowing pool and the world shifted around him, rocks crumbling, the room twisting, everything *changing*.

The vision vanished.

Kelsier died.

It turned out to be far more painful a process than he had anticipated. Instead of a soft fade to nothingness, he felt an awful *tearing* sensation—as if he were a cloth caught between the jaws of two vicious hounds.

He screamed, desperately trying to hold himself together. His will meant nothing. He was rent, ripped, and hurled into a place of endless shifting mists.

He stumbled to his knees, gasping, aching. He wasn't certain what he knelt upon, as downward seemed to just be more mist. The ground rippled like liquid, and felt soft to his touch.

He knelt there, enduring, feeling the pain slowly fade away. At last he unclenched his jaw and groaned.

He was alive. Kind of.

He managed to look up. That same thick greyness shifted all around him. A nothingness? No, he could see shapes in it, shadows. Hills? And high in the sky, some kind of light. A tiny sun perhaps, as seen through dense grey clouds.

Kelsier breathed in and out, then growled, heaving himself to his feet. "Well," he proclaimed, "*that* was thoroughly awful."

It did seem there was an afterlife, which was a pleasant discovery. Did this mean . . . did this mean Mare was still out there somewhere? He'd always offered platitudes, talking to the others about being with her again someday. But deep down he'd never believed, never really thought . . .

The end was not the end. Kelsier smiled again, this time truly excited. He turned about, and as he inspected his surroundings, the mists seemed to withdraw. No, it felt like Kelsier was *solidifying,* entering this place fully. The withdrawal of the mists was more like a clearing of his own mind.

The mists coalesced into shapes. Those shadows he'd mistaken for hills were buildings, hazy and formed of shifting mists. The ground beneath his feet was also mist, a deep vastness, like he was standing on the surface of the ocean. It was soft to his touch, like cloth, and even a little springy.

Nearby lay the overturned prison wagon, but here it was made of mist. That mist shifted and moved, but the wagon retained its form. It was like the mist was trapped by some unseen force into a specific shape. More strikingly, the wagon's prison bars *glowed* on this side. Complementing them, other white-hot pinpricks of light appeared around him, dotting the landscape. Doorknobs. Window latches. Everything in the living world was reflected here in this place, and while most things were shadowy mist, metal instead appeared as a powerful light.

Some of those lights moved. He frowned, stepping toward one, and only then did he recognize that many of the lights were people. He saw each as an intense white glow radiating out from a human form.

Metal and souls are the same thing, he observed. Who would have thought?

As he got his bearings, he recognized what was happening in the living world. Thousands of lights moved, flowing away. The crowd was running from the square. A powerful light, with a tall silhouette, strode in another direction. The Lord Ruler.

Kelsier tried to follow, but stumbled over something at his feet. A misty form slumped on the ground, pierced by a spear. Kelsier's own corpse.

Touching it was like remembering a fond experience. Familiar scents from his youth. His mother's voice. The warmth of lying on a hillside with Mare, looking up at the falling ash.

Those experiences faded and seemed to grow *cold*. One of the lights from the mass of fleeing people—it was hard to make out individuals, with everyone alight—scrambled toward him. At first he thought perhaps this person had seen his spirit. But no, they ran to his corpse and knelt.

Now that she was close, he could make out the details of this figure's features, cut of mist and glowing from deep within.

"Ah, child," Kelsier said. "I'm sorry." He reached out and cupped Vin's face as she wept over him, and found he could feel her. She was solid to his ethereal fingers. She didn't seem able to feel his touch, but he caught a vision of her from the real world, cheeks stained with tears.

His last words to her had been harsh, hadn't they? Perhaps it was a good thing that he and Mare had never had children.

A glowing figure surged from the fleeing masses and grabbed Vin. Was that Ham? Had to be, with that profile. Kelsier stood up and watched them withdraw. He had set plans in motion for them. Perhaps they would hate him for that.

"You let him kill you."

Kelsier spun, surprised to find a person standing beside him. Not a figure made of mist, but a man in strange clothing: a thin wool coat that went down almost to his feet, and beneath it a shirt that laced closed, with a kind of conical skirt. That was tied with a belt that had a bone-handled knife stuck through a loop.

The man was short, with black hair and a prominent nose. Unlike the other people—who were made of light—this man looked normal, like Kelsier. Since Kelsier was dead, did this make the man another ghost?

"Who are you?" Kelsier demanded.

"Oh, I think you know." The man met Kelsier's eyes, and in them Kelsier saw eternity. A cool, calm eternity—the eternity of stones that saw generations pass, or of careless depths that didn't notice the changing of days, for light never reached them anyway.

"Oh, hell," Kelsier said. "There's actually a God?"

"Yes."

Kelsier decked him.

It was a good, clean punch, thrown from the shoulder while he brought his other arm up to block a counterstrike. Dox would be proud.

God didn't dodge. Kelsier's punch took him right across the face, connecting with a satisfying *thud*. The punch tossed God to the ground, though when he looked up he seemed more shocked than pained.

Kelsier stepped forward. "What the hell is wrong with you? You're real, and you're letting *this* happen?" He waved toward the square where—to his horror—he saw lights winking out. The Inquisitors were attacking the crowd.

"I do what I can." The fallen figure seemed to distort for a moment, bits of him expanding, like mists escaping an enclosure. "I do . . . I do what I can. It is in motion, you see. I . . ."

Kelsier recoiled a step, eyes widening as God *came apart*, then pulled back together.

Around him, other souls made the transition. Their bodies stopped glowing, then their souls lurched into this land of mists: stumbling, falling, as if ejected from their bodies. Once they arrived, Kelsier saw them in color. The same man—God—appeared near each of them. There were suddenly over a dozen versions of him, each identical, each speaking to one of the dead.

The version of God near Kelsier stood up and rubbed his jaw. "Nobody has ever done that before."

"What, really?" Kelsier asked.

"No. Souls are usually too disoriented. Some do run, though." He looked to Kelsier.

Kelsier made fists. God stepped back and—amusingly—reached for the knife at his belt.

Well, Kelsier wasn't going to attack him, not again. But he *had* heard the challenge in those words. Would he run? Of course not. Where would he run to?

Nearby, an unfortunate skaa woman lurched into the afterlife, then almost immediately *faded*. Her figure stretched, transforming to a white mist that was pulled toward a distant, dark point. That was how it looked, at least, though the point she stretched toward wasn't a place—not really. It was . . . Beyond. A location that was somehow distant, pointing away from him no matter where he moved.

She stretched, then faded away. Other spirits in the square followed.

Kelsier spun on God. "What's happening?"

"You didn't think *this* was the end, did you?" God asked, waving toward the shadowy world. "This is the in-between step. After death and before . . ."

"Before what?"

"Before the Beyond," God said. "The Somewhere Else. Where souls must go. Where *yours* must go."

"I haven't gone yet."

"It takes longer for Allomancers, but it will happen. It is the natural progress of things, like a stream flowing toward the ocean. I'm here not to make it occur, but to comfort you as you go. I see it as a kind of . . . duty that comes with my position." He rubbed the side of his face and gave Kelsier a glare that said what he thought of his reception.

Nearby, another pair of people faded into the eternities. They seemed to accept it, stepping into the stretching nothingness with relieved, welcoming smiles. Kelsier looked at those departing souls.

"Mare," he whispered.

"She went Beyond. As you will."

Kelsier looked toward that point Beyond, the point toward which all the dead were being drawn. He felt it, faintly, begin to tug on him as well.

No. Not yet.

"We need a plan," Kelsier said.

"A plan?" God asked.

"To get me out of this. I might need your help."

"There *is* no way out of this."

"That's a terrible attitude," Kelsier said. "We'll never get anything done if you talk like that."

He looked at his arm, which was—disconcertingly—starting to blur, like ink on a page that had been accidentally brushed before it dried. He felt a *draining*.

He started walking, forcing himself into a stride. He wouldn't just stand there while eternity tried to suck him away.

"It is natural to feel uncertain," God said, falling into step beside him. "Many are anxious. Be at peace. The ones you left behind will find their own way, and you—"

"Yes, great," Kelsier said. "No time for lectures. Talk to me. Has anyone ever resisted being pulled into the Beyond?"

"No." God's form pulsed, unraveling again before coming back together. "I've told you already."

Damn, Kelsier thought. *He seems one step from falling apart himself.*

Well, you had to work with what you had. "You've got to have some kind of idea what I could try, Fuzz."

"What did you call me?"

"Fuzz. I've got to call you something."

"You could try 'My Lord,'" Fuzz said with a huff.

"That's a terrible nickname for a crewmember."

"Crewmember . . ."

"I need a team," Kelsier said, still striding through the shadowy version of Luthadel. "And as you can see, my options are limited. I'd rather have Dox, but he's got to go deal with the man who is claiming to be you. Besides, the initiation to this particular team of mine is a killer."

"But—"

Kelsier turned, taking the smaller man by the shoulders. Kelsier's arms were blurring further, drawn away like water being pulled into the current of an invisible stream.

"Look," Kelsier said quietly, urgently, "you said you were here to comfort me. This is how you do it. If you're right, then nothing I do now will matter. So why not humor me? Let me have one last thrill as I face down the ultimate eventuality."

Fuzz sighed. "It would be better if you accepted what is happening."

Kelsier held Fuzz's gaze. Time was running out; he could *feel* himself sliding toward oblivion, a distant point of nothingness, dark and unknowable. Still he held that gaze. If this creature acted anything like the human he resembled, then holding his eyes—with confidence, smiling, self-assured—would work. Fuzz would bend.

"So," Fuzz said. "You're not only the first to punch me, you're also the first to try to *recruit* me. You are a distinctively strange man."

"You don't know my friends. Next to them I'm normal. Ideas please." He started walking up a street, moving just to be moving. Tenements loomed on either side, made of shifting mists. They looked like the ghosts of buildings. Occasionally a wave—a shimmer of light—would pulse through the ground and buildings, causing the mists to writhe and twist.

"I don't know what you expect me to tell you," Fuzz said, hustling up to walk beside him. "Spirits who come to this place are drawn into the Beyond."

"You aren't."

"I'm a god."

A god. Not just "God." Noted.

"Well," Kelsier said, "what is it about being a god that makes you immune?"

"Everything."

"I can't help thinking you aren't pulling your weight on this team, Fuzz. Come on. Work with me. You indicated that Allomancers last longer. Feruchemists too?"

"Yes."

"People with power," Kelsier said, pointing toward the distant spires of Kredik Shaw. This was the road the Lord Ruler had taken, heading toward his palace. Though the Lord Ruler's carriage was now distant,

Kelsier could still see his soul glowing up there somewhere. Far brighter than the others.

"What about him?" Kelsier said. "You say that everyone has to bend to death, but obviously that isn't true. He is immortal."

"He's a special case," Fuzz said, perking up. "He has ways of not dying in the first place."

"And if he did die?" Kelsier pressed. "He'd last even longer on this side than I am, right?"

"Oh, indeed," Fuzz said. "He Ascended, if just for a short time. He held enough of the power to expand his soul."

Got it. Expand my soul.

"I . . ." God wavered, figure distorting. "I . . ." He cocked his head. "What was I saying?"

"About how the Lord Ruler expanded his soul."

"That was delightful," God said. "It was spectacular to watch! And now he is *Preserved*. I am glad you didn't find a way to destroy him. Everyone else passes, but not him. It's wonderful."

"Wonderful?" Kelsier felt like spitting. "He's a tyrant, Fuzz."

"He's unchanging," God said, defensive. "He's a brilliant specimen. So unique. I don't agree with what he does, but one can empathize with the lamb while admiring the lion, can one not?"

"Why not stop him? If you disagree with what he does, then do something about it!"

"Now, now," God said. "That would be hasty. What would removing him accomplish? It would just raise another leader who is more transient—and cause chaos and even more deaths than the Lord Ruler has caused. Better to have stability. Yes. A constant leader."

Kelsier felt himself stretching further. He'd go soon. It didn't seem his new body could sweat, for if it could have his forehead would certainly be drenched by now.

"Maybe you would enjoy watching another do as he did," Kelsier said. "Expand their soul."

"Impossible. The power at the Well of Ascension won't be gathered and ready for more than a year."

"*What?*" Kelsier said. The *Well of Ascension?*

He dredged through his memories, trying to remember the things Sazed had told him of religion and belief. The scope of it threatened to overwhelm him. He'd been playing at rebellion and thrones—focusing on religion only when he thought it might benefit his plans—and all the while, *this* had been in the background. Ignored and unnoticed.

He felt like a child.

Fuzz kept speaking, oblivious to Kelsier's awakening. "But no, you wouldn't be able to use the Well. I've failed at locking him away. I knew I would; he's stronger. His essence seeps out in natural forms. Solid, liquid, gas. Because of how we created the world. He has plans. But are they deeper than my plans, or have I finally outthought him . . . ?"

Fuzz distorted again. His diatribe made little sense to Kelsier. He felt as if it was important, but it just wasn't *urgent*.

"Power is returning to the Well of Ascension," Kelsier said.

Fuzz hesitated. "Hm. Yes. Um, but it's far, far away. Yes, too far for you to go. Too bad."

God, it turned out, was a terrible liar.

Kelsier seized him, and the little man cringed.

"Tell me," Kelsier said. "Please. I can feel myself stretching away, falling, being pulled. Please."

Fuzz yanked out of his grip. Kelsier's fingers . . . or rather, his soul's fingers . . . weren't working as well any longer.

"No," Fuzz said. "No, it is not right. If you touched it, you might just add to his power. You will go as all others."

Very well, Kelsier thought. *A con, then.*

He let himself slump against the wall of a ghostly building. He sighed, settling down in a seated position, back to the wall. "All right."

"See, there!" Fuzz said. "Better. Much better, isn't it?"

"Yes," Kelsier said.

God seemed to relax. With discomfort, Kelsier noticed God was still leaking. Mist slipped away from his body at a few pinprick points. This creature was like a wounded beast, placidly going about its daily life while ignoring the bite marks.

Remaining motionless was hard. Harder than facing down the Lord

Ruler had been. Kelsier wanted to run, to scream, to scramble and move. That sensation of being drawn away was *horrible*.

Somehow he feigned relaxation. "You asked," he said, as if very tired and having trouble forcing it out, "me a question? When you first appeared?"

"Oh!" Fuzz said. "Yes. You let him kill you. I had not expected that."

"You're God. Can't you see the future?"

"To an extent," Fuzz said, animated. "But it is cloudy, so cloudy. Too many possibilities. I did not see this among them, though it was probably there. You must tell me. Why *did* you let him kill you? At the end, you just stood there."

"I couldn't have gotten away," Kelsier said. "Once the Lord Ruler arrived, there was no escaping. I had to confront him."

"You didn't even fight."

"I used the Eleventh Metal."

"Foolishness," God said. He started pacing. "That was Ruin's influence on you. But what was the point? I can't understand why he wanted you to have that useless metal." He perked up. "And that *fight*. You and the Inquisitor. Yes, I've seen many things, but that was unlike any other. Impressive, though I wish you hadn't caused such destruction, Kelsier."

He returned to pacing, but seemed to have more of a spring to his step. Kelsier hadn't expected God to be so . . . human. Excitable, even energetic.

"I saw something," Kelsier said, "as the Lord Ruler killed me. The person as he might once have been. His past? A version of his past? He stood at the Well of Ascension."

"Did you? Hmm. Yes, the metal, flared during the moment of transition. You got a glimpse of the Spiritual Realm, then? His Connection and his past? You were using Ati's essence, unfortunately. One shouldn't trust it, even in a diluted form. Except . . ." He frowned, cocking his head, as if trying to remember something he'd forgotten.

"Another god," Kelsier whispered, closing his eyes. "You said . . . you trapped him?"

"He will break free eventually. It's inevitable. But the prison isn't my last gambit. It can't be."

Perhaps I should *just let go,* Kelsier thought, drifting.

"There now," God said. "Farewell, Kelsier. You served *him* more often than you did me, but I can respect your intentions, *and* your remarkable ability to Preserve yourself."

"I saw it," Kelsier whispered. "A cavern high in the mountains. The Well of Ascension . . ."

"Yes," Fuzz said. "That's where I put it."

"But . . ." Kelsier said, stretching, "he moved it. . . ."

"Naturally."

What would the Lord Ruler do, with a source of such power? Hide it far away?

Or keep it very, very close? Near to his fingertips. Hadn't Kelsier seen furs, like the ones he'd seen the Lord Ruler wearing in his vision? He'd seen them in a room, past an Inquisitor. A building within a building, hidden within the depths of the palace.

Kelsier opened his eyes.

Fuzz spun toward him. "What—"

Kelsier heaved himself to his feet and started running. There wasn't much *self* to him left, just a fuzzy blurred image. The feet that he ran upon were distorted smudges, his form a pulled-out, unraveling piece of cloth. He barely found purchase upon the misty ground, and when he stumbled against a building, he *pushed* through it, ignoring the wall as one might a stiff breeze.

"So you *are* a runner," Fuzz said, appearing beside him. "Kelsier, child, this accomplishes nothing. I suppose I should have expected nothing less from you. Frantically butting against your destiny until the last moment."

Kelsier barely heard the words. He focused on the run, on resisting that grip *hauling* him backward, into the nothing. He raced the grip of death itself, its cold fingers closing around him.

Run.

Concentrate.

Struggle to *be.*

The flight reminded him of another time, climbing through a pit, arms bloodied. He would *not be taken!*

The pulsing became his guide, that wave that washed periodically through the shadowy world. He sought its source. He barreled through buildings, crossed thoroughfares, ignoring both metal and the souls of men until he reached the grey mist silhouette of Kredik Shaw, the Hill of a Thousand Spires.

Here, Fuzz seemed to grasp what was going on.

"You zinc-tongued raven," the god said, moving beside him without effort while Kelsier ran with everything he had. "You're not going to reach it in time."

He was running through mists again. Walls, people, buildings faded. Nothing but dark, swirling mists.

But the mists had never been his enemy.

With the thumping of those pulses to guide him, Kelsier strained through the swirling nothingness until a pillar of light exploded before him. It was there! He could see it, burning in the mists. He could almost touch it, almost . . .

He was losing it. Losing himself. He could move no more.

Something seized him.

"Please . . ." Kelsier whispered, falling, sliding away.

This is not right. Fuzz's voice.

"You want to see something . . . spectacular?" Kelsier whispered. "Help me live. I'll *show* you . . . *spectacular*."

Fuzz wavered, and Kelsier could sense the divinity's hesitance. It was followed by a sense of purpose, like a lamp being lit, and laughter.

Very well. Be Preserved, Kelsier. Survivor.

Something shoved him forward, and Kelsier merged with the light.

Moments later he blinked awake. He lay in the misty world still, but his body—or, well, his spirit—had re-formed. He lay in a pool of light like liquid metal. He could feel its warmth all around him, invigorating.

He could make out a misty cavern outside the pool; it seemed to be made of natural rock, though he couldn't tell for certain, because it was all mist on this side.

The pulsing surged through him.

"The power," Fuzz said, standing beyond the light. "You are now part of it, Kelsier."

"Yeah," Kelsier said, climbing to his feet, dripping with radiant light. "I can feel it, thrumming through me."

"You are trapped with him," Fuzz said. He seemed shallow, wan, compared to the powerful light that Kelsier stood amid. "I warned you. This is a prison."

Kelsier settled down, breathing in and out. "I'm alive."

"According to a very loose definition of the word."

Kelsier smiled. "It'll do."

2

I MMORTALITY proved to be far more frustrating than Kelsier had
anticipated.

Of course, he didn't know if he was *truly* immortal or not. He
didn't have a heartbeat—which was only unnerving when he noticed
it—and didn't need to breathe. But who could say if his soul aged or not
in this place?

In the hours following his survival, Kelsier inspected his new home.
God was right, it *was* a prison. The pool he was in grew deep at the
center point, and was filled with liquid light that seemed a reflection
of something more . . . potent on the other side.

Fortunately, though the Well was not wide, only the very center was
deeper than he was tall. He could stay around the perimeter and only be
in the light up to his waist. It was thin, thinner than water, and easy to
move through.

He could also step out of this pool and its attached pillar of light, settling onto the rocky side. Everything in this cavern was made of mist,
though the edges of the Well . . . He seemed to see the stone better
here, more fully. It appeared to have some actual color to it. As if this
place were part spirit, like him.

He could sit on the edge of the Well, legs dangling into the light. But if he tried to walk too far from the Well, misty wisps of that same power trailed him and held him back, like chains. They wouldn't let him get more than a few feet from the pool. He tried straining, pushing, dashing and throwing himself out, but nothing worked. He always pulled up sharply once he got a few feet away.

After several hours of trying to break free, Kelsier slumped on the side of the Well, feeling . . . exhausted? Was that even the right word? He had no body, and felt no traditional signs of tiredness. No headache, no strained muscles. But he *was* fatigued. Worn out like an old banner allowed to flap in the wind through too many rainstorms.

Forced to relax, he took stock of what little he could make out of his surroundings. Fuzz was gone; the god had been distracted by something a short time after Kelsier's Preservation, and had vanished. That left Kelsier with a cavern made of shadows, the glowing pool itself, and some pillars extending through the chamber. At the other end, he saw the glow of bits of metal, though he couldn't figure out what they were.

This was the sum of his existence. Had he just locked himself away in this little prison for eternity? It seemed an ultimate irony to him that he might have managed to cheat death, only to find himself suffering a fate far worse.

What would happen to his mind if he spent a few decades in here? A few *centuries*?

He sat on the rim of the Well, and tried to distract himself by thinking about his friends. He'd trusted in his plans at the moment of his death, but now he saw so many holes in his plot to inspire a rebellion. What if the skaa didn't rise up? What if the stockpiles he'd prepared weren't enough?

Even if that all worked, so much would ride upon the shoulders of some very ill-prepared men. And one remarkable young woman.

Lights drew his attention, and he leaped to his feet, eager for any distraction. A group of figures, outlined as glowing souls, had entered this room in the world of the living. There was something odd about them. Their eyes . . .

Inquisitors.

Kelsier refused to flinch, though by every instinct he dreaded these creatures. He had bested one of their champions. He would fear them no longer. Instead, he paced his confines, trying to discern what the three Inquisitors were lugging toward him. Something large and heavy, but it didn't glow at all.

A body, Kelsier realized. *Headless.*

Was this the one he'd killed? Yes, it must be. Another Inquisitor was reverently carrying the dead one's spikes, a whole pile of them, all placed together inside a large jar of liquid. Kelsier squinted at it, taking a single step out of his prison, trying to determine what he was seeing.

"Blood," Fuzz said, suddenly standing nearby. "They store the spikes in blood until they can be used again. In that way, they can prevent the spikes from losing their effectiveness."

"Huh," Kelsier said, stepping to the side as the Inquisitors tossed the body into the Well, then dropped in the head. Both evaporated. "Do they do this often?"

"Each time one of their number dies," Fuzz said. "I doubt they even know what they are doing. Tossing a dead body into that pool is beyond meaningless."

The Inquisitors retreated with the spikes of the fallen. Judging by their slumped forms, the four creatures were exhausted.

"My plan," Kelsier said, looking to Fuzz. "How is it going? My crew should have discovered the warehouse by now. The people of the city . . . did it work? Are the skaa angry?"

"Hmmm?" Fuzz asked.

"The revolution, the plan," Kelsier said, stepping toward him. God shifted backward, getting just beyond where Kelsier would be able to reach, hand going to the knife at his belt. Perhaps that punch earlier had been ill-advised. "Fuzz, listen. You have to go nudge them. We'll never have a better chance of overthrowing him."

"The plan . . ." Fuzz said. He unraveled for a moment, before returning. "Yes, there was a plan. I . . . remember I had a plan. When I was smarter . . ."

"The plan," Kelsier said, "is to get the skaa to revolt. It won't matter how powerful the Lord Ruler is, won't matter if he's immortal, once we toss him in chains and lock him away."

Fuzz nodded, distracted.

"Fuzz?"

He shook, glancing toward Kelsier, and the sides of his head unraveled slowly—like a fraying rug, each thread seeping away and vanishing into nothing. "He's killing me, you know. He wants me gone before the next cycle, though . . . perhaps I can hold out. You hear me, Ruin! I'm not dead yet. Still . . . still here . . ."

Hell, Kelsier thought, cold. *God is going insane.*

Fuzz started pacing. "I know you're listening, changing what I write, what I have written. You make our religion all about you. They hardly remember the truth any longer. Subtle as always, you worm."

"Fuzz," Kelsier said. "Could you just go—"

"I needed a sign," Fuzz whispered, stopping near Kelsier. "Something he couldn't change. A sign of the weapon I'd buried. The boiling point of water, I think. Maybe its freezing point? But what if the units change over the years? I needed something that would be remembered always. Something they'll immediately recognize." He leaned in. "Sixteen."

"Six . . . teen?" Kelsier said.

"Sixteen." Fuzz grinned. "Clever, don't you think?"

"Because it means . . ."

"The number of metals," Fuzz said. "In Allomancy."

"There are ten. Eleven, if you count the one I discovered."

"No! No, no, that's stupid. Sixteen. It's the perfect number. They'll see. They have to see." Fuzz started pacing again, and his head returned—mostly—to its earlier state.

Kelsier sat down on the rim of his prison. God's actions were far more erratic than they had been earlier. Had something changed, or—like a human with a mental disease—was God simply better at some times than he was at others?

Fuzz looked up abruptly. He winced, turning his eyes toward the ceiling, as if it were going to collapse on him. He opened his mouth, jaw working, but made no sound.

"What . . ." he finally said. "What have you *done*?"

Kelsier stood up in his prison.

"What have you done?" Fuzz screamed.

Kelsier smiled. "Hope," he said softly. "I have hoped."

"He was perfect," Fuzz said. "He was . . . the only one of you . . . that . . ." He spun suddenly, gazing down the shadowy room beyond Kelsier's prison.

Someone stood at the other end. A tall, commanding figure, not made of light. Familiar clothing, of both white and black, contrasting with itself.

The Lord Ruler. His spirit, at least.

Kelsier stepped up onto the rim of stone around the pool and waited as the Lord Ruler strode toward the light of the Well. He stopped in place when he noticed Kelsier.

"I killed you," the Lord Ruler said. "Twice. Yet you live."

"Yes. We're all aware of how strikingly incompetent you are. I'm glad you're beginning to see it for yourself. That's the first step toward change."

The Lord Ruler sniffed and looked around at the chamber, with its diaphanous walls. His eyes passed over Fuzz, but he didn't give the god much consideration.

Kelsier exulted. She'd done it. She'd actually *done it*. How? What secret had he missed?

"That grin," the Lord Ruler said to Kelsier, "is insufferable. I *did* kill you."

"I returned the favor."

"You *didn't* kill me, Survivor."

"I forged the blade that did."

Fuzz cleared his throat. "It is my duty to be with you as you transition. Don't be worried, or—"

"Be silent," the Lord Ruler said, inspecting Kelsier's prison. "Do you know what you've done, Survivor?"

"I've won."

"You've brought Ruin upon the world. You are a pawn. So proud, like a soldier on the battlefield, confident he controls his own destiny—while ignoring the thousands upon thousands in his rank." He shook his head. "Only a year left. So close. I would have again ransomed this undeserving planet."

"This is just . . ." Fuzz swallowed. "This is an in-between step. After death and before the Somewhere Else. Where souls must go. Where *yours* must go, Rashek."

Rashek? Kelsier looked again at the Lord Ruler. You could not tell a Terrisman by skin tone; that was a mistake many people made. Some Terris were dark, others light. Still, he would have thought . . .

The room filled with furs. This man, in the cold.

Idiot. That was what it meant, of course.

"It was all a lie," Kelsier said. "A trick. Your fabled immortality? Your healing? Feruchemy. But how did you become an Allomancer?"

The Lord Ruler stepped right up to the pillar of light that rose from the prison, and the two stared at one another. As they had on that square above when alive.

Then the Lord Ruler stuck his hand into the light.

Kelsier set his jaw and pictured sudden, horrifying images of spending an eternity trapped with the man who had murdered Mare. The Lord Ruler pulled his hand out, however, trailing light like molasses. He turned his hand over, inspecting the glow, which eventually faded.

"So now what?" Kelsier asked. "You remain here?"

"Here?" The Lord Ruler laughed. "With an impotent mouse and a half-blooded rat? Please."

He closed his eyes, and then he stretched toward that point that defied geometry. He faded, then finally vanished.

Kelsier gaped. "He *left*?"

"To the Somewhere Else," Fuzz said, sitting down. "I should not have been so hopeful. Everything passes, nothing is eternal. That is what Ati always claimed. . . ."

"He didn't have to leave," Kelsier said. "He could have remained. Could have survived!"

"I told you, by this point rational people *want* to move on." Fuzz vanished.

Kelsier remained standing there, at the edge of his prison, the glowing pool tossing his shadow across the floor. He stared into the misty room with its columns, waiting for something, though he wasn't certain what. Confirmation, celebration, a change of some sort.

Nothing. Nobody came, not even the Inquisitors. How had the revolution gone? Were the skaa now rulers of society? He would have liked to see the deaths of the noble ranks, treated—in turn—as they had treated their slaves.

He received no confirmation, no sign, of what was happening above. They didn't know about the Well, obviously. All Kelsier could do was settle down.

And wait.

PART TWO
WELL

1

WHAT Kelsier would have given for a pencil and paper.
Something to write on, some way to pass the time. A means of collecting his thoughts and creating a plan of escape.

As the days passed, he tried scratching notes into the sides of the Well, which proved impossible. He tried unraveling threads from his clothing, then tying knots in them to represent words. Unfortunately, threads vanished soon after he pulled them free, and his shirt and trousers immediately returned to the way they'd looked before. Fuzz, during one of his rare visits, explained that the clothing wasn't real—or rather, it was just an extension of Kelsier's spirit.

For the same reason, he couldn't use his hair or blood to write. He didn't technically have either. It was supremely frustrating, but sometime during his second month of imprisonment he admitted the truth to himself. Writing wasn't all that important. He'd never been able to write while confined to the Pits, but he'd planned all the same. Yes, they had been feverish plans, impossible dreams, but lack of paper hadn't stopped him.

The attempts to write weren't about making plans so much as finding something to do. A quest to soak up his time. It had worked for a few weeks. But in acknowledging the truth, he lost his will to keep trying to find a way to write.

Fortunately, about the time he acknowledged this, he discovered something new about his prison.

Whispering.

Oh, he couldn't *hear* it. But could he "hear" anything? He didn't have ears. He was . . . what had Fuzz said? A Cognitive Shadow? A force of mind, holding his spirit together, preventing it from diffusing. Saze would have had a field day. He loved mystical topics like this.

Regardless, Kelsier *could* sense something. The Well continued to pulse as it had before, sending waves of writhing shock through the walls of his prison and out into the world. Those pulses seemed to be strengthening, a continuous thrumming, like the sense bronze lent one in "hearing" people using Allomancy.

Inside of each pulse was . . . something. Whispers, he called them—though they contained more than just words. They were saturated with sounds, scents, and images.

He saw a book, with ink staining its pages. A group of people sharing a story. Terrismen in robes? Sazed?

The pulses whispered chilling words. *Hero of Ages. The Announcer. Worldbringer.* He recognized those terms from the ancient Terris prophecies mentioned in Alendi's logbook.

Kelsier knew the discomforting truth now. He had *met* a god, which meant there was real depth and reality to faith. Did this mean there was something to that array of religions Saze had kept in his pocket, like playing cards to stack a deck?

You have brought Ruin upon this world. . . .

Kelsier settled into the powerful light that was the Well, and found—with practice—that if he submerged himself in the center right before a pulse, he could ride it a short distance. It sent his consciousness traveling out of the Well to catch glimpses of each pulse's destination.

He thought he saw libraries, quiet chambers where distant Terrismen spoke, exchanging stories and memorizing them. He saw madmen huddled in streets, whispering the words the pulses delivered. He saw a Mistborn man, noble, jumping between buildings.

Something other than Kelsier rode with those pulses. Something directing an unseen work, something interested in the lore of the Terris. It took Kelsier an embarrassingly long time to realize he should try another tack. He dunked himself into the center of the pool, surrounded by the too-thin liquid light, and when the next pulse came he pushed himself in the opposite direction—not along with the pulse, but toward its source.

The light thinned, and he looked into someplace new. A dark expanse that was neither the world of the dead nor the world of the living.

In that other place, he found *destruction*.

Decay. Not blackness, for blackness was too complete, too *whole* to represent this thing he sensed in the Beyond. It was a vast force that would gleefully take something as simple as darkness, then rip it apart.

This force was time infinite. It was the winds that weathered, the storms that broke, the timeless waves running slowly, slowly, slowly to a stop as the sun and the planet cooled to nothing.

It was the ultimate end and destiny of all things. And it was angry.

Kelsier pulled back, throwing himself up out of the light, gasping, trembling.

He had met God. But for every Push, there was a Pull. What was the opposite of God?

What he had seen troubled him so much that he almost didn't return. He almost convinced himself to ignore the terrible thing in the darkness. He nearly blocked out the whispers and tried to pretend he had never seen that awesome, vast destroyer.

But of course he couldn't do that. Kelsier had never been able to resist a secret. This thing, even more than meeting Fuzz, proved that Kelsier had been playing all along at a game whose rules far outmatched his understanding.

That both terrified and excited him.

And so, he returned to gaze upon the thing. Again and again he went, struggling to comprehend, though he felt like an ant trying to understand a symphony.

He did this for weeks, right up until the point when the thing *looked* at him.

Before, it hadn't seemed to notice—as one might not notice the spider hiding inside a keyhole. This time though, Kelsier somehow alerted it. The thing churned in an abrupt change of motion, then *flowed* toward Kelsier, its essence surrounding the place from which Kelsier observed. It rotated slowly about itself in a vortex—like an ocean that began turning around one spot. Kelsier couldn't help but feel that an infinite, vast eye was suddenly *squinting* at him.

He fled, splashing, kicking up the liquid light as he backed away into his prison. He was so alarmed that he felt a phantom *heartbeat* thrumming inside of him, his essence acknowledging the proper reaction to shock and trying to replicate it. That stilled as he settled into his customary seat at the side of the pool.

The sight of that thing turning its attention upon him, the sensation of being tiny in the face of something so vast, deeply troubled Kelsier. For all his confidence and plotting, he was basically nothing. His entire life had been an exercise in unintentional bravado.

Months passed. He didn't return to study the thing Beyond; Kelsier instead waited for Fuzz to visit and check in on him, as he did periodically.

When Fuzz finally arrived, he looked even more unraveled than the last time, mists escaping from his shoulders, a small hole in his left cheek exposing a view into his mouth, his clothing growing ragged.

"Fuzz?" Kelsier asked. "I saw something. This . . . Ruin you spoke of. I think I can watch it."

Fuzz just paced back and forth, not even speaking.

"Fuzz? Hey, are you listening?"

Nothing.

"Idiot," Kelsier tried. "Hey, you're a disgrace to deityhood. Are you paying attention?"

Even an insult didn't work. Fuzz just kept pacing.

Useless, Kelsier thought as a pulse of power left the Well. He happened to catch a glimpse of Fuzz's eyes as the pulse passed.

And in that moment, Kelsier was reminded why he had named this creature a god in the first place. There was an infinity beyond those eyes, a complement to the one trapped here in this Well. Fuzz was the infinity of a note held perfectly, never wavering. The majesty of a painting, frozen and still, capturing a slice of life from a time gone by. It was the power of many, many moments compressed somehow into one.

Fuzz stopped before him and his cheeks unraveled fully, revealing a skeleton beneath that was also unraveling, eyes glowing with eternity. This creature *was* a divinity; he was just a broken one.

Fuzz left, and Kelsier didn't see him for many months. The stillness and silence of his prison seemed as endless as the creatures he had studied. At one point, he found himself planning how to draw the attention of the destructive one, if only to beg it to end him.

It was when he started talking to himself that he really got worried.

"What have you done?"

"I've saved the world. Freed mankind."

"Gotten revenge."

"The goals can align."

"You are a coward."

"I changed the world!"

"And if you're just a pawn of that thing Beyond? Like the Lord Ruler claimed? Kelsier, what if you have no destiny other than to do as you're told?"

He contained the outburst, recovered himself, but the fragility of his own sanity unnerved him. He hadn't been completely sane in the Pits either. In a moment of stillness—staring at the shifting mists that made up the walls of the cavernous room—he admitted a deeper secret to himself.

He hadn't been completely sane *since* the Pits.

That was one reason why he didn't at first trust his senses when someone spoke to him.

"Now *this* I did not expect."

Kelsier shook himself, then turned with suspicion, worried he was hallucinating. It was possible to see all kinds of things in those shifting mists that made up the walls of the cavern, if you stared at them long enough.

This, however, was not a figure made of mist. It was a man with stark white hair, his face defined by angular features and a sharp nose. He seemed vaguely familiar to Kelsier, but he couldn't place why.

The man sat on the floor, one leg up and his arm resting upon his knee. In his hand he held some kind of stick.

Wait . . . no, he wasn't sitting on the floor, but on an object that somehow seemed to be *floating* upon the mists. The white, loglike object sank halfway into the mists of the floor and rocked like a ship on the water, bobbing in place. The rod in the man's hand was a short oar, and his other leg—the one that wasn't up—rested over the side of the log and vanished into the misty ground, visible only as an obscured silhouette.

"You," the man said to Kelsier, "are very bad at doing as you're supposed to."

"Who are you?" Kelsier asked, stepping to the edge of his prison, eyes narrowed. This was no hallucination. He refused to believe his sanity was that far gone. "A spirit?"

"Alas," the man said, "death has never really suited me. Bad for the complexion, you see." He studied Kelsier, lips raised in a knowing smile.

Kelsier hated him immediately.

"Got stuck there, did you?" the man said. "In Ati's prison . . ." He clicked his tongue. "Fitting recompense, for what you did. Poetic even."

"What I did?"

"Destroying the Pits, O scarred one. That was the only perpendicularity on this planet with any reasonable ease of access. This one is *very* dangerous, growing more so by the minute, and difficult to find. By doing as you did, you basically ended traffic through Scadrial. Upended an entire mercantile ecosystem, which I'll admit was fun to watch."

"Who *are* you?" Kelsier said.

"I?" the man said. "I am a drifter. A miscreant. The flame's last breath, made of smoke at its passing."

"That's . . . needlessly obtuse."

"Well, I'm that too." The man cocked his head. "That mostly, if I'm honest."

"And you claim to *not* be dead?"

"If I were, would I need this?" the Drifter said, knocking his oar against the front of his small loglike vessel. It bobbed at the motion, and for the first time Kelsier was able to make out what it was. Arms he'd missed before, hanging down into the mists, obscured. A head that drooped on its neck. A white robe, masking the shape.

"A corpse," he whispered.

"Oh, Spanky here is just a spirit. It's damnably difficult to get about in this subastral—anyone physical risks slipping through these mists and falling, perhaps forever. So many thoughts pool together here, becoming what you see around you, and you need something finer to travel over it all."

"That's horrible."

"Says the man who built a revolution upon the backs of the dead. At least I only need *one* corpse."

Kelsier folded his arms. This man was wary—though he spoke light-heartedly, he watched Kelsier with care, and held back as if contemplating a method of attack.

He wants something, Kelsier guessed. *Something that I have, maybe?* No, he seemed legitimately surprised that Kelsier was there. He had come here, intending to visit the Well. Perhaps he wanted to enter it, access the power? Or did he, perhaps, just want to have a look at the thing Beyond?

"Well, you're obviously resourceful," Kelsier said. "Perhaps you can help me with my predicament."

"Alas," the Drifter said. "Your case is hopeless."

Kelsier felt his heart sink.

"Yes, nothing to be done," the Drifter continued. "You are, indeed, stuck with that face. By manifesting those same features on this side, you show that even your *soul* is resigned to you always looking like one ugly sonofa—"

"Bastard," Kelsier cut in. "You had me for a second."

"Now, that's demonstrably wrong," the Drifter said, pointing. "I believe only one of us in this room is illegitimate, and it isn't me. Unless . . ." He tapped the floating corpse on the head with his oar. "What about you, Spanky?"

The corpse actually mumbled something.

"Happily married parents? Still alive? Really? I'm sorry for their loss." The Drifter looked to Kelsier, smiling innocently. "No bastards on this side. What about yours?"

"The bastard by birth," Kelsier said, "is always better off than the one by choice, Drifter. I'll own up to my nature if you own up to yours."

The Drifter chuckled, eyes alight. "Nice, nice. Tell me, since we're on the topic, which are you? A skaa with noble bearing, or a nobleman with skaa interests? Which half is more *you*, Survivor?"

"Well," Kelsier said dryly, "considering that the relatives of my noble half spent the better part of four decades trying to exterminate me, I'd say I'm more inclined toward the skaa side."

"Aaaah," the Drifter said, leaning forward. "But I didn't ask which you liked more. I asked which you *were*."

"Is it relevant?"

"It's *interesting*," the Drifter said. "Which is enough for me." He reached down to the corpse he was using as a boat, then removed something from his pocket. Something that glowed, though Kelsier couldn't tell if it was something naturally radiant, or just something made of metal.

The glow faded as the Drifter administered it to his vessel, then— covering the motion with a cough, as if to hide from Kelsier what he was doing—furtively applied some of the glow to his oar. When he placed the oar back into the mists, it sent the boat scooting closer to the Well.

"*Is* there a way for me to escape this prison?" Kelsier asked.

"How about this?" the Drifter said. "We'll have an insult battle. Winner gets to ask one question, and the other has to answer truthfully. I'll start. What's wet, ugly, and has scars on its arms?"

Kelsier raised an eyebrow. All of this talk was a distraction, as evidenced by Drifter scooting—again—closer to the prison. *He's going to try to jump for the Well*, Kelsier thought. *Leap in, hoping to be fast enough to surprise me.*

"No guess?" Drifter asked. "The answer is basically anyone who spends time with you, Kelsier, as they end up slitting their wrists, hitting themselves in the face, and then drowning themselves to forget the experience. Ha! Okay, your turn."

"I'm going to murder you," Kelsier said softly.

"I— Wait, *what*?"

"If you step inside here," Kelsier said, "I'm going to murder you. I'll slice the tendons on your wrists so your hands can't do anything more than batter at me uselessly as I kneel against your throat and slowly crush the life out of you—all while I remove your fingers one by one. I'll finally let you breathe a single, frantic gasp—but at that moment I'll shove your middle finger between your lips so that you're forced to suck it down as you struggle for air. You'll go out knowing you choked to death on your own rotten flesh."

The Drifter gaped at him, mouth working soundlessly. "I . . ." he finally said. "I don't think you know how to play this game."

Kelsier shrugged.

"Seriously," Drifter said. "You need some help, friend. I know a guy. Tall, bald, wears lots of earrings. Have a chat with him next—"

The Drifter cut off midsentence and leaped for the prison, kicking off the floating corpse and throwing himself at the light.

Kelsier was ready. As Drifter entered the light, Kelsier grabbed the man by one arm and slung him toward the side of the pool. The maneuver worked, and Drifter seemed to be able to touch the walls and floor here in the Well. He slammed against the wall, sending waves of light splashing up.

As Kelsier tried to punch at Drifter's head while he was stumbling, the man caught himself on the side of the pool and kicked backward, knocking Kelsier's legs out from beneath him.

Kelsier splashed in the light, and he tried to burn metals by reflex. Nothing happened, though there was *something* to the light here. Something familiar—

He managed to get to his feet, and caught Drifter lunging for the center, the deepest part. Kelsier snatched the man by the arm, swinging him away. Whatever this man wanted, Kelsier's instincts said that he shouldn't be allowed to have it. Beyond that, the Well was Kelsier's only asset. If he could hold the man back from what he wanted, subdue him, perhaps it would lead to answers.

The Drifter stumbled, then lunged, trying to grab Kelsier.

Kelsier, in turn, pivoted and buried his fist in the man's stomach. The motion gave him a thrill; after sitting for so long, inactive, it was nice to be able to *do* something.

Drifter grunted at the punch. "All right then," he muttered.

Kelsier brought his fists up, checked his footing, then unleashed a series of quick blows at Drifter's face that *should* have dazed him.

When Kelsier pulled back—not wanting to go too far and hurt the man seriously—he found that Drifter was smiling at him.

That didn't seem a good sign.

Somehow, Drifter shook off the hits he'd taken. He jumped forward, dodged Kelsier's attempted punch, then ducked and *slammed* his fist into Kelsier's kidneys.

It *hurt*. Kelsier lacked a body, but apparently his spirit could feel pain. He let out a grunt and brought up his arms to protect his face, stepping backward in the liquid light. The Drifter attacked, relentless, slamming his fists into Kelsier with no care for the damage he might be doing to himself.

Go to the ground, Kelsier's instincts told him. He dropped one hand and tried to seize Drifter by the arm, planning to send them both down into the light to grapple.

Unfortunately, the Drifter was a little too quick. He dodged and kicked Kelsier's legs from beneath him again, then grabbed him by the throat, slamming him repeatedly—brutally—against the bottom of the shallower part of the prison, splashing him in light that was too thin to be water, but suffocating nonetheless.

Finally Drifter hauled him up, limp. The man's eyes were glowing. "That was unpleasant," Drifter said, "yet somehow still satisfying. Apparently you already being dead means I can hurt you." As Kelsier tried to grab his arm, Drifter slammed Kelsier down again, then pulled him back up, stunned.

"I'm sorry, Survivor, for the rough treatment," Drifter continued. "But you are *not* supposed to be here. You did what I needed you to, but you're a wild card I'd rather not deal with right now." He paused. "If it's any consolation, you should feel proud. It's been centuries since anyone got the drop on me."

He released Kelsier, letting him slump down and catch himself against the side of the prison, half submerged in the light. He growled, trying to pull himself up after Drifter.

Drifter sighed, then proceeded to *kick* at Kelsier's leg repeatedly, shocking him with the pain of it. He screamed, holding his leg. It should have cracked from the force of those kicks, and though it had not, the pain was overwhelming.

"This is a lesson," Drifter said, though it was difficult to hear the words through the pain. "But not the one you might think it is. You don't have a body, and I don't have the inclination to actually injure your soul. That pain is caused by your mind; it's thinking about what *should* be happening to you, and responding." He hesitated. "I'll refrain from making you choke on a chunk of your own flesh."

He walked toward the middle of the pool. Kelsier watched through eyes quivering with pain as Drifter held his hands out to the sides and closed his eyes. He stepped into the center of the pool, the deep portion, and vanished into the light.

A moment later, a figure climbed back out of the pool. Yet this time, the person was shadowy, glowing with inner light like . . .

Like someone in the world of the living. This pool had let Drifter transition from the world of the dead to the real world. Kelsier gaped, following Drifter with his eyes as the man strode past the pillars in the room, then stopped at the other side. Two tiny sources of metal still glowed fiercely there to Kelsier's eyes.

Drifter selected one. It was small, as he could toss it into the air and catch it again. Kelsier could sense the triumph in that motion.

Kelsier closed his eyes and concentrated. No pain. His leg wasn't actually hurt. *Concentrate.*

He managed to make some of the pain fade. He sat up in the pool, rippling light coming up to his chest. He breathed in and out, though he didn't need the air.

Damn. The first person he'd seen in months had thrashed him, then stolen something from the chamber outside. He didn't know what, or why, or even how the Drifter had managed to slip from one world to the next.

Kelsier crawled to the center of the pool, lowering himself down into the deep portion. He stood, his leg still aching faintly, and put his hands to the sides. He concentrated, trying to . . .

To what? Transition? What would that even do to him?

He didn't care. He was frustrated and humiliated. He needed to prove to himself that he wasn't incapable.

He failed. No amount of concentration, visualization, or straining of muscles made him do what the Drifter had managed. He climbed from the pool, exhausted and chastened, and settled on the side.

He didn't notice Fuzz standing there until the god spoke. "What were you *doing*?"

Kelsier turned. Fuzz visited infrequently these days, but when he did come, he always did it unannounced. If he spoke, he often only raved like a madman.

"Someone was just here," Kelsier said. "A man with white hair. He somehow used this Well to pass from the world of the dead to the world of the living."

"I see," Fuzz said softly. "He dared that, did he? Dangerous, with Ruin straining against his bonds. But if anyone were going to try something so foolhardy, it would be Cephandrius."

"He stole something, I think," Kelsier said. "From the other side of the room. A bit of metal."

"Aaah . . ." Fuzz said softly. "I had thought that when he rejected the rest of us, he would stop interfering. I should know better than to trust an implication from him. Half the time you can't trust his outright promises. . . ."

"Who is he?" Kelsier asked.

"An old friend. And no, before you ask, you can't do as he did and transition between Realms. Your ties to the Physical Realm have been severed. You're a kite with no string connecting it to the ground. You cannot ride the perpendicularity across."

Kelsier sighed. "Then why was he able to come to the world of the dead?"

"It's not the world of the dead. It's the world of the mind. Men—all things, truly—are like a ray of light. The floor is the Physical Realm, where that light pools. The sun is the Spiritual Realm, where it begins. This Realm, the Cognitive Realm, is the space between where that beam stretches."

The metaphor barely made any sense to him. *They all know so much,* Kelsier thought, *and I know so little.*

Still, at least Fuzz was sounding better today. Kelsier smiled toward the god, then froze as Fuzz turned his head.

Fuzz was missing half his face. The entire left side was just gone. Not wounded, and there was no skeleton. The complete half smoked, trailing wisps of mist. Half his lips remained, and he smiled back at Kelsier, as if nothing were wrong.

"He stole a bit of my essence, distilled and pure," Fuzz explained. "It can Invest a human, grant him or her Allomancy."

"Your . . . face, Fuzz . . ."

"Ati thinks to finish me," Fuzz said. "Indeed, his knife was placed long ago. I'm already dead." He smiled again, a gruesome expression, then vanished.

Feeling wrung out, Kelsier slumped alongside the pool, lying on the stones—which actually felt a little like real stone, instead of the fluffy softness of everything else made of mist.

He hated this feeling of ignorance. Everyone else was in on some grand joke, and he was the butt. Kelsier stared up at the ceiling, bathed in the glow of the shimmering Well and its column of light. Eventually, he came to a quiet decision.

He would find the answers.

In the Pits of Hathsin, he had awakened to purpose and had determined to destroy the Lord Ruler. Well, he would awaken again. He stood up and stepped into the light, strengthened. The clash of these gods was important, that thing in the Well dangerous. There was more to all of this than he'd ever known, and because of that he had a reason to live.

Perhaps more importantly, he had a reason to stay sane.

2

KELSIER no longer worried about madness or boredom. Each time he grew weary of his imprisonment, he remembered that feeling—that *humiliation*—he'd felt at Drifter's hands. Yes, he was trapped in a space only five or so feet across, but there was *plenty* to do.

First he returned to his study of the thing Beyond. He forced himself to duck beneath the light to face it and meet its inscrutable gaze—he did it until he didn't flinch when it turned its attention on him.

Ruin. A fitting name for that vast sense of erosion, decay, and destruction.

He continued to follow the Well's pulses. These trips gave him cryptic clues to Ruin's motives and plots. He sensed a familiar pattern to the things it changed—for Ruin seemed to be doing what Kelsier himself had done: co-opting a religion. Ruin was manipulating the hearts of the people by changing their lore and books.

That terrified Kelsier. His purpose expanded, as he watched the world through these pulses. He didn't just need to understand, he needed to fight this thing. This horrible force that would end all things, if it could.

He struggled, therefore, with a desperation to understand what he saw. Why did Ruin transform the old Terris prophecies? What was the Drifter—whom Kelsier spotted in very rare pulses—doing up in the Terris Dominance? Who was this mysterious Mistborn to whom Ruin paid so much attention, and was he a threat to Vin?

When he rode the pulses, Kelsier watched for—*craved*—signs of the people he knew and loved. Ruin was keenly interested in Vin, and many of his pulses centered around watching her or the man she loved, that Elend Venture.

The mounting clues worried Kelsier. Armies around Luthadel. A city still in chaos. And—he hated to confront this one—it looked like the Venture boy was *king*. When Kelsier realized this, he was so angry he spent days away from the pulses.

They'd gone and put a *nobleman* in charge.

Yes, Kelsier had saved this man's life. Against his better judgment, he'd rescued the man that Vin loved. Out of love for her, perhaps a twisted paternal sense of duty. The Venture boy hadn't been *too* bad, compared to the rest of his kind. But to give him the throne? It seemed that even Dox was listening to Venture. Kelsier would have expected Breeze to ride whatever wind came his way, but Dockson?

Kelsier fumed, but he could not remain away for long. He hungered for these glimpses of his friends. Though each was only a brief flash—like a single image from eyes blinked open—he clung to them. They were reminders that outside his prison, life continued.

Occasionally he was given a glimpse of someone else. His brother, Marsh.

Marsh *lived*. That was a welcome discovery. Unfortunately, the discovery was tainted. For Marsh was an Inquisitor.

The two of them had never been what one would call familial. They had taken divergent paths in life, but that wasn't the true source of the distance between them—it wasn't even due to Marsh's stern ways butting against Kelsier's glibness, or Marsh's unspoken jealousy for things Kelsier had.

No, the truth was they had been raised knowing that at any point they could be dragged before the Inquisitors and murdered for their half-blooded nature. Each had reacted differently to an entire life spent, essentially, with a death sentence: Marsh with quiet tension and caution, Kelsier with aggressive self-confidence to mask his secrets.

Both had known a single, inescapable truth. If one brother were caught, it meant the other would be exposed as a half-blood and likely killed as well. Perhaps this situation would have brought other siblings together. Kelsier was ashamed to admit that for him and Marsh, it had been a wedge. Each mention of "Stay safe" or "Watch yourself" had been colored by an undercurrent of "Don't screw up, or you'll get me killed." It had been a vast relief when, after their parents' deaths, the two of them had agreed to give up pretense and enter the underground of Luthadel.

At times Kelsier toyed with fantasies of what might have been. Could he and Marsh have integrated fully, becoming part of noble society? Could he have overcome his loathing for them and their culture?

Regardless, he wasn't fond of Marsh. The word "fond" sounded too much of walks in a park or time spent eating pastries. One was fond of a favorite book. No, Kelsier was not *fond* of Marsh. But strangely, he still loved him. He was initially happy to find the man alive, but then perhaps death would have been better than what had been done to him.

It took Kelsier weeks to figure out the reason Ruin was so interested in Marsh. Ruin could *talk* to Marsh. Marsh and other Inquisitors, judging by the glimpses and the sensation he received of words being sent.

How? Why Inquisitors? Kelsier found no answers in the visions he saw, though he did witness an important event.

The thing called Ruin was growing stronger, and it was stalking Vin and Elend. Kelsier saw it clearly in a trip through the pulses. A vision of the boy, Elend Venture, sleeping in his tent. The power of Ruin coalescing, forming a figure, malevolent and dangerous. It waited there until Vin entered, then tried to stab Elend.

As Kelsier lost the pulse, he was left with the image of Vin deflecting the blow and saving Elend. But he was confused. Ruin had waited there specifically until Vin returned.

It hadn't actually wanted to hurt Elend. It had just wanted Vin to see him trying.

Why?

3

I T's a plug," Kelsier said.

Fuzz—Preservation, as the god had said he could be called—sat outside the prison. He was still missing half his face, and the rest of him was leaking in larger patches as well.

These days the god spent more time near the Well, for which Kelsier was grateful. He had been practicing how to pull information from the creature.

"Hmmm?" Preservation asked.

"This Well," Kelsier said, gesturing around him. "It's like a plug. You created a prison for Ruin, but even the most solid of burrows must have an entrance. *This* is that entrance, sealed with your own power to keep him out, since you two are opposites."

"That . . ." Preservation said, trailing off.

"That?" Kelsier prompted.

"That's *utterly wrong*."

Damn, Kelsier thought. He'd spent weeks on that theory.

He was starting to feel an urgency. The pulses of the Well were growing more demanding, and Ruin seemed to be growing increasingly eager in its touch upon the world. Recently the light of the Well had started to act differently, condensing somehow, pulling together. Something was happening.

"We are gods, Kelsier," Preservation said with a voice that trailed off, then grew louder, then trailed off again. "We permeate everything. The rocks are me. The people are me. And him. All things persist, but decay. Ruin . . . and Preservation . . ."

"You told me this was your power," Kelsier said, gesturing again at the Well, trying to get the god back on topic. "That it gathers here."

"Yes, and elsewhere," Preservation said. "But yes, here. Like dew collects, my power gathers in that spot. It is natural. A cycle: clouds, rain, river, humidity. You cannot press so much essence into a system without it congealing here and there."

Great. That didn't tell him anything. He pressed further on the topic, but Fuzz grew quiet, so he tried something else. He needed to keep Preservation talking—to prevent the god from slumping into one of his quiet stupors.

"Are you afraid?" Kelsier asked. "If Ruin gets free, are you afraid he will kill you?"

"Ha," Preservation said. "I've told you. He killed me long, long ago."

"I find that hard to believe."

"Why?"

"Because I'm sitting here talking to you."

"And I'm talking to *you*. How alive are you?"

A good point.

"Death for one such as me is not like death for one such as you," Preservation said, staring off again. "I was killed long ago, when I made the decision to break our promise. But this power I hold . . . it *persists* and it *remembers*. It wants to be alive itself. I have died, but some of me remains. Enough to know that . . . there *were* plans. . . ."

It was no use trying to pry out what those plans were. He didn't remember whatever this "plan" was that he'd made.

"So it's not a plug," Kelsier said. "Then what is it?"

Preservation didn't reply. He didn't even seem to hear.

"You said to me once before," Kelsier continued, speaking more loudly, "that the power exists to be used. That it *needs* to be used. Why?"

Again no answer. He was going to need to try a different tactic. "I looked at him again. Your opposite."

Preservation stood up straight, turning his haunting, half-finished gaze upon Kelsier. Mentioning Ruin often shocked him out of his stupor.

"He is dangerous," Preservation said. "Stay away. My power protects you. Do not taunt him."

"Why? He's locked up."

"Nothing is eternal, not even time itself," Preservation said. "I didn't imprison him so much as *delay* him."

"And the power?"

"Yes . . ." Preservation said, nodding.

"Yes, what?"

"Yes, he will use that. I see." Preservation started, as if realizing—or maybe just recalling—something important. "My power created his prison. My power can unlock it. But how would he find someone who would do it? Who would hold the powers of creation, then *give them away* . . ."

"Which . . . we don't want them to do," Kelsier said.

"No. It will free him!"

"And last time?" Kelsier asked.

"Last time . . ." Preservation blinked, and seemed to come to himself more. "Yes, last time. The Lord Ruler. I made it work last time. I've put her into the spot to do this, but I can hear her thoughts. . . . He's been working on her. . . . So mixed up . . ."

"Fuzz?" Kelsier asked, uncertain.

"I must stop her. Someone . . ." His eyes unfocused.

"What are you doing?"

"Hush," Fuzz said, voice suddenly more commanding. "I'm trying to stop this."

Kelsier looked around, but there was nobody else here. "Who?"

"Do not assume that the me you see here is the only me," Fuzz said. "I am everywhere."

"But—"

"Hush!"

Kelsier hushed, in part because he was happy to see such strength from the god after so long motionless. After some time, however, he slumped down. "No use," Fuzz mumbled. "His tools are stronger."

"So . . ." Kelsier said, testing to see if he'd be hushed again. "Last time. Rashek used the power, instead of . . . what? Giving it up?"

Fuzz nodded. "Alendi would have done the right thing, as he perceived it. Given the power up—but that would have freed Ruin. 'Giving the power up' is a stand-in for giving the power to him. The powers would interpret that as me releasing him. My power, accepting his touch back into the world, directly."

"Great," Kelsier said. "We need a sacrifice then. Someone to take up the powers of eternity, then use them for whatever he wants instead of giving them away. Well, that is a sacrifice *I'm* perfect to make. How do I do it?"

Preservation regarded him. The creature's earlier strength was no more. He was fading, losing his human attributes. He didn't blink anymore, for example, and didn't make a pretense of breathing in before speaking. He could be utterly motionless, lifeless as an iron rod.

"You," Preservation finally said. "Using *my* power. *You.*"

"You let the Lord Ruler do it."

"He tried to save the world."

"As did I."

"You tried to rescue a boatful of people from a fire by sinking the boat, then claiming, 'At least they didn't burn to death.'" God hesitated. "You're going to punch me again, aren't you?"

"Can't reach you, Fuzz," Kelsier said. "The power. *How do I use it?*"

"You can't," Preservation said. "That power is part of the prison. This is what you did by merging your soul to the Well, Kelsier. You wouldn't be able to hold it anyway. You're not Connected enough to me."

Kelsier settled down to think on this, but before he had time to do much, he noticed an oddity. Were those *figures* in the chamber outside? Yes, they were. Living people, marked by their glowing souls. More Inquisitors come to drop off a dead body? He hadn't seen any of them for ages.

Two people stole into the corridor and approached the Well, passing rows of pillars that showed as illusory mist to Kelsier.

"They're here," Preservation said.

"Who?" Kelsier said, squinting. It was difficult to make out details of faces, with those souls glowing. "Is that . . ."

It was Vin.

"What?" Preservation said, looking toward Kelsier, noting his shock. "You thought I was waiting here for nothing? It happens today. The Well of Ascension is full. The time has arrived."

The other figure was the boy, Elend Venture. Kelsier was surprised to find he wasn't angry at the sight. Yes, the crew should have known better than to put a nobleman in charge, but that wasn't really Elend's fault. He'd always been too oblivious to be dangerous.

Besides, whatever the faults of his parentage, this Venture boy had stayed with Vin.

Kelsier folded his arms, watching Venture kneel beside the pool. "If he touches it, I'm going to slap him."

"He will not," Preservation said. "It's for her. He knows it. I've been preparing her. I tried, at least."

Vin turned, and seemed to be looking at God. Yes, she *could* see him. Was there a way Kelsier could use that?

"You tried?" Kelsier said. "Did you explain what she needs to do? Your opposite has been watching her, interacting with her. I've *seen* him doing it. He tried to kill Elend."

"No," Fuzz said, haunted. "He was imitating me. He looked as I do, to them, and tried to kill the boy. Not because he cares about one death, but because he wanted her to distrust me. To think I am her enemy. But can't she tell the difference? Between his hate and destruction, and my peace. I cannot kill. I've never been able to kill. . . ."

"Talk to her!" Kelsier said. "Tell her what she needs to do, Fuzz!"

"I . . ." Preservation shook his head. "I can't get through to her, can't speak to her. I can hear her mind, Kelsier. His lies are there. She doesn't trust me. She thinks she needs to give it up. I've tried to stop this. I left her clues, and then I tried to make someone else stop her. But . . . I've . . . I've failed . . ."

Oh, hell, Kelsier thought. *Need a plan. Quick.*

Vin was going to give up the power. Release the thing. Even without

Preservation's assertions, Kelsier would have known what Vin would do. She was a better person than he had ever been, and she never *had* thought she deserved the rewards she was given. She'd take this power, and she'd assume she had to give it up for the greater good.

But how to change that? If Preservation couldn't speak to her, then what?

Elend stood up and approached Preservation. Yes, the boy could see Preservation too.

"She needs motivation," Kelsier said, an idea clicking in his mind. Ruin had tried to stab Elend, to frighten her.

It was the right idea. He just hadn't gone far enough.

"Stab him," Kelsier said.

"What?" Preservation said, aghast.

Kelsier pushed out of his prison bonds a few steps, approaching Fuzz, who stood just outside. He strained to the absolute limits of his fetters.

"Stab him," Kelsier said. "Use that knife at your belt, Fuzz. They can see you, and you can affect their world. *Stab Elend Venture.* Give her a reason to use the power. She'll want to save him."

"I'm *Preservation*," he said. "The knife . . . I haven't actually drawn it in millennia. You speak of acting like him, as he pretended I would act! It's horrible!"

"You have to!" Kelsier said.

"I can't . . . I . . ." Fuzz reached to his belt, and his hand shimmered. The knife appeared there. He looked down at it, the blade glistening. "Old friend . . ." he whispered at it.

He looked toward Elend, who nodded. Preservation raised his arm, weapon in hand.

Then stopped.

His half face was a mask of pain. "No . . ." he whispered. "I Preserve . . ."

He's not going to do it, Kelsier thought, watching Elend talk to Vin, his posture reassuring. *He can't do it.*

Only one option.

"Sorry, kid," Kelsier said.

Kelsier grabbed Preservation's shimmering arm and *slashed* it across the Venture boy's stomach.

He felt as if he were stabbing his own flesh. Not because of Venture, but because he knew what it would do to Vin. His heart lurched as she rushed to Venture's side, weeping.

Well, he'd saved this boy's life once, so this would make them even. Besides, she would rescue him. She'd *have* to save Elend. She loved him.

Kelsier stepped back, returning to his prison proper, leaving an aghast Preservation to stare at his own hand as he stumbled away from the fallen man.

"Gut wound," Kelsier whispered. "He'll take time to die, Vin. Grab the power. It's *right here*. Use it."

She cradled Venture. Kelsier waited, anxious. If she entered the pool, she'd be able to see Kelsier, wouldn't she? She'd become transcendent, like Preservation. Or would she have to use the power first?

Would that free Kelsier? He had no answers, only an assurance that whatever happened, he could not let that thing Beyond escape. He turned.

And was shocked to find it *there*. He could sense it, pressed against the reality of this world, an infinite darkness. Not just the flimsy imitation of Preservation he'd made before, but the entire vast power. It wasn't in any specific space, but at the same time it was pressed up against reality and watching with a keen interest.

To his horror, Kelsier saw it change, sending forward spines like the spindly legs of a spider. On their end, dangling like a puppet, was a humanoid figure.

Vin . . . it whispered. *Vin* . . .

She looked toward the pool, her posture grieved. Then she left Venture and entered the Well, passing Kelsier without seeing him and reaching the deepest point. She sank slowly into the light. At the last moment, she ripped something glowing from her ear and tossed it out—a bit of metal. Her earring?

Once she sank completely, she did not appear on this side. Instead, a storm began. A rising column of light surrounded Kelsier, blocking him from seeing anything but the raw *energy*. Like a sudden tide, an explosion, an instant sunrise. It was all around him, active, *excited*.

You mustn't do it, child, Ruin said through his humanlike puppet. How could it speak with such a soothing voice? He could see the force behind it, the destruction, but the face it put on was so kindly. *You know what you must do.*

"Don't listen to it, Vin!" Kelsier screamed, but his voice was lost in the roar of the power. He shouted and railed as the voice conned Vin, warning her that if she took the power she'd destroy the world. Kelsier fought through the light, trying to find her, to seize her and explain.

He failed. He failed *horribly*. He couldn't make himself heard, couldn't touch Vin. Couldn't do anything. Even his impromptu plan of stabbing Elend proved foolish, for she released the power. Weeping, flayed, ripped open, she did the most selfless thing he had ever seen.

And in so doing, she doomed them.

The power became a weapon as she released it. It made a spear in the air and ripped a hole through reality and into the place where Ruin waited.

Ruin rushed through that hole to freedom.

4

KELSIER sat on the lip of the now empty Well of Ascension. The light was gone, and with it his prison. He could leave.

He didn't seem to be stretching away and fading. Apparently being part of Preservation's power for a time had expanded Kelsier's soul, letting him linger. Though honestly, he wished he could vanish at this moment.

Vin—glowing and radiant to his eyes—lay beside Elend Venture, clutching him and weeping as his soul pulsed, growing weaker. Kelsier stood up, turning his back toward the sight. For all his cleverness, he'd gone and broken the poor girl's heart.

I must be the smartest idiot around, Kelsier thought.

"It was going to happen," Preservation said. "I thought . . . Maybe . . ." From the corner of his eye, Kelsier saw Fuzz approach Vin, then look down at the fallen Venture.

"I can Preserve him," Preservation whispered.

Kelsier spun. Preservation started waving at Vin, and she stumbled to her feet. She followed the god a few feet to something Elend had dropped, a fallen nugget of metal. Where had that come from?

The Venture boy was carrying it when he entered, Kelsier thought. That was the last bit of metal from the other side of the room, the twin of the one the Drifter had stolen. Kelsier approached as Vin took the nugget of metal, so tiny, and approached Elend, then put it into his mouth. She washed it down with a vial of metal.

Soul and metal became one. Elend's light strengthened, glowing vibrantly. Kelsier closed his eyes, feeling a thrumming sense of peace.

"That was good work, Fuzz," Kelsier said, opening his eyes and smiling at Preservation as the god stepped over to him. Vin's posture manifested incredible joy. "I'm almost ready to think you're a benevolent god."

"Stabbing him was dangerous, painful," Preservation said. "I cannot condone such recklessness. But perhaps it was right, regardless of how I feel."

"Ruin's free," Kelsier said, looking upward. "That thing has escaped."

"Yes. Fortunately, before I died, I put a plan into motion. I can't remember it, but I'm certain that it was brilliant."

"You know, I've said something similar myself on occasion, after a night of drinking." Kelsier rubbed his chin. "I'm free too."

"Yes."

"This is where you joke that you aren't certain which was more dangerous to release. Me or the other one."

"No," Fuzz said. "I know which is more dangerous."

"Failing marks for effort there, I'm afraid."

"But perhaps . . ." Preservation said. "Perhaps I cannot say which is more *annoying*." He smiled. With his face half melted off and his neck starting to go, it was unnerving. Like a happy bark from a crippled puppy.

Kelsier slapped him on the shoulder. "We'll make a solid crewmember out of you yet, Fuzz. For now, I want to get the *hell* out of this room."

PART THREE
SPIRIT

1

KELSIER really wanted something to drink. Wasn't that what you did when you got out of prison? Went drinking, enjoyed your freedom by giving it up to a little booze and a terrible headache?

When alive, he'd usually avoided such levity. He liked to control a situation, not let it control him—but he couldn't deny that he thirsted for something to drink, to numb the experience he'd just been through.

That seemed terribly unfair. No body, but he could still be thirsty?

He climbed from the caverns surrounding the Well of Ascension, passing through misty chambers and tunnels. As before, when he touched something he was able to see what it looked like in the real world.

His footing was firm on the inconstant ground; though it was somewhat springy, like cloth, it held his weight unless he stamped hard—which would cause his foot to sink in like it was pushing through thick mud. He could even pass through the walls if he tried, but it was harder than it had been during his initial run, when he'd been dying.

He emerged from the caverns into the basement of Kredik Shaw, the Lord Ruler's palace. It was even easier than usual to get turned about in this place, as everything was misty to his eyes. He touched the things of mist that he passed, so he could picture his surroundings better. A vase, a carpet, a door.

Kelsier eventually stepped out onto the streets of Luthadel a free—if dead—man. For a time he just walked the city, so relieved to be out of that hole that he was able to ignore the sense of dread he felt at Ruin's escape.

He must have wandered an entire day that way, sitting on rooftops, strolling past fountains. Looking over this city dotted with glowing pieces of metal, like lights hovering in the mists at night. He ended up on top of the city wall, observing the koloss who had set up camp outside the town but—somehow—didn't seem to be killing anyone.

He needed to see if there was a way to contact his friends. Unfortunately, without the pulses—those had stopped when Ruin escaped—to guide him, he didn't know where to start looking. He'd lost track of Vin and Elend in his excitement at leaving the caverns, but he remembered some of what he'd seen through the pulses. That gave him a few places to search.

He ultimately found his crew at Keep Venture. It was the day after the disaster at the Well of Ascension, and they appeared to be holding a funeral. Kelsier strolled through the courtyard, passing among the glowing souls of men, each burning like a limelight. Those he brushed gave him an impression of their appearance. Many he recognized: skaa he'd interacted with, encouraged, uplifted during his final months of life. Others were unfamiliar. A disturbing number of soldiers who had once served the Lord Ruler.

He found Vin at the front, sitting on the steps of Keep Venture, huddled and slumped over. Elend was nowhere to be seen, though Ham stood nearby, arms folded. In the courtyard, somebody waved their hands before the group, giving a speech. Was that Demoux? Leading the people in the funeral service? Those were certainly corpses laid out in the courtyard, their souls no longer shining. He couldn't hear what Demoux was saying, but the presentation seemed clear.

Kelsier settled down on the steps beside Vin. He clasped his hands before himself. "So . . . that went well."

Vin, of course, didn't reply.

"I mean," Kelsier continued, "yes, we ended up releasing a world-ending force of destruction and chaos, but at least the Lord Ruler is dead. Mission accomplished. Plus you still have your nobleman boyfriend, so there's that. Don't worry about the scar on his stomach. It'll make him look more rugged. Mists know, the little bookworker could use some toughening up."

She didn't move, but maintained her slumped posture. He rested his arm across her shoulders and was given a glimpse of her as she looked in the real world. Full of color and life, yet somehow . . . weathered. She seemed so much older now, no longer the child he'd found scamming obligators on the streets.

He leaned down beside her. "I'm going to beat this thing, Vin. I *am* going take care of this."

"And how," Preservation said from the courtyard below the steps, "are you going to accomplish *that*?"

Kelsier looked up. Though he was prepared for the sight of Preservation, he still winced to see him as he was—barely even in human shape any longer, more a dissolved bunch of weaving threads of frayed smoke, giving the vague impression of a head, arms, legs.

"He's free," Preservation said. "That's it. Time up. Contract due. He will take what was promised."

"We'll stop him."

"Stop him? He's the force of entropy, a universal constant. You can't *stop* that any more than you can stop time."

Kelsier stood up, leaving Vin and walking down the steps toward Preservation. He wished he could hear what Demoux was saying to this small crowd of glowing souls.

"If he can't be stopped," Kelsier said, "then we'll slow him. You did it before, right? Your grand plan?"

"I . . ." Preservation said. "Yes . . . There was a plan. . . ."

"I'm free now. I can help you put it into motion."

"Free?" Preservation laughed. "No, you've just entered a larger prison. Tied to this Realm, bound to it. There's nothing you can do. Nothing I can do."

"That—"

"He's watching us, you know," Preservation said, looking upward at the sky.

Kelsier followed his gaze reluctantly. The sky—misty and shifting— seemed so distant. It felt as if it had pulled back from the planet, like people in a crowd shying away from a corpse. In that vastness Kelsier saw something dark, thrashing, writhing upon itself. More solid than mist, like an ocean of snakes, obscuring the tiny sun.

He knew that vastness. Ruin was indeed watching.

"He thinks you're insignificant," Preservation said. "I think he finds you amusing—the soul of Ati that is still in there somewhere would laugh at this."

"He has a soul?"

Preservation didn't respond. Kelsier stepped up to him, passing corpses made of mists on the ground.

"If he is alive," Kelsier said, "then he can be killed. No matter how powerful." *You're proof of that, Fuzz. He's killing you.*

Preservation laughed, a harsh, barking noise. "You keep forgetting which of us is a god and which is just a poor dead shadow. Waiting to expire." He waved a mostly unraveled arm, fingers made of spirals of unwound, misty strings. "Listen to them. Doesn't it embarrass you how they talk? The Survivor? Ha! I Preserved them for millennia. What have *you* done for them?"

Kelsier turned toward Demoux. Preservation appeared to have for- gotten that Kelsier couldn't hear the speech. Intending to go touch Demoux, to get a view of what he looked like now, Kelsier brushed one of the corpses on the ground.

A young man. A soldier, by the looks of it. He didn't know the boy, but he started to worry. He looked back at where Ham was standing— that figure near him would be Breeze.

What of the others?

He grew cold, then started touching corpses, looking for any he rec- ognized. His motions became more frantic.

"What are you seeking?" Preservation asked.

"How many—" Kelsier swallowed. "How many of these were friends of mine?"

"Some," Preservation said.

"Any members of the crew?"

"No," Preservation said, and Kelsier let out a sigh. "No, they died during the initial break-in, days ago. Dockson. Clubs."

A spear of ice shot through Kelsier. He tried to stand up from beside the corpse he'd been inspecting, but stumbled, trying to force out the words. "No. No, not Dox."

Preservation nodded.

"Wh . . . When did it happen? How?"

Preservation laughed. The sound of madness. He showed little of the kindly, uncertain man who had greeted Kelsier when he'd first entered this place.

"Both were murdered by koloss as the siege broke. Their bodies were burned days ago, Kelsier, while you were trapped."

Kelsier trembled, feeling lost. "I . . ." Kelsier said.

Dox. I wasn't here for him. I could have seen him again, as he passed. Talked to him. Saved him maybe?

"He cursed you as he died, Kelsier," Preservation said, voice harsh. "He blamed you for all this."

Kelsier bowed his head. Another lost friend. And Clubs too . . . two good men. He'd lost too many of those in his life, dammit. Far too many.

I'm sorry, Dox, Clubs. I'm sorry for failing you.

Kelsier took that anger, that bitterness and shame, and channeled it. He'd found purpose again during his days in prison. He wouldn't lose it now.

He stood and turned to Preservation. The god—shockingly—cringed as if *frightened*. Kelsier seized the god's form, and in a brief moment was given a vision of the grandness beyond. The pervading light of Preservation that permeated all things. The world, the mists, the metals, the very souls of men. This creature was somehow dying, but his power was far from gone.

He also felt Preservation's pain. It was the loss Kelsier had felt at Dox's death, only magnified thousands of times over. Preservation felt every light that went out, felt them and knew them as a person he had loved.

Around the world they were dying at an accelerated pace. Too much ash was falling, and Preservation only anticipated it increasing. Armies of koloss rampaging beyond control. Death, destruction, a world on its last legs.

And . . . to the south . . . what was *that*? People?

Kelsier held Preservation, in awe at this creature's divine agony. Then Kelsier pulled him close, into an embrace.

"I'm so sorry," Kelsier whispered.

"Oh, Senna . . ." Preservation whispered. "I'm losing this place. Losing them all . . ."

"We are going to stop it," Kelsier said, pulling back.

"It can't be stopped. The deal . . ."

"Deals can be broken."

"Not these kinds of deals, Kelsier. I was able to trick Ruin before, lock him away, by fooling him with our agreement. But that wasn't a breach of contract, more leaving a hole in the agreement to be exploited. This time there are no holes."

"Then we go out kicking and screaming," Kelsier said. "You and me, we're a team."

Preservation seemed to *condense,* his form pulling itself together, threads reweaving. "A team. Yes. A crew."

"To do the impossible."

"Defy reality," Preservation whispered. "Everyone always said you were insane."

"And I always acknowledged that they had a point," Kelsier said. "Thing is, while they were correct to question my sanity, they never did have the right reasoning. It's not my ambition that should worry them."

"Then what should?"

Kelsier smiled.

Preservation, in turn, laughed—a sound that had lost its edge, the harshness gone. "I can't help you do . . . whatever it is you think you're doing. Not directly. I don't . . . think well enough anymore. But . . ."

"But?"

Preservation solidified a little further. "But I know where you'll find someone who can."

2

KELSIER followed a thread of Preservation, like a glowing tendril of mist, through the city. He made sure to look up periodically, confronting that force in the sky, which had boiled through the mists there and was coming to dominate in every direction.

Kelsier would not back down. He would not let this thing intimidate him again. He'd already killed one god. The second murder was always easier than the first.

The tendril of Preservation led him past shadowy tenements, through a slum that somehow looked even more depressing on this side—all crammed together, the souls of men packed in frightened lumps. His crew had saved this city, but many of the people Kelsier passed didn't seem to know it yet.

Eventually the tendril led him out broken city gates to the north, past rubble and corpses being slowly sorted. Past living armies and that fearsome army of koloss, out beyond the city and a short hike along the river to . . . the lake?

Luthadel was built not far from the lake that bore its name, though most of the city's populace determinedly ignored that fact. Lake Luthadel wasn't the swimming or sport kind of lake, unless you fancied bathing in a soupy sludge that was more ash than it was water—and good luck catching what few fish remained after centuries of residing next to a city full of half-starved skaa. This close to the ashmounts, keeping the river and lake navigable had demanded the full-time attention of an entire class of people, the canal workers, a strange breed of skaa who rarely mixed with those from the city proper.

They would have been horrified to find that here on this side, the lake—and actually the river as well—was inverted somehow. Opposite to the way the mists under his feet had a liquid feel to them, the lake rose into a solid mound, only a few inches high but harder and somehow more substantial than the ground he'd become used to walking upon.

In fact, the lake was like a low island rising from the sea of mists. What was solid and what was fluid seemed somehow reversed in this place. Kelsier stepped up to the island's edge, the ribbon of Preservation's essence curling past him and leading onto the island, like a mythical string showing the way home from the grand maze of Ishathon.

Kelsier stuffed his hands in his trouser pockets and kicked at the ground of the island. It was some type of dark, smoky stone.

"What?" Preservation whispered.

Kelsier jumped, then glanced at the line of light. "You . . . in there, Fuzz?"

"I'm everywhere," Preservation said, his voice soft, frail. He sounded exhausted. "Why have you stopped?"

"This is different."

"Yes, it congeals here," Preservation said. "It has to do with the way men think, and where they are likely to pass. Somewhat to do with that, at least."

"But what is it?" Kelsier said, stepping up onto the island.

Preservation said nothing further, and so Kelsier continued toward the center of the island. Whatever had "congealed" here, it was strikingly stonelike. And things grew on it. Kelsier passed scrubby plants sprouting from the otherwise hard ground—not misty, inchoate plants, but real ones full of color. They had broad brown leaves with—curiously— what seemed like *mist* rising from them. None of the plants reached higher than his knees, but there were still far more than he'd expected to find here.

As he passed through a field of the plants, he thought he caught something scurrying between them, rustling leaves in its passing.

The world of the dead has plants and animals? he thought. But that wasn't what Preservation had called it. The Cognitive Realm. How did these plants grow here? What watered them?

The farther he penetrated onto this island, the darker it became. Ruin was covering up that tiny sun, and Kelsier began to miss even the faint glow that had permeated the phantom mists in the city. Soon he was traveling in what seemed like twilight.

Eventually Preservation's ribbon grew thin, then vanished. Kelsier stopped near its tip, whispering, "Fuzz? You there?"

No response, the silence refuting Preservation's claim earlier that he was everywhere. Kelsier shook his head. Perhaps Preservation was listening, but wasn't *there* enough to give a reply. Kelsier continued forward, passing through a place where the plants had grown to waist height, mist rising from their broad leaves like steam from a hot plate.

Finally, ahead he spotted *light*. Kelsier pulled up. He'd fallen into a prowl naturally, led by instincts gained from a life spent on the con, literally since the day of his birth. He had no weapons. He knelt, feeling at the ground for a stone or stick, but these plants weren't big enough to provide anything substantial, and the ground was smooth, unbroken.

Preservation had promised him help, but he wasn't sure how much he trusted what Preservation said. Odd, that living through his own death should make him *more* hesitant to trust in God's word. He took off his belt for a weapon, but it evaporated in his hands and appeared back on his waist. Shaking his head, he prowled closer, approaching near enough to the fire to pick out two people. Alive, and in this Realm, not glowing souls or misty spirits.

The man wore skaa clothing—suspenders, shirt with sleeves rolled up—and tended a small dinner fire. He had short hair and a narrow, almost pinched face. That knife at his belt, nearly long enough to be a sword, would come in very handy.

The other person, who sat on a small folding chair, might have been Terris. There were some among their population who had a skin tone almost as dark as hers, though he'd also met some people from the various southern dominances who were dark. She certainly wasn't wearing Terris clothing—she had on a sturdy brown dress, with a large leather girdle around the waist, and wore her hair woven into tiny braids.

Two. He could handle two, couldn't he? Even without Allomancy or weapons. Regardless, best to be careful. He hadn't forgotten his humiliation at the hands of the Drifter. Kelsier made a careful decision, then stood up, straightened his coat, and strode into their camp.

"Well," he proclaimed, "this has been an unusual few days, I can tell you *that*."

The man at the fire scrambled backward, hand on his knife, gaping. The woman remained seated, though she reached for something at her side. A little tube with a handle on the bottom. She pointed it toward him, treating it like some kind of weapon.

"So," Kelsier said, glancing at the sky with its shifting, writhing mass of too-solid tendrils, "anyone else bothered by the voracious force of destruction in the air above us?"

"Shadows!" the man shouted. "It's *you*. You're dead!"

"Depends on your definition of dead," Kelsier said, strolling over to the fire. The woman trailed him with that odd weapon of hers. "What in the blazes are you *burning* for that fire?" He looked up at the two of them. "What?"

"How?" the man sputtered. "What? When . . ."

". . . Why?" Kelsier added helpfully.

"Yes, why!"

"I have a very delicate constitution, you see," Kelsier said. "And death seemed like it would be *rather* bad for the digestion. So I decided not to participate."

"One doesn't merely *decide* to become a shadow!" the man exclaimed. He had a faintly strange accent, one Kelsier couldn't place. "It's an important rite! With requirements and traditions. This . . . this is . . ." He threw his hands into the air. "This is a *bother*."

Kelsier smiled, meeting the gaze of the woman, who reached for a cup of something warm on the ground beside her. With her other hand she tucked her weapon away, as if it had never been there. She was perhaps in her mid-thirties.

"The Survivor of Hathsin," she said, musing.

"You seem to have me at a disadvantage," Kelsier said. "One problem with notoriety, unfortunately."

"I should assume there are many disadvantages to fame, for a thief. One doesn't particularly wish to be recognized while trying to lift pocketbooks."

"Considering how he's regarded by the people of this domain," the man said, still watching Kelsier with a wary eye, "I'd expect them to be delighted to discover him robbing them."

"Yes," Kelsier said dryly, "they practically lined up for the privilege. Must I repeat myself?"

She considered. "My name is Khriss, of Taldain." She nodded toward the other man, and he reluctantly replaced his knife. "That is Nazh, a man in my employ."

"Excellent," Kelsier said. "Any idea why Preservation would tell me to come talk to you?"

"*Preservation?*" Nazh said, stepping up and seizing Kelsier's arm. So, as with the Drifter, they could indeed touch Kelsier. "You've spoken directly with one of the *Shards?*"

"Sure," Kelsier said. "Fuzz and I go way back." He pulled his arm free of Nazh's grip and grabbed the other folding stool from beside the fire—two simple pieces of wood that folded together, a piece of cloth between them to sit on.

He settled it across from Khriss and sat down.

"I don't like this, Khriss," Nazh said. "He's dangerous."

"Fortunately," she replied, "so are we. The Shard Preservation, Survivor. How does he look?"

"Is that a test to see if I've actually spoken with him," Kelsier said, "or a sincere question as to the creature's status?"

"Both."

"He's dying," Kelsier said, spinning Nazh's knife in his fingers. He'd palmed it during their altercation a moment ago, and was curious to find that though it was made of metal, it didn't glow. "He's a short man with black hair—or he used to be. He's been . . . well, *unraveling.*"

"Hey," Nazh said, eyes narrowing at the knife. He looked at his belt, and the empty sheath. *"Hey!"*

"Unraveling," Khriss said. "So a slow death. Ati doesn't know how to Splinter another Shard? Or he hasn't the strength? Hmm . . ."

"Ati?" Kelsier asked. "Preservation mentioned that name too."

Khriss pointed at the sky with one finger while she sipped at her drink. "That's him. What he's become, at least."

"And . . . what is a Shard?" Kelsier asked.

"Are you a scholar, Mr. Survivor?"

"No," he said. "But I've killed a few."

"Cute. Well, you've stumbled into something far, far bigger than you, your politics, or your little planet."

"Bigger than you can handle, Survivor," Nazh said, swiping back his knife as Kelsier balanced it on his finger. "You should just bow out now."

"Nazh does have a point," Khriss said. "Your questions are dangerous. Once you step behind the curtain and see the actors as the people they are, it becomes harder to pretend the play is real."

"I . . ." Kelsier leaned forward, clasping his hands before him. Hell . . . that fire was warm, but it didn't seem to be *burning* anything. He stared at the flames and swallowed. "I woke up from death after having, deep down, expected there to be no afterlife. I found that God was real, but that he was dying. I need answers. *Please.*"

"Curious," she said.

He looked up, frowning.

"I have heard many stories of you, Survivor," she said. "They often laud your many admirable qualities. Sincerity is never one of those."

"I can steal something else from your manservant," Kelsier said, "if it will make you feel more comfortable that I am what you expected."

"You can try," Nazh said, walking around the fire, folding his arms and obviously trying to look intimidating.

"The Shards," Khriss said, drawing Kelsier's attention, "are not God, but they are *pieces* of God. Ruin, Preservation, Autonomy, Cultivation, Devotion . . . There are sixteen of them."

"Sixteen," Kelsier breathed. "There are fourteen *more* of these things running around?"

"The rest are on other planets."

"Other . . ." Kelsier blinked. "Other *planets.*"

"Ah, see," Nazh said. "You've broken him already, Khriss."

"Other planets," she repeated gently. "Yes, there are dozens of them. Many are inhabited by people much like you or me. There is an original, shrouded and hidden somewhere in the cosmere. I've yet to find it, but I *have* found stories.

"Anyway, there was a God. Adonalsium. I don't know if it was a force or a being, though I suspect the latter. Sixteen people, together, *killed* Adonalsium, ripping it apart and dividing its essence between them, becoming the first who Ascended."

"Who were they?" Kelsier said, trying to make sense of this.

"A diverse group," she said. "With equally diverse motives. Some wished for the power; others saw killing Adonalsium as the only good option left to them. Together they murdered a deity, and became divine themselves." She smiled in a kindly way, as if to prepare him for what came next. "Two of those created this planet, Survivor, including the people on it."

"So . . . my world, and everyone I know," Kelsier said, "is the creation of a pair of . . . half gods?"

"More like fractional gods," Nazh said. "And ones with no particular qualifications for deityhood, other than being conniving enough to murder the guy who had the job before."

"Oh, hell . . ." Kelsier breathed. "No wonder we're all so bloody messed up."

"Actually," Khriss noted, "people are generally like that, no matter who made them. If it's any consolation, Adonalsium originally created the first humans, therefore your gods had a pattern to use."

"So we're copies of a flawed original," Kelsier said. "Not terribly comforting." He looked upward. "And that thing? It used to be human?"

"The power . . . distorts," Khriss said. "There's a person in that somewhere, directing it. Or perhaps just riding it at this point."

Kelsier remembered the puppet Ruin had presented, the shape of a man. Now basically a shell filled with a terrible power. "So what happens if one of these things . . . dies?"

"I'm very curious to see," Khriss said. "I've never viewed it in person, and the past deaths were different. They were each a single, stunning event, the god's power shattered and dispersed. This is more like a strangulation, while those were like a beheading. This should be very instructive."

"Unless I stop it," Kelsier said.

She smiled at him.

"Don't be patronizing," Kelsier snapped, standing up, the stool falling down behind him. "I am going to stop it."

"This world is winding down, Survivor," Khriss said. "It is a true shame, but I know of no way to save it. I came with the hopes that I might be able to help, but I can't even reach the Physical Realm here any longer."

"Someone destroyed the gateway in," Nazh noted. "Someone *incredibly* foolhardy. Brash. Stupid. Didn't—"

"You're overselling it," Kelsier said. "The Drifter told me what I did."

"The . . . who?" Khriss asked.

"Fellow with white hair," Kelsier said. "Lanky, with a sharp nose and—"

"Damn," Khriss said. "Did he get to the Well of Ascension?"

"Stole something there," Kelsier said. "A bit of metal."

"*Damn,*" Khriss said, looking at her servant. "We need to go. I'm sorry, Survivor."

"But—"

"This isn't because of what you just told us," she said, rising and waving for Nazh to help gather their things. "We were leaving anyway. This planet is dying; as much as I wish to witness the death of a Shard, I don't dare risk doing it from up close. We'll observe from afar."

"Preservation thought you'd be able to help," Kelsier said. "Surely there is *something* you can do. Something you can tell me. It can't be over."

"I *am* sorry, Survivor," Khriss said softly. "Perhaps if I knew more, perhaps if I could convince the Eyree to answer my questions . . ." She shook her head. "It will happen slowly, Survivor, over months. But it is coming. Ruin will consume this world, and the man once known as Ati won't be able to stop it. If he even cared to."

"Everything," Kelsier whispered. "Everything I've known. Every person on my . . . my planet?"

Nearby, Nazh bent down and picked up the fire, making it *vanish.* The oversized flame just folded up upon itself in his palm, and Kelsier thought he saw a puff of mist when it did so. Kelsier picked up his stool with one finger, unscrewed the bolt on the bottom, and palmed it into his hand before handing the stool to Nazh.

Nazh then tugged on a hiking pack, tied with scroll cases across the top. He looked to Khriss.

"Stay," Kelsier said, turning back to Khriss. "Help me."

"Help you? I can't even help *myself,* Survivor. I'm in exile, and even if I weren't I wouldn't have the resources to stop a Shard. I probably should never have come." She hesitated. "And I'm sorry, but I cannot invite you to come with us. The eyes of your god will be upon you, Kelsier. He'll know where you are, as you have pieces of him within. It has been dangerous enough to speak here with you."

Nazh handed her a pack, and she slung it over her shoulder.

"I *am* going to stop this," Kelsier told them.

Khriss lifted a hand and curled her fingers in an unfamiliar gesture, bidding him farewell it seemed. She turned away from the clearing and strode away, into the brush. Nazh followed.

Kelsier sank down. They'd taken the stools, so he settled onto the ground, bowing his head. *This is what you deserve, Kelsier,* a piece of him thought. *You wished to dance with the divine and steal from gods. Should you now be surprised that you've found yourself in over your head?*

The sound of rustling leaves made him scramble back to his feet. Nazh emerged from the shadows. The shorter man stopped at the perimeter of the abandoned camp, then cursed softly before stepping forward and removing his side knife, sheath and all, and handing it toward Kelsier.

Hesitant, Kelsier accepted the leatherbound weapon.

"It's a bad state you and yours are in," Nazh said softly, "but I rather like this place. Damnable mists and all." He pointed westward. "They've set up out there."

"They?"

"The Eyree," he said. "They've been at this far longer than we have, Survivor. If someone will know how to help you, it will be the Eyree. Look for them where the land becomes solid again."

"Solid again . . ." Kelsier said. "Lake Tyrian?"

"Beyond. Far beyond, Survivor."

"The *ocean*? That's miles and miles away. Past Farmost!"

Nazh patted him on the shoulder, then turned back to hike after Khriss.

"Is there hope?" Kelsier called.

"What if I told you no?" Nazh said over his shoulder. "What if I said I figured you were damn well ruined, so to speak. Would it change what you were going to do?"

"No."

Nazh raised his fingers to his forehead in a kind of salute. "Farewell, Survivor. Take care of my knife. I'm fond of it."

He vanished into the darkness. Kelsier watched after him, then did the only rational thing.

He ate the bolt he'd taken from the bottom of the stool.

3

THE bolt didn't do anything. He'd hoped he'd be able to make Allomancy work, but the bolt just settled into his stomach—a strange and uncomfortable weight. He couldn't burn it, despite trying. As he walked, he eventually coughed it back up and tossed it away.

He stepped to the transition from the island to the misty ground around Luthadel, and felt a new weight upon him. A doomed world, dying gods, and an entire universe he'd never known existed. His only hope now was . . . to journey to the ocean?

That was farther than he had ever gone, even during his travels with Gemmel. It would take months to walk that far. Did they have months?

He stepped off the island, crossing onto the soft ground of the misted banks. Luthadel loomed in the near distance, a shadowy wall of curling mist.

"Fuzz?" he called. "You out there?"

"I'm everywhere," Preservation said, appearing beside him.

"So you were listening?" Kelsier asked.

He nodded absently, form frayed, face indistinct. "I think . . . Surely I was . . ."

"They mentioned someone called the Eyes Ree?"

"Yes, the I-ree," Preservation said, pronouncing it in a slightly different way. "Three letters. I R E. It means something in their language, these people from another land. The ones who died, but did not. I have felt them crowding at the edges of my vision, like spirits in the night."

"Dead, but alive," Kelsier said. "Like me?"

"No."

"Then what?"

"Died, but did not."

Great, Kelsier thought. He turned toward the west. "They are supposedly at the ocean."

"The Ire built a city," Preservation said, softly. "In a place between worlds . . ."

"Well," Kelsier said, then took a deep breath. "That's where I'm going."

"Going?" Preservation said. "You're leaving me?"

The urgency of those words startled Kelsier. "If these people can help us, then I need to talk to them."

"They can't help us," Preservation said. "They're . . . they're callous. They plot over my corpse like scavenging insects waiting for the last beat of the heart. Don't go. Don't *leave me.*"

"You're everywhere. I can't leave you."

"No. They're beyond me. I . . . I cannot depart this land. I'm too Invested in it, in every rock and leaf." He pulsed, his already indistinct form spreading thinner. "We . . . grow attached easily, and it takes one who is particularly dedicated to leave."

"And Ruin?" Kelsier said, turning toward the west. "If he destroys everything, would he be able to escape?"

"Yes," Preservation said, very softly. "He could go then. But Kelsier, you can't abandon me. We . . . we're a team, right?"

Kelsier rested his hand on the creature's shoulder. Once so confident, now little more than a *smudge* in the air. "I'll be back as soon as I can. If I'm going to stop that thing, I'll need some kind of help."

"You pity me."

"I pity anyone who's not me, Fuzz. A hazard of being the man I am. But you *can* do this. Keep an eye on Ruin, and try to get word to Vin and that nobleman of hers."

"Pity," Preservation repeated. "Is that . . . is that what I've become? Yes . . . Yes, it is."

He reached up with a vaguely outlined hand and seized Kelsier's arm from underneath. Kelsier gasped, then cut off as Preservation grabbed him by the back of the neck with his other hand, locking his gaze with Kelsier's. Those eyes snapped into focus, fuzziness becoming suddenly distinct. A glow burst from them, silvery white, bathing Kelsier and blinding him.

Everything else was vaporized; nothing could withstand that terrible, wonderful light. Kelsier lost form, thought, very being. He transcended *self* and entered a place of flowing light. Ribbons of it exploded from him, and though he tried to scream, he had no voice.

Time didn't pass; time had no relevance here. It was not a place. Location had no relevance. Only Connection, person to person, man to world, Kelsier to god.

And that god was *everything*. The thing he had pitied was the very ground Kelsier walked upon, the air, the metals—his own soul. Preservation *was* everywhere. Beside it, Kelsier was insignificant. An afterthought.

The vision faded. Kelsier stumbled away from Preservation, who stood, placid, a blur in the air—but a representation of so much more. Kelsier put his hand to his chest and was pleased, for a reason he couldn't explain, to find that his heart was beating. His soul was learning to imitate a body, and somehow having a racing heart was comforting.

"I suppose I deserved that," Kelsier said. "Be careful how you use those visions, Fuzz. Reality isn't particularly healthy for a man's ego."

"I would call it very healthy," Preservation replied.

"I saw everything," Kelsier mumbled. "Everyone, everything. My Connection to them, and . . . and . . ."

Spreading into the future, he thought, grasping at an explanation. *Possibilities, so many possibilities . . . like atium.*

"Yes," Preservation said, sounding exhausted. "It can be trying to recognize one's true place in things. Few can handle the—"

"Send me back," Kelsier said, scrambling up to Preservation, taking him by the arms.

"What?"

"*Send me back.* I need to see that again."

"Your mind is too fragile. It will break."

"I broke that damn thing years ago, Fuzz. Do it. Please."

Preservation hesitantly gripped him, and this time his eyes took longer to start glowing. They flashed, his form trembling, and for a moment Kelsier thought the god would dissipate entirely.

Then the glow spurted to life, and in an instant Kelsier was consumed. This time he forced himself to look away from Preservation—though it was less a matter of *looking*, and more a matter of trying to sort through the horrible overload of information and sensation that assaulted him.

Unfortunately, in turning his attention away from Preservation he risked giving it to something else—something equally demanding. There was a second god here, black and terrible, the thing with the spines and spidery legs, sprouting from dark mists and reaching into everything throughout the land.

Including Kelsier.

In fact, his ties to Preservation were trivial by comparison to these hundreds of black fingers which attached him to that thing Beyond. He sensed a powerful satisfaction from it, along with an idea. Not words, just an undeniable fact.

You are mine, Survivor.

Kelsier rebelled at the thought, but in this place of perfect light, truth *had* to be acknowledged.

Straining, soul crumbling before that terrible reality, Kelsier turned toward the tendrils of light spreading into the distance. Possibilities upon possibilities, compounded upon one another. Infinite, overwhelming. The future.

He dropped out of the vision again, and this time fell to his knees panting. The glow faded, and he was again on the banks of Lake Luthadel. Preservation settled down beside him and rested his hand on Kelsier's back.

"I can't stop him," Kelsier whispered.

"I know," Preservation said.

"I could see thousands upon thousands of possibilities. In none of them did I defeat that thing."

"The ribbons of the future are never as useful as . . . as they should be," Preservation said. "I rode them much, in the past. It's too hard to see what is actually likely, and what is just a fragile . . . fragile, distant maybe. . . ."

"I can't stop it," Kelsier whispered. "I'm too like it. Everything I do serves *it*." Kelsier looked up, smiling.

"It broke you," Preservation said.

"No, Fuzz." Kelsier laughed, standing. "No. I can't stop it. No matter what I do, I can't stop it." He looked down at Preservation. "But *she* can."

"He knows this. You were right. He *has* been preparing her, infusing her."

"She can beat it."

"A frail possibility," Preservation said. "A false promise."

"No," Kelsier said softly. "A *hope*."

He held his hand out. Preservation took it and let Kelsier pull him to his feet. God nodded. "A hope. What is our plan?"

"I continue to the west," Kelsier said. "I saw, in the possibilities . . ."

"Do not trust what you saw," Preservation said, sounding far more firm than he had earlier. "It takes an infinite mind to even *begin* to glean information from those tendrils of the future. Even then you are likely to be wrong."

"The path I saw started by me going to the west," Kelsier said. "It's all I can think to do. Unless you have a better suggestion."

Preservation shook his head.

"You need to stay here, fight him off, resist—and try to get through to Vin. If not her, then Sazed."

"He . . . is not well."

Kelsier cocked his head. "Hurt in the fighting?"

"Worse. Ruin tries to break him."

Damn. But what could he do, except continue with his plan? "Do what you can," Kelsier said. "I'll seek these people to the west."

"They *won't* help."

"I'm not going to ask for their help," Kelsier said, then smiled. "I'm going to rob them."

PART FOUR
JOURNEY

1

K ELSIER ran. He needed the urgency, the strength, of being in motion. A man running somewhere had a purpose.

He left the region around Luthadel, jogging alongside a canal for direction. Like the lake, the canal was reversed here—a long, narrow mound rather than a trough.

As he moved, Kelsier tried yet again to sort through the conflicting set of images, impressions, and ideas he'd experienced in that place where he could perceive everything. Vin *could* beat this thing. Of that Kelsier was certain, as certain as he was that he couldn't defeat Ruin himself.

From there however, his thoughts grew more vague. These people, the Ire, were working on something dangerous. Something he could use against Ruin . . . maybe.

That was all he had. Preservation was right; the threads in that place between moments were too knotted, too ephemeral, to give him much beyond a vague impression. But at least it was something he could do.

So he ran. He didn't have time to walk. He wished again for Allomancy, pewter to lend him strength and endurance. He'd had that power for such a short time, compared to the rest of his life, but it had become second nature to him very quickly.

He no longer had those abilities to lean on. Fortunately, without a body he did not seem to tire unless he stopped to think about the fact that he *should* be tiring. That was no problem. If there was one thing Kelsier was good at, it was lying to himself.

Hopefully Vin would be able to hold out long enough to save them all. It was a terrible weight to put on the shoulders of one person. He would lift what portion he could.

I KNOW *this place,* Kelsier thought, slowing his jog as he passed through a small canalside town. A waystop where canalmasters could rest their skaa, have a drink, and enjoy a warm bath for the night. It was one of many that dotted the dominances, all nearly identical. This one could be distinguished by the two crumbling towers on the opposite bank of the canal.

Yes, Kelsier thought, stopping on the street. Those towers were distinctive even in the dreamy, misted landscape of this Realm. Longsfollow. How could he have reached this place already? It was well outside the Central Dominance. How long had he been running?

Time had become a strange thing to him since his death. He had no need for food, and didn't feel tiredness beyond what his mind projected. With Ruin obstructing the sun, and the only light that of the misty ground, it was very difficult to judge the passing of days.

He'd been running . . . for a while. A long while?

He suddenly felt exhausted, his mind numbing, as if suffering the effects of a pewter drag. He groaned and sat down by the side of the canal mound, which was covered in tiny plants. Those plants seemed to grow anywhere water was present in the real world. He'd found them sprouting from misty cups.

Occasionally he'd found other, stranger plants in the landscape between towns—places where the springy ground grew more firm. Places without people: the extended, ashen emptiness between dots of civilization.

He heaved himself to his feet, fighting off the exhaustion. It was all in his head, quite literally. Reluctant to push himself back into a run for the moment, he strolled through Longsfollow. A town had grown up here around the canal stop. Well, a village. Noblemen who ran plantations farther out from the canal would come here to trade and to ship goods in toward Luthadel. It had become a hub of commerce, a bustling civic center.

Kelsier had killed seven men here.

Or had it been eight? He strolled, counting them off. The lord, both of his sons, his wife . . . Yes, seven, counting two guards and that cousin. That was right. He'd spared the cousin's wife, who had been with child.

He and Mare had been renting a room above the general store, over there, pretending to be merchants from a minor noble house. He walked up the steps outside the building, stopping at the door. He rested his fingers on it and sensed it in the Physical Realm, familiar even after all this time.

We had plans! Mare had said as they furiously packed. *How could you do this?*

"They murdered a child, Mare," Kelsier whispered. "Sank her in the canal with stones tied to her feet. Because she spilled their tea. Because she spilled the *damn tea.*"

Oh, Kell, she'd said. *They kill people every day. It's terrible, but it's life. Are you going to bring retribution to* every *nobleman out there?*

"Yes," Kelsier whispered. He made a fist against the door. "I did it. I made the Lord Ruler himself pay, Mare."

And that boiling mass of writhing serpents in the sky . . . that had been the result. He'd seen the truth, in his moment between time with Preservation. The Lord Ruler would have prevented this doom for another thousand years.

Kill one man. Get vengeance, but cause how many more deaths? He and Mare had fled this village. He'd later learned that Inquisitors had come, torturing many of the people they'd known here, killing not a few in their search for answers.

Kill, and they killed in turn. Get revenge, and their vengeance returned tenfold.

You are mine, Survivor.

He gripped at the door handle, but couldn't do more than gain an impression of how it looked. He couldn't move it. Fortunately, he was able to push against the door and force himself through. He stumbled to a stop, and was shocked to see that the room was occupied. A solitary soul—glowing, so it was a person in the real world, not this one—lay on the cot in the corner.

He and Mare had left this place in a hurry, and had been forced to stash some of their possessions in a hole behind a stone in the hearth. Those were gone now; he'd pilfered them after Mare's death, following his escape from the Pits and his training with the strange old Allomancer named Gemmel.

He avoided the person and walked to the small hearth. When he'd returned for that hidden coin, he'd been on his way to Luthadel, his mind overflowing with grand plans and dangerous ideas. He'd retrieved the coin, but had found more than he intended. The pouch of coin, and beside it a journal of Mare's.

"If I'd died," Kelsier said, loudly, "if I'd let myself be pulled into that other place . . . I'd be with Mare now, wouldn't I?"

No reply.

"Preservation!" Kelsier shouted. "Do you know where she is? Did you see her pass into that darkness you spoke of, in that place where people go after this? I'd be with her, wouldn't I, if I'd let myself die?"

Again Preservation didn't reply. His mind certainly wasn't in all places, even if his essence was. Considering how erratic he'd been lately, his mind might not be completely in even *one* place. Kelsier sighed, looking around the small room.

Then he stepped back, realizing that the person on the cot had stood up and was looking about.

"What do you want?" Kelsier snapped.

The figure jumped. Had he *heard* that?

Kelsier walked up to the figure and touched him, gaining a vision of an old beggar, scraggly of beard and wild of eye. The man was muttering to himself, and Kelsier—while touching him—could make some of it out.

"In me head," the man muttered. "Geddouta me head."

"You can hear me," Kelsier said.

The figure jumped again. "Damn whispers," he said. "Geddouta me head!"

Kelsier lowered his hand. He'd seen this, in the pulses. Sometimes the mad whispered the things they had heard from Ruin. But it seemed they could hear Kelsier as well.

Could he use this man? *Gemmel muttered like that sometimes,* Kelsier realized, feeling a chill. *I always thought he was mad.*

Kelsier tried to speak further with the man, but the effort was fruitless. The man kept jumping and muttering, but wouldn't actually respond.

Eventually Kelsier made his way back out of the room. He'd been glad for the madman to distract him from his memories of this place. He fished in his pocket, but then remembered he didn't have the picture of Mare's flower any longer. He'd left it for Vin.

He knew the answer to the questions he'd asked of Preservation just before. In refusing to accept death, Kelsier had also given up returning to Mare. Unless there was nothing beyond the warping. Unless *that* death was real and final.

Surely she couldn't have expected him to just give in, to let the stretching darkness take him? *Everyone else I've seen passed willingly,* Kelsier thought. *Even the Lord Ruler. Why must I insist on remaining?*

Foolish questions. Useless. He couldn't go when the world was in such danger. And he wouldn't just let himself die, not even to be with her.

He left the town, turned his path to the west again, and continued running.

3

KELSIER knelt down beside an old cookfire, no longer burning, represented by a group of shadowy, cold logs in this Realm. He found it was important to stop every few weeks or so to catch a breather. He had been running . . . well, a long time now.

Today he intended to finally crack a puzzle. He seized the misted remains of the old cookfire. Immediately he gained a vision of them in the real world—but he pushed through that, feeling something beyond.

Not just images, but sensations. Almost emotions. Cold wood that somehow remembered warmth. This fire was dead in the real world, but it *wished* it could burn again.

It was a strange sensation, realizing that logs could have wishes. This flame had burned for years, feeding the families of many skaa. Countless generations had sat before this pit in the floor. They'd kept the fire burning almost perpetually. Laughing, savoring their brief moments of joy.

The fire had given them that. It longed to do so again. Unfortunately, the people had left. Kelsier was finding more and more villages abandoned these days. Ashfalls went on longer than usual, and Kelsier had felt occasional trembling in the ground, even in this Realm. Earthquakes.

He could give this fire something. *Burn again,* he told it. *Be warm again.*

It couldn't happen in the Physical Realm, but all things there could manifest here. The fire wasn't actually alive, but to the people who had once lived here, it had been almost so. A familiar, warm friend.

Burn . . .

Light burst from his fingers, pouring out of his hands, a flame appearing there. Kelsier dropped it quickly, stepping back, grinning at the crackling blaze. It looked very much like the fire that Nazh and Khriss had carried with them; the logs themselves had appeared on this side, with dancing flames.

Fire. He'd made *fire* in the world of the dead. *Not bad, Kell,* he thought, kneeling. After taking a deep breath, he pushed his hand into the fire and grabbed the center of the logs, then closed his fist, capturing the bit of mist that made up the essence of that cookfire. It all folded upon itself, vanishing.

He cupped the small handful of mist. He could feel it, like he could feel the ground beneath him. Springy, but real enough as long as he didn't push too hard. He tucked the soul of the cookfire away in his pocket, fairly certain it wouldn't burst alight unless he commanded it to do so.

He left the skaa hovel, stepping out into a plantation. He'd never been here before—this was farther west than he'd traveled with Gemmel. The plantations out here were made of odd rectangular buildings that were low and squat, but each had a large courtyard. He strolled out of this one, entering a street that ran among a dozen similar hovels.

All in all, skaa were better off out here than they were in the inner dominances. It was like saying that a man drowning in beer was better off than one drowning in acid.

Ash fell through the sky. Though he'd not been able to see it during his first days in this Realm, he'd learned to pick it out. It reflected like tiny curling bits of mist, almost invisible. Kelsier broke into a jog, and the ash streamed around him. Some passed through him, leaving him with the impression that *he* was ash. A burned-out husk, a corpse reduced to embers that drifted on the wind.

He passed far too much ash heaped up on the ground. It shouldn't be falling so heavily here. The ashmounts were distant; from what he'd learned in his travels, ash only fell once or twice a month out here. Or at least that was how it had been before Ruin's awakening. Some trees still lived here, shadowy, their souls manifesting as misty forms that glowed like the souls of men.

He approached people on the road who were making westward, toward the coastal towns. Likely their noblemen had already fled that direction, terrified by the sudden increase of ash and the other signs of destruction. As Kelsier passed the people, he stretched out his hand, letting it brush against them and give him impressions of each one.

A young mother lamed by a broken foot, carrying her new baby close to her breast.

An old woman, strong, as old skaa needed to be. The weak were often left to die.

A young, freckled man in a fine shirt. He'd stolen that from the lord's manor, most likely.

Kelsier watched for signs of madness or raving. He'd confirmed that those types could often hear him, though it didn't always require obvious madness. Many seemed unable to make out his specific words, but instead heard him as phantom whispers. Impressions.

He picked up speed, leaving the townspeople behind. He could tell that this was a well-traveled area from the light of the mists beneath him. During his months running, he'd come to understand—and to an extent even accept—the Cognitive Realm. There was a certain freedom to being able to move unhindered through walls. To being able to peek in at the people and their lives.

But he was so lonely.

He tried not to think about it. He focused on his run and the challenge ahead. Because of the way time blended here, it didn't feel to him as if months had passed. Indeed, this experience was far preferable to his sanity-grating year trapped at the Well.

But he missed the people. Kelsier needed people, conversation, friends. Without them he felt dried out. What he wouldn't have given for Preservation, unhinged as he was, to appear and speak to him. Even that white-haired *Drifter* would have been a welcome break from the wasteland of mists.

He tried to find madmen so he could at least have *some* interaction with other living beings, no matter how meaningless.

At least I've gained something, Kelsier thought. A campfire in his pocket. When he got out of this, and he *would* get out of it, he'd certainly have stories to tell.

4

K ELSIER, the Survivor of Death, finally crested one last hill and
beheld an incredible sight spread before him. Land.

It rose from the edge of the mists, an ominous, dark expanse. It felt less alive than the shifting white-grey mists beneath him,
but oh was it a welcome sight.

He let out a long, relieved sigh. These last few weeks had been increasingly difficult. The thought of more running had started to nauseate him,
and the loneliness had him seeing phantoms in the shifting mists, hearing
voices in the lifeless nothing all around.

He was a much different figure from the one who had left Luthadel.
He planted his staff on the ground beside him—he'd recovered that from
the body of a dead refugee in the real world and coaxed it to life, giving
it a new home and a new master to serve. Same for the enveloping cloak
he wore, frayed at the edges almost like a mistcloak.

The pack he carried was different; he'd taken that from an abandoned
store. No master had ever carried it. It considered its purpose to sit on a
shelf and be admired. So far it had still made for a suitable companion.

Kelsier settled down, putting aside his staff and digging into his pack.
He counted off his balls of mist, which he kept wrapped up tight in the

pack. None had vanished this time; that was good. When an object was recovered—or worse, destroyed—in the Physical Realm, its Identity changed and the spirit would return to the location of its body.

Abandoned objects were best. Ones that had been owned for a long while, so they had a strong Identity, but that currently had nobody in the Physical Realm to care for them. He pulled out the ball of mist that was his campfire and unfolded it, bathing in its warmth. It was starting to fray, the logs pocked with misty holes. He could only guess that he'd carried it too far from its origin, and the distance was distressing it.

He pulled out another ball of mist, which unfolded in his hand, becoming a leather waterskin. He took a long drink. It didn't do him any real good; the water vanished soon after being poured out, and he didn't seem to need to drink.

He drank anyway. It felt good on his lips and throat, refreshing. It let him pretend to be alive.

He huddled on that hillside, overlooking the new frontier, sipping at phantom water beside the soul of a fire. His experience in the realm of gods, that moment between time, was a distant memory now . . . but, honestly, it had felt distant from the second he'd fallen out of it. The brilliant Connections and eternity-spanning revelations had immediately faded like mist before the morning sun.

He'd needed to reach this place. Beyond that . . . he had no idea. There were people out there, but how did he find them? And what did he do when he located them?

I need what they have, he thought, taking another pull on the waterskin. *But they won't give it to me.* He knew that for certain. But what was it they had? Knowledge? How could he con someone when he didn't even know if they'd speak his language?

"Fuzz?" Kelsier said, just as a test. "Preservation, you there?"

No reply. He sighed, packing away his waterskin. He glanced over his shoulder toward the direction he'd come from.

Then he scrambled to his feet, ripping his knife from the sheath at his side and spinning about, putting the fire between him and what stood there. The figure wore robes and had bright, flame-red hair. He bore a welcoming smile, but Kelsier could see spines beneath the surface of his skin. Pricking spider legs, thousands of them, pushing against the skin and causing it to pucker outward in erratic motions.

Ruin's puppet. The thing he'd seen the force construct and dangle toward Vin.

"Hello, Kelsier," Ruin said through the figure's lips. "My colleague is unavailable. But I will convey your requests, if you wish it of me."

"Stay back," Kelsier said, flourishing the knife, reaching by instinct for metals he could no longer burn. Damn, he missed that.

"Oh, Kelsier," Ruin said. "Stay back? I'm all around you—the air you pretend to breathe, the ground beneath your feet. I'm in that knife and in your very soul. How exactly am I to 'stay back'?"

"You can say what you wish," Kelsier said. "But you don't own me. I am *not* yours."

"Why do you resist so?" Ruin asked, strolling around the fire. Kelsier walked the other direction, keeping distance between himself and this creature.

"Oh, I don't know," Kelsier said. "Perhaps because you're an *evil force of destruction and pain.*"

Ruin pulled up, as if offended. "That was uncalled for!" He spread his hands. "Death is not evil, Kelsier. Death is necessary. Every clock must wind down, every day must end. Without *me* there is no life, and never could have been. Life is change, and I represent that change."

"And now you'll end it."

"It was a gift I gave," Ruin said, stretching out his hand toward Kelsier. "Life. Wondrous, *beautiful* life. The joy of the new child, the pride of a parent, the satisfaction of a job well done. These are from *me.*

"But it is done now, Kelsier. This planet is an elderly man, having lived his life in full, now wheezing his last breaths. It is not evil to give him the rest he demands. It's a *mercy.*"

Kelsier looked at that hand, which undulated with the pinprick pressing of the spiders inside.

"But who am I talking to?" Ruin said with a sigh, pulling back his hand. "The man who would not accept his own end, even though his soul longed for it, even though his wife longed for him to join her in the Beyond. No, Kelsier. I do not anticipate you will see the necessity of an ending. So continue to think me evil, if you must."

"Would it hurt so much," Kelsier said, "to give us a little more time?"

Ruin laughed. "Ever the thief, looking for what you can get away with. No, a reprieve has been granted time and time again. I assume you have no message for me to deliver, then?"

"Sure," Kelsier said. "Tell Fuzz he's to take something long, hard, and sharp, then ram it up your backside for me."

"As if he could harm even me. You realize that if he were in control, nobody would age? Nobody would think or live? If he had his way you'd all be frozen in time, unable to act lest you harm one another."

"So you're killing him."

"As I said," Ruin replied with a grin. "A mercy. For an old man well past his prime. But if all you plan to do is insult me, I must be going. It's a shame you'll be off on that island when the end comes. I assume you'd like to greet the others when they die."

"It can't be *that* close."

"It is, fortunately. But even if you could have done something to help, you're useless out here. A shame."

Sure, Kelsier thought. *And you came here to tell me that, rather than remaining quietly pleased that I was off being distracted by my quest.*

Kelsier recognized a hook when he saw one. Ruin wanted him to *believe* that the end was very near, that coming out here had been pointless.

Which meant it wasn't.

Preservation said he couldn't leave to go where I'm going, Kelsier thought. *And Ruin is similarly bound, at least until the world is destroyed.*

Maybe, for the first time in months, he'd be able to escape that squirming sky and the eyes of the destroyer. He saluted Ruin, tucked away his fire, then strode down the hill.

"Running, Kelsier?" Ruin said, appearing on the hillside with hands clasped as Kelsier passed him. "You cannot flee your fate. You are tied to this world, and to me."

Kelsier kept on walking, and Ruin appeared at the bottom of the hill, in the same pose.

"Those fools in the fortress won't be able to help you," Ruin noted. "I think that once this world reaches its end, I will pay them a visit. They've existed far too long past what is right."

Kelsier stopped at the edge of the new land of dark stone, like the lake that had become an island. This one was even larger. The ocean had become a continent.

"I will kill Vin while you're gone," Ruin whispered. "I will kill them all. Think about that, Kelsier, on your journey. When you come back, if there's anything left, I might have need of you. Thank you for all you've done on my behalf."

Kelsier stepped out onto the ocean continent, leaving Ruin behind on the shore. Kelsier could almost see the spindly threads of power that animated this puppet, providing a voice to the terrible force.

Damn. Its words were lies. He *knew* that.

They hurt anyway.

PART FIVE
IRE

1

HE'D hoped to have the sun back once Ruin vanished from the sky, but after walking far enough out, he seemed to leave his world behind—and the sun with it. The sky here was nothing but empty blackness. Kelsier eventually managed to use some vines to strap his flagging cookfire to the end of his staff, which became an improvised torch.

It was a strange experience, hiking through the darkened landscape, holding a staff with an entire *campfire* on the top. But the logs didn't fall apart, and the thing wasn't nearly as heavy as it should have been. Not as hot either, particularly if—when bringing it out—he didn't make it manifest fully.

Plant life grew all around him, real to his touch and eyes, though of strange varieties, some with brownish-red fronds and others with wide palms. Many trees—a jungle of exotic plants.

There were some bits of mist in here. If he knelt by the ground and looked for them, he could find little glowing spirits. Fish, sea plants. They manifested here above the ground, though in the ocean on the other side they were probably down within the depths. Kelsier stood up, holding the soul of some kind of massive deep-sea creature—like a fish, only as large as a building—in his hand, feeling its ponderous strength.

That was surreal, but so was his life these days. He dropped the fish's soul and continued onward, hiking through waist-high plants with a blazing staff lighting the way.

As he got farther from the shore, he felt a tugging at his soul. A manifestation of his ties to the world he'd left behind. He knew, without having to experiment, that this tug would ultimately grow strong enough that he wouldn't be able to continue outward.

He could use that. The tugging was a tool that let him judge if he was getting farther from his world, or if he'd gotten turned around in the darkness. Navigation was otherwise next to impossible, now that he didn't have the canals and roadways to guide him.

By judging the pull on his soul, he kept himself pointed directly outward, away from his homeland. He wasn't completely certain that was where he'd find his goal, but it seemed like his best bet.

He hiked through the jungle for days, but then it started to dwindle. Eventually he reached a place where plants grew only in occasional patches. They were replaced with strange formations of rock, like glassy sculptures. The jagged things were often some ten feet or more tall. He didn't know what to make of those. He had stopped passing the souls of fish, and nothing seemed to be alive out here in either Realm.

The pull tugging him backward was growing laborious to fight. He was beginning to worry he'd have to turn around when, at long last, he spotted something new.

A light on the horizon.

2

S NEAKING was a great deal easier when you didn't technically have a body.

Kelsier moved in silence, having dismissed his cloak and staff. He'd left his pack behind, and though there were a few plants out here, he could pass *through* them, not even rustling their leaves.

The lights ahead pulsed from a fortress crafted of white stone. It wasn't a city, but close enough for him. That light had an odd quality; it didn't burn or flicker like a flame. Some kind of limelight? He drew near and pulled up beside one of the odd rock formations that were common out here. It had hooked spikes drooping from it almost like branches.

The very walls of this fortress glowed faintly. Was that mist? It didn't seem to have the same hue to it; it was too blue. Keeping to the shadows of rock formations, Kelsier rounded the building toward a brighter light source at the back.

This turned out to be an enormous glowing cord as thick as a large tree trunk. It pulsed with a slow, rhythmic power, and the light it gave off was the same shade as the walls—only far more brilliant. It seemed to be some kind of energy conduit, and ran off into the far distance, visible in the darkness for miles.

The cord passed into the fortress through a large gate in the back. As Kelsier crept closer, he found that little lines of energy were running across the stone of the wall. They branched smaller and smaller, like a glowing web of veins.

The fortress was tall, imposing, like a keep—but without the ornamentation. It didn't have a separate fortification around it, but its walls were steep and sheer. Guards moved atop the roof, and as one passed, Kelsier pushed himself down into the ground. He was able to sink into it completely, becoming nearly invisible, though that required grabbing hold of the ground and pulling himself downward until only the top of his head was visible.

The guards didn't notice him. He climbed back out of the ground and inched up to the base of the fortress wall. He pressed his hand against the glowing stone and was given the impression of a rocky wall far from here, in another place. An unfamiliar land with striking *green* plants. He gasped, pulling his hand away.

These weren't stones, but the spirits of stones—like his spirit of a fire. They had been brought here and constructed into a building. Suddenly he didn't feel quite so clever at having found himself a staff and a sack.

He touched the stone again, looking at that green landscape. That was what Mare had talked about, a land with an open blue sky. *Another planet,* he decided. *One that didn't suffer our fate.*

For the moment he ignored the image of that place, pushing his fingers through the spirit of the stone. Strangely, the stone resisted. Kelsier gritted his teeth and pushed harder. He managed to get his fingers to sink in about two inches, but couldn't make them go any farther.

It's that light, he thought. It pushed back on him. *Looks a little like the light of souls.*

Well, he couldn't slip through the wall. What now? He retreated into the shadows to consider. Should he try to sneak in one of the gates? He rounded the building, contemplating this for a short time, before suddenly feeling foolish. He hurried forward to the wall again and pressed his hand against the stones, sinking his fingers in a few inches. Then he reached up and did the same with the other hand.

Then he proceeded to scale the wall.

Though he missed Steelpushing, this method proved quite effective. He could grip the wall basically anywhere he wanted, and his form didn't have much weight. Climbing was easy, as long as he maintained his concentration. Those images of a land with green plants were very distracting. Not a speck of ash in sight.

A piece of him had always considered Mare's flower a fanciful story. And while the place looked strange, it also attracted him with its alien beauty. There was something about it that was incredibly inviting. Unfortunately, the wall kept trying to spit his fingers back out, and maintaining his grip took a great deal of attention. He continued moving; he could revel in that luxurious scene of green grass and pleasant hills another time.

One of the upper levels had a window big enough to get through, which was good. The guards on the keep's top would have been difficult to dodge. Kelsier slipped in the window, entering a long stone corridor lit by the spiderwebs of power coursing across the walls, floor, and ceiling.

The energy must keep the stones from evaporating, Kelsier thought. All the souls he'd brought with him had begun to deteriorate, but these stones were solid and unbroken. Those tiny lines of power were somehow sustaining the spirits of the stone, and perhaps as a side effect keeping people like Kelsier from passing through the walls.

He crept down the corridor. He wasn't sure what he was searching for, but he wouldn't have learned anything more by sitting outside and waiting.

The power coursing through this place kept giving him visions of another world—and, he realized with discomfort, the energy seemed to be permeating him. Mixing with his soul's own energy, which had already been touched by the power at the Well. In a few brief moments, he had started to think that place with the green plants looked *normal.*

He heard voices echoing in the hallway, speaking a strange language with a nasal tone. Prepared for this, Kelsier scrambled out a window and clung there, just outside.

A pair of guards hurried through the hallway beside him, and after they passed he peeked in to see that they were wearing long white-blue tabards, pikes at their shoulders. They had fair skin and looked like they could have been from one of the dominances—except for their strange language. They spoke energetically, and as the words washed across him Kelsier thought . . . He thought he could make some of it out.

Yes. They speak the language of open fields, of green plants. Of where these stones came from, and the source of this power . . .

". . . is pretty sure he saw something, sir," one guard was saying.

The words struck Kelsier strangely. On one hand he felt they *should* be indecipherable. On the other hand he instantly knew what they meant.

"How would a Threnodite have made it all the way here?" the other guard snapped. "It defies reason, I tell you."

They passed through the doors at the other end of the hall. Kelsier climbed back into the corridor, curious. Had a guard seen him outside then? This didn't seem like a general alarm, so if he had been spotted, the glimpse had been brief.

He debated fleeing, but decided to follow the guards instead. Though most new thieves tried to avoid guards during an infiltration, Kelsier's experience showed that you generally wanted to tail them—for they'd always stick close to the things that were most important.

He wasn't certain if they could harm him in any way, though he figured it would be best not to find out, so he stayed a good distance back from the guards. After curving through a few stone corridors, they reached a door and went in. Kelsier crept up, cracked it, and was rewarded by the sight of a larger chamber where a small group of guards were setting up a strange device. A large yellow gemstone the size of Kelsier's fist shone in the center, glowing even more brightly than the walls. That gem was surrounded by a lattice of golden metal holding it in place. All told, it was the size of a desk clock.

Kelsier leaned forward, hidden just outside the door. That gemstone . . . that had to be worth a *fortune.*

A different door into the room—one opposite him—slammed open, causing several guards to jump, then salute. The creature that entered seemed . . . well, mostly human. Wizened, dried up, the woman had puckered lips, a bald scalp, and strange silvery-dark skin. She glowed faintly with the same quiet blue-white light as the walls.

"What is this?" the creature snapped in the language of the green plants.

The guard captain saluted. "Probably just a false alarm, ancient one. Maod says he saw something outside."

"Looked like a figure, ancient one," another guard piped up. "Saw it myself. It tested at the wall, sinking its fingers into the stone, but was rebuffed. Then it retreated, and I lost sight of it in the darkness."

So he *had* been seen. Damn. At least they didn't seem to know he'd crept into the building.

"Well, well," the ancient creature said. "My foresight does not seem so foolish now, does it, Captain? The powers of Threnody wish to join the main stage. Engage the device."

Kelsier had an immediate sinking feeling. Whatever that device did, he suspected it would not go well for him. He turned to bolt down the corridor, making for one of the windows. Behind him, the powerful golden light of the gemstone faded.

Kelsier felt nothing.

"Well," the captain said from behind, voice echoing. "Nobody from Threnody within a day's march of here. Looks like a false alarm after all."

Kelsier hesitated in the empty corridor. Then, cautious, he crept back to peek into the room. The guards and the wizened creature all stood around the device, seeming displeased.

"I do not doubt your foresight, ancient one," the guard captain continued. "But I *do* trust my forces on the Threnodite border. There are no shadows here."

"Perhaps," the creature said, resting her fingers on the gemstone. "Perhaps there was someone, but the guard was wrong about it being a Cognitive Shadow. Have the guards be on alert, and leave the device on just in case. This timing strikes me as too opportune to be coincidental. I must speak with the rest of the Ire."

As she said the word, this time Kelsier got a sense of its meaning in the language of the green plants. It meant "age," and he had a sudden impression of a strange symbol made from four dots and some lines that curved, like ripples in a river.

Kelsier shook his head, dispelling the vision. The creature was walking in Kelsier's direction. He scrambled away, barely reaching a window and climbing out as the creature pushed open the door and strode through the hallway.

New plan, Kelsier decided, hanging outside on the wall, feeling completely exposed. *Follow the weird lady giving orders.*

He let her get a distance ahead of him, then entered the corridor and followed silently. She rounded the outer corridor of the fortress before eventually reaching the end of it, where it stopped at a guarded door. She passed inside, and Kelsier thought for a moment, then climbed out another window.

He had to be careful; if the guards above weren't already keeping close watch on the walls, they soon would be. Unfortunately, he doubted he could get through that doorway without bringing every guard in the place down on him. Instead he climbed along the outside of the fortress until he reached the next window past the guarded door. This one was smaller than the others he'd gone through, more like an arrow slit than a true window. Fortunately, it looked into the room the strange woman had entered.

Inside, an entire group of the creatures sat in discussion. Kelsier pressed up against the slit of a window, peeking in, clinging precariously to the wall some fifty feet in the air. The beings all had that same silvery skin, though two were a shade darker than the rest. It was difficult to distinguish individuals among them; they were all so old, the men completely bald, the women nearly so. Each wore the same distinctive robe—white, with a hood that could be pulled up and silver embroidery around the cuffs.

Curiously, the light from the walls was dimmer in the room. The effect was particularly noticeable near where one of the creatures was sitting or standing. It was like . . . they themselves were drawing in the light.

He was at least able to pick out the woman from before, with her wizened lips and long fingers. Her robe had a thicker band of silver. "We must move up our timetable," she was saying to the others. "I do not believe this sighting was a coincidence."

"Bah," said a seated man who held a cup of glowing liquid. "You

always jump at stories, Alonoe. Not every coincidence is a sign of someone drawing upon Fortune."

"And do you disagree that it is best to be careful?" Alonoe demanded.
"We have come too far, worked too hard, to let the prize slip away now."

"Preservation's Vessel *has* nearly expired," another woman said. "Our
window to strike is approaching."

"An entire Shard," Alonoe said. "Ours."

"And if that was an agent of Ruin the guards spotted?" asked the seated
man. "If our plans have been discovered? The Vessel of Ruin could have
his eyes upon us at this very moment."

Alonoe seemed disturbed by this, and she glanced upward as if to
search the sky for the watching eyes of the Shard. She recovered, speaking firmly. "I will take the chance."

"We will draw his anger either way," another of the beings noted. "If
one of us Ascends to Preservation, we will be safe. Only then."

Kelsier chewed on this as the creatures fell silent. *So someone else can
take up the Shard. Fuzz is almost dead, but if someone were to seize his power
as he died . . .*

But hadn't Preservation told Kelsier that such a thing was impossible?
You wouldn't be able to hold my power anyway, Preservation had said.
You're not Connected enough to me.

He'd seen that now firsthand, in the space between moments. Were
these creatures somehow Connected enough to Preservation to take the
power? Kelsier doubted it. So what was their plan?

"We move forward," the seated man said, looking to the others. One
at a time, they nodded. "Devotion protect us. We move forward."

"You won't need Devotion, Elrao," Alonoe said. "You will have *me*."

Over my dead body, Kelsier thought. Or . . . well, something like that.

"The timetable is accelerated then," said Elrao, the man with the cup.
He drank the glowing liquid, then stood. "To the vault?"

The others nodded. Together they left the room.

Kelsier waited until they were gone, then tried pushing himself through
the window. It was too small for a person, but he wasn't completely a
person any longer. He could meld a few inches with the stone, and with
effort he was able to contort his shape and *squeeze* through the wide slit.

He finally tumbled into the room, shoulders popping into their previous shape. The experience left him with a splitting headache. He sat up, back to the wall, and waited for the pain to fade before standing to give this room a thorough ransacking.

He didn't come up with much. A few bottles of wine, a handful of gemstones left casually in one of the drawers. Both were real, not souls pulled through to this Realm.

The room had a door leading into the inner parts of the fortress, and so—after peeking through—he slipped in. This next room looked more promising. It was a bedroom. He rifled through the drawers, discovering several robes like the ones the wizened people had been wearing. And then, in the small table by the hearth, the jackpot. A book of sketches filled with strange symbols like the one he had visualized. Symbols that he felt, vaguely, he could understand.

Yes . . . These were writing, though most of the pages were filled with terms he couldn't begin to comprehend, even once he began to be able to read the symbols themselves. Terms like "Adonalsium," "Connection," "Realmatic Theory."

The end pages, however, described the culmination of the notes and sketches. A kind of arcane device in the shape of a sphere. You could break it and absorb the power within, which would briefly Connect you to Preservation—like the lines he'd seen in the space between moments.

That was their plan. Travel to the location of Preservation's death, prime themselves with this device, and absorb his power—Ascending to take his place.

Bold. Exactly the kind of plan Kelsier admired. And now, he finally knew what he was going to steal from them.

3

THIEVERY was the most authentic form of flattery.

What could be more satisfying than knowing the things you possessed were intriguing, captivating, or valuable enough to provoke another man to risk everything to obtain them? This was Kelsier's purpose in life, to remind people of the value of the things they loved. By taking them away.

These days, he didn't care for the *little* thieveries. Yes, he'd pocketed the gemstones he'd found up above, but that was more out of pragmatism than anything else. Ever since the Pits of Hathsin, he hadn't been interested in stealing common possessions.

No, these days he stole something far greater. Kelsier stole dreams.

He crouched outside the fortress, hidden between two spires of twisting black rock. He now understood the purpose of creating such a powerful building, here at the reaches of Preservation and Ruin's dominion. That fortress protected a vault, and inside that vault lay an incredible opportunity. The seed that would make a person, under the right circumstances, into a god.

Getting to it would be nearly impossible. They'd have guards, locks, traps, and arcane devices he couldn't plan for or expect. Sneaking in and robbing that vault would test his skills to their utmost, and even then he was likely to fail.

He decided not to try.

That was the thing about big, defended vaults. You couldn't realistically leave most possessions in them forever. Eventually you had to use what you guarded—and that provided men such as Kelsier with an opportunity. And so he waited, prepared, and planned.

It took a week or so—counting days by judging the schedules of the guards—but at long last an expedition sallied forth from the keep. The grand procession of twenty people rode on horseback, holding aloft lanterns.

Horses, Kelsier thought, slipping through the darkness to keep pace with the procession. *Hadn't expected that.*

Well, they weren't moving terribly quickly even with the mounts. He was able to keep up with them easily, particularly since he didn't tire as he had when alive.

He counted five of the wizened ancients and a force of fifteen soldiers. Curiously, each of the ancients was dressed almost exactly the same, in their similar robes with hoods up and leather satchels over their shoulders, the same style of saddlebags on each horse.

Decoys, Kelsier decided. *If someone attacks, they can split up. Their enemy might not know which of them to follow.*

Kelsier could use that, particularly since he was relatively certain who carried the Connection device. Alonoe, the imperious woman who seemed to be in charge, wasn't the type to let power slip through her spindly fingertips. She intended to become Preservation; letting one of her colleagues carry the device would be too risky. What if they got ideas? What if they used it themselves?

No, she'd have the weapon on her somewhere. The only question was how to get it from her.

Kelsier gave it some time. Days of travel through the darkened landscape, keeping pace with the caravan while he planned.

There were three basic types of thievery. The first involved a knife to the throat and a whispered threat. The second involved pilfering in the night. And the third . . . well, that was Kelsier's favorite. It involved a tongue coated with zinc. Instead of a knife it used confusion, and instead of prowling it worked in the open.

The best kind of thievery left your target uncertain whether anything had happened at all. Getting away with the prize was all well and good, but it didn't mean much if the city guard came pounding on your door the next day. He'd rather escape with half as many boxings, but the confidence that his trickery wouldn't be discovered for weeks to come.

And the *real* trophy was to pull off a heist so clever, the target didn't ever discover you'd taken something from them.

Each "night" the caravan made camp in an anxious little cluster of bedrolls around a campfire much like the one in Kelsier's pack. The ancients got out jars of light, drinking and restoring the luminance to their skin. They didn't chat much; these people seemed less like friends and more like a group of noblemen who considered one another allies by necessity.

Soon after their meal each night, the ancients retired to their bedrolls. They set guards, but didn't sleep in tents. Why would you need a tent out here? There was no rain to keep off, and practically no wind to block. Just darkness, rustling plants, and a dead man.

Unfortunately, Kelsier couldn't figure out a way to get to the weapon. Alonoe slept with her satchel in her hands, watched over by two guards. Each morning she checked to make sure the weapon was still there. Kelsier managed to get a glimpse of it one morning, and saw the glowing light inside, making him reasonably certain her satchel wasn't a decoy.

Well, that would come. His first step was to sow a little misdirection. He waited for an appropriate night, then pushed himself down into the ground, sinking his essence beneath the surface. Then he pulled himself through the rock. It was like swimming through very thick liquid dirt.

He came up near where Alonoe had just settled down to sleep, and stuck only his lips out of the ground. *Dox would have had a fit of laughter seeing this*, Kelsier thought. Well, Kelsier was far too arrogant to worry about his pride.

"So," he whispered to Alonoe in her own language, "you presume to hold Preservation's power. You think you'll fare better than he did at resisting me?"

He then pulled himself down under the ground. It was black as night under there, but he could hear the thumping of feet and the cries of shock from what he'd said. He swam out a distance, then lifted an ear from the ground.

"It was Ruin!" Alonoe was saying. "I swear, it must have been his Vessel. Speaking to me."

"So he does know," said another of the ancient ones. Kelsier thought it was Elrao, the man who had challenged her back in the fortress.

"Your wards were supposed to prevent this!" Alonoe said. "You told me they'd stop him from sensing the device!"

"There are ways for him to know of us without having sensed the orb, Alonoe," another female said. "My art is exacting."

"How he found us is not the problem," Elrao said. "The question is why he hasn't destroyed us."

"Preservation's Vessel still lives," the other woman said, musing. "That might be preventing Ruin's direct interference."

"I don't like it," Elrao said. "I think we should turn back."

"We have committed," Alonoe replied. "We press forward. No quarreling."

The stir in the camp eventually quieted down and the ancient ones turned back to their bedrolls, though more of the guards stayed awake than usual. Kelsier smiled, then pushed himself over beside Alonoe's head again.

"How would you like to die, Alonoe?" he whispered to her, then ducked beneath the earth.

This time they didn't go back to sleep. The next day it was a bleary-eyed party that set off across the dark landscape. That night, Kelsier prodded them again. And again. He made the next week a hell for the group, whispering to different members, promising them terrible things. He was quite proud of the various ways he came up with to distract, frighten, and unnerve them. He didn't get a chance to grab Alonoe's satchel—if anything, they were more careful with it than they had been. He did manage to snatch one of the other ones while they were breaking down camp one morning. It was empty save for a fake glass orb.

Kelsier continued his campaign of discord, and by the time the group reached the jungle of strange trees their patience had unraveled. They snapped at one another and spent less time each morning or night resting. Half the party was convinced they should turn back, though Alonoe insisted that the fact that "Ruin" only *spoke* to them was proof he couldn't stop them. She pressed the increasingly divided group forward, into the trees.

Which was exactly where Kelsier wanted them. Staying ahead of the horses would be easy in this snarl of a jungle, where he could pass through foliage as if it weren't there. He slipped on ahead and set up a little surprise for the group, then came back to find them bickering again. Perfect.

He pushed himself into the center of one of the trees, keeping only his hand outside, tucked at the back, holding the knife that Nazh had given him. As the line of horses passed, he reached out and swiped one of the animals on the flank.

The creature let out a scream of pain, and chaos broke out in the line. The people near the front—their nerves taut from a week spent being tormented by Kelsier's whispers—gave their horses their heads. Soldiers shouted, warning they were under attack. Ancient ones urged their beasts in different directions, some collapsing as the animals tripped in the underbrush.

Kelsier darted through the jungle, catching up to those in the front. Alonoe had kept her horse mostly under control, but it was even darker in these trees than outside, and the lanterns jostled wildly as the animals moved. Kelsier dashed past Alonoe to a point ahead where he'd strung his cloak between two trees and lashed it in place with vines.

He climbed a tree and reached into the cloak as the front of the line— haggard and reduced in numbers—arrived. He'd lashed his fire inside the cloak, and he brought it alive as they neared. The result was a burning, cloaked figure, appearing suddenly in the air above the already frazzled group.

They screamed, calling that Ruin had found them, and split apart, running their horses in a chaotic jumble—some in one direction, some in another.

Kelsier dropped to the ground and slipped through the darkness, staying parallel to Alonoe and the guard who managed to remain with her. The woman soon caught her horse in a snarl of undergrowth. Perfect. Kelsier ducked away and recovered his stash of supplies, then threw on one of the robes he'd found in the fortress. He scrambled through the brush, the robe catching on things, until he was just close enough for Alonoe to see.

Then he stepped out where she could see him and called to her, waving his hand. Thinking she'd found a larger group of her people, she and her lone guard trotted their horses toward him. That, however, only served to draw them away from the rest of the group. Kelsier led her farther from the others, then ducked away into the darkness, losing her and leaving her and her guard isolated.

From there he scrambled through the dark underbrush toward the rest of the group, his phantom heart pounding.

This. He'd *missed* this.

The con. The excitement of playing people like flutes, twisting them about themselves, tying their minds in knots. He hurried through the forest, listening to the shouts of fright, the calls of soldiers to one another, the snorts and cries of the horses. The patch of dense vegetation had become demonic disharmony.

Nearby, one of the wizened men was gathering soldiers and his colleagues, calling for them to keep their heads, and started leading them back in the direction they'd come, perhaps to regroup with those who had been lost when the line first scattered.

Kelsier—still wearing the robe and holding his stolen satchel over his shoulder—lay down on the ground in their path, and waited until someone spotted him.

"There!" a guard said. "It's—"

Kelsier sank himself down into the ground, leaving the robe and satchel behind. The guard screamed at the sight of one of the ancients apparently *melting* to nothing.

Kelsier crept up out of the ground a short distance away as the group gathered around his robe and satchel. "She *disintegrated,* ancient one!" the guard said. "I watched it with my own eyes."

"That's one of Alonoe's robes," a woman whispered, hand pulled to her breast in shock.

Another of the ancients looked in the satchel. "Empty," he said. "Merciful Domi . . . What were we thinking?"

"Back," Elrao said. "Back! Everyone get your horses! We're leaving. Curse Alonoe and this idea of hers!"

They were gone in moments. Kelsier strolled through the forest, stepping up beside the discarded robe—which they'd left—listening to the main bulk of the expedition crash through the jungle in their haste to escape him.

He shook his head, then took a short walk through the underbrush to where Alonoe and her lone guard were now trying to follow the sounds of the main body. They were doing a pretty good job of it, all things considered.

When the ancient one wasn't looking, Kelsier grabbed the guard around the neck and hauled him into the darkness. The man thrashed, but Kelsier got him in a quick lock and hold, knocking the man out without too much trouble. He pulled the body back quietly, then returned to find the solitary ancient one standing with lantern in hand beside her horse, turning frantically.

The jungle had become eerily still. "Hello?" she called. "Elrao? Riina?"

Kelsier waited in shadow as the calls became more and more frantic. Eventually the woman's voice gave out. She slumped down in the forest, exhausted.

"Leave it," Kelsier whispered.

She looked up, red-eyed, frightened. Ancient or not, she could obviously still feel fear. Her eyes darted to one side, then the other, but he was too well hidden for her to spot him.

"*Leave it*," Kelsier repeated.

He didn't need to ask again. She nodded, trembling, then took off her satchel and opened it, dumping out a large glass orb. The light from it was brilliant, and Kelsier had to step back lest it reveal him. Yes, there was power in that orb, great power. It was filled with glowing liquid that was far purer, and far brighter, than what the ancients had been drinking.

Exhaustion evident in her every move, the woman went to climb back onto her horse.

"Walk," Kelsier commanded.

She looked toward the darkness, searching, but didn't see him. "I . . ." she said, then licked her wizened lips. "I could serve you, Vessel. I—"

"*Go,*" Kelsier ordered.

Wincing, she unhooked the saddlebags and—lethargically—threw them over her shoulder. He didn't stop her. She probably needed those jars of glowing liquid to survive, and he didn't want her dead. He just wanted her to be slower than her companions. Once she found them, they might compare stories and realize they'd been had.

Or perhaps not. Alonoe struck out into the jungle. Hopefully they'd all conclude that Ruin had indeed bested them. Kelsier waited until she was gone, then strolled over and picked up the large glass orb. It showed no discernible way of being opened, other than shattering it.

He held the glowing orb before him and shook it, gazing at the incredible, mesmerizing liquid light within.

That was the most fun he'd had in ages.

PART SIX
HERO

1

Kelsier ran across a broken world. The trouble had been apparent the moment he left the ocean, stepping back onto the misty ground that made up the Final Empire. Here he'd found the wreckage of a coastal city. Smashed buildings, shattered streets. The entire city seemed to have *slid* into the ocean, a fact he wasn't able to fully piece together until he stood above the town and noticed the shadowy remains of buildings sticking from the ocean island farther up the coast.

From there it only grew worse. Empty towns. Vast piles of ash, which manifested on this side as rolling hills that he ran across for a time before realizing what they were.

Several days into his run home, he passed a small village where a few glowing souls huddled together in a building. As he watched, horrified, the roof collapsed, dumping ash on them. Three glows winked out immediately, and the souls of three ashen skaa appeared in the Cognitive Realm, their strings to the physical world cut.

Preservation didn't appear to greet them.

Kelsier grabbed one of them, an aged woman who—as he took her hand—started and looked at him with wide eyes. "Lord Ruler!"

"No," Kelsier said. "But close. What is happening?"

She started to stretch away. Her companions had already vanished.

"It's ending . . ." she whispered. "All ending . . ."

And she was gone. Kelsier was left holding empty air, disturbed.

He started running again. He'd felt guilty leaving the horse behind in the forest, but surely the animal was better off there than it would have been here.

Was he too late? Was Preservation already dead?

He ran himself hard, the heft of the glass orb weighing down his pack. Perhaps it was the urgency, but his course became even more single-minded than it had been during his trip out. He didn't want to see the failing world, the death all around him. Compared to that the exhaustion of the run was preferable, and so he sought it, running himself ragged.

He traveled for days upon days. Weeks upon weeks. Never stopping, never looking. Until . . .

Kelsier.

He jolted to a halt on a field of windswept ash. He had the distinct impression of mist in the physical world. Glowing mist. *Power.* He could not see that here, but he could sense it all around him.

"Fuzz?" he said, raising a hand to his forehead. Had he imagined that voice?

Not that way, Kelsier, the voice said, sounding distant. But yes, it *was* Preservation. *We aren't . . . aren't . . . there. . . .*

The crushing weight of fatigue hit Kelsier. Where was he? He spun about, looking for some kind of landmark, but those were difficult to find out here. The ash had buried the canals; a few weeks back he remembered swimming down through the ground to find them. Lately . . . he'd just been running. . . .

"Where?" Kelsier demanded. "Fuzz?"

So . . . tired . . .

"I know," Kelsier whispered. "I know, Fuzz."

Fadrex. Come to Fadrex. You are close. . . .

Fadrex City? Kelsier had been there before, in his youth. It was just south of . . .

There. Just barely visible in the Cognitive Realm, he made out the shadowy tip of Mount Morag in the distance. That direction was north.

He turned his back toward the ashmount and ran for everything he was worth. It seemed a brief eyeblink before he reached the city and was given a welcome, warming sight. Souls.

The city was alive. Guards in the towers and on the tall rock formations surrounding the city. People in the streets, sleeping in their beds, clogging the buildings with beautiful, shining light. Kelsier walked right through the city gates, entering a wonderful, radiant city where people still fought on.

In the warmth of that glow, he knew he was not too late.

Unfortunately, his was not the only attention focused here. He had resisted looking upward during his run, but he could not help but do so now, confronting the churning, boiling mass. Shapes like black snakes slithered across one another, stretching to the horizon in all directions. It was watching. It was here.

So where was Preservation? Kelsier walked through the city, basking in the presence of other souls, recovering from his extended run. He stopped at one street corner, then spotted something. A tiny line of light, like a very long piece of hair, near his feet. He knelt, picking at it, and found that it stretched all the way along the street—impossibly thin, glowing faintly, yet too strong for him to break.

"Fuzz?" Kelsier said, following the strand, finding where it connected to another—it seemed a lattice that spread through the whole city.

Yes. I . . . I'm trying. . . .

"Nice work."

I can't talk to them . . . Fuzz said. *I'm dying, Kelsier. . . .*

"Hang on," Kelsier said. "I've found something; it's here in my pack. I took it from those creatures you mentioned. The Eyree."

I do not sense anything, Fuzz said.

Kelsier hesitated. He didn't want to reveal the object to Ruin. Instead he picked up the thread, which had enough slack for him to slip it into the pack and press it against the orb.

"How about that?"

Ahh . . . Yes . . .

"Can this help you somehow?"

No, unfortunately.

Kelsier felt his heart sink further.

The power . . . the power is hers. . . . But Ruin has her, Kelsier. I can't . . . I can't give it. . . .

"Hers?" Kelsier asked. "Vin? Is she here?"

The thread vibrated in Kelsier's fingers like the string of an instrument. Waves came along it from one direction.

Kelsier followed them, noticing again how Preservation had covered this city with his essence. Perhaps he figured that if he was going to be strung out anyway, he should lie down like a protective blanket.

Preservation led him to a small city square clogged with glowing souls and bits of metal on the walls. They glowed so brightly, particularly in contrast to the darkness of his months out alone. Was one of these souls Vin?

No, they were beggars. He moved among them, feeling at their souls with his fingertips, catching glimpses of them in the other Realm. Huddled in the ash, coughing and shivering. The fallen men and women of the Final Empire, the people even the common skaa tended to dismiss. For all his grand plans, he hadn't made the lives of these people better, had he?

He stopped in place.

That last beggar, sitting against an old brick wall . . . there was something about him. Kelsier backed up, touching the beggar's soul again, seeing a vision of a man with hands and face wrapped in bandages, white hair sticking out from beneath. Stark white hair, a fact not quite hidden by the ash that had been rubbed into it.

Kelsier felt a sudden shock, a painful *spike* that ran up his fingers into his soul. He jumped back as the beggar glanced his direction.

"You!" Kelsier said. "Drifter!"

The beggar shifted in place, but then glanced another direction, searching the square.

"What are you doing here?" Kelsier demanded.

The glowing figure gave no response.

Kelsier whipped his hand back and forth, trying to shake out the pain. His fingers had actually gone *numb*. What had that been? And how had the white-haired Drifter managed to affect him in *this* Realm?

A small glowing figure landed on a rooftop nearby.

"Oh, *hell*," Kelsier said, looking from Vin to the Drifter. He responded immediately, throwing himself toward the wall of the building and climbing desperately up it to Vin's side. "Vin. Vin, stay *away* from that man."

Of course yelling was pointless. She couldn't hear him.

Still, Kelsier seized her by the shoulders, seeing her in the Physical Realm. When had she grown so confident, so knowing? Those shoulders of hers had once cringed, but now they gave her the posture of a woman fully in control. Those eyes that had once widened in wonder were now narrowed with keen perception. Her hair was longer, but her slight build somehow seemed far more *powerful* than it had when he'd first met her.

"Vin," Kelsier said. "Vin! Listen, please. That man is trouble. Don't approach him. Don't—"

Vin cocked her head, then leaped off the roof, *away* from the Drifter.

"Hell," Kelsier said. "Did she actually hear me?"

Or was it a coincidence? Kelsier leaped after Vin, tossing himself carelessly from the building. He didn't have Allomancy, but he was light, and could fall without getting hurt. He landed softly and sprinted across the springy ground, tailing Vin as best he could, running *through* buildings, ignoring walls, trying to stay close. She still got ahead of him.

Kelsier . . . Preservation's voice whispered at him.

Something thrummed through him, a familiar jolt of power, a warmth within. It reminded him of burning metals. Preservation's own essence, empowering him.

He ran faster, jumped farther. It wasn't true Allomancy, but instead was something more raw and primal. It surged through Kelsier, warming his soul, letting him reach Vin—who had stopped in the street before a large building. Soon after he reached her, she took off again down the street, but this time Kelsier managed to keep pace, barely.

And she knew he was there. He could sense it in the way she leaped, trying to shake a tail, or at least catch sight of one. She was good, but this was a game he'd been playing for decades before she was born.

She *could* sense him. Why? How?

She sped up and he followed, with difficulty. His motions were clumsy;

he had Preservation pushing him along, but he didn't have the finesse of true Allomancy. He couldn't Push or Pull; he merely jumped, grabbing hold of the shadowed walls of buildings, then throwing himself off in prowling leaps.

Still, he grinned widely. He hadn't realized how much he had missed training with Vin in the mists, matching himself against another Mistborn, watching his protégé inch toward excellence. She was good now. Fantastic even. Remarkable at judging the force of each Push, at balancing her own weight against her anchors.

This was energy; this was excitement. Almost he forgot the troubles he faced. Almost this was enough. If he could dance the mists with Vin at night, then finding a way to recapture his life in the Physical Realm might not matter so much.

They hit an intersection and turned toward the city's perimeter. Vin bounded ahead on lines of steel; Kelsier hit the ground, thrumming with Preservation's power, and prepared to jump.

Something descended around him. A blackness of shredding spikes, of spider-leg scratches in the air, of jet-black mist.

"Well," Ruin said from all sides. "Well, well. Kelsier? How did I not see you earlier?"

The power suffocated him, pushing him toward the ground. Ahead, a small figure bounded after Vin, created of black mist and pulsing with a similar rhythm to what Kelsier had displayed. A decoy of some sort.

Like he did before, Kelsier thought. *Imitating Fuzz to trick Vin.* He struggled, frustrated, against his bonds.

Preservation, in turn, whimpered like a child in Kelsier's mind, then withdrew from him. The warming power faded from within Kelsier. Remarkably, as the power dampened, so did Ruin's ability to hold Kelsier down. Ruin's strength became less oppressive, and Kelsier was able to struggle to his feet and push through the veil of sharp mists, stumbling onto the street.

"Where *have* you been?" Ruin asked. The power behind Kelsier condensed, forming into the shape of the man he'd seen before, with the red hair. The motions beneath the man's skin were more subdued this time.

"Here and there," Kelsier said, glancing after Vin. He'd never catch up to her now. "I thought I'd see the sights. Find out what death has to offer."

"Ah, very coy. Did you visit the Ire? And got turned away from them, I assume. Yes, I can guess at that. What I want to know is why you returned. I thought for certain you would flee. Your part in this is done; you did what I needed you to."

Kelsier set down his pack, hopefully keeping hidden the orb of light inside. He walked forward, strolling around Ruin's manifestation. "My part?"

"The Eleventh Metal," Ruin said, amused. "You think that was a co-incidence? A story nobody else had heard of, a secret way to kill an im-mortal emperor? It fell right in your lap."

Kelsier took it in stride. He'd already figured that Gemmel had been touched by Ruin, that Kelsier himself had been a pawn of the creature. *But why could Vin hear me?* What was he missing? He looked after Vin again.

"Ah," Ruin said. "The child. You still think she's going to defeat me, do you? Even after she set me free?"

Kelsier spun toward Ruin. Damn. How much did the creature know? Ruin smiled and stepped up to Kelsier.

"Leave Vin alone," Kelsier hissed.

"Leave her alone? She's mine, Kelsier. Just as you are. I've known that child since the day of her birth, and have been preparing her for even longer."

Kelsier gritted his teeth.

"So cute," Ruin said. "You actually thought this was all your idea, didn't you? The fall of the Final Empire, the end of the Lord Ruler . . . recruiting Vin in the first place?"

"Ideas are never original," Kelsier said. "Only one thing is."

"And what is that?"

"Style," Kelsier said.

Then he punched Ruin across the face.

Or he tried to. Ruin evaporated as his fist drew close, and a copy of him formed beside Kelsier a moment later. "Ah, Kelsier," he said. "Was that wise?"

"No," Kelsier said. "It was merely thematic. Leave her alone, Ruin."

Ruin smiled at him in a pitying way, then a thousand spindly, needle-like black spikes shot from the creature's body, ripping through the robes that made up its clothing. They pierced Kelsier like spears, fraying his soul, bringing a blinding wave of pain.

He screamed, falling to his knees. It was like the stretching when he'd first entered this place, only *forced, intrusive.*

He dropped to the ground, spasming, his soul leaking curls of mist. The spikes were gone, as was Ruin. But of course the creature was never *truly* gone. It watched from that undulating sky, covering everything.

Nothing can be destroyed, Kelsier, Ruin's voice whispered, intruding directly into his mind. *That's something humans can't understand. All things merely change, break down, become something new . . . something perfect. Preservation and I, we're two sides to the same coin, really. For when I am done, he shall finally have his desired stillness, unchangingness. And there won't be anything, body or soul, to disturb it.*

Kelsier breathed in and out, using familiar motions from when he'd been alive to calm himself. Finally he groaned and rolled to his knees.

"You deserved that," Preservation noted, his voice distant.

"Sure did," Kelsier said, stumbling to his feet. "It was worth trying anyway."

2

Over the next few days, Kelsier tried to replicate his success in getting Vin to listen to him. Unfortunately, Ruin was watching for him now. Each time Kelsier got close, Ruin interfered, surrounding him, holding him back. Choking him with black smoke and driving him away.

Ruin seemed amused to keep Kelsier around the periphery of Vin's camp outside Fadrex, and didn't drive him away. But anytime Kelsier tried to speak directly with her, Ruin punished him. Like a parent slapping a child's hand for getting too close to the flame.

It was infuriating, more so because of the way Ruin's words dug at him. Everything Kelsier had accomplished had merely been part of this *thing's* master plan to be freed. And the creature *did* have some kind of hold on Vin. It could appear to her, as reinforced by how it led her away from the camp one day, in a sudden motion that confused Kelsier.

He tried to follow, running after the phantom that Ruin had made. It bounded like a Mistborn and Vin followed, obviously convinced that she'd discovered a spy. They left the camp behind entirely.

Kelsier slowed, feeling useless, standing on the misty ground outside the city and watching them vanish into the distance. She could sense that thing, and as long as it was here it overshadowed Kelsier. He'd never be able to speak with her.

Ruin's reason for leading Vin away soon manifested. Something launched an assault on Vin and Elend's army of koloss. Kelsier figured it out from the bustling of the camp, and was able to reach the scene faster than the people in the Physical Realm. It looked like siege equipment had been rolled out onto a ridge above where the koloss camped.

It rained down death upon the beasts. Kelsier couldn't do anything but watch as the sudden attack killed thousands of them. He couldn't feel any real regret when the koloss were destroyed, but it did seem a waste.

The koloss raged in frustration, unable to reach their enemy. Curiously, their souls started to appear in the Cognitive Realm.

And they were human.

Not koloss at all, but *people*, dressed in a variety of outfits. Many were skaa, but there were soldiers, merchants, and even nobility among them. Both male and female.

Kelsier gaped. He had never quite known what koloss were, but he had not expected this. Common people, made beasts somehow? He rushed among the dying souls as they faded.

"What happened to you," he demanded of one woman. "How did this happen to you?"

She regarded him with a bemused expression. "Where," she said, "where am I?"

In a moment she was gone. It seemed the transition was too much of a shock. The others showed similar confusion, holding out their hands as if surprised to find themselves human again—though not a few seemed relieved. Kelsier watched as thousands of these figures appeared, then faded away. It was a slaughter on the other side, stones crashing down all around. One passed right through Kelsier before rolling away, breaking bodies.

He could use this, but he would need something specific. Not a skaa peasant, or even a crafty lord. He needed someone who . . .

There.

He dashed through fading spirits and dodged between the glowing souls of creatures not yet dead, making for a particular spirit who had just appeared. Bald, with tattoos circling his eyes. An obligator. This man seemed less surprised by events, and more resigned. By the time Kelsier arrived, the lanky obligator was already starting to stretch away.

"How?" Kelsier demanded, counting on the obligator to understand more about the koloss. "How did this happen to you?"

"I don't know," the man said.

Kelsier felt his heart sink.

"The beasts," the man continued, "should have known better than to take an obligator! I was their keeper, and they did this to me? This world is ruined."

Should have known better? Kelsier clutched the obligator's shoulder as the man stretched toward nothingness. "How? Please, *how* is it done? Men become koloss?"

The obligator looked to him and, vanishing, said one word.

"Spikes."

Kelsier gaped again. Around him on the misty plain, souls blazed bright, flashed, and were dumped into this Realm—before finally fading to nothing. Like human bonfires being extinguished.

Spikes. Like Inquisitor spikes?

He walked to the slumped-over corpses of the dead and knelt, inspecting them. Yes, he could see it. Metal glowed on this side, and among those corpses were little spikes—like embers, small but glowing fiercely.

They were much harder to make out on the living koloss, because of the way the soul blazed, but it seemed to him that the spikes pierced into the soul. Was that the secret? He shouted at a pair of koloss, and they looked toward him, then glanced about, confused.

The spikes transform them, Kelsier thought, *like Inquisitors. Is that how they're controlled? Through piercings in the soul?*

What of madmen? Were their souls cracked open, allowing something similar? Troubled, he left the field and its dying, although the battle—or rather the slaughter—seemed to be ending.

Kelsier crossed the misty field outside Fadrex, then lingered out here alone, away from the souls of men until Vin returned, trailed by a shadow she didn't seem to know was there this time. She passed by, then disappeared into the camp.

Kelsier settled down near one of the little tendrils of Preservation, and touched it. "He has his fingers in everything, doesn't he, Fuzz?"

"Yes," Preservation said, his voice frail, tiny. "See."

Something appeared in Kelsier's mind, a sequence of images: Inquisitors listening with heads raised toward Ruin's voice. Vin in the creature's shadow. A man he didn't know sitting on a burning throne and watching Luthadel, a twisted smile on his lips.

Then, little Lestibournes. Spook wore a burned cloak that seemed too big for him, and Ruin crouched nearby, whispering with Kelsier's *own voice* into the poor lad's ear.

After him, Kelsier saw Marsh standing among falling ash, spiked eyes staring sightlessly across the landscape. He didn't seem to be moving; the ash was piling up on his shoulders and head.

Marsh . . . Seeing his brother like that made Kelsier sick. Kelsier's plan had required Marsh to join the obligators. He had deduced what must have happened next. Marsh's Allomancy had been noticed, as had the fervent way he lived his life.

Passion and care. Marsh had never been as capable as Kelsier. But he had always, *always* been a better man.

Preservation showed him dozens of others, mostly people in power leading their followers to doom, laughing and dancing as ash piled high and crops withered in the mists. Each one was a person either pierced by metal or influenced by people around them who were pierced by metal. He should have made the connection back at the Well of Ascension, when he'd seen in the pulses that Ruin could speak to Marsh and the other Inquisitors.

Metal. It was the key to everything.

"So much destruction," Kelsier whispered at the visions. "We can't survive this, can we? Even if we stop Ruin, we are doomed."

"No," Preservation said. "Not doomed. Remember . . . hope, Kelsier. You said, I . . . I . . . am . . ."

"I am hope," Kelsier whispered.

"I cannot save you. But we must trust."

"In what?"

"In the man I was. In the . . . the plan . . . The sign . . . and the Hero . . ."

"Vin. He has her, Fuzz."

"He doesn't know as much as he thinks," Preservation whispered. "That is his weakness. The . . . weakness . . . of all clever men . . ."

"Except me, of course."

Preservation had enough spark left to chuckle at that, which did Kelsier some good. He stood up, dusting off his clothing. Which was somewhat pointless, seeing as how there was no dust here—not to mention no actual clothing. "Come now, Fuzz, when have you known me to be wrong?"

"Well, there was—"

"Those don't count. I wasn't fully myself back then."

"And . . . when did you become . . . fully yourself?"

"Only just now," Kelsier said.

"You could . . . you could use that excuse . . . anytime. . . ."

"Now you're catching on, Fuzz." Kelsier put his hands on his hips. "We use the plan you set in motion when you were sane, eh? All right then. How can I help?"

"Help? I . . . I don't . . ."

"No, be decisive. Bold! A good crewleader is always sure of himself, even when he isn't. *Especially* when he isn't."

"That doesn't make . . . sense. . . ."

"I'm dead. I don't need to make sense anymore. Ideas? You're crewleader now."

". . . Me?"

"Sure. Your plan. You're in charge. I mean, you *are* a god. That should count for something, I suppose."

"Thank you for . . . finally . . . acknowledging that. . . ."

Kelsier deliberated, then set his pack on the ground. "You're sure this can't help? It builds links between people and gods. I'd think it could heal you or something."

"Oh, Kelsier," Preservation said. "I've told you that I am dead already. You cannot . . . save me. Save my . . . successor instead."

"Then I will give it to Vin. Would that help?"

"No. You must tell . . . her. You can reach . . . through the gaps in souls . . . when I cannot. Tell her that she must not trust . . . pierced by metal. You must free her to take . . . my power. All of it."

"Right," Kelsier said, tucking away the glass globe. "Free Vin. Easy."

He just had to find a way past Ruin.

3

S o, Midge," Kelsier whispered to the dozing man. "You got that?"

"Mission . . ." the scruffy soldier mumbled. "Survivor . . ."

"You can't trust anyone pierced by metal," Kelsier said. "Tell her that. Those exact words. It's a mission for you from the Survivor."

The man snorted awake; he was supposed to have been on watch, and he stumbled to his feet as his replacement approached. Kelsier regarded the glowing beings, anxious. It had taken precious days—during which Ruin had kept him far from Vin—to search out someone in the army who was touched in the head, someone with that distinctive soul of madness.

It wasn't that they were broken, as he had once guessed. They were merely . . . open. This man, Midge, seemed perfect. He responded to Kelsier's words, but he wasn't so unhinged that the others ignored him.

Kelsier followed Midge eagerly through camp to one of the cookfires, where Midge started chatting, animatedly, with the others there.

Tell them, Kelsier thought. *Spread the news through camp. Let Vin hear it.*

Midge continued speaking. Others stood up around the fire. They were listening! Kelsier touched Midge, trying to hear what he was saying. He couldn't make it out though, until a thread of Preservation touched him—then the words started to vibrate through his soul, faintly audible to his ears.

"That's right," Midge said. "He talked to me. Said I'm special. Said we shouldn't trust none of you. I'm holy, and you just ain't."

"What?" Kelsier snapped. "Midge, you *idiot.*"

It went downhill from there. Kelsier stepped back as men around the cookfire squabbled and started shoving one another, then began a full-on brawl. With a sigh, Kelsier settled down on the misty shadow of a boulder and watched several days' worth of work evaporate.

Someone laid a hand on his shoulder, and he glanced toward Ruin, who had appeared there.

"Careful," Kelsier said, "you'll get *you* on my shirt."

Ruin chuckled. "I was worried, leaving you alone, Kelsier. But it seems you've been serving me well in my absence." One of the brawlers punched Demoux right across the face, and Ruin winced. "Nice."

"Needs to follow through more," Kelsier mumbled. "You need to really commit to a punch."

Ruin smiled a deep, knowing, insufferable smile. *Hell,* Kelsier thought. *I hope that's not what I look like.*

"You must realize by now, Kelsier," Ruin said, "that anything you do, I will counter. Struggle serves only Ruin."

Elend Venture arrived on the scene, gliding on a Steelpush that Kelsier envied, looking properly regal. That boy had grown into more of a man than Kelsier had ever expected he would. Despite that stupid beard.

Kelsier frowned. "Where is Vin?"

"Hm?" Ruin said. "Oh, I have her."

"Where?" Kelsier demanded.

"Away. Where I can keep her in hand." He leaned toward Kelsier. "Good job wasting time on the madman." He vanished.

I absolutely hate that man, Kelsier thought. Ruin . . . he was no more impressive, deep down, than Preservation was. *Hell,* Kelsier thought, *I'm better at this god stuff than they are.* At least he had inspired people.

Including Midge and the rest of the brawlers, unfortunately. Kelsier stood up from the rock and finally acknowledged a fact he'd been wanting to avoid. He couldn't do anything here, not with Ruin so focused on Vin and Elend right now. Kelsier had to get to someone else. Sazed maybe? Or perhaps Marsh. If he could get through to his brother while Ruin was distracted . . .

He had to hope that the wards on that orb would shade him from the dark god's eyes, as they had when Kelsier had first arrived at Fadrex. He needed to leave this place, strike out, lose Ruin's interest and then try to contact Marsh or Spook, get them to relay a message to Vin.

It hurt him to leave her behind in Ruin's clutches, but there was nothing more he could do.

Kelsier left that very hour.

4

KELSIER was nowhere in particular when God finally died.

He couldn't place the location. No town nearby, at least not one that hadn't been buried in ash. He had intended to head toward Luthadel, but with all the landmarks covered over—and with no sun to guide him—he wasn't certain he'd been going the right direction.

The land trembled, the misty ground quivering. Kelsier pulled up short, looking at the sky, at first expecting that Ruin was causing this tremor.

Then he felt it. Perhaps it was the small Connection he had to Preservation from his time at the Well of Ascension. Or maybe it was the piece inside him that the god had placed, the piece inside them all. The light of the soul.

Whatever the reason, Kelsier felt the end like a long, drawn-out sigh. It sent a chill up his spine, and he scrambled to find a thread of Preservation. They had been all over the ground earlier in his trip, but now he found nothing.

"Fuzz!" he screamed. "Preservation!"

Kelsier . . . The voice vibrated through him. *Goodbye.*

"Hell, Fuzz," Kelsier said, searching the sky. "I'm sorry. I . . ." He swallowed.

Odd, the voice said. *After all these years appearing for others as they died, I never expected . . . that my own passing would be so cold and lonely. . . .*

"I'm here for you," Kelsier said.

No. You weren't. Kelsier, he's splitting my power. He's breaking it apart. It will be gone . . . Splintered. . . . He'll destroy it.

"Like hell he will," Kelsier said, dropping his pack. He reached inside, gripping the glowing orb filled with liquid.

It's not for you, Kelsier, Preservation said. *It's not yours. It belongs to another.*

"I'll get it to her," Kelsier said, taking up the sphere. He drew in a deep breath, then used Nazh's knife to smash the orb, spraying his arm and body with the glowing liquid.

Lines like threads burst out from him. Glowing, effulgent. Like the lines from burning steel or iron, except they pointed at everything.

Kelsier! Preservation said, his voice strengthening. *Do better than you have before! They called you their god, and you were casual with their faith! The hearts of men are NOT YOUR TOYS.*

"I . . ." Kelsier licked his lips. "I understand. My Lord."

Do better, Kelsier, Preservation commanded, his voice fading. *If the end comes, get them below ground. It might help. And remember . . . remember what I told you, so long ago. . . . Do what I cannot, Kelsier. . . .*

SURVIVE.

The word vibrated through him, and Kelsier gasped. He knew that feeling, remembered that exact command. He'd heard that voice in the Pits. Waking him, driving him forward.

Saving him.

Kelsier bowed his head as he felt Preservation fade, finally, and stretch into the darkness.

Then, full of borrowed light, Kelsier seized the threads spinning around him and *Pulled.* The power resisted. He didn't know why—he had only a rudimentary understanding of what he was doing. Why did the power attune to some people and not others?

Well, he'd Pulled on stubborn anchors before. He yanked with all his might, drawing the power toward him. It struggled, defying him almost like it was alive . . . until . . .

It broke, flooding into him.

And Kelsier, the Survivor of Death, Ascended.

With a cry of exultation, he felt the power flow through him, like Allomancy a hundred times over. A feverish, molten, burning energy that washed through his soul. He laughed, rising into the air, expanding, becoming everywhere and everything.

What is this? Ruin's voice demanded.

Kelsier found himself confronted by the opposing god, their forms extending into eternity—one the icy coolness of life frozen, unmoving; the other the scrabbling, crumbling, violent blackness of decay. Kelsier grinned as he felt utter and complete *shock* from Ruin.

"What was it," Kelsier asked, "that you said before? Anything I can do, you will counter? How about this?"

Ruin raged, power flaring in a cyclone of anger. The persona cracked apart, revealing the *thing*, the raw energy that had plotted and planned for so long, only to be stopped now. Kelsier's grin widened, and he imagined— with delight—the sensation of ripping apart this monster that had killed Preservation. This useless, outdated waste of energy. Crushing it would be so *satisfying*. He willed his boundless power to attack.

And nothing happened.

Preservation's power resisted him still. It shied away from his murderous intent, and push though he would, he couldn't make it hurt Ruin.

His enemy vibrated, quivering, and the shaking became a sound like laughter. The churning dark mists recovered, transforming back into the image of a deific man stretching through the sky. "Oh, Kelsier!" Ruin cried. "You think I mind what you have done? Why, I'd have chosen for *you* to take the power! It's perfect! You're merely an aspect of me, after all."

Kelsier gritted his teeth, then stretched forth fingers made of rushing wind, as if to grab Ruin and *throttle* him.

The creature merely laughed louder. "You can barely control it," Ruin said. "Even assuming it could harm me, you couldn't accomplish such a task. Look at you, Kelsier! You haven't form or shape. You're not alive, you're an *idea*. A *memory* of a man holding the power will never be as potent as a real one with ties to all three Realms."

Ruin shoved him aside with ease, though Kelsier felt a *crackling* at the thing's touch. These powers reacted to one another like flame and water. That made Kelsier certain there *was* a way to use the power he held to destroy Ruin. If he could figure it out.

Ruin turned his attention from Kelsier, and so Kelsier took to trying to acquaint himself with the power. Unfortunately, each thing he tried was met with resistance—both from Ruin's energy and from the power of Preservation itself. He could see himself now, in the Spiritual Realm—and those black lines were still there, tying him to Ruin.

The power he held didn't like that at all. It tumbled inside him, churning, trying to break free. He could hold on, but he knew that if he let go, it would escape him and he would never be able to recapture it.

Still, it was grand to be more than just a spirit. He could see into the Physical Realm again, though metal continued to glow brightly to his eyes. It was a relief to be able to see something other than misty shadows and glowing souls.

He wished that view were more encouraging. Endless seas of ash. Very few cities, dug out like craters. Burning mountains that spewed not only ash, but lava and brimstone. The land had cracked, creating rifts.

He tried not to think of that, but of the people. He could feel them, like he felt the very crust and core of the planet. He easily found which ones had souls that were open to him, and eagerly he swung down in. Surely among these he could find one who could deliver a message to Vin.

Yet they didn't seem to be able to hear him, no matter how he whispered to them. It was frustrating and baffling. He held the powers of eternity. How could he have lost the ability he'd had before, the ability to communicate with his people?

Around him, Ruin laughed.

"You think your predecessor didn't try that?" Ruin asked. "Your power cannot leak through those cracks, Preservation. It tries too hard to shore them up, to protect them. Only *I* can widen cracks."

Whether his reasoning was correct or not, Kelsier couldn't tell. But he did confirm time and time again that madmen could no longer hear him.

However, now *he* could hear people.

Everyone, not just the mad. He could hear their thoughts like voices—their hopes, their worries, their terrors. If he focused too long on them, directed his attention to a city, the multitude of thoughts threatened to overwhelm him. It was a buzz, a rush, and he found it difficult to separate individuals from the mess.

Above it all—land, cities, ash—hung the mists. They coated everything, even in the daytime. While trapped entirely in the Cognitive Realm, he hadn't seen how pervasive they were.

That's power, he thought, gazing upon it. *My power. I should be able to hold that, manipulate it.*

He couldn't. That left Ruin far stronger than he was. Why had Preservation left the mists untouched like that? It was still part of him, of course, but it was like . . . like a diffused army, spread as scouts throughout the kingdom, rather than gathered for war.

Ruin wasn't so inhibited. Kelsier could see his power at work now, revealed in ways that had been too grand for him to recognize before Ascending. Ruin ripped open the tops of ashmounts, holding them pried apart, letting death spew forth. He touched koloss all across the empire, driving them to murderous frenzies. When they ran out of people to kill, he gleefully turned them against one another.

He had hold of multiple people in every remaining city. His machinations were incredible—complex, subtle. Kelsier couldn't even follow all the threads, but the result was obvious: chaos.

Kelsier could do nothing about it. He held unimaginable power, yet he was *still* impotent. But importantly, Ruin had to *act* to counter him.

That was an important revelation. He and Ruin were both everywhere; their souls were the very bones of the planet. But their attention . . . that could only be divided so far.

If Kelsier tried to change things where Ruin was focused, he always lost. When Kelsier tried to stop the ashmounts, Ruin's arms ripping them open were stronger than his trying to seal them. When he tried to bolster Vin's armies with a sense of encouragement, Ruin acted like a blockade, keeping him away.

In a desperate attempt, he made a push to approach Vin herself. He wasn't certain what he could do, but he wanted to try battering Ruin away—push himself, and see what he was capable of doing.

He threw everything he had into it, straining against Ruin—feeling the friction of their essences meeting as he drew nearer to Vin, who was locked in a room within the palace of Fadrex. His essence meeting Ruin's caused shocks through the land, trembles. An earthquake.

He was able to draw close. He could feel Vin's mind, hear her thoughts. She knew so little—like he had known so little when he'd begun this. She didn't know about Preservation.

The clashing pushed Kelsier's essence away, ripping Preservation back from him, exposing his core—like a grinning skull as the flesh was torn free. A soul lined with darkness, but which was *Connected* to Vin somehow. Tied to her by the inscrutable lines that made up the Spiritual Realm.

"Vin!" he shouted, in agony, straining. The fight between him and Ruin caused the earthquake to intensify, and Ruin exulted in that destruction. It weakened his attention for a brief moment.

"Vin!" Kelsier said, getting closer. "Another god, Vin! There's another force!"

Confusion. She didn't see. Something leaked from Kelsier, drawing toward her. And with a shock, Kelsier saw a terrible sight, something he'd never suspected. A glowing spot of metal in Vin's ear, so similar to the color of her brilliant soul that he had missed it until he'd gotten very close.

Vin was spiked.

"What's the first rule of Allomancy, Vin!" Kelsier screamed. "The first thing I taught you!"

Vin looked up. Had she *heard*?

"Spikes, Vin!" Kelsier began. "You can't trust—"

Ruin returned and shoved Kelsier with a fierce burst of power, interrupting him. To hold on longer would have meant letting Ruin rip the power of Preservation away from him completely, and so he let himself go.

Ruin shoved him out of the building, out of the city entirely. Their clash brought incredible pain to Kelsier, and he couldn't help bearing the impression that—divine though he was—he was *limping* as he left the city.

Ruin was too focused on this place. Too strong here. He had almost all of his attention pointed at Vin and this city of Fadrex. He was even bringing in Marsh.

Maybe . . .

Kelsier tried to get close to Marsh, focusing his attention on his brother. Those same lines were there as had been with Vin, lines of Connection linking Kelsier's soul to his brother. Perhaps he could get through to Marsh too.

Unfortunately, Ruin spotted this too easily, and Kelsier was too weakened—too sore—from the previous clash. Ruin rebuffed him with ease, but not before Kelsier heard something emanating from Marsh.

Remember yourself, Marsh's thoughts whispered. *Fight, Marsh, FIGHT. Remember who you are.*

Kelsier felt a swelling of pride as he fled from Ruin. Something within Marsh, something of his brother, had survived. However, there was nothing Kelsier could do to help now. Whatever Ruin wanted in Fadrex, Kelsier would have to let him have it. To confront Ruin here was impossible, for Ruin could best Kelsier in a direct confrontation.

Fortunately, Kelsier had made a career of knowing when to avoid a fair fight. The con was on, and when the house guard was alert, your best bet was to lie low for a while.

Ruin watched Fadrex so intently, it would leave chinks elsewhere.

5

Do better, Kelsier.

He watched and waited. He could be careful.

The hearts of men are not your toys.

He floated, becoming the mists, observing how Ruin moved his pieces. The Inquisitors were his primary hands. Ruin positioned them deliberately.

The weakness of all clever men.

An opening. Kelsier needed an opening.

Survive.

Ruin thought he was in control all across the Final Empire. So sure of himself. But there were holes. He was devoting less and less attention to the broken city of Urteau, with its empty canals and starving people. One of his threads revolved around a young man who wore cloth wrapping his eyes and a burned cloak on his back.

Yes, Ruin thought he had this city in hand.

But Kelsier . . . Kelsier *knew* that boy.

Kelsier focused his attention on Spook as the young man—overwhelmed and driven to the brink of madness—stumbled onto a stage before a crowd. Ruin had driven him to this point by wearing Kelsier's form. He was trying to make an Inquisitor of the boy, while at the same time setting up the city to burn in riots and bedlam.

But his actions in this city were like so many others. His attention was too divided, with his only real focus on Fadrex. He worked in Urteau, but didn't *prioritize* it. He'd already set his plans in motion: Ruin the hopes of this people, burn the city to the ground. All it required was for a confused boy to commit a murder.

Spook stood onstage, prepared to kill in front of the crowd. Kelsier drew his attention in like a puff of mist, careful, quiet. He was the pulsing of the boards beneath Spook's feet, he was the air being breathed, he was the flame and fire.

Ruin was here, raging, demanding that Spook murder. It wasn't the careful, smiling persona. This was a purer, rawer form of the power. This piece of him had little of Ruin's attention, and he hadn't brought his full power to bear.

It didn't notice Kelsier as he drew back from the power, exposing his own soul and drawing it close to Spook. Those lines were there, the lines of familiarity, family, and Connection. Strangely, they were even *stronger* for Spook than they'd been for Marsh and Vin. Why would that be?

Now, you must kill her, Ruin said to Spook.

Under that anger, Kelsier whispered to Spook's broken soul. *Hope.*

You want power, Spook? Ruin thundered. *You want to be a better Allomancer? Well, power must come from somewhere. It is never free. This woman is a Coinshot. Kill her, and you can have her ability. I will give it to you.*

Hope, Kelsier said.

Back and forth. *Kill.* Ruin sent impressions, words. *Murder, destroy. Ruin.*

Hope.

Spook reached for the metal at his chest.

No! Ruin shouted, sounding shocked. *Spook, do you want to go back to being normal? Do you want to be useless again? You'll lose your pewter, and go back to being weak, like you were when you let your uncle die!*

Spook looked at Ruin, grimaced, then cut into his body and pulled the spike free.

Hope.

Ruin screamed in denial, his figure fuzzing, spider-leg knives spearing out of the broken shape he wore. Destruction sprouted from the figure and became black mist.

Spook sank down onto the platform, slumping to his knees, then fell forward. Kelsier knelt and held him, drawing Preservation's power back to himself. "Oh, Spook," he whispered. "You poor, poor child."

He could feel the youth's spirit sputtering. *Broken.* Cracked through to the core. The boy's thoughts drifted to Kelsier. Thoughts of a woman he loved. Thoughts of his own failures. Confused thoughts.

Deep down, this boy had been following Ruin because he'd wished so desperately for Kelsier to guide him. He'd tried so hard to be like Kelsier himself.

It twisted Kelsier about, seeing the faith of this youth. Faith in him. Kelsier, the Survivor.

A pretend god.

"Spook," Kelsier whispered, touching Spook's soul with his own again. He choked on the words, but forced them out. "Spook, her city is burning."

Spook trembled.

"Thousands will die in the flames," Kelsier whispered. He touched the boy's cheek. "Spook, child. You want to be like me? Really like me? Then fight when you are beaten!"

Kelsier looked up at the spiraling, churning form of Ruin, angered. More of Ruin's attention was focusing in this direction. It would soon rebuff Kelsier.

Beating it here was only a small victory, but it was proof. This thing could be resisted. Spook had done it.

And would do it again.

Kelsier looked down at the child in his arms. No, not a child any longer. He opened himself to Spook, and spoke a single, all-powerful command.

"Survive!"

Spook screamed, burning his metal, startling himself to lucidity. Kelsier stood up, triumphant. Spook lurched to his knees, his spirit strengthening.

"Whatever you do," Ruin said to Kelsier, as if seeing him there for the first time, "I counter."

The force of destruction exploded outward, sending tendrils of darkness into the city. He didn't push Kelsier away. Kelsier wasn't certain if that was because his attention was still too focused elsewhere, or if he just didn't care whether Kelsier stayed to witness the end of this city.

Fires. Death. Kelsier saw the thing's plan in a flashing moment: Burn this city to the ground, extinguish all signs of Ruin's failure. End the people here.

Spook was already moving, confronting the people around him, giving orders as if he were the Lord Ruler himself. And was that . . .

Sazed!

Kelsier felt a comforting warmth upon seeing the quiet Terrisman stepping up to Spook. Sazed always had answers. But here he looked haggard, confused, *exhausted*.

"Oh, my friend," Kelsier whispered. "What has he done to you?"

The group obeyed Spook's orders, rushing off. Spook lagged behind them, walking down the street. Kelsier could see the threads of the future, in the Spiritual Realm. Coated in darkness, a city destroyed. Possibilities ending.

But a few lines of light remained. Yes, it was still possible. First this boy had to save his city.

"Spook," Kelsier said, forming himself a body of power. Nobody could see him, but that didn't matter. He fell into step beside Spook, who practically stumbled along. One foot after the other, barely moving.

"Keep moving," Kelsier encouraged. He could feel this man's pain, his anguish and confusion. His faith battered. And somehow, through Connection, Kelsier could talk to him as he'd not been able to do to others.

Kelsier shared in Spook's exhaustion with each trembling, agonized step. He whispered the words over and over. *Keep moving.* It became a mantra. Spook's young woman arrived, helping him. Kelsier walked on his other side. *Keep moving.*

Blessedly, he did. Somehow the exhausted young man stumbled all the way to a burning building. He stopped outside, where Sazed had been forced to shy away. Kelsier read their attitudes in the slump of their shoulders, the fear in their eyes, reflecting flames. He heard their thoughts, pulsing from them, quiet and afraid.

This city was doomed, and they knew it.

Spook let the others pull him back from the fires. Emotions, memories, ideas rose from the boy.

Kelsier didn't care about me, Spook thought. *He didn't think of me. He remembered the others, but not me. Gave them jobs to do. I didn't matter to him. . . .*

"I named you, Spook," Kelsier whispered. "You were my friend. Isn't that enough?"

Spook stopped in place, pulling against the grip of the others.

"I'm sorry," Kelsier said, weeping, "for what you must do. Survivor."

Spook pulled from the grip of the others. And as Ruin raged above, sputtering and screaming—finally bringing in his attention to begin forcing Kelsier back—this young man entered the flames.

And saved the city.

6

KELSIER sat on a strange, verdant field. Green grass everywhere. So odd. So beautiful.

Spook walked over and settled down next to him. The boy removed the cloth from his eyes and shook his head, then ran his fingers through his hair. "What is this?"

"Half dream," Kelsier said, plucking a piece of grass and chewing on it.

"Half dream?" Spook asked.

"You're almost dead, kid," Kelsier said. "Smashed your spirit up pretty good. Lots of cracks." He smiled. "That let me in."

There was more to it. This young man was special. At the very least, their relationship was special. Spook believed in him as no other had.

Kelsier thought on this as he plucked another piece of grass and chewed on it.

"What are you doing?" Spook asked.

"It looks so strange," Kelsier said. "Like Mare always said it would."

"So you're *eating* it?"

"Chewing it, mostly," Kelsier said, then spat it to the side. "Just curious."

Spook puffed in and out. "Doesn't matter. None of this matters. You're not real."

"Well, that's partially right," Kelsier said. "I'm not completely real. Haven't been since I died. But then I'm also a god now . . . I think. It's complicated."

Spook looked at him, frowning.

"I needed someone I could chat with," Kelsier said. "I needed you. Someone who was broken, but who had resisted *him*."

"The other you."

Kelsier nodded.

"You always were so harsh, Kelsier," Spook said, staring out over the rolling green fields. "I could see that deep down, you *really* hated the nobility. I thought that hatred was why you were so strong."

"Strong like scar tissue," Kelsier whispered. "Functional, but stiff. It's a strength I'd rather you never need."

Spook nodded, and seemed to understand.

"I'm proud of you, kid," Kelsier said, giving him a fond punch to the arm.

"I almost ruined everything," he said, eyes downcast.

"Spook, if you knew how many times *I've* almost destroyed a city, you'd be embarrassed to talk like that. Hell, you barely even broke that place. They've put out the fires, rescued most of the population. You're a hero."

Spook looked up, smiling.

"Here's the thing, kid," Kelsier said. "Vin doesn't know."

"Know what?"

"The spikes, Spook. I can't get the message to her. She needs to know. And Spook, she . . . she has a spike in her too."

"Lord Ruler . . ." Spook whispered. "Vin?"

Kelsier nodded. "Listen to me. You're going to wake soon. I need you to remember this part, even if you forget everything else about the dream. When the end comes, get people underground. Send a message to Vin. Scratch the message in metal, for anything not set in metal cannot be trusted.

"Vin needs to know about Ruin and his false faces. She needs to know about the spikes, that metal buried within a person lets Ruin whisper to them. Remember it, Spook. Don't trust anyone pierced by metal! Even the smallest bit can taint a man."

Spook began to fuzz, waking.

"Remember," Kelsier said. "Vin is hearing Ruin. She doesn't know who to trust, and that's why you absolutely must get that message sent, Spook. The pieces of this thing are all spinning about, cast to the wind. You have a clue that nobody else does. Send it flying for me."

Spook nodded as he woke up.

"Good lad," Kelsier whispered, smiling. "You did well, Spook. I'm proud."

7

A MAN left Urteau, forging outward through the mists and the ash, starting the long trip toward Luthadel.

Kelsier didn't know this man, Goradel, personally. However, the power knew him. Knew how he'd joined the Lord Ruler's guards as a youth, hoping for a better life for himself and his family. This was a man whom Kelsier, if he'd been given the chance, would have killed without mercy.

Now Goradel might just save the world. Kelsier soared behind him, feeling the anticipation of the mists build. Goradel carried a metal plate bearing the secret.

Ruin rolled across the land like a shadow, dominating Kelsier. He laughed as he saw Goradel fighting through the ash, piled as high as snow in the mountains.

"Oh, Kelsier," Ruin said. "This is the best you can do? All that work with the child in Urteau, for this?"

Kelsier grunted as tendrils of Ruin's power sought out a pair of hands and brought them calling. In the real world hours passed, but to the eyes of gods time was a mutable thing. It flowed as you wished it to.

"Did you ever play card tricks, Ruin?" Kelsier asked. "Back when you were a common man?"

"I was never a common man," Ruin said. "I was but a Vessel awaiting my power."

"So what did that Vessel do with its time?" Kelsier asked. "Play card tricks?"

"Hardly," Ruin said. "I was a far better man than that."

Kelsier groaned as Ruin's hands eventually arrived, soaring high through the falling ash. A figure with spikes through his eyes, lips drawn back in a sneer.

"I was pretty good at card tricks," Kelsier said softly, "when I was a child. My first cons were with cards. Not three-card spin; that was too simple. I preferred the tricks where it was you, a deck of cards, and a mark who was watching your every move."

Below, Marsh struggled with—then finally slaughtered—the hapless Goradel. Kelsier winced as his brother didn't just murder, but reveled in the death, driven to madness by Ruin's taint. Strangely, Ruin worked to hold him *back*. As if in the moment, he'd lost control of Marsh.

Ruin was careful not to let Kelsier get too close. He couldn't even draw near enough to hear his brother's thoughts. Ruin laughed as, awash in the gore of the murder, Marsh finally retrieved the letter Spook had sent.

"You think," Ruin said, "you're so clever, Kelsier. Words in metal. I can't read them, but my minion can."

Kelsier sank down as Marsh felt at the plate Spook had ordered carved, reading the words out loud for Ruin to hear. Kelsier formed a body for himself and knelt in the ash, slumping forward, beaten.

Ruin formed beside him. "It's all right, Kelsier. This is the way things were *meant* to be. The reason they were created! Do not mourn the deaths that come to us; celebrate the lives that have passed."

He patted Kelsier, then evaporated. Marsh stumbled to his feet, ash sticking to the still-wet blood on his clothing and face. He then leaped after Ruin, following his master's call. The end was approaching quickly now.

Kelsier knelt by the corpse of the fallen man, who was slowly being covered in ash. Vin had spared him, and Kelsier had gotten him killed after all. He reached into the Cognitive Realm, where the man's spirit had stumbled in the place of mist and shadows, and was now looking skyward.

Kelsier approached and clasped the man's hand. "Thank you," he said. "And I'm sorry."

"I've failed," Goradel said as he stretched away.

It twisted Kelsier inside, but he didn't dare contradict the man. *Forgive me.*

Now, to be quiet. Kelsier let himself drift again, spread out. No longer did he try to stop Ruin's influence. In withdrawing, he saw that he *had* been helping a tiny bit. He'd held back some earthquakes, slowed the flow of lava. An insignificant amount, but at least he'd done something.

Now he let it go and gave Ruin free rein. The end accelerated, twisting about the motions of one young woman, who arrived back in Luthadel at the advent of a storm.

Kelsier closed his eyes, feeling the world hush, as if the land itself were holding its breath. Vin fought, danced, and pushed herself to the limits of her abilities—and then beyond. She stood against Ruin's assembled might of Inquisitors, and fought with such majesty that Kelsier was astonished. She was better than the Inquisitor he'd fought, better than any man he'd seen. Better than Kelsier himself.

Unfortunately, against an entire murder of Inquisitors, it was not nearly enough.

Kelsier forced himself to hold back. And *hell,* was it difficult. He let Ruin reign, let his Inquisitors beat Vin to submission. The fight was over too soon, and ended with Vin broken and defeated, at Marsh's mercy.

Ruin stepped close, whispering to her. *Where is the atium, Vin?* he said. *What do you know of it?*

Atium? Kelsier drew himself near as Marsh knelt by Vin and prepared to hurt her. Atium. Why . . .

It all came together for him. Ruin wasn't complete either. There in the broken city of Luthadel—rain washing down, ash clogging the streets, Inquisitors roosting and watching with expressionless spiked eyes—Kelsier understood.

Preservation's plan. It could work!

Marsh snapped Vin's arm, and grinned.

Now.

Kelsier hit Ruin with the full strength of his power. It wasn't much, and he was a poor master of it. But it *was* unexpected, and it drew away Ruin's attention. The powers met, and the friction—the opposition—caused them to grind.

Pain coursed through Kelsier. The ground throughout the city trembled.

"Kelsier, Kelsier," Ruin said.

Below, Marsh laughed.

"Do you know," Kelsier said, "why I always won at card tricks, Ruin?"

"Please," Ruin said. "Does this matter?"

"It's because," Kelsier said, grunting in pain, his power taut, "I could always. Force. People to choose. The card *I wanted them to.*"

Ruin paused, then looked down. The letter—delivered by Goradel not to Vin, but to Marsh—did its job.

Marsh ripped free Vin's earring.

The world froze. Ruin, vast and immortal, looked on with complete and utter horror.

"You made the wrong one of us into your Inquisitor, Ruin," Kelsier hissed. "You shouldn't have picked the *good* brother. He always *did* have a nasty habit of doing what was right instead of what was smart."

Ruin looked to Kelsier, turning his full, incredible attention on him.

Kelsier smiled. Gods, it appeared, could still fall for a classic misdirection con.

Vin reached to the mists, and Kelsier felt the power within him tremble, eager. This was what they'd been meant for; this was their purpose. He felt Vin's yearning, and felt her question. Where had she felt this power before?

Kelsier rammed himself against Ruin, the powers clashing, exposing his soul. His darkened, battered soul.

"The power came from the Well of Ascension, of course," Kelsier said to Vin. "It's the same power, after all. Solid in the metal you fed to Elend. Liquid in the pool you burned. And vapor in the air, confined to night. Hiding you. Protecting you . . ."

Kelsier took a deep breath. He felt Preservation's energy being ripped from him. He felt Ruin's fury pummeling him, flaying him, ravenous to destroy him. For one last moment he felt the world. The farthest ashfall, the people in the distant south, the curling winds, and the life straining—struggling—to continue on this planet.

Then Kelsier did the most difficult thing he'd ever done.

"Giving you power!" he roared to Vin, letting go of Preservation's essence so she could take it up.

Vin drew in the mists.

And Ruin's full fury came against Kelsier, slamming him down, ripping into his soul. Tearing him apart.

8

KELSIER was cloven asunder with a rending, pervasive pain—like that of a bone being pulled from a socket. He tumbled, unable to see or think—unable to do more than scream at the attack.

He ended up someplace surrounded by mist, blind to anything beyond its shifting. Death, for real this time? No . . . but he was very close. He could feel the stretching coming upon him again, coaxing him, trying to pull him toward that distant point where everyone else had gone.

He wanted to go. He hurt *so much*. He wanted it all to end, to go away. Everything. He just wanted it to stop.

He had felt this despair before, in the Pits of Hathsin. He didn't have Preservation's voice to guide him now, as he had then, but—weeping, trembling—he sank his hands into the misty expanse around him and *held on*. Clinging to it, refusing to go. Denying that force that called to him, promising peace and an ending.

Eventually it stilled, and the stretching sensation faded away. He had held the power of deity. The final death could not take him unless he wanted it to.

Or unless he was completely destroyed. He shuddered in the mists, thankful for their embrace, but still uncertain where he was—and uncertain why Ruin hadn't finished the job. He'd planned to; Kelsier had felt that. Fortunately, Kelsier's destruction had become an afterthought in the face of a new threat.

Vin. She'd done it! She'd Ascended!

Groaning, Kelsier pulled himself upward, finding he'd been hit so hard by Ruin's attack that he'd been driven far down into the springy, misty ground of the Cognitive Realm. He was able to pull himself out, with difficulty, and collapsed onto the surface. His soul was distorted, mangled, like a body struck by a boulder. It leaked dark smoke from a thousand holes.

As he lay there it slowly re-formed, and the pain—at long last—faded. Time had passed. He didn't know how much, but it had been hours upon hours. He wasn't in Luthadel. De-Ascending—then being crushed by Ruin's power—had flung his soul far from the city.

He blinked phantom eyes. Above him the sky was a tempest of white and black tendrils, like clouds attacking one another. In the distance he could hear something that made the Realm tremble. He forced himself to his feet and walked, eventually cresting a hill where he saw—below—that figures made of light were locked in battle. A war, men against koloss.

Preservation's plan. He'd seen it, understood it in those last moments. Ruin's body was atium. The plan was to create something special and new—people who could *burn away* Ruin's body in an attempt to get rid of it.

Below, men fought for their lives, and he saw them transcending the Physical Realm because of the body of the god that they burned. Above, Ruin and Preservation clashed. Vin did a much better job of it than Kelsier had; she had the full power of the mists, and beyond that there was something *natural* about the way she held that power.

Kelsier dusted himself off and adjusted his clothing. Still the same shirt and trousers he'd been wearing during his fight with the Inquisitor long ago. What had happened to his pack and the knife Nazh had given him? Those were lost somewhere on the endless fields of ash between here and Fadrex.

He crossed through the battle, stepping out of the way of raging koloss and transcendent men who could see into the Spiritual Realm, if only in a very limited way.

Kelsier reached the top of a hill and stopped. On another hill beyond, distant but close enough to make out, Elend Venture stood among a pile of corpses, clashing with Marsh. Vin hovered above, expansive and incredible, a figure of glowing light and awesome power—like an inspiration for the sun and clouds.

Elend Venture raised his hand, and then *exploded* with light. Lines of white scattered from him in all directions, lines that drilled through all things. Lines that Connected him to Kelsier, to the future, and to the past.

He's seeing it fully, Kelsier thought. *That place between moments.*

Elend ended with a sword in Marsh's neck, and looked directly at Kelsier, transcending the three Realms.

Marsh slammed an axe into Elend's chest.

"No!" Kelsier screamed. *"No!"* He stumbled down the hillside, running for Venture. He climbed over corpses, shadowy on this side, and scrambled toward where Elend had died.

He hadn't reached the position yet when Marsh took off Elend's head.

Oh, Vin. I'm sorry.

Vin's full attention coursed around the fallen man. Kelsier pulled to a stop, numb. She would rage. She would lose control. She would . . .

Rise in glory?

He watched, awed, as Vin's strength coalesced. There was no hatred in the thrumming that washed from her, calming all things. Above her Ruin laughed, again assuming he knew so much. That laughter cut off as Vin rose against him, a glorious, radiant spear of power—controlled, loving, compassionate, but *unyielding*.

Kelsier knew then why she, and not he, had needed to do this.

Vin crashed her power against Ruin's, suffocating him. Kelsier stepped up to the top of the hill, watching, feeling a familiarity with that power. A kinship that warmed him deep within as Vin performed the ultimate act of heroism.

She brought destruction to the destroyer.

It ended in an eruption of light. Wisps of mist, both dark and white, streamed down from the sky. Kelsier smiled, knowing that at long last it was finished. In a rush, the mists swirled in twin columns, impossibly high. The powers had been released. They quivered, uncertain, like a storm brewing.

Nobody is holding them. . . .

Kelsier reached out, timid, trembling. He could . . .

Elend Venture's spirit stumbled into the Cognitive Realm beside him, tripping and collapsing to the ground. He groaned, and Kelsier grinned at him.

Elend blinked as Kelsier held out a hand. "I always imagined death," Elend said, letting Kelsier help him to his feet, "as being greeted by everyone I've ever loved in life. I hadn't imagined that would include *you*."

"You need to pay better attention, kid," Kelsier said, looking him over. "Nice uniform. Did you *ask* them to make you look like a cheap knockoff of the Lord Ruler, or was it more an accident?"

Elend blinked. "Wow. I hate you already."

"Give it time," Kelsier said, slapping him on the back. "For most that eventually fades to a sense of mild exasperation." He looked at the power still coursing around them, then frowned as a figure made of glowing light scrambled across the field. Its shape was familiar to him. It stepped up to Vin's corpse, which had fallen to the ground.

"Sazed," Kelsier whispered, then touched him. He was not prepared for the rush of emotion brought on by seeing his friend in this state. Sazed was frightened. Disbelieving. Crushed. Ruin was dead, but the world was still ending. Sazed had thought that Vin would save them. Honestly, so had Kelsier.

But it seemed there was yet another secret.

"It's him," Kelsier whispered. "He's the Hero."

Elend Venture placed a hand on Kelsier's shoulder. "You need to pay better attention," he noted. "Kid." He pulled Kelsier away as Sazed reached for the powers, one with each hand.

Kelsier stood in awe of the way they combined. He'd always seen these powers as opposites, yet as they swirled around Sazed it seemed that they actually *belonged* to one another. "How?" he whispered. "How is he Connected to them both, so evenly? Why not just Preservation?"

"He has changed, this last year," Elend said. "Ruin is more than death and destruction. It is peace with these things."

The transformation continued, but awesome though it was, Kelsier's attention was drawn by something else. A coalescing of power near him on the hilltop. It formed into the shape of a young woman who slipped easily into the Cognitive Realm. She didn't so much as stumble, which was both appropriate and horribly unfair.

Vin glanced at Kelsier and smiled. A welcoming, warm smile. A smile of joy and acceptance, which filled him with pride. How he wished he'd been able to find her earlier, when Mare was still alive. When she'd needed parents.

She went to Elend first, and seized him in a long embrace. Kelsier glanced at Sazed, who was expanding to become everything. Well, good for him. It was a tough job; Sazed could have it.

Elend nodded to Kelsier, and Vin walked over. "Kelsier," she said to him, "oh, Kelsier. You always did make your own rules."

Hesitant, he didn't embrace her. He reached out his hand, feeling oddly reverent. Vin took it, the tips of her fingers curling into his palm.

Nearby another figure had coalesced from the power, but Kelsier ignored him. He stepped closer to Vin. "I . . ." What did he say? Hell, he didn't know.

For once, he didn't know.

She embraced him, and he found himself weeping. The daughter he'd never had, the little child of the streets. Though she was still small, she'd outgrown him. And she loved him anyway. He held his daughter close against his own broken soul.

"You did it," he finally whispered. "What nobody else could have done. You gave yourself up."

"Well," she said, "I had such a good example, you see."

He pulled her tight and held her for a moment longer. Unfortunately, he eventually had to let go.

Ruin stood up nearby, blinking. Or . . . no, it wasn't Ruin any longer. It was just the Vessel, Ati. The man who had held the power. Ati ran his hand through his red hair, then looked about. "Vax?" he said, sounding confused.

"Excuse me," Kelsier said to Vin, then released her and trotted over to the red-haired man.

Whereupon he decked the man across the face, laying him out completely.

"Excellent," Kelsier said, shaking his hand. At his feet, the man looked at him, then closed his eyes and sighed, stretching away into eternity.

Kelsier walked back to the others, passing a figure in Terris robes standing with hands clasped before him, draping sleeves covering them. "Hey," Kelsier said, then looked at the sky and the glowing figure there. "Aren't you . . ."

"Part of me is," Sazed replied. He looked to Vin and Elend and held out his hands, one toward each of them. "Thank you both for this new beginning. I have healed your bodies. You can return to them, if you wish."

Vin looked to Elend. To Kelsier's horror, he had begun to stretch out. He turned toward something Kelsier couldn't see, something Beyond, and smiled, then stepped in that direction.

"I don't think it works that way, Saze," Vin said, then kissed him on the cheek. "Thank you." She turned, took Elend's hand, and began to stretch toward that unseen, distant point.

"Vin!" Kelsier cried, grabbing her other hand, clutching it. "No, Vin. You held the power. You don't have to go."

"I know," she said, looking back over her shoulder at him.

"Please," Kelsier said. "Don't go. Stay. With me."

"Ah, Kelsier," she said. "You have a lot to learn about love, don't you?"

"I know love, Vin. Everything I've done—the fall of the empire, the power I've given up—that was all *about* love."

She smiled. "Kelsier. You are a great man, and should be proud of what you've done. And you do love. I know you do. But at the same time, I don't think you understand it."

She turned her gaze toward Elend, who was vanishing, only his hand—in hers—still visible. "Thank you, Kelsier," she whispered, looking back at him, "for all you have done. Your sacrifice was amazing. But to do the things you had to do, to defend the world, you had to become something. Something that worries me.

"Once, you taught me an important lesson about friendship. I need to return that lesson. A last gift. You need to know, you need to ask. How much of what you've done was about love, and how much was about proving something? That you hadn't been betrayed, bested, beaten? Can you answer honestly, Kelsier?"

He met her eyes, and saw the implicit question.

How much was about us? it asked. *And how much was about you?*

"I don't know," he said to her.

She squeezed his hand and smiled—that smile she'd never have been able to give when he first found her.

That, more than anything, made him proud of her.

"Thank you," she whispered again.

Then she let go of his hand and followed Elend into the Beyond.

9

THE land shook and groaned as it died, and was reborn.

Kelsier walked it, hands shoved in his pockets. He strolled through the end of the world, power spraying in all directions, giving him visions of all three Realms.

Fires burned from the heavens. Stones crashed together, then ripped back apart. Oceans boiled, and their steam became a new mist in the air.

Still Kelsier walked. He walked as if his feet could carry him from one world to the next, from one life to the next. He didn't feel abandoned, but he did feel alone. Like he was the only man left in all the world, and the last witness of eras.

Ash was consumed by a land of stones made liquid. Mountains crashed from the ground behind Kelsier, in rhythm to his footsteps. Rivers washed down from the heights and oceans filled. Life sprang up, trees sprouting and shooting toward the sky, making a forest around him. Then that passed, and he was in a desert, quickly drying, sand boiling from the depths of the land as Sazed created it.

A dozen different settings passed him in an eyeblink, the land growing in his wake, his shadow. Kelsier finally stopped on a lofty highland plateau overlooking a new world, winds from three Realms ruffling his clothing. Grass grew beneath his feet, then blossoms sprouted. Mare's flowers.

He knelt and bowed his head, resting his fingers on one of them.

Sazed appeared beside him. Slowly, Kelsier's vision of the real world faded, and he was trapped again in the Cognitive Realm. All became mist around him.

Sazed sat down next to him. "I will be honest, Kelsier. This is not the end I had in mind when I joined your crew."

"The rebellious Terrisman," Kelsier said. Though he was in the world of mist, he could see clouds—vaguely—in the real world. They passed beneath his feet, surging around the base of the mountain. "You were a living contradiction even then, Saze. I should have seen it."

"I can't bring them back," Sazed said softly. "Not yet . . . perhaps not ever. The Beyond is a place I can't reach."

"It's all right," Kelsier said. "Do me a favor. Will you see what you can do for Spook? His body is in rough shape. He's pushed it too hard. Fix him up a little? Maybe make him Mistborn while you're at it. They're going to need some Allomancers in the world that comes."

"I'll consider it," Sazed said.

They sat there together. Two friends at the edge of the world, at the end and start of time. Eventually, Sazed stood and bowed to Kelsier. A reverent motion for one who was himself divine.

"What do you think, Saze?" Kelsier asked, staring out over the world. "Is there a way for me to get out of this, and live again in the Physical Realm?"

Sazed hesitated. "No. I do not think so." He patted Kelsier on the shoulder, then vanished.

Huh, Kelsier thought. *He holds the powers of creation in twain, a god among gods.*

And he's still a terrible liar.

EPILOGUE

S POOK felt uncomfortable living in a mansion when everyone else had so little. But they had insisted—and besides, it wasn't much of a mansion. Yes, it was a log house of two stories, when most lived in shanties. And yes, he had his own room. But that room was small, and it felt muggy at night. They didn't have glass for windows, and if he left the shutters open, insects got in.

This perfect new world had a disappointing amount of normalcy to it.

He yawned, closing his door. The room held a cot and a desk. No candles or lamps; they didn't yet have the resources to spare those. His head was full of Breeze's instructions on how to be a king, and his arms hurt from training with Ham. Beldre would expect him for dinner shortly.

Downstairs a door thumped, and Spook jumped. He kept expecting loud noises to hurt his ears more than they did, and even after all these weeks he still wasn't used to walking around with his eyes uncovered. On his desk one of his aides had left a little writing board—they didn't have paper—scratched on with charcoal, listing a few of his appointments for the next day. And at the bottom was a quick note.

I finally got the smith to make this as you requested, though he was timid about handling Inquisitor spikes. Not sure why you want it so much, Your Majesty. But here you go.

At the base of the board was a tiny spike shaped like an earring. Hesitant, Spook picked it up and held it before him. Why *did* he want this, again? He remembered something, whispers in his dreams. *Get a spike forged, an earring. An old Inquisitor spike will work. You can find one in the caverns that used to be beneath Kredik Shaw. . . .*

A dream? He considered, then—perhaps against his better judgment—jabbed the thing through his ear.

Kelsier appeared in the room with him.

"Gah!" Spook said, leaping back. "You! You're dead. Vin killed you. Saze's book says—"

"It's okay, kid," Kelsier said. "I'm the real one."

"I . . ." Spook stammered. "It . . . Gah!"

Kelsier walked over and put his arm around Spook's shoulders. "See, I knew this would work. You've got them both now. Broken mind, Hemalurgic spike. You can see just enough into the Cognitive Realm. That means we can work together, you and I."

"Oh hell," Spook said.

"Now, don't be like that," Kelsier said. "Our work is important. *Vital.* We're going to unravel the mysteries of the universe. The cosmere, as it is called."

"What . . . what do you mean?"

Kelsier smiled.

"I think I'm going to be sick," Spook said.

"It's a big, big place out there, kid," Kelsier said. "Bigger than I ever knew. Ignorance almost lost us everything. I'm not going to let that happen again." He tapped at Spook's ear. "While dead, I had an opportunity. My mind expanded, and I learned some things. My focus wasn't on these spikes; I think I could have worked it all out, if it had been. I still learned enough to be dangerous, and the two of us are going to figure the rest out."

Spook pulled back. He was his own man now! He didn't need to just do whatever Kelsier said. Hell, he didn't even know if this really *was* Kelsier. He'd been fooled once before.

"Why?" Spook demanded. "Why would I care?"

Kelsier shrugged. "The Lord Ruler was immortal, you know. By a combination of the powers, he managed to make himself unable to age—unable to die, under most circumstances. You're Mistborn, Spook. Halfway there. Aren't you curious about what else is possible? I mean, we have a little pile of Inquisitor spikes, and nothing to do with them. . . ."

Immortal.

"And you?" Spook asked. "What do you get from this?"

"Nothing big," Kelsier said. "Just a little thing. Someone once explained my problem. My string has been cut, the thing holding me to the physical world." His smile broadened. "Well, we're just going to have to find me a new string."

POSTSCRIPT

I started planning this story while writing the original trilogy. By then, I'd pitched the idea of a "trilogy of trilogies" to my editor. (This is the idea that Mistborn, as a series, would change epochs and tech levels as the Cosmere matured.) I also knew that Kelsier would be playing a major role in future books in the series.

I'm not opposed to letting characters die; I believe that every series I've done has had some major, permanent casualties among viewpoint characters. At the same time, I was well aware that Kelsier's story was not finished. The person he was at the end of the first volume had learned some things, but hadn't completed his journey.

So, early on I began planning how to bring him back. I saturated *The Hero of Ages* with hints as to what he was doing behind the scenes, and even managed to slip in a few earlier hints here and there. I made very clear to fans who asked me that Kelsier was never good at doing what he was supposed to.

I am very aware of character resurrection as a dangerous trope, the balance of which I'm still figuring out. I didn't think this one was particularly controversial, in part because of the foreshadowing I'd done. But I do want death to be a very real danger, or consequence, in my stories.

That said, Kelsier from the start was coming back—though at times I wavered on whether I was going to write this story or not. I was worried that if I wrote it out, it would feel disjointed, as so much time passes and so many different phases of storytelling had to occur. I started writing for it a few years before I finally published it, tweaking scenes off and on, here and there.

Once I wrote *The Bands of Mourning*, it became clear to me that I'd need to get an explanation to readers out sooner rather than later. This set me to working on the story more diligently. In the end, I'm very pleased with how it turned out. It is a little disjointed, as I worried. However, the chance to finally talk about some of the behind-the-scenes stories going on in the Cosmere was very rewarding, both for myself and for fans.

To forestall questions, I do know what Kelsier and Spook were up to directly following this story. And I also know what Kelsier was doing during the era of the Wax and Wayne books. (There are some hints in those, as the original books have hints at this story.)

I can't promise that I'll write *Secret History 2* or *3*. There's already a lot on my plate. However, the possibility is in the back of my mind.

THE
TALDAIN
SYSTEM

THE TALDAIN SYSTEM

TALDAIN is one of the most bizarre planets in the cosmere, a fact that, in turn, feels bizarre to me. Having grown up on Taldain's Darkside, there is a part of me—even all these years later—that instinctively feels that the way of this planet is the normal, natural one.

Taldain is a tidally locked planet trapped between the gravitational forces of two stars in a binary system. The smaller star is a weak white dwarf that, enveloped in a particulate ring, is barely visible from the dark side of the planet. Those of us originating from this side of the planet consider a uniform darkness (what most might consider a twilight similar to the sky just after a sun has set) to be the natural state.

Our planet is not grim, and assumptions otherwise are simple ignorance. The ultraviolet light that shines through the ring causes a certain reflective luminescence in much of the plant and animal life. Indeed, the few visitors to the planet that I've met often found it somewhere between striking and garish.

On the other side of the planet is Dayside, which faces the larger of the two stars, a blue-white supergiant around which the dwarf orbits. The sun is a dominating fixture of Dayside, which is primarily a vast sandy desert, with most of the flora and fauna living beneath the surface.

For years we assumed that our Shard, Autonomy, had Invested only Dayside, through the sunlight itself. We know now it is not as simple as this, though the mechanism is best explained under those assumptions. The Investiture beats down from the sky, and is absorbed by a microflora that grows like a lichen on the surface of the sand, giving it its brilliant white color (when fully Invested) or deep blackness (when that Investiture is depleted).

Giving water to the tiny plant causes a chain reaction of sudden growth, energy, and Realmic transition. Certain people can control this reaction, using the water from their own bodies to forge a brief Cognitive bond. They can draw Investiture (in very small amounts) directly from the Spiritual Realm, and use that to control the sand.

Though the effect is dramatic, the actual power used is quite small. This is a magic more about finesse than raw strength.

Dayside is home to two prominent cultures, while Darkside is more hospitable and varied. The flora and fauna of both sides are remarkable, though currently prospective visitors are—unfortunately—unable to experience them directly. Autonomy's policy of isolationism in recent times (in direct contrast to her interference with other planets, I might add) has prevented travel to and from Taldain for many, many years.

A fact of which I am all too aware.

WHITE SAND

This excerpt of the 2016 graphic novel is followed by the beginning of the 1999 draft that formed the basis of the graphic adaptation.

SO...

...*THE MASTRELL'S PATH.* REMIND ME AGAIN WHY I THOUGHT THIS WOULD BE A *SMART IDEA?*

WHITE SAND

STORY: BRANDON SANDERSON
SCRIPT: RIK HOSKIN
ART: JULIUS GOPEZ
COLORS: ROSS CAMPBELL
LETTERS: MARSHALL DILLON
EDITS: RICH YOUNG

I GUESS I'VE ALWAYS BEEN TRYING TO PROVE SOMETHING TO MY FATHER, THE LORD MASTRELL.

"AND THIS ONE, SENIOR MASTRELL TENDEL? DOES HE SHOW *PROMISE?*"

"YES, LORD MASTRELL. HE'S ONE IN A VERY STRONG GROUP THIS YEAR."

WELL, CHILD? TELL THE LORD MASTRELL YOUR NAME.

TRAIBEN, SIR.

NOW SHOW US YOUR MASTERY SO FAR.

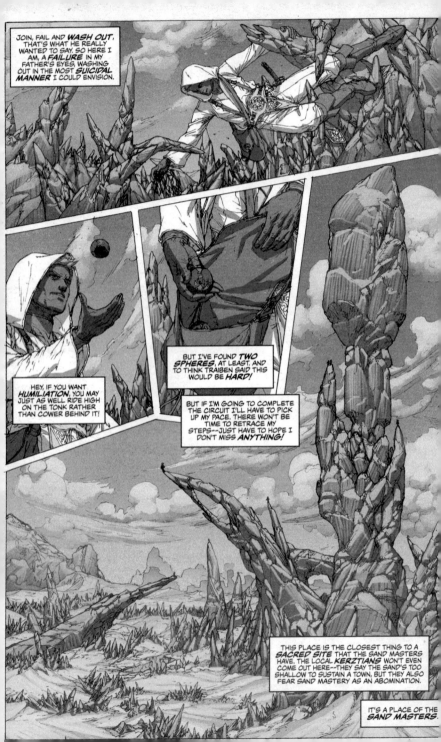

JOIN, FAIL AND *WASH OUT*, THAT'S WHAT HE REALLY WANTED TO SAY. SO HERE I AM, A *FAILURE* IN MY FATHER'S EYES, WASHING OUT IN THE MOST *SUICIDAL MANNER* I COULD ENVISION.

HEY, IF YOU WANT *HUMILIATION*, YOU MAY JUST AS WELL RIDE HIGH ON THE TONK RATHER THAN COWER BEHIND IT!

BUT I'VE FOUND *TWO SPHERES*, AT LEAST. AND TO THINK TRAIBEN SAID THIS WOULD BE *HARD!*

BUT IF I'M GOING TO COMPLETE THE CIRCUIT I'LL HAVE TO PICK UP MY PACE. THERE WON'T BE TIME TO RETRACE MY STEPS--JUST HAVE TO HOPE I DON'T MISS *ANYTHING!*

THIS PLACE IS THE CLOSEST THING TO A *SACRED SITE* THAT THE SAND MASTERS HAVE. THE LOCAL *KERZTIANS* WON'T EVEN COME OUT HERE--THEY SAY THE SAND'S TOO SHALLOW TO SUSTAIN A TOWN, BUT THEY ALSO FEAR SAND MASTERY AS AN ABOMINATION.

IT'S A PLACE OF THE *SAND MASTERS*.

NEW STUDENTS ARE ASSIGNED THEIR POSITION BASED ON THEIR *ABILITY.*

OKAY, *BIG DROP.* BIGGER THAN I WAS EXPECTING, BUT THIS IS THE PATH ALL RIGHT--MARKER FLAG CONFIRMS IT. *SO NOW THE REAL TEST BEGINS.*

MY PALTRY ABILITY PLUNGED ME TO A SOCIAL POSITION AT THE BOTTOM OF A CHASM *TWICE AS DEEP* AS THIS ONE.

TO SAND MASTERS, *POWER IS EVERYTHING.* I LEARNED THAT YOUNG, AS SOON AS I WAS INDUCTED INTO THE DIEM.

BUT THE WAY *I* SEE THINGS...

...THERE'S *ABILITY*...

...AND THEN THERE'S *CONTROL*.

SURE, THE WAY I DO IT MAY NOT BE *FLASHY*--

--BUT IT GETS THE *JOB DONE*.

ONCE USED, SAND'S NO LONGER WHITE--IT'S *BLACK*. THAT MEANS ITS ENERGY IS SPENT.

IT'S A GOOD REMINDER THAT IT'S NOT JUST THE SAND'S ENERGY I HAVE TO WATCH OUT HERE--IT'S *MINE*.

MY MOUTH IS *DRY*. THE FIRST SIGN OF DEHYDRATION. SAND MASTERY DOESN'T JUST TAKE *STRENGTH*--IT REQUIRES *WATER*, SUCKING THE PRECIOUS LIQUID FROM THE BODY OF A MASTER.

THEY DON'T REALLY **SEE**--
THEY **FEEL**. THE KERZTIANS
BELIEVE THAT THEY EVEN
SPEAK TO THE SAND

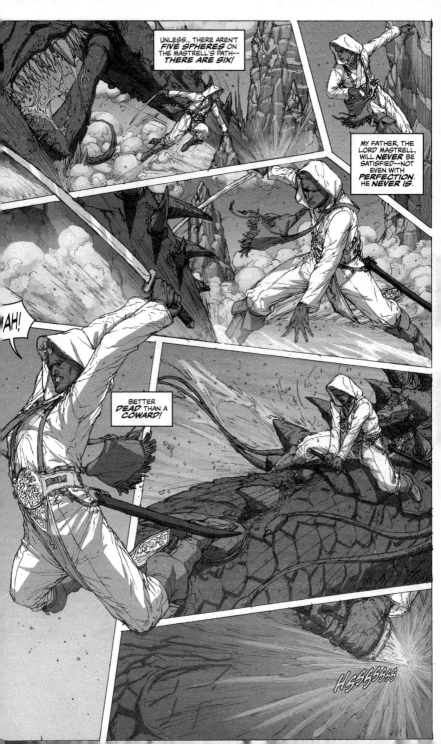

PROLOGUE

THE wind caressed the stark dunes with a whispering touch, catching fine grains of sand between its fingers and bearing them forth like thousands of tiny charioteers. The sand, like the dunes it sculpted, was bone white. It had been bleached by the sun's harsh stare—a stare that never slackened, for here, in the empire of the white sand, the sun never set. It hung motionless, neither rising nor falling, ever watching the dunes like a jealous monarch.

Praxton could feel the wind-borne grains of sand biting into his cheek. He pulled up the hood of his robe, but it seemed to make little difference. He could still feel the particles attacking the side of his face like furious insects. The sand masters would have to hurry—the winds could whip the Kerla sands from stagnation to a whirling typhoon in a matter of minutes.

A dozen forms stood a short distance away, clothed in brown robes. They had their hoods pulled up against the wind, but it was easy to tell from their small frames that they were children, barely into their second decade of life. The boys stood uncomfortably, shuffling with nervous feet as the winds whipped at their robes. They knew how important this day was. They couldn't understand as Praxton did; they couldn't know how many times they would look back on the event, how often the results of the testing would determine the course of their lives. Still, they could sense the significance of what was about to happen.

At the bidding of a white-robed mastrell, the boys reached into their robes and pulled out small cloth bags. Praxton watched the event with a stern face—the face he usually wore—presiding over the ceremony as Lord Mastrell, leader of the sand masters. He watched with emotionless eyes as each boy pulled a handful of white sand from within his bag. They had to hold tightly to keep the increasingly powerful wind from tearing the sand away and scattering it across the Kerla.

Praxton frowned, as if his simple displeasure could force the wind to abate. The testing took place close to the mountain KraeDa—one of the few places in the Kerla where stone jutted free from the sand. Here the wind was usually blocked by both mountain and surrounding cliffs.

He shook his head, taking his mind off the wind as the first boy began the testing. Two mastrells stood before him, instructing him in quiet voices that were lost upon the wind. Praxton saw the results, even if he couldn't hear the voices—the boy stared at the sand in his hand for a moment, a brief flutter of wind revealing the look of concentration on his face. The sand, cupped protectively in his open palm, began to glow faintly for a moment, then turned a dull black, like the charred remnants of a fire.

"A good start," one of the senior mastrells, Tendel, muttered from behind him. Praxton nodded silently—Tendel was correct; it was a good sign. The boy—Praxton thought he recognized him as Traiben, son of a lower sand master—had been able to make the sand glow bright enough to be seen even from a short distance, which meant he had at least moderate power.

The testing continued, some of the boys producing glows similar to Traiben's, some barely managing to turn the sand black. Overall, however, it was an unusually strong batch. They would bring much strength to the Diem.

There was a sudden flash, one so bright that it produced an explosive crack loud enough to be heard even over the wind. Praxton blinked in surprise, trying to clear the bright afterimage from his eyes. The two mastrells performing the test stood stunned before a small child with a shaking hand.

Tendel whistled beside Praxton. "I haven't seen one so powerful in years," the old mastrell said. "Who is that?"

"Drile," Praxton said despite himself. "Son of Reenst Rile."

"A profitable catch in more than one way, then," Tendel noted.

The testing mastrells recovered from their surprise and moved on to the next, and final, boy. Despite his age, his determined calmness, and his stern nature, Praxton felt his heart beat a little more quickly as the final child listened to their instructions.

Oh please, he felt himself mutter in a half-conscious prayer. He was not a religious man, but this was his final opportunity. He had failed so many times before. . . .

The boy looked at his sand. His hood had fallen to the wind, and his face, round and topped with a pile of short blond hair, adopted a look of total concentration. Praxton held his breath, waiting, excited in spite of himself.

The boy stared at the sand, his teeth clenched. Praxton felt his excitement dribble away as nothing happened. Finally, the sand gave a very weak glimmer—one so dark Praxton couldn't be certain he hadn't just imagined it—then faded to a dun black.

Though he knew he betrayed no look of disappointment, Praxton felt the senior mastrells around him grow stiff with anticipation.

"I'm . . . sorry, Lord Mastrell," Tendel said beside him.

"It is nothing," Praxton replied with a dismissive wave of his hand. "Not every boy is meant to be a sand master."

"But . . . this was your last son," Tendel pointed out—a rather unnecessary acknowledgment, in Praxton's estimation.

"Take them away," Praxton ordered in a loud voice. *So, this will be my legacy,* he thought to himself. *A Lord Mastrell who couldn't produce a single sand master child. I will be remembered as the man who married a woman from Darkside, thereby sullying his line.*

He sighed, continuing. "Those who have skill may enter the Diem; the rest will choose another Profession."

The sand masters moved quickly, their feet sinking easily into the swirling, fine-grained dunes beneath. They were eager to seek refuge from the furious elements. One form, however, did not follow the white-robed mastrells. Small and slight of frame, the boy stood in the increasingly violent wind. His robe whipped around him, writhing like a beast in the throes of a gruesome death.

"Kenton," Praxton said under his breath.

"I will be a sand master!" the young boy said, his voice barely audible over the wind. A short distance away the line of retreating mastrells and boys paused, several heads turning in surprise.

"You have no talent for sand mastery, boy!" Praxton spat, waving for the group to continue moving. They made only a perfunctory show of obeying the order. Few people ever challenged the Lord Mastrell, especially not young boys. Such a sight was worth standing in a sandstorm to watch.

"The Law says I have enough!" Kenton rebutted, his small voice nearly a scream.

Praxton frowned. "You've studied the Law, have you, boy?"

"I have."

"Then you know that I am the only one who can grant advancement in the Diem," Praxton said, growing more and more furious at the challenge to his authority. It looked bad to be confronted by a child, especially his own son. "The Lord Mastrell must give his approval before any sand master can increase in rank."

"Every rank but the first!" Kenton shouted back.

Praxton paused, feeling his rage build. Everything beat against him—the insufferable wind, the boy's insolence, the other sand masters' eyes. . . . The worst of it was his own knowledge. Knowledge that the boy was right. Anyone who could make the sand glow was technically allowed to join the Diem. Boys with less power than Kenton had become sand masters. Of course, none of them had been children of the Lord Mastrell. If Kenton joined the Diem, his inability would weaken Praxton's authority by association.

The boy continued to stand, his posture determined. The windblown sand was piling around his legs, burying him up to the knees in a shifting barrow.

"You will not find it easy in the Diem, boy," Praxton hissed. "By the sands, see reason!"

Kenton did not move.

Praxton sighed. "Fine!" he declared. "You may join."

Kenton smiled in victory, pulling his legs free from the dune and scrambling over to join the line of students. Praxton watched motionlessly as the boy moved.

The buffeting wind tore at his robes, sand scraping its way into his eyes and between his lips. Such discomfort would be little compared to the pain Kenton would soon know—the Diem was a place of unforgiving politics, and sheer power was often the means by which a sand master was judged. No, life would not be easy for one so weak, especially since his father was so powerful. No matter what Praxton did, the other students would resent Kenton for supposed coddlings or favoritism.

Oblivious to the trials ahead of him, the young boy made his way to the caves a short distance away. It appeared as if Praxton's final child would also prove to be his largest embarrassment.

CHAPTER ONE

I T almost seemed to Kenton as if the sands were breathing. Heat from the immobile sun reflected off the grains, distorting the air—making the dunes seem like they were composed of tiny coals, white-hot with energy. In the distance, Kenton could hear wind moaning through crevices in the rock. There was only one place in the enormous dune-covered expanse of the Kerla that such rock protrusions could be found: here, beside Mount KraeDa, in the place sacred to the sand masters. Everywhere else the sands were far too deep.

Kenton, now a man, once again stood before a group of mastrells. In many ways he was very similar to the boy who had stood in this exact place eight years before. He had the same close-cropped blondish hair, the same roundish face and determined expression, and—most importantly—the same look of rebellious conviction in his eyes. He now wore the white robes of a sand master, but, unlike most others of his kind, he wore no colored sash. His sash was plain white—the sign of a student who hadn't yet been assigned a rank in the Diem. Tied at his waist was another oddity—a sword. He was the only person in the group of sand masters who was armed.

"Don't tell me you intend to go through with this foolishness?" the man in front of Kenton demanded. Praxton, looking older than the sand itself, stood at the head of the Diem's twenty gold-sashed mastrells. Though he had seen barely sixty years, Praxton's skin was dry, wrinkled like a fruit that had been left out in the sun. Like most sand masters, he wore no beard.

Kenton looked back defiantly, something he had grown very good at doing over the last eight years. Praxton regarded his son with a mixture of disgust and embarrassment. Then, with a sigh, the old man did something unexpected. He moved away from the rest of the mastrells, who stood silently on the rock plateau. Kenton watched with confusion as Praxton waved him over, standing far enough away from the others that the two could have a private conversation. For once, Kenton did as commanded, moving over to hear what the Lord Mastrell had to say.

Praxton looked back at the mastrells, then turned back to Kenton. His eyes only briefly shot down at the sword tied at Kenton's waist before coming up to stare him in the eyes.

"Look, boy," Praxton said, his voice cracking slightly as he spoke. "I have suffered your insolence and games for eight years. The Sand Lord only knows how much trouble you've caused. Why must you constantly defy me?"

Kenton shrugged. "Because I'm good at it?"

Praxton scowled.

"Lord Mastrell," Kenton continued, more serious but no less defiant. "Once a sand master has accepted a rank, he's forever frozen in that place."

"So?" Praxton demanded.

Kenton didn't answer. He had refused advancement four times now, a move that had made him into a fool and a novelty before the rest of the Diem. Inept students were sometimes forced to spend five years as an acolent, but never in the history of sand mastery had anyone remained a student for eight.

Praxton sighed again, reaching down to take a sip of water from his qido. "All right, boy," Praxton finally said. "Despite the pain—despite the shame—I will admit that you've worked hard. The Sand Lord knows you haven't any talent to speak of, but at least you did something with the small amount you have. Give up this stupid decision to run the Path, and tomorrow I'll offer you the rank of fen."

Fen. It was the next to lowest of the nine sand master ranks; only underfen—the rank Kenton had been offered the four previous years—was beneath it.

"No," Kenton said. "I think I want to be a mastrell."

"*Aisha!*" Praxton cursed.

"Don't swear now, Father," Kenton suggested. "Wait until I run the Path successfully. Then what will you do?"

Kenton's defiant words were more optimistic than his heart, however. Even as his father raged, Kenton felt the questions resurfacing.

What on the sands am I doing? Eight years ago no one thought I could even be a sand master, and now I've been offered a respectable rank in the Diem. It isn't what I wanted, but . . .

"Boy, you're inept enough to make the Hundred Idiots look brilliant. Running the Mastrell's Path won't prove anything. It's meant for mastrells—not for simple acolents."

"The Law doesn't say a student cannot run it," Kenton said, thoughts of his inadequacy still strong in his mind.

"I won't make you a mastrell," Praxton warned. "Even if you find all five spheres, I won't do it. The Path is not a test or a proof. Mastrells run it if they want to, but only after they've been advanced. Your success will mean nothing. You'll never be a mastrell—you aren't even worthy to be a sand master!"

Praxton's words burned away Kenton's doubts like water in the sun. If there was one person who could fuel Kenton's sense of defiance, it was Praxton.

"Then I'll be an acolent until the day I die, Lord Mastrell," Kenton replied, folding his arms.

"You can't be a mastrell," Praxton reiterated. "You don't have the power."

"I don't believe in power, Father. I believe in ability. I can do anything a mastrell can; I just have different methods." It was an old argument, one he had been making for the last eight years.

"Can you slatrify?"

Kenton paused. No, that was one thing he couldn't do. Slatrification, the ability to change sand into water, was the ultimate art of sand mastery. It was wildly different from sand mastery's other abilities, and none of Kenton's creativity or ingenuity could replicate it.

"There have been mastrells who couldn't slatrify," Kenton replied weakly.

"Only two," Praxton replied. "And both were able to control over two dozen ribbons of sand at once. How many can you control, boy?"

Kenton ground his teeth. It was a direct question, however, and he couldn't refuse to respond. "One," he finally admitted.

"One," Praxton repeated. "One ribbon. I've never known a mastrell who couldn't control at least fifteen. You're telling me you can do as much with one as they can with fifteen? Why can't you see how preposterous that is?"

Kenton smiled slightly. *Thank you for the encouragement, Father.* "Well, I'll just have to prove it to you then, Lord Mastrell," he said with a mocking bow, turning away from his father.

"The Path was meant for mastrells, boy," Praxton's cracking voice repeated behind him. "Most of them don't even use it—it's too dangerous."

Kenton ignored the old man, instead approaching another sand master who was standing a short distance away. His short frame cast no shadow, for the sun was directly overhead here, in the jagged rocklands south of Mount KraeDa. The sand master was bald and had a slightly fat, oval face. Around his waist was tied the yellow sash of an undermastrell, the rank directly below mastrell. The man smiled as Kenton approached.

"Are you sure you want to do this, Kenton?"

Kenton nodded. "Yes, Elorin, I do."

"Your father's objections are well founded," Elorin cautioned. "The Mastrell's Path was created by a group of men with inflated egos who wanted very desperately to prove themselves better than their peers. It was designed for those with massive power. Mastrells have died running it before."

"I understand," Kenton said, but inwardly he was curious. No one who had run the Path was allowed to reveal its secrets, and for all his studying, Kenton hadn't been able to determine what could be so dangerous about a simple race through the Kerla. Was it the lack of water? Steep cliffs? Neither should have provided much of a challenge to well-trained sand masters.

Elorin continued. "All right then. The Lord Mastrell has asked me to mediate your run. A group of us will watch as you move through the Path, evaluating your progress and making certain you don't cheat. We cannot help you unless you ask, and if we do the intervention will end your run where it stands."

The shorter man reached into his white sand master's robes, pulling out a small red sphere. "There are five of these hidden on the Path," he explained. "Your goal is to find all five. You may start when I say so. You have until the moon passes behind the mountain and reappears on the other side. The test is over the moment you either run out of time or find the fifth sphere."

Kenton looked up. The moon circled the sky once per day, hovering just above the horizon the entire time. Soon it would pass behind Mount KraeDa. He would probably have about an hour, a hundred minutes, to run the Path.

"So I don't have to make it back to the starting point?" Kenton clarified.

Elorin shook his head. "The moment the moon reappears, your run is over. We will count the spheres you have found, and that is your score."

Kenton nodded.

"You may not take your qido with you," Elorin informed him, reaching out a hand to take Kenton's water bottle from his side.

"The sword too," Praxton called from behind, his lips curled downward in their characteristic look of disapproval.

"That is not in the rules, old man," Kenton objected, his hand falling to the hilt.

"A true sand master has no need of such a clumsy weapon," Praxton argued.

"It's not in the rules," Kenton repeated.

"He is right, Lord Mastrell," Elorin agreed. He was frowning too—as kind as the undermastrell was, even he didn't agree with Kenton's insistence on carrying a sword. In the eyes of most sand masters, weapons were crass things, meant for lowly Professions such as soldiers.

Praxton rolled his eyes in a look of frustration, but made no further objections. A few minutes later the last bit of the moon's sphere disappeared behind the mountain.

"May the Sand Lord protect you, young Kenton," Elorin offered.

The Path started simply enough, and Kenton quickly found the first two spheres. The red sandstone globes had been so easy to locate, in fact, that he began to worry that he had missed something. Unfortunately, Kenton knew that he didn't have time to go back and recheck his steps. Either he found them all on the first try, or he failed.

That determination drove Kenton forward as he ran across the top of a rock ledge. Around him the strange formations of stone jutted from the sand floor, some rising hundreds of feet into the air, others barely breaking the surface. The scenery was familiar to him—the sand masters came to this place every year to choose new members and award merits to old ones. It was almost a sacred place, though sand masters tended to be irreligious. None of the Kerla's Kerztian inhabitants came to this place—its sand was far too shallow to sustain a town. In fact, few even knew of its existence. It was a place of the sand masters.

And, for four years, it had been a place of embarrassment—to Kenton at least. Four years of standing before the entire population of the Diem, presenting himself for an advancement that would not be granted. He knew that most of the others considered him a fool—an arrogant fool. At times, he wondered if they might be right. Why did he keep pushing for a rank he did not deserve? Why not be satisfied with what Praxton was willing to give him?

Life in the Diem had not been easy for Kenton. Sand master society was ancient and stratified—new students were immediately given positions of leadership and favor based on their power. Those with lesser ability were made the virtual servants and attendants of those more talented—and such was a situation that continued up through the entire sand master hierarchy.

To them, power was everything. Kenton had watched the other acolents in his group, and seen how easily sand mastery came to them. They didn't have to stretch themselves, didn't have to learn how to control their sand. Their answer to any problem was to throw a dozen ribbons at it and hope it went away. Today, Kenton intended to prove that there was a better way.

Kenton paused, stopping abruptly. He had run out of ground—directly in front of him the sand-covered earth ended in a steep chasm. It rose again perhaps fifty feet away. He could barely make out a flag flapping on the other side of the gorge—a marker to indicate the direction he was to take.

And so the real test begins, Kenton thought, reaching down to grab a handful of sand from the ground. Another sand master, one more powerful, could have leapt the chasm, propelling himself through the air on a stream of sand. Kenton didn't have that option.

So, instead, he jumped off the cliff.

He plummeted toward the ground, his white robes flapping in the sudden wind. He didn't look down, instead concentrating on the sand clutched in his fist.

The sand burst to life.

With an explosion of light, the sand changed from bone white to shimmering mother-of-pearl. Kenton opened his hand as he fell, commanding the sand to move. It shot forward, forming into a ribbon of light that extended from his palm toward the quickly approaching dunes below.

When the sand had reached the ground, he commanded it to gather mass from the dunes below and move back up. A second later there was a shimmering line of mastered sand extending from Kenton to the ground. He was still falling, but as he commanded the sand to push, his descent slowed. The sand worked like a shimmering coil, slowing him more and more as he approached the ground. He came to a stop just a foot above the surface of the dunes, then stepped off the ribbon and dropped to the ground. As he did so, he released the ribbon from his control, and the shimmering sand immediately darkened and fell dead. No longer white, it was now a dull black, its energy spent.

Kenton jogged along the bottom of the ravine, forcing himself not to slow despite the fatigue of sand mastery. He was beginning to regret his insistence on bringing his sword—the weapon seemed to grow more and more heavy as he ran, dragging at his side.

Going along the bottom of the chasm instead of jumping was costing him precious time. He had already wasted about sixty minutes of his hour. He licked his lips, which were growing dry. Sand mastery didn't just take strength, it required water, sucking the precious liquid from the body of the sand master. A sand master had to be careful not to master to the point that his body took permanent damage from dehydration.

Kenton reached the second cliff and looked up, gathering his strength. In the distance he could see a group of white-robed forms. The mastrells, evaluating his progress. Even at a distance, Kenton could sense the finality in their postures. They assumed he was stuck—it was well known that Kenton could barely lift himself a few feet with his sand. Of course, that much in itself was amazing—no other sand master could do so much with only a single ribbon. Amazing or not, however, it wasn't enough to get him to the top of the cliff, which was at least a hundred feet tall.

The mastrells were turning their heads, discussing among themselves in voices far too distant to hear. Ignoring them, Kenton reached down and grabbed another handful of sand. He called it to life, feeling it begging to squirm and shimmer in his hand. The sand shone brightly—more brightly, even, than that of a mastrell. Kenton could only control one ribbon, but it was by far the most powerful ribbon any sand master had ever created.

This had better work . . . Kenton thought to himself.

He let the sand slip forward, dropping to the ground like a stream of water. There, he gathered more sand, calling to life as much as he could handle—enough to make a thin string perhaps twenty feet long. This time, however, he didn't form the sand into the ribbon. Instead he created a step.

He couldn't lift himself very far, true. The higher a sand master lifted himself in the air, the more sand was required, and Kenton could only control a relatively small amount. He could, however, hold himself in place.

Taking a breath, he stepped onto his small platform of sand, pressing his body against the rough stone cliff face. Then, holding on as best he could and not looking down, he began to inch sideways, dropping sand off one edge of the platform and replacing it on the other. He concentrated on making his sand cling to the cliff wall, slipping in cracks and holding to its imperfections, rather than pushing it against the ground. Slowly, Kenton moved to the side, sloping his platform of sand just enough that he moved in a diagonal direction up the wall.

He must have looked incredibly silly. Sand masters were supposed to flow and dance, soaring through the air in clouds of radiant sand, not creep up the side of a wall like a sleepy sandling. Still, the process worked, and barely a few minutes later he was nearing the top of the chasm. It was then that he noticed something—a small ledge about ten feet down the side of the cliff. Perched on the ledge was a small red sphere.

Kenton smiled in triumph, maladroitly climbing onto the top of the ledge. He then shook his rectangle of sand into a ribbon and sent it to collect the sphere. Guided by his commands, the rope of sand wrapped around the sphere and brought it back to its master. There were only two spheres left to find. Unfortunately, he had just over thirty minutes to do so.

The group of mastrells watched him with dumbfounded frowns as he jogged past the marking flag and located the next one in the distance. The rocks were growing more and more frequent now, forming caverns and walls of stone. Kenton moved along on the sandy ground, his eyes searching for any hints of red. The next sphere couldn't be far away—if he guessed right, the Path wound in a circle, and he was nearing the place where he had started. For a moment, his horror returned—had he missed two entire spheres?

A short distance away several lines of glimmering sand marked his silent followers. True to mastrell form, each of them was making a huge display of power, gathering as many ribbons of sand around them as they could manage. While it wasn't actually possible to fly with sand mastery, powerful mastrells could launch themselves in extended leaps that could span hundreds of feet. Each jumping mastrell left a trail of sand behind him—sand pushing against the ground to form a means of propulsion.

The mastrells stopped atop a pillar of rock a short distance away. Kenton slowed his jog to a walk, watching them with careful eyes. The place they landed looked too predetermined to be random—the sphere had to be somewhere close. Kenton searched around him, his eyes seeking out shadows and places that could hide one of the diminutive spheres. Unfortunately, there was no shortage of options.

A short distance away a large wall-like section of rock extended from the sand. It was filled with fist-sized holes, each one extending back into darkness. With a sinking feeling, Kenton realized that this was his next test.

Any one of them could hold a sphere! he thought with an internal moan. If he had been able to control two dozen ribbons, searching through the holes would have taken no time at all. However, using his single ribbon to do the same would probably take longer than he had left.

Yet, it appeared as if that were his only choice. Sighing, Kenton brought a handful of sand to life. Perhaps he would get lucky and choose the right hole. He paused, however, as he prepared to send the ribbon forth. There had to be a better way.

His eyes skimmed the rock wall. Ironically, one thing he had learned from his lack of ability was that sometimes sand mastery wasn't the answer. His eyes almost passed over the solution before his brain registered it. A small pile of black sand. There were only two things that could change sand from white to black—water or sand mastery.

Kenton smiled, approaching the discolored sand. It wasn't pure black, more of a dull grey. It had probably been recharging in the sunlight for a couple of hours now—a few more and it would be completely indistinguishable from the white sand around it. Kenton raised his eyes from the sand, looking at the wall directly above it. Just over his head he noticed a trail of black grains sitting on the lip of one of the holes.

Kenton reached into the hole, retrieving the red sandstone sphere that was hidden in its depths. Though there was a smile on his lips when he turned to look back at the mastrells, inwardly Kenton was worried. If the sand master who had hidden the spheres hadn't been careless—if he had used his hands instead of sand mastery—Kenton would never have found the sphere.

Still, he couldn't help feeling a sense of satisfaction as the mastrells jumped away, twisting ribbons of sand carrying them into the air. Now there was only one sphere left. If Kenton found it, he would have succeeded in a task that baffled many mastrells.

As he moved to begin running again, Kenton noticed that one of the mastrells had stayed behind. Even though the column of rock was far away, somehow Kenton knew that the stooped-over form belonged to his father. The wind wailed through rock hollows around Kenton as he stared up at Praxton's face.

The Lord Mastrell was not pleased. Kenton stared at him for a long moment, trying to project his defiance. Eventually, Praxton raised his hands, summoning a dozen strings of sand from the floor below. They twisted around him like living creatures, their bright translucent glow shifting from color to color in the way of mastered sand. When Praxton jumped, the ribbons threw him into the air, and Kenton was left alone beside the rock wall.

One more. Kenton took a deep breath and started to move again. He was running out of time—not only would the moon soon reappear, but he was beginning to feel the effects of his sand mastery. His mouth was parched, refusing to salivate, and his eyes were beginning to burn. His brow, which had been slick with sweat during the beginning of the run, was now crusted with salty residue. The price a sand master had to pay, the fuel that his art burned, was the water from his own body.

The dry mouth and eyes were the first signs that he was getting close to doing permanent damage to himself. The first thing a sand master learned was to keep track of his water, to pace himself so he didn't overmaster. Students who even approached the point of overmastery were severely punished.

If only I could slatrify, he thought, not for the first time. There was a reason the ability to change sand into water was the most valuable of sand mastery's skills.

Casting such thoughts aside, Kenton continued to jog. The rock walls were rising high around him again. Even as he began to think the area looked familiar, he rounded a corner and stopped. Up ahead he could just barely make out the rock plateau where he had begun the Path. The mastrells stood atop it, waiting for him to approach.

Kenton paused with a groan, leaning against the smooth rock wall.

His breath was beginning to come with more and more difficulty; both running and sand mastery sapped strength, and his dry throat made each breath painful. The mastrells held his qido and its water—he anticipated that first drink with such ferocity that he almost didn't care that he had failed.

And he had failed. Somewhere, back on the Path, he had missed one of the spheres. He had done well—four out of five was a respectable number. Some of the mastrells he knew had only found three. Unfortunately, Kenton couldn't afford anything less than perfection. Praxton wouldn't see the four spheres his son had found, but the one he had missed.

Kenton rested the back of his head against the rock for a moment. He briefly considered turning back to try to find the sphere, but he probably only had ten minutes left. That was barely enough time to make it back to the rock wall where he had found the last sphere. He opened his eyes and stood upright. He knew he had done better than anyone could have assumed.

Kenton kicked away the windblown sand that had gathered at his feet, striding out into the middle of the basin. Realistically, he knew that even a successful run of the Path wouldn't have changed Praxton's mind. The Lord Mastrell was as harsh as the sands themselves; few things impressed him.

Kenton picked up a handful of sand—he would have to use his step method to climb up the back of the rock basin and join the mastrells. He only paused for a moment to regard the strange rock formation around him. The sides were smooth and steep, almost forming a pit with a sand-filled bottom, perhaps fifty feet across. How many years had it taken the Kerla's dry winds to carve such an odd bowl-like formation?

Kenton froze, his abrupt stop kicking up a small spray of sand. As his eyes had scanned the basin, they fell on something so dumbfounding it almost caused him to trip in surprise. There, sitting in the middle of the circular flooring of sand, was a speck of red. It sat like a drop of blood, stark against the white background. Ripples in the sand had caused him to miss it earlier, but now there was no mistaking the red sphere.

Kenton looked up at the mastrells with confusion. They stood along the rim of the basin, their white robes fluttering, as if in unison, before the wind.

Something's wrong. There had to be more—some test. This was the last sphere. It should have been the most difficult to find.

Only a moment later he felt the sand begin to shift beneath his feet.

"Aisha!" Kenton yelped in surprise, jumping backward. It couldn't be . . .

The sand near the sphere began to churn like boiling water. There was something beneath it—something that was rising.

Deep sand! Kenton thought with shock. The sand-filled pit must go down farther than he had assumed.

A black form burst from the ground, burying the sphere in a wave of sand. Kenton gasped in amazement as he regarded the creature that slid from the ground. Sand streamed like water off the twenty-foot-tall monstrosity's carapace as it rose into the air. Its body was formed of bulbous, chitinous segments stacked on top of one another. A pair of arms sprouted from each "waist" where segments met, arms that were tipped with thick, jagged claws. Its head—if that was the right term—was little more than a box with deep black spots instead of eyes, with no visible mouth. The worst thing was, Kenton knew that the bulk of the creature's body was probably still hidden beneath the sands.

He was so busy staring that he was almost crushed as the creature swiped a claw in his direction. Kenton yelped, dodging to the side, dashing toward the wall of the basin. The sandling's body was huge—perhaps ten feet wide. Kenton was going to have a difficult time staying out of its way.

His body, invigorated by adrenaline and excitement, no longer responded sluggishly. His heart began to race, but his mind worked even faster. Kenton had read of deep sandlings, and even seen drawings of them, but he had never visited deep sand in person. Few people—even Kerztians—were foolish enough to wander onto deep sand. Mentally, he ran through the catalogue of deep sandlings he had studied, but this one didn't seem to fit any of the descriptions. Kenton dodged again as the sandling reached for him. The creature seemed to glide through the sand as if it were water—Kenton could barely see the thousands of tiny hairlike tentacles that lined the beast's carapace, the means by which it moved.

All observation was abandoned as the creature's claw slammed down in front of him. Kenton dropped to the sand, barely rolling out of the way as a second claw swiped through the air above him. The creature was incredibly fast—there was a reason deep sand was regarded with terror. The creatures that lurked within its depths were said to be nearly indestructible.

Kenton rolled to his feet, thankful for the hours he had spent sparring with soldiers from the Tower. His movements were quick and dexterous as he whipped his sword free with his left hand and grabbed a handful of sand in the other.

"We cannot intercede unless you ask!" a voice came from above. Kenton didn't spare a look upward, instead focusing on his foe. The creature had eyespots on each side of its head—it would not be easy to surprise. Of course, sandlings were said to have poorly developed sight. Their true sense was the sand itself. It was more than an ability to feel movement; for some reason sandlings could sense the location of even a completely still body. The Kerztians said deep sandlings could actually speak with the sand, though few from Lossand gave credence to their mysticisms.

"Didn't you hear me?" the voice repeated as Kenton dodged again. "Ask us to bring you out!" It belonged to Elorin. Kenton ignored him, calling his sand to life as he spun away from a claw. He raised his sword, deflecting a second attack. The creature's strength was such that his parry barely seemed to do much good, but it did allow him to dodge the attack just long enough to strike.

Even as he turned, Kenton raised his fist, commanding his sand forward. The sand tore out of his palm, streaking toward the sandling's head. It extended like a spear from Kenton's hand, leaving a glowing trail behind. The sand moved so quickly it seemed to scream in the air— Kenton might not be able to control dozens of lines at once, but when it came to a single ribbon, he was unmatched. No sand master could move sand with half as much speed or precision.

The sand snapped against the creature's shell of a head and immediately lost its luster, spraying to the sides like a stream of water hitting a stone wall. Kenton stood in confusion, so stunned that the creature's next attack took him in the side, throwing him back against the stone wall and ripping a deep gash in his shoulder. Kenton's sword dropped to the sand, slipping from stunned fingers.

The sandling was terken. It was impervious to sand mastery.

Kenton cursed again, feeling blood begin to flow from his shoulder. He had, of course, read of terken creatures, but they were supposed to be extremely rare. Only the most ancient and feared of deep sandlings—creatures said to be protected by the Sand Lord himself—had terken shells. How had one come to live here, in the middle of shallow sands and rock formations?

Regardless, it was obvious what he was supposed to do. All sandlings, whether from the deep sands or not, had one powerful weakness: water. The liquid could dissolve their carapaces, melting away their shell and skin, leaving behind nothing but sludge.

It made sense. The final challenge in the Mastrell's Path would test the most powerful of sand mastery's skills—the ability to change sand into water. With slatrification, a sand master could melt away the sandling's shell with barely a thought. Unfortunately, Kenton couldn't slatrify. Suddenly Elorin's suggestion that he escape made a great deal of sense.

Kenton cast his speculations aside, concentrating on staying alive. He was moving more and more slowly; he could feel himself weakening. Trying to ignore the pain of his shoulder, he stooped as he ran, grabbing another handful of sand. As the next attack came he used the mastered sand to give himself a boost, jumping high into the air and tumbling over the claws.

Kenton dropped heavily to the sand, then scrambled in the direction of the sandling's original position. Somewhere in that sand was the sphere. He didn't really need to kill the sandling; he just needed to find the sphere and get away.

He released his sand, dropping it to the ground black and stale. Instead, he placed his hand on the ground near where he had last seen the sphere. He called ribbon after ribbon to life, commanding them to jump away and then releasing them. Sand flew from the ground where he knelt; he commanded and released ribbons in such quick succession that it almost seemed like he could control more than one at a time.

Unfortunately, the sandling did not leave him to his digging. Kenton's jump had confused it, but it quickly reoriented itself. It came at him, the only sound of its movement that of sand rubbing against sand. Kenton continued to dig until the last moment, then dashed away, running desperately. He could feel the dryness on his skin, and each time he blinked his lids seemed to stick to his eyes. His lungs were beginning to burn, and his breaths came painfully. He was approaching the last of his water reserves—he would probably even be chastised for going this far. *For the good of the Diem, one mustn't even come close to over-mastery,* the familiar teaching claimed. It was time to give up.

Just as he made the determination to escape, however, he saw it. Resting beside the far wall of the basin was a speck of red, brighter than the dark drops of his own blood that ran behind him. Crying out, Kenton switched directions, ducking beneath the sandling's arms and dashing so close to its body that he could smell the sulfurous pungency of its carapace.

And, as he ran by the creature, feeling the sand slither beneath his feet from the sandling's motion, he noticed an incredulous sight. There, trapped between two bowl-like chinks in the sandling's carapace, was another red sphere.

Kenton continued his dash, his mind confused. He stopped beside the wall, digging in the sand until his fingers found something round and hard. He pulled the sphere free, looking at it with a frown, then turned his eyes back on the sandling. From this angle he could see it distinctly—a red sphere, just like the five he had already found. There weren't five spheres on the Path, but six.

Kenton dropped the sphere into the pouch at his side, then turned eyes up to the edge of the cliff. Directly above he could see the faces of twenty mastrells looking down at him. He could escape now; his time was probably all but up anyway. He had won—he had found all five spheres. What was he waiting for?

For some reason he looked back at the sandling. Its shell and skin were terken, but its insides . . .

Kenton knew his father wouldn't be satisfied with perfection—he never was. Praxton would demand more. Well, Kenton would give him more.

The mastrells cried out in surprise as Kenton dashed away from the wall, his face resolute.

"Idiot boy!" Praxton's voice sounded behind him.

Kenton brought sand to life, whipping it past the creature and using it to snatch his discarded sword from the sand floor. The blade flashed through the air, carried on fingers of sand. Kenton caught it as he ducked beneath the sandling's first attack, grabbing a second handful of sand as he came up barely inches from the creature's chest.

With a cry of determination, Kenton slammed his sword into the creature's side. The blade slipped off a segment of carapace and crunched through a less-protected line of skin, digging deeply into the soft area between plates. Kenton jammed the weapon in with all the strength he had left.

Suddenly, his sword jerked, then ripped free from his hands, blasted backward by a powerful force. A loud hissing sound exploded from the cut. He had pierced the skin. Kenton caught a faceful of acrid gas— what sandlings had instead of blood—just before one of the monster's legs caught him full in the chest, flinging him into the air.

Even as he soared away from the creature, Kenton called the sand in his fist to life. He commanded it forward, driving it with all of his skill. Kenton slammed against the rock wall at the same time that his sand hit the creature's chest, yet he did not release control of his ribbon. He felt his body slump to the ground, but ignored the pain, commanding his sand to find the cut, to wiggle past the terken carapace into the creature's cavernous insides. He had to fight against air pressure and his own approaching unconsciousness, but he refused to release the sand.

He felt it break through, the resistance of the air pressure suddenly vanishing. With a final surge of effort, Kenton ordered the ribbon around wildly, slicing it through organs inside the monster's chest. The sandling began to shake and spasm as Kenton commanded the sand to move vaguely upward. A second later Kenton found the head, and the sandling grew rigid in a sudden motion, throwing sand in all directions. Then, as silent in death as it had been in life, the creature slumped to the side, its corpse sinking slightly in the sand before coming to a rest.

Kenton didn't know where he found the strength to stumble to his feet and cross the sand. He only vaguely remembered retrieving his sword and using it to pry the sixth sphere free from the creature's carapace.

One image remained stark in his mind, however—that of looking up at the ridge and seeing his father's hard, angry face. Just behind the Lord Mastrell, the enormous Mount KraeDa towered in the distance. As Kenton watched, the silvery edge of the moon began to peek out from behind the mountain.

POSTSCRIPT

I was thinking that *Mistborn: Secret History* was the story in this collection that had the longest time between original idea and final publication, but then I remembered that this is in here.

What to say about *White Sand*? I'm thrilled to, at long last, be publishing this graphic novel. (And I'm very thankful to Dynamite, the publisher, for letting us include this excerpt in the collection.) *White Sand* started very long ago as a simple image: finding a body buried in the sand. The novel was the first I ever wrote—and also the eighth, as I started it over from scratch to try again once I'd learned more about writing. The excerpt you have here is from the 1999 version, not the 1995 version.

It's been a long, long road to publication for this story. I'm still very enamored of the world, and consider it a major part of the Cosmere. (The fact that Khriss is an important figure in the unfolding of these things should indicate that.) However, it was getting hard to plan when I'd be able to squeeze the novel in. I still have to finish so many books, I had no idea where to slot this trilogy in. Then Dynamite came to us and suggested the graphic novel. I was up for this from the get-go, as it was a way to get a canonical version of the story on shelves for readers faster than my schedule would otherwise allow.

As for the scene in question—well, you can see from it that my writing style starting with my very first book was focused on magic systems. At that point, I was reading a lot of The Wheel of Time and other similar books. I loved how powerful the characters were, but I wanted to create something that showed off someone who *wasn't* particularly powerful in the magic. Kenton was born out of me trying to figure out a magic where finesse would be as valuable as raw strength, and sand mastery grew completely out of that.

The idea of a test he had to complete (one many believed he wouldn't be able to pass) using the magic seemed the perfect way to show this off. Indeed, it worked out great—and boy does it pop off the page in graphic novel form. Of all my magic systems, this one seems the best for this medium, because it's so visual.

THE
THRENODITE
SYSTEM

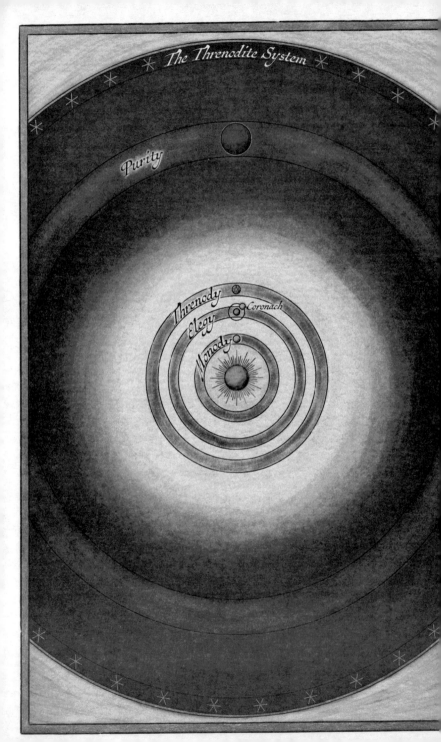

THE THRENODITE SYSTEM

THE Threnodite system is a site warped by an ancient conflict. Long ago, soon after the Shattering, Odium clashed with (and mortally wounded) the Shard Ambition here. Ambition would later be Splintered, though that final act took place in a different location.

The direct clash between two Shards of Adonalsium had a profound effect on the planets of this system. Though the actual battle took place in the vast space between planets—and though the true contest happened mostly in other Realms—the ripples of destruction and change washed through the system. Investigations into how this changed the other planets of the system have been fruitless, as none of them have perpendicularities to allow physical visitation.

Fortunately I have personal access to someone from Threnody, the third planet in the system. Judging by the records that Nazh has provided, I have concluded that some measure of Investiture must have existed on this planet before the battle between Shards. However, the waves of destruction—carrying ripped-off chunks of Ambition's power—twisted both the people and the planet of Threnody.

The planet is home to two separate continents. The larger of the two has been abandoned to something known as "the Evil," a force that even Nazh can speak of only in vague terms. A creeping darkness, a terrible force that consumed the entirety of the continent, feasting upon the souls of men. I do not know how much of this is metaphoric, and how much literal. Expeditions sent from the smaller continent to explore have vanished, and the place is dangerous to visit even in the Cognitive Realm.

The smaller continent is a frontier, mostly unexplored and unnamed, with several bastions of civilization. I have visited one of the largest of these, and even it feels unfinished—set up haphazardly by refugees flee-ing across the ocean, lacking some basic necessities. They focused on making it a fortress first, and a home second. This makes sense, as the people there live in constant fear that the Evil will find a way across the ocean.

Or perhaps they fear the spirits of the dead. People on Threnody are afflicted with a particular ailment that—upon death—sometimes turns them into what we call a Cognitive Shadow. I will leave aside the nature of whether or not a Cognitive Shadow is actually the soul of the person—this is a question for a theologian or a philosopher.

I can, however, explain what is happening magically. A spirit infused with extra Investiture will often imprint upon that very power. Much as the spren of Roshar become self-aware over time because of people's focus on the Surges as being alive, this excess Investiture can attain the ability to remain sapient after being separated from its Physical form.

Locally they think of these things as ghosts, though really they are instantiations of self-aware (well, in this case, barely self-aware) Investi-ture. This is an area deserving of more research. Unfortunately, visiting the planet is difficult, as there is no stable perpendicularity—only very unstable ones that cannot be predicted easily, and have a somewhat morbid origin.

SHADOWS
FOR
SILENCE
IN THE
FORESTS of HELL

THE one you have to watch for is the White Fox," Daggon said, sipping his beer. "They say he shook hands with the Evil itself, that he visited the Fallen World and came back with strange powers. He can kindle fire on even the deepest of nights, and no shade will dare come for his soul. Yes, the White Fox. Meanest bastard in these parts for sure. Pray he doesn't set his eyes on you, friend. If he does, you're dead."

Daggon's drinking companion had a neck like a slender wine bottle and a head like a potato stuck sideways on the top. He squeaked as he spoke, a Lastport accent, voice echoing in the eaves of the waystop's common room. "Why . . . why would he set his eyes on me?"

"That depends, friend," Daggon said, looking about as a few overdressed merchants sauntered in. They wore black coats, ruffled lace poking out the front, and the tall-topped, wide-brimmed hats of fortfolk. They wouldn't last two weeks out here in the Forests.

"It depends?" Daggon's dining companion prompted. "It depends on what?"

"On a lot of things, friend. The White Fox is a bounty hunter, you know. What crimes have you committed? What have you done?"

"Nothing." That squeak was like a rusty wheel.

"Nothing? Men don't come out into the Forests to do 'nothing,' friend."

His companion glanced from side to side. He'd given his name as Earnest. But then, Daggon had given his name as Amity. Names didn't mean a whole lot in the Forests. Or maybe they meant everything. The right ones, that was.

Earnest leaned back, scrunching down that fishing-pole neck of his as if trying to disappear into his beer. He'd bite. People liked hearing about the White Fox, and Daggon considered himself an expert. At least, he was an expert at telling stories to get ratty men like Earnest to pay for his drinks.

I'll give him some time to stew, Daggon thought, smiling to himself. *Let him worry.* Earnest would ply him for more information in a bit.

While he waited, Daggon leaned back, surveying the room. The merchants were making a nuisance of themselves, calling for food, saying they meant to be on their way in an hour. That *proved* them to be fools. Traveling at night in the Forests? Good homesteader stock would do it. Men like these, though . . . they'd probably take less than an hour to violate one of the Simple Rules and bring the shades upon them. Daggon put the idiots out of his mind.

That fellow in the corner, though . . . dressed all in brown, still wearing his hat despite being indoors. That fellow looked truly dangerous. *I wonder if it's him,* Daggon thought. So far as he knew, nobody had ever seen the White Fox and lived. Ten years, over a hundred bounties turned in. Surely someone knew his name. The authorities in the forts paid him the bounties, after all.

The waystop's owner, Madam Silence, passed by the table and deposited Daggon's meal with an unceremonious thump. Scowling, she topped off his beer, spilling a sudsy dribble onto his hand, before limping off. She was a stout woman. Tough. Everyone in the Forests was tough. The ones that survived, at least.

He'd learned that a scowl from Silence was just her way of saying hello. She'd given him an extra helping of venison; she often did that. He liked to think that she had a fondness for him. Maybe someday . . .

Don't be a fool, he thought to himself as he dug into the heavily gravied food and took a few gulps of his beer. Better to marry a stone than Silence Montane. A stone showed more affection. Likely she gave him the extra slice because she recognized the value of a repeat customer. Fewer and fewer people came this way lately. Too many shades. And then there was Chesterton. Nasty business, that.

"So . . . he's a bounty hunter, this Fox?" The man who called himself Earnest seemed to be sweating.

Daggon smiled. Hooked right good, this one was. "He's not just a bounty hunter. He's *the* bounty hunter. Though the White Fox doesn't go for the small-timers—and no offense, friend, but you seem pretty small-time."

His friend grew more nervous. What *had* he done? "But," the man stammered, "he wouldn't come for me—er, pretending I'd done something, of course—anyway, he wouldn't come in here, would he? I mean, Madam Silence's waystop, it's protected. Everyone knows that. Shade of her dead husband lurks here. I had a cousin who saw it, I did."

"The White Fox doesn't fear shades," Daggon said, leaning in. "Now, mind you, I don't *think* he'd risk coming in here—but not because of some shade. Everyone knows this is neutral ground. You've got to have some safe places, even in the Forests. But . . ."

Daggon smiled at Silence as she passed him by, on the way to the kitchens again. This time she didn't scowl at him. He was getting through to her for certain.

"But?" Earnest squeaked.

"Well . . ." Daggon said. "I could tell you a few things about how the White Fox takes men, but you see, my beer is nearly empty. A shame. I think you'd be very interested in how the White Fox caught Makepeace Hapshire. Great story, that."

Earnest squeaked for Silence to bring another beer, though she bustled into the kitchen and didn't hear. Daggon frowned, but Earnest put a coin on the side of the table, indicating he'd like a refill when Silence or her daughter returned. That would do. Daggon smiled to himself and launched into the story.

Silence Montane closed the door to the common room, then turned and pressed her back against it. She tried to still her racing heart by breathing in and out. Had she made any obvious signs? Did they know she'd recognized them?

William Ann passed by, wiping her hands on a cloth. "Mother?" the young woman asked, pausing. "Mother, are you—"

"Fetch the book. Quickly, child!"

William Ann's face went pale, then she hurried into the back pantry. Silence clutched her apron to still her nerves, then joined William Ann as the girl came out of the pantry with a thick, leather satchel. White flour dusted its cover and spine from the hiding place.

Silence took the satchel and opened it on the high kitchen counter, revealing a collection of loose-leaf papers. Most had faces drawn on them. As Silence rifled through the pages, William Ann moved to the peephole for spying into the common room.

For a few moments, the only sound to accompany Silence's thumping heart was that of hastily turned pages.

"It's the man with the long neck, isn't it?" William Ann asked. "I remember his face from one of the bounties."

"That's just Lamentation Winebare, a petty horse thief. He's barely worth two measures of silver."

"Who, then? The man in the back, with the hat?"

Silence shook her head, finding a sequence of pages at the bottom of her pile. She inspected the drawings. *God Beyond,* she thought. *I can't decide if I want it to be them or not.* At least her hands had stopped shaking.

William Ann scurried back and craned her neck over Silence's shoulder. At fourteen, the girl was already taller than her mother. A fine thing to suffer, a child taller than you. Though William Ann grumbled about being awkward and lanky, her slender build foreshadowed a beauty to come. She took after her father.

"Oh, God *Beyond,*" William Ann said, raising a hand to her mouth. "You mean—"

"Chesterton Divide," Silence said. The shape of the chin, the look in the eyes . . . they were the same. "He walked right into our hands, with four of his men." The bounty on those five would be enough to pay her supply needs for a year. Maybe two.

Her eyes flickered to the words below the pictures, printed in harsh, bold letters. **Extremely dangerous. Wanted for murder, rape, extortion.** And, of course, there was the big one at the end: **And assassination.**

Silence had always wondered if Chesterton and his men had intended to kill the governor of the most powerful fort city on this continent, or if it had been an accident. A simple robbery gone wrong. Either way, Chesterton understood what he'd done. Before the incident, he had been a common—if accomplished—highway bandit.

Now he was something greater, something far more dangerous. Chesterton knew that if he were captured, there would be no mercy, no quarter. Lastport had painted Chesterton as an anarchist, a menace, and a psychopath.

Chesterton had no reason to hold back. So he didn't.

Oh, God Beyond, Silence thought, looking at the continuing list of his crimes on the next page.

Beside her, William Ann whispered the words to herself. "He's out there?" she asked. "But where?"

"The merchants," Silence said.

"*What?*" William Ann rushed back to the peephole. The wood there—indeed, all around the kitchen—had been scrubbed so hard that it had been bleached white. Sebruki had been cleaning again.

"I can't see it," William Ann said.

"Look closer." Silence hadn't seen it at first either, even though she spent each night with the book, memorizing its faces.

A few moments later William Ann gasped, raising her hand to her mouth. "That seems so *foolish* of him. Why is he going about perfectly visible like this? Even in disguise."

"Everyone will remember just another band of fool merchants from the fort who thought they could brave the Forests. It's a clever ruse. When they vanish from the paths in a few days, it will be assumed—if anyone cares to wonder—that the shades got them. Besides, this way Chesterton can travel quickly and in the open, visiting waystops and listening for information."

Was this how Chesterton discovered good targets to hit? Had they come through her waystop before? The thought made her stomach turn. She had fed criminals many times; some were regulars. Every man was probably a criminal out in the Forests, if only for ignoring taxes imposed by the fortfolk.

Chesterton and his men were different. She didn't need the list of crimes to know what they were capable of doing.

"Where's Sebruki?" Silence said.

William Ann shook herself, as if coming out of a stupor. "She's feeding the pigs. Shadows! You don't think they'd recognize her, do you?"

"No," Silence said. "I'm worried she'll recognize them." Sebruki might only be eight, but she could be shockingly—disturbingly—observant.

Silence closed the book of bounties. She rested her fingers on the satchel's leather.

"We're going to kill them, aren't we?" William Ann asked.

"Yes."

"How much are they worth?"

"Sometimes, child, it's not about what a man is worth." Silence heard the faint lie in her voice. Times were increasingly tight, with the price of silver from both Bastion Hill and Lastport on the rise.

Sometimes it wasn't about what a man was worth. But this wasn't one of those times.

"I'll get the poison." William Ann left the peephole and crossed the room.

"Something light, child," Silence cautioned. "These are dangerous men. They'll notice if things are out of the ordinary."

"I'm not a fool, Mother," William Ann said dryly. "I'll use fenweed. They won't taste it in the beer."

"Half dose. I don't want them collapsing at the table."

William Ann nodded, entering the old storage room, where she closed the door and began prying up floorboards to get to the poisons. Fenweed would leave the men cloudy-headed and dizzy, but wouldn't kill them.

Silence didn't dare risk something more deadly. If suspicion ever came back to her waystop, her career—and likely her life—would end. She needed to remain, in the minds of travelers, the crotchety but fair innkeeper who didn't ask too many questions. Her waystop was a place of perceived safety, even for the roughest of criminals. She bedded down each night with a heart full of fear that someone would realize a suspicious number of the White Fox's bounties stayed at Silence's waystop in the days preceding their demise.

She went into the pantry to put away the bounty book. Here, too, the walls had been scrubbed clean, the shelves freshly sanded and dusted. That child. Who had heard of a child who would rather clean than play? Of course, given what Sebruki had been through . . .

Silence could not help reaching onto the top shelf and feeling the crossbow she kept there. Silver boltheads. She kept it for shades, and hadn't yet turned it against a man. Drawing blood was too dangerous in the Forests. It still comforted her to know that in case of a true emergency, she had the weapon at hand.

Bounty book stowed, she went to check on Sebruki. The child was indeed caring for the pigs. Silence liked to keep a healthy stock, though of course not for eating. Pigs were said to ward away shades. She used any tool she could to make the waystop seem more safe.

Sebruki knelt inside the pig shack. The short girl had dark skin and long, black hair. Nobody would have taken her for Silence's daughter, even if they hadn't heard of Sebruki's unfortunate history. The child hummed to herself, scrubbing at the wall of the enclosure.

"Child?" Silence asked.

Sebruki turned to her and smiled. What a difference one year could make. Once, Silence would have sworn that this child would never smile again. Sebruki had spent her first three months at the waystop staring at walls. No matter where Silence had put her, the child had moved to the nearest wall, sat down, and stared at it all day. Never speaking a word. Eyes dead as those of a shade . . .

"Aunt Silence?" Sebruki asked. "Are you well?"

"I'm fine, child. Just plagued by memories. You're . . . cleaning the *pig shack* now?"

"The walls need a good scrubbing," Sebruki said. "The pigs do so like it to be clean. Well, Jarom and Ezekiel prefer it that way. The others don't seem to care."

"You don't need to clean so hard, child."

"I like doing it," Sebruki said. "It feels good. It's something I can do. To help."

Well, it was better to clean the walls than stare blankly at them all day. Today, Silence was happy for anything that kept the child busy. Anything, so long as she didn't enter the common room.

"I think the pigs will like it," Silence said. "Why don't you keep at it in here for a while?"

Sebruki eyed her. "What's wrong?"

Shadows. She was so observant. "There are some men with rough tongues in the common room," Silence said. "I won't have you picking up their cussing."

"I'm not a child, Aunt Silence."

"Yes you are," Silence said firmly. "And you'll obey. Don't think I won't take a switch to your backside."

Sebruki rolled her eyes, but went back to work and began humming to herself. Silence let a little of her grandmother's ways out when she spoke with Sebruki. The child responded well to sternness. She seemed to crave it, perhaps as a symbol that someone was in control.

Silence wished she actually were in control. But she was a Forescout— the surname taken by her grandparents and the others who had left Homeland first and explored this continent. Yes, she was a Forescout, and she'd be damned before she'd let anyone know how absolutely powerless she felt much of the time.

Silence crossed the backyard of the large inn, noting William Ann inside the kitchen mixing a paste to dissolve in the beer. Silence passed her by and looked in on the stable. Unsurprisingly, Chesterton had said they'd be leaving after their meal. While a lot of folk sought the relative safety of a waystop at night, Chesterton and his men would be accustomed to sleeping in the Forests. Even with the shades about, they would feel more comfortable in a camp of their own devising than they would in a waystop bed.

Inside the stable, Dob—the old stable hand—had just finished brushing down the horses. He wouldn't have watered them. Silence had a standing order to not do that until last.

"This is well done, Dob," Silence said. "Why don't you take your break now?"

He nodded to her with a mumbled, "Thank'ya, mam." He'd find the front porch and his pipe, as always. Dob hadn't two wits to rub together, and he hadn't a clue about what she really did at the waystop, but he'd been with her since before William's death. He was as loyal a man as she'd ever found.

Silence shut the door after him, then fetched some pouches from the locked cabinet at the rear of the stable. She checked each one in the dim light, then set them on the grooming table and heaved the first saddle onto its owner's back.

She was near finished with the saddling when the door eased open. She froze, immediately thinking of the pouches on the table. Why hadn't she stuffed them in her apron? Sloppy!

"Silence Forescout," a smooth voice said from the doorway.

Silence stifled a groan and turned to confront her visitor. "Theopolis," she said. "It's not polite to sneak about on a woman's property. I should have you thrown out for trespassing."

"Now, now. That would be rather like . . . the horse kicking at the man who feeds him, hmmm?" Theopolis leaned his gangly frame against the doorway, folding his arms. He wore simple clothing, no markings of his station. A fort tax collector often didn't want random passers to know of his profession. Clean-shaven, his face always had that same patronizing smile on it. His clothing was too clean, too new to be that of one who lived out in the Forests. Not that he was a dandy, nor was he a fool. Theopolis was dangerous, just a different kind of dangerous from most.

"Why are you here, Theopolis?" she said, hefting the last saddle onto the back of a snorting roan gelding.

"Why do I always come to you, Silence? It's not because of your cheerful countenance, hmmm?"

"I'm paid up on taxes."

"That's because you're mostly exempt from taxes," Theopolis said. "But you haven't paid me for last month's shipment of silver."

"Things have been a little dry lately. It's coming."

"And the bolts for your crossbow?" Theopolis asked. "One wonders if you're trying to forget about the price of those silver boltheads, hmmm? And the shipment of replacement sections for your protection rings?"

His whining accent made her wince as she buckled the saddle on. Theopolis. Shadows, what a day!

"Oh my," Theopolis said, walking over to the grooming table. He picked up one of the pouches. "What are these, now? That looks like wetleek sap. I've heard that it glows at night if you shine the right kind of light upon it. Is this one of the White Fox's mysterious secrets?"

She snatched the pouch away. "Don't say that name," she hissed.

He grinned. "You have a bounty! Delightful. I have always wondered how you tracked them. Poke a pinhole in that, attach it to the underside of the saddle, then follow the dripping trail it leaves? Hmmm? You could probably track them a long way, kill them far from here. Keep suspicion off the little waystop?"

Yes, Theopolis was dangerous, but she needed *someone* to turn in her bounties for her. Theopolis was a rat, and like all rats he knew the best holes, troughs, and crannies. He had connections in Lastport, and had managed to get her the money in the name of the White Fox without revealing her.

"I've been tempted to turn you in lately, you know," Theopolis said. "Many a group keeps a betting pool on the identity of the infamous Fox. I could be a rich man with this knowledge, hmmm?"

"You're already a rich man," she snapped. "And though you're many things, you are not an idiot. This has worked just fine for a decade. Don't tell me you'd trade wealth for a little notoriety?"

He smiled, but did not contradict her. He kept half of what she earned from each bounty. It was a fine arrangement for Theopolis. No danger to him, which was how she knew he liked it. He was a civil servant, not a bounty hunter. The only time she'd seen him kill, the man he'd murdered couldn't fight back.

"You know me too well, Silence," Theopolis said with a laugh. "Too well indeed. My, my. A bounty! I wonder who it is. I'll have to go look in the common room."

"You'll do nothing of the sort. Shadows! You think the face of a tax collector won't spook them? Don't you go walking in and spoiling things."

"Peace, Silence," he said, still grinning. "I obey your rules. I am careful not to show myself around here often, and I don't bring suspicion to you. I couldn't stay today anyway; I merely came to give you an offer. Only now you probably won't need it! Ah, such a pity. After all the trouble I went to in your name, hmmm?"

She felt cold. "What help could you possibly give me?"

He took a sheet of paper from his satchel, then carefully unfolded it with too-long fingers. He moved to hold it up, but she snatched it from him.

"What is this?"

"A way to relieve you of your debt, Silence! A way to prevent you from ever having to worry again."

The paper was a writ of seizure, an authorization for Silence's creditors—Theopolis—to claim her property as payment. The forts claimed jurisdiction over the roadways and the land to either side of them. They did send soldiers out to patrol them. Occasionally.

"I take it back, Theopolis," she spat. "You most certainly *are* a fool. You'd give up everything we have for a greedy land snatch?"

"Of course not, Silence. This wouldn't be giving up anything at all! Why, I *do* so feel bad seeing you constantly in my debt. Wouldn't it be more efficient if I took over the finances of the waystop? You would remain working here, and hunting bounties, as you always have. Only, you would no longer have to worry about your debts, hmmm?"

She crumpled the paper in her hand. "You'd turn me and mine into slaves, Theopolis."

"Oh, don't be so dramatic. Those in Lastport have begun to worry that such an important waypoint as this is owned by an unknown element. You are drawing attention, Silence. I should think that is the last thing you want."

Silence crumpled the paper further in her hand, fist tight. Horses shuffled in their stalls. Theopolis grinned.

"Well," he said. "Perhaps it won't be needed. Perhaps this bounty of yours is a big one, hmmm? Any clues to give me, so I don't sit wondering all day?"

"Get out," she whispered.

"Dear Silence," he said. "Forescout blood, stubborn to the last breath. They say your grandparents were the first of the first. The first people to come scout this continent, the first to homestead the Forests . . . the first to stake a claim on hell itself."

"Don't call the Forests that. This is my home."

"But it is how men saw this land, before the Evil. Doesn't that make you curious? Hell, land of the damned, where the shadows of the dead made their home. I keep wondering: Is there really a shade of your departed husband guarding this place, or is it just another story you tell people? To make them feel safe, hmmm? You spend a fortune in silver. That offers the real protection, and I never *have* been able to find a record of your marriage. Of course, if there wasn't one, that would make dear William Ann a—"

"*Go.*"

He grinned, but tipped his hat to her and stepped out. She heard him climb into the saddle, then ride off. Night would soon fall; it was probably too much to hope that the shades would take Theopolis. She'd long suspected that he had a hiding hole somewhere near, probably a cavern he kept lined with silver.

She breathed in and out, trying to calm herself. Theopolis was frustrating, but he didn't know everything. She forced her attention back to the horses and got out a bucket of water. She dumped the contents of the pouches into it, then gave a hearty dose to the horses, who each drank thirstily.

Pouches that dripped sap in the way Theopolis indicated would be too easy to spot. What would happen when her bounties removed their saddles at night and found the pouches? They'd know someone was coming for them. No, she needed something less obvious.

"How am I going to manage this?" she whispered as a horse drank from her bucket. "Shadows. They're reaching for me on all sides."

Kill Theopolis. That was probably what Grandmother would have done. She considered it.

No, she thought. *I won't become that. I won't become her.* Theopolis was a thug and a scoundrel, but he had not broken any laws, nor had he done anyone direct harm that she knew. There had to be rules, even out here.

There had to be lines. Perhaps in that respect, she wasn't so different from the fortfolk.

She'd find another way. Theopolis only had a writ of debt; he had been required to show it to her. That meant she had a day or two to come up with his money. All neat and orderly. In the fort cities, they claimed to have civilization. Those rules gave her a chance.

She left the stable. A glance through the window into the common room showed her William Ann delivering drinks to the "merchants" of Chesterton's gang. Silence stopped to watch.

Behind her, the Forests shivered in the wind.

Silence listened, then turned to face them. You could tell fortfolk by the way they refused to face the Forests. They averted their eyes, never looking into the depths. Those solemn trees covered almost every inch of this continent, those leaves shading the ground. Still. Silent. Animals lived out there, but fort surveyors declared that there were no predators. The shades had gotten those long ago, drawn by the shedding of blood.

Staring into the Forests seemed to make them . . . retreat. The darkness of their depths withdrew, the stillness gave way to the sound of rodents picking through fallen leaves. A Forescout knew to look the Forests straight on. A Forescout knew that the surveyors were wrong. There *was* a predator out there. The Forest itself was one.

Silence turned and walked to the door into the kitchen. Keeping the waystop had to be her first goal, so she was committed to collecting Chesterton's bounty now. If she couldn't pay Theopolis, she had little faith that everything would stay the same. He'd have a hand around her throat, as she couldn't leave the waystop. She had no fort citizenship, and times were too tight for the local homesteaders to take her in. No, she'd *have* to stay and work the waystop for Theopolis, and he would squeeze her dry, taking larger and larger percentages of the bounties.

She pushed open the door to the kitchen. It—

Sebruki sat at the kitchen table holding the crossbow in her lap.

"God Beyond!" Silence gasped, pulling the door closed as she stepped inside. "Child, what are you—"

Sebruki looked up at her. Those haunted eyes were back, eyes void of life and emotion. Eyes like a shade's.

"We have visitors, Aunt Silence," Sebruki said in a cold, monotone voice. The crossbow's winding crank sat next to her. She had managed to load the thing and cock it, all on her own. "I coated the bolt's tip with blackblood. I did that right, didn't I? That way, the poison will kill him for sure."

"Child . . ." Silence stepped forward.

Sebruki turned the crossbow in her lap, holding it at an angle to support it, one small hand on the trigger. The point turned toward Silence.

Sebruki stared ahead, eyes blank.

"This won't work, Sebruki," Silence said, stern. "Even if you were able to lift that thing into the common room, you wouldn't hit him—and even if you did, his men would kill us all in retribution!"

"I wouldn't mind," Sebruki said softly. "So long as I got to kill him. So long as I pulled the trigger."

"You care nothing for us?" Silence snapped. "I take you in, give you a home, and this is your payment? You steal a weapon? You *threaten* me?"

Sebruki blinked.

"What is wrong with you?" Silence said. "You'd shed blood in this place of sanctuary? Bring the shades down upon us, beating at our protections? If they got through, they'd kill everyone under my roof! People I've promised safety. How *dare* you!"

Sebruki shook, as if coming awake. Her mask broke and she dropped the crossbow. Silence heard a snap, and the catch released. She felt the bolt pass within an inch of her cheek, then break the window behind.

Shadows! Had the bolt grazed Silence? Had Sebruki *drawn blood*? Silence reached up with a shaking hand, but blessedly felt no blood. The bolt hadn't hit her.

A moment later Sebruki was in her arms, sobbing. Silence knelt down, holding the child close. "Hush, dear one. It's all right. It's all right."

"I heard it all," Sebruki whispered. "Mother never cried out. She knew I was there. She was strong, Aunt Silence. That was why I could be strong, even when the blood came down. Soaking my hair. I heard it. *I heard it all.*"

Silence closed her eyes, holding Sebruki tight. She herself had been the only one willing to investigate the smoking homestead. Sebruki's father had stayed at the waystop on occasion. A good man. As good a man as was left after the Evil took Homeland, that was.

In the smoldering remains of the homestead, Silence had found the corpses of a dozen people. Each family member had been slaughtered by Chesterton and his men, right down to the children. The only one left had been Sebruki, the youngest, who had been shoved into the crawl space under the floorboards in the bedroom.

She'd lain there, soaked in her mother's blood, soundless even as Silence found her. She'd only discovered the girl because Chesterton had been careful, lining the room with silver dust to protect against shades as he prepared to kill. Silence had tried to recover some of the dust that had trickled between the floorboards, and had run across eyes staring up at her through the slits.

Chesterton had burned thirteen different homesteads over the last year. Over fifty people murdered. Sebruki was the only one who had escaped him.

The girl trembled as she heaved with sobs. "Why . . . Why?"

"There is no reason. I'm sorry." What else could she do? Offer some foolish platitude or comfort about the God Beyond? These were the Forests. You didn't survive on platitudes.

Silence did hold the girl until her crying began to subside. William Ann entered, then stilled beside the kitchen table, holding a tray of empty mugs. Her eyes flickered toward the fallen crossbow, then at the broken window.

"You'll kill him?" Sebruki whispered. "You'll bring him to justice?"

"Justice died in Homeland," Silence said. "But yes, I'll kill him. I promise it to you, child."

Stepping timidly, William Ann picked up the crossbow, then turned it, displaying its now broken bow. Silence breathed out. She should never have left the thing where Sebruki could get to it.

"Care for the patrons, William Ann," Silence said. "I'll take Sebruki upstairs."

William Ann nodded, glancing at the broken window again.

"No blood was shed," Silence said. "We will be fine. Though if you get a moment, see if you can find the bolt. The head is silver." This was hardly a time when they could afford to waste money.

William Ann stowed the crossbow in the pantry as Silence carefully set Sebruki on a kitchen stool. The girl clung to her, refusing to let go, so Silence relented and held her for a time longer.

William Ann took a few deep breaths, as if to calm herself, then pushed back out into the common room to distribute drinks.

Eventually, Sebruki let go long enough for Silence to mix a draught. She carried the girl up the stairs to the loft above the common room, where the three of them made their beds. Dob slept in the stable and the guests in the nicer rooms on the second floor.

"You're going to make me sleep," Sebruki said, regarding the cup with reddened eyes.

"The world will seem a brighter place in the morning," Silence said. *And I can't risk you sneaking out after me tonight.*

The girl reluctantly took the draught, then drank it down. "I'm sorry. About the crossbow."

"We will find a way for you to work off the cost of fixing it."

That seemed to comfort Sebruki. She was a homesteader, Forests born. "You used to sing to me at night," Sebruki said softly, closing her eyes, lying back. "When you first brought me here. After . . . After . . ." She swallowed.

"I wasn't certain you noticed." Silence hadn't been certain Sebruki noticed anything, during those times.

"I did."

Silence sat down on the stool beside Sebruki's cot. She didn't feel like singing, so she began humming. It was the lullaby she'd sung to William Ann during the hard times right after her birth.

Before long, the words came out, unbidden:

"Hush now, my dear one . . . be not afraid. Night comes upon us, but sunlight will break. Sleep now, my dear one . . . let your tears fade. Darkness surrounds us, but someday we'll wake. . . ."

She held Sebruki's hand until the child fell asleep. The window by the bed overlooked the courtyard, so Silence could see as Dob brought out Chesterton's horses. The five men in their fancy merchant clothing stomped down off the porch and climbed into their saddles.

They rode in a file out onto the roadway; then the Forests enveloped them.

One hour after nightfall, Silence packed her rucksack by the light of the hearth.

Her grandmother had kindled that hearth's flame, and it had been burning ever since. She'd nearly lost her life lighting the fire, but she hadn't been willing to pay any of the fire merchants for a start. Silence shook her head. Grandmother always had bucked convention. But then, was Silence any better?

Don't kindle flame, don't shed the blood of another, don't run at night. These things draw shades. The Simple Rules, by which every homesteader lived. She'd broken all three on more than one occasion. It was a wonder she hadn't been withered away into a shade by now.

The fire's warmth seemed a distant thing as she prepared to kill. Silence glanced at the old shrine, really just a closet, that she kept locked. The flames reminded her of her grandmother. At times, she thought of the fire *as* her grandmother. Defiant of both the shades and the forts, right until the end. She'd purged the waystop of other reminders of Grandmother, all save the shrine to the God Beyond. That was set behind a locked door beside the pantry, and next to the door had once hung her grandmother's silver dagger, symbol of the old religion.

That dagger was etched with the symbols of divinity as a warding. Silence now carried it in a sheath at her side, not for its wardings, but because it was silver. One could never have too much silver in the Forests.

She packed the sack carefully, first putting in her medicine kit and then a good-sized pouch of silver dust to heal withering. She followed that with ten empty sacks of thick burlap, tarred on the inside to prevent their contents from leaking. Finally, she added an oil lamp. She wouldn't want to use it, as she didn't trust fire. Fire could draw shades. However, she'd found it useful to have on prior outings, so she brought it. She'd only light it if she ran across someone who already had a fire started.

Once done, she hesitated, then went to the old storage room. She removed the floorboards and took out the small, dry-packed keg that lay beside the poisons.

Gunpowder.

"Mother?" William Ann asked, causing her to jump. She hadn't heard the girl enter the kitchen.

Silence nearly dropped the keg in her startlement, and that nearly stopped her heart. She cursed herself for a fool, tucking the keg under her arm. It couldn't explode without fire. She knew that much.

"Mother!" William Ann said, looking at the keg.

"I probably won't need it."

"But—"

"I know. Hush." She walked over and placed the keg into her sack. Attached to the side of the keg, with cloth stuffed between the metal arms, was her grandmother's firestarter. Igniting gunpowder counted as kindling flames, at least in the eyes of the shades. It drew them almost as quickly as blood did, day or night. The early refugees from Homeland had discovered that in short order.

In some ways, blood was easier to avoid. A simple nosebleed or issue of blood wouldn't draw the shades; they wouldn't even notice. It had to be the blood of another, shed by your hands—and they would go for the one who shed the blood first. Of course, after that person was dead, they often didn't care who they killed next. Once enraged, shades were dangerous to all nearby.

Only after Silence had the gunpowder packed did she notice that William Ann was dressed for traveling in trousers and boots. She carried a sack like Silence's.

"What do you think you're about, William Ann?" Silence asked.

"You intend to kill five men who had only half a dose of fenweed by yourself, Mother?"

"I've done similar before. I've learned to work on my own."

"Only because you didn't have anyone else to help." William Ann slung her sack onto her shoulder. "That's no longer the case."

"You're too young. Go back to bed; watch the waystop until I return."

William Ann showed no signs of budging.

"Child, I told you—"

"Mother," William Ann said, taking her arm firmly, "you aren't a *youth* anymore! You think I don't see your limp getting worse? You can't do everything by yourself! You're going to have to start letting me help you sometime, dammit!"

Silence regarded her daughter. Where had that fierceness come from? It was hard to remember that William Ann, too, was Forescout stock. Grandmother would have been disgusted by her, and that made Silence proud. William Ann had actually had a childhood. She wasn't weak, she was just . . . normal. A woman could be strong without having the emotions of a brick.

"Don't you cuss at your mother," Silence finally told the girl.

William Ann raised an eyebrow.

"You may come," Silence said, prying her arm out of her daughter's grip. "But you *will* do as you are told."

William Ann let out a deep breath, then nodded eagerly. "I'll warn Dob we're going." She walked out, adopting the natural slow step of a homesteader as she entered the darkness. Even though she was within the protection of the waystop's silver rings, she knew to follow the Simple Rules. Ignoring them when you were safe led to lapses when you weren't.

Silence got out two bowls, then mixed two different types of glow-paste. When finished, she poured them into separate jars, which she packed into her sack.

She stepped outside into the night. The air was crisp, chill. The Forests had gone silent.

The shades were out, of course.

A few of them moved across the grassy ground, visible by their own soft glow. Ethereal, translucent, the ones nearby right now were old shades; they barely had human forms any longer. The heads rippled, faces shifting like smoke rings. They trailed waves of whiteness about an arm's length behind them. Silence had always imagined that as the tattered remains of their clothing.

No woman, not even a Forescout, looked upon shades without feeling a coldness inside of her. The shades were about during the day, of course; you just couldn't see them. Kindle fire, draw blood, and they'd come for you even then. At night, though, they were different. Quicker to respond to infractions. At night they also responded to rapid motions, which they never did during the day.

Silence took out one of the glowpaste jars, bathing the area around her in a pale green light. The light was dim, but was even and steady, unlike torchlight. Torches were unreliable, since you couldn't relight them if they went out.

William Ann waited at the front with the lantern poles. "We will need to move quietly," Silence told her while affixing the jars to the poles. "You may speak, but do so in a whisper. I said you will obey me. You will, in all things, immediately. These men we're after . . . they will kill you, or worse, without giving the deed a passing thought."

William Ann nodded.

"You're not scared enough," Silence said, slipping a black covering around the jar with the brighter glowpaste. That plunged them into darkness, but the Starbelt was high in the sky today. Some of that light would filter down through the leaves, particularly if they stayed near the road.

"I—" William Ann began.

"You remember when Harold's hound went mad last spring?" Silence asked. "Do you remember that look in the hound's eyes? No recognition? Eyes that lusted for the kill? Well, that's what these men are, William Ann. Rabid. They need to be put down, same as that hound. They won't see you as a person. They'll see you as meat. Do you understand?"

William Ann nodded. Silence could see that she was still more excited than afraid, but there was no helping that. Silence handed William Ann the pole with the darker glowpaste. It had a faint blue light to it but didn't illuminate much. Silence put the other pole to her right shoulder, sack over her left, then nodded toward the roadway.

Nearby, a shade drifted toward the boundary of the waystop. When it touched the thin barrier of silver on the ground, the silver crackled like sparks and drove the thing backward with a sudden jerk. The shade floated the other way.

Each touch like that cost Silence money. The touch of a shade ruined silver. That was what her patrons paid for: a waystop whose boundary had not been broken in over a hundred years, with a long-standing tradition that no unwanted shades were trapped within. Peace, of a sort. The best the Forests offered.

William Ann stepped across the boundary, which was marked by the curve of the large silver hoops jutting from the ground. They were anchored below by concrete so you couldn't just pull one up. Replacing an overlapping section from one of the rings—she had three concentric ones surrounding her waystop—required digging down and unchaining the section. It was a lot of work, which Silence knew intimately. A week didn't pass that they didn't rotate or replace one section or another.

The shade nearby drifted away. It didn't acknowledge them. Silence didn't know if regular people were invisible to them unless the rules were broken, or if the people just weren't worthy of attention until then.

She and William Ann moved out onto the dark roadway, which was somewhat overgrown. No road in the Forests was well maintained. Perhaps if the forts ever made good on their promises, that would change. Still, there was travel. Homesteaders traveling to one fort or another to trade food. The grains grown out in Forest clearings were richer, tastier than what could be produced up in the mountains. Rabbits and turkeys caught in snares or raised in hutches could be sold for good silver.

Not hogs. Only someone in one of the forts would be so crass as to eat a pig.

Anyway, there *was* trade, and that kept the roadway worn, even if the trees around did have a tendency to reach down their boughs—like grasping arms—to try to cover up the pathway. Reclaim it. The Forests did not like that people had infested them.

The two women walked carefully and deliberately. No quick motions. Walking so, it seemed an eternity before something appeared on the road in front of them.

"There!" William Ann whispered.

Silence released her tension in a breath. Something glowing blue marked the roadway in the light of the glowpaste. Theopolis's guess at how she tracked her quarries had been a good one, but incomplete. Yes, the light of the paste also known as Abraham's Fire did make drops of wetleek sap glow. By coincidence, wetleek sap *also* caused a horse's bladder to loosen.

Silence inspected the line of glowing sap and urine on the ground. She'd been worried that Chesterton and his men would set off into the Forests soon after leaving the waystop. That hadn't been likely, but still she'd worried.

Now she was sure she had the trail. If Chesterton cut into the Forests, he'd do it a few hours after leaving the waystop, to be more certain their cover was safe. She closed her eyes and breathed a sigh of relief, then found herself offering a prayer of thanks by rote. She hesitated. Where had that come from? It had been a long time.

She shook her head, rising and continuing down the road. By drugging all five horses, she got a steady sequence of markings to follow.

The Forests felt . . . dark this night. The light of the Starbelt above didn't seem to filter through the branches as well as it should. And there seemed to be more shades than normal, prowling between the trunks of trees, glowing just faintly.

William Ann clung to her lantern pole. The child had been out in the night before, of course. No homesteader looked forward to doing so, but none shied away from it either. You couldn't spend your life trapped inside, frozen by fear of the darkness. Live like that, and . . . well, you were no better off than the people in the forts. Life in the Forests was hard, often deadly. But it was also free.

"Mother," William Ann whispered as they walked. "Why don't you believe in God anymore?"

"Is this really the time, girl?"

William Ann looked down as they passed another line of urine, glowing blue on the roadway. "You always say something like that."

"And I'm usually trying to avoid the question when you ask it," Silence said. "But I'm also not usually walking the Forests at night."

"It just seems important to me now. You're wrong about me not being afraid enough. I can hardly breathe, but I do know how much trouble the waystop is in. You're always so angry after Master Theopolis visits. You don't change our border silver as often as you used to. One out of two days, you don't eat anything but bread."

"And you think this has to do with God . . . why?"

William Ann kept looking down.

Oh, shadows, Silence thought. *She thinks we're being punished.* Fool girl. Foolish as her father.

They passed the Old Bridge, walking its rickety wooden planks. When the light was better, you could still pick out timbers from the New Bridge down in the chasm below, representing the promises of the forts and their gifts, which always looked pretty but frayed before long. Sebruki's father had been one of those who had come put the Old Bridge back up.

"I believe in the God Beyond," Silence said, after they reached the other side.

"But—"

"I don't worship," Silence said, "but that doesn't mean I don't believe. The old books, they called this land the home of the damned. I doubt that worshipping does any good if you're already damned. That's all."

William Ann didn't reply.

They walked another good two hours. Silence considered taking a shortcut through the woods, but the risk of losing the trail and having to double back felt too dangerous. Besides. Those markings, glowing a soft blue-white in the unseen light of the glowpaste . . . those were something *real*. A lifeline of light in the shadows all around. Those lines represented safety for her and her children.

With both of them counting the moments between urine markings, they didn't miss the turnoff by much. A few minutes walking without seeing a mark, and they turned back without a word, searching the sides of the path. Silence had worried this would be the most difficult part of the hunt, but they easily found where the men had turned into the Forests. A glowing hoofprint formed the sign; one of the horses had stepped in another's urine on the roadway, then tracked it into the Forests.

Silence set down her pack and opened it to retrieve her garrote, then held a finger to her lips and motioned for William Ann to wait by the road. The girl nodded. Silence couldn't make out much of her features in the darkness, but she did hear the girl's breathing grow more rapid.

Being a homesteader and accustomed to going out at night was one thing. Being alone in the Forests . . .

Silence took the blue glowpaste jar and covered it with her handkerchief. Then she took off her shoes and stockings and crept out into the night. Each time she did this, she felt like a child again, going into the Forests with her grandfather. Toes in the dirt, testing for crackling leaves or twigs that would snap and give her away.

She could almost hear his voice giving instructions, telling her how to judge the wind and use the sound of rustling leaves to mask her as she crossed noisy patches. He'd loved the Forests until the day they'd claimed him. *Never call this land hell,* he had said. *Respect the land as you would a dangerous beast, but do not hate it.*

Shades slid through the trees nearby, almost invisible with nothing to illuminate them. She kept her distance, but even so, she occasionally turned to see one of the things drifting past her. Stumbling into a shade could kill you, but that kind of accident was uncommon. Unless enraged, shades moved away from people who got too close, as if blown by a soft breeze. So long as you were moving slowly—and you *should* be—you would be all right.

She kept the handkerchief around the jar except when she wanted to check specifically for any markings. Glowpaste illuminated shades, and shades that glowed too brightly might give warning of her approach.

A groan sounded nearby. Silence froze, heart practically bursting from her chest. Shades made no sound; that had been a man. Tense, silent, she searched until she caught sight of him, well hidden in the hollow of a tree. He moved, massaging his temples. The headaches from William Ann's poison were upon him.

Silence considered, then crept around the back of the tree. She crouched down, then waited a painful five minutes for him to move. He reached up again, rustling the leaves.

Silence snapped forward and looped her garrote around his neck, then pulled tight. Strangling wasn't the best way to kill a man in the Forests. It was so slow.

The guard started to thrash, clawing at his throat. Shades nearby halted.

Silence pulled tighter. The guard, weakened by the poison, tried to kick at her with his legs. She shuffled backward, still holding tightly, watching those shades. They looked around like animals sniffing the air. A few of them started to dim, their own faint natural luminescence fading, their forms bleeding from white to black.

Not a good sign. Silence felt her heartbeat like thunder inside. *Die, damn you!*

The man finally stopped jerking, motions growing more lethargic. After he trembled one final time and fell still, Silence waited there for a painful eternity, holding her breath. Finally the shades nearby faded back to white, then drifted off in their meandering directions.

She unwound the garrote, breathing out in relief. After a moment to get her bearings, she left the corpse and crept back to William Ann.

The girl did her proud; she'd hidden herself so well that Silence didn't see her until she whispered, "Mother?"

"Yes," Silence said.

"Thank the God Beyond," William Ann said, crawling out of the hollow where she'd covered herself in leaves. She took Silence by the arm, trembling. "You found them?"

"Killed the man on watch," Silence said with a nod. "The other four should be sleeping. This is where I'll need you."

"I'm ready."

"Follow."

They moved back along the path Silence had taken. They passed the heap of the lookout's corpse, and William Ann inspected it, showing no pity. "It's one of them," she whispered. "I recognize him."

"Of course it's one of them."

"I just wanted to be sure. Since we're . . . you know."

Not far beyond the guard post, they found the camp. Four men in bedrolls slept amid the shades as only true Forestborn would ever try. They had set a small jar of glowpaste at the center of the camp, inside a pit so it wouldn't glow too brightly and give them away, but it was enough light to show the horses tethered a few feet away on the other side of the camp. The green light also showed William Ann's face, and Silence was shocked to see not fear but intense anger in the girl's expression. She had taken quickly to being a protective older sister to Sebruki. She was ready to kill after all.

Silence gestured toward the rightmost man, and William Ann nodded. This was the dangerous part. On only a half dose, any of these men could still wake to the noise of their partners dying.

Silence took one of the burlap sacks from her pack and handed it to William Ann, then removed her hammer. It wasn't some war weapon, like her grandfather had spoken of. Just a simple tool for pounding nails. Or other things.

Silence stooped over the first man. Seeing his sleeping face sent a shiver through her. A primal piece of her waited, tense, for those eyes to snap open.

She held up three fingers to William Ann, then lowered them one at a time. When the third finger went down, William Ann shoved the sack over the man's head. As he jerked, Silence pounded him hard on the side of the temple with the hammer. The skull cracked and the head sank in a little. The man thrashed once, then grew limp.

Silence looked up, tense, watching the other men as William Ann pulled the sack tight. The shades nearby paused, but this didn't draw their attention as much as the strangling had. So long as the sack's lining of tar kept the blood from leaking out, they should be safe. Silence hit the man's head twice more, then checked for a pulse. There was none.

They carefully did the next man in the row. It was brutal work, like slaughtering animals. It helped to think of these men as rabid, as she'd told William Ann earlier. It did not help to think of what the men had done to Sebruki. That would make her angry, and she couldn't afford to be angry. She needed to be cold, quiet, and efficient.

The second man took a few more knocks to the head to kill, but he woke more slowly than his friend. Fenweed made men groggy. It was an excellent drug for her purposes. She just needed them sleepy, a little disoriented. And—

The next man sat up in his bedroll. "What . . . ?" he asked in a slurred voice.

Silence leaped for him, grabbing him by the shoulders and slamming him to the ground. Nearby shades spun about as if at a loud noise.

Silence pulled her garrote out as the man heaved at her, trying to push her aside, and William Ann gasped in shock.

Silence rolled around, wrapping the man's neck. She pulled tight, straining while the man thrashed, agitating the shades. She almost had him dead when the last man leaped from his bedroll. In his dazed alarm, he chose to dash away.

Shadows! That last one was Chesterton himself. If he drew the shades . . .

Silence left the third man gasping and threw caution aside, racing after Chesterton. If the shades withered him to dust, she'd have *nothing*. No corpse to turn in meant no bounty.

The shades around the campsite faded from view as Silence reached Chesterton, catching him at the perimeter of the camp by the horses. She desperately tackled him by the legs, throwing the groggy man to the ground.

"You bitch," he said in a slurred voice, kicking at her. "You're the inn-keeper. You poisoned me, you *bitch*!"

In the forest, the shades had gone completely black. Green eyes burst alight as they opened their earthsight. The eyes trailed a misty light.

Silence battered aside Chesterton's hands as he struggled.

"I'll pay you," he said, clawing at her. "I'll pay you—"

Silence slammed her hammer into his arm, causing him to scream. Then she brought it down on his face with a crunch. She ripped off her sweater as he groaned and thrashed, somehow wrapping it around his head and the hammer.

"William Ann!" she screamed. "I need a bag. A bag, girl! Give me—"

William Ann knelt beside her, pulling a sack over Chesterton's head as the blood soaked through the sweater. Silence reached to the side with a frantic hand and grabbed a stone, then smashed it into the sack-covered head. The sweater muffled Chesterton's screams, but also muf-fled the rock. She had to beat again and again.

He finally fell still. William Ann held the sack against his neck to keep the blood from flowing out, her breath coming in quick gasps. "Oh, God Beyond. Oh, *God* . . ."

Silence dared look up. Dozens of green eyes hung in the forest, glowing like little fires in the blackness. William Ann squeezed her eyes shut and whispered a prayer, tears leaking down her cheeks.

Silence reached slowly to her side and took out her silver dagger. She remembered another night, another sea of glowing green eyes. Her grandmother's last night. *Run, girl! RUN!*

That night, running had been an option. They'd been close to safety. Even then, Grandmother hadn't made it. She might have, but she hadn't.

That night horrified Silence. What Grandmother had done. What Silence had done . . . Well, tonight she had only one hope. Running would not save them. Safety was too far away.

Slowly, blessedly, the eyes started to fade away. Silence sat back and let the silver knife slip out of her fingers to the ground.

William Ann opened her eyes. "Oh, God Beyond!" she said as the shades faded back into view. "A miracle!"

"Not a miracle," Silence said. "Just luck. We killed him in time. Another second, and they'd have enraged."

William Ann wrapped her arms around herself. "Oh, shadows. Oh, shadows. I thought we were dead. Oh, shadows."

Suddenly, Silence remembered something. The third man. She hadn't finished strangling him before Chesterton ran. She stumbled to her feet, turning.

He lay there, immobile.

"I finished him off," William Ann said. "Had to strangle him with my hands. My hands . . ."

Silence glanced back at her. "You did well, girl. You probably saved our lives. If you hadn't been here, I'd never have killed Chesterton without enraging the shades."

The girl still stared out into the woods, watching the placid shades. "What would it take?" she asked. "For you to see a miracle instead of a coincidence?"

"It would take a miracle, obviously," Silence said, picking up her knife. "Instead of just a coincidence. Come on. Let's put a second sack on these fellows."

William Ann joined her, lethargic as she helped put sacks on the heads of the bandits. Two sacks each, just in case. Blood was the most dangerous. Running drew shades, but slowly. Fire enraged them immediately, but it also blinded and confused them.

Blood, though . . . blood shed in anger, exposed to the open air . . . a single drop could make the shades slaughter you, and then everything else within their sight.

Silence checked each man for a heartbeat, just in case, and found none. They saddled the horses and heaved the corpses, including the lookout, into the saddles and tied them in place. They took the bedrolls and other equipment too. Hopefully the men would have some silver on them. Bounty laws let Silence keep what she found unless there was specific mention of something stolen. In this case, the forts just wanted Chesterton dead. Pretty much everyone did.

Silence pulled a rope tight, then paused.

"Mother!" William Ann said, noticing the same thing. Leaves rustling out in the Forests. They'd uncovered their jar of green glowpaste to join that of the bandits, so the small campsite was well illuminated as a gang of eight men and women on horseback rode in through the Forests.

They were from the forts. The nice clothing, the way they kept looking into the Forests at the shades . . . Fortfolk for certain. Silence stepped forward, wishing she had her hammer to look at least a little threatening. That was still tied in the sack around Chesterton's head. It would have blood on it, so she couldn't get it out until that dried or she was in someplace very, *very* safe.

"Now, look at this," said the man at the front of the newcomers. "I couldn't believe what Tobias told me when he came back from scouting, but it appears to be true. All five men in Chesterton's gang, killed by a couple of Forest homesteaders?"

"Who are you?" Silence asked.

"Red Young," the man said with a tip of the hat. "I've been tracking this lot for the last four months. I can't thank you enough for taking care of them for me." He waved to a few of his people, who dismounted.

"Mother!" William Ann hissed.

Silence studied Red's eyes. He was armed with a cudgel, and one of the women behind him had one of those new crossbows with the blunt tips. They cranked fast and hit hard, but didn't draw blood.

"Step away from the horses, child," Silence said.

"But—"

"Step away." Silence dropped the rope of the horse she was leading. Three fort city people gathered up the ropes, one of the men leering at William Ann.

"You're a smart one," Red said, leaning down and studying Silence. One of his women walked past, towing Chesterton's horse with the man's corpse slumped over the saddle.

Silence stepped up, resting a hand on Chesterton's saddle. The woman towing it paused, then looked at her boss. Silence slipped her knife from its sheath.

"You'll give us something," Silence said to Red, knife hand hidden. "After what we did. One quarter, and I don't say a word."

"Sure," he said, tipping his hat to her. He had a fake kind of grin, like one in a painting. "One quarter it is."

Silence nodded. She slipped the knife against one of the thin ropes that held Chesterton in the saddle. That gave her a good cut on it as the woman pulled the horse away. Silence stepped back, resting her hand on William Ann's shoulder while covertly moving the knife back into its sheath.

Red tipped his hat to her again. In moments, the bounty hunters had retreated back through the trees toward the roadway.

"One quarter?" William Ann hissed. "You think he'll pay it?"

"Hardly," Silence said, picking up her pack. "We're lucky he didn't just kill us. Come on." She moved out into the Forests. William Ann walked with her, both moving with the careful steps the Forests demanded. "It might be time for you to return to the waystop, William Ann."

"And what are you going to do?"

"Get our bounty back." She was a Forescout, dammit. No prim fort man was going to steal from her.

"You mean to cut them off at the white span, I assume. But what will you do? We can't fight so many, Mother."

"I'll find a way." That corpse meant freedom—*life*—for her daughters. She would not let it slip away like smoke between the fingers. They entered the darkness, passing shades that had, just a short time before, been almost ready to wither them. Now the shades drifted away, completely indifferent toward their flesh.

Think, Silence. Something is very wrong here. How had those men found the camp? The light? Had they overheard her and William Ann talking? They'd claimed to have been chasing Chesterton for months. Shouldn't she have caught wind of them before now? These men and women looked too crisp to have been out in the Forests for months trailing killers.

It led to a conclusion she did not want to admit. One man had known she was hunting a bounty today and had seen how she was planning to track that bounty. One man had cause to see that bounty stolen from her.

Theopolis, I hope I'm wrong, she thought. *Because if you're behind this . . .*

Silence and William Ann trudged through the guts of the Forest, a place where the gluttonous canopy above drank in all of the light, leaving the ground below barren. Shades patrolled these wooden halls like blind sentries. Red and his bounty hunters were of the forts. They would keep to the roadways, and that was her advantage. The Forests were no friend to a homesteader, no more than a familiar chasm was any less dangerous a drop.

But Silence was a sailor on this abyss. She could ride its winds better than any fortdweller. Perhaps it was time to make a storm.

What homesteaders called the "white span" was a section of roadway lined by mushroom fields. It took about an hour through the Forests to reach the span, and Silence was feeling the price of a night without sleep by the time she arrived. She ignored the fatigue, tromping through the field of mushrooms, holding her jar of green light and giving an ill cast to trees and furrows in the land.

The roadway bent around through the Forests, then came back this way. If the men were heading toward Lastport or any of the other nearby forts, they would come this direction. "You continue on," Silence said to William Ann. "It's only another hour's hike back to the waystop. Check on things there."

"I'm not leaving you, Mother."

"You promised to obey. Would you break your word?"

"And you promised to let me help you. Would you break yours?"

"I don't need you for this," Silence said. "And it will be dangerous."

"What are you going to do?"

Silence stopped beside the roadway, then knelt, fishing in her pack. She came out with the small keg of gunpowder. William Ann went as white as the mushrooms.

"Mother!"

Silence untied her grandmother's firestarter. She didn't know for certain if it still worked. She'd never dared compress the two metal arms, which looked like tongs. Squeezing them together would grind the ends against one another, making sparks, and a spring at the joint would make them come back apart.

Silence looked up at her daughter, then held the firestarter up beside her head. William Ann stepped back, then glanced to the sides, toward nearby shades.

"Are things really that bad?" the girl whispered. "For us, I mean?"

Silence nodded.

"All right then."

Fool girl. Well, Silence wouldn't send her away. The truth was, she probably *would* need help. She intended to get that corpse. Bodies were heavy, and there wasn't any way she'd be able to cut off just the head. Not out in the Forests, with shades about.

She dug into her pack, pulling out her medical supplies. They were tied between two small boards, intended to be used as splints. It was not difficult to tie the two boards to either side of the firestarter. With her hand trowel, she dug a small hole in the roadway's soft earth, about the size of the powder keg.

She then opened the plug to the keg and set it into the hole. She soaked her handkerchief in the lamp oil, stuck one end in the keg, then positioned the firestarter boards on the road with the end of the kerchief next to the spark-making heads. After covering the contraption with some leaves, she had a rudimentary trap. If someone stepped on the top board, that would press it down and grind out sparks to light the kerchief. Hopefully.

She couldn't afford to light the fire herself. The shades would come first for the one who made the fire.

"What happens if they don't step on it?" William Ann asked.

"Then we move it to another place on the road and try again," Silence said.

"That could shed blood, you realize."

Silence didn't reply. If the trap was triggered by a footfall, the shades wouldn't see Silence as the one causing it. They'd come first for the one who triggered the trap. But if blood was drawn, they would enrage. Soon after, it wouldn't matter who had caused it. All would be in danger.

"We have hours of darkness left," Silence said. "Cover your glowpaste."

William Ann nodded, hastily putting the cover on her jar. Silence inspected her trap again, then took William Ann by the shoulder and pulled her to the side of the roadway. The underbrush was thicker there, as the road tended to wind through breaks in the canopy. People sought out places in the Forests where they could see the sky.

The bounty hunters came along eventually. Silent, illuminated by a jar of glowpaste each. Fortfolk didn't talk at night. They passed the trap, which Silence had placed on the narrowest section of roadway. She held her breath, watching the horses pass, step after step missing the lump that marked the board. William Ann covered her ears, hunkering down.

A hoof hit the trap. Nothing happened. Silence released an annoyed breath. What would she do if the firestarter was broken? Could she find another way to—

The explosion struck her, the wave of force shaking her body. Shades vanished in a blink, green eyes snapping open. Horses reared and whinnied, men and women yelling.

Silence shook off her stupefaction, grabbing William Ann by the shoulder and pulling her out of hiding. Her trap had worked better than she'd assumed; the burning rag had allowed the horse who had triggered the trap to take a few steps before the blast hit. No blood, just a lot of surprised horses and confused people. The little keg of gunpowder hadn't done as much damage as she'd anticipated—the stories of what gunpowder could do were often as fanciful as stories of the Homeland—but the sound had been incredible.

Silence's ears rang as she fought through the confused fortfolk, finding what she'd hoped to see. Chesterton's corpse lay on the ground, dumped from saddleback by a bucking horse and a frayed rope. She grabbed the corpse under the arms and William Ann took the legs. They moved sideways into the Forests.

"Idiots!" Red bellowed from amid the confusion. "Stop her! It—"

He cut off as shades swarmed the roadway, descending upon the men. Red had managed to keep his horse under control, but now he had to dance it back from the shades. Enraged, they had turned pure black, though the blast of light and fire had obviously left them dazed. They fluttered about, like moths at a flame. Green eyes. A small blessing. If those turned red . . .

One bounty hunter, standing on the road and spinning about, was struck. His back arched, black-veined tendrils crisscrossing his skin. He dropped to his knees, screaming as the flesh of his face shrank around his skull.

Silence turned away. William Ann watched the fallen man with a horrified expression.

"Slowly, child," Silence said in what she hoped was a comforting voice. She hardly felt comforting. "Carefully. We can move away from them. William Ann. Look at me."

The girl turned to look at her.

"Hold my eyes. Move. That's right. Remember, the shades will go to the source of the fire first. They are confused, stunned. They can't smell fire like they do blood, and they'll look from it to the nearest rapid motion. Slowly, easily. Let the scrambling fortfolk distract them."

The two of them eased into the Forests with excruciating deliberateness. In the face of so much chaos, so much danger, their pace felt like a crawl. Red organized a resistance. Fire-crazed shades could be fought, destroyed, with silver. More and more would come, but if the bounty hunters were clever and lucky, they'd be able to destroy those nearby and then move slowly away from the source of the fire. They could hide, survive. Maybe.

Unless one of them accidentally drew blood.

Silence and William Ann stepped through a field of mushrooms that glowed like the skulls of rats and broke silently beneath their feet. Luck was not completely with them, for as the shades shook off their disorientation from the explosion, a pair of them on the outskirts turned and struck out toward the fleeing women.

William Ann gasped. Silence deliberately set down Chesterton's shoulders, then took out her knife. "Keep going," she whispered. "Pull him away. Slowly, girl. *Slowly*."

"I won't leave you!"

"I will catch up," Silence said. "You aren't ready for this."

She didn't look to see if William Ann obeyed, for the shades—figures of jet black streaking across the white-knobbed ground—were upon her. Strength was meaningless against shades. They had no real substance. Only two things mattered: your speed and not letting yourself be frightened.

Shades *were* dangerous, but so long as you had silver, you could fight. Many a man died because he ran, drawing even more shades, rather than standing his ground.

Silence swung at the shades as they reached her. *You want my daughter, hellbound?* she thought with a snarl. *You should have tried for the fortfolk instead.*

She swept her knife through the first shade, as Grandmother had taught. *Never creep back and cower before shades. You're Forescout blood. You claim the Forests. You are their creature as much as any other. As am I. . . .*

Her knife passed through the shade with a slight tugging feeling, creating a shower of bright white sparks that sprayed out of the shade. The shade pulled back, its black tendrils writhing about one another.

Silence spun on the other. The pitch sky let her see only the thing's eyes, a horrid green, as it reached for her. She lunged.

Its spectral hands were upon her, the icy cold of its fingers gripping her arm below the elbow. She could feel it. Shade fingers had substance; they could grab you, hold you back. Only silver warded them away. Only with silver could you fight.

She rammed her arm in farther. Sparks shot out its back, spraying like a bucket of washwater. Silence gasped at the horrid, icy pain. Her knife slipped from fingers she could no longer feel. She lurched forward, falling to her knees as the second shade fell backward, then began spinning about in a mad spiral. The first one flopped on the ground like a dying fish, trying to rise, its top half falling over.

The cold of her arm was so *bitter*. She stared at the wounded arm, watching the flesh of her hand wither upon itself, pulling in toward the bone.

She heard weeping.

You stand there, Silence. Grandmother's voice. Memories of the first time she'd killed a shade. *You do as I say. No tears! Forescouts don't cry. Forescouts DON'T CRY.*

She had learned to hate her that day. Ten years old, with her little knife, shivering and weeping in the night as her grandmother had enclosed her and a drifting shade in a ring of silver dust.

Grandmother had run around the perimeter, enraging it with motion. While Silence was trapped in there. With death.

The only way to learn is to do, Silence. And you'll learn, one way or another!

"Mother!" William Ann said.

Silence blinked, coming out of the memory as her daughter dumped silver dust on the exposed arm. The withering stopped as William Ann, choking against her thick tears, dumped the entire pouch of emergency silver over the hand. The metal reversed the withering, and the skin turned pink again, the blackness melting away in sparks of white.

Too much, Silence thought. William Ann had used all of the silver dust in her haste, far more than one wound needed. It was difficult to summon any anger, for feeling flooded back into her hand and the icy cold retreated.

"Mother?" William Ann asked. "I left you, as you said. But he was so heavy, I didn't get far. I came back for you. I'm sorry. I came back for you!"

"Thank you," Silence said, breathing in. "You did well." She reached up and took her daughter by the shoulder, then used the once-withered hand to search in the grass for Grandmother's knife. When she brought it up, the blade was blackened in several places, but still good.

Back on the road, the fortfolk had made a circle and were holding off the shades with silver-tipped spears. The horses had all fled or been consumed. Silence fished on the ground, coming up with a small handful of silver dust. The rest had been expended in the healing. Too much.

No use worrying about that now, she thought, stuffing the handful of dust in her pocket. "Come," she said, hauling herself to her feet. "I'm sorry I never taught you to fight them."

"Yes you did," William Ann said, wiping her tears. "You've told me all about it."

Told. Never shown. *Shadows, Grandmother. I know I disappoint you, but I won't do it to her. I can't. But I am a good mother. I* will *protect them.*

The two left the mushrooms, taking up their grisly prize again and tromping through the Forests. They passed more darkened shades floating toward the fight. All of those sparks would draw them. The fortfolk were dead. Too much attention, too much struggle. They'd have a thousand shades upon them before the hour was out.

Silence and William Ann moved slowly. Though the cold had mostly retreated from Silence's hand, there was a lingering . . . something. A deep shiver. A limb touched by the shades wouldn't feel right for months.

That was far better than what could have happened. Without William Ann's quick thinking, Silence could have become a cripple. Once the withering settled in—that took a little time, though it varied—it was irreversible.

Something rustled in the woods. Silence froze, causing William Ann to stop and glance about.

"Mother?" William Ann whispered.

Silence frowned. The night was so black, and they'd been forced to leave their lights. *Something's out there,* she thought, trying to pierce the darkness. *What are you?* God Beyond protect them if the fighting had drawn one of the Deepest Ones.

The sound did not repeat. Reluctantly, Silence continued on. They walked for a good hour, and in the darkness Silence hadn't realized they'd neared the roadway again until they stepped onto it.

Silence heaved out a breath, setting down their burden and rolling her tired arms in their joints. Some light from the Starbelt filtered down upon them, illuminating something like a large jawbone to their left.

458 · BRANDON SANDERSON

The Old Bridge. They were almost home. The shades here weren't even agitated; they moved with their lazy, almost butterfly, gaits.

Her arms felt so sore. That body felt as if it were getting heavier every moment. People often didn't realize how heavy a corpse was. Silence sat down. They'd rest for a time before continuing on. "William Ann, do you have any water left in your canteen?"

William Ann whimpered.

Silence started, then scrambled to her feet. Her daughter stood beside the bridge, and something dark stood behind her. A green glow suddenly illuminated the night as the figure took out a small vial of glowpaste. By that sickly light, Silence could see that the figure was Red.

He held a dagger to William Ann's neck. The fort man had not fared well in the fighting. One eye was now a milky white, half his face blackened, his lips pulled back from his teeth. A shade had gotten him across the face. He was lucky to be alive.

"I figured you'd come back this way," he said, the words slurred by his shriveled lips. Spittle dripped from his chin. "Silver. Give me your silver."

His knife . . . it was common steel.

"*Now!*" he roared, pulling the knife closer to William Ann's neck. If he so much as nicked her, the shades would be upon them in heartbeats.

"I only have the knife," Silence lied, taking it out and tossing it to the ground before him. "It's too late for your face, Red. That withering has set in."

"I don't care," he hissed. "Now the body. Step away from it, woman. Away!"

Silence stepped to the side. Could she get to him before he killed William Ann? He'd have to grab that knife. If she sprang just right . . .

"You killed my crew," Red growled. "They're dead, all of them. God, if I hadn't rolled into the hollow . . . I had to *listen* to it. Listen to them being slaughtered!"

"You were the only smart one," she said. "You couldn't have saved them, Red."

"Bitch! You killed them."

"They killed themselves," she whispered. "You come to my Forests, take what is mine? It was your crew or my children, Red."

"Well, if you want your child to live through this, you'll stay very still. Girl, pick up that knife."

Whimpering, William Ann knelt. Red mimicked her, staying just behind her, watching Silence, holding the knife steady. William Ann picked up the knife in trembling hands.

Red pulled the silver knife from William Ann, then held it in one hand, the common knife at her neck in the other. "Now, the girl is going to carry the corpse, and you're going to wait right there. I don't want you coming near."

"Of course," Silence said, already planning. She couldn't afford to strike right now. He was too careful. She would follow through the Forests, along the road, and wait for a moment of weakness. Then she'd strike.

Red spat to the side.

Then a padded crossbow bolt shot from the night and took him in the shoulder, jolting him. His blade slid across William Ann's neck, and a dribble of blood ran down it. The girl's eyes widened in horror, though it was little more than a nick. The danger to her throat wasn't important.

The blood was.

Red tumbled back, gasping, hand to his shoulder. A few drops of blood glistened on his knife. The shades in the Forests around them went black. Glowing green eyes burst alight, then deepened to crimson.

Red eyes in the night. Blood in the air.

"Oh, hell!" Red screamed. "Oh, *hell*." Red eyes swarmed around him. There was no hesitation here, no confusion. They went straight for the one who had drawn blood.

Silence reached for William Ann as the shades descended. Red grabbed the girl and shoved her through a shade, trying to stop it. He spun and dashed the other direction.

William Ann passed through the shade, her face withering, skin pulling in at the chin and around the eyes. She stumbled through the shade and into Silence's arms.

Silence felt an immediate, overwhelming panic.

"No! Child, no. No. *No . . .*"

William Ann worked her mouth, making a choking sound, her lips pulling back toward her teeth, her eyes open wide as her skin tightened and her eyelids shriveled.

Silver. I need silver. I can save her. Silence snapped her head up, clutching William Ann. Red ran down the roadway, slashing the silver dagger all about, spraying light and sparks. Shades surrounded him. Hundreds, like ravens flocking to a roost.

Not that way. The shades would finish with him soon and would look for flesh—any flesh. William Ann still had blood on her neck. They'd come for her next. Even without that, the girl was withering fast.

The dagger wouldn't be enough to save William Ann. Silence needed dust, silver dust, to force down her daughter's throat. Silence fumbled in her pocket, coming out with the small bit of silver dust there.

Too little. She *knew* that would be too little. Her grandmother's training calmed her mind, and everything became immediately clear.

The waystop was close. She had more silver there.

"M . . . Mother . . ."

Silence heaved William Ann into her arms. Too light, the flesh drying. Then she turned and ran with everything she had across the bridge.

Her arms stung, weakened from having hauled the corpse so far. The corpse . . . she couldn't lose it!

No. She couldn't think on that. The shades would have it, as warm enough flesh, soon after Red was gone. There would be no bounty. She had to focus on William Ann.

Silence's tears felt cold on her face as she ran, wind blowing her. Her daughter trembled and shook in her arms, spasming as she died. She'd become a shade if she died like this.

"I won't lose you!" Silence said into the night. "Please. I won't lose you. . . ."

Behind her, Red screamed a long, wailing screech of agony that cut off at the end as the shades feasted. Near her, other shades stopped, eyes deepening to red.

Blood in the air. Eyes of crimson.

"I hate you," Silence whispered into the air as she ran. Each step was agony. She *was* growing old. "I hate you! What you did to me. What you did to us."

She didn't know if she was speaking to Grandmother or the God Beyond. So often, they were the same in her mind. Had she ever realized that before?

Branches lashed at her as she pushed forward. Was that light ahead? The waystop?

Hundreds upon hundreds of red eyes opened in front of her. She stumbled to the ground, spent, William Ann like a heavy bundle of branches in her arms. The girl trembled, her eyes rolled back in her head.

Silence held out the small bit of silver dust she'd recovered earlier. She longed to pour it on William Ann, save her a little pain, but she knew with clarity that was a waste. She looked down, crying, then took the dust and made a small circle around the two of them. What else could she do?

William Ann shook with a seizure as she rasped, drawing in breaths and clawing at Silence's arms. The shades came by the dozens, huddling around the two of them, smelling the blood. The flesh.

Silence pulled her daughter close. She should have gone for the knife after all; it wouldn't heal William Ann, but she could have at least fought with it.

Without that, without anything, she failed. Grandmother had been right all along.

"Hush now, my dear one . . ." Silence whispered, squeezing her eyes shut. "Be not afraid."

Shades came at her frail barrier, throwing up sparks, making Silence open her eyes. They backed away, then others came, beating against the silver, their red eyes illuminating writhing black forms.

"Night comes upon us . . ." Silence whispered, choking at the words, ". . . but sunlight will break."

William Ann arched her back, then fell still.

"Sleep now . . . my . . . my dear one . . . let your tears fade. Darkness surrounds us, but someday . . . we'll wake. . . ."

So tired. *I shouldn't have let her come.*

If she hadn't, Chesterton would have gotten away from her, and she'd have probably fallen to the shades then. William Ann and Sebruki would have become slaves to Theopolis, or worse.

No choices. No way out.

"Why did you send us here?" she screamed, looking up past hundreds of glowing red eyes. "What is the point?"

There was no answer. There was never an answer.

Yes, that *was* light ahead; she could see it through the low tree branches in front of her. She was only a few yards from the waystop. She would die, like Grandmother had, mere paces from her home.

She blinked, cradling William Ann as the tiny silver barrier failed.

That . . . that branch just in front of her. It had such a very odd shape. Long, thin, no leaves. Not like a branch at all. Instead, like . . .

Like a crossbow bolt.

It had lodged into the tree after being fired from the waystop earlier in the day. She remembered facing down that bolt earlier, staring at its reflective end.

Silver.

Silence Montane crashed through the back door of the waystop, hauling a desiccated body behind her. She stumbled into the kitchen, barely able to walk, and dropped the silver-tipped bolt from a withered hand.

Her skin continued to pull tight, her body shriveling. She had not been able to avoid withering, not when fighting so many shades. The crossbow bolt had merely cleared a path, allowing her to push forward in a last, frantic charge.

She could barely see. Tears streamed from her clouded eyes. Even with the tears, her eyes felt as dry as if she had been standing in the wind for an hour while holding them wide open. Her lids refused to blink, and she couldn't move her lips.

She had . . . powder. Didn't she?

Thought. Mind. What?

She moved without thought. Jar on the windowsill. In case of broken circle. She unscrewed the lid with fingers like sticks. Seeing them horrified a distant part of her mind.

Dying. I'm dying.

She dunked the jar of silver powder in the water cistern and pulled it out, then stumbled to William Ann. She fell to her knees beside the girl, spilling much of the water. The rest she dumped on her daughter's face with a shaking arm.

Please. Please.

Darkness.

"We were sent here to be strong," Grandmother said, standing on the cliff edge overlooking the waters. Her whited hair curled in the wind, writhing like the wisps of a shade.

She turned back to Silence, and her weathered face was covered in droplets of water from the crashing surf below. "The God Beyond sent us. It's part of the plan."

"It's so easy for you to say that, isn't it?" Silence spat. "You can fit anything into that nebulous *plan*. Even the destruction of the world itself."

"I won't hear blasphemy from you, child." A voice like boots stepping in gravel. She walked toward Silence. "You can rail against the God Beyond, but it will change nothing. William was a fool and an idiot. You are better off. We are *Forescouts*. We *survive*. We will be the ones to defeat the Evil, someday." She passed Silence by.

Silence had never seen a smile from Grandmother, not since her husband's death. Smiling was wasted energy. And love . . . love was for the people back in Homeland. The people who'd perished from the Evil.

"I'm with child," Silence said.

Grandmother stopped. "William?"

"Who else?"

Grandmother continued on.

"No condemnations?" Silence asked, turning, folding her arms.

"It's done," Grandmother said. "We are Forescouts. If this is how we must continue, so be it. I'm more worried about the waystop, and meeting our payments to those damn forts."

I have an idea for that, Silence thought, considering the lists of bounties she'd begun collecting. *Something even you wouldn't dare. Something dangerous. Something unthinkable.*

Grandmother reached the woods and looked at Silence, scowled, then pulled on her hat and stepped into the trees.

"I will not have you interfering with my child," Silence called after her. "I will raise my own as I will!"

Grandmother vanished into the shadows.

Please. Please.

"I *will*!"

I won't lose you. I won't . . .

Silence gasped, coming awake and clawing at the floorboards, staring upward.

Alive. She was alive!

Dob the stableman knelt beside her, holding the jar of powdered silver. She coughed, lifting fingers—plump, the flesh restored—to her neck. It was hale, though ragged from the flakes of silver that had been forced down her throat. Her skin was dusted with black bits of ruined silver.

"William Ann!" she said, turning.

The child lay on the floor beside the door. William Ann's left side, where she'd first touched the shade, was blackened. Her face wasn't too bad, but her hand was a withered skeleton. They'd have to cut that off. Her leg looked bad too. Silence couldn't tell how bad without tending the wounds.

"Oh, child . . ." Silence knelt beside her.

But the girl breathed in and out. That was enough, all things considered.

"I tried," Dob said. "But you'd already done what could be done."

"Thank you," Silence said. She turned to the aged man, with his high forehead and dull eyes.

"Did you get him?" Dob asked.

"Who?"

"The bounty."

"I . . . yes, I did. But I had to leave him."

"You'll find another," Dob said in his monotone, climbing to his feet. "The Fox always does."

"How long have you known?"

"I'm an idiot, mam," he said. "Not a fool." He bowed his head to her, then walked away, slump-backed as always.

Silence climbed to her feet, then groaned, picking up William Ann. She lifted her daughter to the rooms above and saw to her.

The leg wasn't as bad as Silence had feared. A few of the toes would be lost, but the foot itself was hale enough. The entire left side of William Ann's body was blackened, as if burned. That would fade, with time, to grey.

Everyone who saw her would know exactly what had happened. Many men would never touch her, fearing her taint. This might just doom her to a life alone.

I know a little about such a life, Silence thought, dipping a cloth into the water bin and washing William Ann's face. The youth would sleep through the day. She had come very close to death, to becoming a shade herself. The body did not recover quickly from that.

Of course, Silence had been close to that too. She, however, had been there before. Another of Grandmother's preparations. Oh, how she hated that woman. Silence owed who she was to how that training had toughened her. Could she be thankful for Grandmother and hateful, both at once?

Silence finished washing William Ann, then dressed her in a soft nightgown and left her in her bunk. Sebruki still slept off the draught Silence had given her.

So she went downstairs to the kitchen to think difficult thoughts. She'd lost the bounty. The shades would have had at that body; the skin would be dust, the skull blackened and ruined. She had no way to prove that she'd taken Chesterton.

She settled against the kitchen table and laced her hands before her. She wanted to have at the whiskey instead, to dull the horror of the night.

She thought for hours. Could she pay Theopolis off some way? Borrow from someone else? Who? Maybe find another bounty. But so few people came through the waystop these days. Theopolis had already given her warning, with his writ. He wouldn't wait more than a day or two for payment before claiming the waystop as his own.

Had she really gone through so much, still to lose?

Sunlight fell on her face and a breeze from the broken window tickled her cheek, waking her from her slumber at the table. Silence blinked, stretching, limbs complaining. Then she sighed, moving to the kitchen counter. She'd left out all of the materials from the preparations last night, her clay bowls thick with glowpaste that still shone faintly. The silver-tipped crossbow bolt lay by the back door where she'd dropped it. She'd need to clean up and get breakfast ready for her few guests. Then, think of *some* way to . . .

The back door opened and someone stepped in.

. . . to deal with Theopolis. She exhaled softly, looking at him in his clean clothing and condescending smile. He tracked mud onto her floor as he entered. "Silence Montane. Nice morning, hmmm?"

Shadows, she thought. *I don't have the mental strength to deal with him right now.*

He moved to close the window shutters.

"What are you doing?" she demanded.

"Hmmm? Haven't you warned me before that you loathe that people might see us together? That they might get a hint that you are turning in bounties to me? I'm just trying to protect you. Has something happened? You look awful, hmmm?"

"I know what you did."

"You do? But, see, I do many things. About what do you speak?"

Oh, how she'd like to cut that grin from his lips and cut out his throat, stomp out that annoying Lastport accent. She couldn't. He was just so blasted *good* at acting. She had guesses, probably good ones. But no proof.

Grandmother would have killed him right then. Was she so desperate to prove him wrong that she'd lose everything?

"You were in the Forests," Silence said. "When Red surprised me at the bridge, I assumed that the thing I'd heard—rustling in the darkness—had been him. It wasn't. He implied he'd been waiting for us at the bridge. That thing in the darkness, it was you. *You* shot him with the crossbow to jostle him, make him draw blood. Why, Theopolis?"

"Blood?" Theopolis said. "In the night? And you *survived*? You're quite fortunate, I should say. Remarkable. What else happened?"

She said nothing.

"I have come for payment of debt," Theopolis said. "You have no bounty to turn in then, hmmm? Perhaps we will need my document after all. So kind of me to bring another copy. This really will be wonderful for us both. Do you not agree?"

"Your feet are glowing."

Theopolis hesitated, then looked down. There, the mud he'd tracked in shone very faintly blue in the light of the glowpaste remnants.

"You followed me," she said. "You *were* there last night."

He looked up at her with a slow, unconcerned expression. "And?" He took a step forward.

Silence backed away, her heel hitting the wall behind her. She reached around, taking out the key and unlocking the door behind her. Theopolis grabbed her arm, yanking her away as she pulled open the door.

"Going for one of your hidden weapons?" he asked with a sneer. "The crossbow you keep on the pantry shelf? Yes, I know of that. I'm disappointed, Silence. Can't we be civil?"

"I will never sign your document, Theopolis," she said, then spat at his feet. "I would sooner die, I would sooner be put out of house and home. You can take the waystop by force, but I will *not* serve you. You can be damned, for all I care, you bastard. You—"

He slapped her across the face. A quick but unemotional gesture. "Oh, do shut up."

She stumbled back.

"Such dramatics, Silence. I can't be the only one to wish you lived up to your name, hmmm?"

She licked her lip, feeling the pain of his slap. She lifted her hand to her face. A single drop of blood colored her fingertip when she pulled it away.

"You expect me to be frightened?" Theopolis asked. "I know we're safe in here."

"Fort city fool," she whispered, then flipped the drop of blood at him. It hit him on the cheek. "Always follow the Simple Rules. Even when you think you don't have to. And I wasn't opening the pantry, as you thought."

Theopolis frowned, then glanced over at the door she had opened. The door into the small old shrine. Her grandmother's shrine to the God Beyond.

The bottom of the door was rimmed in silver.

Red eyes opened in the air behind Theopolis, a jet-black form coalescing in the shadowed room. Theopolis hesitated, then turned.

He didn't get to scream as the shade took his head in its hands and drew his life away. It was a newer shade, its form still strong despite the writhing blackness of its clothing. A tall woman, hard of features, with curling hair. Theopolis opened his mouth, then his face withered away, eyes sinking into his head.

"You should have run, Theopolis," Silence said.

His head began to crumble. His body collapsed to the floor.

"Hide from the green eyes, run from the red," Silence said, retrieving the silver-tipped crossbow bolt from where it lay by the back door. "Your rules, Grandmother."

The shade turned to her. Silence shivered, looking into those dead, glassy eyes of a matriarch she loathed and loved.

"I hate you," Silence said. "Thank you for making me hate you." She held the crossbow bolt before her, but the shade did not strike. Silence edged around, forcing the shade back. It floated away from her, back into the shrine lined with silver at the bottom of its three walls, where Silence had trapped it years ago.

Her heart pounding, Silence closed the door, completing the barrier, and locked it again. No matter what happened, that shade left Silence alone. Almost, she thought it remembered. And almost, Silence felt guilty for trapping that soul inside the small closet for all these years.

Silence found Theopolis's hidden cave after six hours of hunting.

It was about where she'd expected it to be, in the hills not far from the Old Bridge. It included a silver barrier. She could harvest that. Good money there.

Inside the small cavern, she found Chesterton's corpse, which Theopolis had dragged to the cave while the shades killed Red and then hunted Silence. *I'm so glad, for once, you were a greedy man, Theopolis.*

She would have to find someone else to start turning in bounties for her. That would be difficult, particularly on short notice. She dragged the corpse out and threw it over the back of Theopolis's horse. A short hike took her back to the road, where she paused, then walked up and located Red's fallen corpse, withered down to just bones and clothing.

She fished out her grandmother's dagger, scored and blackened from the fight. It fit back into the sheath at her side. She trudged, exhausted, back to the waystop and hid Chesterton's corpse in the cold cellar out behind the stable, beside where she'd put Theopolis's remains. She hiked back into the kitchen. Beside the shrine's door where her grandmother's dagger had once hung, she had placed the silver crossbow bolt that Sebruki had unknowingly sent her.

What would the fort authorities say when she explained Theopolis's death to them? Perhaps she could claim to have found him like that. . . .

She paused, then smiled.

"Looks like you're lucky, friend," Daggon said, sipping at his beer. "The White Fox won't be looking for you anytime soon."

The spindly man, who still insisted his name was Earnest, hunkered down a little farther in his seat.

"How is it you're still here?" Daggon asked. "I traveled all the way to Lastport. I hardly expected to find you here on my path back."

"I hired on at a homestead nearby," said the slender-necked man. "Good work, mind you. Solid work."

"And you pay each night to stay here?"

"I like it. It feels peaceful. The homesteads don't have good silver protection. They just . . . let the shades move about. Even inside." The man shuddered.

Daggon shrugged, lifting his drink as Silence Montane limped by. Yes, she was a healthy-looking woman. He really *should* court her, one of these days. She scowled at his smile and dumped his plate in front of him.

"I think I'm wearing her down," Daggon said, mostly to himself, as she left.

"You will have to work hard," Earnest said. "Seven men have proposed to her during the last month."

"What!"

"The reward!" the spindly man said. "The one for bringing in Chesterton. Lucky woman, Silence Montane, finding the White Fox's lair like that."

Daggon dug into his meal. He didn't much like how things had turned out. That dandy Theopolis had been the White Fox all along? Poor Silence. How had it been, stumbling upon his cave and finding him inside, all withered away?

"They say that this Theopolis spent his last strength killing Chesterton," Earnest said, "then dragging him into the hole. Theopolis withered before he could get to his silver powder. Very like the White Fox, always determined to get the bounty, no matter what. We won't soon see a hunter like him again."

"I suppose not," Daggon said, though he'd much rather that the man had kept his skin. Now who would Daggon tell his tales about? He didn't fancy paying for his own beer.

Nearby, a greasy-looking fellow rose from his meal and shuffled out of the front door, looking half drunk already, though it was only noon.

Some people. Daggon shook his head. "To the White Fox," he said, raising his drink.

Earnest clinked his mug to Daggon's. "The White Fox, meanest bastard the Forests have ever known."

"May his soul know peace," Daggon said, "and may the God Beyond be thanked that he never decided we were worth his time."

"Amen," Earnest said.

"Of course," Daggon said, "there *is* still Bloody Kent. Now *he's* a right nasty fellow. You'd better hope he doesn't get your number, friend. And don't you give me that innocent look. These are the Forests. Everybody here has done something, now and then, that you don't want others to know about. . . ."

POSTSCRIPT

This story started when George R. R. Martin leaned over at a book signing the two of us were doing and said, "Hey, do you do short fiction?"

I told him I did *long* short fiction. He then invited me into one of his anthologies—which was a true honor. The anthologies he and Gardner Dozois do are kind of a "who's who" of speculative fiction writers, and though George is famous for his novels these days, he's always been known in the industry for his editorial skills. (Gardner, by the way, is equally famous—so it's a real privilege to get an invitation from them.)

I thought a long time about the nature of an anthology called *Dangerous Women*. I worried that stories submitted to it might fall into the trope of making women dangerous all in the same way. (This turned out to not be the case, fortunately.) I didn't want to write just another clichéd story about a femme fatale, or a woman soldier who was basically a man with breasts.

What other ways could someone be dangerous? I knew early on that I wanted my protagonist to be a middle-aged mother. Threnody was a fully built world already, as I knew it was important to the Cosmere. I toyed with setting the story there, and the final piece came when I was doing genealogy for religious purposes and ran across a woman named Silence.

Who would name their daughter Silence? It seemed one of those beautifully Puritan names that wouldn't fly in most settings—but it was perfect for Threnody. (Someday, someone will pull out of us what Nazh's real name is.) The story grew from there.

A few cool notes about this story. First, the rules for how to deal with the ghosts are (vaguely) based on Jewish laws of what you can and can't do on the Sabbath. Isaac, our tireless cartographer, named the planet

Threnody (he named Nazh as well). The frame story with the men in Silence's inn was nearly cut two or three times—even Gardner was skeptical about it when he started reading. In the end, it proved worth its space because of the punch it gives transitioning into Silence's viewpoint, and because of the nice way it wraps up the story at the end. I think it's necessary, but it also means the story starts with what I consider a weaker section.

You'll see more of this world in the future, most likely.

THE
DROMINAD
SYSTEM

The Drominad System

Seventh of the Sun

Sixth of the Sun

Fifth of the Sun

asteroid belt

Fourth of the Sun

Third of the Sun

Second of the Sun

First of the Sun

First of the First

THE DROMINAD SYSTEM

THERE are many planets in the cosmere that are inhabited, but upon which no Shards currently reside. Though the lives, passions, and beliefs of the people are, of course, important regardless of which planet they reside on, only a few of these planets have relevance to the greater cosmere at large.

This is mostly due to the fact that travel on and off the planets (at least in the Physical Realm) is dependent upon perpendicularities—places where a person can transition from Shadesmar onto the planet itself. If a world doesn't have a perpendicularity, then it can be studied from the Cognitive Realm, but cannot truly be visited.

In general, perpendicularities are created by the presence of a Shard on the planet. The concentration of so much Investiture on the Cognitive and Physical Realms creates points of . . . friction, where a kind of tunneling exists. At these points, Physical matter, Cognitive thought, and Spiritual essence become one—and a being can slide between Realms.

The existence of a perpendicularity (which often take the form of pools of concentrated power on the Physical Realm) on a planet is a hallmark of a Shard's presence. This is what makes First of the Sun so interesting.

The system, nicknamed Drominad, has a remarkable three planets inhabited by fully developed human societies. (There is also a fourth planet in the habitable zone.) This is unique in the cosmere; only the Rosharan system can rival it, and there one of the planets is inhabited solely by Splinters.

All four of these planets have water as a dominant feature. And one of them, the first planet, has a perpendicularity.

I have not been able to discover why, or how, this perpendicularity exists. There is certainly no Shard residing in the system. I cannot say what is happening, only that this feature must hint at things that occurred in the past of the planet. There is likely Investiture here somewhere as well, though I have not yet had a chance to investigate First of the Sun myself. The area around the perpendicularity is extremely dangerous, and the few expeditions sent there from Silverlight have not returned.

SIXTH
OF THE
DUSK

D EATH hunted beneath the waves. Dusk saw it approach, an enormous blackness within the deep blue, a shadowed form as wide as six narrowboats tied together. Dusk's hands tensed on his paddle, his heartbeat racing as he immediately sought out Kokerlii.

Fortunately, the colorful bird sat in his customary place on the prow of the boat, idly biting at one clawed foot raised to his beak. Kokerlii lowered his foot and puffed out his feathers, as if completely unmindful of the danger beneath.

Dusk held his breath. He always did, when unfortunate enough to run across one of these things in the open ocean. He did not know what they looked like beneath those waves. He hoped to never find out.

The shadow drew closer, almost to the boat now. A school of slimfish passing nearby jumped into the air in a silvery wave, spooked by the shadow's approach. The terrified fish showered back to the water with a sound like rain. The shadow did not deviate. The slimfish were too small a meal to interest it.

A boat's occupants, however . . .

It passed directly underneath. Sak chirped quietly from Dusk's shoulder;

the second bird seemed to have some sense of the danger. Creatures like the shadow did not hunt by smell or sight, but by sensing the minds of prey. Dusk glanced at Kokerlii again, his only protection against a danger that could swallow his ship whole. He had never clipped Kokerlii's wings, but at times like this he understood why many sailors preferred Aviar that could not fly away.

The boat rocked softly; the jumping slimfish stilled. Waves lapped against the sides of the vessel. Had the shadow stopped? Hesitated? Did it sense them? Kokerlii's protective aura had always been enough before, but . . .

The shadow slowly vanished. It had turned to swim downward, Dusk realized. In moments, he could make out nothing through the waters. He hesitated, then forced himself to get out his new mask. It was a modern device he had acquired only two supply trips back: a glass faceplate with leather at the sides. He placed it on the water's surface and leaned down, looking into the depths. They became as clear to him as an undisturbed lagoon.

Nothing. Just that endless deep. *Fool man,* he thought, tucking away the mask and getting out his paddle. *Didn't you just think to yourself that you never wanted to see one of those?*

Still, as he started paddling again, he knew that he'd spend the rest of this trip feeling as if the shadow were down there, following him. That was the nature of the waters. You never knew what lurked below.

He continued on his journey, paddling his outrigger canoe and reading the lapping of the waves to judge his position. Those waves were as good as a compass for him—once, they would have been good enough for any of the Eelakin, his people. These days, just the trappers learned the old arts. Admittedly, though, even *he* carried one of the newest compasses, wrapped up in his pack with a set of the new sea charts— maps given as gifts by the Ones Above during their visit earlier in the year. They were said to be more accurate than even the latest surveys, so he'd purchased a set just in case. You could not stop times from changing, his mother said, no more than you could stop the surf from rolling.

It was not long, after the accounting of tides, before he caught sight of the first island. Sori was a small island in the Pantheon, and the most commonly visited. Her name meant "child"; Dusk vividly remembered training on her shores with his uncle.

It had been long since he'd burned an offering to Sori, despite how well she had treated him during his youth. Perhaps a small offering would not be out of line. Patji would not grow jealous. One could not be jealous of Sori, the least of the islands. Just as every trapper was welcome on Sori, every other island in the Pantheon was said to be affectionate of her.

Be that as it may, Sori did not contain much valuable game. Dusk continued rowing, moving down one leg of the archipelago his people knew as the Pantheon. From a distance, this archipelago was not so different from the homeisles of the Eelakin, now a three-week trip behind him.

From a distance. Up close, they were very, very different. Over the next five hours, Dusk rowed past Sori, then her three cousins. He had never set foot on any of those three. In fact, he had not landed on many of the forty-some islands in the Pantheon. At the end of his apprenticeship, a trapper chose one island and worked there all his life. He had chosen Patji—an event some ten years past now. Seemed like far less.

Dusk saw no other shadows beneath the waves, but he kept watch. Not that he could do much to protect himself. Kokerlii did all of that work as he roosted happily at the prow of the ship, eyes half closed. Dusk had fed him seed; Kokerlii did like it so much more than dried fruit.

Nobody knew why beasts like the shadows only lived here, in the waters near the Pantheon. Why not travel across the seas to the Eelakin Islands or the mainland, where food would be plentiful and Aviar like Kokerlii were far more rare? Once, these questions had not been asked. The seas were what they were. Now, however, men poked and prodded into everything. They asked, "Why?" They said, "We should explain it."

Dusk shook his head, dipping his paddle into the water. That sound—wood on water—had been his companion for most of his days. He understood it far better than he did the speech of men.

Even if sometimes their questions got inside of him and refused to go free.

After the cousins, most trappers would have turned north or south, moving along branches of the archipelago until reaching their chosen island. Dusk continued forward, into the heart of the islands, until a shape loomed before him. Patji, largest island of the Pantheon. It towered like a wedge rising from the sea. A place of inhospitable peaks, sharp cliffs, and deep jungle.

Hello, old destroyer, he thought. *Hello, Father.*

Dusk raised his paddle and placed it in the boat. He sat for a time, chewing on fish from last night's catch, feeding scraps to Sak. The black-plumed bird ate them with an air of solemnity. Kokerlii continued to sit on the prow, chirping occasionally. He would be eager to land. Sak seemed never to grow eager about anything.

Approaching Patji was not a simple task, even for one who trapped his shores. The boat continued its dance with the waves as Dusk considered which landing to make. Eventually, he put the fish away, then dipped his paddle back into the waters. Those waters remained deep and blue, despite the proximity to the island. Some members of the Pantheon had sheltered bays and gradual beaches. Patji had no patience for such foolishness. His beaches were rocky and had steep drop-offs.

You were never safe on his shores. In fact, the beaches were the most dangerous part—upon them, not only could the horrors of the land get to you, but you were still within reach of the deep's monsters. Dusk's uncle had cautioned him about this time and time again. Only a fool slept on Patji's shores.

The tide was with him, and he avoided being caught in any of the swells that would crush him against those stern rock faces. Dusk approached a partially sheltered expanse of stone crags and outcroppings, Patji's version of a beach. Kokerlii fluttered off, chirping and calling as he flew toward the trees.

Dusk immediately glanced at the waters. No shadows. Still, he felt naked as he hopped out of the canoe and pulled it up onto the rocks, warm water washing against his legs. Sak remained in her place on Dusk's shoulder.

Nearby in the surf, Dusk saw a corpse bobbing in the water.

Beginning your visions early, my friend? he thought, glancing at Sak.

The Aviar usually waited until they'd fully landed before bestowing her blessing.

The black-feathered bird just watched the waves.

Dusk continued his work. The body he saw in the surf was his own. It told him to avoid that section of water. Perhaps there was a spiny anemone that would have pricked him, or perhaps a deceptive undercurrent lay in wait. Sak's visions did not show such detail; they gave only warning.

Dusk got the boat out of the water, then detached the floats, tying them more securely onto the main part of the canoe. Following that, he worked the vessel carefully up the shore, mindful not to scrape the hull on sharp rocks. He would need to hide the canoe in the jungle. If another trapper discovered it, Dusk would be stranded on the island for several extra weeks preparing his spare. That would—

He stopped as his heel struck something soft as he backed up the shore. He glanced down, expecting a pile of seaweed. Instead he found a damp piece of cloth. A shirt? Dusk held it up, then noticed other, more subtle signs across the shore. Broken lengths of sanded wood. Bits of paper floating in an eddy.

Those fools, he thought.

He returned to moving his canoe. Rushing was never a good idea on a Pantheon island. He did step more quickly, however.

As he reached the tree line, he caught sight of his corpse hanging from a tree nearby. Those were cutaway vines lurking in the fernlike treetop. Sak squawked softly on his shoulder as Dusk hefted a large stone from the beach, then tossed it at the tree. It thumped against the wood, and sure enough, the vines dropped like a net, full of stinging barbs.

They would take a few hours to retract. Dusk pulled his canoe over and hid it in the underbrush near the tree. Hopefully, other trappers would be smart enough to stay away from the cutaway vines—and therefore wouldn't stumble over his boat.

Before placing the final camouflaging fronds, Dusk pulled out his pack. Though the centuries had changed a trapper's duties very little, the modern world did offer its benefits. Instead of a simple wrap that left his legs and chest exposed, he put on thick trousers with pockets on the legs and a buttoning shirt to protect his skin against sharp branches and leaves. Instead of sandals, Dusk tied on sturdy boots. And instead of a tooth-lined club, he bore a machete of the finest steel. His pack contained luxuries like a steel-hooked rope, a lantern, and a firestarter that created sparks simply by pressing the two handles together.

He looked very little like the trappers in the paintings back home. He didn't mind. He'd rather stay alive.

Dusk left the canoe, shouldering his pack, machete sheathed at his side. Sak moved to his other shoulder. Before leaving the beach, Dusk paused, looking at the image of his translucent corpse, still hanging from unseen vines by the tree.

Could he really have ever been foolish enough to be caught by cutaway vines? Near as he could tell, Sak only showed him plausible deaths. He liked to think that most were fairly unlikely—a vision of what could have happened if he'd been careless, or if his uncle's training hadn't been so extensive.

Once, Dusk had stayed away from any place where he saw his corpse. It wasn't bravery that drove him to do the opposite now. He just . . . needed to confront the possibilities. He needed to be able to walk away from this beach knowing that he could still deal with cutaway vines. If he avoided danger, he would soon lose his skills. He could not rely on Sak too much.

For Patji would try on every possible occasion to kill him.

Dusk turned and trudged across the rocks along the coast. Doing so went against his instincts—he normally wanted to get inland as soon as possible. Unfortunately, he could not leave without investigating the origin of the debris he had seen earlier. He had a strong suspicion of where he would find their source.

He gave a whistle, and Kokerlii trilled above, flapping out of a tree nearby and winging over the beach. The protection he offered would not be as strong as it would be if he were close, but the beasts that hunted minds on the island were not as large or as strong of psyche as the shadows of the ocean. Dusk and Sak would be invisible to them.

About a half hour up the coast, Dusk found the remnants of a large camp. Broken boxes, fraying ropes lying half submerged in tidal pools, ripped canvas, shattered pieces of wood that might once have been walls. Kokerlii landed on a broken pole.

There were no signs of his corpse nearby. That could mean that the area wasn't immediately dangerous. It could also mean that whatever might kill him here would swallow the corpse whole.

Dusk trod lightly on wet stones at the edge of the broken campsite. No. Larger than a campsite. Dusk ran his fingers over a broken chunk of wood, stenciled with the words *Northern Interests Trading Company*. A powerful mercantile force from his homeland.

He had told them. He had *told* them. Do not come to Patji. Fools. And they had camped here on the beach itself! Was nobody in that company capable of listening? He stopped beside a group of gouges in the rocks, as wide as his upper arm, running some ten paces long. They led toward the ocean.

Shadow, he thought. *One of the deep beasts.* His uncle had spoken of seeing one once. An enormous . . . *something* that had exploded up from the depths. It had killed a dozen krell that had been chewing on ocean-side weeds before retreating into the waters with its feast.

Dusk shivered, imagining this camp on the rocks, bustling with men unpacking boxes, preparing to build the fort they had described to him. But where was their ship? The great steam-powered vessel with an iron hull they claimed could rebuff the attacks of even the deepest of shadows? Did it now defend the ocean bottom, a home for slimfish and octopus?

There were no survivors—nor even any corpses—that Dusk could see. The shadow must have consumed them. He pulled back to the slightly safer locale of the jungle's edge, then scanned the foliage, looking for signs that people had passed this way. The attack was recent, within the last day or so.

He absently gave Sak a seed from his pocket as he located a series of broken fronds leading into the jungle. So there were survivors. Maybe as many as a half dozen. They had each chosen to go in a different direction, in a hurry. Running from the attack.

Running through the jungle was a good way to get dead. These company types thought themselves rugged and prepared. They were wrong.

He'd spoken to a number of them, trying to persuade as many of their "trappers" as possible to abandon the voyage.

It had done no good. He wanted to blame the visits of the Ones Above for causing this foolish striving for progress, but the truth was the companies had been talking of outposts on the Pantheon for years. Dusk sighed. Well, these survivors were likely dead now. He should leave them to their fates.

Except . . . The thought of it, outsiders on Patji, it made him shiver with something that mixed disgust and anxiety. They were *here*. It was wrong. These islands were sacred, the trappers their priests.

The plants rustled nearby. Dusk whipped his machete about, leveling it, reaching into his pocket for his sling. It was not a refugee who left the bushes, or even a predator. A group of small, mouselike creatures crawled out, sniffing the air. Sak squawked. She had never liked meekers.

Food? the three meekers sent to Dusk. *Food?*

It was the most rudimentary of thoughts, projected directly into his mind. Though he did not want the distraction, he did not pass up the opportunity to fish out some dried meat for the meekers. As they huddled around it, sending him gratitude, he saw their sharp teeth and the single pointed fang at the tips of their mouths. His uncle had told him that once, meekers had been dangerous to men. One bite was enough to kill. Over the centuries, the little creatures had grown accustomed to trappers. They had minds beyond those of dull animals. Almost he found them as intelligent as the Aviar.

You remember? he sent them through thoughts. *You remember your task?*

Others, they sent back gleefully. *Bite others!*

Trappers ignored these little beasts; Dusk figured that maybe with some training, the meekers could provide an unexpected surprise for one of his rivals. He fished in his pocket, fingers brushing an old stiff piece of feather. Then, not wanting to pass up the opportunity, he got a few long, bright green and red feathers from his pack. They were mating plumes, which he'd taken from Kokerlii during the Aviar's most recent molting.

He moved into the jungle, meekers following with excitement. Once he neared their den, he stuck the mating plumes into some branches, as if they had fallen there naturally. A passing trapper might see the plumes and assume that Aviar had a nest nearby, fresh with eggs for the plunder. That would draw them.

Bite others, Dusk instructed again.

Bite others! they replied.

He hesitated, thoughtful. Had they perhaps seen something from the company wreck? Point him in the right direction. *Have you seen any others?* Dusk sent them. *Recently? In the jungle?*

Bite others! came the reply.

They were intelligent . . . but not *that* intelligent. Dusk bade the animals farewell and turned toward the forest. After a moment's deliberation, he found himself striking inland, crossing—then following—one of the refugee trails. He chose the one that looked as if it would pass uncomfortably close to one of his own safecamps, deep within the jungle.

It was hotter here beneath the jungle's canopy, despite the shade. Comfortably sweltering. Kokerlii joined him, winging up ahead to a branch where a few lesser Aviar sat chirping. Kokerlii towered over them, but sang at them with enthusiasm. An Aviar raised around humans never quite fit back in among their own kind. The same could be said of a man raised around Aviar.

Dusk followed the trail left by the refugee, expecting to stumble over the man's corpse at any moment. He did not, though his own dead body did occasionally appear along the path. He saw it lying half eaten in the mud or tucked away in a fallen log with only the foot showing. He could never grow too complacent, with Sak on his shoulder. It did not matter if Sak's visions were truth or fiction; he needed the constant reminder of how Patji treated the unwary.

He fell into the familiar, but not comfortable, lope of a Pantheon trapper. Alert, wary, careful not to brush leaves that could carry biting insects. Cutting with the machete only when necessary, lest he leave a trail another could follow. Listening, aware of his Aviar at all times, never outstripping Kokerlii or letting him drift too far ahead.

The refugee did not fall to the common dangers of the island—he cut across game trails, rather than following them. The surest way to encounter predators was to fall in with their food. The refugee did not know how to mask his trail, but neither did he blunder into the nest of firesnap lizards, or brush the deathweed bark, or step into the patch of hungry mud.

Was this another trapper, perhaps? A youthful one, not fully trained? That seemed something the company would try. Experienced trappers were beyond recruitment; none would be foolish enough to guide a group of clerks and merchants around the islands. But a youth, who had not yet chosen his island? A youth who, perhaps, resented being required to practice only on Sori until his mentor determined his apprenticeship complete? Dusk had felt that way ten years ago.

So the company had hired itself a trapper at last. That would explain why they had grown so bold as to finally organize their expedition. *But Patji himself?* he thought, kneeling beside the bank of a small stream. It had no name, but it was familiar to him. *Why would they come here?*

The answer was simple. They were merchants. The biggest, to them, would be the best. Why waste time on lesser islands? Why not come for the Father himself?

Above, Kokerlii landed on a branch and began pecking at a fruit. The refugee had stopped by this river. Dusk had gained time on the youth. Judging by the depth the boy's footprints had sunk in the mud, Dusk could imagine his weight and height. Sixteen? Maybe younger? Trappers apprenticed at ten, but Dusk could not imagine even the company trying to recruit one so ill trained.

Two hours gone, Dusk thought, turning a broken stem and smelling the sap. The boy's path continued on toward Dusk's safecamp. How? Dusk had never spoken of it to anyone. Perhaps this youth was apprenticing under one of the other trappers who visited Patji. One of them could have found his safecamp and mentioned it.

Dusk frowned, considering. In ten years on Patji, he had seen another trapper in person only a handful of times. On each occasion, they had both turned and gone a different direction without saying a word. It was the way of such things. They would try to kill one another, but they didn't do it in person. Better to let Patji claim rivals than to directly stain one's hands. At least, so his uncle had taught him.

Sometimes, Dusk found himself frustrated by that. Patji would get them all eventually. Why help the Father out? Still, it was the way of things, so he went through the motions. Regardless, this refugee was making directly for Dusk's safecamp. The youth might not know the proper way of things. Perhaps he had come seeking help, afraid to go to one of his master's safecamps for fear of punishment. Or . . .

No, best to avoid pondering it. Dusk already had a mind full of spurious conjectures. He would find what he would find. He had to focus on the jungle and its dangers. He started away from the stream, and as he did so, he saw his corpse appear suddenly before him.

He hopped forward, then spun backward, hearing a faint hiss. The distinctive sound was made by air escaping from a small break in the ground, followed by a flood of tiny yellow insects, each as small as a pinhead. A new deathant pod? If he'd stood there a little longer, disturbing their hidden nest, they would have flooded up around his boot. One bite, and he'd be dead.

He stared at that pool of scrambling insects longer than he should have. They pulled back into their nest, finding no prey. Sometimes a small bulge announced their location, but today he had seen nothing. Only Sak's vision had saved him.

Such was life on Patji. Even the most careful trapper could make a mistake—and even if they didn't, death could still find them. Patji was a domineering, vengeful parent who sought the blood of all who landed on his shores.

Sak chirped on his shoulder. Dusk rubbed her neck in thanks, though her chirp sounded apologetic. The warning had come almost too late. Without her, Patji would have claimed him this day. Dusk shoved down those itching questions he should not be thinking, and continued on his way.

He finally approached his safecamp as evening settled upon the island. Two of his tripwires had been cut, disarming them. That was not surprising; those were meant to be obvious. Dusk crept past another deathant nest in the ground—this larger one had a permanent crack as an opening they could flood out of, but the rift had been stoppered with a smoldering twig. Beyond it, the nightwind fungi that Dusk had spent years cultivating here had been smothered in water to keep the spores from escaping. The next two tripwires—the ones not intended to be obvious—had *also* been cut.

Nice work, kid, Dusk thought. He hadn't just avoided the traps, but disarmed them, in case he needed to flee quickly back this direction. However, someone really needed to teach the boy how to move without being trackable. Of course, those tracks could be a trap unto themselves—an attempt to make Dusk himself careless. And so, he was extra careful as he edged forward. Yes, here the youth had left more footprints, broken stems, and other signs. . . .

Something moved up above in the canopy. Dusk hesitated, squinting. A *woman* hung from the tree branches above, trapped in a net made of jellywire vines—they left someone numb, unable to move. So, one of his traps had finally worked.

"Um, hello?" she said.

A woman, Dusk thought, suddenly feeling stupid. *The smaller foot-print, lighter step . . .*

"I want to make it perfectly clear," the woman said. "I have no intention of stealing your birds or infringing upon your territory."

Dusk stepped closer in the dimming light. He recognized this woman. She was one of the clerks who had been at his meetings with the company. "You cut my tripwires," Dusk said. Words felt odd in his mouth, and they came out ragged, as if he'd swallowed handfuls of dust. The result of weeks without speaking.

"Er, yes, I did. I assumed you could replace them." She hesitated. "Sorry?"

Dusk settled back. The woman rotated slowly in her net, and he noticed an Aviar clinging to the outside—like his own birds, it was about as tall as three fists atop one another, though this one had subdued white and green plumage. A streamer, which was a breed that did not live on Patji. He did not know much about them, other than that like Kokerlii, they protected the mind from predators.

The setting sun cast shadows, the sky darkening. Soon, he would need to hunker down for the night, for darkness brought out the island's most dangerous of predators.

"I promise," the woman said from within her bindings. What was her name? He believed it had been told to him, but he did not recall. Something untraditional. "I really don't want to steal from you. You remember me, don't you? We met back in the company halls?"

He gave no reply.

"Please," she said. "I'd really rather not be hung by my ankles from a tree, slathered with blood to attract predators. If it's all the same to you."

"You are not a trapper."

"Well, no," she said. "You may have noticed my gender."

"There have been female trappers."

"One. One female trapper, Yaalani the Brave. I've heard her story a hundred times. You may find it curious to know that almost every society has its myth of the female role reversal. She goes to war dressed as a man, or leads her father's armies into battle, or traps on an island. I'm convinced that such stories exist so that parents can tell their daughters, 'You are not Yaalani.'"

This woman spoke. A lot. People did that back on the Eelakin Islands. Her skin was dark, like his, and she had the sound of his people. The slight accent to her voice . . . he had heard it more and more when visiting the homeisles. It was the accent of one who was educated.

"Can I get down?" she asked, voice bearing a faint tremor. "I cannot feel my hands. It is . . . unsettling."

"What is your name?" Dusk asked. "I have forgotten it." This was too much speaking. It hurt his ears. This place was supposed to be soft.

"Vathi."

That's right. It was an improper name. Not a reference to her birth order and day of birth, but a name like the mainlanders used. That was not uncommon among his people now.

He walked over and took the rope from the nearby tree, then lowered the net. The woman's Aviar flapped down, screeching in annoyance, favoring one wing, obviously wounded. Vathi hit the ground, a bundle of dark curls and green linen skirts. She stumbled to her feet, but fell back down again. Her skin would be numb for some fifteen minutes from the touch of the vines.

She sat there and wagged her hands, as if to shake out the numbness. "So . . . uh, no ankles and blood?" she asked, hopeful.

"That is a story parents tell to children," Dusk said. "It is not something we actually do."

"Oh."

"If you had been another trapper, I would have killed you directly, rather than leaving you to avenge yourself upon me." He walked over to her Aviar, which opened its beak in a hissing posture, raising both wings as if to be bigger than it was. Sak chirped from his shoulder, but the bird didn't seem to care.

Yes, one wing was bloody. Vathi knew enough to care for the bird, however, which was pleasing. Some homeislers were completely ignorant of their Aviar's needs, treating them like accessories rather than intelligent creatures.

Vathi had pulled out the feathers near the wound, including a blood feather. She'd wrapped the wound with gauze. That wing didn't look good, however. Might be a fracture involved. He'd want to wrap both wings, prevent the creature from flying.

"Oh, Mirris," Vathi said, finally finding her feet. "I tried to help her. We fell, you see, when the monster—"

"Pick her up," Dusk said, checking the sky. "Follow. Step where I step."

Vathi nodded, not complaining, though her numbness would not have passed yet. She collected a small pack from the vines and straightened her skirts. She wore a tight vest above them, and the pack had some kind of metal tube sticking out of it. A map case? She fetched her Aviar, who huddled happily on her shoulder.

As Dusk led the way, she followed, and she did not attempt to attack him when his back was turned. Good. Darkness was coming upon them, but his safecamp was just ahead, and he knew by heart the steps to approach along this path. As they walked, Kokerlii fluttered down and landed on the woman's other shoulder, then began chirping in an amiable way.

Dusk stopped, turning. The woman's own Aviar moved down her dress away from Kokerlii to cling near her bodice. The bird hissed softly, but Kokerlii—oblivious, as usual—continued to chirp happily. It was fortunate his breed was so mind-invisible, even deathants would consider him no more edible than a piece of bark.

"Is this . . ." Vathi said, looking to Dusk. "Yours? But of course. The one on your shoulder is not Aviar."

Sak settled back, puffing up her feathers. No, her species was not Aviar. Dusk continued to lead the way.

"I have never seen a trapper carry a bird who was not from the islands," Vathi said from behind.

It was not a question. Dusk, therefore, felt no need to reply.

This safecamp—he had three total on the island—lay atop a short hill following a twisting trail. Here, a stout gurratree held aloft a single-room structure. Trees were one of the safer places to sleep on Patji. The treetops were the domain of the Aviar, and most of the large predators walked.

Dusk lit his lantern, then held it aloft, letting the orange light bathe his home. "Up," he said to the woman.

She glanced over her shoulder into the darkening jungle. By the lantern-light, he saw that the whites of her eyes were red from lack of sleep, despite the unconcerned smile she gave him before climbing up the stakes he'd planted in the tree. Her numbness should have worn off by now.

"How did you know?" he asked.

Vathi hesitated, near to the trapdoor leading into his home. "Know what?"

"Where my safecamp was. Who told you?"

"I followed the sound of water," she said, nodding toward the small spring that bubbled out of the mountainside here. "When I found traps, I knew I was coming the right way."

Dusk frowned. One could not hear this water, as the stream vanished only a few hundred yards away, resurfacing in an unexpected location. Following it here . . . that would be virtually impossible.

So was she lying, or was she just lucky?

"You wanted to find me," he said.

"I wanted to find *someone*," she said, pushing open the trapdoor, voice growing muffled as she climbed up into the building. "I figured that a trapper would be my only chance for survival." Above, she stepped up to one of the netted windows, Kokerlii still on her shoulder. "This is nice. Very roomy for a shack on a mountainside in the middle of a deadly jungle on an isolated island surrounded by monsters."

Dusk climbed up, holding the lantern in his teeth. The room at the top was perhaps four paces square, tall enough to stand in, but only barely. "Shake out those blankets," he said, nodding toward the stack and setting down the lantern. "Then lift every cup and bowl on the shelf and check inside of them."

Her eyes widened. "What am I looking for?"

"Deathants, scorpions, spiders, bloodscratches . . ." He shrugged, putting Sak on her perch by the window. "The room is built to be tight, but this is Patji. The Father likes surprises."

As she hesitantly set aside her pack and got to work, Dusk continued up another ladder to check the roof. There, a group of bird-size boxes, with nests inside and holes to allow the birds to come and go freely, lay arranged in a double row. The animals would not stray far, except on special occasions, now that they had been raised with him handling them.

Kokerlii landed on top of one of the homes, trilling—but softly, now that night had fallen. More coos and chirps came from the other boxes. Dusk climbed out to check each bird for hurt wings or feet. These Aviar pairs were his life's work; the chicks each one hatched became his primary stock-in-trade. Yes, he would trap on the island, trying to find nests and wild chicks—but that was never as efficient as raising nests.

"Your name was Sixth, wasn't it?" Vathi said from below, voice accompanied by the sound of a blanket being shaken.

"It is."

"Large family," Vathi noted.

An ordinary family. Or, so it had once been. His father had been a twelfth and his mother an eleventh.

"Sixth of what?" Vathi prompted below.

"Of the Dusk."

"So you were born in the evening," Vathi said. "I've always found the traditional names so . . . uh . . . *descriptive*."

What a meaningless comment, Dusk thought. *Why do homeislers feel the need to speak when there is nothing to say?*

He moved on to the next nest, checking the two drowsy birds inside, then inspecting their droppings. They responded to his presence with happiness. An Aviar raised around humans—particularly one that had lent its talent to a person at an early age—would always see people as part of their flock. These birds were not his companions, like Sak and Kokerlii, but they were still special to him.

"No insects in the blankets," Vathi said, sticking her head up out of the trapdoor behind him, her own Aviar on her shoulder.

"The cups?"

"I'll get to those in a moment. So these are your breeding pairs, are they?"

Obviously they were, so he didn't need to reply.

She watched him check them. He felt her eyes on him. Finally, he spoke. "Why did your company ignore the advice we gave you? Coming here was a disaster."

"Yes."

He turned to her.

"Yes," she continued, "this whole expedition will likely be a disaster—a disaster that takes us a step closer to our goal."

He checked Sisisru next, working by the light of the now-rising moon. "Foolish."

Vathi folded her arms before her on the roof of the building, torso still disappearing into the lit square of the trapdoor below. "Do you think that our ancestors learned to wayfind on the oceans without experiencing a few disasters along the way? Or what of the first trappers? You have knowledge passed down for generations, knowledge learned through trial and error. If the first trappers had considered it too 'foolish' to explore, where would you be?"

"They were single men, well-trained, not a ship full of clerks and dockworkers."

"The world is changing, Sixth of the Dusk," she said softly. "The people of the mainland grow hungry for Aviar companions; things once restricted to the very wealthy are within the reach of ordinary people. We've learned so much, yet the Aviar are still an enigma. Why don't chicks raised on the homeisles bestow talents? Why—"

"Foolish arguments," Dusk said, putting Sisisru back into her nest. "I do not wish to hear them again."

"And the Ones Above?" she asked. "What of their technology, the wonders they produce?"

He hesitated, then he took out a pair of thick gloves and gestured toward her Aviar. Vathi looked at the white and green Aviar, then made a comforting clicking sound and took her in two hands. The bird suffered it with a few annoyed half bites at Vathi's fingers.

Dusk carefully took the bird in his gloved hands—for him, those bites would not be as timid—and undid Vathi's bandage. Then he cleaned the wound—much to the bird's protests—and carefully placed a new bandage. From there, he wrapped the bird's wings around its body with another bandage, not too tight, lest the creature be unable to breathe.

She didn't like it, obviously. But flying would hurt that wing more, with the fracture. She'd eventually be able to bite off the bandage, but for now, she'd get a chance to heal. Once done, he placed her with his other Aviar, who made quiet, friendly chirps, calming the flustered bird.

Vathi seemed content to let her bird remain there for the time, though she watched the entire process with interest.

"You may sleep in my safecamp tonight," Dusk said, turning back to her.

"And then what?" she asked. "You turn me out into the jungle to die?"

"You did well on your way here," he said, grudgingly. She was not a trapper. A scholar should not have been able to do what she did. "You will probably survive."

"I got lucky. I'd never make it across the entire island."

Dusk paused. "Across the island?"

"To the main company camp."

"There are *more* of you?"

"I . . . Of course. You didn't think . . ."

"What happened?" *Now who is the fool?* he thought to himself. *You should have asked this first.* Talking. He had never been good with it.

She shied away from him, eyes widening. Did he look dangerous? Perhaps he had barked that last question forcefully. No matter. She spoke, so he got what he needed.

"We set up camp on the far beach," she said. "We have two ironhulls armed with cannons watching the waters. Those can take on even a deepwalker, if they have to. Two hundred soldiers, half that number in scientists and merchants. We're determined to find out, once and for all, why the Aviar must be born on one of the Pantheon Islands to be able to bestow talents.

"One team came down this direction to scout sites to place another fortress. The company is determined to hold Patji against other interests. I thought the smaller expedition a bad idea, but had my own reasons for wanting to circle the island. So I went along. And then, the deep-walker . . ." She looked sick.

Dusk had almost stopped listening. Two *hundred* soldiers? Crawling across Patji like ants on a fallen piece of fruit. Unbearable! He thought of the quiet jungle broken by the sounds of their racketous voices. The sound of humans yelling at each other, clanging on metal, stomping about. Like a city.

A flurry of dark feathers announced Sak coming up from below and landing on the lip of the trapdoor beside Vathi. The black-plumed bird limped across the roof toward Dusk, stretching her wings, showing off the scars on her left. Flying even a dozen feet was a chore for her.

Dusk reached down to scratch her neck. It was happening. An invasion. He had to find a way to stop it. Somehow . . .

"I'm sorry, Dusk," Vathi said. "The trappers are fascinating to me; I've read of your ways, and I respect them. But this was *going* to happen someday; it's inevitable. The islands *will* be tamed. The Aviar are too valuable to leave in the hands of a couple hundred eccentric woodsmen."

"The chiefs . . ."

"All twenty chiefs in council agreed to this plan," Vathi said. "I was there. If the Eelakin do not secure these islands and the Aviar, someone else will."

Dusk stared out into the night. "Go and make certain there are no insects in the cups below."

"But—"

"*Go,*" he said, "and make *certain* there are no insects in the cups below!"

The woman sighed softly, but retreated into the room, leaving him with his Aviar. He continued to scratch Sak on the neck, seeking comfort in the familiar motion and in her presence. Dared he hope that the shadows would prove too deadly for the company and its iron-hulled ships? Vathi seemed confident.

She did not tell me why she joined the scouting group. She had seen a shadow, witnessed it destroying her team, but had still managed the presence of mind to find his camp. She was a strong woman. He would need to remember that.

She was also a company type, as removed from his experience as a person could get. Soldiers, craftsmen, even chiefs he could understand. But these soft-spoken scribes who had quietly conquered the world with a sword of commerce, they baffled him.

"Father," he whispered. "What do I do?"

Patji gave no reply beyond the normal sounds of night. Creatures moving, hunting, rustling. At night, the Aviar slept, and that gave opportunity to the most dangerous of the island's predators. In the distance a nightmaw called, its horrid screech echoing through the trees.

Sak spread her wings, leaning down, head darting back and forth. The sound always made her tremble. It did the same to Dusk.

He sighed and rose, placing Sak on his shoulder. He turned, and almost stumbled as he saw his corpse at his feet. He came alert immediately. What was it? Vines in the tree branches? A spider, dropping quietly from above? There wasn't supposed to be anything in his safecamp that could kill him.

Sak screeched as if in pain.

Nearby, his other Aviar cried out as well, a cacophony of squawks, screeches, chirps. No, it wasn't just them! All around . . . echoing in the distance, from both near and far, wild Aviar squawked. They rustled in their branches, a sound like a powerful wind blowing through the trees.

Dusk spun about, holding his hands to his ears, eyes wide as corpses appeared around him. They piled high, one atop another, some bloated, some bloody, some skeletal. Haunting him. Dozens upon *dozens*.

He dropped to his knees, yelling. That put him eye-to-eye with one of his corpses. Only this one . . . this one was not quite dead. Blood dripped from its lips as it tried to speak, mouthing words that Dusk did not understand.

It vanished.

They all did, every last one. He spun about, wild, but saw no bodies. The sounds of the Aviar quieted, and his flock settled back into their nests. Dusk breathed in and out deeply, heart racing. He felt tense, as if at any moment a shadow would explode from the blackness around his camp and consume him. He anticipated it, felt it coming. He wanted to run, run *somewhere*.

What had that been? In all of his years with Sak, he had never seen anything like it. What could have upset all of the Aviar at once? Was it the nightmaw he had heard?

Don't be foolish, he thought. *This was different, different from anything you've seen. Different from anything that has been seen on Patji.* But what? What had changed . . .

Sak had not settled down like the others. She stared northward, toward where Vathi had said the main camp of invaders was setting up.

Dusk stood, then clambered down into the room below, Sak on his shoulder. "What are your people doing?"

Vathi spun at his harsh tone. She had been looking out of the window, northward. "I don't—"

He took her by the front of her vest, pulling her toward him in a two-fisted grip, meeting her eyes from only a few inches away. *"What are your people doing?"*

Her eyes widened, and he could feel her tremble in his grip, though she set her jaw and held his gaze. Scribes were not supposed to have grit like this. He had seen them scribbling away in their windowless rooms. Dusk tightened his grip on her vest, pulling the fabric so it dug into her skin, and found himself growling softly.

"Release me," she said, "and we will speak."

"Bah," he said, letting go. She dropped a few inches, hitting the floor with a thump. He hadn't realized he'd lifted her off the ground.

She backed away, putting as much space between them as the room would allow. He stalked to the window, looking through the mesh screen at the night. His corpse dropped from the roof above, hitting the ground below. He jumped back, worried that it was happening again.

It didn't, not the same way as before. However, when he turned back into the room, his corpse lay in the corner, bloody lips parted, eyes staring sightlessly. The danger, whatever it was, had not passed.

Vathi had sat down on the floor, holding her head, trembling. Had he frightened her that soundly? She did look tired, exhausted. She wrapped her arms around herself, and when she looked at him, there was a cast to her eyes that hadn't been there before—as if she were regarding a wild animal let off its chain.

That seemed fitting.

"What do you know of the Ones Above?" she asked him.

"They live in the stars," Dusk said.

"We at the company have been meeting with them. We don't understand their ways. They look like us; at times they talk like us. But they have . . . rules, laws that they won't explain. They refuse to sell us their marvels, but in like manner, they seem forbidden from taking things from us, even in trade. They promise it, someday when we are more advanced. It's like they think we are children."

"Why should we care?" Dusk said. "If they leave us alone, we will be better for it."

"You haven't seen the things they can do," she said softly, getting a distant look in her eyes. "We have barely worked out how to create ships that can sail on their own, against the wind. But the Ones Above . . . they can sail the skies, sail the *stars themselves*. They know so much, and they won't *tell* us any of it."

She shook her head, reaching into the pocket of her skirt. "They are after something, Dusk. What interest do we hold for them? From what I've heard them say, there are many other worlds like ours, with cultures that cannot sail the stars. We are not unique, yet the Ones Above come back here time and time again. They *do* want something. You can see it in their eyes. . . ."

"What is that?" Dusk asked, nodding to the thing she took from her pocket. It rested in her palm like the shell of a clam, but had a mirror-like face on the top.

"It is a machine," she said. "Like a clock, only it never needs to be wound, and it . . . shows things."

"What things?"

"Well, it translates languages. Ours into that of the Ones Above. It also . . . shows the locations of Aviar."

"*What?*"

"It's like a map," she said. "It points the way to Aviar."

"That's how you found my camp," Dusk said, stepping toward her.

"Yes." She rubbed her thumb across the machine's surface. "We aren't supposed to have this. It was the possession of an emissary sent to work with us. He choked while eating a few months back. They *can* die, it appears, even of mundane causes. That . . . changed how I view them.

"His kind have asked after his machines, and we will have to return them soon. But this one tells us what they are after: the Aviar. The Ones Above are always fascinated with them. I think they want to find a way to trade for the birds, a way their laws will allow. They hint that we might not be safe, that not everyone Above follows their laws."

"But why did the Aviar react like they did, just now?" Dusk said, turning back to the window. "Why did . . ." *Why did I see what I saw? What I'm still seeing, to an extent?* His corpse was there, wherever he looked. Slumped by a tree outside, in the corner of the room, hanging out of the trapdoor in the roof. Sloppy. He should have closed that.

Sak had pulled into his hair like she did when a predator was near.

"There . . . is a second machine," Vathi said.

"Where?" he demanded.

"On our ship."

The direction the Aviar had looked.

"The second machine is much larger," Vathi said. "This one in my hand has limited range. The larger one can create an enormous map, one of an entire island, then *write* out a paper with a copy of that map. That map will include a dot marking every Aviar."

"And?"

"And we were going to engage the machine tonight," she said. "It takes hours to prepare—like an oven, growing hot—before it's ready. The schedule was to turn it on tonight just after sunset so we could use it in the morning."

"The others," Dusk demanded, "they'd use it without you?"

She grimaced. "Happily. Captain Eusto probably did a dance when I didn't return from scouting. He's been worried I would take control of this expedition. But the machine isn't harmful; it merely locates Aviar."

"Did it do *that* before?" he demanded, waving toward the night.

504 · BRANDON SANDERSON

"When you last used it, did it draw the attention of all the Aviar? Discomfort them?"

"Well, no," she said. "But the moment of discomfort has passed, hasn't it? I'm sure it's nothing."

Nothing. Sak quivered on his shoulder. Dusk saw death all around him. The moment they had engaged that machine, the corpses had piled up. If they used it again, the results would be horrible. Dusk knew it. He could *feel* it.

"We're going to stop them," he said.

"What?" Vathi asked. "*Tonight?*"

"Yes," Dusk said, walking to a small hidden cabinet in the wall. He pulled it open and began to pick through the supplies inside. A second lantern. Extra oil.

"That's insane," Vathi said. "Nobody travels the islands at night."

"I've done it once before. With my uncle."

His uncle had died on that trip.

"You can't be serious, Dusk. The nightmaws are out. I've heard them."

"Nightmaws track minds," Dusk said, stuffing supplies into his pack. "They are almost completely deaf, and close to blind. If we move quickly and cut across the center of the island, we can be to your camp by morning. We can stop them from using the machine again."

"But why would we *want* to?"

He shouldered the pack. "Because if we don't, it will destroy the island."

She frowned at him, cocking her head. "You can't know that. Why do you think you know that?"

"Your Aviar will have to remain here, with that wound," he said, ignoring the question. "She would not be able to fly away if something happened to us." The same argument could be made for Sak, but he would not be without the bird. "I will return her to you after we have stopped the machine. Come." He walked to the floor hatch and pulled it open.

Vathi rose, but pressed back against the wall. "I'm staying here."

"The people of your company won't believe me," he said. "You will have to tell them to stop. You are coming."

Vathi licked her lips in what seemed to be a nervous habit. She glanced to the sides, looking for escape, then back at him. Right then,

Dusk noticed his corpse hanging from the pegs in the tree beneath him. He jumped.

"What was that?" she demanded.

"Nothing."

"You keep glancing to the sides," Vathi said. "What do you think you see, Dusk?"

"We're going. Now."

"You've been alone on the island for a long time," she said, obviously trying to make her voice soothing. "You're upset about our arrival. You aren't thinking clearly. I understand."

Dusk drew in a deep breath. "Sak, show her."

The bird launched from his shoulder, flapping across the room, landing on Vathi. She turned to the bird, frowning.

Then she gasped, falling to her knees. Vathi huddled back against the wall, eyes darting from side to side, mouth working but no words coming out. Dusk left her to it for a short time, then raised his arm. Sak returned to him on black wings, dropping a single dark feather to the floor. She settled in again on his shoulder. That much flying was difficult for her.

"What was *that*?" Vathi demanded.

"Come," Dusk said, taking his pack and climbing down out of the room.

Vathi scrambled to the open hatch. "No. Tell me. What *was* that?"

"You saw your corpse."

"All about me. Everywhere I looked."

"Sak grants that talent."

"There is no such talent."

Dusk looked up at her, halfway down the pegs. "You have seen your death. That is what will happen if your friends use their machine. Death. All of us. The Aviar, everyone living here. I do not know why, but I know that it *will* come."

"You've discovered a new Aviar," Vathi said. "How . . . When . . . ?"

"Hand me the lantern," Dusk said.

Looking numb, she obeyed, handing it down. He put it into his teeth and descended the pegs to the ground. Then he raised the lantern high, looking down the slope.

The inky jungle at night. Like the depths of the ocean.

He shivered, then whistled. Kokerlii fluttered down from above, landing on his other shoulder. He would hide their minds, and with that, they had a chance. It would still not be easy. The things of the jungle relied upon mind sense, but many could still hunt by scent or other senses.

Vathi scrambled down the pegs behind him, her pack over her shoulder, the strange tube peeking out. "You have two Aviar," she said. "You use them both at once?"

"My uncle had three."

"How is that even possible?"

"They like trappers." So many questions. Could she not think about what the answers might be before asking?

"We're actually going to do this," she said, whispering, as if to herself. "The jungle at night. I should stay. I should refuse . . ."

"You've seen your death if you do."

"I've seen what you claim is my death. A new Aviar . . . It has been centuries." Though her voice still sounded reluctant, she walked after him as he strode down the slope and passed his traps, entering the jungle again.

His corpse sat at the base of a tree. That made him immediately look for what could kill him here, but Sak's senses seemed to be off. The island's impending death was so overpowering, it seemed to be smothering smaller dangers. He might not be able to rely upon her visions until the machine was destroyed.

The thick jungle canopy swallowed them, hot, even at night; the ocean breezes didn't reach this far inland. That left the air feeling stagnant, and it dripped with the scents of the jungle. Fungus, rotting leaves, the perfumes of flowers. The accompaniment to those scents was the sounds of an island coming alive. A constant crinkling in the underbrush, like the sound of maggots writhing in a pile of dry leaves. The lantern's light did not seem to extend as far as it should.

Vathi pulled up close behind him. "Why did you do this before?" she whispered. "The other time you went out at night?"

More questions. But sounds, fortunately, were not too dangerous.

"I was wounded," Dusk whispered. "We had to get from one safe-camp to the other to recover my uncle's store of antivenom." Because Dusk, hands trembling, had dropped the other flask.

"You survived it? Well, obviously you did, I mean. I'm surprised, is all."

She seemed to be talking to fill the air.

"They could be watching us," she said, looking into the darkness. "Nightmaws."

"They are not."

"How can you know?" she asked, voice hushed. "Anything could be out there, in that darkness."

"If the nightmaws had seen us, we'd be dead. That is how I know." He shook his head, sliding out his machete and cutting away a few branches before them. Any could hold deathants skittering across their leaves. In the dark, it would be difficult to spot them, and so brushing against foliage seemed a poor decision.

We won't be able to avoid it, he thought, leading the way down through a gully thick with mud. He had to step on stones to keep from sinking in. Vathi followed with remarkable dexterity. *We have to go quickly. I can't cut down every branch in our way.*

He hopped off a stone and onto the bank of the gully, and there passed his corpse sinking into the mud. Nearby, he spotted a second corpse, so translucent it was nearly invisible. He raised his lantern, hoping it wasn't happening again.

Others did not appear. Just these two. And the very faint image . . . yes, that was a sinkhole there. Sak chirped softly, and he fished in his pocket for a seed to give her. She had figured out how to send him help. The fainter images were immediate dangers—he would have to watch for those.

"Thank you," he whispered to her.

"That bird of yours," Vathi said, speaking softly in the gloom of night, "are there others?"

They climbed out of the gully, continuing on, crossing a krell trail in the night. He stopped them just before they wandered into a patch of deathants. Vathi looked at the trail of tiny yellow insects, moving in a straight line.

"Dusk?" she asked as they rounded the ants. "Are there others? Why haven't you brought any chicks to market?"

"I do not have any chicks."

"So you found only the one?" she asked.

Questions, questions. Buzzing around him like flies.

Don't be foolish, he told himself, shoving down his annoyance. *You would ask the same, if you saw someone with a new Aviar.* He had tried to keep Sak a secret; for years, he hadn't even brought her with him when he left the island. But with her hurt wing, he hadn't wanted to abandon her.

Deep down, he'd known he couldn't keep his secret forever. "There are many like her," he said. "But only she has a talent to bestow."

Vathi stopped in place as he continued to cut them a path. He turned back, looking at her alone on the new trail. He had given her the lantern to hold.

"That's a mainlander bird," she said. She held up the light. "I knew it was when I first saw it, and I assumed it wasn't an Aviar, because mainlander birds can't bestow talents."

Dusk turned back and continued cutting.

"You brought a mainlander chick to the Pantheon," Vathi whispered behind. "And it *gained a talent.*"

With a hack he brought down a branch, then continued on. Again, she had not asked a question, so he needed not answer.

Vathi hurried to keep up, the glow of the lantern tossing his shadow before him as she stepped up behind. "Surely someone else has tried it before. Surely . . ."

He did not know.

"But why would they?" she continued, quietly, as if to herself. "The Aviar are special. Everyone knows the separate breeds and what they do. Why assume that a fish would learn to breathe air, if raised on land? Why assume a non-Aviar would become one if raised on Patji. . . ."

They continued through the night. Dusk led them around many dangers, though he found that he needed to rely greatly upon Sak's help. *Do not follow that stream, which has your corpse bobbing in its waters. Do not touch that tree; the bark is poisonous with rot. Turn from that path. Your corpse shows a deathant bite.*

Sak did not speak to him, but each message was clear. When he stopped to let Vathi drink from her canteen, he held Sak and found her trembling. She did not peck at him as was usual when he enclosed her in his hands.

They stood in a small clearing, pure dark all around them, the sky shrouded in clouds. He heard distant rainfall on the trees. Not uncommon, here.

Nightmaws screeched, one then another. They only did that when they had made a kill or when they were seeking to frighten prey. Often, krell herds slept near Aviar roosts. Frighten away the birds, and you could sense the krell.

Vathi had taken out her tube. Not a scroll case—and not something scholarly at all, considering the way she held it as she poured something into its end. Once done, she raised it like one would a weapon. Beneath her feet, Dusk's body lay mangled.

He did not ask after Vathi's weapon, not even as she took some kind of short, slender spear and fitted it into the top end. No weapon could penetrate the thick skin of a nightmaw. You either avoided them or you died.

Kokerlii fluttered down to his shoulder, chirping away. He seemed confused by the darkness. Why were they out like this, at night, when birds normally made no noise?

"We must keep moving," Dusk said, placing Sak on his other shoulder and taking out his machete.

"You realize that your bird changes everything," Vathi said quietly, joining him, shouldering her pack and carrying her tube in the other hand.

"There will be a new kind of Aviar," Dusk whispered, stepping over his corpse.

"That's the *least* of it. Dusk, we assumed that chicks raised away from these islands did not develop their abilities because they were not around others to train them. We assumed that their abilities were innate, like our ability to speak—it's inborn, but we require help from others to develop it."

"That can still be true," Dusk said. "Other species, such as Sak, can merely be trained to speak."

"And your bird? Was it trained by others?"

"Perhaps." He did not say what he really thought. It was a thing of trappers. He noted a corpse on the ground before them.

It was not his.

He held up a hand immediately, stilling Vathi as she continued on to ask another question. What was *this*? The meat had been picked off much of the skeleton, and the clothing lay strewn about, ripped open by animals that feasted. Small, funguslike plants had sprouted around the ground near it, tiny red tendrils reaching up to enclose parts of the skeleton.

He looked up at the great tree, at the foot of which rested the corpse. The flowers were not in bloom. Dusk released his breath.

"What is it?" Vathi whispered. "Deathants?"

"No. Patji's Finger."

She frowned. "Is that . . . some kind of curse?"

"It is a name," Dusk said, stepping forward carefully to inspect the corpse. Machete. Boots. Rugged gear. One of his colleagues had fallen. He *thought* he recognized the man from the clothing. An older trapper named First of the Sky.

"The name of a person?" Vathi asked, peeking over his shoulder.

"The name of a tree," Dusk said, poking at the corpse's clothing, careful of insects that might be lurking inside. "Raise the lamp."

"I've never heard of that tree," she said skeptically.

"They are only on Patji."

"I have read a lot about the flora on these islands. . . ."

"Here you are a child. Light."

She sighed, raising it for him. He used a stick to prod at pockets on the ripped clothing. This man had been killed by a pack of tuskrun, larger predators—almost as large as a man—that prowled mostly by day. Their movement patterns were predictable unless one happened across one of Patji's Fingers in bloom.

There. He found a small book in the man's pocket. Dusk raised it, then backed away. Vathi peered over his shoulder. Homeislers stood so *close* to each other. Did she need to stand right by his elbow?

He checked the first pages, finding a list of dates. Yes, judging by the last date written down, this man was only a few days dead. The pages after that detailed the locations of Sky's safecamps, along with explanations of the traps guarding each one. The last page contained the farewell.

I am First of the Sky, taken by Patji at last. I have a brother on Suluko. Care for them, rival.

Few words. Few words were good. Dusk carried a book like this himself, and he had said even less on his last page.

"He wants you to care for his family?" Vathi asked.

"Don't be stupid," Dusk said, tucking the book away. "His birds."

"That's sweet," Vathi said. "I had always heard that trappers were incredibly territorial."

"We are," he said, noting how she said it. Again, her tone made it seem as if she considered trappers to be like animals. "But our birds might die without care—they are accustomed to humans. Better to give them to a rival than to let them die."

"Even if that rival is the one who killed you?" Vathi asked. "The traps you set, the ways you try to interfere with one another . . ."

"It is our way."

"That is an awful excuse," she said, looking up at the tree.

She was right.

The tree was massive, with drooping fronds. At the end of each one was a large closed blossom, as long as two hands put together. "You don't seem worried," she noted, "though the plant seems to have killed that man."

"These are only dangerous when they bloom."

"Spores?" she asked.

"No." He picked up the fallen machete, but left the rest of Sky's things alone. Let Patji claim him. Father did so like to murder his children. Dusk continued onward, leading Vathi, ignoring his corpse draped across a log.

"Dusk?" Vathi asked, raising the lantern and hurrying to him. "If not spores, then how does the tree kill?"

"So many questions."

"My life is about questions," she replied. "And about answers. If my people are going to work on this island . . ."

He hacked at some plants with the machete.

"It *is* going to happen," she said, more softly. "I'm sorry, Dusk. You can't stop the world from changing. Perhaps my expedition will be defeated, but others will come."

"Because of the Ones Above," he snapped.

"They may spur it," Vathi said. "Truly, when we finally convince them we are developed enough to be traded with, we will sail the stars as they do. But change will happen even without them. The world is progressing. One man cannot slow it, no matter how determined he is."

He stopped in the path.

You cannot stop the tides from changing, Dusk. No matter how determined you are. His mother's words. Some of the last he remembered from her.

Dusk continued on his way. Vathi followed. He would need her, though a treacherous piece of him whispered that she would be easy to end. With her would go her questions, and more importantly her answers. The ones he suspected she was very close to discovering.

You cannot change it. . . .

He could not. He hated that it was so. He wanted so badly to protect this island, as his kind had done for centuries. He worked this jungle, he loved its birds, was fond of its scents and sounds—despite all else. How he wished he could prove to Patji that he and the others were worthy of these shores.

Perhaps. Perhaps then . . .

Bah. Well, killing this woman would not provide any real protection for the island. Besides, had he sunk so low that he would murder a helpless scribe in cold blood? He would not even do that to another trapper, unless they approached his camp and did not retreat.

"The blossoms can think," he found himself saying as he turned them away from a mound that showed the tuskrun pack had been rooting here. "The Fingers of Patji. The trees themselves are not dangerous, even when blooming—but they attract predators, imitating the thoughts of a wounded animal that is full of pain and worry."

Vathi gasped. "A *plant*," she said, "that broadcasts a mental signature? Are you certain?"

"Yes."

"I need one of those blossoms." The light shook as she turned to go back.

Dusk spun and caught her by the arm. "We must keep moving."

"But—"

"You will have another chance." He took a deep breath. "Your people will soon infest this island like maggots on carrion. You will see other trees. Tonight, we must *go*. Dawn approaches."

He let go of her and turned back to his work. He had judged her wise, for a homeisler. Perhaps she would listen.

She did. She followed behind.

Patji's Fingers. First of the Sky, the dead trapper, should not have died in that place. Truly, the trees were not that dangerous. They lived by opening many blossoms and attracting predators to come feast. The predators would then fight one another, and the tree would feed off the corpses. Sky must have stumbled across a tree as it was beginning to flower, and got caught in what came.

His Aviar had not been enough to shield so many open blossoms. Who would have expected a death like that? After years on the island, surviving much more terrible dangers, to be caught by those simple flowers. It almost seemed a mockery, on Patji's part, of the poor man.

Dusk and Vathi's path continued, and soon grew steeper. They'd need to go uphill for a while before crossing to the downward slope that would lead to the other side of the island. Their trail, fortunately, would avoid Patji's main peak—the point of the wedge that jutted up the easternmost side of the island. His camp had been near the south, and Vathi's would be to the northeast, letting them skirt around the base of the wedge before arriving on the other beach.

They fell into a rhythm, and she was quiet for a time. Eventually, atop a particularly steep incline, he nodded for a break and squatted down to drink from his canteen. On Patji one did not simply sit, without care, upon a stump or log to rest.

Consumed by worry, and not a little frustration, he didn't notice what Vathi was doing until it was too late. She'd found something tucked into a branch—a long colorful feather. A mating plume.

Dusk leaped to his feet.

Vathi reached up toward the lower branches of the tree.

A set of spikes on ropes dropped from a nearby tree as Vathi pulled the branch. They swung down as Dusk reached her, one arm thrown in the way. A spike hit, the long, thin nail ripping into his skin and jutting out the other side, bloodied, and stopping a hair from Vathi's cheek.

She screamed.

Many predators on Patji were hard of hearing, but still that wasn't wise. Dusk didn't care. He yanked the spike from his skin, unconcerned with the bleeding for now, and checked the other spikes on the drop-rope trap.

No poison. Blessedly, they had not been poisoned.

"Your arm!" Vathi said.

He grunted. It didn't hurt. Yet. She began fishing in her pack for a bandage, and he accepted her ministrations without complaint or groan, even as the pain came upon him.

"I'm so sorry!" Vathi sputtered. "I found a mating plume! That meant an Aviar nest, so I thought to look in the tree. Have we stumbled across another trapper's safecamp?"

She was babbling out words as she worked. Seemed appropriate. When he grew nervous, he grew even more quiet. She would do the opposite.

She was good with a bandage, again surprising him. The wound had not hit any major arteries. He would be fine, though using his left hand would not be easy. This would be an annoyance. When she was done, looking sheepish and guilty, he reached down and picked up the mating plume she had dropped.

"This," he said with a harsh whisper, holding it up before her, "is the symbol of your ignorance. On the Pantheon Islands, nothing is easy, nothing is simple. That plume was placed by another trapper to catch someone who does not deserve to be here, someone who thought to find an easy prize. You cannot be that person. Never move without asking yourself, is this too easy?"

She paled. Then she took the feather in her fingers.

"Come."

He turned and walked on their way. That was the speech for an apprentice, he realized. Upon their first major mistake. A ritual among trappers. What had possessed him to give it to her?

She followed behind, head bowed, appropriately shamed. She didn't realize the honor he had just paid her, if unconsciously. They walked onward, an hour or more passing.

By the time she spoke, for some reason, he almost welcomed the words breaking upon the sounds of the jungle. "I'm sorry."

"You need not be sorry," he said. "Only careful."

"I understand." She took a deep breath, following behind him on the path. "And I *am* sorry. Not just about your arm. About this island. About what is coming. I think it inevitable, but I do wish that it did not mean the end of such a grand tradition."

"I . . ."

Words. He hated trying to find words.

"It . . . was not dusk when I was born," he finally said, then hacked down a swampvine and held his breath against the noxious fumes that it released toward him. They were only dangerous for a few moments.

"Excuse me?" Vathi asked, keeping her distance from the swampvine. "You were born . . ."

"My mother did not name me for the time of day. I was named because my mother saw the dusk of our people. The sun will soon set on us, she often told me." He looked back to Vathi, letting her pass him and enter a small clearing.

Oddly, she smiled at him. Why had he found those words to speak? He followed into the clearing, concerned at himself. He had not given those words to his uncle; only his parents knew the source of his name.

He was not certain why he'd told this scribe from an evil company. But . . . it did feel good to have said them.

A nightmaw broke through between two trees behind Vathi.

The enormous beast would have been as tall as a tree if it had stood upright. Instead it leaned forward in a prowling posture, powerful legs behind bearing most of its weight, its two clawed forelegs ripping up the ground. It reached forward its long neck, beak open, razor-sharp and deadly. It looked like a bird—in the same way that a wolf looked like a lapdog.

He threw his machete. An instinctive reaction, for he did not have time for thought. He did not have time for fear. That snapping beak—as tall as a door—would have the two of them dead in moments.

His machete glanced off the beak and actually cut the creature on the side of the head. That drew its attention, making it hesitate for just a moment. Dusk leaped for Vathi. She stepped back from him, setting the butt of her tube against the ground. He needed to pull her away, to—

The explosion deafened him.

Smoke bloomed around Vathi, who stood—wide-eyed—having dropped the lantern, oil spilling. The sudden sound stunned Dusk, and he almost collided with her as the nightmaw lurched and fell, skidding, the ground *thumping* from the impact.

Dusk found himself on the ground. He scrambled to his feet, backing away from the twitching nightmaw mere inches from him. Lit by flickering lanternlight, it was all leathery skin that was bumpy like that of a bird who had lost her feathers.

It was dead. Vathi had killed it.

She said something.

Vathi had *killed* a nightmaw.

"Dusk!" Her voice seemed distant.

He raised a hand to his forehead, which had belatedly begun to prickle with sweat. His wounded arm throbbed, but he was otherwise tense. He felt as if he should be running. He had never wanted to be so close to one of these. *Never.*

She'd actually killed it.

He turned toward her, his eyes wide. Vathi was trembling, but she covered it well. "So, that worked," she said. "We weren't certain it would, even though we'd prepared these specifically for the nightmaws."

"It's like a cannon," Dusk said. "Like from one of the ships, only in your *hands*."

"Yes."

He turned back toward the beast. Actually, it *wasn't* dead, not completely. It twitched, and let out a plaintive screech that shocked him, even with his hearing muffled. The weapon had fired that spear right into the beast's chest.

The nightmaw quaked and thrashed a weak leg.

"We could kill them all," Dusk said. He turned, then rushed over to Vathi, taking her with his right hand, the arm that wasn't wounded.

"With those weapons, we could kill them *all*. Every nightmaw. Maybe the shadows too!"

"Well, yes, it has been discussed. However, they are important parts of the ecosystem on these islands. Removing the apex predators could have undesirable results."

"Undesirable results?" Dusk ran his left hand through his hair. "They'd be gone. All of them! I don't care what other problems you think it would cause. They would all be *dead*."

Vathi snorted, picking up the lantern and stamping out the fires it had started. "I thought trappers were connected to nature."

"We are. That's how I know we would all be better off without any of these things."

"You are disabusing me of many romantic notions about your kind, Dusk," she said, circling the dying beast.

Dusk whistled, holding up his arm. Kokerlii fluttered down from high branches; in the chaos and explosion, Dusk had not seen the bird fly away. Sak still clung to his shoulder with a death grip, her claws digging into his skin through the cloth. He hadn't noticed. Kokerlii landed on his arm and gave an apologetic chirp.

"It wasn't your fault," Dusk said soothingly. "They prowl the night. Even when they cannot sense our minds, they can smell us." Their sense of smell was said to be incredible. This one had come up the trail behind them; it must have crossed their path and followed it.

Dangerous. His uncle always claimed the nightmaws were growing smarter, that they knew they could not hunt men only by their minds. *I should have taken us across more streams,* Dusk thought, reaching up and rubbing Sak's neck to soothe her. *There just isn't time. . . .*

His corpse lay wherever he looked. Draped across a rock, hanging from the vines of trees, slumped beneath the dying nightmaw's claw . . .

The beast trembled once more, then amazingly it lifted its gruesome head and let out a last screech. Not as loud as those that normally sounded in the night, but bone-chilling and horrid. Dusk stepped back despite himself, and Sak chirped nervously.

Other nightmaw screeches rose in the night, distant. That sound . . . he had been trained to recognize that sound as the sound of death.

"We're going," he said, stalking across the ground and pulling Vathi away from the dying beast, which had lowered its head and fallen silent.

"Dusk?" She did not resist as he pulled her away.

One of the other nightmaws sounded again in the night. Was it closer? *Oh, Patji, please,* Dusk thought. *No. Not this.*

He pulled her faster, reaching for his machete at his side, but it was not there. He had thrown it. He took out the one he had gathered from his fallen rival, then dragged her out of the clearing, back into the jungle, moving quickly. He could no longer worry about brushing against deathants.

A greater danger was coming.

The calls of death came again.

"Are those getting *closer*?" Vathi asked.

Dusk did not answer. It was a question, but he did not know the answer. At least his hearing was recovering. He released her hand, moving more quickly, almost at a trot—faster than he ever wanted to go through the jungle, day or night.

"Dusk!" Vathi hissed. "Will they come? To the call of the dying one? Is that something they do?"

"How should I know? I have never known one of them to be killed before." He saw the tube, again carried over her shoulder, lit by the light of the lantern she carried.

That gave him pause, though his instincts screamed at him to keep moving and he felt a fool. "Your weapon," he said. "You can use it again?"

"Yes," she said. "Once more."

"*Once* more?"

A half dozen screeches sounded in the night.

"Yes," she replied. "I only brought three spears and enough powder for three shots. I tried firing one at the shadow. It didn't do much."

He spoke no further, ignoring his wounded arm—the bandage was in need of changing—and towing her through the jungle. The calls came again and again. Agitated. How did one escape nightmaws? His Aviar clung to him, a bird on each shoulder. He had to leap over his corpse as they traversed a gulch and came up the other side.

How do you escape them? he thought, remembering his uncle's training. *You don't draw their attention in the first place!*

They were fast. Kokerlii would hide his mind, but if they picked up his trail at the dead one . . .

Water. He stopped in the night, turning right, then left. Where would he find a stream? Patji was an island. Fresh water came from rainfall, mostly. The largest lake . . . the only one . . . was up the wedge. Toward the peak. Along the eastern side, the island rose to some heights with cliffs on all sides. Rainfall collected there, in Patji's Eye. The river was his tears.

It was a dangerous place to go with Vathi in tow. Their path had skirted the slope up the heights, heading across the island toward the northern beach. They were close. . . .

Those screeches behind spurred him on. Patji would just have to forgive him for what came next. Dusk seized Vathi's hand and towed her in a more eastern direction. She did not complain, though she did keep looking over her shoulder.

The screeches grew closer.

He ran. He ran as he had never expected to do on Patji, wild and reckless. Leaping over troughs, around fallen logs coated in moss. Through the dark underbrush, scaring away meekers and startling Aviar slumbering in the branches above. It was foolish. It was crazy. But did it matter? Somehow, he knew those other things would not claim him. The kings of Patji hunted him; lesser dangers would not dare steal from their betters.

Vathi followed with difficulty. Those skirts were trouble, but she caught up to him each time Dusk had to occasionally stop and cut their way through underbrush. Urgent, frantic. He expected her to keep up, and she did. A piece of him—buried deep beneath the terror—was impressed. This woman would have made a fantastic trapper. Instead she would probably destroy all trappers.

He froze as screeches sounded behind, so close. Vathi gasped, and Dusk turned back to his work. Not far to go. He hacked through a dense patch of undergrowth and ran on, sweat streaming down the sides of his face. Jostling light came from Vathi's lantern behind; the scene before him was one of horrific shadows dancing on the jungle's boughs, leaves, ferns, and rocks.

This is your fault, Patji, he thought with an unexpected fury. The screeches seemed almost on top of him. Was that breaking brush he could hear behind? *We are your priests, and yet you hate us! You hate all.*

Dusk broke from the jungle and out onto the banks of the river. Small by mainland standards, but it would do. He led Vathi right into it, splashing into the cold waters.

He turned upstream. What else could he do? Downstream would lead closer to those sounds, the calls of death.

Of the Dusk, he thought. *Of the Dusk.*

The waters came only to their calves, bitter cold. The coldest water on the island, though he did not know why. They slipped and scrambled as they ran, best they could, upriver. They passed through some narrows, with lichen-covered rock walls on either side twice as tall as a man, then burst out into the basin.

A place men did not go. A place he had visited only once. A cool emerald lake rested here, sequestered.

Dusk towed Vathi to the side, out of the river, toward some brush. Perhaps she would not see. He huddled down with her, raising a finger to his lips, then turned down the light of the lantern she still held. Nightmaws could not see well, but perhaps the dim light would help. In more ways than one.

They waited there, on the shore of the small lake, hoping that the water had washed away their scent—hoping the nightmaws would grow confused or distracted. For one thing about this place was that the basin had steep walls, and there was no way out other than the river. If the nightmaws came up it, Dusk and Vathi would be trapped.

Screeches sounded. The creatures had reached the river. Dusk waited in near darkness, and so squeezed his eyes shut. He prayed to Patji, whom he loved, whom he hated.

Vathi gasped softly. "What . . . ?"

So she had seen. Of course she had. She was a seeker, a learner. A questioner.

Why must men ask so many questions?

"Dusk! There are Aviar here, in these branches! Hundreds of them." She spoke in a hushed, frightened tone. Even as they awaited death itself, she saw and could not help speaking. "Have you seen them? What is this place?" She hesitated. "So many juveniles. Barely able to fly . . ."

"They come here," he whispered. "Every bird from every island. In their youth, they must come here."

He opened his eyes, looking up. He had turned down the lantern, but it was still bright enough to see them roosting there. Some stirred at the light and the sound. They stirred more as the nightmaws screeched below.

Sak chirped on his shoulder, terrified. Kokerlii, for once, had nothing to say.

"Every bird from every island . . ." Vathi said, putting it together. "They all come here, to this place. Are you certain?"

"Yes." It was a thing that trappers knew. You could not capture a bird before it had visited Patji.

Otherwise it would be able to bestow no talent.

"They come here," she said. "We knew they migrated between islands. . . . Why do they come here?"

Was there any point in holding back now? She would figure it out. Still, he did not speak. Let her do so.

"They gain their talents here, don't they?" she asked. "How? Is it where they are trained? Is this how you made a bird who was not an Aviar into one? You brought a hatchling here, and then . . ." She frowned, raising her lantern. "I recognize those trees. They are the ones you called Patji's Fingers."

A dozen of them grew here, the largest concentration on the island. And beneath them, their fruit littered the ground. Much of it eaten, some of it only halfway so, bites taken out by birds of all stripes.

Vathi saw him looking, and frowned. "The fruit?" she asked.

"Worms," he whispered in reply.

A light seemed to go on in her eyes. "It's not the birds. It never has been . . . it's a parasite. They carry a parasite that bestows talents! That's why those raised away from the islands cannot gain the abilities, and why a mainland bird you brought here could."

"Yes."

"This changes everything, Dusk. Everything."

"Yes."

Of the Dusk. Born during that dusk, or bringer of it? What had he done?

Downriver, the nightmaw screeches drew closer. They had decided to search upriver. They were clever, more clever than men off the islands thought them to be. Vathi gasped, turning toward the small river canyon.

"Isn't this dangerous?" she whispered. "The trees are blooming. The nightmaws will come! But no. So many Aviar. They can hide those blossoms, like they do a man's mind?"

"No," he said. "All minds in this place are invisible, always, regardless of Aviar."

"But . . . how? Why? The worms?"

Dusk didn't know, and for now didn't care. *I am trying to protect you, Patji!* Dusk looked toward Patji's Fingers. *I need to stop the men and their device. I know it! Why? Why do you hunt me?*

Perhaps it was because he knew so much. Too much. More than any man had known. For he had asked questions.

Men. And their questions.

"They're coming up the river, aren't they?" she asked.

The answer seemed obvious. He did not reply.

"No," she said, standing. "I won't die with this knowledge, Dusk. I *won't*. There must be a way."

"There is," he said, standing beside her. He took a deep breath. *So I finally pay for it.* He took Sak carefully in his hand, and placed her on Vathi's shoulder. He pried Kokerlii free too.

"What are you doing?" Vathi asked.

"I will go as far as I can," Dusk said, handing Kokerlii toward her. The bird bit with annoyance at his hands, although never strong enough to draw blood. "You will need to hold him. He will try to follow me."

"No, wait. We can hide in the lake, they—"

"They will find us!" Dusk said. "It isn't deep enough by far to hide us."

"But you can't—"

"They are nearly here, woman!" he said, forcing Kokerlii into her hands. "The men of the company will not listen to me if I tell them to turn off the device. You are smart, you can make them stop. You can reach them. With Kokerlii you can reach them. Be ready to go."

She looked at him, stunned, but she seemed to realize that there was no other way. She stood, holding Kokerlii in two hands as he pulled out the journal of First of the Sky, then his own book that listed where his Aviar were, and tucked them into her pack. Finally, he stepped back into the river. He could hear a rushing sound downstream. He would have to go quickly to reach the end of the canyon before they arrived. If he could draw them out into the jungle even a short ways to the south, Vathi could slip away.

As he entered the stream, his visions of death finally vanished. No more corpses bobbing in the water, lying on the banks. Sak had realized what was happening.

She gave a final chirp.

He started to run.

One of Patji's Fingers, growing right next to the mouth of the canyon, was blooming.

"Wait!"

He should not have stopped as Vathi yelled at him. He should have continued on, for time was so slim. However, the sight of that flower—along with her yell—made him hesitate.

The flower . . .

It struck him as it must have struck Vathi. An idea. Vathi ran for her pack, letting go of Kokerlii, who immediately flew to his shoulder and started chirping at him in annoyed chastisement. Dusk didn't listen. He yanked the flower off—it was as large as a man's head, with a large bulging part at the center.

It was invisible in this basin, like they all were.

"A flower that can think," Vathi said, breathing quickly, fishing in her pack. "A flower that can draw the attention of predators."

Dusk pulled out his rope as she brought out her weapon and prepared it. He lashed the flower to the end of the spear sticking out slightly from the tube.

Nightmaw screeches echoed up the cavern. He could see their shadows, hear them splashing.

He stumbled back from Vathi as she crouched down, set the weapon's butt against the ground, and pulled a lever at the base.

The explosion, once again, nearly deafened him.

Aviar all around the rim of the basin screeched and called in fright, taking wing. A storm of feathers and flapping ensued, and through the middle of it, Vathi's spear shot into the air, flower on the end. It arced out over the canyon into the night.

Dusk grabbed her by the shoulder and pulled her back along the river, into the lake itself. They slipped into the shallow water, Kokerlii on his shoulder, Sak on hers. They left the lantern burning, giving a quiet light to the suddenly empty basin.

The lake was not deep. Two or three feet. Even crouching, it didn't cover them completely.

The nightmaws stopped in the canyon. His lanternlight showed a couple of them in the shadows, large as huts, turning and watching the sky. They were smart, but like the meekers, not as smart as men.

Patji, Dusk thought. *Patji, please . . .*

The nightmaws turned back down the canyon, following the mental signature broadcast by the flowering plant. And, as Dusk watched, his corpse bobbing in the water nearby grew increasingly translucent.

Then faded away entirely.

Dusk counted to a hundred, then slipped from the waters. Vathi, sodden in her skirts, did not speak as she grabbed the lantern. They left the weapon, its shots expended.

The calls from the nightmaws grew farther and farther away as Dusk led the way out of the canyon, then directly north, slightly downslope. He kept expecting the screeches to turn and follow.

They did not.

The company fortress was a horridly impressive sight. A work of logs and cannons right at the edge of the water, guarded by an enormous iron-hulled ship. Smoke rose from it, the burning of morning cookfires. A short distance away, what must have been a dead shadow rotted in the sun, its mountainous carcass draped half in the water, half out.

He didn't see his own corpse anywhere, though on the final leg of their trip to the fortress he had seen it several times. Always in a place of immediate danger. Sak's visions had returned to normal.

Dusk turned back to the fortress, which he did not enter. He preferred to remain on the rocky, familiar shore—perhaps twenty feet from the entrance—his wounded arm aching as the company people rushed out through the gate to meet Vathi. Their scouts on the upper walls kept careful watch on Dusk. A trapper was not to be trusted.

Even standing here, some twenty feet from the wide wooden gates into the fort, he could smell how wrong the place was. It was stuffed with the scents of men—sweaty bodies, the smell of oil, and other, newer scents that he recognized from his recent trips to the homeisles. Scents that made him feel like an outsider among his own people.

The company men wore sturdy clothing, trousers like Dusk's but far better tailored, shirts and rugged jackets. Jackets? In Patji's heat? These people bowed to Vathi, showing her more deference than Dusk would have expected. They drew hands from shoulder to shoulder as they started speaking—a symbol of respect. Foolishness. Anyone could make a gesture like that; it didn't mean anything. True respect included far more than a hand waved in the air.

But they did treat her like more than a simple scribe. She was better placed in the company than he'd assumed. Not his problem anymore, regardless.

Vathi looked at him, then back at her people. "We must hurry to the machine," she said to them. "The one from Above. We must turn it off."

Good. She would do her part. Dusk turned to walk away. Should he give words at parting? He'd never felt the need before. But today, it felt . . . wrong not to say something.

He started walking. Words. He had never been good with words.

"Turn it off?" one of the men said from behind. "What do you mean, Lady Vathi?"

"You don't need to feign innocence, Winds," Vathi said. "I know you turned it on in my absence."

"But we didn't."

Dusk paused. What? The man sounded sincere. But then, Dusk was no expert on human emotions. From what he'd seen of people from the home-isles, they could fake emotion as easily as they faked a gesture of respect.

"What *did* you do, then?" Vathi asked them.

"We . . . opened it."

Oh no . . .

"Why would you do that?" Vathi asked.

Dusk turned to regard them, but he didn't need to hear the answer. The answer was before him, in the vision of a dead island he'd misinterpreted.

"We figured," the man said, "that we should see if we could puzzle out how the machine worked. Vathi, the insides . . . they're complex beyond what we could have imagined. But there are seeds there. Things we could—"

"No!" Dusk said, rushing toward them.

One of the sentries above planted an arrow at his feet. He lurched to a stop, looking wildly from Vathi up toward the walls. Couldn't they see? The bulge in mud that announced a deathant den. The game trail. The distinctive curl of a cutaway vine. Wasn't it *obvious*?

"It will destroy us," Dusk said. "Don't seek . . . Don't you see . . . ?"

For a moment, they all just stared at him. He had a chance. Words. He needed *words*.

"That machine is deathants!" he said. "A den, a . . . Bah!" How could he explain?

He couldn't. In his anxiety, words fled him, like Aviar fluttering away into the night.

The others finally started moving, pulling Vathi toward the safety of their treasonous fortress.

"You said the corpses are gone," Vathi said as she was ushered through the gates. "We've succeeded. I will see that the machine is not engaged on this trip! I promise you this, Dusk!"

"But," he cried back, "it was never *meant* to be engaged!"

The enormous wooden gates of the fortress creaked closed, and he lost sight of her. Dusk cursed. Why hadn't he been able to explain?

Because he didn't know how to talk. For once in his life, that seemed to matter.

Furious, frustrated, he stalked away from that place and its awful smells. Halfway to the tree line, however, he stopped, then turned. Sak fluttered down, landing on his shoulder and cooing softly.

Questions. Those questions wanted into his brain.

Instead he yelled at the guards. He demanded they return Vathi to him. He even pled.

Nothing happened. They wouldn't speak to him. Finally, he started to feel foolish. He turned back toward the trees, and continued on his way. His assumptions were probably wrong. After all, the corpses *were* gone. Everything could go back to normal.

. . . Normal. Could anything *ever* be normal with that fortress looming behind him? He shook his head, entering the canopy. The dense humidity of Patji's jungle should have calmed him.

Instead it annoyed him. As he started the trek toward another of his safecamps, he was so distracted that he could have been a youth, his first time on Sori. He almost stumbled straight onto a gaping deathant den; he didn't even notice the vision Sak sent. This time, dumb luck saved him as he stubbed his toe on something, looked down, and only then spotted both corpse and crack crawling with motes of yellow.

He growled, then sneered. "Still you try to kill me?" he shouted, looking up at the canopy. "Patji!"

Silence.

"The ones who protect you are the ones you try hardest to kill," Dusk shouted. "Why!"

The words were lost in the jungle. It consumed them.

"You deserve this, Patji," he said. "What is coming to you. You *deserve to be destroyed*!"

He breathed out in gasps, sweating, satisfied at having finally said those things. Perhaps there was a purpose for words. Part of him, as traitorous as Vathi and her company, was *glad* that Patji would fall to their machines.

Of course, then the company itself would fall. To the Ones Above. His entire people. The world itself.

He bowed his head in the shadows of the canopy, sweat dripping down the sides of his face. Then he fell to his knees, heedless of the nest just three strides away.

Sak nuzzled into his hair. Above, in the branches, Kokerlii chirped uncertainly.

"It's a trap, you see," he whispered. "The Ones Above have rules. They can't trade with us until we're advanced enough. Just like a man can't, in good conscience, bargain with a child until they are grown. And so, they have left their machines for us to discover, to prod at and poke. The dead man was a ruse. Vathi was *meant* to have those machines.

"There will be explanations, left as if carelessly, for us to dig into and learn. And at some point in the near future, we will build something like one of their machines. We will have grown more quickly than we should have. We will be childlike still, ignorant, but the laws from Above will let these visitors trade with us. And then, they will take this land for themselves."

That was what he should have said. Protecting Patji was impossible. Protecting the Aviar was impossible. Protecting their entire *world* was impossible. Why hadn't he explained it?

Perhaps because it wouldn't have done any good. As Vathi had said . . . progress would come. If you wanted to call it that.

Dusk had arrived.

Sak left his shoulder, winging away. Dusk looked after her, then cursed. She did not land nearby. Though flying was difficult for her, she fluttered on, disappearing from his sight.

"Sak?" he asked, rising and stumbling after the Aviar. He fought back the way he had come, following Sak's squawks. A few moments later, he lurched out of the jungle.

Vathi stood on the rocks before her fortress.

Dusk hesitated at the brim of the jungle. Vathi was alone, and even the sentries had retreated. Had they cast her out? No. He could see that the gate was cracked, and some people watched from inside.

Sak had landed on Vathi's shoulder down below. Dusk frowned, reaching his hand to the side and letting Kokerlii land on his arm. Then he strode forward, calmly making his way down the rocky shore, until he was standing just before Vathi.

She'd changed into a new dress, though there were still snarls in her hair. She smelled of flowers.

And her eyes were terrified.

He'd traveled the darkness with her. Had faced nightmaws. Had seen her near to death, and she had not looked this worried.

"What?" he asked, finding his voice hoarse.

"We found instructions in the machine," Vathi whispered. "A manual on its workings, left there as if accidentally by someone who worked on it before. The manual is in their language, but the smaller machine I have . . ."

"It translates."

"The manual details how the machine was constructed," Vathi says. "It's so complex I can barely comprehend it, but it seems to explain concepts and ideas, not just give the workings of the machine."

"And are you not happy?" he asked. "You will have your flying machines soon, Vathi. Sooner than anyone could have imagined."

Wordless, she held something up. A single feather—a mating plume. She had kept it.

"Never move without asking yourself, is this too easy?" she whispered. "You said it was a trap as I was pulled away. When we found the manual, I . . . Oh, Dusk. They are planning to do to us what . . . what we are doing to Patji, aren't they?"

Dusk nodded.

"We'll lose it all. We can't fight them. They'll find an excuse, they'll *seize* the Aviar. It makes perfect sense. The Aviar use the worms. We use the Aviar. The Ones Above use us. It's inevitable, isn't it?"

Yes, he thought. He opened his mouth to say it, and Sak chirped. He frowned and turned back toward the island. Jutting from the ocean, arrogant. Destructive.

Patji. Father.

And finally, at long last, Dusk understood.

"No," he whispered.

"But—"

He undid his pants pocket, then reached deeply into it, digging around. Finally, he pulled something out. The remnants of a feather, just the shaft now. A mating plume that his uncle had given him, so many years ago, when he'd first fallen into a trap on Sori. He held it up, remembering the speech he'd been given. Like every trapper.

This is the symbol of your ignorance. Nothing is easy, nothing is simple.

Vathi held hers. Old and new.

"No, they will not have us," Dusk said. "We will see through their traps, and we will not fall for their tricks. For we have been trained by the Father himself for this very day."

She stared at his feather, then up at him.

"Do you really think that?" she asked. "They are cunning."

"They may be cunning," he said. "But they have not lived on Patji. We will gather the other trappers. We will not let ourselves be taken in."

She nodded hesitantly, and some of the fear seemed to leave her. She turned and waved for those behind her to open the gates to the building. Again, the scents of mankind washed over him.

Vathi looked back, then held out her hand to him. "You will help, then?"

His corpse appeared at her feet, and Sak chirped warningly. *Danger.* Yes, the path ahead would include much danger.

Dusk took Vathi's hand and stepped into the fortress anyway.

POSTSCRIPT

The original version of this story had Dusk referring to himself as "Sixth," which was super confusing to readers. I liked it because it was so different, but in the end I relented to the feedback I was getting—because it was the right thing to do. Not only is "Dusk" more important thematically than "Sixth," it's way easier to keep track of in a sentence.

For those who don't know, this story was brainstormed on an episode of Writing Excuses. We did four episodes where we brainstormed together, then one of us took that idea and wrote a story on it. The initial brainstorming session we did for me ended up failing; I just wasn't excited about the story. So we tried again, and this was the result.

This is the only story in the anthology where the world wasn't built into the original Cosmere plan. I did, however, leave myself room in my Cosmere outline for a handful of worlds I hadn't defined yet—as I knew I'd eventually have stories I wanted to tell that didn't fit on a planet with a Shard. Our brainstorming session on air wasn't specifically for a Cosmere story, but as I worked on the outline, I was intrigued by the idea of using symbiosis (in a new way) for a Cosmere Investiture.

I quickly fell in love with the idea, and the resulting story. You'll likely see more from the people of this planet, though there are no plans for another story or novel in the world. If you can't tell from the Alcatraz books and the Horneater culture in the Stormlight Archive, I have a fascination with Polynesian culture. The concept of wayfinding through the lapping of waves is just one of those things that won't leave me alone, and the ability to write about a character out on his own on the ocean—isolated in multiple ways—was intriguing to me. Also, considering how many talkative characters I do in books, it was a pleasure to try something new in someone like Dusk.

This is the farthest forward, timeline-wise, of any of the stories in this collection. So, at the time of Khriss's writing of the introduction to the system, the events of this story haven't actually taken place yet.

If you'd like to read the original brainstorming sessions in print form, along with early drafts of this story, they're available (along with the three stories written by the other hosts of Writing Excuses: Mary Robinette Kowal, Dan Wells, and Howard Tayler) in an anthology called *Shadows Beneath*.

THE
ROSHARAN
SYSTEM

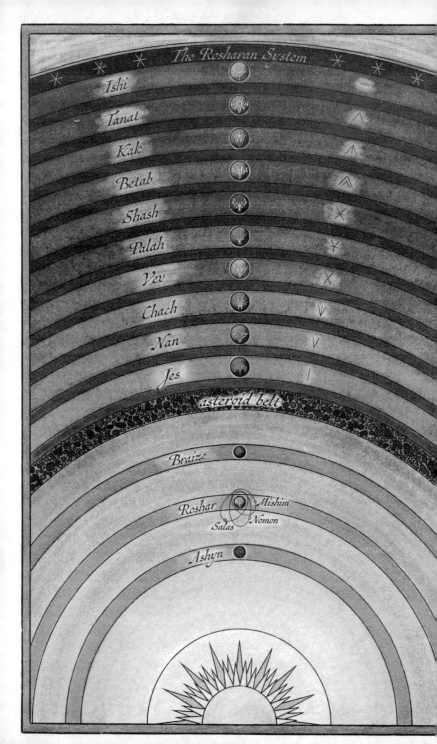

THE ROSHARAN SYSTEM

ROSHAR (which—characteristic of the dominant confidence of its people—is the name of a planet, a system, *and* the main continent on the planet) is a busy place. As empty as the Scadrian system seems, this one always feels crowded to me. A series of enormous gas giants crowd the outer reaches of the system, though nobody has been able to observe them directly, as their manifestation on Shadesmar is minor.

There are a whopping *three* planets in the habitable zone, all of which are inhabited to one extent or another. There is Ashyn, the burning planet, which suffered a cataclysm long ago. People here live in very small pockets of survivability, including the famous floating cities. Farthest out of the three is Braize, which despite being cold and inhospitable to men is home to an ecosystem of self-aware Splinters. (The local parlance would call them spren.) I believe it's possible some of these are actually Cognitive Shadows, but research here is difficult and dangerous, so I will hold back on theorizing for the moment.

The showpiece of the system is, of course, the middle planet of Roshar itself. At 0.7 cosmere standard in gravitation and 0.9 in size—and possessing a high-oxygen environment—Roshar is home to a diverse and unique ecology containing dramatic megafauna and fascinating symbiotic relationships between creatures (both humanoid and not) and Splinters of Investiture.

The most dramatic of these is the relationship between humans and self-aware spren, which is the basis for the magic of Surgebinding. This magic has strong roots in natural physics, with the spren being personifications of the forces themselves (called Surges locally). Gravitation, the strong axial force, surface tension . . . these things have come alive, as have more abstract notions such as transformation and transportation.

However, this pattern (the bonding of spren to human) is merely an expansion of what already exists in the nature of the planet. Gargantuan crustaceans grow to incredible size without collapsing under their own weight not just through the nature of the planet, but through symbiosis with spren. Certain animals obtain flight through similar means, and there is even a race of equines that—through the spren bond—have adapted to life on the planet and obtained a high enough level of self-awareness to nearly be named a sapient species.

I will not speak on the relationship of Roshar's divergent ecology here, as that is a topic too large to address in a simple survey such as this one. However, travelers to the planet should be made aware of the storms. Life on Roshar has been shaped over millennia by massive, Invested storms, which pose a danger that cannot be overstated.

These storms, by my best guess, predate the arrival of the Shards Honor and Cultivation—as do many of the spren. However, the presence of the Shards molded and transformed the planet's nature to the point that it is difficult to distinguish what is pre-Shattering in origin, and what is a newer development. Surely, many of the spren that now exist on the planet have arisen from the friction between Honor, Cultivation, and Odium.

Odium. Be aware that this system is the current habitation of the Shard of Odium on the Physical and Cognitive Realms. This Shard undoubtedly caused the Splintering of Devotion, Dominion, Honor, and perhaps others throughout the cosmere.

Visitors to Roshar should know that fire will respond unusually because of the high-oxygen environment, which I believe is part of the reason that an alternative light source was developed during the early days of humanoid life on the planet. Be aware that lengths and times mentioned in essays and stories about the world usually use local measurements. A Rosharan year is longer than cosmere standard, and a Rosharan foot is larger than cosmere standard. It is difficult not to feel very small, at times, on this domineering, majestic tempest of a planet.

EDGEDANCER

This story takes place after and contains spoilers for *Words of Radiance*.

1

LIFT prepared to be awesome.

She sprinted across an open field in northern Tashikk, a little more than a week's travel from Azimir. The place was overgrown with brown grass a foot or two high. The occasional trees were tall and twisty, with trunks that looked like they were made of interwoven vines, and branches that pointed upward more than out.

They had some official name, but everyone she knew called them drop-deads because of their springy roots. In a storm, they'd fall over flat and just lie there. Afterward they'd pop back up, like a rude gesture made at the passing winds.

Lift's run startled a group of axehinds who had been grazing nearby; the lean creatures leaped away on four legs with the two front claws pulled in close to the body. Good eating, those beasties. Barely any shell on them. But for once, Lift wasn't in the mood to eat.

She was on the *run*.

"Mistress!" Wyndle, her pet Voidbringer, called. He took the shape of a vine, growing along the ground beside her at superfast speed, matching her pace. He didn't have a face at the moment, but could speak anyway. Unfortunately.

"Mistress," he pled, "can't we please just *go back*?"

Nope.

Lift became awesome. She drew on the stuff inside of her, the stuff that made her glow. She Slicked the soles of her feet with it, and leaped into a skid.

Suddenly, the ground didn't rub against her at all. She slid as if on ice, whipping through the field. Grass startled all around her, curling as it yanked down into stone burrows. That made it bow before her in a wave.

She zipped along, wind pushing back her long black hair, tugging at the loose overshirt she wore atop her tighter brown undershirt, which was tucked into her loose-cuffed trousers.

She slid, and felt free. Just her and the wind. A small windspren, like a white ribbon in the air, started to follow her.

Then she hit a rock.

The stupid rock held firm—it was held in place by little tufts of moss that grew on the ground and stuck to things like stones, holding them down as shelter against the wind. Lift's foot flashed with pain and she tumbled in the air, then hit the stone ground face-first.

Reflexively, she made her face awesome—so she kept right on going, skidding on her cheek until she hit a tree. She stopped there, finally.

The tree slowly fell over, playing dead. It hit the ground with a shivering sound of leaves and branches.

Lift sat up, rubbing her face. She'd cut her foot, but her awesomeness plugged up the hole, healing it plenty quick. Her face didn't even hurt much. When a part of her was awesome, it didn't rub on what it touched, it just kind of . . . glided.

She still felt stupid.

"Mistress," Wyndle said, curling up to her. His vine looked like the type fancy people would grow on their buildings to hide up parts that didn't look rich enough. Except he had bits of crystal growing out of him along the vine's length. They jutted out unexpectedly, like toenails on a face.

When he moved, he didn't wiggle like an eel. He actually grew, leaving a long trail of vines behind him that would soon crystallize and decay into dust. Voidbringers were strange.

He wound around himself in a circle, like rope coiling, and formed a small tower of vines. And then something grew from the top: a face that formed out of vines, leaves, and gemstones. The mouth worked as he spoke.

"Oh, mistress," he said. "Can't we stop playing out here, *please*? We need to get back to Azimir!"

"Go back?" Lift stood up. "We just escaped that place!"

"Escaped! The *palace*? Mistress, you were an honored guest of the emperor! You had everything you wanted, as much food, as much—"

"All lies," she declared, hands on hips. "To keep me from noticin' the truth. They was going to *eat* me."

Wyndle stammered. He wasn't so frightening, for a Voidbringer. He must have been like . . . the Voidbringer all the other ones made fun of for wearing silly hats. The one that would correct all the others, and explain which fork they had to use when they sat down to consume human souls.

"Mistress," Wyndle said. "Humans do *not* eat other humans. You were a guest!"

"Yeah, but *why*? They gave me too much stuff."

"You saved the emperor's life!"

"That should've been good for a few days of freeloading," she said. "I once pulled a guy out of prison, and he gave me five whole days in his den for free, and a nice handkerchief too. *That* was generous. The Azish letting me stay as long as I wanted?" She shook her head. "They wanted something. Only explanation. They was going to starvin' eat me."

"But—"

Lift started running again. The cold stone, perforated by grass burrows, felt good on her toes and feet. No shoes. What good were shoes? In the palace, they'd started offering her heaps of shoes. And nice clothing—big, comfy coats and robes. Clothing you could get lost in. She'd liked wearing something soft for once.

Then they'd started asking. Why not take some lessons, and learn to read? They were grateful for what she'd done for Gawx, who was now Prime Aqasix, a fancy title for their ruler. Because of her service, she could have tutors, they said. She could learn how to wear those clothes properly, learn how to write.

It had started to consume her. If she'd stayed, how long would it have been before she wasn't Lift anymore? How long until she'd have been gobbled up, another girl left in her place? Similar face, but at the same time all new?

She tried using her awesomeness again. In the palace, they had talked about the recovery of ancient powers. Knights Radiant. The binding of Surges, natural forces.

I will remember those who have been forgotten.

Lift Slicked herself with power, then skidded across the ground a few feet before tumbling and rolling through the grass.

She pounded her fist on the stones. Stupid ground. Stupid awesomeness. How was she supposed to stay standing, when her feet were slipperier than if they'd been coated in oil? She should just go back to paddling around on her knees. It was so much easier. She could balance that way, and use her hands to steer. Like a little crab, scooting around this way and that.

They were elegant things of beauty, Darkness had said. *They could ride the thinnest rope, dance across rooftops, move like a ribbon on the wind. . . .*

Darkness, the shadow of a man who had chased her, had said those things in the palace, speaking of those who had—long ago—used powers like Lift's. Maybe he'd been lying. After all, he'd been preparing to murder her at the time.

Then again, why lie? He'd treated her derisively, as if she were nothing. Worthless.

She set her jaw and stood up. Wyndle was still talking, but she ignored him, instead taking off across the deserted field, running as fast as she could, startling grass. She reached the top of a small hill, then jumped and coated her feet with power.

She started slipping immediately. The air. The air she pushed against when moving was holding her back. Lift hissed, then coated her *entire self* in power.

She sliced through the wind, turning sideways as she skidded down the side of the hill. Air slid off her, as if it couldn't find her. Even the sunlight seemed to melt off her skin. She was between places, here but not. No air, no ground. Just pure motion, so fast that she reached grass before it had time to pull away. It flowed around her, its touch brushed aside by her power.

Her skin started to glow, tendrils of smoky light rising from her. She laughed, reaching the bottom of the small hill. There she leaped some boulders.

And ran face-first into another tree.

The bubble of power around her popped. The tree toppled over—and, for good measure, the two next to it decided to fall as well. Perhaps they thought they were missing out on something.

Wyndle found her grinning like a fool, staring up at the sun, spread out on the tree trunk with her arms interwoven with the branches, a single golden gloryspren—shaped like an orb—circling above her.

"Mistress?" he said. "Oh, mistress. You were *happy* in the palace. I saw it in you!"

She didn't reply.

"And the emperor," Wyndle continued. "He'll miss you! You didn't even tell him you were going!"

"I left him a note."

"A note? You learned to write?"

"Storms, no. I ate his dinner. Right out from under the tray cover while they was preparing to bring it to him. Gawx'll know what that means."

"I find that doubtful, mistress."

She climbed up from the fallen tree and stretched, then blew her hair out of her eyes. Maybe she *could* dance across rooftops, ride on ropes, or . . . what was it? Make wind? Yeah, she could do that one for sure. She hopped off the tree and continued walking through the field.

Unfortunately, her stomach had a few things to say about how much awesomeness she'd used. She ran on food, even more than most folks. She could draw some awesomeness from everything she ate, but once it was gone, she couldn't do anything incredible again until she'd had more to eat.

Her stomach rumbled in complaint. She liked to imagine that it was cussing at her something awful, and she searched through her pockets. She'd run out of the food in her pack—she'd taken a *lot*—this morning. But hadn't she found a sausage in the bottom before tossing the pack?

Oh, right. She'd eaten that while watching those riverspren a few hours ago. She dug in her pockets anyway, but only came out with a handkerchief that she'd used to wrap up a big stack of flatbread before stuffing it in her pack. She shoved part of the handkerchief into her mouth and started chewing.

"Mistress?" Wyndle asked.

"Mie hab crubs onnit," she said around the handkerchief.

"You shouldn't have been Surgebinding so much!" He wound along on the ground beside her, leaving a trail of vines and crystals. "And we *should* have stayed in the palace. Oh, how did this happen to me? I should be gardening right now. I had the most *magnificent* chairs."

"Shars?" Lift asked, pausing.

"Yes, chairs." Wyndle wound up in a coil beside her, forming a face that tilted toward her at an angle off the top of the coil. "While in Shadesmar, I had collected the most magnificent selection of the souls of chairs from your side! I cultivated them, grew them into grand crystals. I had some Winstels, a nice Shober, *quite* the collection of spoonbacks, even a throne or two!"

"Yu gurdened *shars*?"

"Of course I gardened chairs," Wyndle said. His ribbon of vine leaped off the coil and followed her as she started walking again. "What else would I garden?"

"Fwants."

"Plants? Well, we have them in Shadesmar, but I'm no *pedestrian* gardener. I'm an artist! Why, I was planning an entire exhibition of sofas when the Ring chose me for this atrocious duty."

"Smufld gramitch mragnifude."

"Would you take that out of your mouth?" Wyndle snapped.

Lift did so.

Wyndle huffed. How a little vine thing huffed, Lift didn't know. But he did it all the time. "Now, what were you trying to say?"

"Gibberish," Lift said. "I just wanted to see how you'd respond." She stuffed the other side of the handkerchief into her mouth and started sucking on it.

They continued on with a sigh from Wyndle, who muttered about gardening and his pathetic life. He certainly was a strange Voidbringer. Come to think of it, she'd never seen him act the least bit interested in consuming someone's soul. Maybe he was a vegetarian?

They passed through a small forest, really just a corpse of trees, which was a strange term, since she never seemed to find any bodies in them. These weren't even drop-deads; those tended to grow in small patches, but each apart from the others. These had branches that wound around one another as they grew, dense and intertwined to face the highstorms.

That was basically the way to do it, right? Everyone else, they wound their branches together. Braced themselves. But Lift, she was a drop-dead. Don't intertwine, don't get caught up. Go your own way.

Yes, that was definitely how she was. That was why she'd had to leave the palace, obviously. You couldn't live your life getting up and seeing the same things every day. You had to keep moving, otherwise people started to know who you were, and then they started to expect things from you. It was one step from there to being gobbled up.

She stopped right inside the trees, standing on a pathway that someone had cut and kept maintained. She looked backward, northward, toward Azir.

"Is this about what happened to you?" Wyndle asked. "I don't know a lot about humans, but I *believe* it was natural, disconcerting though it might appear. You aren't wounded."

Lift shaded her eyes. The wrong things were changing. She was supposed to stay the same, and the world was supposed to change around her. She'd asked for that, hadn't she?

Had she been lied to?

"Are we . . . going back?" Wyndle asked, hopeful.

"No," Lift said. "Just saying goodbye." Lift shoved her hands in her pockets and turned around before continuing through the trees.

2

YEDDAW was one of those cities Lift had always meant to visit. It was in Tashikk, a strange place even compared to Azir. She'd always found everyone here too polite and reserved. They also wore clothing that made them hard to read.

But everyone said that you had to see Yeddaw. It was the closest you could get to seeing Sesemalex Dar—and considering *that* place had been a war zone for basically a billion years, she wasn't likely to ever get there.

Standing with hands on hips, looking down at the city of Yeddaw, she found herself agreeing with what people said. This *was* a sight. The Azish liked to consider themselves grand, but they only plastered bronze or gold or something over all their buildings and pretended that was enough. What good did that do? It just reflected her own face at her, and she'd seen that too often to be impressed by it.

No, *this* was impressive. A majestic city cut *out of the starvin' ground*.

She'd heard some of the fancy scribes in Azir talk about it—they said it was a new city, created only a hunnerd years back by hiring the Imperial Shardblades out of Azir. Those didn't spend much time at war, but were instead used for making mines or cutting up rocks and stuff. Very practical. Like using the royal throne as a stool to reach something on the high shelf.

She really shouldn't have gotten yelled at for that.

Anyway, they'd used those Shardblades here. This had once been a large, flat plain. Her vantage on a hilltop, though, let her make out hundreds of trenches cut in the stone. They interconnected, like a huge maze. Some of the trenches were wider than others, and they made a vague spiral toward the center, where a large moundlike building was the only part of the city that peeked up over the surface of the plain.

Above, in the spaces between trenches, people worked fields. There were virtually no structures up there; everything was down below. People *lived* in those trenches, which seemed to be two or three stories deep. How did they avoid being washed away in highstorms? True, they'd cut large channels leading out from the city—ones nobody seemed to live in, so the water could escape. Still didn't seem safe, but it *was* pretty cool.

She could hide really well in there. That was why she'd come, after all. To hide. Nothing else. No other reason.

The city didn't have walls, but it did have a number of guard towers spaced around it. Her pathway led down from the hills and joined with a larger road, which eventually stopped in a line of people awaiting permission to get into the city.

"How on Roshar did they manage to cut away so much rock!" Wyndle said, forming a pile of vines beside her, a twisting column that took him high enough to be by her waist, face tilted toward the city.

"Shardblades," Lift said.

"Oh. Ooooh. Those." He shifted uncomfortably, vines writhing and twisting about one another with a scrunching sound. "Yes. Those."

She folded her arms. "I should get me one of those, eh?"

Wyndle, strangely, groaned loudly.

"I figure," she explained, "that Darkness has one, right? He fought with one when he was trying to kill me and Gawx. So I ought to find one."

"Yes," Wyndle said, "you should do just that! Let us pop over to the market and pick up a legendary, all-powerful weapon of myth and lore, worth more than many kingdoms! I hear they sell them in bushels, following spring weather in the east."

"Shut it, Voidbringer." She eyed his tangle of a face. "You know something about Shardblades, don't you?"

The vines seemed to wilt.

"You *do*. Out with it. What do you know?"

He shook his vine head.

"Tell me," Lift warned.

"It's forbidden. You must discover it on your own."

"That's what I'm doing. I'm discovering it. From you. Tell me, or I'll *bite* you."

"*What?*"

"I'll bite you," she said. "I'll gnaw on you, Voidbringer. You're a vine, right? I eat plants. Sometimes."

"Even assuming my crystals wouldn't break your teeth," Wyndle said, "my mass would give you no sustenance. It would break down into dust."

"It's not about sustenance. It's about torture."

Wyndle, surprisingly, met her expression with his strange eyes grown from crystals. "Honestly, mistress, I don't think you have it in you."

She growled at him, and he wilted further, but didn't tell her the secret. Well, storms. It was good to see him have a backbone . . . or, well, the plant equivalent, whatever that was. Backbark?

"You're supposed to obey me," she said, shoving her hands in her pockets and heading along the path toward the city. "You ain't following the rules."

"I am indeed," he said with a huff. "You just don't know them. And I'll have you know that I am a gardener, and not a soldier, so I'll *not* have you hitting people with me."

She stopped. "Why would I hit anyone with you?"

He wilted so far, he was practically shriveled.

Lift sighed, then continued on her way, Wyndle following. They merged with the larger road, turning toward the tower that was a gateway into the city.

"So," Wyndle said as they passed a chull cart, "this is where we were going all along? This city cut into the ground?"

Lift nodded.

"You could have told me," Wyndle said. "I've been worried we'd be caught outside in a storm!"

"Why? It ain't raining anymore." The Weeping, oddly, had stopped. Then started again. Then stopped again. It was acting downright strange, like regular weather, rather than the long, long mild highstorm it was supposed to be.

"I don't know," Wyndle said. "Something is wrong, mistress. Something in the world. I can feel it. Did you hear what the Alethi king wrote to the emperor?"

"About a new storm coming?" Lift said. "One that blows the wrong way?"

"Yes."

"The noodles all called that silly."

"Noodles?"

"The people who hang around Gawx, talking to him all the time, telling him what to do and trying to get me to wear a robe."

"The *viziers* of *Azir*. Head clerks of the empire and advisors to the Prime!"

"Yeah. Wavy arms and blubbering features. Noodles. Anyway, they thought that angry guy—"

"—Highprince Dalinar Kholin, de facto king of Alethkar and most powerful warlord in the world right now—"

"—was makin' stuff up."

"Maybe. But don't you feel something? Out there? Building?"

"A distant thunder," Lift whispered, looking westward, past the city, toward the far-off mountains. "Or . . . or the way you feel after someone drops a pan, and you see it falling, and get ready for the clatter it will make when it hits."

"So you do feel it."

"Maybe," Lift said. The chull cart rolled past. Nobody paid any attention to her—they never did. And nobody could see Wyndle but her, because *she* was *special*. "Don't your Voidbringer friends know about this?"

"We're not . . . Lift, we're spren, but my kind—cultivationspren—are not very important. We don't have a kingdom, or even cities, of our own. We only moved to bond with you because the Cryptics and the honorspren and everyone were starting to move. Oh, we've jumped *right* into the sea of glass feet-first, but we barely know what we're doing! Everyone who had any idea of how to accomplish all this died centuries ago!"

He grew along the road beside her as they followed the chull cart, which rattled and shook as it bounced down the roadway.

"Everything is wrong, and nothing makes sense," Wyndle continued. "Bonding to you was supposed to be more difficult than it was, I gather. Memories come to me fuzzily sometimes, but I do remember more and more. I didn't go through the trauma we all thought I'd endure. That might be because of your . . . unique circumstances. But mistress, listen to me when I say something big is coming. This was the wrong time to leave Azir. We were secure there. We'll need security."

"There isn't time to get back."

"No. There probably isn't. At least we have shelter ahead."

"Yeah. Assuming Darkness doesn't kill us."

"Darkness? The Skybreaker who attacked you in the palace and came very close to murdering you?"

"Yeah," Lift said. "He's in the city. Didn't you hear me complaining that I needed a Shardblade?"

"In the city . . . in Yeddaw, where we're *going right now*?"

"Yup. The noodles have people watching for reports of him. A note came in right before we left, saying he'd been spotted in Yeddaw."

"Wait." Wyndle zipped forward, leaving a trail of vines and crystal behind. He grew up the back of the chull cart, curling onto its wood right in front of her. He made a face there, looking at her. "Is *that* why we left all of a sudden? Is *that* why we're here? Did you come *chasing* that monster?"

"Course not," Lift said, hands in her pockets. "That would be stupid."

"Which you are not."

"Nope."

"Then *why* are we *here*?"

"They got these pancakes here," she said, "with things cooked into them. Supposed to be super tasty, and they eat them during the Weeping. Ten varieties. I'm gonna steal one of each."

"You came all this way, leaving behind luxury, to eat some pancakes."

"Really *awesome* pancakes."

"Despite the fact that a deific Shardbearer is here—a man who went to great lengths to try to execute you."

"He wanted to stop me from using my powers," Lift said. "He's been seen other places. The noodles looked into it; they're fascinated by him. Everyone pays attention to that bald guy who collects the heads of kings, but *this* guy has been murdering his way across Roshar too. Little people. Quiet people."

"And we came here why?"

She shrugged. "Seemed like as good a place as any."

He let himself slide off the back of the cart. "As a point of fact, it most expressly is *not* as good a place as any. It is demonstrably worse for—"

"You sure I can't eat you?" she asked. "That would be super convenient. You got lots of extra vines. Maybe I could nibble on a few of those."

"I assure you, mistress, that you would find the experience *thoroughly* unappealing."

She grunted, stomach growling. Hungerspren appeared, like little brown specks with wings, floating around her. That wasn't odd. Many of the folks in line had attracted them.

"I got two powers," Lift said. "I can slide around, awesome, and I can make stuff grow. So I could grow me some plants to eat?"

"It would almost certainly take more energy in Stormlight to grow the plants than the sustenance would provide, as determined by the laws of the universe. And before you say anything, these are laws that even *you* cannot ignore." He paused. "I think. Who knows, when *you're* involved?"

"I'm *special*," Lift said, stopping as they finally reached the line of people waiting to get into the city. "Also, hungry. More hungry than special, right now."

She poked her head out of the line. Several guards stood at the ramp down into the city, along with some scribes wearing the odd Tashikki clothing. It was this *loooong* piece of cloth that they wrapped around themselves, feet to forehead. For being a single sheet, it was really complex: it wound around both legs and arms individually, but also wrapped back around the waist sometimes to create a kind of skirt. Both the men and the women wore the cloths, though not the guards.

They sure were taking their time letting people in. And there sure were a lot of people waiting. Everyone here was Makabaki, with dark eyes and skin—darker than Lift's brownish tan. And a lot of those waiting were families, wearing normal Azish-style clothing. Trousers, dirty skirts, some with patterns. They buzzed with exhaustionspren and hungerspren, enough to be distracting.

She'd have expected mostly merchants, not families, to be waiting here. Who were all these people?

Her stomach growled.

"Mistress?" Wyndle asked.

"Hush," she said. "Too hungry to talk."

"Are you—"

"Hungry? Yes. So shut up."

"But—"

"I bet those guards have food. People always feed guards. They can't properly hit folks on the head if they're starvin'. That's a *fact*."

"Or, to offer a counterproposal, you could simply *buy* some food with the spheres the emperor allotted you."

"Didn't bring them."

"You didn't . . . you didn't *bring the money*?"

"Ditched it when you weren't looking. Can't get robbed if you don't have money. Carrying spheres is just asking for trouble. Besides." She narrowed her eyes, watching the guards. "Only fancy people have money like that. We normal folk, we have to get by some other way."

"So now you're normal."

"Course I am," she said. "It's everyone else that's weird."

Before he could reply, she ducked underneath the chull wagon and started sneaking toward the front of the line.

3

TALLEW, you say?" Hauka asked, holding up the tarp covering the suspicious pile of grain. "From Azir?"

"Yes, of course, officer." The man sitting on the front of the wagon squirmed. "Just a humble farmer."

With no calluses, Hauka thought. *A humble farmer who can afford fine Liaforan boots and a silk belt.* Hauka took her spear and started shoving it into the grain, blunt end first. She didn't run across any contraband, or any refugees, hidden in the grain. So that was a first.

"I need to get your papers notarized," she said. "Pull your cart over to the side here."

The man grumbled but obeyed, turning his cart and starting to back the chull into the spot beside the guard post. It was one of the only buildings erected here above the city, along with a few towers spaced where they could lob arrows at anyone trying to use the ramps or set up position to siege.

The farmer with the wagon backed his cart in very, very carefully—as they were near the ledge overlooking the city. Immigrant quarter. Rich people didn't enter here, only the ones without papers. Or the ones who hoped to avoid scrutiny.

Hauka rolled up the man's credentials and walked past the guard post. Scents wafted out of that; lunch was being set up, which meant the people in line had an even longer wait ahead of them. An old scribe sat in a seat near the front of the guard post. Nissiqqan liked to be out in the sun.

Hauka bowed to him; Nissiqqan was the deputy scribe of immigration on duty for today. The older man was wrapped head-to-toe in a yellow shiqua, though he'd pulled the face portion down to expose a furrowed face with a cleft chin. They were in home lands, and the need to cover up before Nun Raylisi—the enemy of their god—was minimal. Tashi supposedly protected them here.

Hauka herself wore a breastplate, cap, trousers, and a cloak with her family and studies pattern on them. The locals accepted an Azish like her with ease—Tashikk didn't have much in the way of its own soldiers, and her credentials of achievement were certified by an Azimir vizier. She could have gotten a similar officer's job with the local guard anywhere in the greater Makabaki region, though her credentials *did* make clear she wasn't certified for battlefield command.

"Captain?" Nissiqqan said, adjusting his spectacles and looking at the farmer's credentials as she proffered them. "Is he refusing to pay the tariff?"

"Tariff is fine and in the strongbox," Hauka said. "I'm suspicious though. That man's no farmer."

"Smuggling refugees?"

"Checked in the grain and under the cart," Hauka said, looking over her shoulder. The man was all smiles. "It's new grain. A little overripe, but edible."

"Then the city will be glad to have it."

He was right. The war between Emul and Tukar was heating up. Granted, everyone was always saying that. But things *had* changed over the last few years. That god-king of the Tukari . . . there were all sorts of wild rumors about him.

"That's it!" Hauka said. "Your Grace, I'll bet that man has been in Emul. He's been raiding their fields while all the able-bodied men are fighting the invasion."

Nissiqqan nodded in agreement, rubbing his chin. Then he dug through his folder. "Tax him as a smuggler *and* as a fence. I believe . . . yes, that will work. Triple tariff. I'll earmark the extra tariffs to be diverted to feeding refugees, per referendum three-seventy-one-sha."

"Thanks," Hauka said, relaxing and taking the forms. Say what you would of the strange clothing and religion of the Tashikki, they certainly did know how to draft solid civil ordinances.

"I have spheres for you," Nissiqqan noted. "I know you've been asking for infused ones."

"Really!" Hauka said.

"My cousin had some out in his sphere cage—pure luck that he'd forgotten them—when that unpredicted highstorm blew through."

"Excellent," Hauka said. "I'll trade you for them later." She had some information that Nissiqqan would be very interested in. They used that as currency here in Tashikk, as much as they did spheres.

And storms, some lit spheres would be nice. After the Weeping, most people didn't have any, which could be storming inconvenient—as open flame was forbidden in the city. So she couldn't do any reading at night unless she found some infused spheres.

She walked back to the smuggler, flipping through forms. "We'll need you to pay this tariff," she said, handing him a form. "And then this one too."

"A fencing permit!" the man exclaimed. "And smuggling! This is thievery!"

"Yes, I believe it is. Or was."

"You can't prove such allegations," he said, slapping the forms with his hand.

"Sure," she said. "If I could *prove* that you crossed the border into Emul illegally, robbed the fields of good hardworking people while they were distracted by the fighting, then carted it here without proper permits, I'd simply seize the whole thing." She leaned in. "You're getting off easily. We both know it."

He met her eyes, then looked nervously away and started filling out the forms. Good. No trouble today. She liked it when there was no trouble. It—

Hauka stopped. The tarp on the man's wagon was rustling. Frowning, Hauka whipped it backward, and found a young *girl* neck-deep in the grain. She had light brown skin—like she was Reshi, or maybe Herdazian—and was probably eleven or twelve years old. She grinned at Hauka.

She hadn't been there before.

"This stuff," the girl said in Azish, mouth full of what appeared to be uncooked grain, "tastes terrible. I guess that's why we make stuff out of it first." She swallowed. "Got anything to drink?"

The smuggler stood up on his cart, sputtering and pointing. "She's ruining my goods! She's *swimming* in it! Guard, do something! There's a dirty refugee in my *grain*!"

Great. The paperwork on this was going to be a nightmare. "Out of there, child. Do you have parents?"

"Course I do," the girl said, rolling her eyes. "Everyone's got parents. Mine'r'dead though." She cocked her head. "What's that I smell? That wouldn't be . . . pancakes, would it?"

"Sure," Hauka said, sensing an opportunity. "Sun Day pancakes. You can have one, if you—"

"Thanks!" The girl leaped from the grain, spraying it in all directions, causing the smuggler to cry out. Hauka tried to snatch the child, but somehow the girl wiggled out of her grip. She leaped over Hauka's hands, then bounded forward.

And landed right on Hauka's shoulders.

Hauka grunted at the sudden weight of the girl, who jumped off her shoulders and landed behind her.

Hauka spun about, off-balance.

"Tashi!" the smuggler said. "She stepped on your *storming shoulders*, officer."

"Thank you. Stay here. Don't move." Hauka straightened her cap, then dashed after the child, who brushed past Nissiqqan—causing him to drop his folders—and entered into the guard chamber. Good. There weren't any other ways out of that post. Hauka stumbled up to the doorway, setting aside her spear and taking the club from her belt. She didn't want to hurt the little refugee, but some intimidation wouldn't be out of order.

The girl slid across the wooden floor as if it were covered in oil, passing right under the table where several scribes and two of Hauka's guards were eating. The girl then stood up and knocked the entire thing on its side, startling everyone backward and dumping food to the floor.

"Sorry!" the girl called from the mess. "Didn't mean to do that." Her head popped up from beside the overturned table, and she had a pancake sticking half out of her mouth. "These aren't bad."

Hauka's men leaped to their feet. Hauka lunged past them, trying to reach around the table to grab the refugee. Her fingers brushed the arm of the girl, who wiggled away again. The child pushed against the floor and slid right between Rez's legs.

Hauka lunged again, cornering the girl on the side of the guard chamber.

The girl, in turn, reached up and wiggled through the room's single slotlike window. Hauka gaped. Surely that wasn't big enough for a person, even a small one, to get through so easily. She pressed herself against the wall, looking out the window. She didn't see anything at first; then the girl's head poked down from above—she'd gotten onto the roof somehow.

The girl's dark hair blew in the breeze. "Hey," she said. "What kind of pancake *was* that, anyway? I've gotta eat all ten."

"Get back in here," Hauka said, reaching through to try to grab the girl. "You haven't been processed for immigration."

The girl's head popped back upward, and her footsteps sounded on the roof. Hauka cursed and scrambled out the front, trailed by her two guards. They searched the roof of the small guard post, but saw nothing.

"She's back in here!" one of the scribes called from inside.

A moment later, the girl skidded out along the ground, a pancake in each hand and another in her mouth. She passed the guards and scrambled toward the cart with the smuggler, who had climbed down and was ranting about his grain getting soiled.

Hauka leaped to grab the child—and this time managed to get hold of her leg. Unfortunately, her two guards reached for the girl too, and they tripped, falling in a jumbled mess right on top of Hauka.

She hung on though. Puffing from the weight on her back, Hauka clung tightly to the little girl's leg. She looked up, holding in a groan.

The refugee girl sat on the stone in front of her, head cocked. She stuffed one of the pancakes into her mouth, then reached behind herself, her hand darting toward the hitch where the cart was hooked to its chull. The hitch came undone, the hook popping out as the girl tapped it on the bottom. It didn't resist a bit.

Oh, storms no.

"Off me!" Hauka screamed, letting go of the girl and pushing free of the men. The stupid smuggler backed away, confused.

The cart rolled toward the ledge behind, and she doubted the wooden fence would keep it from falling. Hauka leaped for the cart in a burst of energy, seizing it by its side. It dragged her along with it, and she had terrible visions of it plummeting down over the ledge into the city, right on top of the refugees of the immigrant quarter.

The cart, however, slowly lurched to a halt. Puffing, Hauka looked up from where she stood, feet pressed against the stones, holding onto the cart. She didn't dare let go.

The girl was there, on top of the grain again, eating the last pancake. "They really are good."

"Tuk-cake," Hauka said, feeling exhausted. "You eat them for prosperity in the year to come."

"People should eat them all the time then, you know?"

"Maybe."

The girl nodded, then stood to the side and kicked open the tailgate of the cart. In a rush, the grain *slid* out of the cart.

It was the strangest thing she'd ever seen. The pile of grain became like liquid, flowing out of the cart even though the incline was shallow. It . . . well, it *glowed* softly as it flowed out and rained down into the city.

The girl smiled at Hauka.

Then she jumped off after it.

Hauka gaped as the girl fell after the grain. The two other guards finally woke up enough to come help, and grabbed hold of the cart. The smuggler was screaming, angerspren boiling up around him like pools of blood on the ground.

Below, the grain billowed in the air, sending up dust as it poured into the immigrant quarter. It was rather far down, but Hauka was pretty sure she heard shouts of delight and praise as the food blanketed the people there.

Cart secure, Hauka stepped up to the ledge. The girl was nowhere to be seen. Storms. Had she been some kind of spren? Hauka searched again but saw nothing, though there was this strange black dust at her feet. It blew away in the wind.

"Captain?" Rez asked.

"Take over immigration for the next hour, Rez. I need a break."

Storms. How on Roshar was she ever going to explain *this* in a report?

4

L IFT wasn't supposed to be able to touch Wyndle. The Voidbringer
kept saying things like "I don't have enough presence in this
Realm, even with our bond" and "you must be stuck partially in
the Cognitive." Gibberish, basically.

Because she *could* touch him. That was very useful at times. Times
like when you'd just jumped off a short cliff, and needed something to
hold on to. Wyndle yelped in surprise as she leaped, then he immediately shot down the side of the wall, moving faster than she fell. He was
finally learning to pay attention.

Lift grabbed ahold of him like a rope, one that she halfway held to as
she fell, the vine sliding between her fingers. It wasn't much, but it did
help slow her descent. She hit harder than would have been safe for
most people. Fortunately, she was awesome.

She extinguished the glow of her awesomeness, then dashed to a
small alleyway. People crowded around behind her, praising various
Heralds and gods for the gift of the grain. Well, they could speak like
that if they wanted, but they all seemed to know the grain hadn't come
from a god—not directly—because it was snatched up quicker than a
pretty whore in Bavland.

In minutes, all that was left of an entire cartload of grain was a few husks blowing in the wind. Lift settled in the alleyway's mouth, inspecting her surroundings. It was like she'd dropped from noonday straight into dusk. Long shadows everywhere, and things smelled wet.

The buildings were cut right into the stone—doorways, windows, and everything bored out of the rock. They painted the walls these bright colors, often in columns to differentiate one "building" from another. People swarmed all about, chatting and stomping and coughing.

This was the good kind of life. Lift liked being on the move, but she didn't like being alone. Solitary was different from alone. She stood up and started walking, hands in pockets, trying to look in all directions at once. This place was amazing.

"That was quite generous of you, mistress," Wyndle said, growing along beside her. "Dumping that grain, after hearing that the man who had it was a thief."

"That?" Lift said. "I just wanted something soft to land on if you were snoozing."

The people she passed wore a variety of attire. Mostly Azish patterns or Tashikki shiquas. But some were mercenaries, probably either Tukari or Emuli. Others wore rural clothing with a lighter coloring, probably from Alm or Desh. She liked those places. Few people had tried to kill her in Alm or Desh.

Unfortunately, there wasn't much to steal there—unless you liked eating mush, and this strange meat they put in everything. It came from some beast that lived on the mountain slopes, an ugly thing with dirty hair all over it. Lift thought they tasted disgusting, and *she'd* once tried to eat a *roofing tile*.

Anyway, on this street there seemed to be far fewer Tashikki than there were foreigners—but what had they called this above? Immigrant quarter? Well, she probably wouldn't stick out here. She even passed a few Reshi, though most of these were huddled near alleyway shanties, wearing little more than rags.

That was an oddity about this place, for sure. It had shanties. She hadn't seen those since leaving Zawfix, which had them inside of old mines. Most places, if people tried to build homes out of shoddy material . . .

well it would all just get blown away in the first highstorm and leave them sitting on the chamber pot, looking stupid with no walls.

Here, the shanties were confined to smaller roadways, which stuck out like spokes from this larger one, connecting it to the next large road in line. Many of these were so packed with hanging blankets, people, and improvised houses that you couldn't see the opening on the other side.

Oddly though, it was all up on stilts. Even the most rickety of constructions was up four feet or so in the air. Lift stood at the mouth of one alleyway, hands in pockets, and looked down along the larger slot. As she'd noted earlier, each wall of the city was also a set of shops and homes cut right into the rock, painted to separate them from their neighbors. And for all of them, you had to walk up three or four steps cut into the stone to get in.

"It's like the Purelake," she said. "Everything's up high, like nobody wants to touch the ground 'cuz it's got some kind of nasty cough."

"Wise," Wyndle said. "Protection from the storms."

"The waters should still wash this place away," Lift said.

Well, they obviously didn't, or the place wouldn't be here. She continued strolling down the road, passing lines of homes cut into the wall, and strings of other homes smushed between them. Those shanties looked inviting—warm, packed, full of life. She even saw the green, bobbing motes of lifespren floating along among them, something you usually only saw when there were lots of plants. Unfortunately, she knew from experience that sometimes no matter how inviting a place looked, it wouldn't welcome a foreigner urchin.

"So," Wyndle said, crawling along the wall next to her head, leaving a trail of vines behind him. "You have gotten us here, and—remarkably—avoided incarceration. What now?"

"Food," Lift said, her stomach grumbling.

"You just ate!"

"Yeah. Used up all the energy getting away from the starvin' guards though. I'm hungrier than when I started!"

"Oh, Blessed Mother," he said in exasperation. "Why didn't you simply *wait* in *line* then?"

"Wouldn't have gotten any food that way."

"It doesn't matter, since you burned all the food into Stormlight, then jumped off a wall!"

"But I got to eat pancakes!"

They wove around a group of Tashikki women carrying baskets on their arms, yammering about Liaforan handicrafts. Two unconsciously covered their baskets and gripped the handles tight as Lift passed.

"I can't believe this," Wyndle said. "I *cannot* believe this is my existence. I was a gardener! Respected! Now, everywhere I go, people look at us as if we're going to pick their pockets."

"Nothing in their pockets," Lift said, looking over her shoulder. "I don't think shiquas even *have* pockets. Those baskets though . . ."

"Did you know we were considering bonding this nice cobbler man instead of you? A very kindly man who took care of children. I could have lived quietly, helping him, making shoes. I could have done an entire *display* of shoes!"

"And the danger that is coming," Lift said. "From the west? If there really *is* a war?"

"Shoes are important to war," Wyndle said, spitting out a splatter of vines on the wall about him—she wasn't sure what that was supposed to mean. "You think the Radiants are going to fight barefoot? We could have made them shoes, that nice old cobbler and me. Wonderful shoes."

"Sounds boring."

He groaned. "You *are* going to slam me into people, aren't you? I'm going to be a weapon."

"What nonsense are you talking about, Voidbringer?"

"I suppose I need to get you to say the Words, don't I? That's my job? Oh, this is *miserable*."

He often said things like this. You probably had to be messed-up in the brain to be a Voidbringer, so she didn't hold it against him. Instead, she dug in her pocket and brought out a little book. She held it up, flipping through the pages.

"What's that?" Wyndle asked.

"I pinched it from that guard post," she said. "Thought I might be able to sell it or something."

"Let me see that," Wyndle said. He grew down the side of the wall, then up around her leg, twisted around her body, and finally along her arm onto the book. It tickled, the way his main vine shot out tiny creepers that stuck to her skin to keep it in place.

On the page, he spread out other little vines, completely growing over the book and between its pages. "Hmmm. . . ."

Lift leaned back against the wall of the slot as she worked. She didn't feel like she was in a city, she felt like she was in a . . . tunnel that led to one. Sure, the sky was open and bright overhead, but this street felt so isolated. Usually in a city you could see ripples of buildings, towering off away from you. You could hear shouts from several streets over.

Even clogged with people—more people than seemed reasonable—this street felt isolated. A strange little cremling crawled up the wall beside her. Smaller than most, it was black, with a thin carapace and a strip of fuzzy brown on its back that seemed spongy. Cremlings were strange in Tashikk, and they only got stranger the farther west you went. Closer to the mountains, some of the cremlings could even *fly*.

"Hmm, yes," Wyndle said. "Mistress, this book is likely worthless. It's only a logbook of times the guards have been on duty. The captain, for example, records when she leaves each day—ten on the dot, by the wall clock—replaced by the night watch captain. One visit to the Grand Indicium each week for detailed debriefing of weekly events. She's fastidious, but I doubt anyone will be interested in buying her logbook."

"Surely someone will want it. It's a book!"

"Lift, books have value based on what is *in* them."

"I know. Pages."

"I mean what's on the pages."

"Ink?"

"I mean what the ink *says*."

She scratched her head.

"You really should have listened to those writing coaches in Azir."

"So . . . no trading this for food?" Her stomach growled, attracting more hungerspren.

"Not likely."

Stupid book—and stupid people. She grumbled and tossed the book over her shoulder.

It hit a woman carrying a basket of yarn, unfortunately. She yelped.

"You!" a voice shouted.

Lift winced. A man in a guard's uniform was pointing at her through the crowd.

"Did you just assault that woman?" the guard shouted at her.

"Barely!" Lift shouted back.

The guard came stalking toward her.

"Run?" Wyndle asked.

"Run."

She ducked into an alley, prompting further shouts from the guard, who came barreling in after her.

5

Roughly a half hour later, Lift lay on a stretched-out tarp atop a shanty, puffing from an extended run. That guard had been *persistent.*

She swung idly on the tarp as a wind blew through the shantied alleyway. Beneath, a family talked about the miracle of an entire cart of grain suddenly being dumped in the slums. A mother, three sons, and a father, all together.

I will remember those who have been forgotten. She'd sworn that oath as she'd saved Gawx's life. The right Words, important Words. But what did they mean? What about her mother? Nobody remembered her.

There seemed far too many people out there who were being forgotten. Too many for one girl to remember.

"Lift?" Wyndle asked. He'd made a little tower of vines and leaves that blew in the wind. "Why haven't you ever gone to the Reshi Isles? That's where you're from, right?"

"It's what Mother said."

"So why not go visit and see? You've been halfway across Roshar and back, to hear you talk. But never to your supposed homeland."

She shrugged, staring up at the late-afternoon sky, feeling the wind.

It smelled fresh, compared to the stench of being down in the slots. The city wasn't ripe, but it was thick with contained smells, like animals locked up.

"Do you know why we had to leave Azir?" Lift said softly.

"To chase after that Skybreaker, the one you call Darkness."

"No. We're not doing that."

"Sure."

"We left because people started to know who I am. If you stay in the same place too long, then people start to recognize you. The shop-keepers learn your name. They smile at you when you enter, and already know what to get for you, because they remember what you need."

"That's a bad thing?"

She nodded, still staring at the sky. "It's worse when they think they're your friend. Gawx, the viziers. They make assumptions. They think they know you, then start to expect things of you. Then you have to be the person everyone thinks you are, not the person you actually are."

"And who is the person you actually are, Lift?"

That was the problem, wasn't it? She'd known that once, hadn't she? Or was it just that she'd been young enough not to care?

How did people know? The breeze rocked her perch, and she snuggled up, remembering her mother's arms, her scent, her warm voice.

The pangs of a growling stomach interrupted her, the needs of the now strangling the wants of the past. She sighed and stood up on the tarp. "Come on," she said. "Let's go find some urchins."

6

GOTTA lunks," the little girl said. She was grimy, with hands that probably hadn't been washed since she'd gotten old enough to pick her own nose. She was missing a lot of teeth. Too many for her age. "The marm, she gotta lunks good."

"Gotta lunks for smalls?"

"Gotta lunks for smalls," the girl said to Lift, nodding. "But gotta snaps too. Biga stone, that one, and eyes is swords. Don't lika smalls, but gotta lunks for them. Real nogginin, that."

"Maybe for outsida cares?" Lift said. "Lika the outsida, they gotta light for her, ifn she given lunks for smalls?"

"Maybe," the girl said. "Maybe that right. But it might be nogginin, but it's wrack too. I say that. Real wrack."

"Thanks," Lift said. "Here." She gave the girl her handkerchief, as promised. In trade for the information.

The girl wrapped it around her head and gave Lift a gap-toothed grin. People liked trading information in Tashikk. It was kind of their thing.

The grimy little girl paused. "That lighta above, the lunks from the sky. I heard loudin about it. That was you, outsida, eh?"

"Yeah."

The girl turned as if to leave, but then reconsidered and put a hand on Lift's arm.

"You," the girl said to Lift. "Outsida?"

"Yeah."

"You listenin'?"

"I'm listenin'."

"People, they don't listen." She smiled at Lift again, then finally scuttled away.

Lift settled back on her haunches in the alleyway across from some communal ovens—a vast, hollowed-out cavern in the wall with huge chimneys cut upward. They burned the rockbud husks from the farms, and anyone could come cook in the central ovens there. They couldn't have fires in their own places. From what Lift had heard, early in the city's life they'd had a fire blaze through the various slums and kill *tons* of people.

In the alleys you didn't see smoke trails, only the occasional pinprick of spherelight. It was supposed to be the Weeping, and most spheres had gone dun. Only those who had spheres out, by luck, during that unexpected highstorm a few days ago would have light.

"Mistress," Wyndle said, "that was the strangest conversation I've *ever* heard, and I once grew an entire garden for some keenspren."

"Seemed normal to me. Just a kid on the street."

"But the way you talked!" Wyndle said.

"What way?"

"With all those odd words and terms. How did you know what to say?"

"It just felt right," Lift said. "Words is words. Anyway, she said that we could get food at the Tashi's Light Orphanage. Same as the other one we talked to."

"Then why haven't we gone there?" Wyndle asked.

"Nobody likes the woman who runs it. They don't trust her; say that she's starvin' mean. That she only gives away food in the first place because she wants to look good for the officials that watch the place."

"To turn your phrase back at you, mistress, food is food."

"Yeah," Lift said. "It's just . . . what's the challenge of eating a lunch someone *gives* you?"

"I'm certain you will survive the indignity, mistress."

Unfortunately, he was right. She was too hungry to produce any awesomeness, which meant being a regular child beggar. She didn't move though, not yet.

People, they don't listen. Did Lift listen? She did usually, didn't she? Why did the little urchin girl care, anyway?

Hands in pockets, Lift rose and picked her way through the crowded slot street, dodging the occasional hand that tried to swat or punch her. People here did something strange—they kept their spheres in rows, strung on long strings, even if they put them in pouches. And all the money she saw had holes in the bottoms of the glass spheres, so you could do that. What if you had to count out exact change? Would you unstring the whole starvin' bunch, then string them up again?

At least they used spheres. People farther toward the west, they just used chips of gemstone, sometimes embedded in hunks of glass, sometimes not. Starvin' easy to lose, those were.

People got so mad when she lost spheres. They were strange about money. Far too concerned with something that you couldn't eat—though Lift figured that was probably the point of using spheres instead of something rational, like bags of food. If you actually traded food, everyone would eat up all their money and then where would society be?

The Tashi's Light Orphanage was a corner building, cut into a place where two streets met. The main face pointed onto the large thoroughfare of the immigrant quarter, and was painted bright orange. The other side faced a particularly wide alleyway mouth that had some rows of seats cut into the sides, making a half circle, like some kind of theater—though it was broken in the center for the alleyway. That strung out into the distance, but it didn't look quite as derelict as some others. Some of the shanties even had doors, and the belching that echoed from within the alley sounded almost refined.

She'd been told by the urchins not to approach from the street side, which was for officials and real people. Urchins were to approach from the alleyway side, so Lift neared the stone benches of the little amphitheater—where some old people in shiquas were sitting—and knocked on the door. A section of the stone above it was carved and painted gold and red, though she couldn't read the letters.

A youth pulled open the door. He had a flat, wide face, like Lift had learned to associate with people who weren't born quite the same as other folk. He looked her over, then pointed at the benches. "Sit there," he said. "Food comes later."

"How much later?" Lift said, hands on hips.

"Why? You got *appointments*?" the young man asked, then smiled. "Sit there. Food comes later."

She sighed, but settled down near where the old people were chatting. She got the impression that they were people from farther in the slum who came out here, to the open circle cut into the mouth of the alleyway, where there were steps to sit on and a breeze.

With the sun getting closer to setting, the slots were falling deeper and deeper into shadow. There wouldn't be many spheres to light it up at night; people would probably go to bed earlier than they normally did, as was common during the Weeping. Lift huddled on one of the seats, Wyndle writhing up beside her. She stared at the stupid door to the stupid orphanage, her stupid stomach growling.

"What was wrong with that young man who answered the door?" Wyndle asked.

"Dunno," Lift said. "Some people are just born like that."

She waited on the steps, listening to some Tashikki men from the slums chat and chuckle together. Eventually a figure skulked into the mouth of the alleyway—it seemed to be a woman, wrapped all in dark cloth. Not a true shiqua. Maybe a foreigner trying to wear one, and hide who she was.

The woman sniffled audibly, holding the hand of a large child, maybe ten or eleven years old. She led him to the doorstep of the orphanage, then pulled him into a hug.

The boy stared ahead, sightless, drooling. He had a scar on his head, healed mostly, but still an angry red.

The woman bowed her head, then her back, and slunk away, leaving the boy. He just sat there, staring. Not a baby in a basket; no, that was a children's tale. This was what actually happened at orphanages, in Lift's experience. People left children who were too big to keep caring for, but couldn't take care of themselves or contribute to the family.

"Did she . . . just leave that boy?" Wyndle asked, horrified.

"She's probably got other children," Lift said softly, "she can barely keep fed. She can't spend all her time looking after one like that, not any longer." Lift's heart twisted inside her and she wanted to look away, but couldn't.

Instead, she stood up and walked over toward the boy. Rich people, like the viziers in Azir, had a strange perspective on orphanages. They imagined them full of saintly little children, plucky and good-hearted, eager to work and have a family.

In Lift's experience though, orphanages had far more like this boy. Kids who were tough to care for. Kids who required constant supervision, or who were confused in the head. Or those who could get violent.

She hated how rich people made up this romantic dream of what an orphanage should be like. Perfect, full of sweet smiles and happy singing. Not full of frustration, pain, and confusion.

She sat down next to the boy. She was smaller than he was. "Hey," she said.

He looked to her with glazed eyes. She could see his wound better now. The hair hadn't grown back on the side of his head.

"It's going to be all right," she said, taking his hand in hers.

He didn't reply.

A short time later, the door into the orphanage opened, revealing a shriveled-up weed of a woman. Seriously. She looked like the child of a broom and a particularly determined clump of moss. Her skin drooped off her bones like something you'd hack up after catching crud in the slums, and she had spindly fingers that Lift figured might be twigs she'd glued in place after her real ones fell off.

The woman put hands on hips—amazingly, she didn't break any bones in the motion—and looked the two of them over. "An idiot and an opportunist," she said.

"Hey!" Lift said, scrambling up. "He's not an idiot. He's just hurt."

"I was describing you, child," the woman said, then knelt beside the boy with the hurt head. She clicked her tongue. "Worthless, worthless," she muttered. "I can see through your deception. You won't last long here. Watch and see." She gestured backward, and the young man Lift had seen earlier came out and took the hurt boy by the arm, leading him into the orphanage.

Lift tried to follow, but twigs-for-hands stepped in front of her. "You can have three meals," the woman told her. "You pick when you want them, but after three you're done. Consider yourself lucky I'm willing to give anything to one like you."

"What's that supposed to mean?" Lift demanded.

"That if you don't want rats on your ship, you shouldn't be in the business of feeding them." The woman shook her head, then moved to pull the door shut.

"Wait!" Lift said. "I need somewhere to sleep."

"Then you came to the right place."

"Really?"

"Yes, those benches usually clear out once it gets dark."

"Stone *benches*?" Lift said. "You want me to sleep on stone benches?"

"Oh, don't whine. It's not even raining any longer." The woman shut the door.

Lift sighed, looking toward Wyndle. A moment later, the young man from before opened the door and tossed something out to her—a large baked roll of clemabread, thick and granular, with spicy paste at the center.

"Don't suppose you have a pancake?" Lift asked him. "I've got a goal to eat—"

He shut the door. Lift sighed, but settled down on the stone benches near some old men, and started gobbling it up. It wasn't particularly good, but it was warm and filling. "Storming witch," she muttered.

"Don't judge her too harshly, child," said one of the old men on the benches. He wore a black shiqua, but had pulled back the part that wrapped the face, exposing a grey mustache and eyebrows. He had dark brown skin with a wide smile. "It is difficult to be the one that handles everyone else's problems."

"She doesn't have to be so mean."

"When she isn't, then children congregate here begging for hand-outs."

"So? Isn't that kind of the *point* of an orphanage?" Lift chewed on the roll. "Sleep on the rock benches? I should go steal her pillow."

"I think you'd find her ready to deal with feisty urchin thieves."

"She ain't never faced *me* before. I'm *awesome*." She looked down at the rest of her food. Of course, if she used her awesomeness, she'd just end up hungry again.

The man laughed. "They call her the Stump, because she won't be blown by any storm. I don't think you'll get the best of her, little one." He leaned in. "But I have information, if you are interested in a trade."

Tashikki and their secrets. Lift rolled her eyes. "Ain't got nothing left to trade."

"Trade me your time, then. I will tell you how to get on the Stump's good side. Maybe earn yourself a bed. In turn, you answer a question for me. Is this a deal?"

Lift cocked an eyebrow at him. "Sure. Whatever."

"Here is my secret. The Stump has a little . . . hobby. She is in the business of trading spheres. An exchanging business, so to speak. Find someone who wants to trade with her, and she will handsomely reward you."

"Trade spheres?" Lift said. "Money for money? What is the point of that?"

He shrugged. "She works hard to cover it up. So it must be important."

"What a lame secret," Lift said. She popped the last of the roll into her mouth, the clemabread breaking apart easily—it was almost more of a mush.

"Will you still answer my question?"

"Depends on how lame *it* is."

"What body part do you feel that you are most like?" he asked. "Are you the hand, always busy doing work? Are you the mind, giving direction? Do you feel that you are more of a . . . leg, perhaps? Bearing up everyone else, and rarely noticed?"

"Yeah. Lame question."

"No, no. It is of most importance. Each person, they are but a piece of something larger—some grand organism that makes up this city. This is the philosophy I am building, you see."

Lift eyed him. Great. Angry twig running an orphanage; weird old man outside it. She dusted off her hands. "If I'm anything, I'm a nose. 'Cuz I'm filled with all kinds of weird crud, and you never know what's gonna fall out."

"Ah . . . interesting."

"That wasn't meant to be helpful."

"Yes, but it was honest, which is the cornerstone of a good philosophy."

"Yeah. Sure." Lift hopped off the stone benches. "As fun as it was talkin' crazy stuff with you, I got somewhere important to be."

"You do?" Wyndle asked, rising from where he'd been coiled up on the bench beside her.

"Yup," Lift said. "I've got an *appointment*."

7

LIFT was worried she'd be late. She'd never been good with time.

Now, she could keep the important parts straight. Sun up, sun down. Blah blah. But the divisions beyond that . . . well, she'd never found those to be important. Other people did though, so she hurried through the slot.

"Are you going to find spheres for that woman at the orphanage?" Wyndle said, zipping along the ground beside her, weaving between the legs of people. "Get on her good side?"

"Of course not," Lift said, sniffing. "It's a scam."

"It is?"

"Course it is. She's probably launderin' spheres for criminals, takin' them as 'donations,' then givin' others back. Men'll pay well to clean up their spheres, particularly in places like this, where you got scribes looking over your shoulder all the starvin' time. Course, it might not be *that* scam. She might be guiltin' people into giving her donations of infused spheres, traded for her dun ones. They'll feel sympathetic, because she talks about her poor children. Then she can trade infused spheres to the moneychangers and make a small profit."

"That's *shockingly* unscrupulous, mistress!"

Lift shrugged. "What *else* are you going to do with orphans? Gotta be good for something, right?"

"But profiting off people's emotions?"

"Pity can be a powerful tool. Anytime you can make someone else feel something, you've got power over them."

"I . . . guess?"

"Gotta make sure that never happens to me," Lift said. "It's how you stay strong, see."

She found her way back to the place where she'd entered the slots, then from there poked around until she found the ramp up to the entrance of the city. It was long and shallow, for driving wagons down, if you needed to.

She crawled up it a ways, just enough to get a glimpse at the guard post. There was still a line up there, grown longer than when she'd been in it. Many people were actually making camp on the stones. Some enterprising merchants were selling them food, clean water, and even tents.

Good luck, Lift thought. Most of the people in that line looked like they didn't own much besides their own skins, maybe an exotic disease or two. Lift retreated. She wasn't awesome enough to risk another encounter with the guards. Instead she settled down in a small cleft in the rock at the bottom of the ramp, where she watched a blanket merchant pass. He was using a strange little horse—it was shaggy and white, and had horns on its head. Looked like those animals that were terrible to eat out west.

"Mistress," Wyndle said from the stone wall beside her head, "I don't know much about humans, but I do know a bit about plants. You're remarkably similar. You need light, water, and nourishment. And plants have roots. To anchor them, you see, during storms. Otherwise they blow away."

"It's nice to blow away sometimes."

"And when the great storm comes?"

Lift's eyes drifted toward the west. Toward . . . whatever was building there. *A storm that blows the wrong way*, the viziers had said. *It can't be possible. What game are the Alethi playing?*

A few minutes later, the guard captain walked down the ramp. The woman practically dragged her feet, and as soon as she was out of sight of the guard post, she let her shoulders slump. Looked like it had been a rough day. What could have caused that?

Lift huddled down, but the woman didn't so much as look at her. Once the captain passed, Lift climbed to her feet and scuttled after.

Tailing someone through this town proved easy. There weren't nearly as many hidden nooks or branching paths. As Lift had guessed, now that it was getting dark, the streets were clearing. Maybe there would be an upswing in activity once the first moon got high enough, but for now there wasn't enough light.

"Mistress," Wyndle said. "What are we doing?"

"Just thought I'd see where that woman lives."

"But why?"

Unsurprisingly, the captain didn't live too far from her guard post. A few streets inward, likely far enough to be outside the immigrant quarter but close enough for the place to be cheaper by association. It was a large set of rooms carved into the rock wall, marked by a window for each one. Apartments, rather than one single "building." It did look pretty strange—a sheer rock face, broken by a bunch of shutters.

The captain entered, but Lift didn't follow. Instead, she craned her neck upward. Eventually one of the windows near the top shone with spherelight, and the captain pushed open the shutters for some fresh air.

"Hm," Lift said, squinting in the darkness. "Let's head up that wall, Voidbringer."

"Mistress, you could call me by my name."

"I could call you lotsa stuff," Lift said. "Be glad I don't got much of an imagination. Let's go."

Wyndle sighed, but curved up the outside of the captain's tenement. Lift climbed, using his vines as foot- and handholds. This took her up past a number of windows, but only a few of them were lit. One pair of windows on the same side helpfully had a washing line draped between them, and Lift snatched a shiqua. Nice of them to leave it out, up high enough that only she could get to it.

She didn't stop at the captain's window, which Wyndle seemed to find surprising. She went all the way up to the top and eventually climbed out onto a field of treb, a grain that grew in bunches inside hard pods on vines. The farmers here grew them in little slits in the stone, just under a foot wide. The vines would bunch up in there, and grow pods that got wedged so they didn't tumble free in storms.

The farmers were done for the day, leaving piles of weeds to get carried away in the next storm—whenever that came. Lift settled down on the lip of the trench, looking out over the city. It was pinpricked by spheres. Not many, but more than she'd have expected. That made illumination shine up from the slots, like they were cracks in something bright at the center. How must it look when people had more infused spheres? She imagined bright columns of light shining up from the holes.

Below, the captain closed her window and apparently hooded her spheres. Lift yawned. "You don't need sleep, right, Voidbringer?"

"I do not."

"Then keep an eye on that building. Wake me up anytime someone goes into it, or if that captain comes out."

"Could you at least tell me *why* we're spying on a captain of the city watch?"

"What else are we going to do?"

"Anything else?"

"Boring," Lift said, then yawned again. "Wake me up, okay?"

He said something, likely a complaint, but she was already drifting off.

It seemed like only moments before he nudged her awake.

"Mistress?" he said. "Mistress, I find myself in awe of your ingenuity, and your stupidity, both at once."

She yawned, shifting on her stolen shiqua blanket and swatting at some lifespren that were floating around. She hadn't dreamed, thankfully. She hated dreams. They either showed her a life she couldn't have, or a life that terrified her. What was the good of either one?

"Mistress?" Wyndle asked.

She stirred, sitting up. She hadn't realized that she'd picked a spot surrounded by and overgrown with vines, and they'd gotten stuck in her clothing. What was she doing up here again? She ran her hand through her hair, which was snarled and sticking out in all sorts of directions.

Sunlight was peeking up over the horizon, and farmers were already out working again. In fact, now that she'd sat up out of the nest of vines, a few had turned to regard her with baffled looks. It probably wasn't often you found a little Reshi girl sleeping by a cliff in your field. She grinned and waved at them.

"Mistress," Wyndle said. "You told me to warn you if someone went into the building."

Right. She started, remembering what she'd been doing, the fog leaving her mind. "And?" she asked, urgent.

"And Darkness himself, the man who almost killed you in the royal palace, just entered the building below us."

Darkness himself. Lift felt a spike of alarm and gripped the edge of the cliff, barely daring to peek over. She'd wondered if he would come.

"You *did* come to the city chasing him," Wyndle said.

"Pure coincidence," she mumbled.

"No it's not. You showed off your powers to that guard captain, *knowing* that she'd write a report about what she saw. And you knew that would draw Darkness's attention."

"I can't search a whole city for one man; I needed a way to get him to come to me. Didn't expect him to find this place so quickly though. Must have some scribe watching reports."

"But *why*?" Wyndle said, his voice almost a whine. "Why are you looking for him? He's dangerous."

"Obviously."

"Oh, mistress. It's crazy. He—"

"He kills people," she said softly. "The viziers have tracked him. He murders people that don't seem to be connected. The viziers are confused, but I'm not." She took a deep breath. "He's hunting someone in this city, Wyndle. Someone with powers . . . someone like me."

Wyndle trailed off, then slowly let out an "aaahh" of understanding.

"Let's get down to her window," Lift said, ignoring the farmers and climbing over the cliff's edge. It was still dark in the city, which was waking up slowly. She shouldn't be too conspicuous until things got busier.

Wyndle helpfully grew down in front of her, giving her something to cling to. She wasn't completely sure what drove her. Maybe it was the lure of finding someone else like her, someone who could explain what she was and why her life made no sense these days. Or maybe she just didn't like the idea of Darkness stalking someone innocent. Somebody who, like her, hadn't done anything wrong—well, nothing big—except for having powers he thought they shouldn't.

She pressed her ear against the shutters of the captain's room. Within, she distinctly heard *his* voice.

"A young woman," Darkness said. "Herdazian or Reshi."

"Yes, sir," the captain said. "Do you mind? Can I see your papers again?"

"You will find them in order."

"I just . . . special operative of the prince? I've never heard of the title before."

"It is an ancient but rarely used designation," Darkness said. "Explain exactly what this child did."

"I—"

"Explain again. To me."

"Well, she gave us quite the runaround, sir. Slipped into our guard post, knocked over our things, stole some food. The big crime was when she dumped that grain into the city. I'm sure she did it on purpose; the merchant has already filed suit against the city guard for willful neglect of duty."

"His case is weak," Darkness said. "Because he hadn't yet been approved for admittance into the city, he didn't come under your jurisdiction. If anything he needs to file against the highway guard, and classify it as banditry."

"That's what I told him!"

"You are not to be blamed, Captain. You faced a force you cannot understand, and which I am not at liberty to explain. I need details, however, as proof. Did she glow?"

"I . . . well . . ."

"Did she *glow*, Captain."

"Yes. I swear, I am of sound mind. I wasn't simply seeing things, sir. She glowed. And the grain glowed too, faintly."

"And she was slippery to the touch?"

"Slicker than if she had been oiled, sir. I've never felt anything like it."

"As anticipated. Here, sign this."

They made some shuffling noises. Lift clung there, ear to the wall, heart pounding. Darkness had a Shardblade. If he suspected she was out here, he could stab through the wall and cut her clean in half.

"Sir?" the guard captain said. "Could you tell me what's going on here? I feel lost, like a soldier on a battlefield who can't remember which banner is hers."

"It is not material for you to know."

"Um . . . yes, sir."

"Watch for the child. Have others do the same, and report to your superiors if she is discovered. I will hear of it."

"Yes, sir."

Footsteps marked him walking for the door. Before he left, he noted something. "Infused spheres, Captain? You are lucky to have them, these days."

"I traded for them, sir."

"And dun ones in the lantern on the wall."

"They ran out weeks ago, sir. I haven't replaced them. Is this . . . relevant, sir?"

"No. Remember your orders, Captain." He bade her farewell.

The door shut. Lift scrambled up the wall again—trailed by a whimpering Wyndle—and hid there on the top, watching as Darkness stepped out onto the street below. Morning sunlight warmed the back of her neck, and she couldn't keep herself from trembling.

A black and silver uniform. Dark skin, like he was Makabaki, with a pale patch on one cheek: a birthmark shaped like a crescent.

Dead eyes. Eyes that didn't care if they were looking at a man, a chull, or a stone. He tucked some papers into his coat pocket, then pulled on his long-cuffed gloves.

"So we've found him," Wyndle whispered. "Now what?"

"Now?" Lift swallowed. "Now we follow him."

8

TAILING Darkness was a far different experience from tailing the captain. For one, it was daylight now. Still early morning, but light enough that Lift had to worry about being spotted. Fortunately, encountering Darkness had completely burned away the fog of sleepiness she'd felt upon awaking.

At first she tried to stay on the tops of the walls, in the gardens above the city. That proved difficult. Though there were some bridges up here crossing over the slots, they weren't nearly as common as she needed. Each time Darkness hit an intersection she had a shiver of fear, worrying he'd turn down a path she couldn't follow without somehow leaping over a huge gap.

Eventually she took the more dangerous route of scrambling down a ladder, then chasing after him within a trench. Fortunately, it seemed that people in here expected some measure of jostling as they moved through the streets. The confines weren't completely cramped—many of the larger streets had plenty of space. But those walls did enhance the feeling of being boxed in.

Lift had lots of practice with this sort of thing, and she kept the tail inconspicuous. She didn't pick any pockets, despite several fine opportunities—people who were practically holding their pouches up, demanding them to be taken. If she hadn't been following Darkness, she might have grabbed a few for old times' sake.

She didn't use her awesomeness, which was running out anyway. She hadn't eaten since last night, and if she didn't use the power, it eventually vanished. Took about half a day; she didn't know why.

She dodged around the figures of farmers heading to work, women carrying water, kids skipping to their lessons—where they'd sit in rows and listen to a teacher while doing some menial task, like sewing, to pay for the education. Suckers.

People gave Darkness lots of space, moving away from him like they would a guy whose backside couldn't help but let everyone know what he'd been eating lately. She smiled at the thought, climbing along the top of some boxes beside a few other urchins. Darkness, though, he wasn't that *normal.* She had trouble imagining him eating, or anything like that.

A shopkeeper chased them down off the boxes, but Lift had gotten a good look at Darkness and was able to scurry after him, Wyndle at her side.

Darkness never paused to consider his route, or to look at the wares of street vendors. He seemed to move too quickly for his own steps, like he was melting from shadow to shadow as he strode. She nearly lost sight of him several times, which was bizarre. She'd always been able to keep track of where people were.

Darkness eventually reached a market where they sure had a lot of fruit on display. Looked like someone had planned a really, really big food fight, but had decided to call it off and were reluctantly selling their ammunition. Lift helped herself to a purple fruit—she didn't know the name—while the shopkeeper was staring, uncomfortably, at Darkness. As people did. It—

"Hey!" the shopkeeper shouted. "Hey, stop!"

Lift spun, tucking her hand behind her back and dropping the fruit—which she kicked with her heel into the crowd. She smiled sweetly.

But the shopkeeper wasn't looking at her. He was looking at a different opportunist, a girl a few years Lift's senior, who had swiped a whole basket of fruit. The young woman bolted the moment she was spotted, leaning down and clinging to the basket. She sprinted deftly through the crowd.

Lift heard herself whimper.

No. Not that way. Not toward—

Darkness snatched the young woman from the crowd. He flowed toward her almost as if he were liquid, then seized her by the shoulder with the speed of a snapping rat trap. She struggled, battering against him, though he remained stiff and didn't seem to notice or mind the attack. Still holding to her, he bent and picked up the basket of fruit, then carried it toward the shop, dragging the thief after him.

"Thank you!" the shopkeeper said, taking back the basket and looking over Darkness's uniform. "Um, officer?"

"I am a special deputized operative, granted free jurisdiction throughout the kingdom by the prince," Darkness said, removing a sheet of paper from his coat pocket and holding it up.

The girl grabbed a piece of fruit from the basket and threw it at Darkness, bouncing it off his chest with a splat. He didn't respond to this, and didn't even flinch as she bit his hand. He just tucked away the document he'd been showing the shopkeeper. Then he looked at her.

Lift knew what it was like to meet those cold, glassy eyes. The girl in his grip cringed before him, then seemed to panic, reaching to her belt, yanking out her knife and brandishing it. She tried a desperate swing at Darkness's arm, but he easily slapped the weapon away with his empty hand.

Around them, the crowd had sensed that something was off. Though the rest of the market was busy, this one section grew still. Lift pulled back beside a small, broken cart—built narrow for navigating the slots— where several other urchins were betting on how long it would be before Tiqqa escaped "this time."

As if in response to this, Darkness summoned his Shardblade and rammed it through the struggling girl's chest.

The long blade sank up to its hilt as he pulled her onto it, and she gasped, eyes going wide—then shriveling and burning out, letting twin trails of smoke creep toward the sky.

The shopkeeper screamed, hand to his chest. He dropped the basket of fruit.

Lift squeezed her eyes closed. She heard the corpse drop to the ground, and Darkness's too-calm voice as he said, "Give this form to the market watch, who will dispose of the body and take your statement. Let me witness the time and date . . . here. . . ."

Lift forced her eyes open. The two urchins beside her gaped in horror, mouths wide. One started crying with a disbelieving whine.

Darkness finished filling out the form, then prodded the shopkeeper, forcing the man to witness it as well in pen, and write a short description of what had happened.

That done, Darkness nodded and turned to go. The shopkeeper—fruit spilled at his feet, a stack of boxes and baskets to his side—stared at the corpse, papers held limply in his fingers. Then angerspren boiled up around him, like red pools on the ground.

"Was that *necessary*!" he demanded. "Tashi . . . Tashi above!"

"Tashi doesn't care much for what you do here," Darkness said as he walked away. "In fact, I'd pray that he doesn't reach your city, as I doubt you'd like the consequences. As for the thief, she would have enjoyed imprisonment for her theft. The punishment prescribed for assaulting an officer with a bladed weapon, however, is death."

"But . . . *But that was barbaric!* Couldn't you have just . . . taken off her hand or . . . or . . . something?"

Darkness stopped, then looked back at the shopkeeper, who cringed.

"I have tried that, where the law allows discretion in punishments," Darkness said. "Removing a hand leads to a high rate of recidivism, as the thief is left unable to do most honest work, and therefore must steal. In such a case, I could make crime worse instead of reducing it."

He cocked his head, looking from the shopkeeper to the corpse, as if confused why anyone would be bothered by what he had done. Without further concern for the matter, he turned and continued on his way.

Lift stared, stunned, then—heedless of being seen—forced away her shock and ran to the fallen girl. She grabbed the body by the shoulders and leaned down, breathing out her awesomeness—the light that burned inside her—and imparting it to the dead young woman.

For a moment it seemed to be working. She saw something, a luminescence in the shape of a figure. It vibrated around the corpse, quivering.
Then it puffed away, and the body remained on the ground, immobile,
eyes burned.

"No . . ." Lift said.

"Too much time passed for this one, mistress," Wyndle said softly.
"I'm sorry."

"Gawx was longer."

"Gawx wasn't slain by a Shardblade," Wyndle said. "I . . . I think that
humans don't die instantly, most of the time. Oh, my memory. Too
many holes, mistress. But I do know that a Shardblade, it is different.
Maybe if you'd reached this one right after. Yes, you'd have been able to
then. It was just too long. And you don't have enough power, either way."

Lift knelt on the stones, drained. The body didn't even bleed.

"She *did* draw a knife on him," Wyndle said, his voice small.

"She was terrified! She saw his eyes and panicked." She gritted her
teeth, then snarled and climbed to her feet. She scrambled over to the
shopkeeper, who jumped back as Lift seized two of his fruits and stared
him right in the eyes as she took a big, juicy bite of one and chewed.

Then she chased after Darkness.

"Mistress . . ." Wyndle said.

She ignored him. She followed after the heartless creature, the murderer. She managed to find him again—he left an even bigger wake of
disturbed people behind him now. She caught sight of him as he left the
market, going up a set of steps, then walking through a large archway.

Lift followed carefully, and peeked out into an odd section of the city.
They'd carved a large, conical chunk out of the stone here. It was deep a
ways, and was filled with water.

It was a really, really big cistern. A cistern as big as several houses, to
collect rain from the storms.

"Ah," Wyndle said. "Yes, separated from the rest of the city by a raised
rim. Rainwater in the streets will flow outward, rather than toward this
cistern, keeping it pure. In fact, it seems that most of the streets have a
slope to them, to siphon water outward. Where does it go from there
though?"

Whatever. She inspected the big cistern, which did have a neat bridge running across it. The thing was so big that you needed a bridge, and people stood on it to lower buckets on ropes down into the water.

Darkness didn't take the path across the bridge; there was a ledge running around the outside of the cistern also, and there were fewer people on it. He obviously wanted to take the route that involved less jostling.

Lift hesitated at the entrance into the place, fighting with her frustration, her sense of powerlessness. She earned a curse or two as she accidentally blocked traffic.

Her name was Tiqqa, Lift thought. *I will remember you, Tiqqa. Because few others will.*

Below, the large cistern pool rippled from the many people drawing water from it. If she followed Darkness around the ledge, she'd be in the open with nobody between them.

Well, he didn't look behind himself very often. She just had to risk it. She took a step along the path.

"Don't!" Wyndle said. "Mistress, stay hidden. He has eyes you cannot see."

Fine. She joined the flow of people moving down the steps. This was the shorter route, but there were a *lot* of people on the bridge. In the bustle, because of her shortness, she lost sight of Darkness.

Sweat prickled on the back of her neck, cold. If she couldn't see him, she felt certain—irrationally—that he was now watching her. She pictured again and again how he'd emerged from the market to grab the thief, a supernatural ease to his movements. Yes, he knew things about people like Lift. He'd spoken of her powers with familiarity.

Lift drew upon her awesomeness. She didn't make herself Slick, but she let the light suffuse her, pep her up. The power felt like it was alive sometimes. The essence of eagerness, a spren. It drove her forward as she dodged and squeezed through the crowd of people on the bridge.

She reached the other side of the bridge, and saw no sign of Darkness on the ledge. Storms. She left through the archway on the other side, slipping back into the city proper and entering a large crossroads.

Shiqua-wrapped Tashikkis passed in front of her, interrupted occasionally by Azish in colorful patterns. This was certainly a better part of town. Light from the rising sun sparkled off painted sections of the walls, here displaying a grand mural of Tashi and the Nine binding the world. Some of the people she passed had parshman slaves, their marbled skin black and red. She hadn't seen many of those here, not as many as in Azir. Maybe she just hadn't been in rich enough sections of the city.

Lots of the buildings here had small trees or ornamental shrubs in front of them. They were bred and cultivated to be lazy, so their leaves didn't pull in despite the near crowds.

Read those crowds . . . Lift thought. *The people. Where are the people being strange?*

She scrambled through the crossroads, intuiting the way. Something about how people stood, where they looked. There was a ripple here. The waves of a passing fish, silent but not still.

She turned a corner, and caught a brief glimpse of Darkness striding up a set of stairs beside a row of small trees. He stepped into a building, then shut the door.

Lift crept up beside the building Darkness had entered, her face brushing the leaves of the trees, causing them to pull in. They were lazy, but not so stupid that they wouldn't move if touched.

"What are these 'eyes' you say he has?" she asked as Wyndle wound up beside her. "The ones I can't see."

"He will have a spren," Wyndle said. "Like me. It's likely invisible to you and anyone else but him. Most are, on this side, I think. I don't remember all the rules."

"You sure are dumb some of the time, Voidbringer."

He sighed.

"Don't worry," Lift said. "I'm dumb *most* of the time." She scratched her head. The steps ended at a door. Did she dare open it and slip in? If she was going to learn anything about Darkness and what he was doing in the city, she'd have to do more than find out where he lived.

"Mistress," Wyndle said, "I might be stupid, but I can say with certainty that you're *not* a match for that creature. There are many Words you haven't spoken."

"Course I haven't said those kinds of words," Lift said. "Don't you ever listen to me? I'm a sweet, innocent little girl. I ain't going to talk about bollocks and jiggers and stuff. I'm not *crass*."

Wyndle sighed. "Not *those* kinds of words. Mistress, I—"

"Oh, hush," Lift said, squatting beside the trees lining the front of the building. "We have to get in there and see what he's up to."

"Mistress, please don't get yourself killed. It would be *traumatic*. Why, I think it would take me months and months to get over it!"

"That's faster than I'd get over it." She scratched at her head. She couldn't hang on the side of the building and listen at Darkness, like she had at the guard captain's place. Not in a fancy part of town, and not in the middle of the day.

Besides, she had loftier goals today than just eavesdropping. She had to actually break into this place to do what she needed to do here. But how? It wasn't like these buildings had back doors. They were cut directly into the rock. She could maybe get in one of the front windows, but that sure would be suspicious.

She glanced at the passing crowds. People in cities, they'd notice something like an urchin breaking in through a window. Something that looked like trouble. But other times they'd ignore the most obvious things in front of their own noses.

Maybe . . . She did have awesomeness left from that fruit she'd eaten. She eyed a shuttered window about five or six feet up. That would be on the first story of the building, but it was up somewhat high, because everything was built up a ways in this city.

Lift hunkered down and let some of her awesomeness out. The little tree beside her stretched and popped softly. Leaves budded, unfurled, and gave a good morning yawn. Branches reached toward the sky. Lift took her time, filling in the tree's canopy, letting it get large enough to obscure the window. Around her feet, seeds from storm-blown rockbuds puffed up like little hot buns. Vines wrapped around her ankles.

Nobody passing on the street noticed. They'd cuff an urchin for scratching her butt in a suspicious manner, but couldn't be bothered with a miracle. Lift sighed, smiling. The tree would cover her as she broke in through that window, if she moved carefully. She let her awesomeness continue to trickle out, comforting the tree, making it even more lazy. Lifespren popped up, little glowing green motes that bobbed around her.

She waited for a lull in the passing crowds, then hopped up and grabbed a branch, hauling herself into the tree. The tree, drinking of her awesomeness, didn't pull its leaves back in. She felt safe here surrounded by the branches, which smelled rich and heady, like the spices used for broth. Vines wrapped around the tree branches, sprouting leaves, much as Wyndle did.

Unfortunately, her power was almost out. A couple pieces of fruit didn't provide much. She pressed her ear against the window's thick stormshutters, and didn't hear anything from the room beyond. Safe in the tree, she softly rattled the stormshutters with her palms, using the sound to pick out where the latch was.

See. I can listen.

But of course, this wasn't the right kind of listening.

The window was latched with some kind of long bar on the other side, probably fitted into slots across the back of the shutters. Fortunately, these stormshutters weren't as tight as those in other towns; they probably didn't need to be, down here safe in the trenches. She let the vines wind around the branches, drinking of her Stormlight, then twist around her arms and squeeze through cracks in the shutters. The vines stretched up the inside of the shutters, pressing up the bar that held the shutters closed, and . . .

And she was in. She used the last of her awesomeness to coat the hinges of the shutters, so they slid against one another without a hint of a sound. She slipped into a boxlike stone room, lifespren pouring in behind her, dancing in the air like glowing whispermill seeds.

"Mistress!" Wyndle said, growing in onto the wall. "Oh, mistress. That was *delightful*! Why don't we forget this entire mess with the Skybreakers, and go . . . why . . . why, go *run a farm*! Yes, a farm. A lovely farm. You could sculpt plants every day, and eat until you were ready to burst! And . . . Mistress?"

Lift padded through the room, noting a rack of swords by the wall, sheathed and deadly. Sparring leathers on the floor near the corner. The smell of oil and sweat. There was no door in the doorway, and she peeked out into a dark hallway, listening.

There was a three-way intersection here. Hallways lined with rooms led to her left and right, and then a longer hallway led straight forward, into darkness. Voices echoed from that direction.

That hallway in front of her cut deeper into the stone, away from windows—and from exits. She glanced right instead, toward the building's entrance. An old man sat in a chair there, near the door, wearing a white and black uniform of the type she'd only seen on Darkness and his men. He was mostly bald, except for a few wisps of hair, and had beady eyes and a pinched face—like a shriveled-up fruit that was trying to pass for human.

He stood up and checked a little window in the door, watching the crowd outside with suspicion. Lift took the opportunity to scuttle into the hallway to her left, where she ducked into the next room over.

This looked more promising. Though it was dim with the stormshutters closed, it seemed like some kind of workroom or den. Lift eased open the shutters for a little light, then did a quick search. Nothing obvious on the shelves full of maps. Nothing on the writing table but some books and a rack of spanreeds. There was a trunk by the wall, but it was locked. She was beginning to despair when she smelled something.

She peeked out of the doorway. That guard had wandered off; she could hear him whistling somewhere, alongside the sound of a stream of liquid in a chamber pot.

Lift slipped farther down the corridor to her left, away from the guard. The next room in line was a bedroom with a door that was cracked open. She slipped in and found a stiff coat hanging on a peg right inside—one with a circular fruit stain on the front. Darkness's jacket for sure.

Below it, sitting on the floor, was a tray with a metal covering—the type fancy people put over plates so they wouldn't have to look at food while it got cold. Underneath, like the emerald treasures of the Tranquiline Halls, Lift found three plates of pancakes.

Darkness's breakfast. Mission accomplished.

She started stuffing her face with a vengeful enthusiasm.

Wyndle made a face from vines beside her. "Mistress? Was this all . . . was this all so you could *steal his food*?"

"Yeph," Lift said, then swallowed. "Course it is." She took another bite. That'd show him.

"Oh. Of course." He sighed deeply. "I suppose this is . . . this is pleasant, then. Yes. No swinging about of innocent spren, stabbing them into people and the like. Just . . . just stealing some food."

"*Darkness's* food." She'd stolen from a palace, and the starvin' emperor of Azir. She'd needed *something* interesting to try next.

It felt good to finally get enough food to fill her stomach. One of the pancakes was salty, with chopped-up vegetables. Another tasted sweet. The third variety was fluffier, almost without any substance to it, though there was some kind of sauce to dip it in. She slurped that down—who had time for dipping?

She ate every scrap, then settled back against the wall, smiling.

"So, we came all this way," Wyndle said, "and tracked the most dangerous man we've ever met, merely so you could steal his breakfast. We didn't come here to do . . . to do anything more, then?"

"Do you want to do something more?"

"Storms, no!" Wyndle said. He twisted his little vine face around, looking toward the hallway. "I mean . . . every moment we spend in here is dangerous."

"Yup."

"We should run. Go found a farm, like I said. Leave him behind, though he's likely tracking someone in this city. Someone like us, someone who can't fight him. Someone he will murder before they even start to grasp their powers . . ."

They sat in the room, empty tray beside them. Lift felt her awesomeness begin to stir within her again.

"So," she asked. "Guess we go spy on them, eh?"

Wyndle whimpered, but—shockingly—nodded.

<h1 style="text-align:center">9</h1>

"Just try not to die too violently, mistress," Wyndle said as she crept closer to the sounds of people talking. "A nice rap on the head, rather than a disemboweling."

That voice was definitely Darkness. The sound of it gave her chills. When the man had confronted her in the Azish palace, he'd been dispassionate, even as he half apologized for what he was about to do.

"I hear that suffocation is nice," Wyndle said. "Though in such a case, don't look at me as you expire. I'm not sure I could handle it."

Remember the girl in the market. Steady.

Storms, her hands were trembling.

"I'm not sure about falling to your death," Wyndle added. "Seems like it might be messy, but at the same time at least there wouldn't be any *stabbing*."

The hallway ended at a large chamber lit by diamonds that gave it a calm, easy light. Not chips, not even spheres. Larger, unset gemstones. Lift crouched by the half-open door, hidden in shadows.

Darkness—wearing a stiff white shirt—paced before two underlings in uniforms in black and white, with swords at their waists. One was a Makabaki man with a round, goofish face. The other was a woman with skin a shade lighter—she looked like she might be Reshi, particularly with that long dark hair she kept in a tight braid. She had a square face, strong shoulders, and *way* too small a nose. Like she'd sold hers off to buy some new shoes, and was using one she'd dug out of the trash as a replacement.

"Your excuses do not befit those who would join our order," Darkness was saying. "If you would earn the trust of your spren, and take the step from initiate to Shardbearer, you must dedicate yourselves. You must prove your worth. Earlier today I followed a lead that each of you missed, and have discovered a second offender in the city."

"Sir!" the Reshi woman said. "I prevented an assault in an alleyway! A man was being accosted by thugs!"

"While this is well," Darkness said, still pacing back and forth in a calm, even stroll, "we must be careful not to be distracted by petty crimes. I realize that it can be difficult to remain focused when confronted by a fracture of the codes that bind society. Remember that greater matters, and greater crimes, must be our primary concern."

"Surgebinders," the woman said.

Surgebinders. People like Lift, people with awesomeness, who could do the impossible. She hadn't been afraid to sneak into a palace, but huddled by that door—looking in at the man she had named Darkness— she found herself terrified.

"But . . ." said the male initiate. "Is it really . . . I mean, shouldn't we *want* them to return, so we won't be the only order of Knights Radiant?"

"Unfortunately, no," Darkness said. "I once thought as you, but Ishar made the truth clear to me. If the bonds between men and spren are reignited, then men will naturally discover the greater power of the oaths. Without Honor to regulate this, there is a small chance that what comes next will allow the Voidbringers to again make the jump between worlds. That would cause a Desolation, and even a small chance that the world will be destroyed is a risk that we cannot take. Absolute fidelity to the mission Ishar gave us—the greater law of protecting Roshar—is required."

"You're wrong," a voice whispered from the darkness. "You may be a god . . . but you're still wrong."

Lift nearly jumped clear out of her own skin. Storms! There was a guy sitting just inside the doorway, *right next to where she was hiding.* She hadn't seen him—she'd been too fixated on Darkness.

He sat on the floor, wearing tattered white clothing. His hair was short, a brown fuzz, as if he'd kept it shaved until recently. He had pale, ghostly skin, and held a long sword in a silvery sheath, pommel resting against his shoulder, length stretching alongside his body and legs. He held his arms draped around the sheath, as if it were a child's toy to hug.

He shifted in his place, and . . . storms, he left a soft white *afterimage* behind him, like you get when staring at a bright gemstone for too long. It faded away in a moment.

"They're already back," he whispered, speaking with a smooth, airy Shin accent. "The Voidbringers have already returned."

"You are mistaken," Darkness said. "The Voidbringers are not back. What you saw on the Shattered Plains are simply remnants from millennia ago. Voidbringers who have been hiding among us all this time."

The man in white looked up, and Lift shied away. His movement left another afterimage that glowed briefly before fading. Storms. White clothing. Strange powers. Shin man with a bald head. Shardblade.

This was the starvin' *Assassin in White*!

"I saw them return," the assassin whispered. "The new storm, the red eyes. You are wrong, Nin-son-God. You are wrong."

"A fluke," Darkness said, his voice firm. "I contacted Ishar, and he assured me it is so. What you saw are a few listeners who remain from the old days, ones free to use the old forms. They summoned a cluster of Voidspren. We've found remnants of them on Roshar before, hiding."

"The storm? The new storm, of red lightning?"

"It means nothing," Darkness said. He did not seem to mind being challenged. He didn't seem to mind anything. His voice was perfectly even. "An oddity, to be sure."

"You're wrong. So wrong . . ."

"The Voidbringers have not returned," Darkness said firmly. "Ishar has promised it, and he will not lie. We must do our duty. You are questioning, Szeth-son-Neturo. This is not good; this is weakness. To question is to accept a descent into inactivity. The only path to sanity and action is to choose a code and to follow it. This is why I came to you in the first place."

Darkness turned, striding past the others. "The minds of men are fragile, their emotions mutable and often unpredictable. The *only* path to Honor is to stick to your chosen code. This was the way of the Knights Radiant, and is the way of the Skybreakers."

The man and woman standing nearby both saluted. The assassin just bowed his head again, closing his eyes, holding to that strange silver-sheathed Shardblade.

"You said that there is a second Surgebinder in the city," the woman said. "We can find—"

"She is mine," Darkness said evenly. "You will continue your mission. Find the one who has been hiding here since we arrived." He narrowed his eyes. "If we don't stop one, others will congregate. They clump together. I have often found them making contact with one another, these last five years, if I leave them alone. They must be drawn to each other."

He turned toward his two initiates; he seemed to ignore the assassin except when spoken to. "Your quarry will make mistakes—they will break the law. The other orders always did consider themselves beyond the reach of the law. Only the Skybreakers ever understood the importance of boundaries. Of picking something external to yourself and using it as a guide. Your minds cannot be trusted. Even my mind—especially my mind—cannot be trusted.

"I have given you enough help. You have my blessing and you have our commission granting us authority to act in this city. You will find the Surgebinder, you will discover their sins, and you will bring them judgment. In the name of all Roshar."

The two saluted again, and the room suddenly darkened. The woman began glowing with a phantom light, and she blushed, looking sheepishly toward Darkness. "I'll find them, sir! I have an investigation in progress."

"I have a lead too," the man said. "I'll have the information by tonight for certain."

"Work together," Darkness said. "This is not a competition. It is a test to measure competence. I'm giving you until sunset, but after that I can wait no longer. Now that others have begun arriving, the risk is too great. At sunset, I will deal with the issue myself."

"Bollocks," Lift whispered. She shook her head, then scuttled back along the hallway, away from the group of people.

"Wait," Wyndle said, following. "Bollocks? I thought you claimed you didn't say words like—"

"They've all got 'em," Lift said. "'Cept the girl, though with that face I can't be certain. Anyway, what I said wasn't crass, 'cuz it was just an *observation*." She hit the intersection of corridors, and peeked to the left. The old man on watch was dozing. That let Lift slip across, into the room where she'd first entered. She climbed out into the tree, then closed the shutters.

In seconds she'd run around a corner into an alleyway, where she let herself slide down until she was sitting with her back against the stone, her heart pounding. Farther into the alleyway here, a family ate pancakes in a somewhat nice shanty. It had two whole walls.

"Mistress?" Wyndle said.

"I'm hungry," she complained.

"You just ate!"

"That was catching me up for spending so much getting into that starvin' building." She squeezed her eyes closed, containing her worry.

Darkness's voice was so cold.

But they're like me. They glow like me. They're . . . awesome, like I am? What in Damnation is going on?

And the Assassin in White. Was he going to go off and kill Gawx?

"Mistress?" Wyndle coiled around her leg. "Oh, mistress. Did you hear what they called him? Nin? That's a name of Nalan, the Herald! That can't be true. They went away, didn't they? Even we have legends about that. If that creature is truly one of them . . . oh, Lift. What are we going to do?"

"I don't know," she whispered. "I don't know. Storms . . . why am I even here?"

"I believe I've been asking that since—"

"Shut it, Voidbringer," she said, forcing herself to roll over and get to her knees. Deeper into the cramped alley, the father of the family reached for a cudgel while the wife tugged the curtain closed on the front of their hovel.

Lift sighed, then went wandering back toward the immigrant quarter.

10

WHEN she arrived at the orphanage, Lift finally figured out why it had been set up next to this open space at the mouth of the alleyway. The orphanage caretaker—the Stump, as she'd been called—had opened the doors and let the children out. They played here, in the most boring playground ever. A set of amphitheater steps and some open floor.

The children seemed to love it. They ran up and down the steps, laughing and giggling. Others sat in circles on the ground, playing games with painted pebbles. Laughterspren—like little silver fish that zipped through the air, this way and that—danced in the air some ten feet up, a whole school of the starvin' things.

There were lots of children, younger on average than Lift had assumed. Most, as she had been able to guess, were the kind that were different in the head, or they were missin' an arm or leg. Things like that.

Lift idled near the wide alleyway mouth, near where two blind girls played a game. One would drop rocks of a variety of sizes and shapes, and the other would try to guess which was which, based on how they sounded when they hit the ground. The group of old men and women in shiquas from the day before had again gathered at the back of the half-moon amphitheater seats, chatting and watching the children play.

"I thought you said orphanages were miserable," Wyndle said, coating the wall beside her.

"Everyone gets happy for a little while when you let them go outside," Lift said, watching the Stump. The wizened old lady was scowling as she pulled a cart through the doors toward the amphitheater. More clemabread rolls. Delightful. Those were only *slightly* better than gruel, which was only *slightly* better than cold socks.

Still, Lift joined the others who got in line to accept their roll. When her turn came, the Stump pointed to a spot beside the cart and didn't speak a word to her. Lift stepped aside, lacking the energy to argue.

The Stump made sure every child got a roll, then studied Lift before handing her one of the last two. "Your second meal of three."

"Second!" Lift snapped. "I ain't—"

"You got one last night."

"I didn't ask for it!"

"You ate it." The Stump pushed the cart away, eating the last of the rolls herself.

"Storming witch," Lift muttered, then found a spot on the stone seats. She sat apart from the regular orphans; she didn't want to be talked at.

"Mistress," Wyndle said, climbing the steps to join her. "I don't believe you when you say you left Azir because they were trying to dress you in fancy clothing and teach you to read."

"Is that so," she said, chewing on her roll.

"You liked the clothing, for one thing. And when they tried to give you lessons, you seemed to enjoy the game of always being gone when they came looking. They weren't forcing you into anything; they were merely offering opportunities. The palace was *not* the stifling experience you imply."

"Maybe not for me," she admitted.

It was for Gawx. They expected all *kinds* of things of the new emperor. Lessons, displays. People came to watch him eat every meal. They even got to watch him sleeping. In Azir, the emperor was owned by the people, like a friendly stray axehound that seven different houses fed, all claiming her as their own.

"Maybe," Lift said, "I just didn't want people expecting so much from me. If you get to know people too long, they'll start depending on you."

"Oh, and you can't bear responsibility?"

"Course I can't. I'm a starvin' street urchin."

"One who came here chasing down what *appears* to be one of the Heralds themselves, gone mad and accompanied by an assassin who has murdered *multiple* world monarchs. Yes, I believe that you *must* be avoiding responsibility."

"You giving me lip, Voidbringer?"

"I think so? Honestly, I don't know what that term means, but judging by your tone, I'd say that I'm probably giving you lip. And you probably deserve it."

She grunted in response, chewing on her food. It tasted terrible, as if it had been left out all night.

"Mama always told me to travel," Lift said. "And go places. While I'm young."

"And that's why you left the palace."

"Dunno. Maybe."

"Utter nonsense. Mistress, what is it really? Lift, what do you *want*?"

She looked down at the half-eaten roll in her hand.

"Everything is changing," she said softly. "That's okay. Stuff changes. It's just that, I'm not supposed to. I *asked* not to. She's supposed to give you what you ask."

"The Nightwatcher?" Wyndle asked.

Lift nodded, feeling small, cold. Children played and laughed all around, and for some reason that only made her feel worse. It was obvious to her, though she'd tried ignoring it for years, that she *was* taller than she'd been when she'd first sought out the Old Magic three years ago.

She looked beyond the kids, toward the street passing out front. A group of women bustled past, carrying baskets of yarn. A prim Alethi man strode in the other direction, with straight black hair and an imperious attitude. He was at least a foot taller than anyone else on the street. Workers moved along, cleaning the street, picking up trash.

In the alleyway mouth, the Stump had deposited her cart and was disciplining a child who had started hitting others. At the back of the amphitheater seats, the old men and women laughed together, one pouring cups of tea to pass around.

They all seemed to just . . . know what to do. Cremlings knew to scuttle, plants knew to grow. Everything had its place.

"The only thing I've ever known how to do was hunt food," Lift whispered.

"What's that, mistress?"

It had been hard, at first. Feeding herself. Over time, she'd figured out the tricks. She'd gotten good at it.

But once you weren't hungry all the time, what did you *do*? How did you *know*?

Someone poked at her arm, and she turned to see that a kid had scooted up beside her—a lean boy with his head shaved. He pointed at her half-eaten roll and grunted.

She sighed and gave it to him. He ate eagerly.

"I know you," she said, cocking her head. "You're the one whose mother dropped him off last night."

"Mother," he said, then looked at her. "Mother . . . come back when?"

"Huh. So you *can* talk," Lift said. "Didn't think you could, after all that staring around dumbly last night."

"I . . ." The boy blinked, then looked at her. No drooling. Must be a good day for him. A grand accomplishment. "Mother . . . come back?"

"Probably not," Lift said. "Sorry, kid. They don't come back. What's your name?"

"Mik," the boy said. He looked at her, confused, as if searching—and failing—to figure out who she was. "We . . . friends?"

"Nope," Lift said. "You don't wanna be my friend. My friends end up as emperors." She shivered, then leaned in. "People *pick his nose* for him."

Mik looked at her blankly.

"Yeah. I'm serious. They pick his nose. Like, he's got this woman who does his hair, and I peeked in, and I saw her sticking something up his nose. Like little tweezers she used to grab his boogies or something." Lift shivered. "Being an emperor is real strange."

The Stump dragged over one of the kids who'd been fighting and plopped him on the stone. Then, oddly, she gave him some earmuffs—like it was cold or something. He put them on and closed his eyes.

The Stump paused, looking toward Lift and Mik. "Making plans on how to rob me?"

"What?" Lift said. "No!"

"One more meal," the woman said, holding up a finger. Then she stabbed it toward Mik. "And when you go, take that one. I *know* he's faking."

"Faking?" Lift turned toward Mik, who blinked, dazed, as if trying to follow the conversation. "You're not serious."

"I can see through it when urchins are feigning illness in order to get food," the Stump snapped. "That one's no idiot. He's pretending." She stomped away.

Mik wilted, looking down at his feet. "I miss Mother."

"Yeah," Lift said. "Nice, eh?"

Mik looked at her, frowning.

"We get to remember ours," Lift said, standing. "That's more than most like us get." She patted him on the shoulder.

A short time later, the Stump called that playtime was over. She herded the kids into the orphanage for naps, though many were too old for that. The Stump gave Mik a displeased eye as he entered, but let him in.

Lift remained in her seat on the stone, then smacked her hand at a cremling that had been inching across the step nearby. Starvin' thing dodged, then clicked its chitin legs as if laughing. They sure did have strange cremlings here. Not like the ones she was used to at all. Weird how you could forget you were in a different country until you saw the cremlings.

"Mistress," Wyndle said, "have you decided what we're going to do?"

Decide. Why did she have to decide? She usually just *did* things. She'd taken challenges as they'd arisen, gone places for no reason other than that she hadn't seen them before.

The old people who had been watching the children slowly rose, like ancient trees releasing their branches after a storm. One by one they trailed off until only one remained, wearing a black shiqua with the wrap pulled down to expose a face with a grey mustache.

"Ey," Lift called to him. "You still creepy, old man?"

"I am the man I was made to be," he said back.

Lift grunted, climbing from her spot and strolling over to him. Some of the kids from before had left their pebbles, with painted colors that were rubbing off. A poor kid's imitation of glass marbles. Lift kicked at them.

"How do you know what to do?" she asked the man, her hands shoved in her pockets.

"About what, little one?"

"About *everything*," Lift said. "Who tells you how to decide what to do with your time? Was it your parents who showed you? What's the secret?"

"The secret to what?"

"To being human," Lift said softly.

"That," the man said, chuckling, "I don't think I know. At least not better than you do."

Lift looked at the sky, up along slotlike walls, scraped clean of vegetation but painted a dark green, as if in imitation of it.

"It is strange," the man said. "People get such a small amount of time. So many I've known say it—as soon as you feel you're getting a handle on things, the day is done, the night falls, and the light goes out."

Lift looked at him. Yup. Still creepy. "I guess when you're old and stuff, you get to thinkin' about being dead. Kind of like when a fellow's got to piss, he starts thinkin' about finding a convenient alleyway."

The man chuckled. "Your life may pass, but the organism that is the city will continue on. Little nose."

"I'm *not* a nose," Lift said. "I was being cheeky."

"Nose, cheek. Both are on the face."

Lift rolled her eyes. "That's not what I meant either."

"What are you then? An ear, perhaps?"

"Dunno. Maybe."

"No. Not yet. But close."

"Riiight," Lift said. "And what are you?"

"I change, moment by moment. One moment I am the eyes that inspect so many people in this city. Another moment I am the mouth, to speak the words of philosophy. They spread like a disease—and so at times I *am* the disease. Most diseases live. Did you know that?"

"You're . . . not really talking about what you're talking about, are you?" Lift said.

"I believe that I am."

"Great." Of all the people she'd chosen to ask about how to be a responsible adult, she'd picked the one with vegetable soup in place of brains. She turned to go.

"What will you make for this city, child?" the man asked. "That is part of my question. Do you choose, or are you simply molded by the greater good? And are you, as a city, a district of grand palaces? Or are you a slum, unto yourself?"

"If you could see inside me," Lift said, turning and walking backward so she faced the old man on the steps, "you wouldn't say things like that."

"Because?"

"Because. At least slums know what they was built for." She turned and joined the flow of people on the street.

11

I don't think you understand how this is supposed to work," Wyndle said, curling along the wall beside her. "Mistress, you . . . don't seem interested in evolving our relationship."

She shrugged.

"There are Words," Wyndle said. "That's what we call them, at least. They're more . . . ideas. Living ideas, with power. You have to let them into your soul. Let *me* into your soul. You heard those Skybreakers, right? They're looking to take the next step in their training. That's when . . . you know . . . they get a Shardblade. . . ."

He smiled at her, the expression appearing in successive patterns of his growing vines along the wall as they chased her. Each image of the smile was slightly different, grown one after another beside her, like a hundred paintings. They made a smile, and yet none of them *was* the smile. It was, somehow, all of them together. Or perhaps the smile existed in the spaces between the images in the succession.

"There's only one thing I know how to do," Lift said. "And that's steal Darkness's lunch. Like I came to do in the first place."

"And, um, didn't we do that already?"

"Not his food. His lunch." She narrowed her eyes.

"Ah . . ." Wyndle said. "The person he's planning to execute. We're going to snatch them away from him."

Lift strolled along a side street, and ended up passing into a garden: a bowl-like depression in the stone with four exits down different roads. Vines coated the leeward side of the wall, but they slowly gave way to brittels on the other side, shaped like flat plates for protection, but with planty stems that crept out and around the sides and up toward the sunlight.

Wyndle sniffed, crossing to the ground beside her. "Barely any cultivation. Why, this is no garden. Whoever maintains this should be reprimanded."

"I like it," Lift said, lifting her hand toward some lifespren, which bobbed over her fingertips. The garden was crowded with people. Some were coming and going, while others lounged about, and still others begged for chips. She hadn't seen many beggars in the city; likely there were all *kinds* of rules and regulations about when you could do it and how.

She stopped, hands on hips. "People here, in Azir and Tashikk, they *love* to write stuff down."

"Oh, most certainly," Wyndle said, curling around some vines. "Mmm. Yes, mistress, these at least are fruit vines. I suppose that is better; it's not *completely* haphazard."

"And they love information," Lift said. "They love tradin' it with one another, right?"

"Most certainly. That is a distinguishing factor of their cultural identity, as your tutors said in the palace. You weren't there. I went to listen in your place."

"What people write can be important, at least to them," Lift said. "But what would they do with it all when they're done with it? Throw it out? Burn it?"

"Throw it out? Mother's vines! No, no, no. You can't just go throwing things out! They might be useful later on. If it were me, I'd find someplace safe for them, and keep them pristine in case I needed them!"

Lift nodded, folding her arms. They'd have his same attitude. This city, with everyone writing notes and rules, then offering to sell everyone else ideas all the time . . . Well, in some ways this place was like a *whole city* of Wyndles.

Darkness had told his hunters to find someone who was doing strange stuff. Awesome stuff. And in this city they wrote down what kids had for *breakfast*. If somebody had seen something strange, they'd have written it down.

Lift scampered through the garden, brushing vines with her toes and causing them to writhe away. She hopped up onto a bench beside a likely target, an older woman in a brown shiqua, with the head portions pulled up and down to show a middle-aged face wearing makeup and displaying hints of styled hair.

The woman wrinkled her nose immediately, which was unfair. Lift had taken a bath back a week or so in Azir, and it had had soap and everything.

"Shoo," the woman said, waving fingers at her. "I've no money for you. Shoo. Go away."

"Don't want money," Lift said. "I've got a *deal* to make. For information."

"I want nothing from you."

"I can give you nothing," Lift said, relaxing. "I'm good at that. I'll go away, and give you nothing. You just gotta answer a question for me."

Lift hunched there on the bench, not moving. Then she scratched herself on the behind. The woman fussed, looking like she was going to leave, and Lift leaned in.

"You are disobeying beggar regulations," the woman snapped.

"Ain't beggin'. I'm tradin'."

"Fine. What do you want to know?"

"Is there a place," Lift said, "in this city where people stuff all the things they wrote down, to keep them safe?"

The woman frowned, then raised her hand and pointed along a street, which led straight for a distance, toward a moundlike bunker that rose from the center of the city. It was big enough to tower over the rest of the stuff around it, peeking up above the tops of the trenches.

"You mean like the Grand Indicium?" the woman asked.

Lift blinked, then cocked her head.

The woman took the opportunity to flee to a different part of the garden.

"Has that always been there?" Lift asked.

"Um, yes," Wyndle said. "Of course it has."

"Really?" Lift scratched her head. "Huh."

12

WYNDLE's vines wove up the side of an alleyway, and Lift climbed, not caring if she drew attention. She hauled herself over the top edge into a field where farmers watched the sky and grumbled. The seasons had gone insane. It was supposed to be raining constantly—a bad time to plant, as the water would wash away the seed paste.

Yet it hadn't rained for days. No storms, no water. Lift walked along, passing farmers who spread paste that would grow to tiny polyps, which would eventually grow to the size of large rocks and fill to bursting with grain. Mash that grain—either by hand or by storm—and it made new paste. Lift had always wondered why she didn't grow polyps inside her stomach after eating, and nobody had ever given her a straight answer.

The confused farmers worked with their shiquas pulled up to their waists. Lift passed, and she tried to listen. To hear.

This was supposed to be their one time of year where they didn't have to work. Sure, they planted some treb to grow in cracks, as it could survive flooding. But they weren't supposed to have to plant lavis, tallew, or clema: much more labor-intensive—but also more profitable—crops to cultivate.

Yet here they were. What if it rained tomorrow, and washed away all this effort? What if it never rained again? The city cisterns, which were glutted with water from the weeks of Weeping, would not last forever. They were so worried, she caught sight of some fearspren—shaped like globs of purple goo—gathering around the mounds upon which the men planted.

As a counterpoint, lifespren broke off from the growing polyps and bobbed over to Lift, trailing in her wake. A swirling, green-glowing dust. Ahead of her, the Grand Indicium rose like the head of a bald man seen peeking above the back of the chair he was sitting in. It was a huge rounded mass of stone.

Everything in the city revolved around this central point. Streets turned in this direction, curling up to it, and as Lift drew close, she could see that an enormous swath of stone had been cut away around the Indicium. The round bunker wasn't much to look at, but it sure did seem secure from the storms.

"Yes, the land *does* slope away from this central point," Wyndle noted. "This focus had to be the highest point of the city anyway—and I guess they figured they'd just accept that, and make the central knob into a fortress."

A fortress for books. People could be so strange. Below, crowds of people—most of them Tashikki—flowed in and out of the building, which had numerous screwlike sloped walkways leading up to it.

Lift settled down on the edge of the wall, feet hanging over. "Kinda looks like the tip of some guy's dangly bits. Like some fellow had such a short sword, everyone felt so sorry for him they said, 'Hey, we'll make a *huge* statue to it, and even though it's tiny, it'll look real big!'"

Wyndle sighed.

"That wasn't crude," Lift noted. "That was being poetic. Ol' Whitehair said you can't be crass, so long as you're talkin' 'bout art. Then you're being elegant. That's why it's okay to hang pictures of naked ladies in a palace."

"Mistress, wasn't this the man who got himself *intentionally* swallowed by a Marabethian greatshell?"

"Yup. Crazy as a box full of drunk minks, that one. I miss him." She liked to pretend he hadn't actually gotten eaten. He'd winked at her as he'd jumped into the greatshell's gaping maw, shocking the crowd.

Wyndle piled around on himself, forming a face—eyes made of crystals, lips formed of a tiny network of vines. "Mistress, what is our plan?"

"Plan?"

He sighed. "We need to get into that building. Are you just going to do whatever strikes you?"

"Obviously."

"Might I offer some suggestions?"

"Long as it doesn't involve sucking someone's soul, Voidbringer."

"I'm not— Look, mistress, that building is an archive. Knowing what I do of this region, the rooms in there will be filled with laws, records, and reports. Thousands upon thousands upon thousands of them."

"Yeah," she said, making a fist. "Among all that, they'll have written down strange stuff for sure!"

"And how, precisely, are we going to find the specific information we want?"

"Easy. You're gonna read it."

". . . Read it."

"Yup. We'll get in there, you'll read their books and stuff, and then we'll decide where strange events were. That will lead us to Darkness's lunch."

". . . Read it *all*."

"Yup."

"Do you have any idea how much information is likely held in that place?" Wyndle said. "There will be hundreds of thousands of reports and ledgers. And to state it explicitly, yes, that's a number more than ten, so you can't count to it."

"I'm not an idiot," she snapped. "I got toes too."

"It's still far more than I can read. I can't sift through all of that information for you. It's impossible. Not going to happen."

She eyed him. "All right. Maybe I can get you *one* soul. Perhaps a tax collector . . . 'cept they ain't human. Would they work? Or would you need, like, three of them to make up one normal person's soul?"

"Mistress! I'm not *bargaining*!"

"Come on. Everyone knows Voidbringers like a good deal. Does it have to be someone important? Or can it be some dumb guy nobody likes?"

"I don't *eat souls*," Wyndle exclaimed. "I'm not trying to haggle with you! I'm stating facts. I *can't read* all the information in that archive! Why can't you just see that—"

"Oh, calm your tentacles," Lift said, swinging her feet, bouncing her heels against the rock cliff. "I hear you. Can't help but hear you, considering how much you whine."

Behind, the farmers were asking whose daughter she was, and why she wasn't running them water like kids were supposed to. Lift scrunched up her face, thinking. "Can't wait until night and sneak in," she muttered. "Darkness wants the poor person killed by then. 'Sides, I bet those scribes work nights. They feed off ink. Why sleep when you could be writin' up some new law about how many fingers people can use to hold a spoon?

"They know their stuff though. They sell it all over the place. The viziers were always writing to them to get some answer to something. Mostly news around the world." She grinned, then stood up. "You're right. We gotta do this differently."

"Yes indeed."

"We gotta be *smart* about it. *Devious.* Think like a Voidbringer."

"I didn't say—"

"Stop complaining," Lift said. "I'm gonna go steal some important-looking clothes."

13

LIFT liked soft clothing. These supple Azish coat and robes were the wardrobe equivalent of silky pudding. It was good to remember that life wasn't only about scratchy things. Sometimes it was about soft pillows, fluffy cake. Nice words. Mothers.

The world couldn't be completely bad when it had soft clothes. This outfit was big for her, but that was okay. She liked it loose. She snuggled into the robes, sitting in the chair, crossing her hands in her lap, wearing a cap on her head. The entire costume was marked by bright colors woven in patterns that meant very important things. She was pretty sure of that, because everyone in Azir wouldn't shut up about their patterns.

The scribe was fat. She needed, like, three shiquas to cover her. Either that or a shiqua made for a horse. Lift wouldn't have thought that they'd give scribes so much food. What did they need so much energy for? Pens were really light.

The woman wore spectacles and kept her face covered, despite being in lands that knew Tashi. She tapped her pen against the table. "*You're* from the palace in Azir."

"Yup," Lift said. "Friend of the emperor. I call him Gawx, but they changed his name to something else. Which is okay, because Gawx is kind of a dumb name, and you don't want your emperor to sound dumb." She cocked her head. "Can't stop that if he starts talking though."

On the ground beside her, Wyndle groaned softly.

"Did you know," Lift said, leaning in to the scribe, "that they've got someone who *picks his nose* for him?"

"Young lady, I believe you are wasting my time."

"That's pretty insulting," Lift said, sitting up straight in her seat, "considering how little you people seem to do around here."

It was true. This whole building was full of scribes rushing this way and that, carrying piles of paper to one windowless alcove or another. They even had this spren that hung out here, one Lift had only seen a couple of times. It looked like little ripples in the air, like a raindrop in a pond—only without the rain, and without the pond. Wyndle called them concentrationspren.

Anyway, they had so much starvin' paper in the place that they needed parshmen to cart it about for them! One passed in the hallway outside, a woman carrying a large box of papers. Those would be hauled to one of a billion scribes who sat at tables, surrounded by blinking spanreeds. Wyndle said they were answering inquiries from around the world, passing information.

The scribe with Lift was a slightly more important one. Lift had gotten into the room by doing as Wyndle suggested: not talking. The viziers did that kind of thing too. Nodding, not saying anything. She'd presented the card, where she'd sketched the words that Wyndle had formed for her with vines.

The people at the front had been intimidated enough to lead her through the hallways to this room, which was larger than others—but it still didn't have any windows. The wall had a brownish yellow stain on the white paint though, and you could pretend it was sunlight.

On the other wall was a shelf that held a really long rack of spanreeds. A few Azish tapestries hung at the back. This scribe was some kind of liaison with the government over in Azir.

Once in the room though, Lift had been forced to talk. She couldn't avoid that anymore. She just needed to be persuasive.

"What unfortunate person," the large scribe asked, "did you mug to get that clothing?"

"Like I'd take it off someone while they were *wearing* it," Lift said, rolling her eyes. "Look. Just pull out one of those glowing pens and write to the palace. Then we can get on to the important stuff. My Voidbringer says you got *tons* of papers in here we're gonna have to look through."

The woman stood up. Lift could practically hear her chair breathe a sigh of relief. The woman pointed toward the door dismissively, but at that moment a lesser scribe—spindly, and wearing a yellow shiqua and a strange brown and yellow cap—entered and whispered in the woman's ear.

She looked displeased. The newcomer shrugged awkwardly, then hurried back out. The fat woman turned to eye Lift. "Give me the names of the viziers you know in the palace."

"Well, there's Dalky—she's got a funny nose, like a spigot. And Big A, I can't say his real name. It's got those choking sounds in it. And Daddy Sag-butt, he's not really a vizier. They call him a scion, which is a different kind of important. Oh! And Fat Lips! She's in charge of them. She doesn't really have fat lips, but she hates it when I call her that."

The woman stared at Lift. Then she turned and walked to the door. "Wait here." She stepped outside.

Lift leaned over toward the ground. "How'm I doin'?"

"Terribly," Wyndle said.

"Yeah. I noticed."

"It's almost as if," Wyndle said, "it would have been *useful* to learn how to talk politely, like the viziers kept telling you."

"Blah blah," Lift said, going to the door and listening. Outside, she could faintly hear the scribes talking.

". . . matches the description given by the captain of the immigration watch to search for in the city . . ." one of them said. "She showed up right here! We've sent to the captain, who luckily is here for her debriefing . . ."

"Damnation," Lift whispered, pulling back. "They're on to us, Voidbringer."

"I should never have helped you with this insane idea!"

Lift crossed the room to the racks of spanreeds. They were all labeled. "Get over here and tell me which one we need."

Wyndle grew up the wall and sent vines across the nameplates. "My, my. These are important reeds. Let's see . . . third one over, it will go to the royal palace scribes."

"Great," Lift said, grabbing it and scrambling onto the table. She set it into the right spot on the board—she'd seen this done tons of times—and twisted the ruby on the top of the reed. It was answered immediately; palace scribes weren't often away from their reeds. They'd sooner give up their fingers.

Lift grabbed the spanreed and placed it against the paper. "Uh . . ."

"Oh, for Cultivation's sake," Wyndle said. "You didn't pay attention at all, did you?"

"Nope."

"Tell me what you want to say."

She said it out, and he again made vines grow across the table in the right shapes. Pen gripped in her fist, she copied the words, one stupid letter at a time. It took *forever*. Writing was ridiculous. Couldn't people just talk? Why invent a way where you didn't have to actually see people to tell them what to do?

This is Lift, she wrote. *Tell Fat Lips I need her. I'm in trouble. And somebody get Gawx. If he's not having his nose picked right—*

The door opened and Lift yelped, twisting the ruby and scrambling off the table.

Beyond the door was a large gathering of people. Five scribes, including the fat one, and three guards. One was the woman who ran the guard post into the city.

Storms, Lift thought. *That was fast.*

She ducked toward them.

"Careful!" the guard shouted. "She's slippery!"

Lift made herself awesome, but the guard shoved the scribes into the room and started pushing the door shut behind her. Lift got between their legs, Slick and sliding easily, but slammed right into the door as it closed.

The guard lunged for her. Lift yelped, coating herself with awesomeness so that when she got grabbed, her wide-sleeved Azish coat came off, leaving her in a robelike skirt with trousers underneath, and then her normal shirts.

She scuttled across the ground, but the room wasn't large. She tried to scramble around the perimeter, but the guard captain was right on her.

"Mistress!" Wyndle cried. "Oh, mistress. Don't get stabbed! Are you listening? Avoid getting hit by anything sharp! Or blunt, actually!"

Lift growled as the other guards slipped in, then quickly shut the door. One prowled around on either side of the room.

She dodged one way, then the other, then punched at the shelf with the spanreeds, causing the scribe to scream as several toppled over.

Lift bolted for the door. The guard captain tackled her, and another piled on top of *her*.

Lift squirmed, making herself awesome, squeezing through their fingers. She just had to—

"Tashi," a scribe whispered. "God of Gods and Binder of the World!" Awespren, like a ring of blue smoke, burst out around her head.

Lift popped out of the grips of the guards, stepping up to stand on one of their backs, which gave her a good view of the desk. The spanreed was writing.

"Took them long enough," she said, then hopped off the guards and sat in the chair.

The guard stood up behind her, cursing.

"Stop, Captain!" the fat scribe said. She looked at the spindly scribe in yellow. "Go get another spanreed to the Azish palace. Get two! We need confirmation."

"For what?" the scribe said, walking to the desk. The guard captain joined them, reading what the pen wrote.

Then, slowly, all three looked up at Lift with wide eyes.

"'To whom it may concern,'" Wyndle read, spreading his vines up onto the table over the paper. "'It is decreed that I—Prime Aqasix Yanagawn the First, emperor of all Makabak—proclaim that the young woman known as Lift is to be shown every courtesy and measure of respect.

"'You will obey her as you would myself, and bill to the imperial account any charges that might be incurred by her . . . foray in your city.

What follows is a description of the woman, and two questions only she can answer, as proof of authentication. But know this—if she is harmed or impeded in any way, you will know imperial wrath.'"

"Thanks, Gawx," Lift said, then looked up at the scribes and guards. "That means you gotta do what I say!"

"And . . . what is it you want?" the fat scribe asked.

"Depends," Lift said. "What were you going to have for lunch today?"

14

THREE hours later, Lift sat in the center of the fat scribe's desk, eating pancakes with her hands and wearing the spindly scribe's hat.

A swarm of lesser scribes searched through reports on the ground in front of her, piles of books scattered about like broken crab shells after a fine feast. The fat scribe stood beside the desk, reading to Lift from the spanreed that wrote Gawx's end of their conversation. The woman had finally pulled down her face wrap, and it turned out she was pretty and a lot younger than Lift had assumed.

"'I'm worried, Lift,'" the fat scribe read to her. "'*Everyone* here is worried. There are reports coming in from the west now. Steen and Alm have seen the new storm. It's happening like the Alethi warlord said it would. A storm of red lightning, blowing the wrong direction.'"

The woman looked up at Lift. "He's right about that, um . . ."

"Say it," Lift said.

"Your Pancakefulness."

"Rolls right off the tongue, doesn't it?"

"His Imperial Excellency is correct about the arrival of a strange new storm. We have independent confirmation of that from contacts in

Shinovar and Iri. An enormous storm with red lightning, blowing in from the west."

"And the monsters?" Lift said. "Things with red eyes in the darkness?"

"Everything is in chaos," the scribe said—her name was Ghenna. "We've had trouble getting straight answers. We had some inkling of this, from reports on the east coast when the storm struck there, before blowing into the ocean. Most people thought those reports exaggerated, and that the storm would blow itself out. Now that it has rounded the planet and struck in the west . . . Well, the prince is reportedly preparing a diktat of emergency for the entire country."

Lift looked at Wyndle, who was coiled on the desk beside her. "Voidbringers," he said, voice small. "It's happening. Sweet virtue . . . the Desolations *have* returned. . . ."

Ghenna went back to reading the spanreed from Gawx. "'This is going to be a disaster, Lift. Nobody is ready for a storm that blows the wrong direction. Almost as bad, though, are the Alethi. How do the Alethi know so much about it? Did that warlord of theirs summon it somehow?'" Ghenna lowered the paper.

Lift chewed on her pancake. It was a dense variety, with mashed-up paste in the center that was too sticky and salty. The one beside it was covered in little crunchy seeds. Neither were as good as the other two varieties she'd tried over the last few hours.

"When's it going to hit?" Lift asked.

"The storm? It's hard to judge, but it's slower than a highstorm, by most reports. It might arrive in Azir and Tashikk in three or four hours."

"Write this to Gawx," Lift said around bites of pancake. "'They got good food here. These pancakes, with lots of variety. One has sugar in the center.'"

The scribe hesitated.

"Write it," Lift said. "Or I'll make you call me more silly names."

Ghenna sighed, but complied.

"'Lift,'" she read as the spanreed wrote the next line from Gawx, who undoubtedly had about fifteen viziers and scions standing around telling him what to say, then writing it when he agreed. "'This isn't the time for idle conversation about food.'"

"Sure it is," Lift replied. "We gotta remember. Storm might be coming, but people will still need to eat. The world ends tomorrow, but the day after that, people are going to ask what's for breakfast. That's your job."

"'And what about the stories of something worse?'" he wrote back. "'The Alethi are warning about parshmen, and I'm doing what I can on such short notice. But what of the Voidbringers they say are in the storms?'"

Lift looked at the room packed with scribes. "I'm workin' on that part," she said. As Ghenna wrote it, Lift stood up, wiping her hands on her fancy robes. "Hey, all you smart people. Whatcha found?"

The scribes looked up at her. "Mistress," one said, "we don't have *any* idea what we're even looking for."

"Strange stuff!"

"What kind of 'strange stuff'?" asked the scribe in yellow, the spindly fellow who looked silly and balding without a hat. "Unusual things happen every day in the city! Do you want the report of the man who claims his pig was born with two heads? What about the man who says he saw the shape of Yaezir in the lichen on his wall? The woman who had a premonition her sister would fall, and then she fell?"

"Nah," Lift said. "That's *normal* strange."

"What's abnormal strange, then?" he asked, exasperated.

Lift started glowing. She called upon her awesomeness, so much that it started radiating out of her skin, like she was a starvin' sphere.

Beside her, the seeds on top of her uneaten pancake sprouted, growing long, twisting vines that curled around one another and spat out leaves.

"Somethin' like this," Lift said, then glanced to the side. Great. She'd ruined the pancake.

The scribes stared at her in awe, so she clapped loudly, sending them back to their work. Wyndle sighed, and she knew what he must be thinking. Three hours, and nothing relevant so far. He'd been right—yeah, they wrote stuff down in this city. That was the problem. They wrote it *all* down.

"There's another message from the emperor for you," Ghenna said. "Um, Your Pancake . . . Storms that sounds stupid."

Lift grinned, then looked over at the paper. The words were written in a flowing, elegant hand. Probably Fat Lips.

"'Lift,'" Ghenna read. "'Are you going to come back? We miss you here.'"

"Even Fat Lips?" Lift asked.

"'Vizier Noura misses you too. Lift, this is your home now. You don't need to live on the streets anymore.'"

"What am I supposed to do there, if I do come back?"

"'Anything you want,'" Gawx wrote. "'I promise.'"

That was the problem.

"I don't know what I'm gonna do yet," she said, feeling strangely . . . isolated, despite the roomful of people. "We'll see."

Ghenna eyed her at that. She apparently thought that what the emperor of Azir wanted, he should get—and little Reshi girls shouldn't make a habit of denying him.

The door cracked open, and the guard captain from the city watch peeked in. Lift leaped off the desk, running over to her, then hopping up to see what she was holding. A report. Great. More words.

"What did you find?" Lift said eagerly.

"You are right," the captain said. "One of my colleagues in the quarter's watch has been watching the Tashi's Light Orphanage. The woman who runs it—"

"The Stump," Lift said. "Meanest thing. Eats the bones of children for afternoon snack. Once had a staring contest with a painting and won."

"—is being investigated. She's running some kind of money-laundering scheme, though the details are confusing. She's been seen trading spheres for ones of lesser value, a practice that would end with her bankrupt, if she didn't have another income scheme. The report says she takes money from criminal enterprises as donations, then secretly transfers them to other groups, after taking a cut, to help confuse the trail of spheres. There's more too. In any case, the children are a front to keep attention away from her practices."

"I told you," Lift said, snatching the paper. "You should arrest her and spend all her money on soup. Give me half, for tellin' you where to look, and I won't tell nobody."

The guard raised her eyebrows.

"We can write down that we did it, if you want," Lift said. "That'll make it *official.*"

"I'll ignore the suggestions of bribery, coercion, extortion, and state embezzlement," the captain said. "As for the orphanage, I don't have jurisdiction over it, but I assure you my colleagues will be moving against this . . . Stump soon."

"Good enough," Lift said, climbing back up on the desk before her legion of scribes. "So what have you found? Anybody glowing, like they're some stormin' benevolent force for good or some such crem?"

"This is too large a project to spring on us without warning!" the fat scribe complained. "Mistress, this is the sort of research we normally have *months* to work on. Give us three weeks, and we can prepare a detailed report!"

"We ain't got three weeks. We barely got three hours."

It didn't matter. Over the next few hours, she tried cajoling, threatening, dancing, bribing, and—as a last-ditch, crazy option—remaining perfectly quiet and letting them read. As the time slipped away, they found nothing and everything at the same time. There were *tons* of vague oddities in the guard reports: stories of a man surviving a fall from too high, a complaint of strange noises outside a woman's window, spren acting odd every morning outside a woman's house unless she left out a bowl of sugar water. Yet none of them had more than one witness, and in each case the guard had found nothing specifically strange other than hearsay.

Each time a weirdness came up, Lift itched to scramble out the door, squeeze through a window, and go running to find the person involved. Each time, Wyndle cautioned patience. If all these reports were true, then basically every person in the city would have been a Surgebinder. What if she ran off chasing one of the hundred reports that were due to ordinary superstition? She'd spend hours and find nothing.

Which was exactly what she felt like she was doing. She was annoyed, impatient, *and* out of pancakes.

"I'm sorry, mistress," Wyndle said as they rejected a report about a Veden woman who claimed her baby had been "blessed by Tashi Himself to have lighter skin than his father, to make him more comfortable interacting with foreigners."

"I don't think any of these is more likely a sign than the one before. I'm beginning to feel we just need to pick one and hope we get lucky."

Lift hated luck, these days. She was having trouble convincing herself that she hadn't hit an unlucky age of her life, so she'd given up on luck. She'd even traded her lucky sphere for a piece of hog's cheese.

The more she thought of it, the more that *luck* seemed the opposite of being *awesome*. One was something you did; the other was something that happened to you no matter what you did.

Course, that didn't mean luck didn't exist. You either believed in that, or you believed in what those Vorin priests were always saying—that poor people was *chosen* to be poor, on account of them being too dumb to ask the Almighty to make them born with heaps of spheres.

"So what do we do?" Lift said.

"Pick one of these accounts, I guess," Wyndle said. "Any of them. Except maybe that one about the baby. I suspect that the mother might not be honest."

"Ya think?"

Lift looked over the papers spread before her—papers she couldn't read, each detailing a report of some vague curiosity. Storms. Pick the right one and she could save a life, maybe find someone else who could do what she did.

Pick the wrong one, and Darkness or his servants would execute an innocent. Quietly, with nobody to witness their passing or to remember them.

Darkness. She hated him, suddenly. With a seething ferocity that startled even her with its intensity. She didn't think she'd ever actually *hated* anyone before. Him though . . . those cold eyes that seemed to refuse all emotion. She hated him more for the fact that it seemed like he did what he did without a shred of guilt.

"Mistress?" Wyndle asked. "What do you choose?"

"I can't choose," she whispered. "I don't know how."

"Just pick one."

"I can't. I don't make choices, Wyndle."

"Nonsense! You do it every day."

"No. I just . . ." She went where the winds blew. Once you made a decision, you were committed. You were saying you thought this was *right*.

The door to their chamber was flung open. A guard there, one Lift didn't recognize, was sweating and puffing. "Status Five emergency diktat from the prince, to be disseminated through the nation immediately. State of emergency in the city. Storm blowing from the wrong direction, projected to hit within two hours.

"All people are to get off the streets and go to storm bunkers, and parshmen are to be imprisoned or exiled into the storm. He wants the alleys of Yeddaw and slot cities evacuated, and orders government officials to report to their assigned bunkers to do head counts, draft reports, and mediate confusion or evacuation disputes. Find a draft of these orders posted at each muster station, with copies being distributed now."

The scribes in the room looked up from their work, then immediately began packing away books and ledgers.

"Wait!" Lift said as the runner moved on. "What are you doing?"

"You've just gotten overruled, little one," Ghenna said. "Your research will have to be put on hold."

"How long!"

"Until the prince decides to step down our state of emergency," she said, quickly gathering the spanreeds from her shelf and packing them in a padded case.

"But, the emperor!" Lift said, grabbing a note from Gawx and wagging it. "He said to help me!"

"We'll gladly help you to a storm bunker," the guard captain said.

"I need help with this problem! He *ordered* you to obey!"

"We, of course, listen to the emperor," Ghenna said. "We will listen very well."

But not necessarily obey. The viziers had explained this. Azir might *claim* to be an empire, and most of the other countries in the region played along. Just like you might play along with the kid who says he's team captain during a game of rings. As soon as his demands grew too extravagant though, he might find himself talking to an empty alleyway.

The scribes were remarkably efficient. It wasn't too long before they'd ushered Lift into the hallway, burdened her with a handful of reports she couldn't read, then split to run to their various duties. They left her with one junior sub-scribe who couldn't be much older than Lift; her job was to show Lift to a storm bunker.

Lift ditched the girl at the first junction she could, scuttling down a side path as the girl explained the emergency to a bleary-eyed old scholar in a brown shiqua. Lift stripped off her nice Azish clothing and dumped it in a corner, leaving her in trousers, shirt, and unbuttoned overshirt. From there she set off into a less-populated section of the building. In the large corridors, scribes gathered and shouted at one another. She wouldn't have expected such a ruckus from a bunch of dried-up old men and women with ink for blood.

It was dark in here, and Lift found reason to wish she hadn't traded away her lucky sphere. The hallways were marked by rugs with Azish patterns to differentiate them, but that was about it. Periodic sphere lanterns lined the walls, but only every fifth one had an infused sphere in it. Everyone was still starvin' for Stormlight. She spent a good minute holding to one, chewing on its latch and trying to get it undone, but they were locked up tight.

She continued down the hallway, passing room after room, each stuffed with paper—though there weren't as many bookshelves as Lift had expected to find. It wasn't like a library. Instead there were walls full of drawers that you could pull open to find stacks of pages.

The longer she walked the quieter it became, until it was like she was walking through a mausoleum—for trees. She crinkled up the papers in her hand and shoved them in her pocket. There were so many, she couldn't properly get her hand in as well.

"Mistress?" Wyndle said from the floor beside her. "We don't have much time."

"I'm thinkin'," Lift said. Which was a lie. She was trying to *avoid* thinkin'.

"I'm sorry the plan didn't work," Wyndle said.

Lift shrugged. "You don't want to be here anyway. You want to be off gardening."

"Yes, I had the most lovely gallery of boots planned," Wyndle said.

"But I suppose . . . I suppose we can't sit around preparing gardens while the world ends, can we? And if I'd been placed with that nice Iriali, I wouldn't be here, would I? And that Radiant you're trying to save, they'd be as good as dead."

"Probably as good as dead anyway."

"But still . . . still worth trying, right?"

Stupid cheerful Voidbringer. She glanced at him, then pulled out the wads of paper. "These are useless. We gotta start over with a new plan."

"And with much less time. Sunset is coming, along with that storm. What do we do?"

Lift dropped the papers. "Somebody knows where to go. That woman who was talkin' to Darkness, his apprentice, she said she had an investigation going. Sounded confident."

"Huh," Wyndle said. "You don't suppose her investigation involved . . . a bunch of scribes searching records, do you?"

Lift cocked her head.

"That would be the smart thing to do," Wyndle said. "I mean, even *we* came up with it."

Lift grinned, then ran back in the direction she'd come from.

15

Y ES," the fat scribe said, flustered after looking through a book. "It was Bidlel's team, room two-three-two. The woman you describe hired them two weeks ago for an undisclosed project. We take the secrecy of our clients *very* seriously." She sighed, closing the book. "Barring imperial mandate."

"Thanks," Lift said, giving the woman a hug. "Thanksthanksthanksthanks."

"I wish I knew what all this meant. Storms . . . you'd think I would be the one who got told everything, but half the time I get the sense that even kings are confused by what the world throws at them." She shook her head and looked to Lift, who was still hugging her. "I *am* going to my assigned station now. You'd be wise to seek shelter."

"Surewillgreatbye," Lift said, letting go and dashing out of the room full of ledgers. She scurried through the hallway, directly *away* from the steps down to the Indicium's storm shelter.

Ghenna poked her head out into the hallway. "Bidlel will have already evacuated! The door will be locked." She paused. "Don't break anything!"

"Voidbringer," Lift said, "can you find whatever number she just said?"

"Yes."

"Good. 'Cuz I don't got that many toes."

They hurried through the cavernous Indicium, which was already feeling empty. Only a half hour or so since the diktat—Wyndle was keeping track—and everyone was on their way out. People locked the doors in the advent of a storm, and moved on to safe places. For those with regular homes, those homes would do, but for the poor that meant storm bunkers.

Poor parshmen. There weren't many in the city, not as many as in Azimir, but by the prince's orders they were being gathered and turned out. Left for the storm, which Lift considered hugely unfair.

Nobody listened to her complaints about that though. And Wyndle implied . . . well, they might be turning into Voidbringers. And he would know.

Still didn't seem fair. She wouldn't leave *him* out in a storm. Even if he claimed it probably wouldn't hurt them.

She followed Wyndle's vines as he led her up two floors, then started counting off rows. The floor on this level was of painted wood, and it felt weird to walk on it. Wooden floors. Wouldn't they break and fall through? Wooden buildings always felt so flimsy to her, and she stepped lightly just in case. It—

Lift frowned, then crouched down, looking one way, then the other. What was that?

"Two-Two-One . . ." Wyndle said. "Two-Two-Two . . ."

"Voidbringer!" Lift hissed. "Shut up."

He twisted about, creeping up the wall near her. Lift pressed her back against the wall, then ducked around a corner into a side corridor and pressed her back against that wall instead.

Booted feet thumped on the carpet. "I can't believe you call *that* a lead," a woman's voice said. Lift recognized it as Darkness's trainee. "Weren't you in the guard?"

"Things work differently in Yezier," a man snapped. The other trainee. "Here, everyone is too coy. They should just say what they mean."

"You expect a Tashikki street informant to be *perfectly clear*?"

"Sure. Isn't that his job?"

The two strode past, and thankfully didn't glance down the side hall toward Lift. Storms, those uniforms—with the high boots, stiff Eastern jackets, and large-cuffed gloves—were imposing. They looked like generals on the field.

Lift itched to follow and see where they went. She forced herself to wait.

Sure enough, a few seconds later a quieter figure passed in the hallway. The assassin, clothing tattered, head bowed, with that large sword—it *had* to be some kind of Shardblade—resting on his shoulder.

"I do not know, sword-nimi," he said softly, "I don't trust my own mind any longer." He paused, stopping as if listening to something. "That is not comforting, sword-nimi. No, it is not. . . ."

He trailed after the other two, leaving a faint afterimage glowing in the air. It was almost imperceptible, less pronounced now that he was moving than it had been in Darkness's headquarters.

"Oh, mistress," Wyndle said, curling up to her. "I nearly expired of fright! The way he stopped there in the hallway, I was *sure* he'd seen me somehow!"

At least the hallways were dark, with those sphere lanterns mostly out. Lift nervously slipped into the hallway and followed the group. They stopped at the right door, and one produced a key. Lift had expected them to ransack the place, but of course they wouldn't need to do that—they had legal authority.

Actually, so did she. How bizarre.

Darkness's two apprentices stepped into the room. The Assassin in White remained outside in the hallway. He settled down on the floor across from the doorway, his strange Shardblade across his lap. He sat mostly still, but when he did move, he left that fading afterimage behind.

Lift pulled into the side corridor again, back pressed to the wall. People shouted somewhere distant in the Grand Indecision, calls for people to be orderly.

"I have to get into that room," Lift said. "Somehow."

Wyndle huddled down on the ground, vines tightening around him.

Lift shook her head. "That means getting past the starvin' *assassin* himself. Storms."

"I'll do it," Wyndle whispered.

"Maybe," Lift said, barely paying attention, "I can make some sorta distraction. Send him off chasin' it? But then that would alert the two in the room."

"I'll do it," Wyndle repeated.

Lift cocked her head, registering what he'd said. She glanced down at him. "The distraction?"

"No." Wyndle's vines twisted about one another, tightening into knots. "I'll do it, mistress. I can sneak into the room. I . . . I don't believe their spren will be able to see me."

"You don't know?"

"No."

"Sounds dangerous."

His vines scrunched as they tightened against one another. "You think?"

"Yeah, totally," Lift said, then peeked around the corner. "Something's wrong about that guy in white. Can you get killed, Voidbringer?"

"Destroyed," Wyndle said. "Yes. It's not the same as for a human, but I have . . . seen spren who . . ." He whimpered softly. "Maybe it *is* too dangerous for me."

"Maybe."

Wyndle settled down, coiled about himself.

"I'm going anyway," he whispered.

She nodded. "Just listen, memorize what those two in there say, and get back here quick. If something happens, scream loud as you can."

"Right. Listen and scream. I can listen and scream. I'm good at these things." He made a sound like taking a deep breath, though so far as she knew he didn't need to breathe. Then he shot out into the corridor, a vine laced with crystal that grew along the corner where wall met floor. Little offshoots of green crept off his sides, covering the carpeting.

The assassin didn't look up. Wyndle reached the doorway into the room with the two Skybreaker apprentices. Lift couldn't hear a word of what was being said inside.

Storms, she hated waiting. She'd built her life around not having to wait for anyone or anything. She did what she wanted, when she wanted.

That was the best, right? Everyone should be able to do what they wanted.

Of course if they did that, who would grow food? If the world was full of people like Lift, wouldn't they just leave halfway through planting to go catch lurgs? Nobody would protect the streets, or sit around in meetings. Nobody would learn to write things down, or make kingdoms run. Everyone would scurry about eating each other's food, until it was all gone and the whole heap of them fell over and *died*.

You knew that, a part of her said, standing up inside, hands on hips with a defiant attitude. *You knew the truth of the world even when you went and asked not to get older.*

Being young was an excuse. A plausible justification.

She waited, feeling itchy because she couldn't do anything. What were they saying in there? Had they spotted Wyndle? Were they torturing him? Threatening to . . . cut down his gardens or something?

Listen, a part of her whispered.

But of course she couldn't hear anything.

She wanted to just rush in there, make faces at them all, then drag them on a chase through the starvin' building. That would be better than sitting here with her thoughts, worrying and condemning herself at the same time.

When you were always busy, you didn't have to think about stuff. Like how most people didn't run off and leave when the whim struck them. Like how your mother had been so warm, and kindly, so ready to take care of everyone. It was incredible that anyone on Roshar should be as good to people as she'd been.

She shouldn't have had to die. Least, she should have had someone half as wonderful as she was to take care of her as she wasted away.

Someone other than Lift, who was selfish, stupid.

And lonely.

She tensed up, then prepared to bolt around the corner. Wyndle, however, finally zipped out into the hallway. He grew along the floor at a frantic pace, then rejoined her—leaving a trail of dust by the wall as his discarded vines crumbled.

Darkness's two apprentices left the room a moment later, and Lift pulled back into the side corridor with Wyndle. In the shadows here, she crouched down against the floor, to avoid standing out against the distant light. The woman and man in uniforms strode past a moment later, and didn't even glance down the hallway. Lift relaxed, fingertips brushing Wyndle's vines.

Then the assassin passed by. He stopped, then looked in her direction, hand resting on his sword hilt.

Lift's breath caught. *Don't become awesome. Don't become awesome!* If she used her powers in these shadows, she'd glow and he'd spot her for sure.

All she could do was crouch there as the assassin narrowed his eyes—strangely shaped, like they were too big or something. He reached to a pouch at his belt, then tossed something small and glowing into the hallway. A sphere.

Lift panicked, uncertain if she should scramble away, grow awesome, or just remain still. Fearspren boiled up around her, lit by the sphere as it rolled near her, and she knew—meeting the assassin's gaze—that he could see her.

He pulled his sword out of the sheath a fraction of an inch. Black smoke poured from the blade, dropping toward the floor and pooling at his feet. Lift felt a sudden, terrible nausea.

The assassin studied her, then snapped the sword into its sheath again. Remarkably, he left, following after the other two, that faint afterimage trailing behind him. He didn't speak a word, and his footfalls on the carpet were almost silent—a faint breeze compared to the clomping of the other two, which Lift could still hear farther down the corridor.

In moments, all three of them had entered the stairwell and were gone.

"Storms!" Lift said, flopping backward on the carpet. "Storming Mother of the World and Father of Storms above! He about made me die of fright."

"I know!" Wyndle said. "Did you hear me not-whimpering?"

"No."

"I was too frightened to even make a sound!"

Lift sat up, then mopped the sweat from her brow. "Wow. Okay, well . . . that was something. What did they talk about?"

"Oh!" Wyndle said, as if he'd forgotten completely about his mission. "Mistress, they had an entire study done! Research for weeks to identify oddities in the city."

"Great! What did they determine?"

"I don't know."

Lift flopped back down.

"They talked over a whole lot of things I didn't understand," Wyndle said. "But mistress, *they* know who the person is! They're heading there right now. To perform an execution." He poked at her with a vine. "So . . . maybe we should follow?"

"Yeah, okay," Lift said. "Guess we can do that. Shouldn't be too hard, right?"

16

Turned out it was *way* hard.

She couldn't get too close, as the hallways had grown eerily empty. And there were tons of branching paths, with little side hallways and rooms everywhere. Mix that with the fact that there weren't many spheres on the walls, and it was a real trick to follow the three.

She did it though. She followed them through the whole starvin' place until they reached some doors out into the city. Lift managed to slip out a window near the doors, falling among some plants beside the stairs outside. She huddled there as the three people she'd been tailing stepped out onto the landing overlooking the city.

Storms, but it felt good to be breathing the open air again, though clouds had moved in front of the setting sun. The whole city felt chilly now. In shadow.

And it was empty.

Before, people had been swarming up and down the steps and ramps into the Grand Indishipium. Now they held only a few last-minute stragglers, and even those were rapidly vanishing as they ducked through doorways, seeking shelter.

The assassin turned eyes toward the west. "The storm is coming," he said.

"All the more reason to be quick," the female apprentice said. She took a sphere from her pocket, then held it up before her and sucked in the light. It streamed into her, and she started to glow with awesomeness.

Then she rose into the air.

She rose into the starvin' air itself!

They can fly? Lift thought. *Why in Damnation can't I fly?*

Her companion rose up beside her.

"Coming, assassin?" The woman looked down toward the landing and the man wearing white.

"I've danced that storm once before," he whispered. "On the day I died. No."

"You're never going to make it into the order at this rate."

He remained silent. The two floating people eyed each other, then the man shrugged. The two of them rose higher, then shot out across the city, avoiding the inconvenience of traveling through the trenches.

They could *storming* fly.

"You're the one he's hunting for, aren't you?" the assassin said softly.

Lift winced. Then she stood up and peeked over the side of the landing where the assassin stood. He turned and looked at her.

"I ain't nobody," Lift said.

"He kills nobodies."

"And you don't?"

"I kill kings."

"Which is *totally* better."

He narrowed his eyes at her, then squatted down, sheathed sword held across his shoulders, with hands draped forward. "No. It is not. I hear their screams, their demands, whenever I see shadow. They haunt me, scramble for my mind, wishing to claim my sanity. I fear they've already won, that the man to whom you speak can no longer distinguish what is the voice of a mad raving and what is not."

"Oooookay," Lift said. "But you didn't attack me."

"No. The sword likes you."

"Great. I like the sword too." She glanced at the sky. "Um . . . do you know where they're going?"

"The report described a man who has been spotted vanishing by several people in the city. He will turn down an alleyway, then it will be empty when someone else follows. People have claimed to see his face twisting to become the face of another. My companions believe he is what is called a Lightweaver, and so must be stopped."

"Is that legal?"

"Nin has procured an injunction from the prince, forbidding any use of Surgebinding in the country, save that specifically authorized." He studied Lift. "I believe the Herald's experiences with you were what taught him to go straight to the top, rather than dancing about with local authorities."

Lift traced the direction the other two had gone. That sky was darkening further, an ominous sign.

"He really is wrong, isn't he?" Lift said. "That one you say is a Herald. He says the Voidbringers aren't back, but they are."

"The new storm reveals it," the assassin said. "But . . . who am I to say? I am mad. Then again, I think that the Herald is too. It makes me agree that the minds of men cannot be trusted. That we need something greater to follow, to guide. But not my stone . . . What good is seeking a greater law, when that law can be the whims of a man either stupid or ruthless?"

"Oooookay," Lift said. "Um, you can be crazy all you want. It's fine. I like crazy people. It's real funny when they lick walls and eat rocks and stuff. But before you start dancing, could you tell me where those other two are going?"

"You won't be able to outrun them."

"So no harm in telling me, right?"

The assassin smiled, though the emotion didn't seem to reach his eyes. "The man who can vanish, this presumed Lightweaver, is an old philosopher well known in the immigrant quarter. He sits in a small amphitheater most days, talking to any who will listen. It is near—"

"—the Tashi's Light Orphanage. Storms. I shoulda guessed. He's almost as weird as you are."

"Will you fight them, little Radiant?" the assassin asked. "You, alone, against two journeyman Skybreakers? A Herald waiting in the wings?"

She glanced at Wyndle. "I don't know. But I have to go anyway, don't I?"

17

LIFT engaged her awesomeness. She dug deeply into the power, summoning strength, speed, and Slickness. Darkness's people didn't seem to care if they were witnessed flying about, so Lift decided she didn't care about being seen either.

She leaped away from the assassin, Slicking her feet, then landed on the flat ramp beside the steps that wound up the outside of the building. She intended to shoot down toward the city, sliding along the side of the steps.

Of course, she lasted about a second before her feet shot out in two different directions and she slammed onto the stones crotch-first. She cringed at the flash of pain, but didn't have time for much more, as she fell into a tumble before dropping right off the side of the tall steps.

She crunched down to the bottom a few moments later, landing in a humiliated heap. Her awesomeness prevented her from getting too hurt, so she ignored Wyndle's cries of worry as he climbed down the wall to her. Instead she twisted about, scrambling up onto her hands and knees. Then she took off running toward the slot that would lead her to the orphanage.

She didn't have time to be bad at this! Normal running wouldn't be fast enough. Her enemies were literally *flying*.

She could see, in her mind's eye, how it should be. The entire city sloped away from this central rise with the Grand Indigestion. She should be able to hit a skid, feet Slick, zipping along the mostly empty street. She should be able to slap her hands against walls she passed, outcroppings, buildings, gaining speed with each push.

She should be like an arrow in flight, pointed, targeted, unchecked.

She could see it. But couldn't *do* it. She threw herself into another skid, but again her feet slipped out from under her. This time they went backward and she fell forward, knocking her face against the stone. She saw a flash of white. When she looked up, the empty street wavered in front of her, but her awesomeness soon healed her.

The shadowed street was a major thoroughfare, but it sat forlorn and empty. People had pulled in awnings and street carts, but had left refuse. Those walls crowded her. Everyone knew to stay out of canyons around a storm, or you'd be swept up in floodwaters. They'd gone and built an entire starvin' city in direct, flagrant violation of that.

Behind her in the distance, the sky rumbled. Before that storm hit, a poor, crazy old man was going to get a visit from two self-righteous assassins. She needed to stop it. She *had* to stop it. She couldn't explain why.

Okay, Lift. Be calm. You can be awesome. You've always been awesome, and now you've got this extra awesomeness. Go. You can do it.

She growled and threw herself into a run, then twisted sideways and slid. She *could* and *would*—

This time, she clipped the corner of a wall at an intersection and ended up sprawled on the ground, with feet toward the sky. She knocked her head back against the ground in frustration.

"Mistress?" Wyndle said, curling up to her. "Oh, I do not like the sound of that storm. . . ."

She got up—feeling ashamed and anything *but* awesome—and decided to just run the rest of the way. Her powers did let her run at speed without getting tired, but she could *feel* that it wasn't going to be enough.

It seemed like ages before she stumbled to a stop outside the orphanage, exhaustionspren swirling around her. She'd run out of awesomeness a short time before arriving, and her stomach growled in protest. The amphitheater was empty, of course. Orphanage to her left, built into the solid stones, seats of the little amphitheater in front of her. And beyond it the dark alleyway, wooden shanties and buildings cluttering the view.

The sky had grown dark, though she didn't know whether it was from the advent of dusk or the coming storm.

Deep within the alleyway, Lift heard a low, raw scream of pain. It sent chills up her spine.

Wyndle had been right. The assassin had been right. What was she doing? She couldn't beat two trained and awesome soldiers. She sank down, worn out, right in the middle of the floor of the amphitheater.

"Do we go in?" Wyndle asked from beside her.

"I don't have any power left," Lift whispered. "I used it up running here."

Had that alleyway always felt so . . . deep? With the shadows of the shanties, the draping cloths and jutting planks of wood, the place looked like an extended barricade—with only the narrowest of pathways through. It seemed like an entirely different world from the rest of the city. It was a dark and hidden realm that could exist only in shadows.

She stood up on unsteady feet, then stepped toward the alleyway.

"What are you doing?" a voice shouted.

Lift spun to find the Stump standing in the doorway of the orphanage.

"You're supposed to go to one of the bunkers!" the woman shouted. "Idiot child." She stalked forward and seized Lift by the arm, towing her into the orphanage. "Don't think that just because you're here, I'll take care of you. There's not room for ones like you, and don't give me any pretense about being sick or tired. Everyone's always pretending in order to get at what we have."

Though she said that, she deposited Lift right inside the orphanage, then slammed the large wooden door and threw the bar down. "Be glad I looked out to see who was screaming." She studied Lift, then sighed loudly. "Suppose you'll want some food."

"I have one meal left," Lift said.

"I've half a mind to give it to the other children," the Stump said. "Honestly, after a prank like that. Standing outside screaming? You should have gone to one of the bunkers. If you think that acting forlorn will earn my pity, you are sadly misguided."

She walked off, muttering. The room here, right inside the doors, was large and open, and children sat on mats all round. A single ruby sphere lit them. The children seemed frightened, several holding to one another. One covered his ears and whimpered as thunder sounded outside.

Lift sank down onto an open mat, feeling surreal, out of place. She'd run all the way here, glowing with power, ready to face monsters that flew in the sky. But here . . . here she was just another orphaned urchin.

She closed her eyes, and listened to them.

"I'm frightened. Is the storm going to be long?"

"Why did everyone have to go inside?"

"I miss my mommy."

"What about the gummers in the alley? Will they be all right?"

Their uncertainty thrummed through Lift. She'd been here. After her mother died, she'd been here. She'd been here dozens of times since, in cities all across the land. Places for forgotten children.

She'd sworn an oath to remember people like them. She hadn't *meant* to. It had just kind of happened. Like everything in her life just kind of happened.

"I want control," she whispered.

"Mistress?" Wyndle said.

"Earlier today," she said. "You told me you didn't believe I'd come here for any of the reasons I'd said. You asked me what I wanted."

"I remember."

"I want control," she said, opening her eyes. "Not like a king or anything. I just want to be able to control it, a little. My life. I don't want to get shoved around, by people or by fate or whatever. I just . . . I want it to be me who chooses."

"I know little of the way your world works, mistress," he said, coiling up onto the wall, then making a face that hung out beside her. "But that seems like a reasonable desire."

"Listen to these kids talk. Do you hear them?"

"They're scared of the storm."

"And of the sudden call to hide. And of being alone. So uncertain . . ."

In the other room she could hear the Stump, talking softly to one of her older helpers. "I don't know. It's not the day for a highstorm. I'll put the spheres out up top, just in case. I wish someone would tell us what was happening."

"I don't understand, mistress," Wyndle said. "What is it I'm supposed to get from this observation?"

"Hush, Voidbringer," she said, still listening. Hearing. Then, she paused and opened her eyes. She frowned and stood, crossing the room.

A boy with a scar on his face was talking to one of the other boys. He looked up at Lift. "Hey," he said. "I know you. You saw my mom, right? Did she say when she was coming back?"

What was his name again? "Mik?"

"Yeah," he said. "Look, I don't belong here, right? I don't remember the last few weeks very well, but . . . I mean, I'm not an orphan. I've still got a mom."

It was him, the boy who had been dropped off the night before. *You were drooling then,* Lift thought. *And even at lunch, you were talking like an idiot. Storms. What did I do to you?* She couldn't heal people that were different in the head, or so she'd thought. What was the difference with him? Was it because he had a head wound, and wasn't born this way?

She didn't remember healing him. Storms . . . she said she wanted control, but she didn't even know how to use what she had. Her race to this place proved it.

The Stump strode back in with a large plate and began handing out pancakes to the children. She got to Lift, then handed her two. "This is the last," she said, wagging her finger.

"Thanks," Lift mumbled as the Stump moved on. The pancakes were cold, and unfortunately of a variety she'd already tried—the ones with sweet stuff in the middle. Her favorite. Maybe the Stump wasn't all bad.

She's a thief and a thug, Lift reminded herself as she ate, restoring her awesomeness. *She's laundering spheres and using an orphanage as cover.* But maybe even a thief and a thug could do some good along the way.

"I'm so confused," Wyndle said. "Mistress, what are you thinking?"

She looked toward the thick door to the outside. The old man was surely dead by now. Nobody would care; likely nobody would notice. One old man, found dead in an alley after the storm.

But Lift . . . Lift would remember him.

"Come on," she said. She stepped over to the door. When the Stump's back was turned to scold a child, Lift pushed up the bar and slipped outside.

18

THE hungry sky rumbled above, dark and angry. Lift knew that feeling. Too much time between meals, and looking to eat whatever it could find, never mind the cost.

The storm hadn't fully arrived yet, but from the distant lightning, it seemed that this new storm didn't have a stormwall. Its onset wouldn't be a sudden, majestic event, but instead a creeping advance. It loomed like a thug in an alley, knife out, waiting for prey to wander past.

Lift stepped up to the mouth of the alleyway beside the orphanage, then crept in, passing between shanties that looked far too flimsy to survive highstorms. Even if the city had been built to absolutely minimize winds, there was just so much *junk* in here. A particularly vigorous sneeze could leave half the people in the alley homeless.

They realized it too, as almost everyone here had gone to the storm bunkers. She did catch the odd face peeking suspiciously between rags draped on windows, anticipationspren growing up from the floor beside them like red streamers. They were people too stubborn, or perhaps too crazy, to be bothered. She didn't completely blame them. The government giving sudden, random orders and expecting everyone to hop? That was the sort of thing she usually ignored.

Except they should have seen the sky, heard the thunder. A flash of red lightning lit her surroundings. Today, these people should have listened.

She inched farther into the alleyway, entering a place of undefined shadows. With the clouds overhead—and everyone having taken their spheres away—the place was nearly impenetrable. So silent, the only sound that of the sky. Storms, was the old man actually in here? Maybe he was safe in a bunker somewhere. That scream from earlier could have been something unrelated, right?

No, she thought. *No, it wasn't.* She felt another chill run through her. Well, even if the old man was here, how would she find his body?

"Mistress," Wyndle whispered. "Oh, I don't like this place, mistress. Something's wrong."

Everything was wrong; it had been since Darkness had first stalked her. Lift continued on, past shadows that were probably laundry draped along strings between shanties. They looked like twisted, broken bodies in the gloom. Another flash of lightning from the approaching storm didn't help; the red light it cast made the walls and shanties seem painted with blood.

How long *was* this alleyway? She was relieved when, at last, she stumbled over something on the ground. She reached down, feeling at a clothed arm. A body.

I will remember you, Lift thought, leaning over and squinting, trying to make out the old man's shape.

"Mistress . . ." Wyndle whimpered. She felt him wrap around her leg and tighten there, like a child clinging to his mother.

What was that? She listened as the silence of the alley gave way to a clicking, scraping sound. It encircled her. And for the first time she noticed that the figure she was poking at didn't seem to be wrapped in a shiqua. The cloth on the arm was too stiff, too thick.

Mother, Lift thought, terrified. *What is happening?*

Lightning flashed, granting her a glimpse of the corpse. A woman's face stared upward with sightless eyes. A black and white uniform, painted crimson by the lightning and covered in some kind of silky substance.

Lift gasped and jumped backward, bumping into something behind her—another body. She spun, and the skittering, clicking sounds grew agitated. The next flash of lightning was bright enough for her to make out a body pressed against the wall of the alleyway, tied to part of a shanty, the head rolling to the side. She knew him, just as she knew the woman on the ground.

Darkness's two minions, Lift thought. *They're dead.*

"I heard an interesting idea once, while traveling in a land you will never visit."

Lift froze. It was the old man's voice.

"There are a group of people who believe that each day, when they sleep, they die," the old man continued. "They believe that consciousness doesn't continue—that if it is interrupted, a new soul is born when the body awakes."

Storms, storms, STORMS, Lift thought, spinning around. The walls seemed to be moving, shifting, sliding like they were covered in oil. She tried shying away from the corpses, but . . . she'd lost where they were. Was that the direction she'd come from, or did that lead deeper into this nightmare of an alleyway?

"This philosophy," the old man's voice said, "certainly has its problems, at least to an outside observer. What of memory, and continuity of culture, family, society? Well, the Omnithi teach that each are things you inherit in the morning from the previous soul that inhabited your body. Certain brain structures imprint memories, to help you live your single day of life as best you can."

"What are you?" Lift whispered, looking around frantically, trying to make sense of the darkness.

"What I find most interesting about these people is how they continue to exist at all," he said. "One would assume chaos would follow if each human sincerely believed that they had only one day to live. I wonder often what it says about you that these people with such dramatic beliefs live lives that are—basically—the same as the rest of you."

There, Lift thought, picking him out in the shadows. The shape of a man, though as lightning lit him she could see that he wasn't all there. Chunks were missing from his flesh. His right shoulder ended in a stump, and storms, he was naked, with strange holes in his stomach and thighs. Even one of his eyes was missing. There was no blood though, and in a quick succession of flashes she picked up something climbing his legs. Cremlings.

That was the skittering sound. Thousands upon thousands of cremlings coated the walls, each the size of a finger. Little beasts of chitin and legs clicking away and making that awful buzz.

"The thing about this philosophy is how difficult it is to disprove," the old man said. "How do you know that *you* are the same *you* as yesterday? You would never know if a new soul came to inhabit your body, so long as it had the same memories. But then . . . if it acts the same, and thinks it is you, why would it matter? What is it to be *you,* little Radiant?"

In the flashes of lightning—they were growing more common—she watched one of the cremlings crawl across his face, a bulbous protrusion hanging off its back. The thing crawled *into* the eye hole, and she realized that bulbous part was an eye. Other cremlings swarmed up and began filling in holes, forming the missing arm. Each had a portion on the back that resembled skin. It presented this outward, using its legs to interlock with the many others holding together on the inside of the body.

"To me," he said, "this is all no more than idle theory, as unlike you I do not sleep. At least, not all of me at once."

"What *are* you?" Lift said.

"Just another refugee."

Lift backed away. She didn't care anymore about going back in the direction she had come—so long as she got away from this thing.

"You needn't fear me," the old man said. "Your war is my war, and has been for millennia. Ancient Radiants named me friend and ally before everything went wrong. What wonderful days those were, before the Last Desolation. Days of . . . honor. Now gone, long gone."

"You killed these two people!" Lift hissed.

"In defense of myself." He chuckled. "I suppose that is a lie. They were not capable of killing me, so I can't plead self-defense, any more than a soldier could plead it in murdering a child. But they did ask, in not so many words, for a contest—and I gave it to them."

He stepped toward her, and a flash of lightning revealed him flexing his fingers on his newly formed hand as the thumb—a single cremling, with little spindly legs on the bottom—settled into place, tying itself into the others.

"But you," the thing said, "did not come for a contest, did you? We watch the others. The assassin. The surgeon. The liar. The highprince. But not you. The others all ignore you . . . and that, I hazard to predict, is a mistake."

He took out a sphere, bathing the place in a phantom glow, and smiled at her. She could see the lines crisscrossing his skin where the cremlings had fit themselves together, but they were nearly lost in the wrinkles of an aged body.

This was just the *likeness* of an old man though. A fabrication. Beneath that skin was not blood or muscle. It was hundreds of cremlings, pulling together to form a counterfeit man.

Many, many more of them still scuttled on the walls, now lit by his sphere. Lift could see that she'd somehow made it around the body of the fallen soldier, and was backing into a dead end between two shanties. She looked up. Didn't seem too difficult to climb, now that she had some light.

"If you flee," the thing noted, "he'll kill the one you wanted to save."

"You are just fine, I'm sure."

The monster chuckled. "Those two fools got it wrong. I'm not the one that Nale is chasing; he knows to stay away from me and my kind. No, there's someone else. He stalks them tonight, and *will* complete his task. Nale, madman, Herald of Justice, is not one to leave business unfinished."

Lift hesitated, hands in place on a shanty's eaves, ready to haul herself up and start climbing. The cremlings on the walls—she'd never seen so many at once—scuttled aside, making room for her to pass.

He knew to let her run, if she wanted to. Clever monster.

Nearby, bathed in cool light that seemed bright as a bonfire compared to what she'd stumbled through before, the creature unwrapped a black shiqua. He started winding it around his right arm.

"I like this place," he explained. "Where else would I have the excuse to cover my entire body? I've spent thousands of years breeding my hordelings, and still I can't make them fit together quite *right*. I can pass for human almost as well as a Siah can these days, I'd hazard, but anyone who looks closely finds something off. It's rather frustrating."

"What do you know about Darkness and his plans?" Lift demanded. "And Radiants, and Voidbringers, and *everything*?"

"That's quite the exhaustive list," he said. "And I confess, I am the wrong one to ask. My siblings are more interested in you Radiants. If you ever encounter another of the Sleepless, tell them you've spoken with Arclo. I'm certain it will gain you sympathy."

"That wasn't an answer. Not the kind I wanted."

"I'm not here to answer you, human. I'm here because I'm interested, and you are the source of my curiosity. When one achieves immortality, one must find purpose beyond the struggle to live, as old Axies always said."

"You seem to have found purpose in talkin' a whole bunch," Lift said. "Without being helpful to nobody." She scrambled up on top of the shanty, but didn't go any higher. Wyndle climbed the wall beside her, and the cremlings shied away from him. They could sense him?

"I'm helping with far more than your little personal problem. I'm building a philosophy, one meaningful enough to span ages. You see, child, I can *grow* what I need. Is my mind becoming full? I can breed new hordelings specialized in holding memories. Do I need to sense what is going on in the city? Hordelings with extra eyes, or antennae to taste and hear, can solve that. Given time, I can make for my body nearly anything I need.

"But you . . . you are stuck with only one body. So how do you make it work? I have come to suspect that men in a city are each part of some greater organism they can't see—like the hordelings that make up my kind."

"That's great," Lift said. "But earlier, you said that Darkness was hunting someone *else*? You think he still hasn't killed his prey in the city?"

"Oh, I'm certain he hasn't. He hunts them right now. He will know that his minions have failed."

The storm rumbled above, close. She itched to leave, to find shelter. But . . .

"Tell me," she said. "Who is it?"

The creature smiled. "A secret. And we are in Tashikk, are we not? Shall we trade? You answer me honestly regarding my questions, and I'll give you a hint."

"Why me?" Lift said. "Why not bother someone else with these questions? At another time?"

"Oh, but you're so *interesting*." He wrapped the shiqua around his waist, then down his leg, then back up it, crossing to the other leg. His cremlings coursed around him. Several climbed up his face, and his eyes crawled out, new ones replacing them so that he went from being dark-eyed to light.

He spoke as he dressed. "You, Lift, are different from anyone else. If each city is a creature, then you are a most special organ. Traveling from place to place, bringing change, transformation. You Knights Radiant . . . I must know how you see yourselves. It will be an important corner of my philosophy."

I am special, she thought. *I'm awesome.*

So why don't I know what to do?

The secret fear crept out. The creature kept talking his strange speech: about cities, people, and their places. He praised her, but each offhand comment about how special she was made her wince. A storm was almost here, and Darkness was about to murder in the night. All she could do was crouch in the presence of two corpses and a monster made of little squirming pieces.

Listen, Lift. Are you listening? People, they don't listen anymore.

"Yes, but how did the city of your birth know to create you?" the creature was saying. "I can breed individual pieces to do as I wish. What bred you? And why was this city able to summon you here now?"

Again that question. *Why are you here?*

"What if I'm *not* special," Lift whispered. "Would that be okay too?"

The creature stopped and looked at her. On the wall, Wyndle whimpered.

"What if I've been lying all along," Lift said. "What if I'm not *strictly* awesome. What if I don't know what to do?"

"Instinct will guide you, I'm sure."

I feel lost, like a soldier on a battlefield who can't remember which banner is hers, the guard captain's voice said.

Listening. She was listening, wasn't she?

Half the time, I get the sense that even kings are confused by the world. Ghenna the scribe's voice.

Nobody listened anymore.

I wish someone would tell us what was happening. The Stump's voice.

"What if you're wrong though?" Lift whispered. "What if 'instinct' doesn't guide us? What if everybody is frightened, and nobody has the answers?"

It was the conclusion that had always been too intimidating to consider. It terrified her.

Did it have to, though? She looked up at the wall, at Wyndle surrounded by cremlings that snapped at him. Her own little Voidbringer.

Listen.

Lift hesitated, then patted him. She just . . . she just had to accept it, didn't she?

In a moment, she felt relief akin to her terror. She was in darkness, but well, maybe she'd manage anyway.

Lift stood up. "I left Azir because I was afraid. I came to Tashikk because that's where my starvin' feet took me. But tonight . . . tonight I *decided* to be here."

"What is this nonsense?" Arclo asked. "How does it help my philosophy?"

She cocked her head as a realization struck her, like a jolt of power. *Huh. Fancy that, would you?*

"I . . . didn't heal that boy," she whispered.

"What?"

"The Stump trades spheres for ones of lesser value, probably swapping dun ones for infused ones. She launders money because she *needs the Stormlight;* she probably feeds on it without realizing what she's doing!" Lift looked down at Arclo, grinning. "Don't you see? She takes care of the kids who were born sick, lets them stay. It's because her powers don't know how to heal those. The rest, though, they get better. They do it so suspiciously often that she's started to believe that kids must *come to her faking* to get food. The Stump . . . is a Radiant."

The Sleepless creature met her eyes, then sighed. "We will speak again another time. Like Nale, I am not one to leave tasks unfinished."

He tossed his sphere along the alleyway, and it plinked against stone, rolling back toward the orphanage. Lighting the way for Lift as she jumped down and started running.

19

THE thunder chased her. Wind howled through the city's slots, windspren zipping past her, as if fleeing the advent of the strange storm. The wind pushed against Lift's back, blowing scraps of paper and refuse around her. She reached the small amphitheater at the mouth of the alley, and hazarded a glance behind her.

She stumbled to a stop, stunned.

The storm *surged* across the sky, a majestic and terrible black thunderhead coursing with red lightning. It was enormous, dominating the entire sky, wicked with flashes of inner light.

Raindrops started to pelt her, and though there was no stormwall, the wind was already growing tempestuous.

Wyndle grew in a circle around her. "Mistress? Mistress, oh, this is bad."

She stepped back, transfixed by the boiling mass of black and red. Lightning sprayed down across the slots, and thunder hit her with so much force, it felt as if she should have been flung backward.

"Mistress!"

"Inside," Lift said, scrambling toward the door into the orphanage. It was so dark, she could barely make out the wall. But as she arrived, she immediately noticed something wrong. The door was open.

Surely they'd closed it after she'd left? She slipped in. The room beyond was black, impenetrable, but feeling at the door told her that the bar had been cut right through. Probably from the outside, and with a weapon that sliced wood cleanly. A Shardblade.

Trembling, Lift felt for the cut portion of the bar on the floor, then managed to fit it into place, holding the door closed. She turned in the room, listening. She could hear the whimpers of the children, choked sobs.

"Mistress," Wyndle whispered. "You can't fight him."

I know.

"There are Words that you must speak."

They won't help.

Tonight, the Words were the easy part.

It was hard not to adopt the fear of the children around her. Lift found herself trembling, and stopped somewhere in the center of the room. She couldn't creep along, stumbling over other kids, if she wanted to stop Darkness.

Somewhere distant in the multistory orphanage, she heard thumping. Firm, booted feet on the wooden floors of the second story.

Lift drew in her awesomeness, and started to glow. Light rose from her arms like steam from a hot griddle. It wasn't terribly bright, but in that pure-black room it was enough to show her the children she had heard. They grew quiet, watching her with awe.

"Darkness!" Lift shouted. "The one they call Nin, or Nale! Nakku, the Judge! I'm here."

The thumping above stopped. Lift crossed the room, stepping into the next one and looking up a stairwell. "It's me!" she shouted up it. "The one you tried—and failed—to kill in Azir."

The door to the amphitheater rattled as wind shook it, like someone was outside trying to get in. The footfalls started again, and Darkness appeared at the top of the stairs, holding an amethyst sphere in one hand, a glittering Shardblade in the other. The violet light lit his face from below, outlining his chin and cheeks, but leaving his eyes dark.

They seemed hollow, like the sockets of the creature Lift had met outside.

"I am surprised to see you accept judgment," Darkness said. "I had thought you would remain in presumed safety."

"Yeah," Lift called. "You know, the day the Almighty was handin' out brains to folks? I went out for flatbread that day."

"You come here during a highstorm," Darkness said. "You are trapped in here with me, and I know of your crimes in this city."

"But I got back by the time the Almighty was givin' out looks," Lift called. "What kept you?"

The insult appeared to have no effect, though it was one of her favorites. Darkness seemed to flow like smoke as he started down the stairs, footsteps growing softer, uniform rippling in an unseen wind. Storms, but he looked so *official* in that outfit with the long cuffs, the crisp jacket. Like the very incarnation of law.

Lift scrambled to the right, away from the children, deeper into the orphanage's ground floor. She smelled spices in this direction, and let her nose guide her into a dark kitchen.

"Up the wall," she ordered Wyndle, who grew along it beside the doorway. Lift snatched a tuber from the counter, then grabbed on to Wyndle and climbed. She quieted her awesomeness, becoming dark as she reached the place where wall met ceiling, clinging to Wyndle's thin vines.

Darkness entered below, looking right, then left. He didn't look up, so when he stepped forward, Lift dropped behind him.

Darkness immediately spun, whipping that Shardblade around with a single-handed grip. It sheared through the wall of the doorway and passed a finger's width in front of Lift as she threw herself backward.

She hit the floor and burst alight with awesomeness, Slicking her backside so she slid across the floor away from him, eventually colliding with the wall just below the steps. She untangled her limbs and started climbing the steps on all fours.

"You're an insult to the order you would claim," Darkness said, striding after her.

"Sure, probably," Lift called. "Storms, I'm an insult to my own *self* most days."

"Of course you are," Darkness said, reaching the bottom of the steps. "That sentence has no meaning."

She stuck her tongue out at him. A totally *rational* and *reasonable* way to fight a demigod. He didn't seem to mind, but then, he wouldn't. He had a lump of crusty earwax for a heart. So tragic.

The second floor of the orphanage was filled with smaller rooms, to her left. To her right, another flight of steps led farther upward. Lift dashed left, choking down the uncooked longroot, looking for the Stump. Had Darkness gotten to her? Several rooms held bunks for the children. So the Stump didn't make them sleep in that one big room; they'd probably gathered there because of the storm.

"Mistress!" Wyndle said. "Do you have a plan!"

"I can make Stormlight," Lift said, puffing and drawing a little awesomeness as she checked the room across the hall.

"Yes. Baffling, but true."

"He can't. And spheres are rare, 'cuz nobody expected the storm that came in the middle of the Weeping. So . . ."

"Ah . . . Maybe we wear him down!"

"Can't fight him," Lift said. "Seems the best alternative. Might have to sneak down and get more food though." Where *was* the Stump? No sign of her hiding in these rooms, but also no sign of her murdered corpse.

Lift ducked back into the hallway. Darkness dominated the other end, near the steps. He walked slowly toward her, Shardblade held in a strange reverse grip, with the dangerous end pointing out behind him.

Lift quieted her awesomeness and stopped glowing. She needed to run him out, and maybe make him think she was running low, so he wouldn't conserve.

"I am sorry I must do this," Darkness said. "Once I would have welcomed you as a sister."

"No," Lift said. "You're not really sorry, are you? Can you even *feel* something like sorrow?"

He stopped in the hallway, sphere still gripped before him for light. He actually seemed to be considering her question.

Well, time to move then. She couldn't afford to get cornered, and sometimes that meant charging at the guy with a starvin' Shardblade. He set himself in a swordsman's stance as she dashed toward him, then stepped forward to swing.

Lift shoved herself to the side and Slicked herself, dodging his sword and sliding along the ground to his left. She got past him, but something about it felt too easy. Darkness watched her with careful, discerning eyes. He'd expected to miss her, she was sure of it.

He spun and advanced on her again, stepping quickly to prevent her from getting down the steps to the ground floor. This positioned her near the steps going upward. Darkness seemed to want her to go that direction, so she resisted, backing up along the hallway. Unfortunately, there was only one room on this end, the one above the kitchen. She kicked open the door, looking in. The Stump's bedroom, with a dresser and bedding on the floor. No sign of the Stump herself.

Darkness continued to advance. "You are right. It seems I have finally released myself from the last vestiges of guilt I once felt at doing my duty. Honor has suffused me, changed me. It has been a long time coming."

"Great. So you're like . . . some kind of emotionless spren now."

"Hey," Wyndle said. "That's insulting."

"No," Darkness said, unable to hear Wyndle. "I'm merely a man, perfected." He waved toward her with his sphere. "Men need light, child. Alone we are in darkness, our movements random, based on subjective, changeable minds. But light is pure, and does not change based on our daily whims. To feel guilt at following a code with precision is wasted emotion."

"And other emotion isn't, in your opinion?"

"There are many useful emotions."

"Which you totally feel, all the time."

"Of course I do. . . ." He trailed off, and again seemed to be considering what she'd said. He cocked his head.

Lift jumped forward, Slicking herself again. He was guarding the way down, but she needed to slip past him anyway and head back below. Grab some food, keep him moving up and down until he ran out of power. She anticipated him swinging the sword, and as he did, she shoved herself to the side, her entire body Slick except the palm of her hand, for steering.

Darkness dropped his sphere and moved with sudden, unexpected speed, bursting afire with Stormlight. He dropped his Shardblade, which puffed away, and seized a knife from his belt. As Lift passed, he slammed it down and caught her clothing.

Storms! A normal wound, her awesomeness would have healed. If he'd tried to grab her, she'd have been too Slick, and would have wriggled away. But his knife bit into the wood and caught her by the tail of her overshirt, jerking her to a stop. Slicked as she was, she just kind of bounced and slid back toward him.

He put his hand to the side, summoning his Blade again as Lift frantically scrambled to free herself. The knife had sunk in deeply, and he kept one hand on it. Storms, he was strong! Lift bit his arm, to no effect. She struggled to pull off the overshirt, Slicking herself but not it.

His Shardblade appeared, and he raised it. Lift floundered, half blinded by her shirt, which she had halfway up over her head, obscuring most of her view. But she could feel that Blade descending on her—

Something went *smack,* and Darkness grunted.

Lift peeked out and saw the Stump standing on the steps upward, holding a large length of wood. Darkness shook his head, trying to clear it, and the Stump hit him again.

"Leave my kids alone, you monster," she growled at him. Water dripped from her. She'd taken her spheres up to the top of the building, to charge them. Of course that was where she'd been. She'd mentioned it earlier.

She raised the length of wood above her head. Darkness sighed, then swiped with his Blade, cutting her weapon in half. He pulled his dagger from the ground, freeing Lift. *Yes!*

Then he kicked her, sending her sliding down the hallway on her own Slickness, completely out of control.

"No!" Lift said, withdrawing her Slickness and rolling to a stop. Her vision shook as she saw Darkness turn on the Stump and grab her by the throat, then pull her off the steps and throw her to the ground. The old lady *cracked* as she hit, and fell limp, motionless.

He stabbed her then—not with his Blade, but with his *knife*. Why? Why not finish her?

He turned toward Lift, shadowed by the sphere he'd dropped, more a monster in that moment than the Sleepless thing Lift had seen in the alleyway.

"Still alive," he said to Lift. "But bleeding and unconscious." He kicked his sphere away. "She is too new to know how to feed on Stormlight in this state. You I'll have to impale and wait until you are truly dead. This one though, she can just bleed out. It's happening already."

I can heal her, Lift thought, desperate.

He knew that. He was baiting her.

She no longer had time to run him out of Stormlight. Pointing the Shardblade toward Lift, he was now truly just a silhouette. Darkness. True Darkness.

"I don't know what to do," Lift said.

"Say the Words," Wyndle said from beside her.

"I've said them, in my heart." But what good would they do?

Too few people listened to anything other than their own thoughts. But what good would listening do her here? All she could hear was the sound of the storm outside, lightning making the stones vibrate.

Thunder.

A new storm.

I can't defeat him. I've got to change him.

Listen.

Lift scrambled toward Darkness, summoning all of her remaining awesomeness. Darkness stepped forward, knife in one hand, Shardblade in the other. She got near to him, and again he guarded the steps downward. He obviously expected her either to go that way, or to stop at the Stump's unconscious body and try to heal her.

Lift did neither. She slid past them both, then turned and scrambled up the steps the Stump had come down a short time earlier.

Darkness cursed, swinging for her, but missing. She reached the third floor, and he charged after her. "You're leaving her to die," he warned, giving chase as Lift found a smaller set of steps that led upward. Onto the roof, hopefully. Had to get him to follow . . .

A trapdoor in the ceiling barred her way, but she flung it open. She emerged into Damnation itself.

Terrible winds, broken by that awful red lightning. A horrific tempest of stinging rain. The "rooftop" was just the flat plain above the city, and Lift didn't spot the Stump's sphere cage. The rain was too blinding, the winds too terrible. She stepped from the trapdoor, but had to immediately huddle down, clinging to the rocks. Wyndle formed handholds for her, whimpering, holding her tightly.

Darkness emerged into the storm, rising from the hole in the clifftop. He saw her, then stepped forward, hefting his Shardblade like an axe.

He swung.

Lift screamed. She let go of Wyndle's vines and raised both hands above herself.

Wyndle sighed a long, soft sigh, melting away, transforming into a silvery length of metal.

She met Darkness's descending Blade with her own weapon. Not a sword. Lift didn't know crem about swords. Her weapon was just a silvery rod. It glowed in the darkness, and it blocked Darkness's blow, though his attack left her arms quivering.

Ow, Wyndle's voice said in her head.

Rain beat around them, and crimson lightning blasted down behind Darkness, leaving stark afterimages in Lift's eyes.

"You think you can fight me, child?" he growled, holding his Blade against her rod. "I who have lived immortal lives? I who have slain demigods and survived Desolations? I am the Herald of Justice."

"I will listen," Lift shouted, "to those who have been ignored!"

"What?" Darkness demanded.

"I heard what you said, Darkness! You were trying to prevent the Desolation. Look behind you! Deny what you're seeing!"

Lightning broke the air and howls rose in the city. Across the farmlands, the ruby glare revealed a huddled clump of people. A sorry, sad group. The poor parshmen who had been evicted.

The red lightning seemed to linger with them.

Their eyes were glowing.

"No," Nale said. The storm appeared to withdraw, briefly, around his words. "An . . . isolated event. Parshmen who had . . . who had survived with their forms . . ."

"You've failed," Lift shouted. "It's come."

Nale looked up at the thunderheads, rumbling with power, red light ceaselessly roiling within.

In that moment it seemed, strangely, that something within him emerged. It was stupid of her to think that with everything happening— the rain, the winds, the red lightning—she could see a difference in his eyes. But she swore that she could.

He seemed to focus, like a person waking up from a daze. His sword dropped from his fingers and puffed away into mist.

Then he slumped to his knees. "Storms. Jezrien . . . Ishar . . . It is true. I've failed." He bowed his head.

And he started weeping.

Puffing, feeling clammy and pained by the rain, Lift lowered her rod.

"I failed weeks ago," Nale said. "I knew it then. Oh, God. God the Almighty. It has returned!"

"I'm sorry," Lift said.

He looked to her, face lit red by the continuous lightning, tears mixing with the rain.

"You actually are," he said, then felt at his face. "I wasn't always like this. I *am* getting worse, aren't I? It's true."

"I don't know," Lift said. And then, by instinct, she did something she would never have thought possible.

She hugged Darkness.

He clung to her, this monster, this callous thing that had once been a Herald. He clung to her and wept in the storm. Then, with a crash of thunder, he pushed away from her. He stumbled on the slick rock, blown by the winds, then started to glow.

He shot into the dark sky and vanished. Lift heaved herself to her feet, and rushed down to heal the Stump.

20

So you don't hafta be a sword," Lift said. She sat on the Stump's dresser, 'cuz the woman didn't have a proper desk for her to claim.

"A sword is traditional," Wyndle said.

"But you don't *hafta* be one."

"Obviously not," he said, sounding offended. "I must be metal. There is . . . a connection between our power, when condensed, and metal. That said, I've heard stories of spren becoming bows. I don't know how they'd make the string. Perhaps the Radiant carried their own string?"

Lift nodded, but she was barely listening. Who cared about bows and swords and stuff? This opened all *kinds* of more interesting possibilities.

"I do wonder what I'd look like as a sword," Wyndle said.

"You went around all day yesterday *complainin'* about me hitting someone with you!"

"I don't want to be a sword that one *swings*, obviously. But there is something stately about a Shardblade, something to be displayed. I would make a fine one, I should think. Very regal."

A knock came at the door downstairs, and Lift perked up. Unfortunately, it didn't sound like the scribe. She heard the Stump talking to someone who had a soft voice. The door closed shortly thereafter, and the Stump climbed the steps and entered Lift's room, carrying a large plate of pancakes.

Lift's stomach growled, and she stood up on the dresser. "Now, those are *your* pancakes, right?"

The Stump, looking as wizened as ever, stopped in place. "What does it matter?"

"It matters a *ton*," Lift said. "Those aren't for the kids. You was gonna eat those yourself, right?"

"A dozen pancakes."

"Yes."

"Sure," the Stump said, rolling her eyes. "We'll pretend I was going to eat them all myself." She dropped them onto the dresser beside Lift, who started stuffing her face.

The Stump folded her bony arms, glancing over her shoulder.

"Who was at the door?" Lift asked.

"A mother. Come to insist, ashamed, that she wanted her child back."

"No kidding?" Lift said around bites of pancake. "Mik's mom actually came *back* for him?"

"Obviously she knew her son had been faking his illness. It was part of a scam to . . ." The Stump trailed off.

Huh, Lift thought. The mom couldn't have known that Mik had been healed—it had only happened yesterday, and the city was a mess following the storm. Fortunately, it wasn't as bad here as it could have been. Storms blowing one way or the other, in Yeddaw it didn't matter.

She was starvin' for information about the rest of the empire though. Seemed everything had gone wrong again, just in a new way this time.

Still, it was nice to hear a little good news. *Mik's mom actually came back. Guess it does happen once in a while.*

"I've been healing the children," the Stump said. She fingered her shiqua, which had been stabbed clean through by Darkness. Though she'd washed it, her blood had stained the cloth. "You're sure about this?"

"Yeah," Lift said around a bite of pancakes. "You should have a weird little thing hanging around you. Not me. Something *weirder*. Like a vine?"

"A spren," the Stump said. "Not like a vine. Like light reflected on a wall from a mirror . . ."

Lift glanced at Wyndle, who clung to the wall nearby. He nodded his vine face.

"Sure, that'll do. Congrats. You're a starvin' Knight Radiant, Stump. You've been feasting on spheres and healing kids. Probably makes up some for treatin' them like old laundry, eh?"

The Stump regarded Lift, who continued to munch on pancakes.

"I would have thought," the Stump said, "that Knights Radiant would be more majestic."

Lift scrunched up her face at the woman, then thrust her hand to the side and summoned Wyndle in the shape of a large, shimmering, silvery fork. A Shardfork, if you would.

She stabbed him into the pancakes, and unfortunately he went all the way through them, through the plate, and poked holes in the Stump's dresser. Still, she managed to pry up a pancake.

Lift took a big bite out of it. "Majestic as Damnation's own gonads," she proclaimed, then wagged Wyndle at the Stump. "That's saying it fancy-style, so my fork don't complain that I'm bein' crass."

The Stump seemed to have trouble coming up with a response to that, other than to stare at Lift with her jaw slack. She was rescued from looking dumb by someone pounding on the door below. One of the Stump's assistants opened it, but the woman herself hastened down the steps as soon as she heard who it was.

Lift dismissed Wyndle. Eating with your hands was way easier than eating with a fork, even a *very nice* fork. He formed back into a vine and curled up on the wall.

A short time later, Ghenna—the fat scribe from the Grand Indifference—stepped in. Judging by the way the Stump practically scraped the ground bowing to the woman, Lift judged that maybe Ghenna was more important than she'd assumed. Bet she didn't have a magic fork though.

"Normally," the scribe said, "I don't frequent such . . . domiciles as this. People usually come to me."

"I can tell," Lift said. "You obviously don't walk about very much."

The scribe sniffed at that, laying a satchel down on the bed. "His Imperial Majesty has been somewhat cross with us for cutting off the communication before. But he is understanding, as he must be, considering recent events."

"How's the empire doing?" Lift said, chewing on a pancake.

"Surviving," the scribe said. "But in chaos. Smaller villages were hit the worst, but although the storm was longer than a highstorm, its winds were not as bad. The worst was the lightning, which struck many who were unlucky enough to be out traveling."

She unpacked her tools: a spanreed board, paper, and pen. "His Imperial Majesty was very pleased that you contacted me, and he has already sent a message asking for the details of your health."

"Tell him I ain't eaten nearly enough pancakes," Lift said. "And I got this strange wart on my toe that keeps growin' back when I cut it off—I think because I heal myself with my awesomeness, which is starvin' inconvenient."

The scribe looked to her, then sighed and read the message that Gawx had sent her. The empire would survive, it said, but would take long to recover—particularly if the storm kept returning. And then there was the issue with the parshmen, which could prove an even greater danger. He didn't want to share state secrets over spanreed. Mostly he wanted to know if she was all right.

She kind of was. The scribe took to writing what Lift had told her, which would be enough to tell Gawx that she was well.

"Also," Lift added as the woman wrote, "I found another Radiant, only she's *real* old, and kinda looks like an underfed crab without no shell." She looked to the Stump, and shrugged in a half apology. Surely she knew. She had mirrors, right?

"But she's actually kind of nice, and takes care of kids, so we should recruit her or something. If we fight Voidbringers, she can stare at them in a real mean way. They'll break down and tell her all about that time when they ate all the cookies and blamed it on Huisi, the girl what can't talk right."

Huisi snored anyway. She deserved it.

The scribe rolled her eyes, but wrote it. Lift nodded, finishing off the last pancake, a type with a real thick, almost mealy texture. "Okay," she proclaimed, standing up. "That's nine. What's the last one? I'm ready."

"The last one?" the Stump asked.

"Ten types of pancakes," Lift said. "It's why I came to this starvin' city. I've had nine now. Where's the last one?"

"The tenth is dedicated to Tashi," the scribe said absently as she wrote. "It is more a thought than a real entity. We bake nine, and leave the last in memory of Him."

"Wait," Lift said. "So there's only *nine*?"

"Yes."

"You all *lied* to me?"

"Not in so much—"

"Damnation! Wyndle, where'd that Skybreaker go? He's got to hear about this." She pointed at the scribe, then at the Stump. "He let you go for that whole money-laundering thing on my insistence. But when he hears you been *lying* about *pancakes*, I might not be able to hold him back."

Both of them stared at her, as if they thought they were innocent. Lift shook her head, then hopped off the dresser. "Excuse me," she said. "I gotta find the Radiant refreshment room. That's a fancy way of saying—"

"Down the stairs," the Stump said. "On the left. Same place it was this morning."

Lift left them, skipping down the stairs. Then she winked at one of the orphans watching in the main room before slipping out the front door, Wyndle on the ground beside her. She took a deep breath of the wet air, still soggy from the Everstorm. Refuse, broken boards, fallen branches, and discarded cloths littered the ground, snarling up at the many steps that jutted into the street.

But the city *had* survived, and people were already at work cleaning up. They'd lived their entire lives in the shadow of highstorms. They had adapted, and would continue to adapt.

Lift smiled, and started off along the street.

"We're leaving, then?" Wyndle asked.

"Yup."

"Just like that. No farewells."

"Nope."

"This is how it's going to be, isn't it? We'll wander into a city, but before there's time to put down roots, we'll be off again?"

"Sure," Lift said. "Though this time, I thought we might wander back to Azimir and the palace."

Wyndle was so stunned he let her pass him by. Then he zipped up to join her, eager as an axehound puppy. "Really? Oh, mistress. *Really?*"

"I figure," she said, "that nobody knows what they're doin' in life, right? So Gawx and the dusty viziers, they need me." She tapped her head. "I got it figured out."

"You've got what figured out?"

"Nothing at all," Lift said, with the utmost confidence.

But I will listen to those who are ignored, she thought. *Even people like Darkness, whom I'd rather never have heard. Maybe that will help.*

They wound through the city, then up the ramp, passing the guard captain, who was on duty there dealing with the even *larger* numbers of refugees coming to the city because they'd lost homes to the storm. She saw Lift, and nearly jumped out of her own boots in surprise.

Lift smiled and dug a pancake out of her pocket. This woman had been visited by Darkness because of her. That sort of thing earned you a debt. So she tossed the woman the pancake—which was really more of a pan*ball* at this point—then used the Stormlight she'd gotten from the ones she'd eaten to start healing the wounds of the refugees.

The guard captain watched in silence, holding her pancake, as Lift moved along the line breathing out Stormlight on everyone like she was tryin' to prove her breath didn't stink none.

It was starvin' hard work. But that was what pancakes was for, makin' kids feel better. Once she was done, and out of Stormlight, she tiredly waved and strode onto the plain outside the city.

"That was very benevolent of you," Wyndle said.

Lift shrugged. It didn't seem like it had made much of a difference— just a few people, and all. But they *were* the type that were forgotten and ignored by most.

"A better knight than me might stay," Lift said. "Heal everyone."

"A big project. Perhaps too big."

"And too small, all the same," Lift said, shoving her hands in her pockets, and walked for a time. She couldn't rightly explain it, but she knew that something larger was coming. And she needed to get to Azir.

Wyndle cleared his throat. Lift braced herself to hear him complain about something, like the silliness of walking all the way here from Azimir, only to walk right back two days later.

". . . I was a very *regal* fork, wouldn't you say?" he asked instead.

Lift glanced at him, then grinned and cocked her head. "Y'know, Wyndle. It's strange, but . . . I'm starting to think you might not be a Voidbringer after all."

POSTSCRIPT

Lift is one of my favorite characters from the Stormlight Archive, despite the fact that she has had very little screen time so far. I'm grooming her for a larger role in the future of the series, but this leaves me with some challenges. By the time Lift becomes a main Stormlight character, she'll have already sworn several of the oaths—and it feels wrong not to show readers the context of her swearing those oaths.

In working on Stormlight Three, I also noticed a small continuity issue. By the time we see him again in that book, the Herald Nale will have accepted that his work of many centuries (watching and making sure the Radiants don't return) is no longer relevant. This is a major shift in who he is and in his goals as an individual—and it felt wrong to have him undergo this realization offscreen.

Edgedancer, then, was an opportunity to fix both of these problems—and to give Lift her own showcase.

Part of my love of writing Lift has to do with the way I get to slip character growth and meaningful moments into otherwise odd or silly-sounding phrases. Such as the fact that in the novelette from *Words of Radiance* she says she's been ten for three years (as a joke) can be foreshadowing with a laugh, which then develops into the fact that she actually thinks her aging stopped at ten. (And has good reason to think that.)

This isn't the sort of thing you can do as a writer with most characters.

I also used this story as an opportunity to show off the Tashikki people, who (not having any major viewpoint characters) were likely not going to get any major development in the main series.

The original plan for this novella was for it to be 18,000 words. It ended up at around 40,000. Ah well. That just happens sometimes. (Particularly when you are me.)

Rich Men, Single Women

Pamela Beck and Patti Massman are Hollywood
screenwriters, and authors of the bestselling novel
Fling. The authors are extraordinary storytellers who
know how to capture the contemporary life-style of
today's career woman while tapping into her secret
desire for the perfect man.

Pamela Beck and
Patti Massman

Rich Men,
Single Women

Pan Books
London, Sydney and Auckland

First published in Great Britain in 1988 by
Sidgwick & Jackson Limited
This edition published 1989 by Pan Books Ltd,
Cavaye Place, London SW10 9PG
9 8 7 6 5 4 3 2
© 1988 Pamela Beck and Patti Massman
ISBN 0 330 30761 4

Printed and bound in Great Britain by
Richard Clay Limited, Bungay, Suffolk

Grateful acknowledgement is made for permission to
reprint excerpts from *Breaking Free: 20 Ways to Leave Your Lover*
by William Fezler. Copyright © 1965.
Reprinted by permission of Acropolis Books Ltd, Washington, DC.

Once again, to the men in our lives who have by being
themselves made our lives rich.

Dennis, Brandon, and Dustin Beck
Stephen, Michael, and Brent Massman

Acknowledgments

Ken Ballard, Andrea Bell, Patricia Mendes Caldeira, Alfredo and Shyval Dodds, Cathy Fine, Alex Glant, Elliot Gottfurcht, Lynn Hiller and Bob Hollman for their vivid accounts and insights which enabled us to paint with accuracy and detail the world in which you are about to meet our characters.

. . . And to Susie Nace, who taught us how to read our characters' minds.

To Marjorie Miller whose love, guidance, and inspiration will keep her forever in our hearts.

To our friends at Dell/Delacorte, Carole Baron, Jackie Farber, and Susan Moldow for their great enthusiasm and for the outstanding job we know they will once again perform for us.

To our very special and unique literary agent, Ed Victor, who was *always* available, *always* supportive, and whose understanding and sensitivity to a writer's fragile makeup never failed to keep us going.

To Dennis Beck, our third and silent partner (though not always so silent). We thank you for your editorial advice, your business advice, and for being our general encyclopedia.

And finally another special thank you to all our single friends (although some of you are no longer single) for your frank and valuable input. In fact, you imparted *such* intimate and revealing material in some instances, we've decided to keep your identity confidential. But you know who you are. . . .

Rich Men, Single Women

Chapter 1 ⌒

From rags to riches—it was a modern-day Cinderella story. Only, she didn't slave by the hearth, she slaved over legal memorandums in a Century City law firm, and her rags were not really rags, but knockoffs of designer labels. And, finally, her prince was not really a prince, but a very rich client who fell madly in love with his lovely young female lawyer, a feisty brunette from Brooklyn. And the pair was to live happily ever after in Beverly Hills.

Paige Williams was positively green with envy at the fairy-talelike way things had turned out for her oldest and dearest friend, Kit Thorton.

Reveling in unaccustomed luxury, she looked around the all-white cloudlike bedroom, which seemed to be the perfect backdrop for all this elegant flurry, the age-old ritual of readying the bride. Across the hall in the master suite was the bride, being preened for that long-awaited march down the wedding aisle. Poised at its finish line would be the kind of prize prince Paige herself had nearly given up on finding. He was rich, nice-looking, divorced, *but* with no kids, and according to Kit, he was even a nice guy.

Lucky Kit, Paige thought with a keen awareness of the contrasts that had developed in their lives over the last decade or so since Kit had moved with her family out to California. Their shared childhood in New York felt like a lifetime ago. Paige and Kit had kept up with one another faithfully over the years, scratching out addresses and telephone numbers as they moved through their respective courses: Kit going the route of law school, then joining a prestigious firm in L.A. near her family; Paige going the route of Broadway, pursuing a dream she had never been able to relinquish. It wasn't until recently that she had actually come to terms with the fact that her desire was bigger than her talent. She had the calling all right—it was in her blood —but she didn't have the acting ability to back it up. The truth was, it had been her dancing that had kept food on her table all these years—hamburgers instead of steak.

"I could definitely get used to this," Paige remarked wryly, crossing over to the small antique table that had been laid out with what the bride had casually referred to as snacks. *Some kind of snack,* she thought, coating a light, intentionally bland French cracker with a layer of sour cream, then adding a thick smear of the pearl-gray beluga caviar they had been consuming in great quantities all weekend. She took a bite of it, careful not to lose any crumbs to the woven white carpet beneath her, then sighed, exulting in the exquisite blend of texture, taste, and privilege. It summed up the weekend beautifully.

"Why her and not me? That's what I keep asking myself!" Paige was careful to make it sound like a joke as she addressed Kit's other two bridesmaids. They were all three lounging around in the silk robes Kit had given them as gifts for being part of the wedding party, and Paige wondered if they didn't feel the envy as acutely as she did. Kit's life looked like it was going to be ambrosia from here on in, while they were all struggling in one way or another.

Tori Mitchell, Kit's long-legged raven-haired cousin from Atlanta, glanced up at Paige from behind a thick issue of *Town & Country,* looking like she belonged on its glossy cover. "Poor Kit. She's been as gracious and generous as a person can be, and here we are all jealous as hell!" she exclaimed in her cute Georgia drawl.

The truth was, Paige didn't think Tori had a jealous bone in her long willowy body. Tori's uptight and aggressive mother, on the other hand, who had come out for her niece's wedding, appeared to have enough jealousy to go around for a whole town, certainly for Buckhead, the elite suburb of Atlanta where Tori grew up.

Although Tori was putting on a commendable front, Paige and Kit's other bridesmaid, Susan Kendell Brown, both knew it was *only* a front. They had seen Tori's mother issuing digs all weekend. Her niece had achieved the ultimate, in her eyes, and so could her daughter. Typically Tori's mother passed over the fact that Tori was already in love. Not that Travis Walton didn't warrant being passed over. The object of Tori's love was a married man, separated, but in no great hurry to actually get himself a divorce. Paige couldn't imagine why the pretty brunette put up with him. Between her meddling mother and her married boyfriend, it was miraculous Tori managed to maintain her sanity.

"Well, here's to good old healthy green-as-can-be envy," Paige said, draining what was left of her Dom Perignon and then refilling her fluted glass. "And *please* don't ever say 'poor Kit,' " she insisted.

Susan Kendell Brown, who had been the bride's roommate at law school, chuckled without looking up. Susan was curled into a voluptuous sofa by the unlit delft-tiled fireplace, deep into the work she had brought out with her from her home in Stockton, California—or trying to be. Susan was exactly as Kit had described her: serious, but with a good dry sense of humor, hiding behind tortoise-rimmed glasses that were much too big for her face. "With a little work, she's Christie Brinkley undiscovered," Kit had said affectionately of her small-town friend. Kit had only great admiration for Susan, who had somehow managed to rise above her blue-collar farming-community roots to put herself through law school in spite of great opposition from her family. Now Susan's dishwater-blond hair, which could have done with some lightening, was pulled tight into a terry turban, making her tortoise-framed glasses stand out even more than they ordinarily did. But Kit was right, the potential for being a knockout was definitely there. Paige was eager to see what Susan would look like after being worked on by the "hot" Hollywood hairstylist and makeup team Kit had hired to beautify all of them for the ceremony.

"Would you sit down and relax? You're a nervous wreck," Susan said suddenly, peeling off her glasses as though in response to Paige's thoughts. "You'd think it was *you* getting married."

"Ah, but don't I wish!" Paige said honestly, wandering over to the large French windows that were like picture frames for the enchanting garden view. *Don't we all wish,* she was tempted to add but didn't. It was impossible not to be affected by all the stir and anticipation that was going on throughout every inch of the groom's sprawling eleven-thousand-square-foot Bel Air estate, and Paige gazed out over the expansive grounds below, taking in the bustle of activity where countless crews appeared to be working painstakingly on every last detail. There were caterers, rental crews, flower designers, and even video technicians, angling about, getting it all on tape for posterity.

The setting was so wondrous, with all the dazzling white freesias, the hibiscus, and the oleander. She could almost smell their rich perfume as she stared out, entranced, already envisioning the processional that was to take place on the elegant lower terrace. A white bridge constructed from scaffolding across the pool added a nice dramatic touch. There were plump white water lilies floating on either side of it.

What a production, Paige thought, watching the dozen or so florists who were still hard at work weaving thousands of orchids into an ivy-covered wall. She felt as though she were observing the building of an elaborate outdoor stage set. And, in a sense, she was. Given the staggering budget Kit had described, Paige probably could have come close to launching a Broadway show. She could have even bought herself a decent part in one. But then another thought occurred to her, which came more as a revelation. Given her choice between starring, so to speak, in this "wedding production," which offered only one grand appearance but then a wonderfully rich and easy life afterward, versus a lead role in a musical, something she had been dreaming about for nearly all her life, it struck Paige she would opt for the bride bit. What Kit was about to have—security on a grand scale and a man to share it all with—suddenly seemed like the greater coup. The longevity implied in that dream and the easy existence were tempting.

Paige's dream had lost its luster.

Susan put down her glasses, ready to call it quits. It was impossible to concentrate with Paige roaming back and forth and Tori nervously turning the pages of her magazine. They were all just passing time, closed off from the bustle of the rest of the house, waiting to be transformed into the kind of glamorous bridesmaids that would befit such a wedding. Hairstylists, makeup artists—this was all such a far cry from any wedding to which she had ever been. It was certainly light-years away from her own simple church wedding in Stockton. God, had she ever really been married? Susan felt a wave of sadness and a stab of regret as she looked back. At the time it had seemed like the most perfect union ever conceived. They were high school sweethearts, both voted the most likely to succeed, both voted the one with whom you'd most like to be stuck on a desert island. They thought they would have the most incredible kids. She remembered her mother that day. What a nervous Nellie. She had done all the cooking herself. Her father, naturally, had gotten riproaring drunk. He kept saying it was the happiest day of his life. And he kept crying. Susan's mother had been beside herself with happiness, embracing Susan with thick arms that wobbled like jelly beneath the print voile of the dress she had made for the occasion.

Maybe if she hadn't been accepted into law school a few years later her marriage might have stood a chance.

Now Susan looked down at the tiresome contracts in front of her. Why did she ever promise her boss that she would review these documents when she should have known that Kit would have them busy every waking hour of the day throughout the three-day stretch of prenuptial parties and activities? Their shared suite at the Beverly Hills Hotel, where they were being put up as guests of the bride and groom, had been like Grand Central Station. This had been Susan's first opportunity to even open her briefcase, and she couldn't have been less in the mood.

Not that she was complaining. These had been the best three days she'd had in ages.

So much for good intentions, she concluded, packing up the blue-backed legal briefs and calling it a day. It was just as well, because as she clicked her case closed the doorbell rang, and Susan presumed that this time the arriving staff was for them.

"Beauty crew," Paige confirmed after crossing over to the large bay window that looked out over the circular stone-paved entrance. Susan joined her there just in time to see an attendant speeding away with another Mercedes. It was a 560 SEC that had BLOW DRY on its personalized license plates.

"God, the cars!" Paige said, echoing Susan's thoughts exactly as they looked out over the lineup of flashy cars that had already formed. If all of the workers were arriving in Mercedeses, Ferraris, Porsches, Jaguars, and Rolls-Royces, what would the guests be showing up in? Susan wondered.

Tori tossed aside her magazine and joined them over at the window. "Obviously the caterer's Rolls," she commented, pointing toward a big black Rolls-Royce with EATS on *its* personalized license plates.

Paige had a funny little smile on her face as she moved across the room, back to where the caviar was laid out. "Probably bought it off the deposit from Kit's wedding," she quipped demurely.

"Come in," Susan called out in response to the knock at the door. She moved curiously out of the way, appraising the hip-looking group as they moved boisterously into the bedroom, carrying weighty-looking duffel bags and a big boxlike black case. There was one hairdresser, one makeup artist, and one assistant. The three of them decided to set up shop in the large adjoining bathroom, which was mirrored almost entirely and had great sunlight flooding into it through a domed skylight. The hairdresser's assistant arranged a series of three chairs, then directed each of the women to a particular seat, while the makeup artist heaved her cumbersome case up onto the white marble countertop and then opened it. The jammed case looked complete enough to fill an entire makeup counter in a department store.

Later, seated in front of the mirrored wardrobe in her bra and underwear, her hair and makeup done, stretching on panty hose, Susan sat marveling at her reflection. The makeup artist had succeeded in giving a dazzling, almost unfamiliar quality to her large wide-set eyes. She had even been talked into having her eyelashes dyed, and they fluttered now, dark and full, fringing her eyes and making them stand out like a couple of jewels. She felt almost giddy with the triumph of it all. Her pale skin glowed, and her ordinarily mousy hair gleamed with luster. No wonder all the women in this city seemed so superior-looking. They were being attended to by professionals who, for a steep fee and a large block of time, transformed ordinary looks into magazine-quality extraordinary looks. Susan cringed at the thought of having to do this routinely. She felt great *now,* but what a drain, both in terms of energy and cash. She imagined breezing into her staid Stockton law firm this way and grinned at the astonished reactions she would receive.

The reaction she was really toying with had to do with one man in particular. She wanted to knock the socks off Billy Donahue—William J. Donahue III, now a senior partner in his family's firm, where Susan also worked. He was reasonably bright and *unreasonably* good-looking. For the last couple of years he had been Susan's boyfriend. It was one of those on-again off-again relationships that was based more on convenience for both of them than on love. Susan had been crazy about Billy when they first met. He was charming, fun to be with, and unattached. *Unattached* being the operative word in a small town like Stockton, where most of the available men were ex-husbands of girls with whom she had gone to school. Billy's biggest problem was that he was an incurable player. Actually it wasn't Billy's problem at all. It was Susan's.

What am I doing with my life? she wondered, staring soberly at her now-glamorous reflection. There was no trace there of the anxiety she was beginning to feel. It was not just the rut she was in with Billy. That was symptomatic of everything else. But eventually Susan had to think about direction, to redefine her own. She had met her professional goals, but now where was she headed, besides straight into a brick wall? What about the rest? What about the part of her life that was hanging in the balance—

the part she had abandoned all those years ago and now needed
badly in order to feel whole? She wanted it all. The career, a
husband, children. Not necessarily on the kind of grand scale Kit
was doing it. But that same package nevertheless. Her fingers felt
icy against her skin as she touched the seed-pearl choker at her
throat, which Billy had bought for her last Christmas. It had
been part present, part peace offering after she had found out he
was sleeping with her secretary. Her life was indeed a mess, she
thought, blinking back tears, trying to hold on to her sense of
humor.

"I didn't look this good at my own wedding," she remarked to
Paige and Tori, who were also getting dressed.

"Maybe that's why your marriage didn't last." Paige's bright
green eyes flashed as she flipped a silky cascade of russet-colored
hair off her face and back over her shoulder. It was a fluid movement, as were all her movements. Paige was a professional dancer
working now in the big Broadway musical *Cats*. Kit had said that
she was an incredible dancer, and Susan imagined that she was.
She had that kind of ease with her body, a smooth sensual awareness of her curvy shape, which was poured now into the sexiest-
looking lace undergarment Susan had ever seen. Her body language was as sassy as her wit.

"Now, that's hitting below the belt," Susan responded, laughing, thinking about how much she liked Paige Williams, when
she had been so certain that she would not. Paige, Susan, and
Tori had been hearing about one another for years, but they had
never actually met until this weekend, which had been like one
long slumber party with the three of them becoming fast friends.
As Susan had anticipated, Paige was kind of off-the-wall, dramatic, a bit of a sex kitten, but she was not in the least bit
insubstantial. There was a raw gutsiness about her that Susan
admired, the way she took charge, the way she said what was on
her mind. There was also a winsome exuberance that made her
impossible not to like.

"Tori, you look sensational," Paige exclaimed, stretching a
lacy white garter belt up over her hips, then going over to help
Tori with a button she was having trouble reaching on her dress.
Susan turned curiously to regard the long-legged brunette who

was now, with Paige's assistance, the first one ready. Her short dark hair was styled sleek and very European, accenting her almost oriental eyes, which were slate-colored and seemed to smile mysteriously up at the corners. Stepping into cornflower-blue pumps that matched the background of her dress, Tori whirled around for her friends' inspection. The bare-shouldered pastel chiffon floated up above her knees as she spun in a smooth circle, looking more like a southern society belle than the fast-climbing real estate executive she was.

Always the bridesmaid and never the bride. Damn you, Mother, for joking about it, if, in fact, it was only a joke. And damn you, Travis Walton, for making it so hopelessly true. Tori Mitchell stood out of sight of the large chattering crowd, close behind Paige and Susan under the umbrella of a lush pink cherry blossom tree, waiting in silence for the wedding coordinator to give them their cue. The orchestra had already begun playing warm-up music, and Tori took a deep breath, struggling to lose herself in the restful baroque sound as it rose serenely into the summer air.

She was fighting for composure, trying to strike Travis from her thoughts, trying to quell the resentment.

Lately weddings were having this effect on her. All of her friends seemed to be getting married, and a good many of them were onto their second kids. Tori felt as though she were watching a drawbridge making its gradual ascent. If she didn't make it in time, she would fail to make the crossing altogether. With all of her heart, she wanted to make it with Travis, but there was that alarming sense of time moving too swiftly past her.

"You're throwing good money after bad," was her mother's stock phrase when issuing unsolicited advice on her daughter's relationship. There was that, along with a battery of other comments, none of them ever terribly original, but all of them hard-hitting.

Tori felt her eyes burning and she swallowed deeply. She had tried so hard over the weekend to be cheerful, but it was impossible to get him off of her mind. The constant disappointments were getting out of hand—his broken promises, his bullshit. He

had said he would fly out from Atlanta with her for the wedding.
He had said a lot of things. And she knew after living with him
all these years that she was an idiot to believe him.

Travis Walton wasn't even divorced. She had fallen for a *salesman*. When Tori first met Travis, she was just twenty-two, fresh
out of college, applying for a job at one of Atlanta's prominent
single-family tract home developers. Travis, with his devastating
good looks and his beguiling charm, was already the superstar
salesman there, upholding a record that in the fifteen years since
he had been at the company hadn't been beat. He had started in
on Tori right away, and of course she fell for his line. He was a
pro. At the time Travis had been in the process of filing for a
divorce. And now, seven precious years later, aware that he had
come no closer to concluding that process, Tori felt duped. Her
own rocketing rise within the corporation to her now prestigious
position as director of marketing didn't compensate for the frustration in her personal life. Certainly that kind of success was
exciting, even heady at times. But it wasn't enough. Travis's
friends had known all along. He wasn't ever *really* going to get a
divorce. Supporting his estranged wife and sharing his income
with her were worthwhile insurance against *having to marry
again*. Those were the casual warnings she had heard over the
years and then discarded, believing misguidedly that *she* could
succeed with Travis where her predecessors had failed. So far it
looked like there were no rewards for hanging in there. Just a
trail of wasted time, she thought, feeling her eyes beginning to
burn again and that familiar fullness at the back of her throat.
Determined not to cry, she took a deep breath and held it. In a
few short moments a thousand eyes would be upon her. And she
had that fifty-dollar makeup job to preserve, as well as appearances.

Oh, yes, appearances. Tori knew she was accomplished at that.
Her mother had instilled in her dozens of little tricks to make the
rest of the world think that everything was great—everything
was grand. She had learned to stand tall, keep her head held
high, and her chin and nose tilted up toward God. Well, even if
only temporarily, Tori could at least draw strength from that
posture. And she did so now as an au courant arrangement of

Romeo and Juliet sprang ceremoniously from the orchestra. As the wedding procession stepped into motion Tori noticed a tightening not only in her own shoulders but in Paige's and Susan's as well. What potential groom were they each thinking of? she wondered. What doomed romance or wishful fantasy was being disturbed now by the rush of music and the stern-looking woman in the prim Saint John knit suit who was signaling to them all to begin? Billy Donahue from Stockton for Susan? Someone new from Beverly Hills for Paige? Tori was surprised to see the tears in their eyes when they both turned to share a last look with her before moving forward and into view. She was even more surprised to find herself reaching out and squeezing both their hands. It was an intense moment for all of them, and her pulse skipped a beat when it was her turn to grace the aisle.

Airy exclamations seemed to mingle with the traditional music as she moved solemnly through the garden ceremony. Her cheeks were aching from the pull of a frozen smile as she continued across the festooned bridge, down the regal white runner, across the expanse of bright green grass, and then over to the designated bridal area, which was set up beneath the vast spread of a Japanese elm.

A pause in the music then summoned everyone's rapt attention, and the guests stood in honor of the bride. Kit was breathtaking, and Tori tried to hold back her tears as she watched her cousin, who looked like a dream as she glided down the aisle, dressed in a cloud of white tulle. More than anything else in the world, Tori wanted Travis to be there with her as he had promised he would, to feel the beauty of the moment and to be seduced by it. Then she cursed herself for banking such high hopes on him.

Feeling a pair of familiar eyes upon her, Tori looked out into the sea of smiling, misty-eyed faces and locked gazes with her mother. *What a wedding. What a catch. Leave it to Kit to do things in such elevated style.* That's what her cool, aristocratic-looking mother was thinking. She was absolutely undone that this was happening to her niece and not to her daughter.

* * *

I'm in my element, Paige thought, dancing with abandon to the orchestra's lively rendition of the Pet Shop Boys' new hit song, enjoying the loud pulsating music, the glorious moonlight, and all the admiring glances being cast her way.

There was one man in particular with whom Paige had been playing eye contact games all evening, beguiling glances exchanged in an amusing flirtation. He wasn't especially good-looking, but there was something about him that had piqued Paige's interest. Probably that he looked rich and slightly arrogant, she thought, keeping a watchful eye on him as her dance partner spun her around the crowded floor. That type always appealed to her, the way success did. He was smoking a fat cigar, puffing at it with noble relish.

Paige had already decided that he wasn't going to move from his spot. He was obviously accustomed to people coming to him, and it was going to be up to her to initiate an introduction. But how? She mulled over that enigma as she continued to dance, focusing on her fantasy and spinning it into great romantic proportions. She was feeling gay and brazen, infused with a romantic high that was better than champagne—better than any kind of drug she could imagine. After a smooth though dated disco dip, Paige smiled boldly and was rewarded when he smiled back. With a kind of ridiculous rising excitement she found herself envisioning all kinds of things: flashes of intimate conversation, a fast attraction, moving out to L.A. at his insistence.

Marrying one of Kit's millionaire friends and moving out to sunny California had an enticing ring to it. The city seemed to be teeming with rich, available, good-looking men. With or without her mystery man, the idea definitely merited some thought. When the song wound down to its end, Paige decided she would maneuver her way across the dance floor and inspire a conversation.

But it was suddenly too late. Her unknown prosperous prospect had vanished. Feeling deserted, Paige declined another dance offer, then swooped a canapé off the hors d'oeuvre tray of a passing waiter.

The spread was almost too lavish for words, and Paige wandered around, catching snatches of conversation. Set up all along the periphery of the garden were wondrous-looking food stations, manned by chefs in crisp white jackets and tall hats, shucking oysters, fishing live lobsters out of tanks and preparing them to order, basting exotic meats like reindeer and boar over mesquite grills, carving filet mignon, and serving the inevitable caviar from a caviar bar.

Carrying a plate jammed with delicacies, Paige threaded her way through the mass of expensively dressed guests, back toward her table, where she was glad to find both Tori and Susan. They were laughing and enjoying themselves with a friend of the groom's, a debonair adventurer type named Dustin Brent, who hadn't taken his eyes off Tori the entire weekend. Too bad he was leaving the country for a year to go climb mountains.

"You looked like you were having fun out there," Tori commented, her slate-colored eyes full of appraisal as Paige slid into the seat beside her.

"I was . . ." Paige lifted up a heavenly-looking salmon-covered toast point, then, biting delicately into it, turned to peer through the crowd again. Through the thick throng of people her mystery man was still nowhere to be found. "But my well-designed fantasy just went up in smoke." She sighed, brushing a crumb away from the corner of her mouth and smiling ironically. "Smuggled Cuban cigar smoke, I believe."

Tori and Susan exchanged an amused look with the lanky Dustin Brent. Paige liked the sparkle in his warm brown eyes, the deep lines there that suggested outdoor vigor. "Oh, I do this kind of thing all the time," she confessed to the three of them, raising her wineglass and sipping from it as she went on to explain. "There was this man watching me when I was out there dancing. Not gorgeous, but my type. De Niro, fattened up a bit—" She laughed when Susan made a face. "Anyway, I was fantasizing that he would sweep me off my feet, proclaim mad passionate love at first sight, and produce a *large,* impromptu engagement ring to prove it."

Paige raised her eyebrows in mock emphasis. "I'm great at these kinds of scenarios," she joked as Tori and Susan both broke up laughing. "I'd imagined him insisting that I marry him right away—"

"Wait—I'll go round up the minister before he leaves!" Tori exclaimed in her melodic southern drawl, succumbing to a chocolate she'd had her eye on.

"And don't bother going home to pack," Paige added dramatically, still playing the part of De Niro as Prince Charming. "We'll go out and buy you a whole new wardrobe."

Everyone laughed, except Paige, who drained her glass and turned back toward the dance floor again, feeling her mood beginning to slip. She was thinking about going home, and the thought of having to return to reality had her feeling sobered. She was getting tired of the rat race of New York. Tired of being one of the millions of "pretty but approaching thirty" actress/dancers hoping in a faded way to one day land that choice role in a smash Broadway play. All those high hopes and plunging disappointments, both professional *and* romantic. What was so *great* about a career anyway? she wondered harshly, uneasy about the chunk of years she had invested in her own. Careers, sure, they all had them: Tori, who was head of marketing for one of Atlanta's largest tract home developers, with enough responsibility to give her an ulcer, which it had; and Susan, a labor lawyer, stuck in Stockton, of all places, working arduous hours representing a bunch of farmers. Impressive at first glance, Paige thought ruefully, real estate executive, lawyer, Broadway dancer. They were three thoroughly modern, single, entirely self-sufficient women. But the fact was, all of them had come out to L.A. *alone*.

Paige turned to aim a careful look at Tori and Susan. "I think the three of us should move out here," she said, beginning to feel that rush of adrenaline again. *Why not?* That's what kept running through her mind as she thought about her moneyed surroundings. There was a richness here, an attainable privilege that the people reflected in their smooth bronze complexions and their easy smiles. Everybody she had met here seemed so incredibly friendly, so incredibly affluent. Life appeared easy, clean, blessed with happy weather. It was a perfect place to begin anew, and it was definitely time for change. It was time for good old-fashioned marriage and family with someone like Kit's George, she decided, looking around and just imagining what it would be like to have all this day in and day out. So, George wasn't gorgeous to look at. And he wasn't the funniest guy she had ever met. A large net worth could make up for a multitude of shortcomings, could even cover the cost of fixing a few of them. A child of the sixties who marched for peace, wore Salvation Army blue jeans, and put down anything that even smacked of convention or especially materialism? Hell, yes. Paige was ready for a little convention in her life at this point, a little materialistic indulgence. So, if she couldn't find Mr. Right, she could at least find Mr. Rich. And what better place to find him than in Beverly Hills, where a glimpse into that *net worth* appeared to be on vivid display, with magnificent mansions and rolling lawns, lighted tennis courts, and a Rolls adorning the driveway. The city seemed filled with Georges, and if Kit could find one, so could they.

"Move to L.A.," Tori demurred with a little nervous laugh. "It would sure shock Travis," she said. *Maybe that's what I need to get him to get his damn divorce already . . .*

"The best thing that could ever happen to your relationship with Travis would be for you to move and let him know that he can't get away with not getting a divorce," Paige emphasized, noticing Dustin Brent's surprise and curious interest as he regarded the demure brunette.

"Your boyfriend is married?" he asked.

"Separated," Tori explained, fiddling with her napkin. "Yesterday and today and forever."

Dustin let his eyes linger on Tori for an extra beat before turning to Paige. "What about you?" he asked her. "Is there a boyfriend we'd have to worry about back in New York?"

"Several," Paige lied cheerfully, watching him as he laughed and pulled a cigar from out of his tux pocket, then pointed it at Susan. "And how about you?"

"One. But he's ripe for replacement," she acknowledged.

"I have an interesting proposition for the three of you," he said, flicking his gold Cartier lighter ablaze and drawing thoughtfully on his cigar. "You could all stay at my place and look after the house for me while I'm away. You'd have *your* adventure while I was out having *mine,*" he offered lightheartedly.

All weekend long everyone had been talking about the mountain climbing expedition Dustin Brent was going on. It had been his fantasy for years to climb the highest mountain in each of the seven continents, Mount Everest being the tallest and most difficult, and this year he was going to do it. He and a friend had hired an English colonel who was an expert climber to organize the ambitious expedition, which was to consist of a team of six experienced climbers and twice as many sherpas to carry their supplies and set up camps. They had estimated the timeframe at one year and the cost for Dustin at one million, since he was subsidizing the effort.

"That's the best offer I've had in ages." Susan's blue eyes sparkled as she laughed and leaned back in her chair.

"We accept!" Paige warned him, serious if he was serious.

"I'm completely serious," he replied, stretching out his long lean legs and crossing them casually at the ankles. "Honestly, ask Kit and George. I've been known to do crazier things. Besides, I've gotten to know you all pretty well this weekend—I'm sure my house will still be there when I get back. If not, it's insured," he joked.

Paige could barely contain herself as he went on. What an opportunity. What a perfect opportunity for all three of them. She felt flushed with anticipation and yet strangely anxious, as though this could be the solution to all that was wrong in her life. Fate was finally bailing her out. It was her turn.

"Listen, six months to a year is a long time to rely on hired help," he pointed out. "You girls could make sure the maid didn't quit or throw too many wild parties. Not only do I have the maid to worry about, but there's the gardeners, the poolman, pest control, the burglar alarm going off, the smoke alarm. . . . I think it's an inspired idea to have you house-sit for me."

"Hey, slow down a minute. I can't really move out here—" Tori looked like someone who had been strapped into a roller coaster seat and wanted to get out, quick, before it was too late.

"Why not?" Paige insisted.

"I haven't had *that* much to drink." Tori's cheeks flushed an attractive shade of pink. She looked over at Dustin, who was smiling challengingly back at her. "Paige is crazy. Tell her we're only joking around."

"*I'm* not joking. You're welcome to stay at my house." Dustin reached into his pants pocket and pulled out a set of European-looking car keys. "You're even welcome to my toys. They're also insured. There's a black Aston-Martin Lagonda, a Bronco . . ."

"Are you always this generous?" Tori asked him, intrigued.

"Why not?" he replied, raking back his wavy brown hair without affectation. "You only go around once."

Paige was liking him more and more. "Tori, I think we should at least consider it," she said. "What have you really got to lose?"

Not about to be seduced, Tori slid Dustin's keys back across the table. "A couple of little things. Like, I'm living with somebody, I have a job," she said.

The order in which Tori had declared her priorities did not escape Paige, and she hesitated, measuring her next words. She herself had lived with so many different men over the course of years that the live-in relationship no longer carried with it all the weight it once had. "There're live-in's in L.A.," she said softly. "Jobs—"

"I like my live-in. I like my job."

"Just for six months," Paige suggested, watching the temptation in Tori's eyes. "Take a hiatus from both. C'mon, Tori, go for it. Who knows, maybe you'll get a ring and a raise, both, out of the whole proposition."

Tori wished it were as simple as Paige was making it sound. Even with all the grief she got from Travis, he did serve a purpose. *Aside* from her being impossibly in love with him.

He gave her the illusion of being married, being part of a coupled society. Kids were the only missing link, and security, if she allowed herself to think about it. What she might have had to gain by leaving him was always tempered by the thought of first having to face being alone. And so her threats were never carried out. To Tori the singles scene was a nightmare, full of hollow relationships, games and canned conversations, questions and answers played by rote, and always the unsettling prospect of disappointment and rejection. At least the disappointment and rejection she experienced with Travis were familiar. Her threshold there was established. And she could anticipate the blows.

"What would you do here, Paige?" Susan, who had been sitting quietly, sat forward, her interest piqued. "Try and get into some film work?" She watched Paige deliberate, stabbing at a chunk of lobster with an ornate silver fork.

"Maybe film. Or maybe something else entirely."

"What about the show you're in?" Susan asked, full of admiration for Paige, tempted in her pleasantly inebriated state to throw caution to the winds and join her. The idea was undeniably appealing, especially for someone like Paige, who had the nerve to do it.

"What's one more show?" Paige shrugged thoughtfully. "It's not doing that much to advance my career anyway."

God, could they really just up and move? Susan wondered, feeling a nice warm sense of light-headedness from the idea. The thought of moving to a big city had always unnerved her before. She wasn't good in crowds. She felt claustrophobic without the wide-open spaces in which she had grown up. And city people were always so intimidating to her.

"Think about how much fun we'd have as roommates," Paige was saying.

Roommates. The last female roommate Susan had had was Kit, when they'd shared an apartment together at law school. Now that all seemed like a lifetime ago. Bitter memories of her divorce and the friction with her family were mixed up together with some of her best memories ever. What a good friend Kit had been throughout it all, unquestionably more fun and less demanding than any man she had ever lived with.

"It's really tempting," Susan said, unable to believe she was actually considering it. "I've never been impetuous, not even once in my entire life. I'm not sure I have it in me."

"What would your family say?" Tori asked her curiously.

Susan winced, wary not of what they would say so much, because they wouldn't say much, but instead of what they would think. "They couldn't relate to it," she said, toying uneasily with the edge of the delicate lace tablecloth, reminded of the rare Italian lace she had wanted for her wedding gown but hadn't been able to afford. The irony struck her as she looked out into the sea of lace-covered tables, acutely conscious of her opulent surroundings, the glitz and sophistication.

Would she change? That would be her parents' primary concern. They were always threatened by the prospect of her changing, as though moving up in educational or income strata meant leaving them behind. Over the years they had interpreted her apparent need to be different from them as an affront.

"What about Billy?" Tori asked, hitting a different nerve.

Billy. The shock value alone made it hard to resist. Susan looked over at Paige and grinned, trying to affect her new friend's stagy manner of speech. "Not doing that much to advance my career anyway," she mimicked meaningfully and was rewarded when they all broke up laughing.

Dustin, who was puffing leisurely on his cigar, regarded her seriously. "Kit could probably get you something over at her firm, now that she's married to one of their biggest clients."

"Oh, right," Susan said, laughing. *"Just like that."*

Dustin snapped his fingers and grinned. "Hey, that's how it works."

"God, L.A., of all places." Susan couldn't help but reflect on how she and her friends had always made such fun of L.A.—looked down her nose at it. All that glitter and sparkle. All of the phonies and the fancy cars. San Francisco was what northern Californians called a *real* city. It was *substantial,* unlike L.A. It was where they went for a fix of culture or good food. L.A. was a joke. Or had it all been envy and curiosity? Susan began to wonder, her blue eyes focused meditatively on the graceful white lilies at the center of the table. Wasn't there, in fact, something deeply seductive about all that fast living and what they perceived to be high-voltage glamour? Certainly she was feeling it now as she sat there too tense to speak.

"Wait a minute. Someone's got to bring some levity into this," Tori started to say. She was sitting at an awkward angle with one arm draped over the back of her chair, looking as if she thought they were all nuts.

"Why?" Susan asked, suddenly convinced. "It really is the best offer I've had in ages. Maybe I'm crazy, but moving out here is beginning to sound like a very practical idea—"

"You're going to just up and move? Quit your jobs?" Tori looked over at Dustin, who was watching them all intently. He shrugged as though to say "Don't look at me," clearly enjoying their debate. Tori, beside herself with frustration, turned back to Susan. "How can you do that with a law practice?"

"I'll give them sufficient notice." It seemed easy enough to Susan. "The truth is, there's nothing holding me in Stockton. If anything, it's a lousy place for a single woman my age. Career-wise, I'd unquestionably be better off in a big city."

Tori was at a loss to refute that.

"If you want my vote," Dustin said, stubbing out his cigar and then regarding Tori. "I think it sounds like a lot of fun. You all seem to be in fairly static situations anyway. You're young. You're beautiful. Paige is absolutely right. So you'd find your-selves new jobs here. There're plenty of opportunities. And as far as men go, you'd be the 'new girls in town.' I could think of half a dozen nice-looking, fun, wealthy guys who would be eager to go out with you."

"Honestly, Dustin, you'd really let us stay at your place?" Paige asked seriously, as though needing to make sure this wasn't all breezy cocktail conversation, wanting to tie the offer down.

"It's all yours if you want it. Six months. Maybe a year. We're talking seven continents," Dustin replied, turning to Tori with a kind of raw smile. "Well, are you in or are you out, Georgia Peach?"

"I need to sleep on it." Tori hesitated, turning warm and then hot under his gaze.

"Oh, be a sport and just say yes!" Paige had impulsively taken Tori's hand. She thought Tori looked like she was back on the roller coaster again, but this time beginning to feel the thrill.

And she was.

He's only using you, came a replay of one of her mother's many low-blow remarks. God knows, she had heard enough of them in the last week. *You think he's actually going to marry you? Why should he? He's got the best of both worlds. You clean the apart-ment for him. You cook his meals. You entertain his friends. You sleep with him. And you even split the bills. You're a wife-maid combined, Tori, dear, without the perks.*

Without the perks is right, Tori thought, her decision suddenly made. Paige was one hundred percent right. To hell with Travis.

To hell with her parents. Why not move out to California and show them all? If she stayed in Atlanta, her life would remain exactly as it was. If she had the guts to pick up and move, she would at least be expanding her options. Her fantasy was that Travis would be so upset at her leaving that he would break down and ask her to marry him. But if he failed to do that, then odds were, after all this time, he never would. Her fantasy would have been just that.

Feeling her first burst of courage, Tori hailed a waiter who was passing by, then, grinning her apologies, snatched a full bottle of champagne from his elegant silver tray. "I want to propose a toast," she said, looking straight at Dustin Brent and feeling encouraged by his apparent amusement at her sudden bravado as she poured out a full round. "To our generous host," she went on, lifting her glass and enjoying the astonishment on all three of their faces. "When do we book our flights out?"

"Tori, you're my kind of woman!" Paige let out a little hoot of victory, accepting the glass of champagne Tori was holding out to her and raising it up in her honor. "You've got more guts than you know about yet, Georgia Peach. To men, money, and sunshine," she saluted with her usual verve, picking up the ball from Tori's toast and moving on to pitch it as some kind of allegiance, continuing to wage her campaign for L.A.

Fact: Kit's life looked great.

Fact: Their lives looked lousy.

Why not move to Beverly Hills to meet and marry rich men as Kit had done? The city seemed suddenly full of promise. The three of them would band together in search of a common goal—to extricate themselves from their lousy situations in their respective cities and to move to Beverly Hills to begin fresh. The town had been lucky for Kit; maybe it would be lucky for them.

Dustin sort of shrank down into his seat as he watched them. "It's a good thing I'm getting out of the country," he joked, "or my precious bachelorhood would be in serious jeopardy. I can see that . . ."

Paige laughed and trailed her finger flirtatiously down the row of black onyx studs fastening his tuxedo shirt. "You're not out of the woods yet, love. If one of us is still 'uncoupled' by the time you get back"—she grinned as she reached his waistband—"you could find yourself on dangerous ground."

Paige let her finger tarry there for a moment longer before she removed it and placed it in between her full sultry lips.

Susan couldn't believe her gall and she wondered what on earth Dustin thought of them.

Smiling broadly, he proposed the next toast, wishing all three of them great success and starting off another round of glass-touching.

With their hopes sealed, Susan found herself filled with a kind of weird anticipation about their futures.

Certainly this balmy California evening was going to be a night upon which they would always look back. But how? Hopefully with gratitude and not regret. It was the eve of opportunities about to bloom as they agreed to uproot themselves from their old, neglected soils to chance their futures in a new, undetermined place.

Rich men—single women, Susan thought loosely, just as the orchestra announced that the bride and groom were about to cut the cake, inviting all the guests to join them there on the upper terrace.

She, Tori, and Paige rose up from their seats, looking significantly at one another, incredulous at what they were about to do as Dustin Brent escorted them away from the table.

Chapter 2

Susan had suspected that their glittery plans made on the crest of an evening high, with champagne coloring their senses, would have dissolved in the sobriety of the next day, headaches replacing wild expectations. But they had not.

Now, the night before she was to leave for Los Angeles, Susan stood quietly apart from the small group that had gathered in her honor, sipping the Harvey Wallbanger her father had made, watching them. Her father, Jake Kendell, a heavyset man in his early sixties, was famous in his small, close-knit circle in Stockton for his tangy "sure-to-knock-you-on-your-ass" Harvey Wallbangers. If he even remembered this little farewell dinner he was having for his daughter, Susan thought, it would be a miracle. His beefy face was already animated from inebriation. And the evening had only just begun. He was acting as though he had just won a ten-thousand-dollar lottery. He was behaving like an ass.

"C'mere, you little defector. This shindig's for you," he slurred, motioning her over with a fat arm. Jake was what Susan would ordinarily call a functioning alcoholic, but tonight he was sloppy and crude. It was Sunday, and he had begun pouring alcohol into himself early in the morning, attempting to anesthetize himself against emotion, and failing. Ever since Susan had told her parents about her plan to move to Los Angeles, her father had hardly uttered three words to her.

"Leave her alone, Jake." It was her mother rising quietly to her defense, her words barely audible, but generally carrying some impact. Betsy Kendell's only moments of courage with her domineering husband surfaced at times like these, when she felt she had to intervene on Susan's behalf. Susan threw her a look of gratitude. She was going to miss her a lot.

"Ahhh, you still make the *best*, Betsy." Susan turned to see her old friend Lisa Davis dipping a Dorito chip into a plastic container heaped with guacamole. Her mother smiled, pleased with the compliment. They were all gathered out on the Astroturfed patio of the Kendells' mobile home, seated on woven plastic strip garden chairs, shielded from the still-hot sun by a white metal awning. Neighbors were engaged in similar Sunday night entertainment, and the smell of meat barbecuing permeated the air. Three years ago Susan's parents had decided to move out of the house she had grown up in and into the mobile home park that had become a retirement mecca for many of their friends. Jake hadn't retired yet, but there was talk that he was going to be forced into it sooner than he cared to think. He was one of the oldest cargo supervisors down at Stockton's bustling port, where he had worked for years at a large grain facility.

"Just look at those two. You're still like a couple of newly-weds," Betsy Kendell said as Lisa fed her husband a chip she had prepared for him, sealing her gesture with a kiss. "How long has it been? Thirteen years?" Betsy knew exactly how long it had been, and she caught the chain of uneasy glances that her comment had inadvertently sparked. It was an innocent attempt at just making conversation, and Susan could tell by the look in her mother's eyes that she wished she'd said nothing.

The two childhood friends had gotten married only weeks apart from one another. They had been like sisters all through school, and both thought it was too good to be true when they dated and married best friends. They were right. It was.

When Susan decided to go to law school, everything changed. Ten years ago women born into blue-collar families, raised in farming communities like Stockton, simply didn't do that. Especially when they were *lucky* enough to marry a man with potential, as Susan had. Skip was on the dean's list at the University of the Pacific. He was bright and had ambition.

Collectively Skip, Susan's parents, her in-laws, even Lisa and Buzz, tried to make her feel guilty. What was the urgency about going to law school? Skip didn't intend to need her income. So what was she trying to prove? College was one thing. He wanted a wife who was smart and interesting. But he wanted a *wife*, the definition of which brought them into constant debate, since it appeared to preclude anything she wanted for herself. She remembered all those bitter arguments they used to have and how close she had come to giving in. She wasn't the aggressive women's-libber they accused her of being. And it was a nightmare being at odds with the only people in the world who meant anything to her. Nobody understood that all she really wanted was some control, some choice. The thought of handing over the reins of her future to someone else the way her mother had done with her father was simply inconceivable to Susan. And besides, she really wanted to practice law.

Looking back, Susan knew it had been tough on Skip. He had been subjected to endless remarks about how he had better be careful or she would be making more money than he. There were the inevitable "house-husband" jokes that they had both been too insecure to ignore. When she applied for a scholarship to law school and got it, it was as though his competitive instincts had been challenged and their relationship with it. She was no longer his partner but his opponent, in a game nobody would win.

Her first year at University of the Pacific Law School was a disaster. Skip and his cousin were starting a small rice export business, and she was busy studying. He resented that she wasn't there for him, fulfilling his image of what a wife should be. It didn't take him long to find someone who did. She was a friend of Lisa's younger sister's, and oddly enough, Susan came out of all the unseemly mess as the culprit. If she had been home, fulfilling her wifely obligations, minding the store, so to speak, none of it would have happened. So, midsemester, quiet, reserved, not given to confrontations, Susan made the difficult decision of transferring from University of the Pacific to Hastings Law School in

San Francisco, away from her husband. It was the most daring thing she had ever done, up until now—a choice she still questioned every now and then.

She and Skip were divorced within six months of her leaving him. He remarried only three months after that, and she always wondered if he ever looked back, as she did, and what he thought. Probably she would never know. Those times when they did run into one another he was careful and distant.

Susan moved in to join the rest of the group. She sat down on the one unoccupied chair and leaned forward to dip a celery stick into the guacamole. "Cuts down on the calories," she kidded lightly, looking fondly at her mother, who had a chip loaded with dip in each hand.

Lisa, who was always rail thin and ate like a horse, stuck her tongue out at Susan. "Oh, go for it, Betsy," she said jauntily. "You'll always look petite next to Jake anyway, so who gives a hoot." Going for another chip herself, she turned back to Susan. "So, where's Billy?" she asked gingerly.

Susan's father snorted at the mention of her boyfriend. "Hah!" he said nastily. "He's probably pulling one of his famous no-show acts."

Betsy threw her husband a sharp look. Susan sighed and looked away. There was always so much tension here. She couldn't wait to leave. And why on earth had she invited Billy anyway? Would she never learn?

"Susan, don't get protective of him after all this time," Buzz said, misreading her silence.

"Who's protective?" Susan drained what was left of her drink. "I'm through defending Billy Donahue."

"That'll be the day," Jake sneered.

Susan took a deep breath. *Here they go again.*

"Maybe he'll come by for dessert—" Betsy suggested.

"I don't want that jerk coming over here period!" Jake rose from his chair and went over to the makeshift bar he had set up, where he began putting together another batch of Wallbangers.

"Can we talk about something else?" Susan asked, frustrated, producing a gloomy lull in the conversation.

"Billy's probably going out of his mind," Lisa said finally. "I'm surprised he didn't break down and ask you to marry him."

Susan looked dubious. She had no illusions about Billy.

"What! Are you dreaming?" Jake rolled his eyes.

"Billy's not right for her anyway," Betsy said, putting her arm around her daughter. "Jake, when are you going to stop drinking and start barbecuing the fish?" Jake had caught a ten-pound striped bass that morning, and it was all cleaned and ready to go on a platter.

"When are you going to mind your own business?"

"Mom, Daddy—please knock it off. Can we have one night of no fighting!"

Jake sucked in his gut, attempting to stuff it into his trousers. He was red in the face and his watery gray eyes narrowed bitterly. "What's the matter, Susan? You embarrassed in front of your friends?"

"No . . ." Susan said steadily, feeling thwarted, sorry for him, sorry for her mother.

"Yes, you are. You've always felt embarrassed about me and your mother."

Now Susan stood up to face him. She was tall, but he was much taller, and their awkward proximity had her looking at his barrel of a chest. "That's not true," she insisted, craning her neck to meet his gaze.

"Like hell it ain't."

Susan backed off, astonished at his tone.

"Your mother and me—we break our backs raising you. And you're gonna just up and move away—"

"Dad. I have to do this."

"You have duties here, girl. Your mother counts on you."

Susan was speechless.

"You think you're better than any of us—you always have."

"Jake." Betsy's voice was urgent.

Jake threw a large trembling hand over in Lisa's direction. "What the hell's the matter with marrying someone like Lisa's Buzz? Or ain't he rich enough for you? You just want too much."

"I don't—" Susan started to respond, stung. She turned apologetically to Lisa and Buzz, at a loss for a response.

"You botched up a perfectly good marriage," Jake continued acidly.

"How do *you* know it was a perfectly good marriage?"

"Because I've been around. I may not have your fancy degrees, but I know who's happy and who's not. You goin' to try and tell me that you're happier than Lisa?"

It was true. Lisa probably was happier than she was, if happiness could effectively be measured. With three wonderful kids and a husband who adored her, Lisa practically glowed with contentment. She had a busy life. It seemed she was president of everything: The P.T.A., her son's Little League, assorted local charities. What had Susan held out for? Maybe her father was right. Maybe she *was* chasing rainbows. Always it had seemed to her that her wants were so simple: A job at which she was happy, a man with whom she could share a productive life. But it was true, simple or not, that at least fifty percent of those wants had eluded her.

"Lisa and I are different," Susan said. "Things turned out differently for us."

"Dammit, Jake, leave her alone," Betsy said, going over to her husband.

But he was beyond reprimand, and he shook her roughly away. They were expecting too much from him. Jake was second generation Stockton. His father had worked at the same grain facility at which he now worked, and Jake had always accepted his lot in life. He believed firmly that people ought to stick to their own kind. It wasn't a good idea to begin hanging around with people out of your class. That bred discontentment and envy. Too much exposure was bad. Now everything was changing, getting out of control. His eldest son had also left home and was living in Bangkok as a translator. After flunking out of Berkeley and joining the army, he had gone to study at the army language school at Fort Ord, in Monterey, where he became fluent in Thai, as well as Chinese and German. Jake's middle child was a container engineer, designing and maintaining the standards of containers, boxes, cans, jars, and things of that nature. He still lived in Stockton, but he had Jake's quarrelsome temper and they rarely spoke. It was in Susan that he had placed all of his dreams—small, happy, attainable dreams. Why couldn't she content herself with a life like Lisa's? What was the matter with his kids?

The glass-and-wrought-iron table shook as he slammed his drink down onto it.

Susan could feel him avoiding her glance as he jiggled inside of his pants pocket for his keys, then headed away from them. She thought about going after him, this being her last night. If she had had any idea of what to say, she would have. But with Jake, nobody ever did. His brooding presence was too intimidating. And he left an uneasy stillness in his wake.

The next morning Susan opened her eyes to bright sunlight, striped and glary from under the metal blinds of her parents' mobile home. As she became aware of voices outside she strained to listen, growing tense and alert. All she could make out from the muffled conversation were her father's periodic no's. Most likely her mother was asking him to apologize, to at least say good-bye. He was refusing.

Susan threw off the quilt her mother had made years ago, recognizing many of the little patches as remnants of old clothes she and her brothers had once worn. It was easy to pick out which materials had belonged to her, because her brothers' clothes, by the time they were ready to be discarded, were always more faded, having been passed down from one brother to the next.

Should she brave going outside and facing him, or not? *Yes,* she thought, rising nervously from the squeaky hide-a-bed she had been sleeping in these last few nights. She glanced toward her parents' bedroom, wondering if her father had slept at home or not, or if he had just returned in the morning to change. His lunch pail and hat were now missing from the top of the TV cabinet, where her mother always laid his things. They had been there the night before, before she had fallen asleep.

"Oh, you're up." Her mother sounded surprised as she came into the room through the screen door. It snapped closed behind her as she moved forward, regarding her daughter. Susan's hair was messy around her face, and the old Lanz nightgown she was wearing brought back memories for both of them.

"I wanted to say good-bye—" Susan began tentatively.

"He's his own worst enemy," Betsy said. "Give him time."

Susan looked at her mother, wondering how she had managed all these years with her father.

"You know he's a smart man, Susan. You kids never give him credit for that," Betsy continued, smoothing nonexistent wrinkles from her crisp print housedress.

"He may have been smart at one time, Mom, but he's not smart anymore. He's too busy fighting everything. Everyone. He sounds like—"

Betsy had started to open the blinds, and she stopped, looking hard at Susan. "You just have to understand. You kids intimidate him—"

"*We* intimidate *him*—"

"Yes. That's right. He feels clumsy around you kids. Ignorant. I'm sure he's worried that if you move to L.A., it'll just get worse." The room brightened up as Betsy went back to adjusting the blinds. Susan stood rooted, watching her, wanting to gain strength from her easy wisdom. "It's hard on him—you have to realize that. Whether you like it or not, you kids make him feel like a failure. Dumb. Inadequate. Because you're all reaching for more."

"But shouldn't we be?"

"I'm not saying you shouldn't. I'm saying you need to put yourself in his place, understand how he feels."

Susan's things were piled up on top of her suitcase on the floor, and she went over to begin straightening up, putting to the side a pair of jeans, some socks, and her tennis shoes. "Maybe I should go out to the port to see him before I take off . . ." she said uncertainly.

Betsy bent down beside her to give her a hand. "Let him be, Susan. I know your father." Frowning at the state of disarray of Susan's things, she emptied them onto the floor and began folding them neatly for her. "He loves you," she said as Susan sat hesitating between two shirts, distracted. Betsy pointed to the blue shirt and went on, talking as she worked. "He's going to miss you a lot. But he needs time with this one. The only good thing, as far as he's concerned, is that this cuts Billy out of the picture for a while. But other than that, well, L.A. is a long ways away. And the kind of people you're going to be with are not exactly your dad's cup of tea."

Susan's eyes were moist as she looked at her mother. There *was* a gap, and it was widening all the time. She had a fleeting sensation of her parents coming out to Los Angeles to visit her. The picture she still held in her mind was of Kit and George's lavish home and the opulent life-style she had experienced there. It had been wonderful, exciting. But it was aeons away from the realities that existed in her parents' world in Stockton. What did she want? What was it that she was really seeking? A chill seemed to set in, and Susan shivered, aware that she was driving herself into further conflict. Money? Was that it? For some reason, if that's all it was, she felt ashamed. She also felt confused. Money was enticing, she would be a liar to say that it was not. But inexplicably the images that went along with it made her feel uneasy. They evoked catch words like nouveau riche, plastic. Or was she displaying a form of learned prejudice—more stereotypical brainwashing against L.A.?

Then Susan felt her mother's reassuring hand on her head.

"I think you *should* go. Don't pay any attention to us," she insisted. There were bags below her pale blue eyes, which looked tired and seemed to have shrunk with age. "I'm going to miss the daylights out of you," she said in a choked voice. "But I'll be all right. And so will your father."

Susan sat back heavily onto her heels. Looking gratefully at her mother through a veil of tears, she took her mother's hands in her own and held them. Saying good-bye was a thousand times more difficult than she ever imagined, and it had her feeling torn apart with emotion.

There was that unshakable sadness.

And yet she was so glad to be leaving.

Chapter 3

The truth was, Tori had been hoping Travis would talk her out of going, that he'd finally get his damn divorce and marry her.

But she had had no such luck.

In only three short days she would be on that plane, bidding good-bye to Atlanta—carrying out a version of a threat she had been delivering to Travis for years. It was an ultimatum wagered and lost.

Definitely lost, she thought, dropping mementos of his love into the already full trash can beneath her desk, hesitating over each one and remembering its particular significance. She was at the office, cleaning out her desk, preparing for her departure. Her top right-hand drawer was virtually filled with three and a half years' worth of assorted tokens from Travis with which she hadn't been able to part.

There were notes he had written, photographs, humorous gifts.

Here she was, trying with all her heart to get her life together, her office in order, and herself out of town, and it was typical of Travis to be working on an all-out campaign to wear her down. All week long he had been sending things—extravagant flower arrangements, great stuffed animals, silly bric-a-brac, crazy telegrams.

There were flowers all over her goddamn office, overflowing into her secretary's cubicle, and still more that she had distributed down the hall because she had run out of space.

He couldn't understand why she was ruining what they both thought was a perfect relationship. They had communication, humor, tenderness, just about everything in common, *and* sex that hadn't lost its greatness after nearly seven years.

Travis was forty-three years old. He knew what was *out there.* He thought Tori was making the mistake of a lifetime throwing all they had together away because of some kind of lack of security on her part.

Marriage, what was so damn essential about marriage?

Trust, love, desire, communication, weren't those elements more important, more long lasting, than a lousy piece of paper? Travis had been with Tori longer than he had been with his wife, and he believed fervently that one of the reasons was because they *were not* married.

Tori came upon a picture of the two of them with their arms around each other, slapping a big SOLD sign onto the FOR SALE sign in front of the condo they had bought together only a year ago.

The acquisition in itself had been a big commitment. Tori had seen it as a significant step in the right direction. Travis, on the other hand, had viewed it as a wise investment that he could always turn around.

He needed exit doors that were clearly marked.

Tori lifted the photo out of the drawer, not bothering to block a fresh onslaught of tears, and sat back in her chair, thinking how this all felt like one interminable bad dream. The emptiness she was feeling was so acute that she felt physically ill. Her stomach hurt. Her muscles ached. She felt like she had the flu, when all she really had was a case of being thirty and single, with no prospects toward a goal she suddenly realized she needed to fulfill.

Marriage and kids, it was an American staple. Why did she feel greedy wanting it? Why did she feel as though it would be so difficult to obtain?

Because she wanted marriage, kids, *and* Travis.

Totally out of control, Tori dropped the photograph, now wet from her tears, onto her desk and stared at it. She looked at his wavy brown hair, wanting to run her fingers through its thick mass. She looked at his eyes and caught the lovable, devilish glint that was always there, that always made her forgive him when she had made up her mind never to again. She thought of the Sundays he had brought her breakfast in bed, the tray adorned with flowers he had cut from outside, waking her up by patting her on the rear, then throwing her into the shower and making unforgettable love to her. They had been together for so long, it was as though they were *already* married. If it weren't for wanting children, Tori would definitely have sacrificed a legal union.

A knock at the door broke her thoughts.

Her secretary, Cora Ann, stood sympathetically in the doorway, her newly acquired granny glasses perched on the end of her nose. Cora Ann had been with the company long before Tori. She was an old mother hen, but everyone loved her. Tori followed her glance around the room, where her chrome-and-glass bookcases had been emptied, pictures taken down from the walls, Tori's treasured dhurrie rug rolled and tied into a log behind her desk.

"He's up to thirteen calls today and it's only"—Cora Ann checked the dainty gold watch on her chunky wrist—"twelve o'clock. Good thing he got transferred over to the Peach Tree office, or he'd be sitting on my desk."

Tori looked over at the blinking red light on her phone and felt her resistance beginning to wane. She had been so strong these last couple of weeks, refusing to take his calls, insisting that he move out for the three weeks that it would take to get all of her things in order and wrap up loose ends at work.

She glanced at the phone again, debating, wanting to pick up the line and talk to him.

"What are you gonna do? Not even see him before you go?"

Tori nodded. She was afraid to see him. She had made a commitment to herself, and she couldn't chance breaking down. And yet, in spite of her resolve, she had her hand on the receiver. Maybe *he* was having second thoughts.

Cora Ann buried her nose in a fragrant bouquet of roses and sniffed. "Even *I'm* beginning to feel sorry for him," she admitted.

"He said he's gone back to seeing his psychiatrist again, that he had to call him for Valium, and that he's lost twelve pounds."

Tori looked at her secretary, surprised. "He told you all that?"

"All of a sudden he's my best friend." Cora Ann removed a pencil from behind her ear. "He obviously didn't think you'd really go through with this. Frankly, honey, none of us did."

The red light on the phone continued to flash, urging Tori into submission as she shuffled absently through the neatly sorted stacks on her desk. The light's quickened pulse seemed to match her heartbeat.

"Also, your mother called," Cora Ann said, deliberating through the awkward pause, tapping her pencil onto the pale green steno pad she was always holding. "She wants to know if you can come for dinner tonight. And Mr. Clayton came by just as Travis called. He needs to talk to you about the Clearwater project. He said to stop by his office before you take off today . . ."

Tori couldn't concentrate on a word Cora Ann was saying. All she could think about was picking up the phone and talking to Travis. On top of cramping stomach muscles, she felt a chill and shivered noticeably.

"Just pick up the damn phone," Cora Ann suggested sweetly on her way out the door.

Praying for a capitulation, Tori lifted up the receiver.

She couldn't deny the rush she felt, the unbelievable sense of comfort at hearing his voice. But she held her reaction in reserve. "Travis, *why* are you calling?" she asked him guardedly, her thoughts sinking nostalgically into the past as she glanced down at her crushed white linen dress, which never failed to arouse crazy memories. Travis had bought it for her one evening when they'd been shopping together over at Lenox Mall. They had also bought a fabulous-looking wide belt that slung low over her hips. The belt had cost more than the dress, but Travis had insisted she get it because for some reason the belt turned him on. So did the thought of nailing her in the dressing room.

He had been in rare form that night, following lecherously behind her into the dressing room, ignoring the craggy old saleswoman's disapproving look, which, by the smile on Travis's face, they certainly deserved.

Tori remembered the large three-way mirror and the way he had angled it as he undressed her. First the belt, which he let slip to the floor, then the zipper at the back of the dress, which he undid with his teeth. She hadn't been wearing a bra, only a pair of French net panties he had never seen before, the effects of which had him down on his knees in an instant, moaning his delight as he went straight for them with his mouth. It was all naughty nirvana until their indiscreet foreplay was interrupted by a sharp rap at the door.

"Everything okay in there?" asked the suspicious saleslady.

Everything was fine!

Except now she was on the verge of tears.

"I have to see you, Tori—" Travis was insisting.

"No."

"I have to pick up some stuff at our place anyway—"

"Travis, no. You're not being fair. I can't see you," Tori forced herself to say. She should never have picked up the phone. She couldn't chance breaking down again. "If you need something over at the apartment, go get it now. Anytime before seven o'clock."

There was another long silence. Tori felt as though she could almost hear him thinking.

"How can you leave without seeing me?" he tried again. "Why don't we just have a drink together or something?"

"Travis, I'm hanging up the phone now," she said, shaken.

She looked at the flowers around the room. The gift cards were all the same. "Don't leave me, you silly woman. I love you!" They were *so* Travis—she could feel him saying it as she read each one.

"Dr. Rosto thinks you should give me a little more time, Tori. He thinks you're trying to manipulate me. And that you're making a mistake."

"Screw Dr. Rosto," Tori replied angrily. "I'm not trying to manipulate you. I'm hurt. I love you. I wish things had worked out differently for us. But I feel I'm wasting my time in our relationship. It's a dead-end situation, since I want to get married and you don't. And it's time for me to take control of my life—"

"Eventually I *do* want to remarry—"

"Eventually? We've been living together for six and a half years. More." Tori took a deep breath. She was tired of this conversation. "Dammit, Travis, you're not even divorced yet. Think about that! Why *aren't* you divorced?" Tori was so angry she was shaking. She looked around her office, trying to gain strength from her decision, which was clear in the empty drawers, the vacant walls, the boxes with her personal things. She had made a resolution to move and she was carrying it through.

With her heart breaking, she hung up on him.

The rest of the day passed slowly, uneventfully. There were some final interoffice business meetings, some phone calls, a lot of strained chitchat about how adventurous Tori was to just pick up and move as she was doing.

Only a few days before, Tori had felt indispensable. Nobody at the office seemed to know what they were going to do without her—their young marketing miracle, they called her. The panic about her leaving had naturally been flattering. But now that everything was in order, the machine of the business working smoothly without its missing part, Tori felt as though she were in the way. She felt deflated.

By four o'clock she was considering leaving early, flying out to California tonight. There was no point in coming back to the office to merely hang around. And the sooner she got out of Atlanta the happier she was going to be. She was making a clean break and she needed to do it fast.

"You want me to call the airlines for you, honey?" Cora Ann asked when Tori buzzed her and told her of her decision.

"No. Thanks. *I'll* do it," Tori replied. "I've got nothing else to do."

Then, with her airline ticket taken care of, her farewell hugs distributed, Tori closed the door on that part of her life, got into her car, and headed home one last time, praying with all her heart that Travis would be there to stop her, and then preparing herself in case he was not.

She envisioned dozens of scenarios on the way. One had Travis there declaring how he couldn't possibly live without her. Another had him there with her shouting coldly at him to leave. The possibilities were endless, and she played them all out in her mind as she continued along the lengthy stretch of highway that would take her from the Perimeter, where she worked, to their condo on Lenox Road in Buckhead, sailing against the traffic, since the bulk of the population in Atlanta went the other way. Everywhere she looked there were new developments springing up, many of them ones in which she herself had participated. Highland Estates, that was hers from start to finish. She had even been involved in the land acquisition, since she had gotten the initial lead. The entrance to the models was announced by a big red-and-white banner bearing the company's logo, which she had helped design.

Taking in the bright blue sky, feeling the hot stickiness of the day, Tori let out a deep sigh. It was so strange to be leaving Georgia. The rich-looking red earth that was piled up on the side of the road where another building was going up sent a longing through her. Red Georgia clay; it was like Scarlett feeling connected to the soil of Tara. There really was something about the copper-colored dirt that held a Georgian to his roots, she thought, the red Georgia clay, the dense lushness of the woods that seemed to stretch on forever.

Tori parked her car in the subterranean lot beneath her condominium complex. Then she grabbed her briefcase, maneuvered it on top of the carton she had brought along with her from the office, and with her hands occupied, she shoved her car door closed with her behind. Accustomed to being loaded down with things—her purse, briefcase, groceries, laundry—Tori knew to use her chin to set off the light summoning the elevator. Its great metal jaws opened and swallowed her up.

Travis was sitting on the couch, drinking beer and watching TV, when she opened the door. The sight of him sitting there brought every little nerve ending to the surface. It seemed to be déjà vu from one of the scenarios she had played out during her long drive home, but which one?

Please, God, let it be one of the good ones, she thought, feeling suspended as he stood up and clicked off the set. The twelve-

pound weight loss was apparent in the loose fit of his jeans. His
love handles had all but disappeared, leaving a smooth line at his
waist, making her miss the slight shelf she had found cute and
fun to pinch. She hated herself for wanting him so badly, for
being so weak.

"Why are you here?" she asked stiffly, using her feet to kick
the box inside the door, feeling defensive and wide open for more
disappointment. Travis crossed awkwardly over to help her,
handing her his beer can, then heaving the box up and over to a
clear corner of the room.

"I just wanted to say good-bye—" he began.

"Good-bye," she replied quickly, feeling her heart sink when
he didn't go on.

As he walked toward her again she backed away from him.
"I'm not going to touch you," he promised, carefully extracting
the beer can from her hand without making contact with her
skin. The sad part about it was he didn't need to. The air between
the two of them was charged with sexual chemistry.

"Please leave," she urged, her voice slightly too high.

"There're a few things we're going to have to talk about and
get settled—"

"Talk to Cora Ann. I don't want to have any communication
with you, Travis. Not for a while. I'm not ready for it."

"C'mon, Tori." As he put his hand on her arm she felt herself
trembling. She wanted him to hold her, to scoop her up in his
arms, to carry her into the bedroom and make all this reality
vanish. Instead she yanked roughly away from him.

"Travis, I want you out of here," she shouted. "Just leave.
Haven't you got any decency? Any inkling of how I feel?"

"I know exactly how you feel!" he shouted back at her.

How? Tori thought. *How do I feel? Tell me.*

"You want to be with me. I want to be with you. This is crazy
—your leaving. Give me six months. What's another six months?
Let's see how we both feel then—"

"No," Tori said firmly. "If you don't know now, you *never*
will."

"It's not that simple—"

"For a *normal* person it would be. You just can't ever make a commitment. You can't ever make up your mind. If you feel like you're going to be trapped, if that's how you view it all, then I don't want to be married to you anyway. I don't want to be in the position of feeling like I'm putting a leash on anybody—"

"Then why get married? Why take the chance of ruining a perfectly good relationship? We've got a better thing going than any married couple we know."

"That's just your arrogant opinion of it, Travis." God, why were they fighting about this again? "I'm not trying to talk you into anything. *I* want to get married. *You* don't. Period. The end. So get out of here, *please*. Leave me alone!"

"Would you want someone to stay with you just because of the obligation of marriage?"

"No. Maybe. I don't know," Tori replied, confused. The truth was, maybe she would. If she were older and they had kids, and he wanted to leave, maybe she would want the security of knowing it wouldn't be so easy for him to leave.

"Look, I know you want kids. And that does change things," Travis said, calming down a bit, his tone turning gentler. "So maybe we would. I don't know. If you really wanted them. I know you'd be a good mother. So if you end up pregnant, then we'll get married. But let's just let it play out naturally. . . ."

Travis had his arms around her waist. His fingers were on that belt he couldn't resist. "God, I miss you so much," he was whispering into her ear, bringing her closer into him. His touch made it impossible for her to respond to the resounding message in her brain that was saying *Back away.*

We are getting nowhere, was all Tori could think. She felt dizzy and confused as he held her more tightly than ever, his cheek pressed against hers, telling her how wonderful she smelled. She fought for control as his large mouth covered hers in a kiss she knew she was desperately going to miss. Then she felt herself caving in as his tongue moved sensually along her neck, making her squirm, pressing on until she was finally kissing him back. There was an alarm blaring in her head and her heart was pounding, but it was nothing compared to this burning-hot desire she was feeling for him.

She wanted to disconnect her brain and *simply feel*. She was crying, and he was kissing her tears, diffusing them all over her face.

Then he did what she had wanted him to do all along. He lifted her up into his arms, cradling her as he carried her into the bedroom, stepping around cartons and then easing her down onto the bed, never separating his mouth from hers, moaning into nearly every kiss.

"Goddamn it, Travis," she managed, completely under the spell of him as a wave of fluid rolled beneath them from the water-inflated mattress, conforming to their shape and movement. She thought fleetingly of her mother, and then her airline ticket, as his hands moved over her stomach, unfastening her belt and casting it off onto the hardwood floor, where it landed noisily. Her parents were expecting her for dinner. Her flight was in two and half hours. What was she doing? His hands were caressing her back now, drawing down the zipper of her dress. She wriggled out of it, sighing as his lips touched down hotly onto her stomach. *God, what's the matter with me?* she thought loosely, intensely conscious of his breath warm and velvety there. He had a physical hold on her, and all she wanted in this instant was to be making love with him.

Forget logic, forget what she was raised to believe she needed. The urge right now was more demanding, more intense. She was helping Travis get out of his pants. She was struggling right along with him, with his zipper, getting the jeans down and off. Now they were one, in sync, wanting the same thing. Pleasure blurred with need, and it existed on a level that wiped out logic because it seemed pure and therefore right.

How she wanted to believe those cons of his, those familiar fragments of comfort imploring her to stay. If only she could surrender to life as it was and love him without complication, without worrying about the future and commitments. If only she were twenty-three again and not feeling pressed for time. Tori fought for control one final time as he pushed aside the quilt and another large wave sloshed beneath them. They were now completely undressed, and she was moving her lips down the length of him, feeling him respond as he angled onto his side, cupping her rear end in his hand.

What a state everything was in. What a cluttered mass of contradiction and confusion. From the partially packed cartons that had taken over their small, always impeccably in order condominium to the crazy myriad of flowers that had also been arriving at home, nothing made sense anymore.

With him hard and urgent inside her now, kissing her with the fever of never seeing her again, she closed her eyes and held on to him, moving with the rhythm of their desire, loving him more than she ever wanted to love anyone again. There was a stillness in the room as their bodies slapped tensely against one another. *Ask me to marry you! Dammit. Get your damn divorce and promise me the rest of your life. . . .* Tears washed down Tori's face as she clung to him, on the edge of climaxing, needing the release. Then as she did, and he relaxed into his own ecstasy, he astonished them both with a proposal.

"You're not going to Los Angeles," he gasped, his body still shuddering from orgasm. "To hell with everything; I'm going to marry you."

Tori was too stunned to reply. It wasn't how she had envisioned a proposal, and she wasn't sure she believed him. There had been too many semiproposals from him in the past. *Semi,* because they had always hinged on some distant slippery detail: money, or his getting a divorce. Gun-shy from a history of disappointments, she pulled away and looked at him, trying to read his soul.

"Tori, I mean it this time," he assured her, propping himself up onto his side to face her and taking her hands. "I really do."

Torn between euphoria and deep skepticism, Tori looked away from him to the ice-blue walls they had painted together, the framed poster art. There were photographs of the two of them scattered around the room. And there were the multitude of boxes marked for Beverly Hills. "I want you to marry me," he whispered, holding on even more tightly to her hands. The loving way in which he said it made her heart leap, and she felt giddy with victory.

"What about your divorce, Travis?" It was a question that made them both nervous.

He punched his pillow, folding it in half and arranging it under his head for a cushion. "Don't worry about it. I'll take care of it."

Tori hedged. The moment was so precious, so fragile; she was afraid of shattering it. "Travis, if you let me down again, I'll *never* forgive you." Her small hand formed a fist of nervous energy that she pressed menacingly into his thick chest.

Lying there watching her, he was the picture of innocence, and she felt guilty for not trusting him.

"How about if I swear on the Bible for you? Huh?" He grinned, tracing his index finger along her hips.

"No good. You're a lousy Catholic."

"Okay, then, I'll swear on my mother's life," he relented playfully, getting up onto his knees and tickling her.

"Last week you wanted to kill her—" Tori protested, squirming as he caught her mercilessly under the ribs.

"All right. I'll swear on my Porsche—"

"Travis, this is serious—" Tori said, trying not to laugh. She watched his brown eyes scan the room, then the length of her, as he calculated what to say next.

"Okay, then, what kind of engagement ring do you want?" he asked after a moment, bounding cheerfully out of bed and crossing the planked wood floor to disappear into the bathroom.

Now, that's serious.

"A big one," she replied, smiling in spite of her anxiety.

He uttered something under his breath, then peeked his head around the door. "How big is big?"

"Big enough that the investment will be too great for you to feel comfortable about backing out."

Travis gripped the door as though someone were strangling him, then collected himself to assure her he would be all right. As he kicked the door shut he let out a loud groan.

"I'm worth it," Tori shouted over the noise of the shower being turned on. It wouldn't be nearly as big as Kit's engagement ring. Kit's husband, George, probably earned in a month what it took Travis a full year to earn. But it didn't matter one bit to Tori. She felt happier at this moment than she could ever remember feeling in her life.

Sitting up and raising her long graceful arms into the air, she let out a quiet little cry of excitement. The mirror across the room reflected her joy, and she smiled at the vision there, feeling young, beautiful, and wonderfully righteous for having ignored her parents all these years when they had told her she was throwing away her best years, wasting them with Travis.

A bad marriage bet? Maybe. But they had underestimated their daughter.

The dozen or so boxes cluttering the room seemed to echo that sentiment, and she glanced gratefully at them, not minding in the least the chore of unpacking that lay ahead of her. The boxes had been her artillery. The flowers had been his. And all thanks to Paige and Susan, for without them, none of this would ever have happened. Funny, she really barely knew either one of them, and yet it seemed today that they were her very best friends. She couldn't wait to call them up to share her tremendous news.

Plucking a begonia from out of an arrangement near the bed, she pinned it into her hair. Then she got out of bed, wrapping the sheet around her naked body and dragging it along for effect to join her fiancé in the bathroom.

Chapter 4

The darkened theater was eerie and magical. A spectacle of cat eyes glittered in the blackness of the aisles that were like dark shadows beneath the lighting designer's pale moon. Scintillatingly, from all over the theater at once, the silent cats began to emerge, scampering forms, prowling toward the huge nocturnal junkyard that was now the stage for T. S. Eliot's flighty Jellicle Cats. As the lights came up, the brilliantly designed set sprang to life, revealing a kind of cosmic playground for cats, a fanciful junkyard with the litter of human consumerism all awesomely scaled.

Outfitted in whiskers, electronically glowing eyes, masklike makeup, and a sleek body-stocking cat costume, Paige slithered across the imaginatively constructed stage set of *Cats,* dancing her way through the collage of junk, slinking around the rusty pots and pans, cast-off cereal boxes, archaic appliances, forsaken mops, dismembered bicycle parts, and giant pushed-in toothpaste tubes.

Bigger. Make it count! Shoulders back. Stomach in. Reach. Stretch. That's it. Saucy now. Leap. Quick turn. Crouch. And hold . . . She'd heard the choreographer's commands so frequently, they played in her head with more force than the words of the songs. Jazz, ballet, acrobatics, these were talented cats indeed, felines of every variety, sending limbs and fur flying in Tony-winning fashion.

Paige was sweating from the hot lights and frenzied exertion, dancing as though she were the only one out there, the focus of the beat, the cat to end all cats. With the ritual of the steps now as reflexive as breathing, she added feeling, more feeling than anyone would ever know.

It was cry or dance, because she couldn't believe this was her last time out there. She was walking out on the dream she had grown up with, only partially fulfilled, and at the same time fighting an insane urge to make this final performance night of hers count. How tempting it was to deviate from the choreographed routine they all did now by rote, to break out of the woodwork of the chorus and perform unrestrained. She thought of the late great Isadora Duncan and imagined the freedom she must have felt dancing out the rhythm that was in her soul, in her mind.

What could they do to her? Paige wondered, now on her knees, swinging her shapely behind for effect. Arrest her? Throw her in jail?

And what about the rest of the cast? It would be a feline fiasco, she mused, as a group of alley cats with dramatically sculpted hair and makeup disguising the faces of eighteen-year-olds, curled around her with a convincing snarl. They were like living celluloid of a younger Paige, when her hopes had been as high as the heavens, her drive fierce. Youth. For them the chorus lines still held promise. Now Paige didn't know whether to envy them or pity them. At thirty, the promise felt like a lie.

Paige hoped Cathy, the pretty one on the end, would make it. Cathy was an outstanding talent, with superb technique, great style. And she was sweet. Of course, in the end, the sweetness could be her downfall. She would need to withstand the harsh and cutthroat elements of the theater, an environment that demanded toughness.

Paige had been tough, and tall, and even talented. She had come *close,* as they say, even made it to second understudy once for a big role in *42nd Street.* But the first understudy had been unforgivably healthy—apparently immune to even the slightest common cold, with muscles that never strained. Paige had spent sleepless nights trying to figure out how to get both the star and the first understudy down at the same time so that she could have at least one shot. She had entertained absurd fantasies like drugging their coffee, having them abducted for a day or two. A slight sprained ankle might have done the trick, but it would have been impossible to trip both of them. She had even envisioned inviting them over for dinner the night before a performance and adding Ex-Lax to their chocolate soufflés which she, of course, would refrain from eating.

Paige plotted plenty. But she never played.

Favorite numbers whizzed by, slipping into memories before they were even completed. There was always a kind of sentimental rush that went along with a final night on a show. But this was Paige's final night on *stage*.

Her thoughts jumped to Susan and Tori, and she wondered how they were handling leaving. Susan had sounded excited, committed, and strangely adjusted to the decision. Tori had sounded as though her leaving symbolized her defeat. She needed bolstering, that was for sure. They had exchanged a few quick phone calls back and forth, mostly talking to one another's answering machines, confirming details, all of them wanting to make certain the others were genuinely going through with this, nobody wanting to quit their job or ditch their boyfriend, to find themselves all alone in L.A. They needed each other.

The closing number in *Cats* was fast approaching its extravagantly staged finale, with a swell of music and frantically changing lights accompanying the alley cats' ascent into the heavens on a space machine.

That's me, Paige thought drolly, *moving out of this life and ascending into another*. Sure, there would be that glittery presence of stars there, but was Beverly Hills really going to be heaven?

Paige was facing a flood of second thoughts when the house lights came up, signaling the performance's end. It was as though she were being hit with her own mortality, the conclusion of the show marking with piercing clarity the end of her career. As she ran out with the rest of the cast, holding hands, bowing, smiling to the thunderous applause, she realized she was feeling more emotion than perhaps she had ever felt in her life. It was so much sadness welling up inside her, ready to explode.

She was actually reeling with an unfulfilled longing for that last burst of applause, reserved for the star, to belong to *her*. Once and for all *she* wanted to be the one clutching the prover-bial bouquet of flowers to her heart and weeping with elation over a performance *well done*—because the audience loved her—because she loved herself. It was a vision that would never come to pass.

As the applause swelled, heightening Paige's anxiety, scattered members of the audience began to rise to their feet in standing ovation. Paige watched as others followed suit, a trend the cast had come to expect.

Her own legs felt weak. They ached, and not from any pulled muscles, but from fear. God, she had been so cavalier about it all up until now. But what had made her so brazenly sure of herself? Was she trading one fantasy for another? *Why can't I set normal goals for myself? Because you're not normal,* was the simple re-sponse of a fellow cast member when they'd sat together in the dressing room before the show, Paige applying cat whiskers for the last time. These were her friends, her soul mates, odd and strained as their relationships were, and she squeezed on tightly to their hands as she ran out to take another sweeping bow. She was part of a chain, and she moved more by their motion now than her own. *Stop crying, you jerk,* she told herself, feeling her makeup going all to hell, thick grease paint bleeding together. She couldn't even wipe away the tears with her hands because they were attached to all those other hands.

Earlier today someone had been talking about an opening on a daytime soap. Paige wondered if she should consider postponing her flight a day or two and go for a reading on the part. If she got it, the pay would be good enough to move to the Upper West Side, where she had been dying to live. She could afford to update her portfolio. Enroll in the new Method acting class she had been wanting to take. Maybe go to Europe during hiatus. Get a new wardrobe. And if she got *that* part, there would be others. She would have finally broken in. She would be "network approved."

So long, chorus lines; hello, national TV. She had a *feeling* about this particular part, this show. Maybe it was fate. Maybe just because she was planning on leaving tomorrow and because she was going out for the role strictly on a lark, this time she would actually get it.

The applause was petering out. Paige's heartbeat was escalating. One more reading—what did she really have to lose?

There was her commitment to Tori and Susan. But they could go it without her. And certainly they would understand. If Tori had stayed in Atlanta because Travis had broken down and proposed to her, Paige would have been *happy* for her. Besides, she was doing them both a giant favor, changing their lives for the better. Paige would stay in New York and become a sensation on TV. Susan and Tori would move to Beverly Hills as planned, meet and marry their multimillionaires, and they'd all live happily ever after.

But was that really what Paige wanted? Certainly she could pursue a television career in L.A. as easily, if not more easily than in New York. What happened to her resolve to abandon all that? Paige was having as much trouble letting go of her go-nowhere career as Tori was of her go-nowhere romance.

It was about three in the morning when Paige finally returned home from the farewell party the cast had thrown for her. Her apartment building was dark and hot and smelled from the Chinese take-out joint that was on the ground floor. In the winter the smell was never that apparent. But in July and August the ride up in the shaky little elevator was nauseating, until about the seventh floor. Thankfully, Paige's flat was up on nine.

After unbolting the series of locks on her door, Paige pushed it open and stepped into her now-sparse apartment. Over the weekend she had sold all of her furniture, posters, old clothes, dishes. All that was left in the tiny place was a sleeping bag she had borrowed from the guy across the hall, a pillow, a coffeemaker, the telephone, which was being disconnected tomorrow and was still hooked up to her answering machine, a small pile of clothes, her makeup case, which was open and in great disarray, and two duffel bags packed for L.A.

"I wonder," she said aloud to the empty room, satisfied with her latest plan. She had decided if she didn't go out for that part in the soap, somewhere deep inside she would always believe the part could have been hers, and she would never forgive herself. A friend from the cast knew one of the producers on the show, called him at home, and arranged a reading for Paige. If she got the part, she would stay in New York, and if she didn't get it, she would give up once and for all and be on that plane to California pursuing a brand-new destiny with no regrets.

The red light indicating messages flashed from the answering machine, and she stumbled exhaustedly over to play them back, wrenching off her boots and shedding her clothes onto the floor on her way.

The first message was from Tori, and at the sound of her trusting voice recorded over the crackly long-distance line, Paige felt a fleeting sense of guilt and disloyalty.

But it passed abruptly as she stood there stunned, feeling instead betrayed by Tori's news.

Getting married! Travis had actually buckled and was going to marry her? Paige couldn't believe her ears.

Her first reaction was anger. She was astonished and hurt, as though Tori were deserting them. Then she remembered how *she* was hoping to be the deserter, and she just felt confused, worried about Susan. Susan couldn't move out to L.A. by herself. She would have a nervous breakdown finding herself in that big house, in that big city, on her own.

Paige listened loosely to the rest of Tori's message, which included effusive apologies and then bursts of excitement as she discussed impending wedding plans, struggling to be happy for her. She shoved open the solitary window over where her couch used to be, but the warm dense air offered little relief in the small studio apartment, which felt suddenly more confining than ever.

Great, now what? Paige thought, clicking off the machine in the middle of Tori's cheerful good-bye, wondering if she still had the heart to go for her audition tomorrow. She dropped down onto the bare hardwood floor, missing the faded but pretty Persian rug that had been there. Dammit, why should she feel so responsible for Susan? Susan was a big girl. So if she ended up the only one of the three of them going out to L.A., that wasn't the worst thing either. She was a professional woman, an attorney. And as Susan had said herself, she was much better off in a big city like L.A. than in Stockton.

Sitting cross-legged, stripped down to her underwear, with little beads of perspiration forming on her stomach, Paige felt practically convinced she was going to get the part in the soap. Life worked that way, taking forever to deliver what you were aching to have and then throwing a curve in with it. Tense with the dilemma now posed, she snapped the answering machine back on, wary about what other little zingers might lay in store for her.

"Hi. It's Dustin Brent." Somehow Paige hadn't expected to hear from him again, since they had already worked out all the details of their move, and she held her breath, thinking how strange it would be if he was also calling to bow out. What if he had decided not to go mountain climbing and his house-sitting offer was off?

It was with a start that Paige realized how disappointed she would actually be, and drawing her knees up close to her chest, she listened anxiously as he went on, praying she hadn't jinxed a good thing and triggered this reverse trend.

The sound of Dustin's voice alone made her want to cancel her tryout at the network and head out to California without another thought. It had nothing to do with Susan. It had to do with palm trees, gorgeous weather, and the lure of rich, powerful men like Dustin Brent. A stirring deep within Paige rekindled all that she had been feeling when she had been struck by the urge to move in the first place, and she sighed, deeply relieved when it became clear that he was not calling to rescind his offer.

What the hell had she been thinking?

For the better part of her life she had been pitting herself against the overwhelmingly bad odds of the theater, depositing years into a kind of giant slot machine and waiting for the payout. Small wins, just when she was ready to quit, would sabotage her logic. Broken hopes kept getting pasted back together. But the seams were beginning to show, and she realized now it was time to bow out gracefully while she was still young enough to do something else with her life.

So what if she got this part? The reality was that it was a nice role on a relatively popular soap. But it wasn't going to make her a star.

Paige didn't even *want* to be a star anymore.

What she wanted was a life like Kit's!

"So, I guess tomorrow's the big day," Dustin's voice replayed breezily. "If you let me know which flight you're coming in on, I'll arrange to have you met at the airport. . . ."

With happy resolve Paige replayed the message when it was over.

Susan Kendell Brown had a roommate after all.

As Damon Runyon used to say, "If you rub up against money long enough, some of it may rub up against you."

That's what Paige was thinking as she began to board her flight at Kennedy's TWA terminal, a flight she vowed was going to change her life.

She had woken up that morning feeling great, in spite of only a few hours sleep, liberated from a dream in which she no longer believed and happy because she was finally being entirely honest with herself about what she wanted.

She felt like the million bucks she was looking forward to having as a balance in her checking account soon.

A slender brunette who looked a lot like Tori rushed up to the check-in counter, her arm linked possessively through her male companion's. They were laughing at something, looking enraptured with one another. Of course it wasn't Tori. Tori was in Atlanta, probably also looking enraptured.

Paige had reached Tori early in the morning to congratulate her on her engagement to Travis. She had tried to sound enthused, but Tori had laughed and told her that when it came to real life, she put on an unconvincing performance. Both of them had laughed, feeling a strange attachment to one another, considering the short time they had been acquainted.

"Hey, I hope this guy appreciates what a 'peach' he's getting," Paige had then teased lightly, thinking about how it wasn't going to be the same without Tori.

"I think he does. Thanks to you . . ." Tori had drawled happily in response, her voice trailing off and gaining, in its awkward silence, a more serious note. "Paige, I don't know how to begin to thank you—"

"Name your first kid after me. How's that?" Paige had kidded, moved.

After some more affectionate teasing, they seemed to run out of conversation, each of them wishing the other one luck, wondering when they would meet up again.

It felt odd after having lived her whole life in New York that Paige's only sad good-bye had been to her friend in Georgia.

In New York her friends seemed to be whomever she was working with at the time, and there was always an off-key edge to the friendship because of professional jealousies. Even at the party the cast had thrown for her last night, there had been no teary farewells, no difficult severing of attachments. The relationships were of a different nature; they had to be. They all knew that at any given time they might be up against one another for a role they couldn't live without. The competition was too much to bear and often brought out the worst in all of them. Their closeness would become marred, and although they stuck together, nobody really trusted one another; envy and resentments clung too close to the surface.

The only potentially difficult good-bye Paige envisioned would have been to her father. But, as usual, he was on the road. As a traveling salesman he had represented everything from widgets to eye shadows. Now he was having the time of his life, selling a sexy line of lacy lingerie and, Paige supposed, probably giving half of it away to females he had enticed along the way.

Paige's father, a widower now, was in his late sixties, but still dashing. He was a dreamer and completely irresponsible. Her mother had been the only steady provider in the family, and Paige always knew she should have felt grateful to her, but it hadn't been easy.

For her mother, life had existed as a gray reality. With her father, the color of life was psychedelic, the shades and possibilities endless. While growing up, Paige rarely saw her father because he was always on the road. Yet it was those memorable visits that had always kept her able to see the bright side.

When Paige was eleven, her mother died of a bleeding ulcer. Paige's father said she had worried herself to death over things she couldn't change.

It was on the issue of change that Paige decided she was somewhere in the middle of their genetic pool. She was dreamer enough to believe in her ability to change just about whatever it was she wanted and pragmatic enough to change courses when the dream no longer appeared practical.

Right now Paige believed in change. The challenge was knowing what it was she wanted on the other side.

Being propelled forward and into the airplane by the bulge of passengers, Paige contemplated the series of well-heeled, mostly male passengers settling into first class. She zeroed knowledgeably in on the quality of their shoes and their briefcases, letting her glance ride up critically to assess the tailoring of their suits. One way to insure falling for a guy with a lot of money was to plant herself in their exclusive midst, she was thinking, beginning to debate how she might maneuver a first-class seat for herself.

Everyone knew about airplane romances—the person one might meet and have a flirtation with, if not more, during the several-hour flight to a mutual destination. Five hours of sitting next to a stranger had been known to produce astonishing intimacy.

If Paige had been assigned a window seat or an aisle seat, she might have stayed put. But because of her middle seat, squeezed in between a guy with a cold and a woman the size of a whale, who liked to talk, Paige felt compelled to try for that upgrade. Her oppressive seat assignment became almost a dare—something to read as fate.

In the midst of calculating her move a pretty blond stewardess greeted her in the aisle with effusive compliments on her wild technicolor earrings, which were shaped like flying saucers.

"I love your earrings. Where did you find them?" the stewardess asked as Paige stepped aside so as not to block the flow of passengers still entering.

"Bloomingdale's," Paige replied.

"God, my layovers in New York never seem to be long enough for me to go shopping anymore," the stewardess lamented, looking longingly at them while Paige looked longingly past her into the first-class section, where she noticed passengers already being supplied with French champagne, magazines, and other upgraded service. "Oh, well. Maybe in my next life."

"What about in this life?" Paige suggested shrewdly, turning back to her and looking around to make sure they weren't being overheard. "I'll make you a deal. You get me a seat in first class and the earrings are yours—today."

Paige watched the stewardess laugh, amused, trying to decide whether Paige was serious or not. When she saw that she was, she went over to check what Paige imagined to be a schedule of seating assignments.

Then, eyeing the proposed collateral with obvious temptation, she told Paige she'd be right back. There were two other attendants manning the first-class section, and Paige watched as the pretty blonde whispered something to them, causing them to look her way. Their smiles indicated the kind of "why not?" mentality that appealed to Paige as they signaled her over to a vacant seat.

When the stewardess brought Paige a diet Coke and a menu for the flight, Paige pointed to a familiar-looking man seated across the aisle from her and down a couple rows. "Who's that man? I know I know him from somewhere," she asked, trying to place him.

"Kareem Abdul-Jabbar," the stewardess whispered discreetly, bending down.

Paige actually hadn't noticed the seven-foot-tall athlete seated by the window and she peered around, impressed, thinking she would be even more impressed if she knew anything about basketball. "Not him. The guy sitting next to him," she replied.

"Oh. That's Jerry Buss. He owns the Lakers." The stewardess grinned knowingly at Paige. "Single. Supposed to be a great guy and lots of fun. Want any more profiles?"

"That'll do for now," Paige said, wondering about Buss. Too bad he was so absorbed talking to Jabbar. Once he turned and looked her way, but that was that. It appeared to be a working trip.

The earrings turned out to be a worthwhile exchange anyway.

While the five-hour flight failed to produce a worthwhile airplane romance, it did yield two interesting L.A. contacts who made a point of giving Paige their business cards, along with a gentle easing into the kind of first-class life-style to which Paige planned to become accustomed.

Chapter 5 ~

Dustin Brent's house stood like a monument to Paige's goal.

It was a large Mediterranean-style house set up on a knoll, with a grand Hollywood-fashion circular driveway that was palm lined and had a heavily populated stone fishpond built into the center of it.

As the heavy wrought iron gates spread open, Paige sat back smugly in the flashy black Aston-Martin in which she had been picked up from the airport, finding it hard to believe she was *really* here—that she had maneuvered fantasy into reality—that this amazing palatial spread was to be her new home.

Throughout the lengthy ride she had been playing with different images of what her new *residence* was going to look like, creating vivid pictures in her head. When Evonne, Dustin's secretary, had announced that they were almost there, Paige had tried to guess which house it was going to be. She wouldn't have dared to guess this one. It was too perfect.

In a large round mirror positioned for viewing traffic, she caught sight of herself driving through the posh gates, seated inside the flashy sports car, and she thought, with a little thrill, how so far *everything* was perfect. Aside from the mild disappointment that Dustin wouldn't be there to greet her.

On the drive over, Evonne had told her how she and Dustin had passed somewhere over the Continental United States, where she was flying west and he was flying east, on his way to wind up unexpected business in New York before his departure for Nepal.

Single, loaded, and soon to be out of the country. Too bad!

"I have just enough time to give you a quick tour," Evonne apologized hurriedly when they were inside, her pale saffron skirt and blouse swinging attractively as she walked. With the giant natural clam shell buckle on her belt and her smart silver-and-topaz jewelry, Dustin's pretty red-headed secretary seemed to blend with the soft California decor of the house, which was so much more "done" than Paige would have imagined, considering its inhabitant was a bachelor.

The house looked to be straight out of *Architectural Digest,* and in fact, she was amused to learn a moment later that it was. Angled on a unique fossil-studded stone coffee table in the living room was a copy of the prestigious magazine, a photo from this precise view gracing its famous cover.

Pale pimiento paver tiles on the floor connected the grand-scale rooms, which were monochromatic, the walls painted an earthy sensuous color reminiscent of southern Spain. Expansive uncurtained windows opened out onto luxuriant landscapes. The furniture seemed to be scaled up to accommodate the vastness of the room, solid without being overbearing. There were rattan armchairs, plumply cushioned in white linen, an airy chaise of rattan and cane, and two bold chairs with rolled upholstered arms in subdued shades of melon with white. Along one wall Paige noticed a collection of rare-looking Indian baskets. And then on the other side of the room fishtail palms caught her eye, soaring high into the lofty beamed ceiling, bent as if caught in the middle of gale-force winds.

The Spanish-speaking housekeeper, introduced to Paige as Maria, headed upstairs with the only earthly belongings Paige had retained packed into two new canvas duffel bags, and Paige watched as they disappeared from sight.

"Think you can get used to this?" Evonne teased, moving swiftly past a fat marble sculpture that Paige almost bumped into. A tiny plaque designated the clean Mexican-looking work as *Zuniga. Zuniga almost shattered,* Paige thought with nervous relief, trying to absorb everything in one elongated glance as she followed alongside her elegant tour guide. "Stop me if you have any questions."

"Hmmm. Thanks," Paige said, more than just a little over-whelmed as they passed through the living room and into the equally impressive den, where one full wall was devoted to photo-graphs.

It was an interesting glimpse into Dustin's life, featuring her host, who was practically a stranger, with a variety of friends, celebrities, politicians, and also a number of travel shots. There were photographs of Dustin skiing in Gstaad, Dustin with his arm around an exotic girl in a deserted-looking beach cove, Dus-tin in Japan with an army of Japanese kids, all grinning deliri-ously.

"What are you going to do, with Dustin out of the country for so long and his company sold? Are you going to continue to work for him?" Paige asked Evonne curiously.

"As you may have already guessed, Dustin's a pretty unusual guy, and extraordinarily generous . . ." Evonne smiled, glanc-ing fondly over at a photograph of her boss where he appeared to be smiling back at her. "First of all, he sold his company—but he still has a lot of business interests I'll be keeping an eye on. There'll be some minimal correspondence. But for the most part he says *he's* getting a vacation, so *I* might as well get one, too. When he gets back, we'll both go back to the *grind.*"

"Was he ever married?" Paige asked, noticing how many dif-ferent females were represented in the gallery of photo memories. On closer examination there appeared to be a recurrence of only one.

"Yes. Jana." Evonne's eyes seemed to gravitate to the pretty brunette.

Just as Paige was thinking it was odd that he would have so many pictures of his ex-wife hanging on the wall, Evonne began to explain how his wife had died in a plane crash about five or six years ago, while taking flying lessons. There had been some kind of mechanical failure and the plane had gone down over the Santa Monica mountains. "Dustin didn't even know she was taking lessons," Evonne said, frowning. "She was doing it as a surprise because *he* was into airplanes and loved to fly. Can you imagine?"

Paige looked over at another picture of Dustin, seeing him differently, the gaiety diminished. "How long had they been married?"

"Just a few years. She was really special. Looked a lot like Jennifer O'Neill."

"Did they have kids?"

"No."

"I wonder why he never remarried."

"Jana was a pretty tough act to follow," Evonne said quietly.

They were both looking at a wedding photograph that was off to one side. The simple look of joy on their faces sent a chill through Paige.

Then, changing the subject, Evonne pointed a long manicured finger at the bar, where a bottle of champagne was angled into a silver ice bucket, arranged beside three fluted champagne glasses. "Dustin left that for you and your friends, although I understand there's just to be two of you now. He said since he couldn't be here to toast you all in person, he was toasting you in spirit."

He's going to be a tough act to follow, Paige thought to herself, noticing the expensive Cristal label. Generous was an understatement—giving Evonne six months to a year's semivacation, lending near-strangers his house, his cars. From what she had heard from Kit, he was even subsidizing the other climbers in the mountain climbing expedition. She was dying to ask Evonne if he'd been this generous *before* he sold his business for fifty million dollars. Something told her the answer to that question was yes.

Definitely impressed, Paige followed Evonne into the kitchen, where Dustin Brent's extraordinary taste was also in evidence. Everything was sleek, high-tech, and efficient-looking with black granite countertops, gleaming white cabinets trimmed in stainless steel, and industrial ovens and refrigerator.

One section of the kitchen was devoted entirely to Indian cooking, and Paige poked about, intrigued, as Evonne told her how, after he had spent some time there, Dustin got frustrated with the American preparation of what had become his favorite food, and he flew a chef out from New Delhi to give him private cooking instruction—even installed an authentic tandoor oven. *What a life,* Paige thought as Evonne toyed with a silver-framed topaz earring, then gestured her over toward a wall of cookbooks, explaining how half of them were translations of prized Indian editions.

"He is so obsessive that he once fell madly in love with a Picasso and, cash short, sold a building because he couldn't live without it," Evonne related, grinning, as they mounted a back set of stairs that led up to the second floor. "He loves watches," she added, as though to further prove her point. "Has a hundred and two different kinds, some of which are so rare, I need to keep an updated inventory for insurance. He loves sweaters—has literally pounds of cashmere . . ."

They had entered Dustin's bedroom, which was probably the sexiest bedroom Paige had ever seen. It was plush, large, and masculine, opening up onto a private office, a handsomely furnished gym, a steam room, a Jacuzzi, two huge walk-in closets, and as Paige pointed out with an amused chuckle, there was even a *bed.* There was something sensuously pleasing about the sheer extravagance, the pounds of cashmere sweaters piled neatly one on top of the other in every imaginable color, and the endless rows of shoes, from buttery leathers and snakeskin to sneakers.

Paige envisioned borrowing a couple of those heavenly cashmeres, belting them and sticking in shoulder pads, adding an oversized blazer, and rolling up the sleeves. He even had a couple of interesting hats.

But after a brief tour through Dustin's bedroom, Evonne told Paige that it was to be the only off-limits portion of the house. There were four other bedrooms upstairs, all of them also exquisitely furnished, with bathrooms that seemed larger than her apartment.

Her *former* apartment, Paige reminded herself with a satisfied grin, still considering snatching a cashmere.

Later, standing under a rich spray of temperature-controlled water, lathering her hair in a sumptuous shampoo that smelled of fresh, tart California lemons, and not having to bump her elbows as she did so, Paige decided she was in love.

She was in love with her new life, with this house, with Beverly Hills. She was in love with the endless possibilities that appeared to await her here: Men, money, and sunshine. The recurrent theme prevailed. Something deep inside Paige made her feel like she was going to have it all. And for the first time in ages she felt focused. Focused and optimistic.

Paige stepped out of the shower and wrapped herself in a plush peach-colored towel. Peering into the steamy mirror, rubbing it to create a smudge of visibility, she found herself thinking about Tori and how perfect this particular guest suite would have been for her. It could have aptly been called the Georgia Peach Suite. There was silver-and-peach wallpaper in the bathroom, soft peach suede walls in the bedroom. Even the bed fittings had luxurious sprays of peach-colored palm fronds silkscreened onto them. As Paige entered the spacious peach-perfect room, enjoying the swankiness of it, she heard the doorbell ring.

Susan, at last, she thought, letting her towel drop onto the floor and snatching up her robe. She was only partially into it when she ran out to the staircase landing and saw Maria opening the door.

Looking bedraggled from her long drive from Stockton, Susan walked tentatively into the house, wearing jeans, a preppy-looking T-shirt, tennis shoes, and a look of complete awe on her face. Paige watched as Susan smiled self-consciously at the housekeeper, taking in her surroundings with great curiosity as she handed over her two modest-looking suitcases.

"You must drive like a snail . . ." Paige shouted down, welcoming her friend with a roguish grin. It was a little like being the first roommate to have arrived at the college dorm. Well, on second thought, *not quite.*

Tori caught a glimpse of herself in the mirror as she passed through the lobby of the Ritz Carlton Hotel on her way to meet her mother for lunch. She was glad to see that she looked as good as she felt. The image she reflected was tall, demure, and positively radiant. She had on a pale pink buttery leather pantsuit, the sleeves on her large extensively padded jacket pushed up to just below the elbows, an ivory silk Charmeuse sleeveless shirt, and a chunky silver necklace. Her skin-tight leather pants squeaked quietly as she walked, creating a rhythm to the tune in her head—a jaunty strain from "I'm Getting Married in the Morning." Of course, she wasn't really getting married in the morning, but she was getting married soon. *Soon.* God, it was still so hard to believe.

As she approached the dining room she was greeted by the tinkling sounds of fine china, silver, and crystal. It was one of those electric days, and she could feel heads turning to watch her. She met each pair of eyes with a confident smile, sharing her joy, knowing how infectious it was. Then, as she looked through the plush cactus-toned room that was architecturally high-tech but classical in decor, she spotted her mother already seated, regarding her menu through a pair of tangerine-colored granny glasses that matched her smart tangerine linen suit.

"Hi," Tori issued cheerfully, sliding into a rosewood-framed chair that was being pulled out for her by one of the many hovering waiters.

"Don't you look beautiful," her mother commented, looking up from her leather-bound menu and over her glasses, which were perched on the end of the same fine aristocratic nose that Tori had inherited.

"Thanks," Tori replied. "You look great, too."

Amanda Mitchell always did. Even when she went to the market she looked perfect, hair and makeup done. That was just her way. She believed in always looking one's best. To her, it was a matter of pride and self-respect. Looking especially striking today, her mother glanced down one last time to muse over a selection on her menu, then set it decisively aside, removing her glasses and moving on to the business of her daughter.

"Well, you did it," Amanda said in a congratulatory manner, taking a bite of her celery swivel and saluting Tori with a bright red Bloody Mary. Her elegant face was a mask that Tori had never been very successful at reading. Her mother had sounded pleased when she called to tell her about her engagement to Travis, but her happiness always seemed so controlled.

"Miracle of miracles, right?" Tori smiled. What the hell, she herself was sublimely happy and it would take more than her cynical, frustrated mother to crush her spirits. A waiter came over, and Tori ordered a Mirassou chardonnay that was available by the glass.

"I hate to bring this up, Tori, but when does Travis's divorce become a fait accompli?"

Tori had been waiting for her to bring it up. "He's at his lawyer's right now," she answered, prepared.

Amanda's thoughts seemed to be running in high gear. "Have you set a date?"

"We're hoping for sometime in December. It depends on what Sam says—his attorney."

Amanda's eyebrow arched.

"Look, I know you and Dad aren't exactly crazy about Travis, that you don't trust him. But just be happy for me, okay?" Tori realized she had been wrong about her uncrushable spirits; they were definitely now on the decline. In only a few short moments Amanda had managed to burst her beautiful bubble. Tori sat up straight and looked over toward where the waiter had put in her drink order, suddenly needing it. She studied a porcelain fruit arrangement on the wall.

"We like Travis." Amanda's voice was silky and composed. "It's just that his track record doesn't exactly make me want to run out and bet my life savings on him."

"You never were the betting kind," Tori joked, intent on keeping things light. But Amanda didn't even smile. "Look, Travis takes getting remarried *very* seriously. He made a mistake with his first wife—we all make mistakes—and he's being very cautious this time around."

Amanda opened her mouth to say something, then stopped herself, emitting a clipped sigh. Tori knew it was a trap. That's what Amanda did when she wanted to say something that was most likely out of line.

"What?" Tori asked, in spite of her better judgment, aware that she was falling for old bait.

"Nothing."

Like hell. "C'mon, Mother, what?" Tori insisted impatiently.

Her drink arrived and she took a soothing sip of it, noticing how at all the other tables people seemed to be having such a wonderful time, chatting gaily, waiting for the Ritz Carlton's Friday luncheon fashion show to begin. Anxious for the distraction, she glanced around to see if there were any models yet on the floor. Then, in response to her mother's pregnant silence, she asked tersely, "What is it you're *dying* to say?"

"Do you really think Travis loves you enough?"

Tori felt like standing up and walking out. She looked at her mother, more astonished than angry. "What do you mean *loves me enough*? He wants to marry me—"

"He didn't initiate a proposal—"

"Maybe he's not the initiating type—"

"You gave him an ultimatum, Tori. Marry me or I take off for California—"

"I didn't mean it as an ultimatum, and I didn't present my leaving that way. I had a terrific opportunity to move to California, and I thought why the hell not." Tori fingered the lion-and-crown logo on her wineglass, trying to contain herself. "What did you expect me to do? Just stay? Leave the relationship as it was? *You're* the one who was always complaining about it."

Amanda took a deliberate sip from her drink, not replying right away. "You could have broken up with him but still stayed in Atlanta."

Tori thought, *Why am I even arguing with her? I'm getting married. I'm happy. Who cares what she thinks?* Then she went on anyway. "I still think it would have been the best thing for me to move to California, if things hadn't worked out with Travis. New surroundings, new people, and I'd have been too far away from him to cave in, as I've been *known* to do in the past."

It was a fact that aggravated Amanda to distraction.

"Travis needed a good kick in the pants," Tori went on more tolerantly, since in the end things had worked out as she wanted. It was just going to take a while for the security of that to sink in. "He may *never* have taken the initiative," she continued. "He would have left everything as it was, comfortable. He doesn't care about getting married. *I* do."

"How can you marry someone who doesn't want to marry you?"

"I think he *does* want to marry me."

"He doesn't want to lose you; that's all you really know for sure. He's making this decision under duress. . . ."

Tori couldn't have felt less hungry when their waiter reappeared to take their order. She listened to her mother requesting the cold veal roast with tuna sauce and *viande de Grissons.* It was exactly what Tori had thought she wanted, but her appetite had vanished along with her joy. "I'll have the fresh fruit and cottage cheese," she said, not because it sounded good, but because it was light. Then she decided that her mother was simply being her usual negative self, that Travis did want to marry her, and that she was allowing herself to get psyched out. The purpose of this lunch was to talk about the wedding, not to analyze Travis's motives. After lunch they were on their way to select an engagement ring. That had been Travis's idea. And that's what Tori wanted to focus on. She wanted to go back to feeling elated.

What happened next made it possible. Like a messenger from the heavens above, the waiter returned with a frosty silver ice bucket containing a bottle of Travis's favorite champagne. "Miss Mitchell," he said with a warm smile, as though appreciating the romantic gesture immensely, "compliments of Mr. Travis Walton. He said he'd see you all later at Tiffany's. And something about going easy on a guy. Keep the rock moderate."

Tori let out an audible sigh of relief, thanking the waiter with more gratitude than he could possibly understand. Her confidence flipped back into place, and she eyed her mother, feeling happy and even a little powerful from the win. She wanted to kiss Travis for not letting her down.

Chapter 6

Paige and Susan were already taking full advantage of their gracious new habitat, ensconced in the swirling mist that rose up and out of the steamy outdoor Jacuzzi into the pleasant evening air.

It was a warm lazy summer night, and they had had the best time out at dinner, celebrating their arrival in their new city, talking about the lives they had left behind, speculating about the new lives that lay ahead of them.

"Cliché or no cliché, I think it's really happened. I think I died and went to heaven," Susan said, adjusting her shoulder blades down to the hot rush of water penetrating from the jet, sipping blithely at the champagne Dustin Brent had left for them. She closed her big blue eyes for a moment, sighing pleasurably, then quickly reopened them, half afraid this perfect picture might have vanished. Happily Dustin's immense, breathtakingly landscaped backyard hadn't just been an alcohol-induced hallucination.

Probably enjoying themselves as much as she was, she thought, punchy by now, were the army of crickets who appeared to be out in full force tonight. She watched them darting capriciously in and out of the glow of opalescent lights spread throughout the luscious grounds, where there were lovely beds of flowers, a couple of great old trees with massive branches that looked ripe for climbing, and a large rectangular swimming pool, which gleamed invitingly beneath the moonlight, making it look tempting enough to jump into as soon as the heat from the Jacuzzi got to be too much.

Paige yawned and drained what was left of her drink, reaching over to the nearly empty bottle of champagne and refilling her glass. "I'm getting spoiled. After Kit's wedding, and this, I don't think I'll be able to go back to the cheap stuff," she said, tasting the Cristal with emphasized relish. She maneuvered her bare chest back down beneath the water, grumbling that her breasts weren't large enough to warrant above-water status.

Susan laughed, embarrassed, unaccustomed to Paige's brashness but assuming she would get used to it. Her own breasts, which were certainly smaller than Paige's, were in clear view, and now, self-conscious, she too slid deeper into the water. How could Paige, who had such a ravishing figure, even dream of complaining about it? *It must be hell being an actress and having all that sort of thing count so much,* she thought.

"So, are you going over to Kit's law firm tomorrow?" Paige asked her.

Susan had set up the appointment the moment she had made up her mind to move, and she nodded yes. "Kit also recommended a couple of other firms. I'd like to stay in labor law, and they really don't do that much of it over there. Her firm is mostly entertainment, some real estate . . ."

"Yes, but her firm is *lucky,*" Paige pointed out, grinning as she brought her glass back up to her lips. "It produced George. Don't forget, we've moved out here to upgrade our *personal* lives. Jobs are easy to come by, but I'll wager Georges are not. What do we want to do, meet a bunch of poor laborers?"

Susan laughed again. Paige had had her in stitches all night. "I could represent the other side, you know," she quipped, feeling a little like a traitor as she said it. In Stockton she had always gained such great satisfaction representing people upon whose lives she felt she had a real effect. Her father had often worked under unsatisfactory conditions out on the docks, and even though she had dealt primarily with agricultural labor organizations, she felt a particular zeal about her work.

Paige meanwhile cocked her head to the side as though she had forgotten about the possibility of the other side, and now approved. After thinking about it for a moment longer, she sighed with a distinct look of regret. "I wish I'd gone to law school or business school . . ." she said.

"Why?" Susan asked, amused.

"It's so easy for you," Paige replied levelly. "I have no idea what I'm going to do. I have experience in only one area, and it's an area in which you get almost no credit for your dues paid. Either they like the way you look for the role or they don't. You're so dependent on luck."

"It's not too late. Go to law school."

They were talking through a cloud of alcohol.

"First I'd have to go to college." Paige eyed Susan with a tough little laugh that seemed almost defensive, repositioning herself in front of another jet. "I'd always thought it was a big waste of time," she explained. "I knew exactly what I wanted and I thought sitting in a classroom, fooling around with all that sorority shit, wasn't going to get it for me. I wanted to get out there and work. Money was another factor, since I wasn't exactly an ideal candidate for a scholarship," she conceded woozily.

"So, go back to school now," Susan advised.

But Paige only laughed again. "Can you picture me sitting in a classroom for the five or six years it would take to get a degree that would be of any value?"

Susan couldn't, but clearly neither could Paige. Her green eyes narrowed thoughtfully. "I haven't changed," she admitted honestly, wringing out the wet ends of her long honey-colored hair and twisting it all up into a thick knot. "I still can't sit still like that. It's a function of genetics. You're either born a student, or you're not. Even talking about it for this long makes me feel claustrophobic. *Confined.* Which is how I always felt at school. Like a racehorse being held back and made to wait through a set of tiresome directions when all I wanted to do was run."

Susan watched as Paige let her hair tumble back down beneath her shoulders.

"That was one of the advantages of being an actress," Paige went on, polishing off what was left of her champagne. "You could be a lawyer, doctor, head of some exciting empire, without the dull grind of school or the job itself. You'd get to wear the look, play the role, even speak the language. Then by the time you were good and sick of it, you'd get to throw that identity away and pick up a new one."

"In that case, I guess you must have really gotten into the cat persona, hanging on to it for four and half years," Susan teased, draining what was left from her own glass, then ducking as Paige delivered a curtain of water, fast and hard in her direction.

"Very funny," Paige admonished, laughing and squinting as the wave of water sprayed in both their faces. "As long as you're going to be my roommate, you could be a little more supportive, you know . . ."

"Sorry, I couldn't resist," Susan replied tipsily, still blinking water out of her eyes. She snatched up the bottle of Cristal just as Paige was going for it.

There was a brief silence as Paige waited to reclaim it, seemingly lost in thought. "Oh, hell, I don't want to work anymore, anyway," she said, watching as the last few drops of champagne detached themselves from the neck of the bottle and dribbled into her glass.

"Why? What do you want to do, besides snare yourself some terrifically rich guy?" Susan asked her. Things were definitely starting to get blurry, and she realized she was on her way to becoming absolutely smashed.

"I guess marry him and let him take care of me for the rest of my life. Acting should be as good a background as any for stepping into the role of a high-society wife," Paige allowed, raising an eyebrow and smirking.

"Not a very liberated vocation, Paige," Susan chastised.

"Who do you think you're kidding? *That* kind of liberated I've been since I was twelve years old. Now I'm ready for the ultimate liberation of not having to worry anymore. I'm ready to hand over the reins."

"Just make sure you like the carriage you're getting into."

"Do I look like a girl who would get into the wrong carriage?"

Between the champagne, the heat from the Jacuzzi, and all the excitement of moving, Susan thought she was going to dissolve into another laughing jag. She also thought she was seeing things, and she turned to Paige with a low perplexed giggle. "Do you see what I see? Or am I just too drunk for words?"

As she said it, Paige's mouth dropped open, and they both looked over toward the figure that seemed to have appeared from out of nowhere. It was Tori, still dressed in pale pink leather from earlier that day, with makeup smeared around her eyes, and a pitiful expression on her pretty face.

"I'm just so filled with rage," Tori explained to them later in a broken voice, tears continuing to wash down her face, catching on the ridges of her long dark lashes. She tried to blink them away, looking up toward the sky, which had that middle-of-the-night look to it, the blackness gradually diminishing, the spray of stars growing fainter.

The three of them were well into another bottle of champagne, swacked and lying on lounge chairs by the Jacuzzi. They were wrapped in their host's lush terry robes, of which he kept a fresh supply in the pool house, listening to Tori cry her heart out as she told them of the heartbreak and humiliation she had undergone in the last twenty-four hours.

The day had begun with her feeling higher than she could ever remember feeling. That lofty but precarious pinnacle of euphoria had her feeling powerful and victorious. Exalted from her win. She was Rocky, with her hands flung high in the air and cheering. Feeling invincible. Gloating over her mother's lack of faith in her. Feeling eternally grateful to Travis and allowing herself to love him even more than she had ever thought possible.

She and her mother had gone to Tiffany's as planned and, as Tori tried on one beautiful ring after another, even her iceberg mother had melted and was giving in to the joy that had her daughter nearly delirious.

The small white bright stones symbolized a dream come true. Each little flicker that bounced off the precious stone sparked something significant in Tori's heart. One spark for the wedding scene she had always believed she would have with Travis. Another spark for kids. Memories collecting in advance of the events.

But then her whole world had come tumbling down, her hopes and dreams and happy projections, right along with her pride. While she stood before the elegant counter at Tiffany's with a black velvet tray of diamond rings glistening in front of her and the one she liked best sparkling on her finger, Travis phoned to call the whole thing off.

Falteringly, he had tried to pin it on his attorney. But his meandering excuses rang false and all too familiar—the thrust of his plea, as usual, postponement.

Midway through, Tori had cut him off, catching the impact of her mother's look and knowing deep in her heart that she would never fully recover from this moment.

"If I hadn't had you all to come to, if I hadn't had that blessed airline ticket staring me in the face, my things all packed, I don't know what I'd have done," Tori emphasized in a bewildered fashion. Then she laughed for a moment, more as an effort to stop herself from crying than anything else.

"You know those movies you see where the character's completely lost it—" she sniffed, taking a brief breath again. "Where she stays holed up in her once attractive apartment that's now a complete wreck, as she is, collapsed into an alcoholic stupor until she either kills herself or someone comes to the rescue—well that's how I feel. If I hadn't have had you all, that poor stupid fool would have been me—my scenario down to the letter. Only maybe I'd have gone and bought a gun in the middle of it all, and shot Travis right in the goddamn . . ."

"Balls!" Paige finished for her.

Poor Tori nodded in accord. She held absolutely no resemblance to the cool, composed southern belle they had met at the wedding, and Susan's heart went out to her. Even after consuming nearly a whole bottle of champagne, Tori couldn't seem to get anesthetized. She was shattered beyond words, mesmerized by her own anger. She looked as though she really could have killed Travis. Paige, outspoken as ever, said she should have.

"God, when I think of all those years I wasted with him—" Tori said fervently, sitting up.

"Uh-uhhh. You can't do that—" Paige interrupted, rising and swaying a little as she walked. "You can't think about that. It's history—*he's* history. You've got to bury him."

There was something to the concept of Travis six feet under ground that seemed to cheer Tori up, and for the first time that evening she actually smiled. "I'd like to *really* bury him," she said, pantomiming the act of holding a pistol, extending her arm toward an imaginary target. The champagne had restored some color to her cheeks, and contemplating revenge, instead of just feeling sorry for herself, seemed to bring back the sparkle to her dark, exotic-looking eyes. With a steady arm, she pretended to pull the trigger, jerking back afterward as though the gun had a nice kick to it.

"Good riddance Travis whatever-your-last-name-is . . . was." Paige proclaimed, satisfied, her eyes fixed on the spot where Travis's dead body would have fallen.

"The only proper thing to do now is to hold a funeral for him," Susan joked, playing along with them. Then she snickered, wondering where in a swank place like this she would be able to find a shovel.

"Susan, now that's a great idea," Paige said, looking surprised that it had come from her. Completely blotto by now, she tripped over one of the champagne bottles on her way to scout for a burial spot, her speech reflecting a mounting enthusiasm. "I think it would be an ideal form of therapy," she said. "To figuratively bury the bastard. Enact a funeral."

Tori seemed sold on the idea.

Susan, who had only been joking, thought it an absurd one. There definitely wasn't going to be a dull moment living with these two, and she rose to her feet after Tori did, feeling slightly silly, but enjoying herself as she padded along the cold ground behind them.

Paige was the one to finally locate a shovel. It was in a storage shed outside the pool house. There was also a rake, which they took as well.

With everything so beautifully manicured, it wasn't easy to find a spot that they could in good conscience dig up, but after a while of giddy hunting, they decided on a spot beneath a tree.

Tori's only regret was that it was in the shade. She said she would have preferred that he have to bake in the hot sun instead.

Standing barefoot on the cool, grainy-feeling dirt, in their matching robes, the three of them took turns digging.

"I've never presided over a funeral before, but I'll wing it," Paige declared.

Susan chuckled, then glanced over at Tori, who was staring down miserably at the ground they had messed up.

Paige came over to put her arm around the tearful brunette. "Now," she said gently, "first we need to throw something in there—do you have a picture of Travis, anything else that he's given to you?"

Tori closed her eyes for a moment, her lips pursed tight against tears. She took a deep drink from her champagne glass in an effort to ward off the sobriety she felt seeping back in. "I've got a couple of pictures in my wallet—" she offered, going for another strong swallow.

After she had returned and handed over the collection of wallet-sized photographs, she watched Paige and Susan examining them. Some of them had Tori and Travis together, arm in arm, others had him alone. It was a weird feeling. Part of her wanted them to tell her how "darling" he was. After all, she was sharing with them photographs of the man she loved and was only *trying* to hate. She actually found herself looking over their shoulders, repressing an urge to narrate: *this one was taken at the park at a company picnic when we first started dating . . .*

God, was it possible that she could ever really get over him?

"He's cute," Paige admitted, shuffling through the photos a second time. "But he's dead," she reminded them, jarring Tori as she let the precious mementos drop out of her hand and into the appropriated plot.

Tori was infuriated by her impulse to bend down and retrieve them, and instead handed her glass brusquely over to Paige. "Wait a minute," she said, reaching to unfasten the chain around her neck with fresh determination. "Let's do this thing right." Feeling a renewed sense of anger over what he had done to her, she let the thin gold strand slither down in beside the pictures.

It seemed like a brazen thing to do and she felt fortified by the act, by the approval she was getting from Susan and Paige, who she could see saluting her from out of the corner of her eye. Spurred on, trying to ignore the ache in the pit of her stomach, Tori hurried across the yard again, toward her pile of clothes by the Jacuzzi where she snatched up a pair of great-looking white snakeskin pumps Travis had given to her just a few weeks ago. She was about to add them to the heap, when Paige made a fast seizure.

"Now, let's not get carried away," Paige intercepted, wriggling into the stylish shoes, which appeared to fit, pivoting smoothly around in them to flash a B.A. over Travis's grave.

Tori couldn't have been more astonished at the sight of Paige's bare ass posed so irreverently and she laughed, feeling a hot crimson blush invading her cheeks. "God, Paige, you're wicked," she chided breathlessly. "Positively *disgraceful . . .*" They all shrieked with laughter, collapsing drunkenly into one another's arms until there were tears rolling down their cheeks.

Susan wondered out loud if they weren't all going to be punished for their sacrilege.

Paige simply beamed, clearly too crocked to care. "As long as we're at it," she suggested, "We might as well bury all old ghosts. Travis won't mind sharing his plot, Tori, will he?" Unconcerned whether he would or not, Paige went cheerfully about refilling all their glasses, then threw the empty amber bottle, which was the expensive champagne's trademark, carelessly into the grave alongside Tori's jewelry and photographs. "Susan, you could throw in what's-his-name from Stockton, and I could throw in . . ." Paige giggled, peering down. "Gee, I wonder if there's room down there for my menagerie of failed love affairs?"

"Here, dig a little deeper," Susan remarked, stooping down to retrieve the shovel and handing it back to Paige, who obligingly extracted some additional dirt before launching into her solemn address:

"In memory of our dearly beloved Travis-shithead Walton—"

"She's a natural at this," Tori whispered.

Paige cast a reproachful look their way, then resumed her oratory: "We lay you to rest, beneath the sod . .   ashes to ashes, dust to dust . . . You tried to be a decent human being, but alas,

you failed, leaving in your wake one very distressed individual."
With mock sincerity, Paige looked away from Travis's imaginary
remains, over to Tori for a moment, then back again. "To your
dearly beloved ones gathered here today, I say, 'Rejoice! The son-
of-a-bitch is dead!' "

"What about the other guys in there? We can't forget about
Billy, you know," Susan quipped.

Paige pondered for a moment. Then suddenly remembering
the glass in her hand she raised it up into the air. "Let's toast
them," she suggested expansively. "To . . . Oh, screw 'em.
Let's toast ourselves instead. To *us*! I think we're terrific."

To complete the ceremony, all three women lifted their glasses
and smashed them a bit too heartily against one another's, causing the costly Baccarat crystal to break and fall into the grave.

"I sure hope we find those Beverly Hills billionaires we moved
out here to meet, *soon,*" Paige said grimacing down at the wreckage and wondering how much more in debt they were going to
actually be by the time Dustin Brent returned.

Chapter 7

Paige was among the solo diners lining the south wall of Nate and Al's Delicatessen, the crowded, famous Beverly Hills deli where she had been going every day for breakfast since she arrived in L.A. a week ago. It was a good spot for viewing and eavesdropping. Everyone there chatted casually with the waitresses, who zipped back and forth past their tables, with a large percentage of their customers' morning diets committed to memory. Who took decaf and who took regular. Who was supposed to be watching their cholesterol and who their salt. The small individual banquettes were built close together, so it was easy for Paige to pick up interesting snatches of conversation. The atmosphere was friendly, clublike.

By all accounts, Nate and Al's served as a kind of commissary for the two most prominent industries in town—show biz and real estate—congregating beneath one roof, and often at one table. When the movers and shakers of the small inbred community weren't actually making deals, they were "schmoozing," as Paige had heard it called, picking each other's brains before, during, or after a plate of well-prepared lox, eggs, and onions, and several cups of good hot coffee.

Paige found it entertaining to watch as she brought her own

cup of coffee up to her lips, grateful for the rich aroma and smooth wake-up taste. It was exactly what she needed to make it through another day of pounding the pavements of the job market jungle.

Auditions in New York had been rough, but at least she was well known on the circuit there. She had friends and experience, which afforded her some respect. Trying to get a regular job was a different story. For Tori and Susan, looking for a job was a breeze. Armed with college educations, master's degrees, a doctorate of law for Susan, real estate credentials for Tori, they were exploring all kinds of interesting-sounding alternatives. But Paige was starting at the lowest rung of the ladder, discovering that making a career change without the passport of a college degree or job experience made her practically unemployable. Nobody cared that she had been in this musical or that. This was Hollywood. An out-of-work actress was an out-of-work actress.

Thinking she might meet a steady flow of executive types who occupied the dozens of high-rise buildings in sleek, clean-looking Century City, Paige had begun her search at a Century City employment agency.

Expecting to take them by storm, she had breezed in, looking spectacular, anticipating a surplus of options. Who wouldn't want to hire her? She was bright, attractive, dynamic. She felt capable of doing anything. Just teach her the role and she would play it.

But to her great dismay, she found it did not work like that. If anything, her looks and energy seemed to antagonize the woman processing new applicants. Paige was handed a pile of paperwork, and then herded off into a room filled with other applicants, where she was instructed to fill out the lengthy questionnaire and, afterward, to submit to a ghastly examination.

Full of problematic spatial-relations puzzles, ambiguous multiple-choice probes, the test made her feel like an idiot. It was absurd; she wasn't applying for a job as an aeronautical engineer. So why start examining her on complicated mathematical equations, multiplication and division of percentages and many-figured fractions? Nor was she trying to pass herself off as a historian. After the math portion came the requisitioning of dates of historical events, names of particular battles, where they had been fought, and who had led them. Part three veered off into her absolute worst subject, geography, where they caught her up short on capitals, lakes, even topography of mountains. Who gave a damn about which body of water connected this state or that, or what the capital of Turkey is? Her only concern with mountain heights was in respect to a growing phobia she had developed lately about any kind of heights.

Through a glass window, she had been able to see another group of applicants hunched over typewriters, being tested for speed. After that they would be expected to demonstrate their shorthand skills, as would Paige, even though she had already told them she didn't know shorthand.

Staring helplessly through the window, watching all those fingers flying across the typewriter keys, and positively mortified that she didn't at least have a pocket calculator to cheat a little with on the math portion, Paige slipped the mostly unanswered test papers into her purse. She had been far too embarrassed to leave them behind when she walked coolly out of the room, feeling very "un-cool" inside.

The classifieds had proved equally futile, most of them bogus employment agency plants looking to lure prospective applicants into their offices so they could make commissions off them. The tantalizing job descriptions you *saw* listed and appeared to qualify for just happened to be taken. . . . However, they had others, if you could just come in and interview.

Paige had had it with their interviews. She was perfectly capable of finding a job on her own. Her focus being, exclusively, where to meet rich men.

Today her plan was to hit Rodeo Drive. If she failed to meet a score of rich men there, while working in one of the more pricey boutiques, she figured she could at least befriend some of their rich female clientele who might fix her up.

She was also thinking of interviewing at a couple of the higher-end health clubs to teach dance and aerobics. At least the rich men there would be on the young side and in good shape.

"I still don't know what I'm gonna have," said an elderly man in loud plaid slacks and a short sleeved yellow shirt, who had been sitting in the booth beside Paige's for a while, browsing through the sports section of the newspaper.

"Have *hope*," the waitress said, hurrying past him toward someone else, who was signaling for his check. It was probably a line she used all the time, but Paige was in the kind of mood in which it felt meaningful. *Hope*. What did that mean to her? Finding a job today? Or, better still, finding a wealthy prospect who would eliminate her need to do so?

After parking at Bonwit Teller's, where she was assured of wrangling a free parking validation, Paige crossed Wilshire Boulevard, heading north on Rodeo. From the prominent corner there where Dayton met Rodeo, Giorgio's blinding yellow-and-white striped awning announced the shopping landmark, and Paige decided to make it her first stop.

Could Judith Krantz really have been alluding to this when she wrote *Scruples*? she wondered, disappointed as she entered the cluttered emporium and looked around, sneezing immediately from all the Giorgio cologne being sprayed out into the air of the store's entrance. There were two pretty black girls, dressed alike, standing at the doorway smiling promotional smiles and spraying the heavy scent. Paige smiled back at them. When you're applying for a job, you smile at everyone, just in case they carry some weight in the hiring process. Though it was doubtful the perfume girls would. Over at the counter, to her left as she walked in, were two more perfume girls, and Paige approached them, allowing another couple to edge in front of her, and then hanging back patiently.

The place was jam-packed.

There was glitz all right, but missing was the aura of elegance and haut monde she had expected to see. It wasn't anything like the chic-looking boutiques Kit had taken them to when they had been out to L.A. for the wedding.

The very yellow shop was overflowing with hordes of shoppers who looked to Paige like they had just been dropped off by a tour bus. She half expected to see racks of souvenirs and postcards, sets of Giorgio coasters. Instead, she saw racks of three-thousand-dollar dresses, all squashed together, as though there were a sale going on, but there wasn't.

It was true, everything she had heard about the swank institution existed; there was the long, gleaming oak-paneled bar serving up cocktails and cappuccinos, the famous pool table, the glittery fashion accessories, the astonishing price tags.

But for Paige, the glamorous myth of Giorgio was definitely dispelled, and she walked out without bothering to go any further.

Collecting a series of discouraging No—but do check back's, she maintained her pace, heading doggedly north up Rodeo, refusing to let her confidence erode.

After all, this was something she was doing just for the money, she kept reminding herself. It was temporary; it wasn't a career. So she couldn't let it get her down. It was an interim thing.

It was just that she hadn't counted on it being so tough, she thought, exiting another shop, with her sixth rejection, deciding the next time if they asked her if she had any experience she would lie and say yes.

Then she started debating if she wouldn't be better off taking her portfolio around, getting an L.A. agent. She could try and do some commercials, audition for some soaps, sitcom work . . .

Paige was in the middle of an old but updated daydream, when she strode past Jerry Magnin, Polo, and then another men's store called Mr. Guy. It struck her, as she nearly collided with a good-looking man walking out of the last shop, carrying an armload of packages, that a high class *men's* clothing store could turn out to be the best bet yet. She and the gentleman smiled apologetically at one another, then with renewed spirit, Paige retraced her steps and went to inquire about positions inside all three. The expensive merchandise ranged from hip to designer high-styled, indicating that the men buying them might just gorgeously fit the bill.

Things were looking up; she collected two applications, and then a third at Ted Lapidus, which was for men and women.

On the other side of the street was a striking complex of small individual designer boutiques such as Valentino, Maud Frizon, Krizia, and even a baby boutique sporting big labels and big price tags for little people.

Kit had taken Paige, Tori, and Susan there, on their first day

visiting L.A. Paige remembered it specifically because the name
of the shop was Tori Steele, and they had teased Tori at the time,
that this could have been hers, if she had been lucky enough to
have snared the flamboyant tycoon before the other Tori did.
"It's just a shame," Kit had joked. "Look at all the great dis-
counts you could have gotten for us."

According to an article Kit had read just last week in *Women's
Wear Daily,* the money behind this enterprise came from a fabu-
lously wealthy Texan who married a woman twenty-five or so
years younger than he, and then financed all this as a plaything
for her, not caring at all if it made money or if he dropped a
million bucks on it a year.

It was just the kind of fairy tale Paige envisioned for herself, as
she browsed her way through the series of in-vogue boutiques,
passing from one into the other through connecting interior
doorways. With a tinge of impatience she fingered the luscious
merchandise, regarding the other women in there who were casually trying things on, accumulating great piles of the fine apparel,
culling through their selections. *Soon,* she told herself, watching
them enviously, smiling evasively at the shop girls who were politely offering assistance.

Just as she was going to ask about a job opening, she spotted a
ravishing red jeweled evening gown that she was dying to try on.
She stole a glance at the price tag and nearly laughed out loud,
feeling something else deep in the pit of her stomach. She had to
have this dress. It was ridiculous, really, because it was fifty-five
hundred dollars, but Paige's thoughts were racing, the way they
did when she had already made her mind up about something,
and was hell-bent on making it happen.

Impulsively, she removed it from the rack, and asked to try it
on. It felt extremely heavy.

"I think this is one of the best things in his collection this
year," said the trim, smartly put-together salesgirl, with a heavy
French accent. The *he* she was referring to was Valentino. "I
think it would look *great* on you!"

It sure as hell should, for fifty-five hundred dollars, Paige
thought dryly. *Fifty-five hundred dollars. She was really out of her*

mind. With the salaries she had been looking at, it would take her
forever to accumulate enough cash to even dream of buying it.

But Paige played along, enjoying being treated as a customer
instead of someone trying to get a job.

Once inside the small, mirrored dressing room, she slipped off
her own tight cotton skirt and blouse, then gazed longingly at the
dress before putting it on. Her shoes were all wrong so she kicked
them off, lest they ruin the effect. Then, as though reading her
mind, the saleswoman peeked inside and asked Paige what size
pump she took.

Moments later, Paige emerged from the dressing room, with
the shimmery gown hugging her long curvy shape, wearing a pair
of red satin pumps they had found for her, and looking positively
dazzling. The fabric was thin as air, and the tiny crystal beads
sewn delicately onto it sparkled as she moved, causing a definite
stir within the shop. The dress was strapless, with a well-con-
structed *bustier* that subtly pushed up the bosom. There were
fingerless red jeweled gloves that stretched up just above her
elbows. And a hip-length, loose-fitting red jeweled jacket with
large padded shoulders.

"It's absolutely divine on you, no?" the French saleswoman
effused.

Paige could not have been more in accord, and she grinned like
the cat who had swallowed the canary. It was amazing what a
fifty-five-hundred-dollar garment could do for you, she thought
giddily, unable to take her eyes off her reflection as she spun
demurely around to catch the gown from all angles. As she did
so, the same man she had almost bumped into in front of Mr.
Guy, passed by the front window of the store, and they caught
each other's eye.

He paused to regard her, nodding his head approvingly, playfully, as though he thought she should buy it.

In response, she tilted her head uncertainly, then narrowed her
sly green eyes, her expression querying You think so?

More emphatically this time, he nodded again, shifting his
heavy load of purchases to the other arm. As he did so, Paige
noticed he had acquired an additional shopping bag, this one
from the baby boutique next door.

Married? she wondered, *or maybe divorced and guilty.* She smiled broadly and decided to take a chance, pointing her finger toward him first, and then toward the dress she had on, creating a sign-language motion that was intended to read—You want to buy it for me?

His smile after that was even broader than her own. And she stood there with her hand poised on her hip, daring him. By this time the saleswoman and a few other people standing around had noticed what was going on. It was rather exciting. Nobody really knew if they knew each other or not, but they were dying to know what was going to happen.

"Is that your husband?" the saleswoman finally asked curiously, as though she somehow had already guessed that it was not.

Paige merely shook her head no. Her adrenaline was racing.

"Your boyfriend?"

"Uh-uh. No." She concentrated on the man's eyes, trying to read what was going on behind them. They were brown eyes, round and intelligent-looking, with deep creases beneath them. He looked to be somewhere in his late forties, early fifties. Was he generous? Was he rich? Was he going to walk away or come inside and sweep her off her feet? She almost fainted when he pushed the door open with his shoulder and walked inside.

By now, just about everybody in the shop was standing motionless, watching, some trying to be more subtle than others. If they had seemed blasé a few moments ago, puzzling over which fifteen-hundred-dollar blouse to buy, they weren't blasé now.

"She'll take it," he said, striding confidently toward them.

Paige stood positively dumbstruck. She was always weaving these fantastic episodes, but they didn't really materialize. She would fantasize the scenario, and then the guy would walk away. More likely than that, he wouldn't stop in the first place. At the very most, he'd stop for a brief moment, smile, and then walk on. Paige didn't know what to say. Everyone was standing around like statues, not sure if he was putting them on.

"She looks smashing in it . . ." the saleswoman ventured at last, clearly feeling ill at ease about saying anything at all, but anxious to make the sale.

When Paige felt his hand come to rest on her bare shoulder, she shivered, a delicious chill traveling from where his skin met hers and then coursing out in all directions. Money and power—an aphrodisiac? The world's most sublime.

Paige, who was always overflowing with gab, could not think of one thing to say. This was the part where they were supposed to fade out, in his gorgeous pad, the dress thrown down carelessly onto the floor, the two of them in bed.

There were a couple of plush mauve chairs over by a steel-and-glass table set up for sales transactions, and she watched as he unloaded his purchases onto them, turning gamely back to her afterward. He himself was dressed as though he frequented these shops. He had on a smart-looking black-and-gray twill blazer of a summer weight, handsomely tailored pale gray slacks, an elegant shirt flecked with gray, and an expensive-looking tie that brought it all together. His buttery rich charcoal shoes were positively scuffless. The only jewelry he had on was a Bulgari watch.

"We'll take the shoes, too," he decided, enjoying a few more moments of the suspense he was creating. "Are they comfortable?"

It was the first time he had actually addressed Paige and she swallowed awkwardly, clearing her voice, which seemed to have dried up on her.

"Hmmm. Very," she managed with surprising composure. Inside, she was a flurry of nerves. Who was this man? And why was he playing this game with her? He was like an apparition of her own creation, who had accidentally dropped into her real life. Most bizarre for her was that there were other people observing. Her daydreams had always happened in a bubble of privacy, but this was a daydream occurring out in the open.

Caught up in it, she smiled her most beguiling smile and walked across the room, modeling for him. The dress hugged tight across her hips and rear end, and she caught him appreciating the effect, regarding the shimmery fabric that draped down toward her ankles, restricting her stride somewhat, even though it was slit rather high in the front. The deeply cut red pumps made her legs look incredibly sexy beneath the gown, as they clicked across the black slate floor.

"What about an evening bag?" he asked, winking at Paige, then proceeding to roam the shop in search of one that might satisfy him. There were quite a few scattered around, displayed to accent different outfits. He went over to a particularly pretty one, which was shaped like a large egg, with variegated red-toned rhinestones covering its contoured surface. "Here, catch . . ." he said to Paige, raising his arm up and back, feigning a pass with the jeweled bag, as though it were a football and causing everyone to loudly catch their breath.

Paige broke up laughing. She thought he was the strangest but most intriguing man she had met in ages.

Please don't be married, she thought. The absence of a wedding band was a good sign, but inconclusive.

The saleswomen, from the looks they were exchanging with one another, clearly had to put up with a lot of crazy clientele, rock stars, brat-pack movie stars, the eccentric well-to-do from all over the world. The Frenchwoman assisting Paige hurried over to delicately retrieve the jeweled egg, as though it were a time bomb that needed to be detonated. "Judith Leiber," she said, naming the purse's renowned designer, presumably in justification of its undoubtedly dear price tag. "We just got this one in."

"Would you like that one or a different one?" he asked Paige considerately, maneuvering close enough for her to be able to breathe in the pleasant fragrance of his after-shave. His eyes were only several inches above her own and she felt them studying her, raising dozens of tiny goosebumps as they trailed down her neck, exploring the provocative cut of her neckline, and lingering on the daring exposure of skin there.

Feeling a tremor of excitement, she pursed her lips, considering, trying to sound nonchalant. "Goes great with the dress."

He grinned, then went over and got the purse again, arranging its gold strap over the curve of her shoulder, stealing a touch of flesh from where he shouldn't as he did so.

Her head was swimming by now, and she caught him with a sharp look that was more sportive than discouraging, as she watched him ease innocently out of the gesture. It was time for one of them to make the move. She took the plunge. "So, where are we going?" she asked him offhandedly, looking as if it were a crime not to be going somewhere divinely special indeed.

Their eyes met again, bold young green eyes connecting with savvy, more complicated brown eyes.

She nearly swooned when she saw him reaching into his pants pocket, pulling out a smart snakeskin billfold, and opening it up. "Carnival Night at the Nicky Loomis mansion," he replied with equal offhandedness. "As far as I'm concerned, it's L.A.'s main event."

For Paige it was definitely going to be.

Five and a half grand, phew! The price of his toys was rising sharply. He watched the skinny French broad nonchalantly tallying up the other items. Tack on another twelve hundred for the purse and an even four hundred for the Maud Frizon shoes.

What the hell, this sexy little bombshell in the hot red dress looked like she was going to be worth it. He didn't really give a damn what the total came to; it couldn't touch the kind of dough his wife shelled out regularly for her insatiable clothing appetite. She had a closet the size of this shop, and even with frequent recycling it was crowded. This little number was for him, for his pleasure, a fuck-toy for his frequent business jaunts to L.A. His father-in-law had at last done him a good turn when he expanded their operations to include California.

He never used to tell them he was married. But now he generally did. It wasn't the obstacle it used to be, so why bother with lying? With the proportion of single women to single men so unjustly balanced, women appeared to have a whole new mindset. There was a tough new breed out there bearing little or no conscience about man-stealing. He offered the surplus of single women, if not a serious relationship, a great time, great sex, and always great gifts. This one, like all the others, would probably think she was different, more special, that she could eventually get him to fall in love with her and leave his wife. That methodology seemed to be built into the female psyche. Marriage and kids. If the money didn't come from his wife's family, he might have been susceptible, vulnerable, he had to admit. There was grave temptation in a young, curvy thirty-year-old instead of Alicia, a gorgeous bod like this one, day in and day out, in bed and out of bed, causing other men to lose their minds with envy.

Not that Stan Parker had any right to complain. Already his situation was enviable. His wife, Alicia, was still reasonably attractive, intelligent. She made very few demands on him. And with her inherited wealth he had been accorded power, prestige, and a life he liked a great deal.

This was indeed one of the perks, he thought, enjoying that impressed look on Paige's spectacular face, as he peeled off one bill after another, telling her more about the big annual charity bash he was inviting her to. The party's host, Nicky Loomis, prided himself in throwing the most-looked-forward-to event in L.A.

Raised poor in Omaha, completely self-made, first as a National Football League star; then in his early thirties, taking over a beer empire; and then later going on to fulfill his grandest goals, owning important sports teams and building them into even bigger ones, going against the tide and constructing his own private sports arena for their games, Nicky Loomis had become a kind of living legend in the sports world.

His press dubbed him a wild man, always a girl on each arm wearing miniskirts because he was known to have a thing for miniskirts. His flamboyant ways were tolerated in the highest social stratum only because of his equally flamboyant charitable contributions. Such as this affair, which he held annually on his own private grounds, an estate made famous years ago by its original hotel baron owner. It was an event for which all stars showed up.

Movie moguls. Politicians. Other sports heavyweights and team owners. It would not be at all surprising to see Donald Trump or George Steinbrenner, Jerry Buss, or even Marvin Davis. People flew in from all over.

Since Nicky was a night person, the evenings were known to go on until four or five in the morning, when he would have set up a big breakfast buffet. He loved to party, probably had the best time of anybody there. And what the heck, two thousand bucks a head, a swell time, and the proceeds went to funding research for curing cancer.

Too bad the big bash was a couple of months away, Stan Parker thought, lamenting, watching this remarkable-looking woman watching him.

Too bad he had a plane to catch in a couple of hours and was on his way back home to Philadelphia, not scheduled to return to L.A. until then.

Those daredevil green eyes of hers were teasing him beneath a thick curtain of lashes. She had great-looking thick eyebrows, sandy colored, like her wild mane of hair that touched down almost to her ass. Rich, honey-colored skin, made for touching.

She would *definitely* think she was different from the others, more special, more clever, more capable of luring him away from his wife. Maybe she was.

When she headed for the dressing room to change clothes he decided to add a mysterious touch and leave before she reappeared—or before he broke down and spent the night, missing Alicia's father's birthday party. He would scribble a quick note on the back of a business card, instructing her to hold August sixth.

God, what a great ass she has, he thought as she kicked off the pumps with a rare flair, and then sashayed into the changing room. *Great ass and a great walk. Ol' Nick would probably try to snatch her for himself; she was just his type. Gorgeous and flashy-looking. The only thing missing was the cut-up-to-her-crotch mini-skirt.*

Although Nicky was single and Stan married, Stan still felt she would fare better with him. Nick was strictly only good for a one-night stand.

On a last impulse, he told the salesgirl to wrap up another Judith Leiber evening bag for him to take home to his wife. A couple of little Judith Leiber pillboxes also, the ones shaped like bunnies, with all the rhinestones, for his daughters.

Chapter 8

Travis Walton is sitting on the toilet, with his pants draped down below his knees, his underwear binding his calves, reading a Superman comic book. The elastic on the underwear is worn, stretched out, full of holes. He looks absurd, still wearing a shirt and tie, with a stupid smile on his face from something he just read in the comic strip. The tie has spaghetti sauce on it.

Tori felt a slight but encouraging pull of amusement, as the image of her former lover shifted. Now she had him wearing only his underwear, sweeping the pathways in front of their condo in Atlanta, with all the neighbors outside, watching him and laughing their heads off. A ferocious little mutt begins barking at him and he fights it off, scared out of his wits, holding the yelping animal off with the broom and hollering for help as the dog zips around behind him and takes a hungry bite out of the cotton Jockey shorts stretched across his buns.

"Laugh at your lover. Picture your lover in an absolutely asinine situation. See him sitting on the toilet reading a Superman comic book or cleaning streets in his underwear while the whole world laughs at him."

Bravo, Tori thought to herself, deep into the book Paige and Susan had picked up for her called *Breaking Free: 20 Ways to*

Leave Your Lover. It was a behavioral approach to getting a lover out of one's system, written by a Hollywood hypnotherapist who had treated endless cases of heartache. The author posited that feelings are learned and could thus be unlearned by employing certain behavior modification techniques he had developed.

The point of the section on laughing at your lover was to get the lovesick to see their lovers in a ridiculous and inferior light, to knock them off their pedestal.

Tori had the book positioned discreetly in her lap, on top of a magazine, so that nobody could see the title. She was sitting in the reception room of Bennetton Development Company, waiting to be called upon for a job interview. She was about ten minutes early for her appointment and killing time, trying to exorcise Travis from her heart.

Burying him had helped only temporarily. Then his ghost rose up from its impromptu grave in Beverly Hills to haunt her, invading her soul with memories, conjuring up still vivid sensations —the way she felt when he kissed her, when he held her in his arms, when he made her laugh. Every time the phone rang, she would race to it with that flutter of excitement, her hopes strained, praying that it was him. She went through all these complicated machinations, conjecturing what she would say, what kind of position she would take, the deal she would propose. Her intricately conceived scenarios changed every other minute because she was thinking about him every other minute.

"Act the part of someone who no longer loves their lover," the book advised.

I can't, Tori thought futilely, *I do love him.*

"Imagery is at the heart of many behavior therapy techniques. Imagine you are falling out of love . . . You *are* falling out of love. Imagine it. Think as if it's happening. Pretend you no longer love this person. Images have great power. It's images that put you in love in the first place. The thought of how wonderful he is, how right for you, how appealing, how sensitive, how open, how considerate . . . Change your imagery! Change your self-image. You are a person who is not in love with anyone. See yourself that way . . ."

Tori was trying with all her heart to absorb the words like

medicine, to drink them in and find herself healed by the clear and astute messages contained within the pages.

But as the book said, it wouldn't happen overnight.

"Tori Mitchell?"

Caught by surprise, Tori looked up, self-consciously snapping the book on her lap shut as she did so.

"You're hired."

"What?" Still startled, Tori looked up into the eyes of a tall, divinely attractive man, somewhere in his late thirties, with unstyled hair the color of straw, which touched down in back to the collar of his pink polo shirt. He had a thick, rugged neck, a deep tan, a strong chin, good mouth, a small nose, and sexy peacock blue eyes, which sparkled with arrogance.

Before Tori had a chance to slip it into her briefcase, he was leaning down, examining the book she was trying to conceal in her lap.

She was so embarrassed, she could barely think straight. He laughed, showing off perfect teeth and terrible manners.

His lack of decorum worsened as he swept the book away from her and began leafing through it, regarding her intermittently over the pages as she attempted to snatch it back from him. She knew she was blushing beet-red; her cheeks felt hot as coals, and her pulse was going haywire.

He was chuckling, thoroughly entertained.

"Do you mind?" she asked mortified, finding herself wrestling with him, a perfect stranger, a perfect jackass.

Before she knew it they were standing in a corridor, where he had maneuvered out past the receptionist, through the door, and into the maze of offices. The company was large, occupying a full floor. Tori had followed him, seizing her things and hurrying after him. She had not missed the receptionist's look, and she wondered if this kind of thing went on often. Who was this jerk?

People nodded deferentially to him as they passed by with assorted greetings, checking Tori out, curious.

"By the way, you have a *great* accent," he said, grinning at her as he mimicked her southern lilt. Then he shook his gorgeous head, indicating disapproval. "He's not worth it. Whoever he is . . ."

Tori had calmed down somewhat, aware that she wasn't going to get her book back until he was good and finished with it, anyway. She smiled, a tight, tolerant smile. "Are you finished?"

" 'Make love in your lover's most unflattering position . . .' " He laughed vigorously, his broad athletic-looking shoulders rising up with amusement, the pink knit material accommodating the movement as he looked Tori up and down. "My guess is you don't have an unflattering position," he leered. " 'Recall all abuses . . .' This is pretty kinky stuff."

He was way out of line, and Tori was about to turn and leave. He could keep the damn book, for all she cared.

"I'm sorry. I don't know what happened to my manners," he apologized expansively, stopping her, taking her hand, and introducing himself with the same impetuous air. "Richard Bennetton. Successor to the throne of Bennetton Development Company. You're very pretty."

Tori gave him an icy once-over. He would not release her hand, and she was forced to continue to stand there under his toying gaze. Richard Bennetton. Son of *the* Bennetton. So, this cocky lunatic was the owner's son. It figured.

"Do you conduct all your interviews this way?" she asked him acidly.

"I never do anything the same way twice. It gets boring. So when could you start?"

Tori laughed, in spite of herself. "I don't think we've played out the interview part yet," she said, in a crazy way intrigued by him. He was spoiled but cute, giving a little boost to her badly bruised ego.

"Interview, schminterview. I have uncanny instincts about people. Especially gorgeous brunettes. You want the job? You're hired."

Tori was incredulous. Her résumé was good. But she would wager a week's salary that he had not even read it. "Just like that? Just because I'm a *gorgeous* brunette?"

"I was wildly impressed by your résumé."

Tori laughed again. "Yeah. Sure you were." A disturbing thrill passed through her as he tightened his grip on her hand and drew her closer. Warning signals went off in her head as she thought of

Travis and how impossible it had been working with someone with whom she was involved. Working *for* someone with whom she was involved would make for triple the madness.

Still holding her hand, Richard led her past his secretary's vacant cubicle and into his office, directing her into a seat.

It was a large corner office with a spectacular view of the city. The one wall that did not offer a view was covered in corkboard, with blueprints and attractive color renderings of housing projects pinned to it. Richard went over and sat down in his plush leather chair behind his big black granite desk that was cluttered with paperwork. The only photograph Tori saw was one of Richard standing somberly beside an older man whom he resembled so strongly that Tori presumed it was his father. There were no framed wives to indicate he was married, no evidence of kids.

Richard was leaning back in his chair, twisting a rubber band around his fingers. Her book he had tossed down onto the heap of papers in front of him. "That's the old man," he stated, following her glance over to the picture on the wall, swiveling his chair to get a good look at him. Then he turned back to Tori with a little smirk that was hard to read. "You'll meet him. He still drives us all crazy around here. If you want the job that is . . ."

"I'd like to hear about it first," Tori said, as two lights on his phone lit up at the same time. Leaning back in her chair she could see his secretary still had not returned to her desk, and she wondered how long he would let the phone ring before he picked up a line. Then she heard an out-of-breath female voice muttering to herself, "Hold on a minute," and then a more professional sounding: "Richard Bennetton's office," as the calls were finally answered. Craning her neck, Tori could see his secretary looking completely harassed as she set down onto her desk a mountain of brochures. Cradling the phone against her shoulder and stretching the extension cord, she moved to shut Richard's door, affording the two of them some privacy.

"Your background is in marketing, right?" Richard was saying, ignoring the momentary commotion. "You'd join our marketing department. We've got a new project that's pretty incredible, if I do say so myself." He was leaning so far back in his chair, it looked as if it were going to break. "Our approach is brilliant.

No one's ever done it before. A prospective buyer comes to our showroom, which is on the site, sits down in front of a video screen complete with joy stick, and cruises the property where we're building a series of private, all-custom estates. We've simulated what it'll look like after it's built, using famous estates from Beverly Hills and Hollywood as prototypes. We've got mock-ups of the old place of William Randolph Hearst's mistress, Marion Davies. Douglas Fairbanks. Walt Disney. The Harold Lloyd estate. The Playboy mansion. The Kirkeby estate, where they used to film *The Beverly Hillbillies*. So it's actually a kick. The parcels are all between two and five acres, and the idea is to give the buyers a chance to see what kind of amazing spread they could have on their lot, if they wanted it. We whet their appetite, like you've whet mine."

Tori was trying to take all this seriously. She had heard a great deal about the project and thought it would be exciting to work on. It was Richard who was going to be difficult.

"So, can I buy you lunch?" he asked, rising restlessly to his feet, business abruptly concluded.

Tori hesitated, leery to say the least. "I've got plans," she lied unconvincingly.

He laughed, reading her loud and clear, then tossed her book back over to her. "If you want the job, it's yours," he told her, coming up behind her and touching her hair. "Just don't wait too long. You know how the saying goes: He who hesitates . . ." Richard completed his warning with an insinuating wink that solidified why she would be out of her mind to accept this job.

If she were the client, she would be wondering where all the money came from to pay for all this. Two floors of brand-spanking-new office space on a prime floor in one of downtown Los Angeles' new gorgeous skyscrapers located on recently renovated, prestigious Bunker Hill.

Nothing about Susan's new life in L.A. resembled her former life in Stockton. She had even had to go out and buy all new clothes. Paige and Tori had insisted that she dress for success. They told her she looked like a country bumpkin, drab, dull. No minced words. Plain Jane. Polyester Paula. So now she looked worse still, in her crumpled linen suit they had talked her into. "There's status to wrinkles," Tori had assured her. "The more wrinkles, the better the fabric. Silk, cotton, fine linen. You show me someone without dozens of creases, and I'll show you—"

"Synthetic Sue!" Susan had finished for her, getting the message loud and clear. Starch was out. You can take the girl out of the country, but you can't take the country out of the girl.

She couldn't believe that she was working here, in one of California's largest, most influential labor law firms, representing the enemy. She was going to have to be doing a lot of justifying to herself in order to sleep at night, a penalty for having switched sides from labor to management. She was in the camp of big business now. In a way, it erased some of the hypocrisies she had had to deal with before, the holier-than-thou contention of representing the *people,* when, in fact, often she was merely working with the other corrupt, out-to-conquer kingpins. Labor organizations may have originally begun for the good of the people, but everyone knew the union guns could be as bad, if not worse, than the business guns. In it for their own gains anyway, they were no longer altruistically fighting to help the workers. So who was she kidding; there were bullies on both sides. At least on the side of management, they made no bones about it. They were in business, out to net as much money as possible. Sweatshops were a horror of the past.

There! She sounded like management already. After only one day on the job.

The simple fact was, management paid more than double. In Stockton, representing labor, Susan earned around twenty-two thousand dollars a year. Now her salary was closer to fifty. Plus perks. The reason for this was that union lawyers worked on yearly retainers, whereas management traditionally billed clients by the hour. Hence, the fancy offices, the expensive cars the partners drove, and the first-class travel arrangements when travel was necessary.

So why did she feel so ambivalent, she mused, as she lifted her crumpled linen blazer from the hook on her door and worked it on, catching the shoulder pads on the shoulder pads of her wrinkled silk shirt. Her office was small but nice, infinitely prettier and neater-looking than any office she had had before. It had white grasscloth walls selected by the attorney before her, modern chrome and laminated made-to-look-like-oak furniture, a scaled-down sofa, occasional table, and two chrome upholstered occasional chairs on which clients or colleagues could sit. Susan's only design decision was going to be what poster art to buy for her bare walls, a task she planned to take care of now on her way home from work.

There was a poster shop in Westwood Village that her secretary had recommended, and Susan drove past the wide-stretching campus of UCLA, and then down crowded Galey Avenue trying to find it. The streets were already spilling over with students and devotees of Westwood, and it was not even dark yet. By eight o'clock, the village hangout would be a frenetic urban youth jungle, teeming with teenagers hanging out of loudly honking cars that ranged from their parents' fancy European models (Rollses and Ferraris not being at all uncommon), to beat-up Buicks and VWs from the other side of town. Susan caught sight of a parking spot being vacated and cut over toward it. Good parking spaces, when they were difficult to come by, always made her feel lucky. And she threw on her parking brake in a good mood.

There were some mimes, their faces painted white, lips, cheeks, and eyes done in exaggerated clown-fashion, holding court before a large crowd. Susan edged in to get a closer look. They were quite good, actually, and she laughed, caught up in the show as they acted out a jealous lover routine. One of them played the harmonica, and when the act was over he broke into a playful medley while the other two passed around a hat, collecting money. Susan took a couple of dollars from her wallet and tossed them in.

Feeling a warm glow from having done so, she negotiated a path through the ever-increasing mob and headed up the street, hungry from the various aromas of hamburgers, pizza, and falafel, while keeping an eye out for the poster shop. Dinner wasn't until seven, and the delicious food smells assaulting her senses tempted her to stop for a snack. She, Tori, and Paige had all been invited over to Kit and George's house for a casual barbecue. Afterward the three women were going to a polo match. Not that any of them was particularly into polo, but Paige had decided she was into polo players. If the event proved disappointing, she had culled an extensive itinerary of nightspots for them to investigate over the course of their evenings in L.A. The purpose of doing so was partially to have a good time and meet interesting men—partially to bring Tori out of her slump.

Miraculously, Susan had gotten over her own inamorato, Billy Donahue, the moment she made up her mind she was leaving town. She had felt nothing when they said good-bye, not even a tinge of the triumph she had been certain she would feel when she left him in a cloud of dust from her Mustang, driving off to a new life they both seemed to sense would be far more exciting than the life he led now. She was moving on, changing tracks, growing, stepping boldly into a vast spectrum of challenges that she was eager to meet. Billy Donahue's mold had been set somewhere in his late teens, when he thought he had it all. Maybe he did—then.

Susan suspected Tori's Travis Walton was not all that she had him cracked up to be either, but Tori was blindly obsessed with him, so much so that Susan kept expecting the doorbell to ring and him to be standing there, engagement ring in hand, marriage proposal and apologies spewing forth. The fantasy was so strong within Tori that it seeped from her very being, connecting into those around her. Susan ached for the stunning brunette who, for all her effort, just could not pull herself together. All fantasies should have come to an abrupt halt when Travis had the nerve to instruct his lawyer to call Tori and propose a low-ball offer on her share of the condo the two of them owned.

The poster store was not at all what Susan had expected. It was closer to an adult toy store and she meandered in, browsing, curious about all the imaginative gadgetry. There were molded black-rubber race cars that functioned as telephones, erotic body parts that functioned as erasers, silverplated paperweights that functioned as five-pound dumbbells, Igloo cold-food containers that doubled as stereo speakers for Walkman units, and even speaker telephones with memory dial and radios designed for use in the shower.

There were so many posters on the walls that Susan did not

know where to look first. They were arranged from about knee level clear up to the ceiling, not missing an inch of usable wall space. She could take her pick between the pretty ones, the funny ones, the more avant-garde, as well as the expected reprint staples, Miró and Hockney being the most heavily represented.

Susan was trying to decide between a couple of David Hockney swimming-pool scenes and a Stella racetrack, calculating the cost, when she noticed a set of stairs leading up to a small studio-type loft. Putting her decision on hold, she mounted the floating staircase that was off to the rear of the store and was surprised to find a delightful display of work created by local artists. There were whimsical ceramic pieces, some exquisite glasswork, interesting sculptures, and a long narrow case of expensive-looking handcrafted jewelry. But what made her actually catch her breath and think seriously about making a purchase were the large and colorful works of one artist hung spaciously on the toast-colored walls. The material the artist had used looked to be plastic-coated chicken wire, painted in vibrant colors and formed into abstract designs. Wondering if she might be able to eke one out of her budget which only moments ago had seemed more than adequate, Susan toured the lot of them, trying to determine which one she would choose. Instead of buying a room full of posters, she could buy one special painting and add to it, if need be. Good God, Paige's extravagance was already rubbing off on her.

Standing facing one of the wire collages was a youngish-looking man in worn, tan-colored cords and a UCLA sweat shirt, with old-fashioned wire-rimmed glasses framing his intense blue eyes that seemed to be looking through the piece in front of him. There was something about the way he was standing there, looking so critically at the work, that made Susan think that he was more than just a browsing student, that perhaps he worked there. When he went and lifted the heavy-looking work off the wall and rehung it to his satisfaction, presumably going for perfect alignment, she concluded he was obviously not just a student.

"Excuse me, I was curious how much these go for," she asked him, uncertain if he had even heard her.

He took off his glasses and rubbed his eyes, completely distracted. "Pardon me?" It was a definite double take.

Now that he had spoken, there was a kind of distinguished quality to his voice that caught Susan by surprise and made him seem markedly older. On closer examination there were lines beneath his small but deep blue eyes, a slight setback to his curly blond hair. He had the kind of flared nostrils that she had always found sexy, and she looked away, aware that she had been staring at him. "Do you work here?" she asked, questioning why, if he did not, he had been lifting and rearranging the painting on the wall.

"Oh, no. Well, not really." He smiled pleasantly, appraising her, nonplussed at how confusing his reply had come across.

Susan smiled back at him, feeling awkward, waiting for an explanation. He did not look the part of someone who went around straightening paintings on walls; he did not look that fastidious.

"I'm the artist," he explained with an unassuming shrug, the dimple on his left cheek growing more pronounced. Susan's eyes traveled down to the worn kneecaps of his pants, which looked as though he played ball in them frequently, and did a lot of knee-slides. His being the artist certainly explained his behavior.

"Are you really?" she asked, just to be sure.

He grinned and nodded.

She was definitely intrigued. "I love your work. It's really terrific," she said, looking up at it again with even more enthusiasm. "I was just wondering if I could afford to buy one," she added wryly. "But I suppose I should be talking numbers with someone who works here, not with the artist himself." To her amusement she realized she was flirting with him, which was completely uncharacteristic for her. The funny thing was, it felt good.

"*If* anyone works here," he corrected her, looking around at the nonexistent salespeople, setting off that wonderful dimple again. There were some typed sheets of paper on top of the jewelry case, cataloging the inventory and he picked one up, scanning it briefly before handing it to her. "They're a little lax here," he explained, though unperturbed. "I guess when I'm rich and famous I'll be in a position to complain. Then again, if this keeps up, it's not very likely I'll ever be rich and famous." He laughed as though he could not have cared less about attaining that status. "Thankfully, I don't have to count on their obviously absentee sales force to pay my rent," he added matter-of-factly, indicating the gold-and-blue letters on his sweat shirt. "I'm an economics professor at UCLA."

"Economics?" Susan said, caught by surprise once more. "Not art or art history?" She had come to the conclusion that he was definitely too old to be a student, but a professor would not have occurred to her. Now it seemed befitting.

"I'm a closet artist. It's how I relax. The fellow who owns this place kept seeing my work at the sidewalk art fairs they hold every year in Westwood, and asked me to show here." He leaned in closer to Susan, dropping his voice. "They're asking a ridiculous amount of money. It's embarrassing. If you're really serious about buying something, cut what you see on the page there in half and negotiate with them from that point. But don't say I told you so."

"You may get famous, but I'll wager you're not likely to ever get rich," Susan laughed.

"Oh, I'd just blow it anyway. Besides, did you ever meet anyone rich who was happy?"

"Is that what you teach in your lectures on economics? Must go over real big."

"I teach the *science* of money, not the philosophy of it."

"I see." Susan chuckled. *Paige would not approve,* she thought, amused. Then she remembered that she was supposed to be meeting Paige and Tori over at Kit's and she glanced anxiously at her watch, having to squint repeatedly in order to read what time it was. Paige had talked her into contact lenses on their second day out in Los Angeles, and the left one felt as though it had slipped. The damn things made her eyes water all the time, and they were a nuisance to put in. The hell with vanity; she was going back to her glasses. This artist professor looked alluring enough in his. Besides, years ago she had talked herself into liking the image of herself in glasses. They made her feel more serious.

So much for posters. So much for this adorable professor. "I've got to run," she said regretfully, wishing she could stay and talk to him or see him again. "I guess I'll be back to negotiate—"

"Hot date? Or a husband?" he asked, fishing.

"Hot date," she replied, happy about the way he had asked. She stopped herself from adding that it was with her girlfriends.

"Well, that's certainly less disconcerting than a husband," he replied. "If you're interested in poor, starving artist-professor types, I'd like to call you. We wouldn't exactly be doing Chasens, maybe something more on the order of a picnic by candlelight at the beach, or something like that . . ."

Chasens was where Kit and George's rehearsal dinner for the wedding had been held. It was beautiful, expensive, a key restaurant in town, but candlelight at the beach sounded much more enticing. She looked down at the Xeroxed sheets of paper he had handed her, trailing her finger down the page. "Mark Arent," she read aloud, locating his name, then grinning at him.

Neither of them had been aware that they had neglected to even exchange names, and now Mark asked her for hers.

"Susan Kendell," she said, automatically extending her hand and then feeling foolish for having done so.

"*Can* I call you?" he reiterated. "We can talk about me giving you a good deal on some of this overpriced stuff here . . ." His tone was joking; his eyes were sincere.

"Sure," Susan said, already imagining Paige's mocking reaction. For lack of any scratch paper, she gave him a deposit slip from her checkbook, a quick smile good-bye and then fled.

She felt him watching her all the way down the stairs and out the door. Her cheeks were pink with pleasure, and her smile intensified as she wondered just what she was getting herself into. So much for her Beverly Hills multimillionaire.

Chapter 9

Kit and George's marriage set up a perfect paradigm embodying all they were striving to find, love and money harmoniously coexisting beneath one grand roof. Their new marriage was going swimmingly. The two newlyweds appeared to have it all: challenging careers, interesting friends, an exciting life-style, and, now, the added thrill of a baby to look forward to. At dinner that night Kit had announced to them that she was pregnant.

The Dom Perignon had not yet ceased its flow.

"If all else fails, *then* you can swoon over this bum artist guy, but give yourself a chance," Paige was saying to Susan as the three girls stepped out of Dustin Brent's Aston-Martin, turning it over to the valet parking attendant at the posh Los Angeles Equestrian Center, on their way to attend the polo match. They were all three dressed to be noticed, having been forewarned that an evening at the popular Equidome was as much a fashion event as it was a sporting event. It was also a premier social event, and by Paige's account a perfect place to meet the kind of men they were hoping to meet.

There were the polo players and the polo partyers, all part of the well-to-do horsey set. In the course of her research on where they should go in L.A., Paige had read an article which described a polo player as equal parts machismo and money—an image that immediately caught her interest. A dashing figure in helmet, skintight pants, and knee-high boots who played a fast and furious game while mounted on a horse at swiftest gallop, swooping down to chase a billiard-sized ball lying seven feet from his shoulder in the most dangerous team sport in the world, where half a ton of man and horse were smashing wildly into six other horses and players on a thirty-five-mile-an-hour collision course. That dashing figure, who maintained a high-goal rating, a string of polo ponies, and liked to play within the sport reputed to be the "king of sports, the sport of kings" seemed like a choice candidate.

"*No* artists," Paige asserted, sweeping past her friends, through the bold white arch at the entrance, past the bright white fences that lent the appropriate horsey feeling to the sprawling complex. She was dressed all in white, wearing a tight, ankle-length skirt that opened in front as she walked, showing off her long, tan, bare legs, her new boots. Her blouse was a crisp white cotton man's-style shirt, with big shoulder pads, lots of rhinestone-and-stud work, closed at the throat with a sparkling rhinestone bolo tie. She was the only one of the three of them who had dressed equestrian-style. Tori was wearing a new icy pink linen-and-lace skirt outfit. Susan was in the new black pants and T-shirt Paige had helped her to select at a shop on Melrose. The snug-fitting pants were tucked into boots that were the black variation of Paige's white ones, which they had bought together, and she had on a loose-fitting golden-poppy blazer. "Not even successful artists," Paige maintained. "Because they're too insane. *I* ought to know. I have an extensive history of artist fiascos from which we can all take note. They can't hold on to their money or their success; they're self-destructive; and, most importantly, *you* can't hold on to them."

"He's not an artist. He's an economics professor," Susan said defensively, taking a good deep whiff of the familiar horse scents. Some people complained about the smell, while Susan, associating it with pleasure, loved it. She felt right at home with the barnyard smells, which evoked feelings of happy anticipation within her, made her think of the long, exhilarating rides, the freedom of a good gallop. With it all she found herself growing increasingly excited about seeing her first polo match. Paige was making such a big deal about Mark Arent. You would think the man had proposed to Susan. Who knew if he would even call? Although she hoped he would. She looked over toward Tori for support, but derived not so much as a glance. Tori had been in her own world all night long, and still was. The two job offers she had received today had done little to cheer her, although the first one, with the erratic playboy-son conducting the interview, did not exactly sound kosher to Susan.

"Well, you know the old adage about professors: Those who can't *do*, teach—" Paige had replied smugly, her mean green eyes on a guy wearing a deep-brown leather bomber jacket, a faded blue denim-colored shirt beneath it, and a sexy hairy chest beneath that.

Susan thought he looked rich but dumb. "That's bullshit, Paige," she said. "Some people *like* to teach. It makes them feel good."

"That or they're afraid of going out there, into the real world, and having to compete," Paige countered. They had reached the ticket booth and were standing in line. The arena was in clear view and already crowded. Off to the side was the private bar and grill restaurant they had heard about, with a lovely outdoor patio overlooking the polo field. "It's *safe* within the confines of a university. The students look up to you. You can *profess* all you want and never risk being put to the test. I think you should concentrate more on the stockbroker George is fixing you up with, counselor, *and* on tonight—"

"Yes, I noticed how you gave *me* the stockbroker and maneuvered the producer for yourself," Susan chided lightly, winking at Tori, who had, in turn, been assigned the surgeon.

"You want the producer?" Paige replied, with that smartass smile of hers. "He's yours!"

"What, we're going to swap blind dates?" Susan thought Paige probably would.

"Why not?" Paige answered, as though the thought amused her.

"Because the stockbroker is going to call up expecting to get

Susan-the-lawyer, and the producer is going to call up expecting to get Paige-the-dancer, and what are we going to do, tell them we switched?"

"You could make it all a lot more fun by *not* telling them," Tori commented, letting out a long deep breath as though she had been holding it for several days. "Susan, you could be Paige; and Paige, you could be Susan. That's the beauty of a blind date. They have no idea what you look like, other than that George probably told them that you're both tall and blond, which you both are. I'm the only one who couldn't get away with it."

Paige laughed, glad to see Tori looking alive again. "She just doesn't want to have to throw her doctor into the grab bag."

"Travis hates doctors. It would be so great to go home engaged to one."

"That's the spirit," Paige commended her, jumping topics and leaving Susan with the stockbroker, after all. "Did you see Kit's necklace and earrings? God . . . all those sapphires make getting disfigured for nine months sound appealing," she went on, referring to the gift George had given Kit to celebrate her being pregnant.

"You're not doing half bad yourself, on that score," Susan reminded Paige. "Jeweled designer gowns, et cetera . . . without getting knocked up."

"Without even a first date . . ." Paige threw in, preening.

"What's so bad about getting knocked up? Sounds good to me." Tori opened up her purse and took out her wallet. They were next.

"Nothing, except that I wouldn't fit into that gorgeous dress," Paige remarked.

Susan looked squarely at Tori. "Let's get things rolling with your *doctor* first, huh?" she suggested.

"It wasn't the doctor I had in mind," Tori frowned. The tone of her voice indicated that she had meant it as a joke, but it fell flat.

"Travis is six feet under," Paige reminded her. "Dead and buried. If you're carrying his kid, save your news and tell the doctor it's his."

"I don't want to marry the doctor. I don't even know the

doctor. He probably has buck teeth, and comes up to my belly button. You heard George say how funny he was. Have you ever met a funny, good-looking doctor? They're either good-looking and full of themselves or funny, short, and overweight. Maybe I'll buy a blond wig, and take your producer, Paige."

"Three, please," Susan said drolly to the man behind the ticket counter.

Looking for seats, they passed a series of private boxes. Did the names designated actually sound rich? Or was it just because she expected them to, Susan wondered, reading the little printed signs as she trailed behind Paige and Tori, heading up toward the bleachers. Harold Tanner. John B. Colligan III. *Mark Arent,* she thought to herself with a little squelched chuckle. *Wouldn't that be something?*

The game was actually thrilling to behold, with all the massed tonnage of horses and men charging with breakneck fury up and down the length of the football-sized arena in hot pursuit of one small ball, about as big and elusive as a round bar of soap. With each tenacious *whack* of a mallet, the ponies would slow, stop, change direction, then shoot out in full racing spirit, legs stretched, hooves pounding, at times accelerating to speeds of forty miles an hour in a matter of seconds, sending up billowy clouds of dust in their wake. Attempting to bring a sense of order to the frenzied stampedes and the raucous cheering was the announcer enthusiastically calling out the plays over a loudspeaker, his booming voice competing with bell signals and intermittent organ music. The players wore cotton T-shirts in their team colors. Tonight it was green against blue, sleek-fitting white breeches tucked into high leather boots capped by thick ribbed knee guards and spurs at their ankles.

Tori was thoroughly caught up in the game, cheering out loud, rooting for the team in the green T-shirts because Paige had decided she liked the green team. With the violence of ice hockey, the velocity of racing, the tension of football, the precision and challenge of golf, and the teamwork of basketball, polo was quite a game. Fundamentally it was played a lot like soccer or ice hockey, each team wrestling to gain control of the ball, to finesse it across the playing field and into the goal. But the ferocity with which it was played—astride horses reeling and charging at furious speeds, the players dipping crazily into a melee of flying hooves and flashing sticks to take a shot—made it all that much more enthralling to watch.

They had brought along a pair of binoculars, which George had lent them, and Tori was peering intently through them when the blue team began a sudden and surprising comeback. A player from the green team overconfidently sliced the air with his mallet, intending to finish off the ball, which was only an arm's length from the goal, but missing it entirely. His error was compounded when a player from the blue team surged forward, scooping the ball smoothly off the ground, propelling it in an arc into the air. There was a rough and tumble scuffle as the other players rallied to intercept, but the same "blue bomber," as Tori came to call him, continued to chase the ball, driving it in a relentless volley of forehand strokes, seemingly unstoppable. At full run, a player from the opposing green team angled to the left over the horse's withers and propelled the ball backhand, stealing it away and sending it back again in the opposite direction. But not for long, as the blue bomber pivoted sharply around, catching up to the ball in advance of anyone else. Thrusting his left shoulder forward, employing a scythelike movement, he swung his upraised mallet in a mighty blow, sending the scampering ball at least fifty yards. His mare whinnied and shied uneasily as he prodded its sides, charging maniacally off after the ball again in relentless pursuit.

Up until now, the announcer's commentary had merely blended in with the lively and colorful scenery. But when the name *Richard Bennetton* was repeated several times in connection with the play, Tori nearly fell out of her seat.

The players' heads were protected by wide-rimmed pith helmets or the newer shiny plastic models, while their eyes and faces were shielded by narrow guards, making it difficult to see what anyone looked like.

Which was why it took Tori until the fourth and final chukker, or period of the match, to discover Richard Bennetton was among the players.

Paige must have recognized his name at the exact same moment because she grabbed onto Tori's arm and looked at her with wild bemusement. *Couldn't be the same Richard Bennetton. Or could it?* When his name resounded again loud and clear through the house speakers, Paige yanked the binoculars from Tori's grasp, nearly strangling her with the narrow black cord from which they were hanging.

Trying to pick him up, Paige scanned the field, lingering for a brief moment on the attractive redhead, also riding on the blue team, whose fiery mass of hair tumbled loosely down her back, beneath her bright blue helmet, distinguishing her as the only female player on the field. Paige moved on, studiously roving the field through the lenses of the binoculars until her intended subject entered the frame. Tori was torn between watching Richard, who had just brought the game to such a thrilling climax, and watching Paige, who was smiling as if she had just fallen in love. "Why the hell didn't you go to lunch with him?" Paige whispered under her breath. "He's gorgeous. Rich. And what a great ass," she continued, gesturing toward the tantalizing view of his rear end rising up and out of saddle in a smooth rhythm as he stretched forward to scoop up the ball, the tight white riding pants accentuating his incredibly sexy bottom. "I'd have gone to lunch, taken the job, and we'd be married by now."

"Sure you would have." Susan laughed at Paige's audacity, swiping the binoculars from her to get a look at this Adonis. With all the elaborate headgear, who could tell whether he was gorgeous or not? What she did pick up was an intensity, the way he was going after the ball at full gallop, leaning out of his saddle in order to make shots that appeared to call upon a gymnastic agility just short of trick riding.

Tori, seeing her two friends gaping at him like that, reclaimed the binoculars just in time to see Richard finish off the game in an arresting maneuver. In a vaulting catapult, he drove the ball straight between the posts, making the goal, and winning the match for his team in one swift shot. She turned bright red when she realized that she was on her feet, cheering louder than almost anyone else in the crowd.

* * *

"Horse people—why do they always look wealthy?" Paige asked after the matches, as they edged their way through the crowd, on their way to the disco there.

When neither Susan nor Tori bothered to reply, she answered herself. "They look wealthy because they're horse people, and horse people just look rich."

"Brilliant, Paige," Tori said, giving Susan a look, feeling incredibly nervous at the prospect of running into Richard. Paige and Susan had said they wanted to go dancing at Horses, the Los Angeles Equestrian Center's restaurant-disco they had passed on the way in, or to check out the private club, maybe get some dessert. All Tori wanted was to sneak out as inconspicuously as possible.

Already she was beginning to see some of the polo players coming through, beer in hand, mingling with their friends.

While all scruffy from the field, their team shirts sweaty and clinging, wet towels tied around their necks, their white pants streaked with dirt, they looked far more appealing than the guests who had not played. Maybe it was the invigorated glow coloring their complexions, sending off a raw sexuality, a hearty, rustic radar. She was a bundle of nerves, though she didn't know why. She hadn't even *liked* Richard. He was cocky. Way too arrogant. He had seemed like a jerk. It was just this game that made him seem so alluring, the competence with which he had handled the horse and the reckless danger that at times approached the edge of lunacy.

So why was her heart racing, as though *she* herself had just been out there, her pulse double the rate it should ordinarily be? Why was she rehearsing in her head what she would say to him if they did run into one another? Curt little remarks occurred to her that made her smile. Not that she would ever really deliver any of them. Witty, smartass pearls rarely materialized when she needed them.

Probably he was here with a date. A girlfriend. Probably he was screwing the redhead on his team. She was savage like he was, loved danger like he did. *Paige* could manage a man like Richard Bennetton. But he would make mincemeat of Tori, and Tori knew it.

The entrance to Horses was spilling over with the mob that was too large to contain inside its doors. Paige determined that it was too college-rowdy here anyway, and began steering them away from the noise, and back over toward the arena to the sign which announced Riding and Polo Club—Members Only, where a more subdued, sophisticated-looking crowd was gathered.

"Members *only,*" Tori reminded Paige, deciding Richard Bennetton was more likely to be here than at Horses, and that she would die of embarrassment if he were to come by and see them trying to sneak in. She could not have been more relieved when Susan pointed out an additional sign, set up on a pedestal over by the door, which read Private Party Tonight. Standing only a few feet away from it at the doorway's threshold were two young men with navy blazers, checking names against a printed guest list. Paige watched them for several moments, as though contemplating how to get in anyway.

"May I help you?" asked one of the men, looking over the three of them. Tori could see Paige trying to read the guest list from her upside down perspective as she stalled, smiling at him.

"We were just catching some fresh air before we came in," she replied smoothly.

"Oh." He looked as if he were debating whether to ask her for her name or wait, when a group of people walked briskly up, rattling off their names, and distracting him.

Tori looked past him, into the room, growing more and more curious about Richard, wondering if he was there. There was a brass railing separating the bar area from the dining area. Hors d'oeuvres were being passed by waiters wearing white shirts, black bow ties, and green butcher-style aprons, which matched the hunter-green-and-burgundy decor of the room. It was all very rich-looking, with roomy burgundy leather armchairs arranged by the fireplace, light oak-framed French windows opening onto an outdoor dining patio. Lush green ficus trees with braided roots sprang from bamboo baskets. And the smoky essence of steaks being barbecued could be inhaled all the way outside. It was so crowded it was difficult to see if he was there or not, and just as she was about to give up, half-relieved, half-disappointed, she glimpsed him standing by the bar with his arm around his red-headed teammate, both of them laughing amidst a large group of friends.

"C'mon, let's get out of here," Tori said brusquely to Susan and Paige, raising her voice a notch so as to be heard over the din of band music.

Paige hesitated, then intuitively followed Tori's gaze inside the doors. "Is he in there?" she asked, standing on the toes of her new white cowboy boots to improve her vantage point.

"Yes . . ." Tori nodded distractedly, her eyes glued to him as he took a swig of beer, lustily wiping his mouth afterward with the back of his hand, then winking at the redhead. It was the same wink he had given *her* just this morning.

"Hmmm. With the redhead . . ." Paige observed, frowning upon locating him. "You sound jealous . . ."

Tori shrugged, surprised to find that she was. "Crazy, isn't it?"

Paige looked past her again, into the room. "All depends on how you look at it. What was it that book said on how to get over your lover? 'Find a new lover. . . .' Could be, dear heart, that things are looking up. I'd say ol' Travis is fading from the picture already."

It was the first time Tori had gone a full hour without brooding over Travis, and she smiled at the revelation. Richard Bennetton had his attractive head tilted back while consuming the balance from his beer bottle in one long luxurious guzzle, making her think of a sexy beer commercial. Instead of feeling stung by the queer sense of jealousy she had experienced only a moment ago, she felt oddly released by it.

Maybe Paige was right. Maybe things *were* looking up.

Chapter 10

It was not altogether unlike performing, gyrating her svelte hips to the loud, pulsating music. Only instead of being on a big stage she was on a tiny one, and the bursting-to-capacity audience was on a significantly smaller scale. They were exhausting their limbs, grunting and sweating right along with her, following her expert lead through an intensive workout geared to help them maintain their already extraordinary shapes.

Paige had ended up getting a job at Sports Club/LA, one of the city's more fashionable and expensive health clubs, teaching aerobics classes. After a couple of weeks of hard-core searching, money and hopes wearing thin, a job opened up for her there and she accepted it with relief. One of the other instructors had quit, and Paige had jumped at the position.

"On your stomachs," she cried out now, over the blare of music.

A quick glance at her watch told her that she had only a few minutes more to go before stretching her students out and winding up the class. Twenty more counts to finish off this position, another sequence pressing in the opposite direction, and their glutei maximi would be killing them for the next forty-eight hours each time they went to sit down, making them think reverently of Paige and her wonderful workout. What Paige really hoped to accomplish was to establish some good contacts so she could teach privates, clearing a tax-free sixty-five dollars an hour instead of a pre-tax ten dollars an hour.

Beethoven's Fifth was perfect cool-down material, and Paige led the relieved class through a series of final soothing stretches. Ahhh, time to go home. The pushing-to-the-max stuff that left them short of breath and ready to drop was behind them. Time to unwind, to think about what they were going to do this lovely Friday night, the prelude to their weekend. The old T.G.I.F. still applied.

Paige knew what she was going to do. Tonight was the night she, Tori, and Susan were all going out on the blind dates George and Kit had set up for them, Paige with the producer, Susan with the stockbroker, and Tori with her surgeon.

The three women had already concluded that the best part of these dates was probably going to be the getting each other dressed and ready, and then the comparing-notes session afterward when they could collect like college roommates and laugh, even if they felt like crying. God, it was nice having such good girlfriends again, not just fellow cast members, but real friends. So far, the best part about moving to Beverly Hills was unquestionably Susan and Tori.

When Paige arrived home from the health club, feeling all grimy from her workout and in a quandary over what she should wear that night, she found a massive bouquet of flowers sitting on the entrance hall table.

"From 'Philadelphia' again." Susan had come out of her room and was calling out to Paige from over the elaborate wrought-iron banister, which wrapped dramatically down around the paver-tiled stairs, concluding its spiral in an exotic indoor cactus garden. She was in that horrible old bathrobe of hers again, rubbing her just-washed hair with a towel.

Paige plucked the white gift card from out of the arrangement, trying to suppress the gnawing doubt as to Philadelphia's bachelorhood. He had been sending flowers and gifts of remembrance at least once a week since their encounter on Rodeo. No phone calls, just a steady stream of extravagant tokens accompanied by short, suggestive notes. This one said "Can't wait to see you, beautiful, all wrapped up in that divine red dress, like a Christmas package."

"What he means to say is that he can't wait to unwrap you." Susan had come downstairs and was standing behind Paige, reading the note over her shoulder, smelling of Ivory soap. "Don't you think this man is a little obsessed? All these presents and innuendos?" Susan remarked, pushing her oversized glasses against the bridge of her nose with her index finger. "What did you do to him? Are you sure you told us the whole story?"

"Down to the last detail," Paige reported, lifting up the bouquet and carrying it into the den, where there was another arrangement, slightly wilted, positioned in the center of the coffee table. Removing the old one, she replaced it with the new.

"Sure would make me nervous," Susan said, dipping down to filch a chocolate from the Steuben candy dish beside the flowers. "Let's see, silver handcuffs from Tiffany's . . ." she rattled off dubiously.

"They're not handcuffs. They're wrist-cuffs. They're sterling silver Elsa Peretti bracelets—"

"A snakeskin whip . . ."

"A Judith Leiber *belt*!" Paige laughed, correcting Susan, eyeing the chocolate, which she finally popped into her mouth. "So, the man's into Judith Leiber. The purse he bought me was also hers. You're the perverse one, Susan, reading all these lewd things into very classy designer gifts."

"How about the silk stockings with the red lace garter belt?" Susan queried with a smirk. She had her head tilted to the side, her wet hair spilling down to one shoulder, as she continued to towel dry it. Paige thought her beat-up terry robe looked as if it would disintegrate if it were run through the washing machine one more time.

"Valentino. To match my dress," Paige replied demurely, not missing a beat.

"And what's *his* present?" Tori chimed in, also in her robe, only *hers* was satin-and-lace Dior. Having gained both their attention, Tori swept down the stairs. Of the three of them, this house suited her the best. Susan belonged in something more earthy, ranchlike, less *done.* While Paige felt she belonged in something *more* done, preferring the fun of flash to quiet chic.

"Like the man said, *me.*" Paige derived a kick out of shocking the two of them. "And you need a new robe, kid," she said snidely to Susan. "If you decide to spend the night at the stockbroker's, better borrow one of mine."

"What—sleep with him on the first date?" Susan cried with mock gravity, flipping her hair the other way to dry the other side. "And besides, I like this robe; I like the cut. I've never been able to find another one like it."

"Time to give up, dear heart," Paige teased, poking her finger through a small frayed hole on the side, and tickling Susan. "God, I'm starving," she announced, taking a bite out of a square-shaped chocolate, hoping it was a caramel and not a nougat. "Since I can't eat before my classes, all I've had all day is a glass of apple celery juice. Mr. Producer's not scheduled for another hour and a half—"

"Oh, bad news, Paige," Tori interrupted grimly. "He called about an hour ago to say he can't make it tonight. They're having some problems with the film he's shooting, and he says he's going to be stuck out there until late. He said he'll call tomorrow to reschedule."

Paige went over to dump the older flower arrangement into the trash can behind the bar, pausing as she did so. "Well then, maybe I'll take the stockbroker, after all," she kidded Susan, smiling to hide her disappointment. She was in the mood to go out. Not to stay there all alone in that great big house. Curling up with a good book sounded like internment. Suddenly restless, she tugged open the bar's small refrigerator, looking for something to drink. "I thought he had a rather sexy voice when I talked to him on the phone," she said slyly, relinquishing the cork from an already open bottle of chardonnay and pouring herself a glassful.

"So did I," Susan replied, pointing her finger at Paige, then looking over at Tori. "I think we should lock her in her room until our dates leave. The girl is not to be trusted."

Paige laughed. "Go ahead. Leave me all by my lonesome. With nobody to have dinner with or keep me company . . ."

Eyeing the two of them, she brought the cool glass of wine to her lips.

"I'm sure Maria would sit down and eat with you," Tori joked, referring to the housekeeper, who seemed to be scared to death of the three of them.

"Muchas gracias por nada," Paige replied unsmiling. "Maybe I'll go to a movie. Or brave a nightclub on my own—" The phone rang and she snatched it up.

Maybe it was the producer and there was a change in plans. Maybe it was John Lester, the man whom she had met on her flight out to L.A., whom she had already gone out with a couple of times. Maybe it was the mortgage broker she had met today at Sports Club/LA. "Hello," she said smoothly into the receiver, winking at Tori and Susan, hoping it *was* for her.

The cheerful male voice on the other end did not sound the least bit familiar. "Hi."

"Hi," Paige said back to the undetermined voice, shrugging at the girls. "Who is this?"

"Who's *this*?" Whoever it was, he was a tease.

"You called *me.* So who's *this*?"

"I like a woman who takes a stand. Okay, I'll give you a clue—"

"Is this an obscene phone call?"

"That could be arranged."

Paige removed the phone from her ear and put her hand over the mouthpiece. "Some screwball—"

"Hello . . . hello . . ."

"I'm still here," Paige reassured him, laughing. "Okay, what's my clue? Who the fuck are you, already?"

"This can't be the sweet innocent I met at my office last week —employing such language."

With a vague sense that she might be speaking to Richard Bennetton, Paige shot a look over at Tori. "You're damn straight it's not," she said, her mind rushing ahead. Office? Had she met anyone in an office who would call her? No. "Let me guess. You play a mean game of polo," Paige ventured, not missing the stunned expression that had overtaken her brunette roommate.

"Polo—" Tori's delicate hand flew up to catch her gasp.

"Very good," he said, sounding impressed. "So has she been unable to get me off her mind?"

"I doubt it, but why don't you ask her yourself?" Paige answered, rolling her eyes as she handed a faint-looking Tori the telephone.

Tori was shaking her head. "No, no, no," she whispered, her stomach all in knots. "Take a message. Tell him I'm not here."

But Paige just kept shoving the phone at her. Tori had no idea what to say to him. If she could call him back, she could get her thoughts untangled. Stymied, she watched as Paige and Susan deserted her, heading up the huge staircase, leaving her in the lurch.

"So you're a polo fan as well," he began the conversation. His voice immediately triggered a picture of him in her mind, sitting behind his huge desk, looking up at his father, then looking penetratingly out at her.

"Yes. Well, not really," she answered foolishly. She was trying to get this straight in her mind. Had he seen her at the polo matches? Or was he referring to what Paige had said? If he had seen her there, why had he not come up to her? Then she remembered the redhead. "Paige, my girlfriend who answered the phone, is into polo," she said awkwardly. *Into polo players, anyway.*

"How'd you like the way I saved the day for my team Friday?" he asked, and she wondered if he was intentionally addressing the question she was mulling over in her head. So he *had* seen her. She wondered when. A shiver of excitement passed through her.

"I was impressed," she replied, trying to concentrate on their conversation so that she could respond with some lucidity, some intelligence. *Relax,* she told herself. While it was starting to dawn on her that she should be flattered that he had called, she was having a hard time regaining composure. She was rusty, out of practice. Living with Travis all those years was like being married. It was ages since she had been on a date.

Thankfully, Richard made it easy on her, carrying the conversation with a polish that indicated *he,* clearly, was *not* out of practice. They talked about polo for a while, the warm July weather they were having, the position at his office he thought she should at least be considering, his recent trip to the south of France, and then finally he asked her out on a date.

Replaying it all in her head afterward, she practically floated up the stairs, giggling to herself because their conversation could not have gone better. First, there was tonight's dinner with Kit and George's friend, Dr. Jeffrey Wallerstein. Then next week she had a date with Richard Bennetton, handsome playboy polo player who, from their conversation, she had garnered to be bicontinental, bicoastal, bilingual, but hopefully not bisexual. It all felt like great revenge against Travis. It felt so great that she went directly up to her room to tear up a picture of him that she had been hanging on to, like a recovering alcoholic who stashes away reserve bottles just in case. No more on-the-sly fixes when she opened her wallet, she thought, gaining momentum as she ripped the photo to shreds.

There was one last picture of Travis hidden in the zipper compartment of her suitcase beneath the bed, and she figured she would know she was completely cured when she was able to tear that up as well. *"Destroy all photos,"* the book had said. She was getting there. "Find a new lover." She was trying.

Richard had sounded nicer on the phone than he had at their interview, more congenial, less full of himself. She was actually looking forward to seeing him.

"Well?" Susan asked, standing at her open door, all dressed and looking terrific. Her ash-colored hair fell like a soft mist around her shoulders, and she was dressed in an outfit Paige had lent her. After two failed attempts at wearing something from her own wardrobe, a dress Paige said looked "too prim," then a pair of pants Paige said looked "too Stockton" (even though she had bought them at Macy's in San Francisco), Susan hadn't known what to wear. Her new Melrose outfit was at the cleaners, and she hadn't thought to pick it up. Her other recent L.A. acquisitions, Paige told her, were appropriate for work, but not for evening.

As their resident wardrobe consultant, Paige insisted Susan borrow the new Karusai outfit she had just bought. Although Paige made the least amount of money of the three of them, she definitely had the most clothes, which she was happy to throw into a kind of joint pool for all of them to share.

"Don't you look chic," Tori said to Susan, who spun around uncertainly for a second inspection. *If she would only stand up straight and hold her shoulders back, she would be guaranteed to turn heads,* Tori thought, then decided she probably did anyway. The featherweight silk pants and oversized jacket, each silk-screened with different sweeping, artistic-looking designs, billowed as she turned. Beneath the jacket she was wearing a simple black scoop-neck shirt.

"You don't think it's 'too Paige'?" Susan worried.

"I think it looks great on you," Tori insisted, feeling so high right then that probably anything would have looked great. Giving it a firm second appraisal she decided the outfit looked at least as good on Susan, whose taller frame lent an added elegance.

"So tell me what happened . . ." Susan came inside Tori's bedroom and flopped down onto the bed, watching Tori rush haphazardly around the room, getting dressed with giddy distraction. In the trash can she noticed Travis's torn-to-shreds photograph, and she wondered about it but didn't ask.

"We're going out next week . . ." A pretty flush colored Tori's pale skin. "He *did* see us."

Susan was thrilled for Tori. She had never seen her glow like this. Not that Susan thought it was Richard specifically, more that he had buoyed her confidence. And after that rat in the trash can, boy, did she ever need it. "When? Where?" Susan asked, envying Tori's petite, graceful frame as she slipped into a Matisse-like print silk tank-dress, then bent over searching in her closet for a pair of shoes. The pair Susan suspected Tori was looking for were on the floor right beside her. Susan picked them up and waved them in the air for her to see.

"Thursday night. To a big black-tie birthday party at this private club called Neon. Oh, thanks," she sighed, gratefully taking the high-heeled pumps and wriggling into them. Continuing her conversation with Susan through the mirror, she added a pair of sleek, quill-shaped African ivory earrings, two thick ivory bangles, and an ivory-and-gold ring.

"So are you going to take the job working for him?" Susan asked playfully, adjusting a pillow beneath her arm as she leaned into a more comfortable position. Her date wouldn't be there for another fifteen minutes or so.

"You never know—" Tori replied breezily, finishing herself off with a couple squirts of cologne. "Versace. Want some?" she asked, turning toward Susan.

"Just in case they arrive at the same time, wouldn't want to clash," Susan replied, rising to her feet and accepting the bottle. Closing her eyes, she gave her neck and wrist a quick dousing, then handed the bottle back to Tori, who was standing beside her, the two of them reflected side by side in the opalescent sea-shell-framed mirror. "Great team, aren't we?" Susan said. Tori took her hand and gave it a tight squeeze. Susan, smiling, pointed to the discarded remnants of Travis scattered in the trash can.

Tori laughed. "As Paige would say, 'Fuck him!' "

When the doorbell rang they both shot glances down at their watches. "I'm not nervous, are you?" Susan asked facetiously, drawing a quick breath. This stockbroker guy was probably a creep—most blind dates were—but she had a nervous flutter in her stomach nevertheless. It was getting so "dressed," she thought, that produced the anxiety. It made her feel as if she were about to be on display, as if the stockbroker were shopping and she were the merchandise.

When Susan went downstairs to answer the door, she was stunned to see her artist-professor, mostly hidden behind one of his enormous paintings, standing there waiting for her to invite him in.

"Hi," she said, feeling that nervous flutter intensify. "What is this? What are you doing here?" Her excitement was impossible to contain. *No artists*. Paige's mandate echoed in her head. *Sorry, Paige, this could be love*, Susan thought, looking at the top of his curly blond head.

Mark came into the house and, after some maneuvering, set the painting against a wall. Tori had appeared at the top of the staircase and was watching. Susan signaled for her to come down.

"You look sensational," Mark was saying, unable to take his

eyes off Susan, who felt embarrassed, way overdressed. She wished that she could run upstairs and throw on a pair of jeans like he had on. Wash off all this makeup. No frayed knees this time, she noticed, taking stock of his stiff, new-looking Levi's jeans. In fact, he looked all cleaned up, as though he had gone to a fair amount of trouble for her, wearing a fresh shirt, smelling as if he had just gotten out of the shower.

"Thanks," she replied, full of questions as she looked into his deep blue eyes that were slightly magnified behind his glasses. She wanted to be wearing *her* jeans and *her* glasses, and *not* to be wearing her contact lenses.

"I'm a real sucker for pretty women who like my work," he began almost shyly.

Susan glanced over at Tori, feeling completely overwhelmed.

"I decided I'd rather you have it than let it sit hanging up on a wall in a gallery where nobody was even bothering to try and sell it anyway," he explained.

"Mark, I can't accept this," she said, though she was dying to. Her astonishment at the last few minutes fused with an uneasiness as to what she was going to do when the doorbell rang and the "creepy stockbroker" and the "fat-but-funny surgeon" arrived. Paige, she decided, could have the stockbroker after all. In a daze she remembered to introduce Tori to Mark.

"Nice to meet you. I've heard so much about you," Tori was saying, all southern charm and smiles as she shook Mark's hand. She was genuinely impressed with his work and stepped back to admire it, telling him how terrific she thought it was. Susan could see by Tori's expression that Tori was surprised that it *was* this good, which pleased Susan to no end.

Mark looked flattered, not at Tori's compliments about his work, but that Susan had told her about him.

"Really, Mark, I can't accept this," Susan said again, though she was already imagining how wonderful it would look hung up in her office.

"Well, then how about if you just keep it for me for a while? The truth of the matter is, I have no place else to put it," he teased, the quick dimple on his left cheek giving his sculptured face a friendly warmth that enveloped Susan. "I figured you had wall space in your office and, since you like it, could hold on to it for me."

"What happened to the wall space it occupied only a week ago?" she teased back, shifting her gaze from him to the colorful piece. It was the one she had liked best from the show, the one he had been rehanging.

"After the earthquake, the damn wall shrank," he replied with a funny shrug.

"I see. What earthquake?"

Mark looked over at Tori. "Is she always like this? Are we taking a deposition or something?"

Susan took a deep breath, tempted, but not sure what to do. She wanted to say, At least let me buy it from you, but she also didn't want to insult him. "Look, I feel kind of funny about this. Originally, you were talking about a break on the price. Why don't you just give me a great deal on it?"

"Some guys bring over flowers—I bring paintings. Just say thank you." Mark looked at her quietly, she thought, conscious of Tori's presence beside them. "Actually, I was on my way to see a friend of mine perform at this nightclub out in Trancas Beach, just past Malibu. You both look like you're going out but if you're not, why don't you come along? The place is kind of a dive, but my friend's a great saxophonist, and I'm kind of partial to dives anyway."

As he said it, Susan knew she was going to have a terrible time with the stockbroker. They were going to some supposedly "in" restaurant, where they would probably consume more gourmet pizza and pasta (that's all anyone in L.A. ever seemed to eat), when she would much rather go with Mark to the dive and listen to his musician friend play.

"Uh, we can't," Tori was saying, looking sympathetically over at Susan. "But that's very sweet of you. Maybe a rain check."

Susan thought he looked disappointed. She had to hold herself back from jumping in and saying she would go with him anyway. She was envisioning the beach as a backdrop in all its moonlit splendor. The romantic dive. She would concede just about anything if Paige would go out with the stockbroker in her place.

Tall and blond . . . Help, Paige! Where are you when I need you? Pretend you're me, and go out with the stockbroker—please.

"Oh, listen, it's a Friday night," he was saying. "I figured you'd be busy. But I thought I'd try. And by the way, no strings with my painting. I'm just an eccentric artist who can't resist giving something he's created to someone who is so terrifically enthusiastic."

"Eccentric artist or distinguished professor—how do you keep the identities straight?" Susan kidded, about to veer back to the rain check.

"So, *this* is the professor!"

Susan couldn't help but cringe at the sound of Paige's low, sexy voice. Her cringe intensified at the sight of Paige making her entrance in a hot pink satin kimono that barely covered her ass, wearing matching pink slippers and a saucy smile. So much for Paige saving the day. She was standing at the landing, her hair dripping wet, heightening her appeal. "Sorry for the way I'm dressed," she added. "I didn't know we had company." *Like hell she didn't,* Susan thought to herself, immediately guilty for her quick, jealous reaction. She hadn't missed Mark's speechless look, the way his eyes kept going to Paige's long bare legs. "I didn't hear the doorbell; I must have been in the shower."

"Paige, this is Mark Arent. Mark, Paige Williams," Susan said stiffly, looking over at Tori, who returned her look.

"The Mark Arent . . ." Paige emphasized. Then she headed over to his painting, the hem of her kimono swinging precariously, clearly tantalizing him as she moved about surveying it. "You really did this?" She looked innocently up at Mark, her theatrical moss-green eyes trained to captivate. Paige, who never went out of the house without wearing makeup, had on none. She looked Cover Girl-natural and, unjustly, more his type than Susan herself at the moment, when, God knows, she wasn't at all.

Mark nodded self-consciously, her slave.

"It's fabulous," Paige enthused, flashing that magic smile of hers over at her roommates. Susan wanted to shove her into a closet. Here she should have been feeling grateful to Paige for lending her her clothes, always bolstering her, making her laugh, when now all she felt was a burning resentment that bordered on tears. Paige was reducing the very articulate professor to a bumbling adolescent.

"Thanks . . ." he floundered, gaping at her. His eyes went from Paige to Susan, who accepted his gaze with relief and attempted to hold on to it.

"Do you make a habit of that practice, giving away your work to pretty girls who admire it?" Paige asked him flirtatiously. Susan thought if he did, she did not want to know. She had a horrible, sinking feeling that tonight *she* was going to end up with the stockbroker, Tori with the surgeon, and Paige, the femme fatale, was going to end up with the professor. It was sheer agony waiting to see how Paige would maneuver that.

"Actually, this is a first," Mark answered, and Susan chose to believe him. There was a momentary silence, which he filled by taking stock of his surroundings for the first time. "So who lives here?" he asked with belated curiosity. "All of you?"

"We're house-sitting," Tori answered.

"Pretty nice place," he observed, continuing to look around, perusing the art on the walls with a keen interest. "Who's the owner?"

"A man named Dustin Brent."

Mark had never heard of him. "Where's he now?"

"Off climbing mountains for about nine months or so," Paige said.

"The lives of the rich and famous," Mark remarked, not looking particularly impressed. "Well, sorry you all couldn't make it to see my friend. He does this rock-and-roll-style blues that makes you *need* to dance. Maybe another time."

"Mark . . ." Susan jumped in. This whole thing had turned sour. She knew she was overreacting about Paige and told herself she should just feel flattered that he had come by to see her. It was a great compliment that he'd brought her one of his paintings as a gift. "Listen, as long as you're parking this thing with me," she teased, "couldn't you at least help me hang it? Let me buy you dinner afterward to thank you."

Mark smiled at her. "You name the day," he said.

"I don't even have your number or anything," she said. "Let me get a piece of paper."

When Susan was out of the room, Paige asked Mark, "What friend?" Far from subtle, she went on to elaborate on how much she *loved* rock and roll *and* blues, and how she was the only one of the three of them who was staying home that night with nothing at all to do.

Susan returned just as Mark was suggesting that Paige go get dressed, and join him. Tori frowned at Susan and shrugged. Mark looked completely innocent. And in the midst of it all, the doorbell rang, like a time's-up signal, with the fate of the evening indelibly sealed. Susan and Tori's dates had arrived at exactly the same moment, the pairs less than perfect, but irreversible.

Chapter 11

Dan Sullivan, Susan's stockbroker blind date, had his hair slicked back à la *Miami Vice*. He was wearing a crumpled black, red, and gray linen jacket, fashionably oversized. He had a perfect tan and a build that unquestionably required hours of dedicated maintenance at a health club, probably Paige's Sports Club/LA. The two of them were so hip-looking that Susan barely recognized that she was part of the couple when they passed by a mirror while being led to their table at the fashionable Ivy at the Shore, one of the pricier indoor–outdoor cafés bordering the Ocean Front Promenade in Santa Monica. She, Susan Kendell Brown, didn't belong to that picture, that image she saw reflected in the swank, mirrored wall. That slick Hollywood-looking couple walking in step with her appeared only vaguely familiar. It was Paige's chic Japanese outfit that seemed to go with his, as though they had coordinated it all in advance, black and gray, stylishly large and flowing, that had caused her to do a double take. A handsome couple indeed, but uncomfortably alien. Susan wanted herself back. She wanted Mark back. She wanted to kill Paige.

She didn't consider herself a violent person, and yet she was enraged, sitting here at the white linen-draped table lit attractively by twinkling votive candles, amidst the Casablanca decor, the thick bamboo furniture, the whirling paddle fans, the Palapa straw ceiling, nodding every now and then to what Dan Sullivan was saying, pretending to study her green-and-pink menu, while instead possessed by an ungovernable stream of elaborately conceived, extremely violent fantasies about what she would like to do to her conniving, sexpot roommate. Strangling her seemed infinitely more satisfying than shooting her. The physical act might at least provide some relief from the fury that was consuming her.

After Paige had so artfully inserted herself in Susan's spot, she had pulled Susan aside to ask her if she "minded." *Do I mind? I'd like to kill you with my bare hands.* That's what Susan had wanted to reply. But instead, coward that she was, she had answered with a frosty "No, I don't mind," hoping, foolheartedly, that Paige would possess some modicum of conscience, decency, loyalty, or merely a simple grain of sensitivity, and bow out. Paige was clever enough to have engineered it so that Susan could have gone out with Mark, and she with Dan-the-stockbroker. Clinging to that hope, Susan had kept stalling, waiting for Paige to save the day for her, throwing unsubtle glances intended to suggest the switch. But Paige either didn't pick up on her hints, or didn't care to. They had been standing in the hallway, where there was an antique African blowgun hung on the wall as art. Susan had been tempted to take it down and shoot Paige right through the heart . . . if she had one.

The coup de grace was that the two of them were directly across the street, right at this moment, over at the Santa Monica pier. Mark had said he was taking Paige there to kill time and maybe grab a bite to eat, before heading off to see his friend perform at Trancas.

God, this had to be one of the worst nights of Susan's life. She couldn't even hope to enjoy herself or give Dan Sullivan a fair chance. She wanted to be out on the ratty but romantic-looking pier, eating French fries and sno-cones and winning stuffed animals at game booths, with Mark.

"So what are you going to have?" Dan asked benignly.

A heart attack, she thought gazing across the street at the bright neon sign that wouldn't let her think of anything else but

Mark. The famous old art-deco archway looked brightly alluring in purple, yellow, and green neon, its lively letters conjuring up images of Paige and Mark, walking hand in hand, laughing, flirting, leaning against lampposts and kissing through the sheer fun of it. She pictured Paige abandoning her manic search to find a rich man, falling head over heels in love with love, in love with Mark. The scenario continued bleakly, with Susan marrying someone like Dan, ending up wealthy but miserable. He would probably cheat on her because she wasn't glamorous enough. She would find out, try to live with it for a while. Then, unable to do so, she would divorce him, winding up with some token settlement, a couple of critical years older, and lonely all over again.

"All that?" joked the would-be groom when she forgot to answer. "You must be *really* hungry."

Susan was too full of anger to be hungry. She looked away from the pier and across the table at her date. He had a nice smile that made her feel suddenly weighted with guilt. She smiled back at him, wanting to connect, then looked down at her menu, reading it for the first time. "I was thinking of having the . . ." It was a blur of food descriptions. Why was she so undone over this? She had only just met Mark. Maybe she wouldn't even like him. For all she knew he was boring, self-righteous, a professorial snob. For all she knew Dan Sullivan was the best catch on the West Coast. She and Mark weren't dating, so why shouldn't Paige go out with him? Paige wasn't interested in someone like Mark, anyway. She just hadn't wanted to stay home by herself. And she did love to dance. "Capellini . . . or maybe something from the mesquite grill," Susan replied with effort. Really, what she needed was a drink. The wine Dan had ordered was chilling in a bucket beside the table because, upon tasting it, Dan had decided it wasn't cool enough. Susan eyed it, content to drink it warm. So she would put an ice cube into her glass.

"They're both good choices," Dan said, seemingly intent on her having a good time. "You may want to start with the capellini, then get the lime chicken over mesquite." His smile was boyish. It cut through some of the studied sophistication.

Susan closed her menu. "Would you mind if we traded seats?" she asked. This wasn't working. She wanted to concentrate on him, and it was impossible with the pier looming larger than life right in front of her. He looked at her peculiarly, rose up politely from his chair, and she let out a short sigh of relief, blaming the move on cigarette smoke from the table behind her. Facing the painted brick wall was infinitely better than facing that damn neon sign all night long, illuminating where she wanted to be but was not. She was going to have a good time if it killed her, she vowed, inching around the table and switching places with him. They passed nose to nose through the tight spot, brushing against one another. Then as she slipped into her seat she caught the same stubborn green-and-purple reflection bouncing off her water glass, flickering at her like an inexorable tease. With firm resolve she moved it as far away as possible, into the dimness of a shadow.

Dan Sullivan was forty-five years old. Grew up in Beverly Hills. Went to Beverly High the same time as Richard Dreyfuss, Albert Brooks, Rob Reiner, and assorted other superachievers whose names she didn't recognize, but probably should have. She tried to sound enthusiastic as he continued rattling off his credits as though delivering a prepared speech. She gathered he went on a lot of blind dates. After Beverly High, he went to the University of Southern California. His father owned a stock brokerage firm, which was how he happened into the field. He skied, played golf and tennis at his country club, had an extensive repertoire of "in" restaurants and movies, saw a shrink once a week, did recreational drugs, and drank Corona beer with a twist of lime. The two of them had nothing in common.

When Susan masochistically asked him if he would like to go across the street to the pier after dinner, he looked at her as if she were nuts. He literally laughed at her suggestion as if it were a big joke. "What? Mix with the element?" The pier was "sleaze city," he told her, a rundown, ramshackle eyesore, a crime magnet that would have done the city of Santa Monica a big favor if it had fallen into the ocean during one of the big storms or earthquakes. Seemingly amused by her out-of-town naïveté, he went on pompously to cite that, according to the police department, the crime rate in the dilapidated pier area was five times that of the rest of the city. Then he laughed again, preening about his élitism with a superior smirk, raking his fingers through his *Miami Vice* hairdo, and adding that if perhaps she had brought a gun along with her, or a switchblade, they could conceivably reconsider.

Susan drew her water glass back over into the light again, positioning it to recapture the colorful neon that appealed to her but clearly not to him. Gaining sort of a sick solace, she planned to stare at the glass for the duration of the evening.

They were leaning against a lamppost, kissing like a couple of teenagers. The ramshackle wooden pier beneath them was vibrating from all the people dancing and jumping around to the great fifties' vintage rock-and-roll music being pounded out by the band housed within the three-sided blue-and-white striped tent. Glittery letters on the drum set identified the group as Li'l Elmo and the Cosmos. Their pompadour hairstyles, dark shades, and slick suits were in keeping with their doo-wop mode. "Shake It Up Baby . . ." reverberated through the seaboard air, mixing with the crashing surf just below, the cheering appreciative crowd that was so large it spilled outside the bounds of the tent, onto the crummy, wood-planked walkway. The young, scruffy-looking crowd was in constant motion, infected by the music, dancing, swaying, hands up in the air, bebopping to the can't-stand-still sound of another era. It was so much fun.

"Dance with me," Mark said to Paige in the middle of the best kiss she had had in ages.

"Hmmm, my two favorite things," she murmured breathlessly into his mouth. He tasted like a cherry sno-cone. He looked cute, kind of silly, with his lips stained cherry red from the sweet icy mound. Hers were probably purple.

"Two favorite things? Hmm, what's that?" He put his hands over her head against the ribbed green lamppost, pressing his body into her incredibly seductive one. What a strange night! He had had Susan on his mind all week long, since he met her. And now he was behaving like a teenager with her roommate, completely intoxicated, swooning the way he hadn't done in years. He reminded himself of one of his students. And he kissed her again, with a hard-on that wouldn't quit.

"Kissing and dancing," she replied. "Are you as good at dancing as you are at kissing? Do we have to stop kissing in order to dance?"

"I don't see why," he answered, taking her gaily in his arms and spinning her onto the dance floor.

"You're good," she laughed, her eyes bright as the moon.

"At kissing or dancing?"

"At both!" she conceded as he brought her down deep to the ground in a daring death drop that drew applause.

They were John Travolta and Olivia Newton-John, and the sea of dancers parted to make way for them, whistling, hooting, and clapping their approval. Inspired by having an audience, Paige tried to take over the lead, but Mark overpowered her effort. He was good. Strong. Better than a lot of men she had danced with onstage. *Please, God, don't let me fall for this guy,* she prayed, giggling with delight as he held her close, playing out a scene from some corny musical as he whirled her around until she became so dizzy she had to collapse in his arms. After another outburst of applause, the mobbed and frenetic dance floor closed in on them again. Burning hot and feeling fantastic, they went at it once more, dancing until they were ready to drop.

"Hungry?" Mark asked her as they headed back up the pier, past various restaurants spotted between game booths, past the dozens of pushcart vendors plying the boardwalk, selling everything from hot tamales to baked potato skins to sno-cones. All they had eaten all evening were the sno-cones.

"Hmmm, am I ever," Paige answered, walking backward in front of him, feeling wildly energetic, wildly sexy. How could she do this to Susan? Susan was her roommate, her friend. She just wanted to sleep with Mark one or two times, screw to their hearts' content, and then she would give him back to Susan, for keeps if she wanted him. It was a concept Susan wouldn't understand or forgive in a million years. Paige just wanted a fling with him. To run her fingers through that curly blond hair, to lift the glasses off his sexy, neoclassic-looking face, and put them on the nightstand beside his bed.

She wondered what his bedroom looked like. It was probably small. Sparse. Except for a lot of books. He probably had a small, adjoining studio where he painted. That would be fun too. Maybe they could paint each other.

Paige, you're a terrible person, she told herself. The kimono had been intentional. She just couldn't stop herself upon hearing the male voice emanating from downstairs. There was something fun about teasing, arousing the innocent buck. When she had gotten out of the shower, she had put on her man-sized terry, which she kept on a hook on the back of the bathroom door. Then, when she had emerged from her room and heard Mark, she had run back into her room and hunted for her more provocative hot pink satin number, hoping he wouldn't leave before she made an appearance.

It was nasty. She should feel guilty. She did. A little, but not enough to stop herself from teasing his neck with her tongue until she made him squirm as he pulled her over to a game booth.

For fifty cents the carny hustling the game booth promised the thrill of a lifetime. The gimmick was to slam a sledgehammer down hard onto a metal seesaw-type gismo that had a sickening-looking rubber frog perched on the opposite end. As the hammer made impact with the vacant metal disc, setting the seesaw off-balance, the rubber frog would go flying, hopefully not onto the floor but into a pond of sorts that had plastic lily pads floating about as receptacles. If the frog landed by chance on one of the lily pads, the player won one of the crummy stuffed animals lining the wall. It was a feat Paige knew, from her numerous excursions to Coney Island, to be nearly impossible.

For her maybe, but not impossible for Mark. It turned out he was a whiz at carnival games. Like Paige, he had grown up in New York, and his hangout had been Coney Island where he had set for himself the goal of learning to outsmart the carnies running the always rigged booths. After Paige's frog leaped onto the floor, Mark handed the carny another fifty cents and told her to take note. He bent down low, eyeing the set-up from counter level, then went on to win five efforts out of seven.

Loaded down with prizes, the two of them continued on, touring the booths with far more enthusiasm than the larkish games warranted. Paige came close to winning several times, just enough to keep the thrill alive, and Mark was definitely winning enough to keep the carnies leery of him.

There were all the usual gimmicks, tossing the football through a tire, throwing darts at balloons, pitching coins into glass plates, shooting water pistols into painted clowns' mouths to inflate a balloon and make it pop, throwing balls at stuffed cotton-calico cats, balls at old-fashioned lead milk bottles, and still more balls at a big round metal knob that was rigged, once hit, to dunk a T-shirt-clad woman into a giant tub of water.

After watching for a while, Paige went up to the man running the dunking booth and whispered her impulsive request in his ear. He looked at her as if she were crazy. He could not possibly do what she wanted him to do. Then she handed him a five dollar bill and he changed his mind.

A moment later, Paige had replaced the waterlogged lady and was sitting on the bench herself, challenging the rapidly increasing crowd who, like Mark, most of all, couldn't believe their eyes.

She watched as Mark dropped two quarters into the carny's hand, astonishment registered in his cool blue eyes, determination registered on his mouth as he took in her new cotton dress, following the off-the-shoulder ruffle, down to the tight, dropped waist that hugged her hips. She was barelegged, having cast her shoes off to the side, and she dropped a toe down toward the water, wondering how cold it was.

Bang! The ball missed, although Mark aimed carefully and threw with all his might. Paige almost fell in from surprise and she grasped on tightly to the wooden plank beneath her, regaining her balance and staring reproachfully at her armed attacker. *Bang.* The ball missed again. A shudder of nervous excitement passed through Paige and she smiled, then ducked as the third ball swerved an inch or so from her head. "Sorry," he apologized, then procured another ball and aimed again.

"Hey, give someone else a try," an overweight guy in shorts and ribbed undershirt called out, pressing in front of a hell-bent Mark, and snatching the baseball-sized rubber ball he had just paid for from his hands. "Back of the line, buddy," the guy stated flatly, returning to Mark his fifty cents. If only she had a camera —the look on Mark's face was priceless.

Paige laughed at his reaction. She waved at him, watching as he acquiesced, appraising the line that had grown to be considerable, gamely counting the ranks of noisy contenders while he made his way to the end of the line. Paige was about to climb down, when she was sent shrieking into the water from a ball hurled by the fat guy in the shorts.

She arose blinded by a veil of water, soaking wet, teeth chattering, and thoroughly stunned. Her clothes were plastered to her body. They felt cold against the warm night air. She felt her nipples taut, erect, pressing against the soaking wet cloth of her dress, and she started to look down but then stopped, embarrassed. It was easy enough to imagine the effect. It was registered in the eager eyes of the men waiting to see her get drenched all over again, waiting for a shot at her themselves, their lurid fantasies ignited. She reddened when she realized hers were as well, then quickly sought out Mark in the crowd, signaling for him to help get her the hell down from there. She found him with his arms folded over his chest, looking at her with a strange, knowing smile that made not just her clothes feel transparent but her thoughts as well. This time *he* waved at her.

"Mark," she shouted, teeth still chattering, folding her own arms across her own chest, needing his help in order to get down. But Mark just burst out laughing when someone else purchased three balls and prepared to throw.

"Hey, wait a minute, this is a *joke*—I don't really work here," she said, turning from Mark to the skinny youth about to bomb her, and then to the carny. She couldn't believe what was going on. She was a lunatic for having gotten up here in the first place.

Bang. Paige was released down into the water a second time. And yet she could have sworn the guy missed the knob by yards! As she came up gasping for breath, she eyed the carny, sure that he had somehow maneuvered the drop himself. "Am I going to at least get a cut?" she remarked snidely, laughing herself this time while flipping a curtain of wet hair away from her face. After all that dancing, the water actually felt refreshing. She had given up on being dry.

"You want a cut, you've got a cut," he said, his shifty brown eyes converting to slits as his smile broadened. Tonight could be a windfall for him. His wife was standing nearby, probably already counting the coins in her head. She had a big beach towel wrapped around her husky shoulders. Her platinum hair was beginning to dry. *Break's over, honey,* Paige started to say, when Mark at last decided to come up beside her.

"Had enough?" he teased, removing his glasses and rubbing those gorgeous blue eyes of his.

Paige glared at him in response. But he was so cute that she couldn't keep a straight face.

Reinstating his glasses, he took in her arousing state of dress, and smiled appreciatively until she actually blushed.

A variety of whistles and hoots rose up from the restless crowd.

Paige, ever the performer, looked out at her audience with actressy composure. What the hell, her *Cats* costume had been more revealing than this. She extended her forefinger up into the air and said grinning, "All right, guys, one more shot at this. Better make it count." Then she turned back to the carny, and said playfully under her breath, "But no cheating this time, mister. Mark, watch this guy's hands."

Bang. Midspeech, Paige was sent shrieking down into the water again.

The carny brought both hands up into the air, looking genuinely surprised, declaring his innocence. Paige turned from him over toward his wife who was chuckling away, as though dunking Paige was the most fun thing she had ever done in her life. Still laughing, she went and got a fresh towel and gave it to the soaking wet stand-in. Her husband went and got a big plastic sack filled with stuffed animals and handed Mark, already laden with junk, the whole bag.

The natural thing to do after that seemed to be to walk along the beach, shoes in hand, arms around each other, listening to the surf and falling under its seductive spell. They had taken a couple of blankets from Mark's Jeep and had wrapped themselves in them for warmth. Paige had slipped off her wet dress and borrowed a baseball jersey of his to put on instead. He remarked that it was longer than the little robe number she had been wearing earlier, and she laughed. It was true.

The beach for Paige was soul-stirring. The huge waves of the Pacific exploding, retreating, swelling again, creating a sense of expectancy beneath a moonlit sky as they walked on and on, the noise from the pier growing fainter and fainter until it was only a memory. The smell was salty, fresh. The air felt thick and moist. The sand beneath her bare feet felt soft and tickly, with its surface giving way, conforming to her steps.

Rarely out of Manhattan, Paige was lucky to walk on grass let alone sand, and she reveled in it now, promising herself a seaside residence one day, envisioning the beach as part of her own backyard, the ocean her private wading pool. Drifting off to sleep to the rhythmic sound of the ocean, being transported by it to another world. *Ahhh, what soulful slumber,* she thought. And how convenient for the sandman's faithful delivery, the customary souvenir of a good sleep.

"I'm getting kind of used to you with wet hair," Mark said, his voice gently interrupting the silence. "Second time in one night. When you came downstairs. And now."

"Yeah?" Paige turned to him, lifting the wet mass all to one side, and letting it cascade provocatively over her shoulder. It was getting chillier outside, and she wrapped the blanket more snugly around herself.

"You too cold?" Mark asked, stopping and wrapping himself and his blanket around her for additional warmth.

"Not now," she said, and it was true she was not. His body acted like a heater, infusing her with a splendid warmth, melting the chill, disarming her resolve to not respond to him. He couldn't afford that idyllic place for her at the beach, she reminded herself lamentably. He couldn't afford *her.*

"You look great with wet hair. It's very sexy." Those eyes again as they bore into her own. That exquisite chiseled nose.

Their thighs were touching, her naked icy one against his warm denim-wrapped one. It was so quiet, so still. There was not a soul in sight. She was hot. She was cold. She felt vulnerable and intensely turned on. "Oh, yeah," Paige said again, tracing his cheek with the still chilled tip of her nose. "How sexy?"

"Pretty fucking sexy—" he answered in a low voice. His blanket was like a tent around them.

"Fucking sexy enough to do it right here?" Paige asked.

An exceptionally powerful wave erupted on the shore, causing her to jump. He drew her closer, sinking down onto the sand, spreading out one blanket for them to lie on, the other to cover them up. They were completely entwined beneath it, toasty warm, kissing roughly, then gently, still tasting faintly of sno-cones.

Paige felt another wave of guilt, thinking about Susan, her large blue eyes so innocently reproachful. But then Mark's hand was traveling up her thigh, and she could barely stand the pleasure. His other hand was rising up beneath the baseball jersey, caressing her stomach, her breasts. She, in turn, was struggling with the zipper on his jeans, undoing his shirt, and caressing him.

It figured that his skin would be so damn soft, like the finest silk velvet, so that she couldn't stop touching him. It figured that *his* touch would exceed perfect, gossamer strokes arousing her to new heights, beyond control, beyond any desire to control.

If he were rich, he would climb on top of her, explode in two seconds, and it would be over, with a quick gratuitous peck on the lips, and her left wanting. But Mark was taking his time. He was leisurely attentive, a superlative lover, making her fall deeply in lust with him. Both their heads were hidden beneath the blanket now so that it was pitch-dark, the blackness amplifying the rhythmic sounds of the surf, their luxurious kissing. Her own moan blended exquisitely with his as his soft full lips found her absolute favorite spot to be kissed.

Should she tell him now? Did she dare? Did she dare not? She was dying to make love with him, but eventually she had to set the record straight, explain to him why she had moved out to L.A., why they couldn't possibly get involved. Their sexual indulgence would be for the sheer pleasure of it, but nothing threatening that broached commitment. They could be lovers, friends, intimate friends, but he must be completely aware that she was undeflectable in her intent to meet and marry a rich man and that, for once in her life, come hell or high water, she was going to score a triumphant ten on her goal.

She was fast losing her train of thought. And yet her train of thought was contributing to the excitement. There was something sexual and offbeat about her predicament, reckless and bad. She felt guilty and wildly turned on. She was trembling and quivering all over. God, if she stopped now to confess all this she would be missing the climax of a lifetime. As he lifted the blanket for a moment and let in a chill rush of air she felt herself falling over the border of reason. His warm tongue, the intense heat of his body disturbed by the frigid gust caused her to cry out in utter delight.

Fuck it, she'd tell him later.

Why were the broke ones always the best in bed?

Chapter 12

"When we went into the restaurant all he did was talk about how short he was. By the time we left the restaurant, I thought I was out with a midget," Tori said drolly to Susan.

It was just after four in the morning, and the two of them were sitting in the den drinking coffee and Armagnac, and eating pistachio nuts. Both were still wearing their clothes from the evening before, shoes deposited somewhere in the room, hair and makeup wilted. Their respective blind dates had brought them home around midnight, Susan's a little before, and they had been sitting up talking together ever since. The only one who had not yet made it home was Paige. A fact that had Susan drinking considerably more than she should.

"Oh, c'mon, Tori," she said, helping herself to another glass of the rare, aged Armagnac. The powerful brandy stung as she brought it to her lips, but the taste and the heady feeling it rendered afterward were delicious. "I met him. He wasn't *that* short."

"He was pretty short," Tori argued, yawning, curling up onto the couch with her head resting on a pillow she had fluffed up. "But most of all it was how short he kept *saying* he was. Maybe if he had spent all evening talking about how tall he was, he would have given a more towering impression. By the time dessert arrived I was picturing him requiring a telephone book or one of those kiddie stools in order to be able to reach the surgery table to operate on one of his patients." Her dress was carelessly hiked up so that her long slim legs were in full view, red toenail polish vivid through her stockings as she flexed and then pointed her toes.

Susan chuckled tipsily.

Tori smiled at her own joke. Could it be she was regaining her sense of humor? Please God! It was Richard Bennetton's phone call that had elevated her mood. She was feeling gay and somewhat sought-after. Even the short surgeon had pressed her for a second date. "Better go easy on that stuff, Susan; it's pure firewater," she advised her friend, who was sitting on the adjacent white duck couch, feet crossed at the ankles on the coffee table, bottle still in one hand, shot-glass-sized liqueur glass in the other.

"Tomorrow's Saturday. I can get as drunk as I please," Susan protested, planning on drinking herself into oblivion.

"Not to mention that our liquor tab here is mounting steadily," Tori added, taking the bottle from Susan and pouring a shot of the Armagnac into a fresh cup of coffee. She preferred her firewater diluted.

"Dustin's postcard said to drink and eat whatever we wanted—"

"Even so—"

"Evonne said we would be doing him a favor, clearing room to afford him the pleasure of acquiring more."

"Sounds more like something Paige would say. Are you sure that really came from Evonne?"

"Are you asking *me* to comment on Paige's reliability, trustworthiness, credibility, or character?" Susan slurred, looking miserably at the clock as one of the graceful stainless-steel arms swept forward to indicate 4:14 A.M. She was tempted to call Trancas and find out if they were even still open. In L.A. nothing was still going full swing at four in the morning.

"Maybe they went out with Mark's musician friend afterward," Tori suggested.

Or then again, maybe Paige has gone back with him to his place and they are screwing their brains out, Susan's thoughts countered unhappily.

They both reached over for another handful of nuts at the same time.

"That was such a nice note Dustin sent. Why can't we meet someone like him?" Susan sighed.

Tori sipped her drink, regarding Susan from over the rim of her cup. She was accustomed to thinking of only one man. Now her head contained a menagerie of men. Richard Bennetton. Still ol' Travis, of course. The seemingly short surgeon. Susan's Mark Arent—or was it Paige's Mark Arent? Paige's mysterious gift-bearing suitor from Philadelphia. And not to be left out, Dustin Brent. "We did meet him."

"So which one of us is he swooning over, missing terribly? Which one of us had him tempted to cancel his trip and stay behind to pursue love? Which one of us is he hoping will still be single when he returns?" Susan wondered dreamily, cracking the natural-color shell of a ripe pistachio with her teeth, then dislodging the nut into her mouth.

"Paige!" They answered in aggravated unison, as Susan dropped the remains of her shell into a crystal bowl marked expressly for that purpose.

"I've never really hated anybody before in my life," Susan said. "Not liked them, sure. But never *hate*. I *really* hate Paige. I mean really hate her." Susan tore off the brass clip-on earrings Paige had lent her and threw them down onto the coffee table. "She gives with one hand, then takes with both of hers. I don't care about these clothes. I don't care about these earrings. I feel like such a jerk. Like I can't get mad at her because she's been so bighearted about all this. But how bighearted is she really when she stays out all night with a guy that comes over to see *me*?"

"There's the good news about Paige. And the bad news," Tori rationalized. It was true. There was something so spirited and fun and actually giving about Paige. If you had a problem, it was her problem to tackle as well. She was as intent on solving it as you were, maybe more so because she was so stubborn and had so much energy. The bad news about Paige was that you couldn't quite trust her. She was a true sybarite, completely self-centered.

If stealing your pleasure granted *her* pleasure, she was prone to doing so, as evidenced tonight, probably not at all aware that she had even done anything wrong.

"Yeah? Well I'm real familiar right now with the bad news. Better remind me about some of the good."

"If it weren't for her, we all wouldn't be here now—" Tori said truthfully, her Georgia accent sounding especially pronounced as she rose to Paige's defense.

"What's so great about *here*?" Susan sipped gloomily at her glass of Armagnac, staring down into the deep tawny color as though it contained answers.

"Would you rather be back in Stockton with your life as it was?"

"Now *you* sound like Paige!"

"Getting the runaround from what's-his-name—" Tori pressed on.

"I'm trying to forget—"

"Not caring. And yet wishing you *did* care. You said so yourself, most of the other eligible men there were ex-husbands of the girls with whom you went to school, guys you wouldn't give a second glance to then. It's not just *men* opportunities. Look at your career jump. Look at how much more money you're making here and the possibilities there are for you," Tori continued, overriding Susan's next interruption. "Would you rather be back in your small-town community, going to barbecues at your parents' mobile home? Look, I have nothing against mobile homes, but I just can't picture you content in a small town like that, getting ridiculed for your ambition rather than encouraged and admired for it, stuck in a rut, when there's clearly so much more opportunity for you out here."

Susan felt tears stinging in her eyes and she blinked them back. Maybe she *was* getting a little too drunk. She felt tired and overwrought. She both missed her family and resented them at the same time. Every time she called, they were so aloof, so distant. They didn't want to hear about L.A., her job, her friends, the house in which she was living. Even though she was calling them from the office, not paying for the calls herself, they kept cutting her off, using the long-distance business as an excuse. She was fine. They were fine. That was all they needed to know. Their conversations were more like telegrams, clipped, abbreviated sentences getting to the heart of the message and then out of it just as abruptly. Didn't they care at all? Didn't her mother care? When she had called Lisa and Buzz, her only real friends in Stockton, she had been stung to find a remoteness there as well, cutting remarks about "Tinseltown," digs about her life there. Upon confronting them, she was told that what she was facing was an inevitability that she would have been naive to not have considered. She had moved, which to them translated as moved on. Her life was different from theirs. And therefore she was now different, changed. *What! Overnight? I'm me. I'll always be me.* But even with her oldest and dearest friends, she was butting up against an unforgiving brick wall. And it naturally hurt.

Content—is that what Tori had said? *Content* was such an ambiguous word. Who was really content? If one were healthy, one was supposed to be content. If not, then one was greedy. Susan's mother and father would claim to be content. But Susan would argue that they were not. One could be content for a fraction of time, but not for any duration. It went against the grain of human nature. Even children were incapable of being content for long. Children offered the purest example of contentment as mere illusion. Take an ice-cream cone. It provided pure, sweet, creamy contentment, but then it was either devoured or it melted away, and the child was left no longer content. Contentment was a passing phenomenon in which people put altogether too much stock. Susan could not say that she would rather be back in Stockton, back in her old life. It may have been okay before, but it was definitely not okay now. "What am I supposed to feel, gratitude toward Paige?" she asked resentfully, chugalugging the rest of her brandy, then reaching over to set the empty glass down onto the table. "When she downright steals the man of my dreams—"

Tori looked at her compassionately, running her fingers through her short dark hair, her dark eyes warm and probing. "C'mon, Susan. You don't even know the guy. What kind of a person can he be anyway, to come over to see you, then go out with your roommate and stay out all night, huh?"

"Human. Paige is probably raping him."

Tori opened her mouth to argue, but then had an apparent change of heart and shrugged.

"I hope she contracts herpes. Or something worse."

"Susan!" Tori had to laugh at Susan's uncharacteristic vitriol.

"Well, okay, maybe not something worse. But a mild case of something would serve her right."

"If he's so perfect, why is it you think she could *catch* something from him? Perfect men come with a clean bill of health. Anyway, he's obviously an easy lay," Tori asserted swiftly.

"Thanks to Paige we've established that one. So maybe he has an overactive libido—"

"I *see.* An enlarged libido," Tori intoned. "Now, that can be a real problem—chronic in fact."

"A bigger problem is a guy with a libido that doesn't operate properly. I'd rather have to contend with an enlarged libido than one too weak to get it up," she volleyed.

"We're concentrating on his weaknesses, Susan. *How to Get Over Your Lover and Survive*—remember that? *Weaknesses,* you all kept insisting to me. *Concentrate* on his weaknesses. Now I've given you one to work on; let's focus on it."

"Like you're cured—"

"I'm *improved.* I'm counting on time and Richard Bennetton to cure me. My affliction was born over the course of years," Tori declared dramatically. "It was a fire, raging wild and out of control, definitely destructive and difficult to extinguish. Your little flame should require just a Dixie cup–sized dousing of water, then *poof,* charred a little, but otherwise like it never happened."

Susan laughed, in spite of her frustration, watching Tori gratefully as she leapt up from the couch and strode over to find the manual they had given her. "This *colossal* libido problem of his," Tori continued—tripping over one of Susan's strewn high heels, then recovering with giddy grace—"could make your life miserable. Now, wasn't that what's-his-name's problem, your lawyer-boyfriend in Stockton? I think there might be a pattern emerging here—"

"Billy Donahue," Susan coached this time. She had to laugh because the two men could not have been more different from one another. But she nodded her accord, smiling and submitting to the game. She had never seen Tori so loose, so plucky. Maybe she *was* getting over Travis, miracle of miracles.

"*That's* right, Billy Donahue. Here's another one for you. Mark wears glasses," Tori recalled. "You want your kids to grow up with defective eyes? Bad eyes are genetic."

"Half of that genetic order is already a go, Tori. *I'm* blind as a bat without my glasses."

"Oh, that's right," Tori yielded with an easy laugh. She had to admit, coming up with "weaknesses" for Mark was a strain, but she was trying. His height was good; his build was good; he was obviously bright and talented. So forget the gene arguments. He wasn't terribly loyal, but they had already covered that ground. What they had not covered was that he wasn't exactly in the income bracket they had allegedly moved out here to enter.

Susan, meanwhile, smirked. "You're having a rough time, aren't you. He's pretty nearly perfect, isn't he?"

"Not *so* perfect. As my mother would say, 'he doesn't even have a pot to piss in.' "

"Your genteel southern-belle mother would say that?"

"She would manage to *say* it genteelly. Anyway, there you go. Can't live off love forever. You're making at least twice the income that he is—you think that's good for a relationship?"

"I don't care about that—" Susan really didn't.

"Aha, but *he* would! Don't forget he has that enlarged libido and ego problem. He would care. They all do. They get bitter and nasty and resentful. Like it's your fault you're more successful than they are. They cheat on you to console themselves. Especially the ones with—"

"I know . . . enlarged libidos."

"You *are* catching on. So there's your focus. He's sweet and sexy, but broke and soon to be bitter, out philandering, maybe even gambling away your money, to try and rescue his own situation. He's a dreamer. All artists are dreamers. He'll be dreaming about that big win. And as he loses more and more of your hard-earned money, he'll keep dreaming that he's getting close to Lady Luck. Lady Luck will take the form of a mistress. An adoring, sympathetic student, soft, blond and voluptuous. There'll be a whole slew of them, in all colors and sizes. Tack on the burden of guilt, which he's surely already been carrying around. And then he'll start to drink. It happens to the best of them."

By now Susan and Tori were both laughing uproariously. They had started working on the brandy again, and Tori was grinning and bearing it, and drinking it straight.

"You ought to pass up real estate and consider a writing career," Susan said.

Tori wrinkled her small patrician nose, her eyes welling up with tears from the brandy. "No way. This is wretched stuff. It would never sell," she replied, referring to her story, not the brandy. She was beginning to like the brandy.

"Why? I'm buying it," Susan countered. "And I'm an intelligent, eighties woman. A discriminating, successful lawyer."

"You are that," Tori agreed, sitting beside Susan now, bumping her affectionately with her shoulder. "Okay, so now you want to hear the revenge part, the just-desserts conclusion to my little yarn?" she asked, clearly anxious to finish what she had begun.

"By all means," Susan said, toasting the so far unuttered conclusion in advance.

"Paige gets the broke-but-talented artist-professor she stole from right under your nose. *But,* your revenge is that you end up married to some rich guy you fall for after you recover from Mark, which shouldn't take too long, married with your gorgeous Russian lynx-belly coat, your nanny pushing your divine little baby in the park in a romantic-looking English pram, while Paige ends up barefoot and pregnant, trying to buy caviar with foodstamps!"

It was in the middle of another passionate interlude that Paige finally decided to set the record straight.

Back at his apartment, which was ironically at the beach, in the quaint canal district of Venice (romantic, but more bohemian than Paige had had in mind), after a couple more memorable rounds of lovemaking, Paige set forth the ground rules and the boundaries of their relationship.

They were lying in his romantically proportioned double bed, an antique that had belonged to his grandmother, listening to one of Mahler's later works, when she broached the subject. As envisioned, Paige had removed his glasses, set them on the small, also antique table by his bed, beside a small brass clock. They had passed on Trancas altogether. Paige was too wet to go anywhere and, besides, they were in the mood not to listen to other people's music but to make their own. Mark's room was painted a quiet white, with some drawings framed and hung on the walls. It looked like the sort of bedroom a professor would inhabit. Small, French, and poetic-looking, a fishtail palm flourishing in an attractive clay pot atop another antique piece in the corner, tapestry pillows arranged on a partially upholstered love seat, and books battling for space on the étagère. But it seemed incongruous for an artist who painted bold, vibrantly colorful canvases like the one he had given to Susan.

Still glowing in the aftermath of their lovemaking, Paige touched his brow with her lips, imparting the speech she had been planning.

When she had told him everything, including the part about her admirer in Philadelphia, the charity gala he was taking her to at the Nicky Loomis mansion, he rolled onto his side to face her, tracing her full breast with his forefinger until the nipple rose up hard and taut, taking on a life of its own. Luxuriating in his touch, his presence, the rich, marvelous music of Mahler, she wound up giving vent to far more than just that information. In a pleasant state of frank abandon, she went back to unwrap fragments of her life in New York (it turned out they had grown up within several miles of each other), her mother dying when Paige was only twelve years old, her friendship with Kit, the bride who had been the impetus for the rich-man hunt, her relationship with her father, and her struggle to make it on Broadway.

She talked. He listened, asking questions every now and then, the kind that inspire long, revealing answers, inserting reminiscences of his own. While she spoke more candidly than she ordinarily did, owing probably to his intelligent, easy acceptance, his nonjudgmental interest, he continued his sensual probing of her skin.

He was passing his fingers exquisitely over her arms, massaging her back, stroking her legs, her stomach—fluid motions voluptuously orchestrated with the music that simultaneously turned her on and relaxed her.

At some point, and she was not sure when, their touching became more intense, more sexual, more urgent. They were both up on their sides, thigh to thigh, chest to chest, toes toying with each other's.

The curly blond hair that grew like wild silken vines over his chest felt sublimely sensuous as her fingers wandered through its depth. The words were out, and they were contemplating a kiss, a long passionate one.

Mahler had also grown more intense, provoking their passion further, charging Paige with an electriclike current that shot through her very being. Their tongues were entwined, tasting, teasing, their lips pressing softly together, wiping out any extraneous thoughts.

In her mind, she and Mark were back on the beach again, feeling the damp, salty air, listening to the ocean imparting secrets to the dark, isolated beach, the whispering lull of the waves drawing them into a satisfying void where no one else could follow drowning them in pleasure.

Paige had already discerned how he loved to be stroked, fingertip caresses that aroused his already swollen private parts, inciting him further, while her hand encircled and moved against his shaft, causing him to moan to the swollen crescendo of sound that stirred the air.

He climbed on top of her this time, drawing both of her legs up to his mouth, kissing them alternately, lovingly, as he moved deep inside of her, while her hands slid down to envelop his bulbous underpart, massaging the warm, moist, flaccid skin nested there with those everloving golden curls, moving her hips to keep pace with him.

Every moan of his coursed through her, his excitement ushering her excitement until they were one, seeking the same motion, the same rhythm, the same end.

She could feel him holding back, delaying his momentous outburst, taking her further and further, until she was breathing more erratically, breaths that were harder to grasp, and she had let go of control and thoughts, and was climbing higher and higher, lost in primal sensation. She started to cry out just as he did, their friction increasing until they were both bathed in glorious sweat, fervent in their movements, needing this orgasm to be the best of them all. And it was.

Savoring the feeling of his weight upon her, watching daylight break through in a filtered illumination that edged the curtains, which were not quite wide enough, Paige was torn between being delighted about Mark's facile acceptance of what she had told him, and feeling stung.

In a way, it granted that she would be able to have her cake and eat it, too. She and Mark could sustain an intimate friendship, great sex, support, and fun while she looked around for her rich man to marry. On the other hand, his position wasn't exactly flattering. She wanted it all. She wanted him to adore her, to crave her. And yet to let her be free.

Paige straggled in about ten in the morning. She found Susan asleep on the couch in the den, the book she had been reading surrendered onto the floor beside her. Tori's shoes, linen blazer, purse, and abandoned jewelry were also still downstairs, but Tori herself appeared to have made it upstairs to her bedroom.

The haphazard state of the elegant room told of a long, late night: brandy bottle down considerably, liqueur glasses left out, lipstick-stained coffee cups, drained-to-the-bottom coffee pitcher, the mountain of pistachio shells spilling from out of the crystal bowl over onto the table, and the gallon-sized carton of ice cream that had been polished off.

From the zipper compartment of her purse, Paige brought out a joint she had been squirreling away, since it was so hard to get good grass nowadays, and succumbed to smoking it. Taking a profound drag from the small yellowed-with-time cigarette, she bent down to pick up the book that lay just below Susan's dangling hand.

How to Get Over Your Lover and Survive read the familiar title. *No, not another one,* Paige thought, dismayed. "Susan, you silly jerk, you don't even know the man," she said reproachfully, looking down at Susan's innocent face breathing peacefully from under the cloak of sleep. When she noticed Susan tensing, hugging herself as though she were cold, Paige lifted the pretty, Indian-looking blanket from the arm of the other couch and drew it gently up over Susan while continuing to regard her with aching regret. How could she have done such a thing, she thought, filled with self-recrimination as she stared down at the friend she had betrayed. Growing more and more uncomfortable, Paige squirmed, taking another intense hit of grass, hoping to dull the guilt.

What was she going to say to Susan? *I'm sorry?* She kept struggling to think up an apology, an explanation, but each one she devised sounded more lame, more inadequate than the next. It was like breaking someone's heart and then offering a Band-Aid.

It reminded her of that awful Christmas when Kit had gotten a beautiful china doll from her parents. Paige had been eaten up with jealousy because all she had gotten from her parents were some Colorforms, a plastic egg containing Silly Putty, and a slip because her father had been selling slips that year (and it had been a particularly bad year for him). She still remembered with a nagging clarity how she had pulled Kit's doll away from her and broken it. "Let me just see it. Don't be such a hog," she had shouted, yanking and yanking until she not only pulled the doll away from Kit's tight grasp but had caused it to drop onto the unyielding black-and-white tiled floor that had been in Kit's parents' den, where the Christmas tree was, and it had shattered into a million pieces. Paige had been gripped with guilt for weeks. She used to dream about it. And she remembered how she had cried at the time—they had both been crying their eyes out—while she kept saying she was sorry over and over again. She remembered how helpless she had felt on her knees beside the minute fragments, trying with all her heart to piece them back together when it was clearly an impossibility, yearning to turn back the clock so that it would have never happened and the beautiful china doll would be back as it was. Kit had been heartbroken, but forgiving. It was Paige who had never quite forgiven herself.

Taking a deep drag on the marijuana cigarette, still studying Susan's sincere and lovely face, Paige slumped down into the chair that had Tori's jacket draped over the back of it, experiencing that same sense of futility and helplessness.

What kind of a terrible person was she to have done such a thing? First she tells Susan not to go out with Mark. Then she not only goes out with him but she ends up in bed with him. Never mind that it was just for the fun of it, that her original position on Mark remained intact—he was not the "catch" she was looking to marry. Susan would never understand. And she would certainly never forgive Paige.

Paige considered denying it. Saying they had just been out all night together, fooling around at the pier, then Trancas, jumping from spot to spot. She found she was nearly panicking, trying to think of a way to repair the damage she had done, to redeem herself. For the first time in years, really since Kit had moved to California, Paige finally had girlfriends again, not the kind she had had in the shows, but real friends and she desperately did not want to lose them.

Chapter 13

Someone's birthday party.

Only Madonna's.

All throughout the evening, Richard had been pointing out different celebrities, names and faces which eluded Tori. The guy in the leopard-skin bow tie—he directed *Star Fire*. The girl in the gold lamé Halston—she was in the new Wier film. The guy with the yellow sneakers that matched the yellow flecks in his bow tie and tuxedo cummerbund had just won an Emmy for his appearance in the new musical *Brash Baby James*.

But a birthday party for Madonna, who was romping around quite "unlike a virgin," with true star cadence, who had been cajoled into giving an impromptu performance, had Tori admittedly awed.

The party Richard had taken her to, being held at Neon, the very exclusive, strikingly appointed private club, was unlike any she had ever been to, with everyone dressed to kill in what could only be described as "black-tie hip." Hairdos were extreme, even weird, sculpted and sprayed to sustain their daring shapes. Clothes and jewelry were also avant-garde, some gorgeous to look at, some unique but too bizarre, some vampish and cheap. Variety and high spirits abounded.

Tori's gown fell into the gorgeous category, thanks to Paige, who had pressed Tori into wearing her new, smashing, red Valentino that Philadelphia had bought for her. It was a bold offer, considering the Nicky Loomis affair she was attending with him was scheduled for the following night. Tori was a wreck, fearing she might spill something on it or snag the delicate fabric, but Paige, still zealously trying to make up for what she had done to Susan last week, wouldn't hear of Tori not wearing it.

The first few days after Paige's all-nighter with Mark had been strained, to say the least, with Susan broodingly quiet, Paige nervously noisy, and Tori uncertain how to act, feeling uncomfortably stuck in the middle. After Paige had apologized for the hundredth time, Susan had finally exploded and told her to shut up already. Paige feebly proposed to help repair things with Susan and Mark, resolving not to see him anymore, but Susan maintained that she didn't care.

On Sunday the four of them—Paige, Mark, Susan, and Tori—had all gone together to Susan's law firm to hang the painting he had brought her. A mistake, Tori had thought at first, with Paige and Mark exchanging private looks, Susan trying to act like nothing hurt, and Tori, still in the middle, striving to keep everything light.

After they had finished at Susan's office, Mark had invited them all out to a favorite falafel stand of his in Venice for lunch, then sailing on a friend's boat, which was really far too small for the four of them.

The cramped quarters served to break down the tension, with everyone nearly getting smacked in the head by the boom as the wind changed courses, and they tried to duck and maneuver themselves out of the way. By the time the sun went down, they had arrived at a sort of tentative peace, all of them punchy from being in the sun so long, the motion of the sea imposing a soothing lethargy, so that they were all surprisingly relaxed, laughing, and having a good time.

Susan had burst into tears later, when they arrived back at the house, but Paige never knew that. "I'm just washing it all out of my system," she had said to Tori, looking completely heartbroken. "It probably wouldn't have worked out, anyway. I don't think we have a lot in common. And I've always preferred dark, swarthy men." There was music floating upstairs from an album Paige and Mark had put on. Mark was having dinner there with the three of them, and Susan assured Tori that she could handle it.

Over the course of the week, Paige and Mark had gone on to become an item. "Just friends," she kept telling them, but Tori wondered. Paige was obviously sleeping with him, and, Tori thought, leading him on. But then again, maybe Mark was smarter than all of them. Maybe he glimpsed a side of Paige that they did not. Maybe he was unconvinced by her brash airs and perceived his best strategy to be patience. Wouldn't it be ironic, Tori thought, if her prediction, called in jest, which had Susan ending up with her millionaire and Paige with her penniless professor came to pass?

While Tori was in the midst of getting dressed, Paige had appeared in her doorway, cradling in her arms her entire ruby red collection—gown, gloves, jacket, purse, shoes, plus the earrings, necklace, and bracelet that had followed by UPS—all compliments of Philadelphia. She stood there for a few long moments surveying the scene before her. It was about twenty minutes before Richard was to arrive, and Tori's room looked like "the big one" California was expecting had finally struck, with Tori's bedroom having been at the epicenter of the massive earthquake. Clothes, lingerie, jewelry, shoes, purses, and makeup were strewn everywhere.

Tori herself was standing wearing only a pair of bikini panties, rummaging through what was left in her closet and feeling completely distraught over what to wear, when she heard Paige saying, "What the hell, maybe this will help to soothe my guilty conscience. Though I think I'll have to come up with something a hell of a lot more than just an outfit for Susan."

Caught by surprise Tori turned around, speechless with relief and gratitude as Paige shrugged and said, "I'm repenting any way I can." Before Tori could muster up the will to protest, Paige dropped the whole lavish load onto the bed, issuing an eager, "C'mon, Miss Georgia Peach, hurry up and try it on before he gets here!"

The effect the dress had on Richard had Tori feeling eternally grateful to Paige. Red was unmistakably her color, the way it contrasted with her pale skin and jet-black hair, which was more spiked and more extreme tonight than she ordinarily wore it. And while the cut of the dress was sophisticated, it was also audaciously seductive, the way it molded to her shape, pushing up her bosom, showing off a lot of leg, making her feel both self-conscious and wickedly alluring at the same time, making her flush the same color as the dress when Richard arrived and she opened the door for him.

He had stood there appraising her for what seemed a long time, his eyes full of amused admiration, as though he had been expecting something far more conservative than the skintight red jeweled gown that left little to the imagination. "You're really full of surprises," he had said, approval in his voice as he circled smoothly around her, appreciating the drama of the red creation from all angles. The one thing Tori had wanted to pass up at the last minute, feeling doubly self-conscious, the red jeweled fingerless gloves, which rose up past her elbows, were what he seemed to be the most bowled over about. As he helped her on with the matching red jeweled jacket, his hands grazing her bare shoulders sent a shiver down her spine, which she could have sworn he felt.

He looked divine in his smartly cut tuxedo, as handsomely appealing as he had looked, still sweaty and invigorated, just off the polo field. He had that same luminous glint to his pale blue eyes, she thought, as he escorted her out to his candy-apple red car, enthusiastically identifying it as a late fifties' model four-door Facel Vega, a recent acquisition for his extensive vintage car collection. Polo was only one of his passions, he assured her, as he opened the door for her to climb inside, eagerly pointing out how the car's unique body design had been so avant-garde for its time that in its era it was a magnet for cops. Built near to the ground in front and in back, it created the illusion of going one hundred twenty miles an hour, even when it was standing absolutely still.

A little showy for her taste but interesting, she thought, ducking into the streamlined classic, taking in the gleaming sterling silver appointments inside and the Baccarat crystal perfume bottles mounted in the back sporting fresh pink-and-white speckled tiger lilies. She immediately thought of Travis because he was mad about old cars.

They had gone to dozens of classic car exhibits together, and she recalled how he used to swoon over the various models, making her laugh as he wished aloud in that funny way of his that a fairy godmother would come and perch herself on his shoulder, wave a magic wand, and grant that the car of his choice would be his. Ironically, the object of Travis's fantasies last year had been a silvery gunmetal Facel Vega.

Impulsively, Tori found herself wishing that Travis could see her stepping into the four-door model that would have made his head spin, wishing for the vision to sting him, to cause him regret. Then she sighed, her pleasure of a few moments ago waning because she was the one bearing the regret.

As Richard chivalrously closed the door for her, seeing to it that she was securely inside, she gazed out through the window and up at the sky, struck by how few stars were visible in contrast to her black and glittery sky in Atlanta. Employing a childhood rhyme, silently wishing upon the largest star she could find, which was probably a planet and not a star anyway, she wished solemnly that she would stop caring *what* Travis thought.

Then for just the briefest second, Richard put his hand on her thigh as he slid into the car beside her from the driver's side. It was a strange sensation, considering where her thoughts had been, and she realized this was the first prelude to physical contact that she had had with another man since Travis. Not feeling any sexual attraction to the surgeon, the concept hadn't occurred to her when he had benignly kissed her good night. But Richard's touch was striking another chord, a responsive one, triggering some deeper intuition, a precognitive vision of the two of them together in bed making love. The image was bizarrely clear, a fragment of time, unsettlingly real, playing in her head like a movie trailer in advance of the act, leaving her both excited and at the same time scared to death.

Richard's friends looked a lot like he did. They were gathered around a festively adorned table, which had a tropical-looking

centerpiece fashioned in keeping with the dining room's aquari-
umlike design. The elliptically shaped room evoked the sensation
of being in water, aqua neon reflecting off birds of paradise,
painted glass walls the color of the Caribbean, illuminated by
tubes of flowing neon gas, aqua, raspberry, red, and violet, all in
bright and fluid motion.

Traveling the length of the long oblong wall, framed in the
center of it almost like a living painting, was a tropical garden
containing giant birds of paradise and lush, verdant trees.

It was all very elegant, as were Richard's friends, who seemed
to stand apart from the rest of the crowd.

They were all youngish, jet-set wealthy types, tied to Madonna
through business transactions instead of rock and roll, talking
casually about their Cessnas, their polo, their high-powered investments.

Only one of them was dressed eccentrically. He was a film
producer friend, an old Columbia chum of Richard's who had
just returned from shooting a film in Tibet and was entertaining
the table with horror stories of the erratic endeavor.

Madonna was to be starring in his next film. He was hoping it
would be shot somewhere more civilized, like in Paris, London,
or New York. Or that the cast would at least behave in a more
civilized fashion.

Tori learned that Richard too had tried his hand at producing
several years ago, though, she guessed, not too successfully. She
was getting the impression that if you had money and lived in
L.A., at one time or another producing was a phase you went
through.

"I'm a guy who needs to run fast," Richard confessed to Tori
when a couple of the guys were kidding him about the T and A
picture he had produced a few years back. "Life has a boredom
factor that keeps me always in two places at once. The day after
production stopped, I was already in the real estate business."

The man sitting on the other side of Tori overheard Richard's
comment and laughed. He reached into the breast pocket of his
tux and brought out a buttery leather pouch containing Cuban
cigars. Passing them among his friends, he remarked, "Yeah, be-

cause his old man told him the well was going to run dry if he didn't get a *real* job."

"Hey, give me a break. *Summer Sensation* made money. My old man was just jealous!" Richard cheerfully defended himself, accepting one of the cigars and then drawing it beneath his nose to inhale the aroma.

"But you blew more than it made," the cigar donor admonished. Then he looked directly at Tori. "Richard's idea of producing a picture is he flies everywhere first-class, stays in first-class hotels, *suites* yet, has the most expensive restaurants in town cater the sets, generally marries the star, buying her jewelry that ups the budget by at least forty percent—"

"Fuck you, Jordan. I only married one star—"

"You also only made one picture," laughed a woman who looked like a younger Candice Bergen. "You want to know about Richard? This is a typical *Richardism:* The picture takes place on the beach, right? A good place for a T and A flick, admittedly. But does he shoot it in Santa Monica, like any sensible person shooting a low-budget film? No, he shoots it in the south of France."

"Hey, they have better T's and A's in the south of France," Richard replied, his hands up in the air by way of a disclaimer, a grin on his handsome face. "Sorry, I couldn't resist," he apologized afterward to Tori. "These guys always like to give me a bad time."

"Ah, poor Richard," another one of the women said, blowing him a kiss across the table. "You want to hear another Richardism? He's on the board of our tennis club. As are all the gentlemen seated before you," she added, patting the tablecloth in front of her in a designating fashion. "He happened to miss a board meeting and they made him president."

"Does that mean you're popular?" Tori asked him lightly, not really getting the so-called Richardism.

"No, it means I'm a schmuck," he said laughing. "Administering the fucking club takes up as much time as my real job."

"You *have* a real job?" Someone else chimed in.

"Now come on, guys, you're going to give Tori all the wrong

impressions," Richard said, being a good sport about the whole thing.

"He works very hard," the producer said solemnly. Then he put his hand up in front of his mouth and pretended to choke.

The roasting was brought to an abrupt halt by a parade of white-gloved waiters boasting trays of tall rosy-colored soufflés, the sweet fragrance of the piping-hot confection trailing behind them as they began depositing them in front of Madonna's guests. Silver bowls of rich whipped cream followed. And then a boisterous chorus of "Happy Birthday."

Madonna, laughing gaily, stood up on her chair to take a bow and throw kisses. She was dressed in a black jersey number that fit like Saran Wrap.

"So who wants to go to Argentina next month?" Richard asked, a second spoonful of soufflé poised in front of his mouth.

"What's in Argentina?"

Tori glanced across the table at the two women who had asked in unison.

"Polo ponies," Richard answered, winking at Tori and then leaning in thoughtfully toward her. "See, if you come to work for me, you can do crazy things like take off for three weeks to go to stay on a gorgeous sprawling *estancia* in exciting Argentina," he said in a voice this time that included only her, describing the rambling Spanish-style hacienda that belonged to a friend of his.

Tori laughed, feeling a warmth from his sparkling eyes that were a paler version of the aqua on the walls. "How's that?" she asked, her voice matching the tenor of his, giving in to the flirtation.

"You'll be my assistant. I'll *require* your assistance."

"Hmmm, I thought I'd be working in the marketing department."

"Yes. But for me. I'm thinking of using a South American theme on the next phase of Bel Air Estates. We're putting polo fields onto some of the estates and I thought it might be a clever idea to market them as Bennetton's *estancias,*" he joked. "I'd need you there with me to pick up ideas. We'll want authenticity . . ."

Tori laughed. "Authenticity," she reiterated, smirking as a

waiter refilled her wineglass, waiting for him to finish and depart. "All part of the job—"

Richard lifted his refilled glass and tilted it toward her as she raised her own. "Sounds intriguing, doesn't it," he said, touching her other hand, toying with the small paved-diamond ring on her finger that looked like kids' jewelry in comparison to the rocks the other women were wearing.

"I think I'm looking for something more—" Tori hesitated, watching his tan muscular hand closing over her pale delicate one.

"More *what?*" he asked, interrupting. She felt her chest swell and her cheeks color. He grinned, taking it all in, calculating. "Bennetton is known for its top-flight salaries and perks, you know."

"I think it's the perks that have me alarmed," she noted.

He was moving his hand along hers in slow circular motions. "We have excellent medical insurance. You'd get a car—"

"Vintage, like yours?"

"If you like."

Tori laughed again, feeling little electriclike waves all over.

"We're a great company to work for. We take over Disneyland once a year—just for our employees. You want to go back· to school to take certain classes? We bankroll you. Tax season get you confused? We hire a slew of extra accountants during tax season to help out anyone who needs it. Did I show you our gym? Separate men's and women's. Our Christmas party is unparalleled . . ."

The dizzying currents continued. Tori put down her wineglass, afraid to drink any more. Then she picked it up again, not sure what to do with her free hand. His steadfast gaze had more effect on her than one of those fast spinning rides at an amusement park.

"I'm still waiting for you to say yes . . ."

She was tempted, unnervingly tempted. *Yes, yes, yes.* The reply rolled around in her head. The job she had finally decided to accept was for a stuffy Canadian-based firm. But it was a stable job, and a choice career move. The job for Bennetton could turn out to be a whim. Richard was clearly erratic, and the job itself so undefined. The sensible thing to do would be to say no to Richard. To tell him, thank you very much, but that she held fast to not mixing business with pleasure, that she was already a veteran of that error, and that she had accepted something else.

"I have an idea," Richard exclaimed mysteriously, rising abruptly from his chair before she had managed to say anything at all. In seconds he had taken her hand and was whisking her up from her chair and out of the party, offering only the faintest of good-byes to his pack of puzzled but not surprised friends.

How strange to be in the arms of a man who had grown up with Kennedy, Sinatra, and Andy Warhol at his family dinner table, Tori thought looking out over the view that was a three-hundred-sixty-degree sweep from the beaches of Santa Monica to downtown Los Angeles.

They were standing on the property country-and-western singer Kenny Rogers had purchased for his new home, staring out at the magical city view aglow in a sea of bright, twinkling lights, broken only now and then by random patches of blackness. Richard had driven Tori up to see the three-hundred-twenty-five-acre site for Bennetton's Bel Air Estates in hopes of selling her not only on the job he was offering her but on himself.

The multi-million-dollar private estate community was both opulent and rural at the same time, set up high above the city in its own majestic mountain-carved haven. For 3.5 million dollars, the discriminating customer could acquire a spacious two- to three-acre site overlooking Century City and Beverly Hills, complete with luxuriant landscaping, security, stone streets, and a pad for a tennis court, Richard told her. For the equestrian-inclined, horse facilities and polo fields were also an option.

The detail work that had gone into the project was mindboggling, from the four-thousand-square-foot Italian granite gate-house, which housed the unique laser-disc video selling devices, to the custom-designed curbs, gutters, and sidewalks, all done in a stamped concrete with a stone pattern finish and laid out in meandering curves, to the streetlights, fire hydrants, and Stop signposts painted with a verdigris patina to look like weather-worn copper. The exceptionally lush landscaping, which had a

European look, principally evergreen shrubs and plants accented with plump stalks of powder-blue-and-lilac delphiniums, had been put in ahead of the construction of the homes themselves. This was done to establish the exclusive environment into which a prospective buyer was buying for upward of three million dollars for a piece of raw land. And that was without the house.

Standing on top of the world in their formal evening wear, a faint breeze stirring the late-night air, with Richard seeming suddenly more vulnerable than arrogant, Tori knew that she was indeed sold.

True, Richard was the overindulged son of a powerful real estate magnate, spoiled, as one would imagine, growing up rich and gorgeous to boot. But there was something else about him hidden beneath the cultivated veneer of his privileged roots, some brooding sensitivity, a hurt that made her want to embrace him and make everything perfect, as it looked to be on the outside. He was honest, cut right to the heart of things, and she liked that. He said what attracted him to her was that she was not afraid of him. She thought that was pretty funny since, in fact, she was scared to death of him.

She had never personally known anyone with wealth on this scale. Vintage car collections. Private jets. Being invited to rock stars' birthday parties, with half the guests arriving in chauffeured limousines, was hardly an everyday occurrence for Tori. She would have to stand in line for hours in order to get only average seats to see Madonna in concert, let alone go to her birthday party. Traveling across the world on a whim, the way Richard and his friends apparently did, staying in only the most swank accommodations, needing bodyguards, as he said he had at one time—it was a lot for Tori to take in.

Richard's mother had died when he was twenty-two, when he was away at Columbia University, smoking a lot of dope, snorting a lot of cocaine, dating a lot of international beauty-queen types, driving fast cars, and living under the silver-spoon delusion that the world was his oyster.

He used to fly back and forth between coasts and had what he described to Tori as a first-class operation within first class, making himself a curiosity factor for the stewardesses because of his youth and quiet vulnerability. By the end of each flight, he would have picked up at least one of them, offering a ride in the limo that was awaiting him. From the limo he produced great tapes and dope and then from there seduced his new "friend" into coming back with him to his great brownstone on the Upper East Side, an invitation which no one ever turned down.

Richard's simple joyride life came to an abrupt halt when his mother died. He was too young and too self-centered to have even considered mortality, that she might not always be there for him. He had been in bed with a couple of the stewardesses, as it happened, when he had gotten the news. They were all so ripped out of their minds they ignored the telephone's incessant ringing for the first several hours, hoping in their drugged haze that it would go away, feeling too out of it to be able to carry on any kind of coherent conversation. He almost didn't even answer when he did, except that he couldn't stand the infernal ringing any longer.

His father's secretary had been the one to call, something he had always wondered about, but even to this day never confronted. The words seemed completely unreal; they kept coming at him over and over again, cutting through a thick fog. Maybe it was the drugs; maybe it was just the shock. He had been more out of it than this before, but he had never felt more out of it. A heart attack, had been the shocking news. But there was nothing wrong with his mother's heart. It was the strongest heart he had ever encountered. Maybe it was his father who had had the heart attack, he remembered thinking in a flight of panic. He could have handled it if it were his father.

The painful irony of it was the fact that he would have had an opportunity to see her before she died if only he hadn't been so messed up when the calls had started coming in. By the time he got the news it was too late to get a flight, and he'd had to wait until the following day. That handful of hours had been critical. His mother died only two hours before he reached the hospital and, to this day, he hadn't ever gotten over the guilt and sense of being cheated at never having gotten to say good-bye.

Richard's relationship with his father remained complicated, fraught with anger, competition, and awe. Tori still remembered the way Richard had sat studying his father's picture in his office, the remark he had made about Tori meeting him, as if he were God there at Bennetton.

In retrospect, the remark now seemed razor-edged. It took a lot of fight to amass the kind of wealth Richard's father had amassed, to reach the heights he had reached, and she imagined he was still there presiding at Bennetton Enterprises, exercising his iron will, running the show with his dukes up, proving himself even at the expense of his son. While Richard referred to everything as *his*—*his* property, *his* concept, *his* sales force—Tori suspected that with a father like Elliot Bennetton, Richard was afforded little autonomy. High-powered men with big egos rarely just handed the store over to their sons.

Tori also learned that Richard had been married twice and had twin daughters, age six. His first marriage had been an act of rebellion, carried out when his father became engaged only a year after his mother's death. Richard had wanted to throw a monkey wrench into his father's marital bliss, so he had showed up at their huge wedding with a bride of his own, turning the affair into an unexpected double ceremony. "Guess what she did for a living," Richard had asked Tori sardonically. Tori got it right on the first try. She was a stewardess.

Wife number two was more in keeping with Richard's image. While for a long time he avoided glamour, cover girls and makeup, he wound up falling in love with and marrying a beautiful French actress. She was starring in his T and A picture his friends had been ribbing him about earlier. Along with her beauty, she had that great French style and arrogance. And of course she had great T and A. They had a whirlwind romance, which ended the day of the wedding. After that it was clear she was on a gold-digging expedition. She was very French, very spoiled, and very moody. On the set they had dubbed her the enfant terrible. She tamed down for a while when she became pregnant, but then after she had given birth to her twins, she went right back to the role of spoiled French bitch and played it to the hilt. After a year and a half of this, Richard threw her out. The problem, of course, was the twins. Richard tried to gain custody, but in the end he relented because, with his life-style, being a single father was just too difficult. Chantal, his wife, took the babies back with her to France, where they lived now, taking long vacations to the United States to stay with Richard as part of their custody arrangement.

"So you see I'm not really the best marriage bet—I don't have the best history," Richard told Tori, and she couldn't decipher how he meant it. A warning to detour her from entertaining any nuptial designs on him? Or was he just stating a fact? *Or* was he embarrassed about his record and trying to make light of it?

"I stand forewarned," she replied, disappointed because the sense of intimacy seemed to have been shattered. They were still standing looking out over the city. The temperature had dropped. She had his tux jacket draped over her own gossamer jeweled one.

He drew it tighter around her, lifting her chin to meet his lips. "I didn't mean it that way," he said, kissing her.

Mean it which way? She wondered why they were discussing marriage on a first date, anyway. He had said that he liked to run fast, and she felt suddenly anxious. Which direction was he running? Toward her or away from her? Kissing him was definitely easier than pursuing this confused line of thought. *Kiss me and transport me far, far away, up to a place where thoughts cannot touch me,* she reflected, eager to blot out anything cerebral, craving a release to pure unguarded sensation. But interference from the workings of her mind prevailed, interrupting sensation, breaking it down.

Richard's lips were thinner than Travis's; they felt different as they pressed against her own.

His kiss was not as smooth, nor as leisurely, and she found herself growing frustrated, melancholy, missing Travis's kiss, the way the two of them could stay joined like that for hours, kissing, teasing, touching.

Richard was moving his hand inside her jacket, over the fabric of her gown, cupping her breasts.

She wanted to feel excited, to stop thinking . . . to stop thinking of Travis, but she had no control.

Feigning arousal, she murmured appropriately, touching him back, running her fingers along his neck, which was thick and warm, letting her hand drop down to his elegant white shirt, feeling his form beneath it.

Richard Bennetton was perfection. What on earth was the matter with her?

The pace of his breathing had quickened, and she realized he had no idea how wooden she felt. This should have been so sexy, so romantic, standing on this plateau above the city with its rare and private vantage, their exquisite formal evening wear stirringly incongruous with their earthy surroundings, the rich earth beneath their feet. The fragrance of wild flowers growing up from the still undeveloped plots of land clung heavily in the darkened night air. There was a faint rustling sound from the trees and the activity of crickets, which punctuated the silence.

It should have felt like a dream come true, Tori with her multimillionaire, confiding in her like a little boy, kissing her, wanting her. But whose dream? Was it hers or was it Paige's?

"God, I want to make love to you," Richard said huskily in her ear, his breath hot with desire. She wondered how many women he had taken up to this exact spot and then seduced. It occurred to her that this might just be a variation on the airplane-stewardess maneuver. The thought bothered her and she had to let it out.

"So where's the tapes and the great dope?" she asked warily, though trying to appear playful as she pulled away. "The brownstone on the Upper East Side—" she reminded him.

He looked at her for a brief puzzled moment, then burst into laughter, sweeping her up in his arms and carrying her rather unsteadily toward his gleaming car of another era. Her dress shimmered, caught by the beam of his headlights. "Why, in the auto, of course," he joked, awkwardly opening the door and depositing her inside, then reaching across her to switch on the radio. "Actually they didn't have tape decks in the fifties," he recalled, "and I'm too much of a purist to put one in. I hope this will do."

A news update flashed across the broadcast, and Richard turned the dial until he came upon a song that suited him. They both laughed when they realized it was an old tune of Kenny Rogers'.

"He must know we're here, on his lot—" Tori kidded, running her fingers through the back of Richard's straw-colored hair, which grew low down at the nape of his neck, as was the latest fashion. Short on top, sensuously full in back, very eighties with a touch of nostalgic sixties. She felt him responding as he rolled his head back and closed his eyes for a brief moment, taking thoughtful pleasure in her touch. Not having moved from his position, he was still stretched across her while holding himself up slightly on one elbow so she wouldn't be crushed. They were both listening to the song on the radio, looking into each other's eyes and sharing the irony. If it *had* been a tape, she would have known it was planned. Instead, it felt like a strange and wonderful message of fate. "I remember this song," she said, feeling the need to say something. He seemed to be penetrating her soul through her eyes, recapturing what she had felt for him earlier. His fingers were keeping time with the sultry country-and-western rhythm, lightly grazing the swell of alabaster skin which rose up from the *bustier* of her gown.

Now she was aroused. Now she could feel the pace of *her* breathing quicken, an excited moistening between her thighs. She was aware of her skin heating up, melting, growing sexy and restless for his touch.

"I think you're going to be in trouble," he observed ominously, the corners of his mouth subtly upturned as he continued his study of her.

She didn't know what he meant, but she felt herself blush. There was something very intense, very intoxicating going on here between the two of them, some connection that had her feeling all out of kilter again. It was puzzling because she was unable to grasp the logic of it. There was a smile rising up from deep inside of her that she could not hold back.

"I predict that within three months you're going to be *taking* that bad marriage risk you stood forewarned on," he said, his fingers roaming dangerously lower, tracing deep into her cleavage, trailing down as far as her dress would permit. She could feel her heart pounding, but he wouldn't let her interrupt.

"Here's another warning," he said, leaning in still closer. "When I want something, I always get it. Nothing stands in my way. Nothing at all. I don't have any feelings about what you want. I wouldn't care if you were married. With a boyfriend. I'm aggressive *and* obsessive. I don't stop until I get what I want. And from the moment I laid eyes on you, sitting there reading that stupid book, I wanted you. Boyfriend or no boyfriend, I predict there's going to be a rock on that finger before you even know it." He was holding her left hand up to his lips, forming a band around her vacant wedding-ring finger with his kiss. She blushed, she smiled, she probably turned as red as her dress. His tenacity was heady, challenging even, flattering because it was now directed at her.

Was this another line of his? Or was it for real? She couldn't tell because her already spinning thoughts had picked up still more velocity. He had driven her up here to beguile her into accepting the job offer. Now it appeared the position might be as his wife. A thought passed fleetingly through her mind but evaporated before any words could be formed. He chased the words off with a lingering kiss, smoother than the kisses before, then maneuvered out of the car, coming around to the other side, clearly enjoying her stupefied reaction. "Careful. I warned you that I like to go fast—" he teased when he was in the car beside her behind the burnished rosewood steering wheel.

"You don't even know me," Tori cautiously pointed out.

Grinning, he inserted his key into the ignition and started it up. "Oh, yes, I do," he said, cocksure, as they swayed from side to side, unable to maintain their balance, Tori certainly unable to maintain hers, as the four-door Facel Vega passed over the gravelly unfinished surface of the famous country-and-western singer's mammoth lot, peeling out onto one of the many roads that he personally had christened.

Then she thought of Travis, and her heart slammed into her chest like a heavy lead gong, causing her to lose touch with how she felt altogether as Richard drove the few blocks leading up toward his just-completed house on a hill, one of the first to have been erected in pricey Bennetton Estates.

Chapter 14

"This is the most fucked-up world—everyone's always in love with the wrong person!" Paige observed later, when Tori had returned home from her evening with Richard. It was after having gone up to Richard's house where Tori had made an empty kind of love with him, consumed with thoughts of Travis the entire time, feeling acutely as though she were cheating on him by being there in bed with Richard.

Richard's body had been like aspirin when she needed Demerol: over-the-counter stuff when she needed prescription.

Her whole being literally ached for Travis, a gripping need that had invaded the very essence of her so that each thought she had was overlapped, joined with a thought of him, the concept and the face of Travis unyielding. He was a drug from which she was experiencing painful withdrawal, the high she required in order to feel alive, in order to feel at all. Being there in bed with Richard only heightened her distress, her craving, his unfamiliar naked presence merely producing a more frustrated awareness of what she needed and didn't have.

Damn him. Straight-as-an-arrow Tori, who smoked grass only occasionally but had never experimented with cocaine or anything harder, felt as though she had gone and gotten herself hooked on a drug far worse, a drug infinitely more devastating. Her addiction had her feeling strung out, frantic for her fix, ready to concede to anything in order to get it.

With Richard naked in his big luxurious bed beside her, moaning from her touch, trying to initiate pleasure, *she* remained far away—plea-bargaining with her psyche in a humiliating effort to ward off total trauma. She needed to feel high, to float away in waves of mind-releasing orgasm and promise.

And she did promise. She promised herself—the hell with everything—she was going to call Travis tomorrow. Maybe tonight. She was going to sneak into Richard's football-field-sized bathroom when this was all over and call Travis to tell him exactly how she felt, how she needed him, and how he also needed her.

The hell with marriage; the hell with her pride and babies and all that she had ever imagined for herself. She couldn't take this anymore. Her heart was breaking for the thousandth time, dealing a death blow to her judgment. It had taken two months of seeing Travis nearly every day before she had felt comfortable enough to make love with him. And now on her first date with Richard she was in bed with him, living out some sort of perverse revenge against Travis and feeling as if it had backfired. All she wanted was to move back home to Atlanta, back to Travis. Back to their condo that he was trying to sell. He could keep his blessed marriage to his wife he hadn't seen in years. He could do any damn thing he pleased. She would never harass him about marriage again, never even mention it.

She was reformed.

It had all just been foreplay until now, with Richard trying to make her come, trying to ready her for his eager entry, but his voice beamed her back to earth, back into his bed.

"You're so wet," he had said thickly, in a voice that sounded as washed out as her thoughts, coming in only distantly familiar, passing through the roadblock that was Travis. His body felt even more unfamiliar, looked unfamiliar, golden skin, golden hair, golden boy, when she was accustomed to dark, macho, and middle-class. "You ready?" he had asked considerately, sucking softly at her shoulder, his long, athletic form pressed up against her. They were both up on their sides, facing one another, their thighs tangled as he held one small but shapely breast cupped in the palm of his hand, while she trailed her fingers along his skin, bronzed from so much sun, silky to the touch.

"You're exquisite," he pronounced, repositioning himself so that he could encircle her breast with his mouth, moaning with relish as he drew his hand down again, passing over her stomach, causing *her* to moan.

He was right—she *was* wet, needing the consummation as much as he. She tried to pretend he was Travis, then stopped herself, stubbornly, as she held his rock-hard penis between both hands, creating a double friction that made him cry out.

Tori wanted nothing more than to feel profoundly turned on by Richard, to lose herself in the power of his high-velocity brand of courtship, and to lose *Travis* in the upheaval of its wake. Even if it were all to be a wild and crazy, impetuous mistake, if it wiped out Travis whatever bruises she incurred would be worth it.

And as he flipped her over, onto her stomach, and entered her from behind, she vowed to try.

"God, you feel so fantastic, I'm going to explode," he whispered after about thirty seconds, and then did.

Not exactly the most romantic position, she thought, for their first time together. But at least she didn't have to face him.

"It's just so classic," Paige reflected, watching as Tori somberly switched off the flood of outside lights. "Susan's in love with Mark. Mark's in love with me. I'm in love with the prospect of being filthy rich, which Mark will never be. Richard's falling in love with *you*. But you're stuck in a rut in love with Travis, who's dead and buried in the backyard anyway Everyone always seems to be facing the wrong way."

"Richard's hardly 'in love' with me," Tori corrected her, walking into the powder room and picking up the entire box of Kleenex. "He's used to getting whatever he wants. And since he doesn't *have* me, he wants me."

"I thought you said he *did have* you," Paige teased, noticing Tori's makeup that had looked so perfect a few hours ago when she had helped her apply it, but was now smeared into a charcoal mess around her pretty eyes. When Richard dropped her off she had walked into the entry hall and seen Paige standing there, book in hand, even though it was two in the morning, waiting to see how it all went. In that instant the floodgate had burst, and Tori had dissolved into tears.

"Only my body, not my soul. I guess he wanted both."

"Funny," Paige said. "When you're younger you give your soul and guard your body. When you get older, you give your body and guard your soul."

"I guess when you marry a rich man you're not in love with you give your body and *sell* your soul," Tori philosophized ruefully, pulling out a fistful of Kleenex and blowing her nose.

"Not me. A prostitute sells her body. A fool sells her soul. I sell nothing."

"You sell your body *and* your soul."

"I share my body, and I always guard the hell out of my soul," Paige insisted, laughing. Then she asked sympathetically, "God, was it that bad?"

Tori thought about it for a moment, looking up at Paige from over the shield of Kleenex concealing the rest of her face, looking a little like an Egyptian belly dancer as her dark eyes smiled in a kind of surrender. "No. Actually, I liked him a lot. I'm just all screwed up, that's all. Thanks for the dress, though. It was a show-stopper." Unable to unzip it by herself, she turned her back to Paige for help.

"Yeah, well let's see what kind of magic it works tomorrow night," Paige said, carefully gliding the zipper down the delicate jeweled fabric of the gown.

"I hate to tell you this, but your party's *tonight,*" Tori corrected her, pointing to the predawn hour appearing on Paige's shiny gold counterfeit Rolex. Wishing she were more like Paige, Tori leaned over and gave her a peck on the cheek. Paige always knew exactly what she wanted. She didn't flounder. She was pragmatic. She had a glow about her, even now in the middle of the night, a clear-headed, scrubbed kind of glow in her white terry robe, her lush, honey-colored hair swept up off her face into a ponytail. "Thanks for being here for me," Tori said gratefully to her, "but go on upstairs and get some sleep. Actually, your dress did work magic for me tonight," she added on second thought. "I'm just too dense to appreciate it. And anyway, *you're* always magic—with or without a Valentino." Holding the un-zipped red gown up so that it wouldn't slip off, she gave Paige a light shove in the direction of the staircase. To Paige's lingering look, she replied, "Thanks. It was perfect. I know tonight will be perfect for you. Now get the hell out of here and get some sleep!"

Already imagining the pleasant sensation of her head meeting her pillow, eager to drift off into sweet dreams of this evening's much looked forward to affair—her date with the mysterious Philadelphia—Paige grasped sleepily onto the cold wrought iron of the stair rail, envisioning herself as the belle of the ball, the new girl in town who would turn heads—*Paige Williams, the Enchantress.* Using the stair rail for support, she swung around to head dreamily up the stairs.

Paige Parker, she thought, drowsily trying on her date's last name and smiling because she had always liked alliterations.

Her near-slumber rapture was caught up short by Tori's brusque but unsurprising announcement. "By the way, I ac-cepted the job at Bennetton," Tori offered without expression.

"Good girl," Paige replied, turning to give her friend the thumbs up sign. If only her friend didn't look so desolate, head-ing over toward the bar, toward the bottle of Armagnac they had *all* been using to numb their bouts of excess emotion. "It takes time, you know," Paige noted encouragingly.

Tori nodded, wishing she could put that interminable stretch of time on "fast forward" and get it over with, already.

The Beverly Hills Hotel crowned Sunset Boulevard like a big pink cake, full of sweet legends, conjuring up lofty expectations. It was pink and green and grand. It stood like a marvelous old tribute to the era when Hollywood reigned supreme.

Paige drove up to the hotel in Dustin Brent's shiny black As-ton-Martin Lagonda feeling very gay, very chic as she handed the expensive toy over to the parking attendant and flashed him one of her more beguiling smiles. It was a gorgeous day, the sky a deep blue, the sun a vivid yellow ball, like a kid's crayon drawing where, in the background, you would expect to see purple moun-tains rising up into proud peaks.

Mountains are not purple. They're brown.
Says who?
*Should we teach them reality? Or let their imaginations flourish
without boundaries, without imposed censors?* It had been one of
the arguments of the day when Paige was a kid, freedom versus
control, nobody certain, Spock preaching one thing, then later
trying to take it back. And what they had ended up with was an
entire generation counting on the power to paint mountains any
damn old color they chose.

Speaking of color, Paige was wearing a scribbly slipdress that
had vivid strokes of boysenberry run wild on tawny tangerine. It
was vibrant and very revealing, dipping to a very low V in back.
She hadn't known what color shoes to wear and had finally decided on a pair of high-heeled black patent pumps she had
bought on sale at Charles Jourdan just before she had moved out.
They didn't quite go, but they didn't clash either.

Catching glances from all directions, she swept through the
lobby of the old hotel, appreciating the airy California decor, the
bustle that activated her senses. She thought back to her initial
impression of the hotel, when she had arrived there in June to
stay for Kit's wedding. *June, July, August—what a turning-point
summer. Thank you, dearest Kit,* she thought, feeling eternally
grateful to her old friend as she headed past the bank of phones,
exchanging flirtatious looks with the men there presumably conducting *deals*—"taking" meetings by phone.

There it was, the Polo Lounge. And from inside she saw her
date waving to her. Handsome Philadelphia looking like a dashing Don Juan. He was as smooth as three-star French vanilla ice
cream.

She hadn't been certain that she would even recognize him. It
had been at least a month since they had met, and their bizarre
but memorable exchange had been only about fifteen minutes
total.

"Hi," she said cheerfully, slipping into the booth beside him,
liking his oatmeal linen suit, his crisp white shirt, and his tie that
seemed to blend with her dress. They made a handsome couple
and had drawn stares from the neighboring tables. Now that she
was sitting face to face with him, it all came back. The round,

intelligent-looking brown eyes. The thoughtful creases beneath them that she imagined could make him look kind or tough, depending upon his mood. He had a good head of hair for his age, which she had estimated to be about forty-five. His teeth were capped; she could tell by the color differentiation when he smiled. She also noticed that he still wasn't wearing a wedding band and that there was no tan line there to indicate that he had taken it off for her benefit.

He was taking her in, just as she was taking him in. So she looked past him, through the window and out to the courtyard set up with green-and-pink flowered tablecloths, tempted by the sunshine, musing that she would have preferred to have sat outside in the garden.

"You look gorgeous," he said, placing his hand on her back, reacting to the absence of fabric there. With a faint smile reflecting his surprise, he ventured further, curiously trailing his hand the length of her spine, all the way down until it intersected with the crazy fabric of her dress where he would have had to negotiate with the nylon zipper to go farther. It was all done with the utmost of discretion, his wandering hand protected from view, sandwiched between her young blooming body and the shiny vinyl booth. "Now I know what I want for lunch," he asserted brashly.

She smiled coolly, deciding to play it remote for a while, thinking he appeared a little too eager to collect on his gifts.

But now came the difficult part, what to say to each other. Flirting was easy. Screwing was easy. Carrying on a conversation required work. She had no idea what he was interested in, what he even did for a living. Straight out asking him would sound forced, contrived, idiotic, and maybe even beside the point. She had to set the tone but she didn't know which keys to strike first. Her opening line began to take on blustering proportions, as though her first words would set her into a category in his mind from which it would be impossible to ever climb out. It occurred to her that she was probably already in that category.

Thank goodness the waiter appeared to requisition drink orders just as she had embarked on some fatuous sentence and spared her from having to complete it. Drink talk could be the beginning of small talk, which could lead them into big talk, and then they could relax and have sex. *God, the pressures of first dates.*

Even the simple task of ordering seemed to present an obstacle. What if she ordered alcoholic and he ordered nonalcoholic? She would feel like a lush, drinking at twelve in the afternoon. On the other hand, something alcoholic seemed appropriate, more festive. She considered champagne, then decided it would look too put on; a beer would look too casual. A Bloody Mary seemed like just the right thing if it weren't too potent, but then she determined the high would probably do her good.

"What about you, Mr. Parker? Your usual?" the waiter asked, while making note of Paige's order. The unexpected familiarity with Philadelphia's name and drink caught her by surprise since he had told her that he didn't stay here.

In their one brief telephone conversation (all other communication had been through telegrams and gifts), he had gone on with such elaboration about how he preferred staying at the old Château Marmont, explaining how he liked it because it was more intimate, more romantic, more bohemian, hidden up in the Hollywood Hills, and commenting how over the years it had become known as a kind of a dormitory for Left Bank artists. Screenplays for *The Color Purple, Butch Cassidy and the Sundance Kid,* and *The Day of the Locust* had all been written by writers in hibernation there. Whoopi Goldberg had whooped it up in the lobby there. Garbo had slept there. Belushi had died there. Sting had once stayed up all night performing a concert for the hotel staff.

Not that Stan Parker seemed like the bohemian type. But his plan was for the two of them to go back to the old Château after lunch (he said they didn't have much of a restaurant), relax by the swimming pool, "get to know each other," as he had put it, and then get dressed and go to the affair together.

It sounded like a good plan to Paige.

"So. Tell me about *you,*" Philadelphia said, inching in closer to her after the waiter had disappeared.

The line coming from her would have sounded inane, but she was grateful that he had broken the ice. From him it was fine.

Not clever, but definitely fine. Paige laughed. Her nerves somewhat mollified. "I'm a heart surgeon," she teased. "I work with
research and rare species—"

He laughed, his eyes bright with amusement, his appreciation
of her humor putting them both still more at ease.

The waiter returned with her Bloody Mary, and Stan's
"usual," which looked like bourbon on the rocks. Paige tipped
her glass toward his. "What? You don't believe that I'm a doctor?" she asked, looking at him with mock reproach over the rim
of her spicy red drink.

He shook his head no.

"There was just a big article about me in *Newsweek*," she declared, as though incredulous that he hadn't read it. "About a
breakthrough I made in developing a new kind of laser technology that helps transplant an obscure variety of Japanese gold fish
hearts into Brazilian parakeets, keeping the parakeets alive for at
least two more years. Can you *imagine* what that's going to do
for mankind . . . ? What do *you* do?"

"Me?" He looked as if he would try to top her. "I'm a leader of
a little-known religious sect in New Guinea."

"I thought you said you were from Philadelphia."

"I was born in Mongolia. My father was a fan of W.C. Fields,
so we relocated. Though by the time we got there, W.C. was
already off in Hollywood. Then when I was about eighteen, I got
the word from upstairs and set out to enlighten pygmies."

Paige was all ears. "On what?"

"Vegetarianism—" They both cracked up.

"This is going to be fun," she predicted, wondering what he
really did, grinning at him over the rich green leather-bound
menu the waiter opened and placed in front of her.

And it was. Stan Parker was a lot of fun. He was impulsive.
Funny. Easy to talk to. She learned that he was in the import-
export business and judged that he did exceedingly well. But
unfortunately, the demands of high-powered corporate life presented themselves with a little too much clarity when an untimely phone call interrupted their lunch, demanding his presence at an unforeseen meeting.

He couldn't have been more gracious about it, finishing the meal without hurrying through it, attentive to her, making sure she had had enough. Did she want dessert? Another cup of coffee? After they were all through, he gave her the key to his room at the Château and told her to go on ahead without him, promising that he would join her there just as soon as he could manage to escape.

Paige was pleasantly mulling the whole thing over while lying out by the sparkling blue oval-shaped pool at the Château Marmont, dark shades over her eyes, drinking diet Coke by herself, oiled and soaking up what was left of the midday sun.

"Miss Williams. Telephone for you again."

It had been an hour since Stan's last call, and Paige shielded her eyes as she looked up at the young handsome man attending the pool area. "Thanks," she said, rising up from the low peach-colored chaise and heading over to the house phone, which was contained in a small brick alcove.

"Well," she asked in a silky voice, snapping her bikini into place over her behind from where it had hiked up, grinning with expectation.

The pool attendant, watching her, also grinned. Another one of Stan Parker's gorgeous little numbers. With this one he had truly outdone himself. She was as close to a "10" as they came. He sighed, thinking it must sure be great to be rich and capable of buying anything. Barely able to tear his eyes away from Paige's beautiful ass, he took the bill she had signed, which from her oil had the faint scent of coconuts, dumped it into the trash, and rewrote another, per Mr. Parker's usual instructions. The bill was still charged to the penthouse, but under the timeworn alias "Joe Smith" so that there would be no record for any prying private eyes, should his wife ever get suspicious. God, didn't these stupid chicks smell that the son of a bitch was married? Or did they know and not care?

"I'm going nuts here, thinking of *you there*—" Stan was saying apologetically to Paige. "We're at a stalemate on this thing. Neither side will budge. Are you doing all right?"

"Fine. A little lonely, but very relaxed—"

"Save some of that relaxation for me."

"I think you should just give in already," Paige teased. "What's another million or so? Compared to an afternoon with me—"

She could feel him smiling over the line. "You probably have on one of those really sexy, French-cut bikinis, with the cheeks of your undoubtedly perfect ass in ripe view," he said.

"I do," she replied playfully.

"God, I knew it. And I'm stuck here with a bunch of stuffed shirts. What color is it? Tease my imagination into a complete frenzy."

Paige looked down at her skimpy gumdrop-orange suit, the revealing top, her sensuous hips swelling softly over the sides of the bottoms that were about the width of a licorice stick. "Gumdrop orange," she answered harmlessly.

He sighed again. "You've probably got a great tan. Your skin is probably the color of caramel and just as smooth."

She cuddled in closer to the brick wall. "And you can't have your lawyers take it from here?" she cooed.

He sounded suddenly distracted, as though there were someone else in the background. "Sorry, beautiful, break's over. I ordered up some champagne and caviar. If you're hungry when you get back up to the room, go ahead and open it," he directed hurriedly. "I'll see you just as soon as I possibly can." And abruptly he hung up.

With her hand lingering restlessly on the phone, trying to kill time, Paige decided to call Tori and Susan, hoping to find someone in. The machine picked up and, disappointed, Paige left word telling them how things were going, about Stan's cute sense of humor and his *un-cute* premature departure and delayed return. Then she left the time, telling them to call her back if they got this message within a half hour.

With the sun's power diminishing, the air growing chillier, Paige collected her suntan oil, her magazines, threw on the shirt she had brought along with her and followed the quiet garden path back over toward the castlelike edifice of the Château.

Killing time before heading up to the suite, she passed idly through the grand, recently renovated, European-style lobby, feeling the red tiles of the floor there cool beneath her bare feet.

In any other hotel, she would have felt self-conscious walking around dressed as she was, barefoot. But the Marmont *was,* as Stan had claimed, *different.*

She looked up to the cathedral-like arches looming over the entry arcade, the chandelier swaying there, ghostly, reminiscent of old black-and-white movies, a clock striking midnight, the scampering of unseen feet. It was made of heavy wrought iron fitted with amber-colored glass and it was genuinely eerie, hanging almost precariously from a ceiling painted in bright, fresh shades of aqua, lavender, green, yellow, and orange conceived in a Matisse-like design.

To her right was a sunken lobby, with cathedral windows, Moorish arches, robust blue furniture, like the furniture in Stan's suite, a marvelous old rolltop desk and a mahogany baby grand piano, where a frail, weirded-out-looking guy wearing wire-rimmed glasses and a deep scowl sat agonizing over the keys. He would play a series of notes, frown, then pick up the bottle of beer he had on the seat beside him, take a swig, then start up again. Next to the beer was a yellow pad of paper and a pencil, and she realized that he was composing. Curious if he were somebody famous, she watched for a little while longer. He had to have felt her standing there looking at him, but he didn't turn around even once.

Growing bored, she headed back toward the room, past the small receptionist desk, pausing in front of the antique vitrine that displayed a variety of Château memorabilia behind glass doors. Its contents ranged from Château Marmont postcards, matchbooks, small stacks of *The Hollywood Reporter, Variety, Rolling Stone,* an unexpected collection of antique dolls with painted porcelain faces, and, surprisingly, the flowered jams and Château Marmont T-shirts she had noticed the moody pianist wearing.

After mounting the couple of flights of stairs leading to the penthouse, Paige proceeded into the plush four-room suite, wondering when Philadelphia would call again. He was true to his word, she was glad to see. Set up attractively on the coffee table, along with flowers and two crystal candlesticks, was an unopened tin of Iranian caviar on ice, a plate of miniature toast squares, and, alongside that, a silver ice bucket containing champagne. It was already six o'clock and the sight of the spread made Paige suddenly ravenously hungry. Weak with temptation and nothing in her stomach, she eyed the tin of caviar, debating, but in the end was unable to disturb the perfect picture.

Instead, she decided to bathe and get dressed.

Just as she was measuring a couple capfuls of fragrant oil into her bath, the telephone rang and she rushed across the icy marble floor of the expansive bathroom to catch it, wondering if it was Tori, Susan, or Stan.

"Hi." Her ebullient, sexy reflection bounced off the mirror as she answered the phone, relaxing into friendly disappointment at the sound of Tori's voice on the other end.

"Got in just under the wire—exactly twenty-seven minutes since your call . . . Is he there yet?" Tori asked, a touch of southern-style sympathy in her voice. It was definitely not the distraught, melancholy voice of last night, Paige was glad to note, and she wondered what had caused the change.

"No, this meeting of his sounds like it could go on forever," Paige complained, keeping an eye on her snowy white bath water, which was rapidly filling up, airy bubbles climbing higher and higher under the force of the water.

"Goes with the territory, Paige. You want a rich guy—this is what you get. A lot of absenteeism while they're out keeping those seven figures rolling in—"

"There's always inheritance cases, like your divine, polo-playing Richard Bennetton—"

Tori laughed brightly. "And speaking of whom—guess who's coming for dinner? Guess who happens to *also* be going to Kit and George's little dinner party tonight?"

"No—you're kidding! Oops, hold on a sec." Through the mirror, Paige had caught sight of the tub about to overflow and dropped the phone in order to shut it off in time. She returned a split second later, eager to hear the rest, thinking no wonder Tori sounded so cheerful. "How did that happen?"

"I mentioned to Richard last night that I was going there. He knows them. But only peripherally—"

"And he had the nerve to call them up and invite himself?"

Tori laughed in cheerful confirmation.

"That's pretty flattering," Paige approved, arranging the various gels and creams from her makeup case along the counter, examining her face in the mirror to be sure she hadn't caught too much sun.

"I knew you'd like that. I just got back from Kit's. She's busy redoing her seating arrangements."

"What did George think—"

"I don't think George is too keen on Richard, but Kit said he's just jealous. He wishes *he* were six two, gorgeous, and loaded without having to lift a finger."

"He's got a point. I think I'm jealous, too. So who's Susan's dinner partner?"

Tori started laughing again, southern-style sympathy creeping back into her voice. "I'll give you two clues: *Brylcreem* and . . . Commodities."

It took Paige a moment; but then she groaned as she got it. "Oh, no. Not the *Miami Vice* stockbroker—"

"Kit said she never gave him a fair chance. And you have to admit, it was a pretty tough night for her," Tori charged.

Paige paused quietly at the reference to Mark, who, though practically living at the house, and everyone's "friend," remained a sensitive subject, since he disappeared routinely into Paige's bedroom after hours. Paige had vowed to herself to make it up to Susan. Even to stop seeing Mark, but she couldn't get herself to break it off. He was the other side of what she needed right now. He made her feel good. He made her laugh. And she seemed to fulfill all that for him. Instead she kept hoping Susan would meet and fall for someone else. Someone more in keeping with the prototype they had moved out here to meet.

"Who knows, maybe she'll like him this time around," Tori offered lightly. "Now, listen, go make some more magic with that red dress of yours. It obviously casts powerful spells . . ."

"That was you who cast the spell last night," Paige said, hanging up the receiver with an amused grin.

When her bath was all steamy and ready, she climbed inside, letting her robe drop into a puddle on the floor. All she was missing she thought, closing her eyes and sinking deeper into the hot bubbling depths, inhaling the exotic almost Oriental fragrance of her Opium bath oil, was a glass of champagne—and, of course, her date, the mysterious Philadelphia, who was growing ever more mysterious still.

An hour and a half later, with Paige lying on the bed, dressed, hair and makeup done, attempting to watch a rerun of *The Waltons,* there was still no sign of him. Not even a phone call this time. Every little noise she heard had her fluffing out her hair, altering her position, primed to greet him.

Growing more and more impatient, she got up and began wandering around the suite, straightening up.

The maid had already been in to turn down the bed, but Paige added her own finishing touches, taking her new, bought-for-just-such-an-occasion Dior gown from out of her overnight case and laying it suggestively across the covers, plucking a couple of flowers from one of the vases and arranging them artfully across the pillows. After that, she retrieved her perfume from her makeup case and sprinkled some judiciously over the sheets and pillows until they smelled subtle but wonderful. Then she moved on to lower the lights to a romantic dim, turned on some music, and finally adjusted the draperies to show off the dazzling panoramic view that made the suite so spectacular, especially at night.

Perfect, she thought, canvassing the suite, pleased with her efforts as she made her inspection of it.

When she couldn't think of anything else to do, she crossed restlessly back over to the window, contemplating the garish but still vital Sunset Strip, with its star-spangled glare of visual metaphors, seriously beginning to wonder what had happened to her date. The telephone had remained queerly silent after Tori's call. It was seven-thirty, and she knew the party had already started. Searching for some sign of him in the silvery stream of traffic that hissed around the bend below, she found herself growing increasingly anxious.

Was she being stood up? she speculated uncomfortably, finding the possibility doubtful. After all, she was in *his* room.

Or was it his room? She was beginning to wonder about everything. He had given her the key, true, and she had been signing the incidental drink bills she had charged to the room. But something was off.

When she had gone to lay out his toilet articles, there had been none. When she had opened the closet to take out his dinner jacket and make sure it was pressed, she had found all the closets bare, except for her own few things, which she had put into one. She had been taken aback at this at the time, since her initial understanding had been that he had arrived the evening before. But then she just presumed that she had misunderstood, that instead he had come in early this morning and that his luggage was simply still in the limo.

But now, considering the myriad of small but gnawing puzzles, she wondered. She wondered about all those people addressing him by name at the Beverly Hills Hotel, the formal, almost self-conscious way in which he had said good-bye to her there.

Starting to analyze everything, she flashed back on the way he had slipped around her question about where his meeting was to take place, as though afraid that she might call him there. The way he had evaded just about everything having to with his personal life. The gifts, the telegrams, even dodging giving her his office phone number.

While she realized she might be letting her imagination get the better of her, she couldn't help this feeling that things were not quite adding up, and it struck her with a disheartening jolt that probably he was *married*. "Paige, you idiot," she scolded herself. "What's wrong with you? You move out to California and, all of a sudden, you've lost your grip." It killed her that she had been so unwilling to face up to this now obvious conclusion earlier, that consciously or unconsciously she had been so intent on protecting her fantasies.

Admittedly, Paige had been out with her share of married men, slept with her share of married men, but it was the prospect of his not being forthright with her, snaking around the issue and not saying anything, that shook her. Lying was the one thing she absolutely wouldn't tolerate. If she wanted to fool around with a man who was married (and since she had moved out to California she specifically did *not* want to), it had always needed to be a conscious choice, a fair, joint decision. Right or wrong, *that* she had been able to accept. At least a relationship was possible in that context; there was a straightforwardness, the terms all laid out on the line. But this outdated, male-chauvinist garbage—*let the dumb broad think you're single and she'll put out for you*—infuriated her. Who did he think he was? What kind of *games* did he think he was playing? *Well, just let him discover exactly who he was playing them with,* she thought, fingering the luminous ruby fabric of the gown he had bought for her, catching the glint of her jeweled evening bag on the couch.

Disappointed, feeling like a complete dope, if her hunch was right, and definitely wanting revenge if it was, Paige opened the desk drawer in the living room and pulled out the telephone directory, looking for the telephone number for the Beverly Hills Hotel. When she found it, she picked up the phone and punched out the number, glancing uneasily toward the door. As long as he was this late she hoped he would be a few moments later. She wasn't looking for an overly dramatic confrontation. And that's what she would get if he came in now and heard her on the phone checking him out. If her hunch was correct, she needed time to compose her response.

As the line began to ring, and then the hotel operator answered and put her on hold, she took a deep breath, watching the door through the gilded antique mirror over the desk, finding her thoughts drifting off to Mark. She resisted them immediately, feeling embarrassed, hurt, and immensely frustrated as she stuffed the telephone book back into the drawer.

Did she really want to know? Of course she wanted to know. She had promised herself: *No more married men.* She had moved out here to get married herself and they had to be strictly off-limits, *verboten.* They were a waste of time, a waste of energy, and all too often a waste of heartbreak. Yet she was going to be damned if she wasted this evening. She had been looking forward to it for too long, had too many hopes banking on it. If Stan Parker was married, she would use him exactly as he planned on using her. She would go ahead and go to the party with him—but she just might *leave* with somebody else. *Thanks for the introduction, darling, it's been swell.* That would be in lieu of *him* having the opportunity to say *Thanks for the fun fuck*—"Good evening.

Beverly Hills Hotel." At last the operator had returned back on the line.

"Yes, Mr. Parker's room, please. Stan Parker," Paige requested, drumming one of the engraved hotel pencils on the desk, bracing herself. It was a game of roulette. The little silver ball was spinning, and she was waiting for it to land. Black meant there would be no Stan Parker registered there. Red meant the phone would begin to ring.

What a shit, she thought resentfully when it did, when her luck rolled into the red, setting her on alert. One ring, two rings . . . at the eighth ring she heard him call out her name. Only she was too bummed out for it to register right away that his voice was *not* coming in over the telephone, but that he was actually there turning the key in the door.

"Hi, beautiful. Paige, darling—"

Reacting like a shot to the dull ringing that persisted like bad news in the background, and at the same time to the voice at the door, she touched the receiver down into place just an instant before he appeared in person in the room, disarmingly handsome in an exquisitely-tailored tuxedo.

Chapter 15 ⟫

Miami Vice stockbroker Dan Sullivan was just as dull as Susan remembered from her blind date with him a couple of weeks before. But the dinner partner Kit and George had seated on the other side of her, Jack Wells, was a different story.

He was an anomaly in the otherwise homogeneous crowd of slick, upwardly mobile types seated around the large rectangular dining-room table. There were thirteen of them (uneven because of the last-minute addition of Richard Bennetton), all nattily dressed, chatting casually over flowers and flickering candlelight. Tori was seated directly across from Susan, between Richard Bennetton, who couldn't keep his eyes off Tori, and a husband of one of Kit's friends whom Susan remembered meeting at the wedding. All of Kit's female friends, Susan noted with interest, were professional women. There was Jane Triperton, a photojournalist who worked for *Newsweek*, Leslie Cravitz, a pediatrician, and Brenda Locke, a literary agent. Susan and Tori were the only unmarried women there. And three of the six females were pregnant—Kit, Jane Triperton, and Leslie Cravitz. A sign of the times, Susan thought, looking down at her own flat belly and trying to imagine it in bloom. Leslie and Kit were on baby number one. Jane was embarking on baby number two.

Jane and her husband, Lance Triperton, had been leading most of the "baby talk" conversation, offering advice on which Lamaze class to take, which doctors were said to be "too quick to cut," pros and cons on nursing—did it or did it not mess up the mother's breasts and *insure* needing a postnatal boob job?—where to find unique baby furniture, the best scientifically designed stimulus toys and apparatus, scaled-down Ferraris for one-year-olds, and finally the exchanging of baby-nurse gossip. Jane had compiled an extensive list of private nurses, their phone numbers, and vital statistics and told Kit and Leslie to have their secretaries call her secretary for a copy of the information.

Having babies in upper-crust L.A. was certainly different from having babies in Stockton. Susan glanced across the table at Tori, wondering if she could possibly relate to any of this because *Susan* certainly could not. Postnatal boob jobs, live-in baby nurses, father-and-son Ferraris, Italian cribs . . . She tried to calculate what the cost of having a baby in Beverly Hills must run. No doubt as soon as the live-in nurse moved out, a live-in nanny would move in to take her place.

It was impossible to catch Tori's eye. She and Richard were oblivious of the entire discussion. They were talking softly between themselves, smiling private smiles, sharing private laughs. *Good for you, Tori,* Susan thought, happy for her. Susan liked Richard. Probably he was spoiled—but that wasn't *his* fault. He was charming and obviously intent on wooing Tori, who, Susan thought, was far too skeptical of his attentions. Why shouldn't he be taken by her? She was down-to-earth, smart but not on the warpath to prove it, beautiful without having to try too hard, and aloof. She wasn't falling all over him, as he was probably accustomed to. Plus that southern accent of hers. . . . Susan could see its disarming affect in Richard Bennetton's handsome face.

Jack Wells caught Susan looking and gave her his own private smile, a quiet communication that seemed to link the two of them and, at the same time, mark them apart from the others at the table. It was as though he had read her thoughts, inferred that she was different, and in the same glance communicated to her that he was different as well, and glad of it. She was sure that he had seen through her high-styled floaty silk dress, Paige's bronze leather jacket and boots. He had probably noticed her worrying that she was going to dribble soy sauce on it during the Japanese hors d'oeuvres they had been served sitting around in the den, and probably caught her gagging on the big squishy coral-colored fish eggs. Kit and George had hired a Japanese caterer, and the caterer's native culinary theme was being carried out to the letter, down to the dragon-emblazoned plates, the tinkling background music, the lyrical arrangement of the flowers, the colorful paper lanterns, and the fancy, ivory chopsticks; everything, except that Kit had passed on actually requiring her guests to sit on the floor to eat. Maybe because half the female guests were pregnant.

Susan and Jack had barely spoken to each other all evening, other than to exchange a few pleasantries. *Oh, so you practice law. Oh, so you manufacture surfboards. Good salmon skin roll, isn't it? Super house.* But she had gleaned a sense of him just by watching. There was a bad scar across his left cheekbone. On anyone else at the party she would have assumed it was from a racing car wreck or a bad skiing accident, a trophy-wound inflicted from one of the rich man's sports, something daring and glamorous. But on Jack Wells the keloidal gash brought something tougher to mind, a rough and tumble street fight, the cutting edge of a knife. Like Susan's, his hip California look was strictly camouflage, she was positive, adapted so that they might blend in when they wanted to—just as long as there wasn't another alien there, sensing the difference. She saw it in his moody brown eyes, his gaunt angular cheekbones, the cautious set to his jaw, the way he had stood around earlier taking everything in, absorbing, measuring as though he were, by choice at times, invisible. Although he wasn't conventionally good-looking, she found she was drawn to what she imagined to be his come-up-the-hard-way brand of elegance. He would be smart, maintain few illusions. No silver spoons or prep schools for this hard-core American male. It was marked in his guarded manner, in his wide, hooded eyes which seemed to carry something raw behind them. He was very nearly the definition of cool. And Susan smiled back at him.

"I'd love to have a kid," he volunteered, surprising her, even though it was "baby talk" that had been dominating the general table conversation for the last twenty minutes or so. He put it to her like a wry proposition, his grin friendly, inquiring. "Maybe ten of them."

"Ten kids!" she laughed, picturing bedlam, wondering if he had been an orphan, and therefore craved an enormous family, or a deprived only child. "I hope you're exaggerating," she emphasized, sipping through a smile at her still-warm sake.

"Why? Did I scare you off?"

"Maybe," she replied, giving him a sidelong glance as one of the pretty, kimonoed waitresses slipped between them for a moment to remove her plate, which contained just the barest remnants of vegetable tempura, a few artichoke leaves that had been dipped and fried, and the lone stem of a zucchini flower. "At these rates . . . with a private nurse per baby, ten Italian cribs, ten private school tuitions from nursery on . . . ten reconstructive breast surgeries. Ouch!"

"Ouch! is right," he proclaimed. "I don't know. Where I come from, *drawers* work as well as cribs. They're cozier, even."

He had made her smile again, as she imagined a whole big chest of drawers, each one containing a cute little blanketed baby. Blue for the boys. Pink for the girls. "And where's that?"

"Minnesota."

"Really? I've always imagined Minnesota to be incredibly beautiful."

"Incredibly cold, anyway." He frowned and she wondered what the frown meant. Apart from his not liking the cold.

She moved aside as a fresh plate was set in front of her, accepting a warm, fragrant towel to clean her hands.

"What about you? Where are you from?" he asked.

"Stockton. It's north of San Francisco—"

"I went into a real estate deal up there once. You know, you *look* like a country girl."

"Hmmm . . ." It was her turn to frown.

"It was meant as a compliment."

"You can take the girl out of the country, but you can't take the country out of the girl?" she inquired, looking at him askance. "What sort of real estate deal?"

The face he made indicated that it was not one of his better ones. His shrug implied a casual acceptance of the loss. "So, did you practice law there? In Stockton?"

She smiled fiendishly, knowing that her reply would get the goat of a manufacturer, an owner of a large plant. "I represented the unions—" she revealed.

On cue, he grimaced. "That's the wrong side of the fence to be on."

"It all depends upon whom you happen to be sitting next to," she replied demurely.

"Well, I doubt you'd be sitting next to a labor activist at a posh little dinner party such as this."

"True." She smiled, sizing him up. "Actually, I'm on *your* side of the fence now. Not because of any philosophical conversion," she was quick to add.

"What then? Money?"

"It pays the bills."

He grinned, looking at her with what she took to be tough respect. He was a realist and he liked other realists. "So how does it feel to have switched sides, to be representing *management* now, instead of the *people*?"

"The *people*—" she mocked lightly, knowing he wouldn't believe for a moment that the *union* could ever really be synonymous with the *people*. "The truth?"

"The truth."

"I miss the action of being out in the fields. It's a far cry from reviewing employment contracts for executives, negotiating their perks, their deferred payments, their golden parachutes, and poison pills, which is what I seem to do all day. You can hardly compare going to bat for some executive wanting a Mercedes over a Cadillac versus someone wanting running water or a toilet that he doesn't have to share with thirty other workers."

"Is that what you used to do?" She couldn't tell if he was intrigued or making fun of her.

"That's exactly what I used to do," she said somewhat defensively, thinking back to her old gutsy tactics. "I used to go out to the farms, the nut orchards, with my court order in hand, and argue with these big-gutted field foremen, who'd get angry as hell when they'd see me. But I loved it, chasing down the trucks, getting the poor, uninformed, frightened workers to realize that they could expect and fight for more humane conditions for themselves and their families."

Jack listened quietly, appraising her. She wondered what he was thinking.

"You can't believe how pathetic the conditions are," she went on. "The workers live in filthy sheds or in these dormitorylike structures with twenty to thirty beds all crammed together. One toilet. One wash basin. They're lucky if they have hot water. They're lucky if they have running water, period. Not to mention no health insurance, that they can be fired indiscriminately if they get sick or if someone higher up doesn't like them. No time off for funeral leave. Sure, most of the union leaders aren't really out to make life for the workers more bearable; they don't care if they have hot water or that there are little kids working the fields. But I loved that in the course of serving their *business* interests, I was getting to see a difference being made. It assuaged my sixties' conscience."

"How much *difference* do you really think you made?" Jack asked a touch too condescendingly. "Did you ever go back afterward and see what exactly had been done, not just talked about or promised?"

"Nothing happens overnight. But there were changes. And *yes,* I did go back and see for myself."

He looked doubtful that the changes could have been significant. He also looked as if he had had plenty of problems with the union guns himself, and she sympathized, knowing how miserable it could be on the other side, the kind of harassment he would have undergone. The truth was, she felt she wasn't naive, just that it was an extremely complex issue about which she herself was plenty ambivalent. Just looking at the last several Teamsters' presidents, they had all been in jail, with the exception of Jackie Presser, who had been under investigation for years but had been spared having it go any further because he was an informer for the FBI and on the FBI payroll. Former Teamsters' president Ray Williams had been indicted, tried, and convicted for trying to bribe a senator. Jimmy Hoffa for bribing jurors . . .

Jack refilled both their sake cups with the individual porcelain containers that were at each of their places, then took a thoughtful sip of his own. "Unions are archaic at this point. They served their original purpose, but for the most part they just exploit those whom they originally set out to serve. I say in fifteen years or so there will be no more unions."

Susan raised an eyebrow, studying her dinner partner, noticing the heavy shadow that was developing along his jawline and finding it sexy. He looked like a cross between Dustin Hoffman and Billy Joel; he had the same intense, wiry characteristics. They were even about the same height. "So how did you happen to get into surfboards? You don't look like the surfboard type," she asked, changing the subject.

"I'm not. I hate the ocean—"

"*I* know," she ventured gamely. "It's too cold—"

He pointed his trigger finger at her and smiled, friendly again. "Plus all that sand. You can never get rid of it. It stays in your trunks and between your toes—" His smile broadened and she laughed. "*My* trunks, anyway."

"I love the ocean," she said.

"Well, we must have *something* in common," he joked.

"Horses?" she tried.

"Nope. I'm allergic."

"Tennis?"

"No time."

"Me neither. There, I knew we'd find some common ground," she said, catching a glimpse of what looked to be a tattoo on Jack's forearm, only faintly visible through the fine white cotton of his shirt. It was a hot night, with the arid Santa Ana winds in full gust, and the men had been given clearance from their host to remove their jackets. Curious, but lacking the nerve to stare or ask him about it, she averted her eyes. "What *do* you like to do?"

"Make money," he responded easily. But he put his hand over his forearm, massaging it there as if the muscle were sore, and she wondered what he was thinking—if he had noticed her trying to make out what was beneath the fabric, if there was anything even there.

"Oh, so that's why you like L.A. The land of money worship."
She took another sip from her sake cup.

"A god that pays off at least," he remarked with a steely smile.
"A tangible deity that you can put in your pocket, make multiply, do any damn thing you want with. Buy hot running water
. . . Even use it to help feed poor starving kids or fund research
drives to cure cancer. It's a productive belief. Which god do you
worship?"

She regarded him curiously, not quite able to get a handle on
him. "That's a very serious question," she replied.

"You can worship *me* if you want," he said, this time without a
trace of seriousness.

The conversation all around the table paused as a bowl for the
next course was slipped in front of each guest, the flower vases
rearranged to accommodate hibachi-type cooking units, one set
up between each couple.

"I want you to know that this dish is especially for you, Jack,"
Kit interjected from her end of the table as the petite Japanese
waitresses brought out a series of steaming iron pots that smelled
absolutely mouth-watering. "Those buckwheat noodles you've
told me about . . . *soba*, well, Haruko makes them and they're
divine. At least I think so, but what do I know? I never lived in
Kyoto—"

One of the waitresses giggled and glanced at her cohort. "Neither did Haruko," she confessed.

Susan, growing ever more curious, looked at Jack. "Kyoto?
You lived in Kyoto?"

"After 'Nam," he said casually, seeming to enjoy the awkward
silence his answer produced. Whether it was intentional or not,
or for her benefit or not, he unclasped his hand from his forearm,
and she decided there was definitely some kind of tattoo there,
though she couldn't distinguish what.

Dan Sullivan leaned over to say something to her, and she
nodded, without bothering to really listen. It was something
about having been in Kyoto himself, but she wasn't interested.
He was boring and his experience there would have been boring,
a carbon-copy nonadventure.

Jack Wells, on the other hand, with his scar that lent him

character, his tattoo glimpsed beneath his shirt sleeve, his seemingly out of character money worship, *he* interested her plenty.

As the thick *tanuki soba* noodle soup was served, Jack identified its various ingredients, the seaweed, or *kobu,* the fishcakes, called *kamaboku,* and a couple of the more exotic Japanese spices. He also expounded on the etiquette of slurping, how the appropriate way to eat soup in Japan was to slurp; the louder the slurp, the greater the compliment you were sending to the chef. Everyone at the table laughed at the loud, ill-bred sound of him consuming his favorite dish the Japanese way, with noisy gusto.

But Susan was glad when he subdued his intake of the rich-tasting dish and directed all of his attention back to her, elaborating on the portion of his life that he had spent in Asia. After Vietnam, having fallen under the mysterious Eastern spell, Jack had stayed on in the Orient, living in Singapore for a while, then moving on to Japan. Still undergoing emotional aftershocks from the chaotic violence of Vietnam, where he had served as a member of a little-known U.S. Army unit known as Tunnel Rats, the Asian aura of tranquility, the feeling of restfulness, of absolute serenity, acted as a medicinal balm.

For eleven long months, his responsibility had been to ferret out Viet Cong in a nearly paralyzingly effective and ostensibly impregnable network of subterranean redoubts, where the VC had built an astoundingly advanced tunnel complex humming with factories, hospitals, flag-making workshops, printing plants, theaters for USO-type entertainment, and strategically placed subterranean command posts. He had done combat in this underground maze, armed only with a flashlight, a knife, handgun, grenades, and sharp animal cunning. Not bothering with false modesty, Jack told her how most enlisted Rats lasted only four months and that, in the four-year history from discovery of the tunnels until the end of the war, no more than one hundred GIs were even qualified to wear the TR badge and the jungle fighter's bush hat that distinguished them. The criteria for the treacherous volunteer mission had been compact stature and gargantuan courage. Only five seven, lean and sinewy, Jack said he had been an ideal candidate for the Rats.

The history of the thriving tunnel complex Susan found particularly fascinating since it was ongoing long before the war against which she and her generation had marched. The Reds' triumph over the Americans, Jack explained, was in actuality the culmination of a thirty-year war going all the way back to the forties and fifties when ground was originally broken for these tunnels by the Viet Minh, predecessors of the Viet Cong in plotting a revolt against their French colonial masters. Almost all the tunnels had been excavated by hand, by peasants using spades or hoes, and the power had been generated by pedaling a bicycle. Remarkably, some of the underground structures were four stories deep.

From these tunnels, which were entered by intricately engineered trapdoors, Communist cadres infiltrated the South Vietnamese capital more or less at will, making the American war effort futile and leading inevitably to the fall of Saigon. It was of little consequence that the Americans had the greatest firepower of any army under the sun, because while our U.S. troops were invading, defoliating, and destroying the land above, they couldn't possibly prevail with the Viet Cong manning their base camp from under the earth below their feet, in a two-hundred-mile tunnel complex that, at the peak of the war in the mid-sixties, stretched from the gates of Saigon all the way west to Cambodia.

Jack didn't spare her any of the details. He told her about how they had approached the camouflaged trapdoors as if walking on scorpions, which was too frequently the case, taking unthinkable risks to pump tear gas or napalm into the complex labyrinth, and succeeding only in wiping out a fraction of their target because, every hundred yards or so, the VC had constructed special water traps rigged to seal entire tunnel sections into separate compartments so that only a single sector could be affected. She shivered from the too-vivid pictures he was creating in her head, reacting to the fear and futility he must have felt.

After the war, Jack said he knew he couldn't face going back home. The reality of his life back in the States was too unreal, too jarring. He said he needed an Asian existence for awhile in order to successfully make the transition. And Japan was where he thought he had found his enlightenment.

Even Japanese art was soothing, their music, their design, their immaculate bonsai gardens, which were at once austere and serene. Those eleven months had been too long, too intense, too full of death and insanity. So he had lived in Japan for a couple of years, healing himself, working odd jobs, mostly in hotels catering to American clientele, learning the language, trying to break through the mystery enshrouding the complex and age-old Japanese customs.

But the tranquility wore off in short order, once he had moved back to the States, replaced by a reckless anxiety to make money fast, to catch up. He felt the blow of inflation both in the economy as well as in his age, finding himself a quarter of a century into his life with no money, no college education, no work experience, and nothing hopeful on the horizon. He wanted the art, the beauty, the grace, but he wasn't going to get it without ample cash to first afford him food, shelter, and self-respect. It had to do with a person's worth being measured by dollars, in his mind, because it would buy power and control, an essential he had had to live without in 'Nam, something he would never live without again. Power and control didn't exist in that jungle. You needed wits and brawn and also a hell of a lot of luck in order to survive.

Nobody escaped a war like Vietnam unscathed, and Jack Wells wasn't any different. He didn't lose any limbs, walk with a limp, or lose his sanity, but he was unquestionably a veteran, a veteran who had traded his Lutheran God for the almighty dollar, becoming a devout workaholic, a Wall Street fanatic.

Kit and George's dinner party was a great success, and when the evening broke up Susan had been in great spirits, waiting for Jack to ask her for her telephone number, sure that he would want to ask her out since they had enjoyed talking to one another so much. When he didn't, her ego seemed irreparably wounded and she left crushed.

First Mark, then Jack. What was the matter with her? Maybe she just wasn't in Tori and Paige's league. Maybe it was time to face the music and alter her expectations. What *were* her expectations, anyway? At this very moment, as she slipped into her car alone, without Tori, because Tori had gone with Richard, she decided she had no clue whatsoever, and she burst into tears.

Instead of going home, she decided to drive back to the office. At least there she could feel in her element, in control. *Successful.* The ever-present piles of work on her desk were something she could manage without this painful insecurity, something in which she could thankfully lose herself. Thank God for work, for her career. If she was bombing out socially, at least they loved her at the firm. They found her to be quick and capable, a creative thinker, good for accumulating those extra billable hours because she was often the last to leave at night.

As she pulled out of the driveway, Susan looked at herself in her rearview mirror, more dissatisfied than ever, wishing she looked more like one of her roommates.

Chapter 16

Paige was burning.

But still cool enough to have not confronted him yet. Her arm was looped through Philadelphia's as they threaded their way through the opulent room, through the gay, elegant crowd toward the dance floor, where he whirled her deftly into his arms, a smashing dancer, humming into her ear along with a tune Frank Sinatra had long ago made a household classic. She hadn't solved the puzzle yet, but she would, soon and with flair.

The party was only the most gorgeous she had ever been to. The legendary estate within which it was being held warranted its status. It was a formidable house, where it would be no trick at all to lose five hundred people, with one huge room opening into the next, ad infinitum, where no amount of furniture could possibly make the place look cluttered, let alone cozy. It was full of crystal, candles, and beautifully dressed guests, milling around, dancing, eating, having a grand time. The Carnival Night theme was carried out subtly, lending a festive mood. Paige half expected the thirty-foot ceilings to produce an echo-chamber effect, probably if one walked through the house alone, there would be one. She could imagine the theatrical resounding of footsteps reverberating through the cavernous rooms, unobstructed.

The house felt very forties, conjuring up images of the hotel baron who had once lived there, at the time Hollywood's reigning party giver, and the glittering, glamorous affairs he was known to have held.

What an era, she thought nostalgically, as Philadelphia drew her closer to his tuxedoed chest for a samba, breathing into her ear how exquisitely she moved. He felt so good up close like that, and she almost relaxed. He looked so sublimely handsome in the black-and-white attire that was de rigueur.

If only she were wrong; if only there were an explanation for his being registered at two hotels at once, she reflected, staring out through the romantic series of French doors, which lined the ballroom. They had been left open so that the guests could flow freely out onto the terrace, down the graceful tier of steps, and out into the spectacular stretch of garden, which Paige likened to a miniature Fontainebleau, even though she hadn't yet been to France. Out past the sparkling, brightly lit fountains, which were housed in long, colorful flower beds, was a second dance floor. While the orchestra inside was playing big band sounds from the forties and fifties, outside there was a disco company blasting current hits. Both were loads of fun, and both dance floors were packed.

The popping of flashbulbs interrupted Paige's train of thought, and both she and Philadelphia turned to see which celebrity was being made immortal on film.

Dancing just a few feet away from them she noticed a tall, imposing-looking man with broad shoulders and thinning dappled gray hair. Dancing with him were two women who may have been his daughters, but who she suspected were not from the way they were dressed, both in jazzy miniskirt outfits, one of satin and lace, the other smothered in emerald green sequins. The three of them stopped dancing just long enough to pose for the photographer, each of the two women cuddling in to plant a kiss on each cheek.

"Who's that?" Paige asked curiously.

"Your host," Stan whispered in her ear.

Anxious for a better look, Paige maneuvered in closer. Bulky and bursting with energy, he looked every bit the part of the flamboyant ex-football star. On the way over to the party, Philadelphia had given Paige the full rundown on her sports-mogul host, telling her all about his football career, about how in his early thirties he had gone on to earn his fortune taking over the beer empire for which he had been hired to do sales, then hurled himself right back into his true love, sports, in a way that would put him on the map forever. Acquiring sports teams with only average records, he built them into championship ones, and then constructed his own private sports arena for their games. Paige thought she should have guessed it was he by his doe-eyed, miniskirted dance partners, since he'd been dubbed by the press "a wild man—with a fetish for miniskirt-clad girls half his age, one on each arm."

The illustrious Nicky Loomis was known as much for his flamboyant antics as he was for his sharp business acumen. He was big and powerful-looking, an ape with a brain and an unquenchable sex drive. He was imposing but still boyish, as though he had never really outgrown his football days, which he probably hadn't. She guessed his age at somewhere in his late fifties. He had small lively eyes, slightly bloodshot from too much fast living, and a prominent nose that looked as if it had been busted a couple of times, enhancing his looks rather than detracting from them, adding another layer of character.

When he noticed Paige studying him, he gave her a flirtatious once-over—a ladies' man, cool and secure, good for a one-night stand and a small diamond bauble as payoff. She returned the look, equally cool, trying to establish in a glance that he had met his match, that he would be missing the time of his life if he let this brief eye contact encounter end there.

As Philadelphia steered Paige off in another direction, she felt Nicky Loomis's eyes on her back, tailing her as they sambaed through the thickening crowd, away from him.

It was a sign and she smiled, pleased, a back-up plan beginning to take form in her head. It was time for the unveiling of the facts, time to find out whether or not Philadelphia was single, married, an innocent charmer, or just a snake.

Why would a man take two hotel rooms? She could think of one reason only. If he were married. That was an easy one—no untimely phone calls from the wife and kids coming in when he was in the middle of receiving a blowjob from his mistress.

On the other hand, maybe there was another Stan Parker registered at the Beverly Hills Hotel, Paige thought, remote as the possibility was.

"You want to take a walk?" he asked her, that horny smile appearing on his face again. What did he think? He was going to get laid in the gardens? Not if there's a Mrs. Stan Parker, you're not. Think again.

"It's so incredible out—" he said with that silver tongue of his, taking her hand, and leading her out through a pair of the French doors, out onto the patio, down the stairs, and then in the opposite direction from where the party was set up. Just out the door, she caught Nicky Loomis still watching her and she drew a quick fix of strength from his unmasked interest, slipping him another cool smile with her eyes, allowing just the faintest curve to her lips.

The backyard was positively mammoth, easily large enough to accommodate his own private football field, *with* bleachers, Paige thought, as she and Stan roamed out of sight of the others, accompanied only by the voice of Whitney Houston serenading them through the state-of-the-art outdoor speaker system, the words of the popular song getting to Paige.

It was chilly and he put his tux jacket over her bare shoulders, since she had left the jacket to her dress back at her seat.

They walked for a while not talking, very close together. Paige's brain felt scrambled and she wondered if men, relationships, love, or any offshoots thereof would *ever* be easy for her, if she would ever be lucky.

She wondered if she could ever fall in love with someone who was simultaneously falling in love with her.

She had meant what she had said to Tori, about life being all messed up that way—everyone always in love with the wrong person. Or the *right* person at the wrong time. All she wanted was what Kit and George had found—both of them unattached, available; *him*, rich, fun . . . Like in the movies. Like in the ever-present scenario of her daydreams. Romance, sexual attraction, safe happy love. And a bankroll to weather the storms.

No more struggling with the likes of cute and good-in-the-sack Mark Arents. She had had dozens of Marks and knew only too well how when the sexual feast wore off, all that was left was just another guy who could only barely afford to take her to dinner.

If only Stan Parker would whip her around, take her into his arms, assuage all her worries, tell her it was love at first sight, tell her that he knew by instinct that he had never met anyone like her before and knew he never would again—that they were symbiotic; this was kismet; they were meant for each other.

She wanted him to tell her that he understood the deeper level of her soul that she kept carefully hidden away, the vulnerabilities she masked with such bravado. That he understood why. That he understood her past, without her even having to utter a word.

It happened so frequently and so convincingly in so many books and movies that she knew the whole thing by heart and couldn't accept it not happening in her real life, if she willed it so, if she waited long enough. God knows, she was due. She was thirty. She was tired. She was running out of lines. She needed him to make it simple, to be her Mr. Right.

This is not a play, Paige; this is real life, she told herself, feeling her hopes plunge as she reached down into his tux pockets for warmth and came upon the shapes of what felt like two different hotel keys. One of them she recognized from the Château. The other one she couldn't figure out.

"So what did you think of the Château?" he asked, the timing of his question catching her off guard, causing her to let the keys drop back down into the bottom of the pocket.

"It's great. Terrific," she replied, stumbling distractedly over her answer, not about to remove her hands from their satin-lined position. "You stay there often, you said?" Her question sounded strained, and he looked at her queerly. She smiled to cover up.

"Yes. Fairly often . . ." As though in imitation of her fantasy, he stopped in his tracks and whirled her around so that they were facing one another. Only now, naturally, it all felt false. "God, you look beautiful in that dress. It made me crazy then, and makes me crazy now," he declared, fondling the expensive fabric proprietarily.

Her hands remained shoved down deep in his tux pockets, her hand clenching the keys as she fabricated a smile. She was stumped, trying to think of a way to confront him.

He started running his finger down her cheek, along her chin, then over her lips. *She* wanted to use her lips for talking right now, not for kissing. They were definitely not symbiotic, she decided as he leaned in to kiss her anyway, which she let him do, her thoughts crowding her brain and blocking sensation.

"Warmer?" he asked, stopping to take a breath, his eyes glazed over with longing, his hard-on affecting his speech. He had her tomato-red lipstick smeared all over his mouth.

"Yes," she lied, her heart racing from anxiety. Just ask him flat out. Are you married? *Are you married . . . ?* But the words wouldn't come out. They kissed again, this time with his hands taking liberties, roaming beneath his dinner jacket, over her breasts, down her waist, her hips, slipping down to her thighs.

"God, you do make me crazy," he breathed, filling her mouth with his words. "You have the sexiest body. I was going nuts at those meetings today. I kept thinking of you in your little bikini . . ."

He tugged lightly at her wrists, removing her hands from the safety of his pockets and relocating them onto his swollen erection. "How am I going to go back out there like this . . . ?" he murmured, grappling with her gown, struggling to lift the heavy jeweled fabric up and out of his way so that he could maneuver his hand down into her panty hose to grab her ass. Then groaning and needing more, he lowered his hands down beneath her red lace panties until they were getting at the wetness of her crotch, playing there, and it felt good, even though she had to make him stop.

She was so moist, she knew he was reading that as a *yes, go on.* She tried to wrestle his hands away, but he ignored her effort, probably interpreting it as token resistance, kissing her harder than ever and pressing up against her until she could barely breathe.

Before she knew it he had unzipped his pants and had pulled his very red, very hard penis from out of the opening there, grinning with lustful pride. Her dress was up at her waist now. He had cornered her up against a massive magnolia tree.

With her mind spinning in a thousand different directions, unable to comprehend how this had happened so fast, afraid to flee and afraid not to flee, Paige ducked down, accidentally brushing her cheek against his penis and slipping awkwardly around him. She was breathing erratically, trying to get control of herself, of him, of this tricky situation. "Excuse me," she managed with miraculous calm. She was sweating now. But she held on to his coat because she had to check out the keys in the pocket. "I have to go to the ladies' room," she blurted out.

He looked at her stunned, out of breath, appearing ridiculous with all that lipstick smeared worse than before on his face, his cock at attention standing out from the metal jaws of his zipper.

She let out a nervous chuckle, feeling every bit as ridiculous as he looked as she backed away, wriggling her dress back down into place, trying to correct her own lipstick. "I'm sorry, Stan, but I have to pee."

She moved fast, fearing that he might come after her.

What if she were wrong? What if there were an explanation? Would all this then be funny?

It wasn't easy, hurrying warily down the rock path of the garden in her high heels. But she made it, emerging as inconspicuously as possible, seizing a glass of champagne from the tray of a waiter, trying to appear composed.

Inside the house, looking for a bathroom, she spotted Nicky Loomis again. The miniskirted miracles, she noticed, were gone.

They turned up again, however, in the powder room, fixing their makeup, chatting, taking a break in front of the long stretch of makeup mirror, addressing each other's reflection instead of bothering to turn and look at each other.

On the far side of the ornate pink room, in the corner, there was a sitting room arrangement, with a couple of pink satin love seats and a small, attractively accessorized table between them. Paige sat down, literally gulping her champagne. She brought out the two hotel keys from his pocket and set them down on the table. And there it was, the Beverly Hills Hotel confirmed in engraved gold script.

Not surprising, but not enlightening either, Paige thought, staring down at the two keys, trying to figure out what to do.

In hopes of learning more, she reached into his breast pocket and discovered the smart snakeskin billfold that triggered an instant recall of their romantic, madcap meeting, then a pang of regret that things had turned out this way. Cautiously, she opened the wallet, turning first to see if the two miniskirted miracles were watching her.

They were oblivious. Good.

Swallowing deeply, Paige began examining the wallet's contents, discovering the family photos she had been afraid she would discover smiling through the small transparent jacket directly behind his driver's license and gold American Express card.

She looked closely at the picture of his wife, finding her to be fairly attractive in a prim, expensive, unimaginative sort of way. The Halston suit, the pearls, the smug smile, standing beside her adoring husband, one kid on either side of them. They looked like the perfect family. *Flawed,* she thought, the picture of Philadelphia standing in the garden, saluting her with his erect cock, still fresh in her mind.

Probing further, Paige came upon only more credit cards and a few hundred dollars in cash.

Well, now what?

Now she had to handle this mess and, at the same time, preserve her dignity. Or, anyway, her pride.

"Do you think he can even get it up?" cracked the redhead in the green sequins, standing up and spraying a final cloud of hairspray onto her perm. Paige turned curiously around.

"Honey, I don't think he can get it *down!*" the other one giggled. She couldn't have been older than eighteen. When she caught Paige staring at her, she giggled again and waved a giddy hello. Paige had no doubt of whom they were speaking. Her only surprise was that they didn't already know firsthand.

The redhead had pulled a vial of coke from out of her purse and was twisting off the cap. There was a small spoon rigged to the side, which she removed. "One more for the road—" she explained, dipping the tiny spoon inside and then casually snorting the powder. Some dropped onto her lipstick, and clung there.

"Great dresses," Paige said to them both, taking another swallow of her champagne, thinking.

This time both girls giggled. "Thanks," they said, one just after the other. "Our date's into miniskirts. In case you haven't heard." Paige assured them that she had. The blonde took a couple of snorts of the proffered cocaine, then held it out to Paige, her young eyes bright, alert. "Want some? It's real pure—"

Paige declined. Coke made her too wired; she didn't like the feeling. "Your date . . . You mean your mutual date?" she posed with a smile.

The redhead put her arm around the blonde. "We share everything," she confessed suggestively. They were obviously trying to shock Paige, so she intentionally didn't react.

"So do you two go to a lot of parties like this?" she asked, stalling them off as they were about to turn and go.

The redhead looked at her as if to say *Are you nuts?* "This party is Geritol city. We met last night at a real 'happening' party at the Playboy Mansion."

Even at thirty, Paige felt suddenly very old.

"We'd never even heard of *Nicky Loomis*," the redhead went on in a slinky voice, "but our sources say he's *only* 'Mr. Sports King.' Like he owns just about all the sports teams you can think of here. The StarDome. Anyway, I think he's kind of hot myself—"

"She has a father complex," the blonde explained with a titter, pulling the coke out of her purse again, sharing it, as she had said she shared everything, with her friend.

Paige's eyes went to their hemlines again and she laughed, on the brink of a wild but great idea. It had to do with getting back at Stan. It had to do with getting together with "Mr. Sports King." Paige thought he was rather "hot" herself. She liked this big old house. She liked the fact that "Mr. Sports King" was single. He would be nearly impossible to rope and tame, but, oh, what a catch, if she caught him.

"Listen, would you two like to make some money and have some fun at the same time?"

"Hey, like you just hit on our two favorite things," the redhead said, snorting eagerly at the cocaine and then returning the vial to her friend. "Add in, maybe, sex," she decided.

"Thanks. As a matter of fact, I just might," Paige retorted shrewdly. She had figured out a way to get rid of Philadelphia gracefully, and she was all smiles and good cheer in anticipation. She took his billfold from out of his pocket again and opened it, extracting two one-hundred-dollar bills to help pay for the execution of her plan.

Step one had the blonde running off to get Paige a pair of scissors and a silver domed tray, while she sent the redhead off for a pen, a sheet of paper, and a discreet retrieval of the sequined jacket she had left at her seat.

Once alone, the smile gone from her face, Paige set to work composing the appropriate notes.

The note to Stan, she decided, would say "Sorry you weren't straight with me. As it turns out, I *do* mind that you're married, but my double-your-pleasure stand-ins don't. I'm sure you think of us all as interchangeable units anyway, so have fun. And by the way, don't embarrass yourself or me by coming by the Château Marmont tonight . . . Happily, you do have somewhere else to stay."

The note to Nicky Loomis would simply say "Less is more." What she planned to send along with the note would say the rest.

When the two stoned-out-of-their-minds, bubble-headed teenagers returned carrying the goods, Paige went to work. Appealing to Nicky Loomis's penchant for miniskirts, she had decided to cut off the bottom of her evening gown, and she took a last lingering look before having the nerve to rip into it. The mirror was not a full-length one, so she had to stand on a chair and let the girls help her. All the coke they had consumed didn't exactly help to steady their hands.

"Hey, this is a Valentino. *Concentrate!*" Paige ordered, unable to believe what they were doing to the dress she had never even really dreamed of being able to buy. It was some consolation, as she saw the scissors tearing into the sumptuous fabric, that at least Tori had had a chance to wear it, too.

When they were all through, Paige laid the shimmery jeweled remains of the gown out across the silver tray, adding a huge stalk of red ginger, which she pulled from a flower arrangement, along with the note she had written to Nicky Loomis, which said it all. The shiny domed lid crowned it perfectly.

After the girls had gone—carrying with them the domed tray and some crisp bills for the waiter who was to deliver it, plus the jacket complete with wallet and credit cards, to be returned to Philadelphia—Paige took a final glance at herself in the mirror. It was a good thing she still had great legs, she thought, standing up on her toes so that she was able to view her fifty-five-hundred-dollar miniskirt creation from the knees up. Coping with familiar symptoms of stage fright, she crossed her fingers for luck and headed out.

Partially concealed by a primitive African sculpture, she stood rooted near the doorway, watching as Nicky humorlessly regarded the waiter handing him the domed tray. He eyed it as though there were a bomb planted beneath the cover. Relief flooded through her when his apprehension turned into boyish pleasure as the glitter of material was revealed and he scooped up the note, hooting unselfconsciously to the friends circled around him. This man was all mischief himself; Paige could see that, as he hooted again after reading the inscribed message, holding on to the big stalk of ginger, the remnants of her gown, and looking around for the balance of it.

When he saw her, sort of in hiding, there was a click of recognition. Paige felt her heart do a flip, and she scooted out through the entry, past pedigreed antique paneling, which she felt compelled to touch, past magnificent carved corbels, exotic paintings, colorful Chinese porcelains, and mounted ostrich eggs, tripping over an upturned corner of an Aubusson rug, recovering and floating out the door, out past the power of personal treasures demonstrated on a scale she had never before seen. A glance over at Philadelphia already out on the dance floor gesticulating with the two replacements Paige had sent him served to reconfirm her decision.

In no time, Nicky Loomis was outside beside Paige. His eyes took in her face briefly, then cut down to her revamped gown, pausing there with keen interest. It wasn't often she had to crane her neck to such a degree, but he was so incredibly tall. So incredibly powerful-looking. His bullish looks made Philadelphia appear too tame, too suavely handsome.

"I think I'd like to get to know you better," Nicky said softly.

"Not here," she replied, feeling bold and happy with her exchange thus far.

He was amused but careful. "The Bel Air Hotel's convenient—" he said, gesturing with his large hand, a heavy star sapphire ring on his finger catching a glint of light.

But Paige smiled cunningly, reaching over to intercept the rest of his sentence, touching her index finger to his lips. "Tonight's *my* treat," she said with that same sultry smile, well aware that a man like Nicky Loomis was not used to being "treated," certainly not by his dates. He would be used to taking care of everything, initiating everything, paying for everything, but that was all part of Paige's strategy. She wanted to throw him off, set herself apart. The miniskirt was going to be her only concession.

And that was different, a ploy, a brash and daring statement applied to arouse his interest, which it clearly had. She wanted to be careful not to fit into any of Nicky Loomis's patterns, particularly the one-night-stand pattern about which she had already been forewarned.

Playfully, Paige snatched the car keys from his hand and helped herself into the driver's seat of his Rolls-Royce. Before he could even say *boo,* she had completely taken charge and she drove out of the private gates of his fairy-tale castle, with him silent by her side, heading down Sunset, down the Strip, toward another castle, toward the Château Marmont.

He wants to lay me so badly that he's letting me call the shots, she thought gloating behind the steering wheel, at least for now, anyway.

The look on Nicky Loomis's face as he walked through the penthouse, noticing the caviar, the champagne, the flowers, the music, the dimmed lighting, the bed turned down, the spectacular nighttime view illuminating the suite through the open drapes, made Paige's heart leap.

He was positively bowled over. She could see it in his expression as he turned to her. "Did you plan this?"

Her mouth curved into an involuntary grin. Thank God for Philadelphia, she thought, forgiving him completely. Thank God he had popped for the penthouse, ordered up this incredible spread. Thank God he had been tied up all day and been too late to partake of it. Thank God he had brought her to Nicky Loomis's party. And thank God for the ruby red dress . . .

"Who else would have?" she teased, joining her beloved Philadelphia in the sin of omission, joining Nicky on the couch.

Heady with success, Paige opened the bottle of champagne herself and filled up the two fluted glasses. He just sat back watching in open astonishment, relaxed, enjoying whatever game it was she was playing, and letting her play it to the hilt. He had his big arms spread over the back of the couch, one thick leg stretched rigidly out, close to hers, the other bent at the knee, in slouch jock fashion. He had loosened the bow tie at his throat and unbuttoned the first couple of buttons of his elegant white shirt. "I think I like being seduced for a change," he observed, accepting the glass of champagne as she handed it to him, filling the room with his presence.

Paige smiled again. *Less is more,* she reminded herself, believing that to be her best course. She wanted to say very little, keep him at bay, and not blow the image she had extemporaneously lucked into, seeing how he obviously liked it. Instead of struggling over a reply or another line of conversation, she busied herself with opening the tin of beluga caviar.

"So . . . I have some questions—" Nicky began, biting into the beluga-smeared cracker she had prepared for him.

"You do?" she asked, using her bottle-green eyes to get to him, to maintain control.

He laughed. "About a dozen of them."

She sipped innocently at her champagne, still not taking her eyes off of him, cooperative. "Fire away," she offered, prepared to dodge.

"Who were you with at the party tonight?"

She gave him a smug, noncommittal smile. "Stan Parker."

"Stan Parker," he reiterated, mulling the name over for recognition. Paige could see that he was coming up blank. She had already known from Philadelphia that the two men had happily never met. "He was your *date*?"

"Hmmm," she nodded. "And now he's with *your* date . . . or, rather, dates, plural."

Nicky's already small eyes appeared to grow smaller as he appraised Paige, studying her as she scooped out another good-sized dollop of the caviar and smeared it onto a second cracker for him. "Should I ask you how you arranged *that*?" he inquired, vastly entertained.

"If you like—"

He considered for a moment, hesitating before popping the second canapé into his mouth. "Did this Stan Parker guy *know* you were going to ditch him? Did he know about your . . . *designs* on the evening—"

"You mean my designs on you?" Paige interrupted, savoring the unique taste of the caviar, squishing the little eggs up against the roof of her mouth with her tongue and relishing the exquisite flavor that oozed from them as they burst.

He looked flattered. "Have I ever met you before? Have *we* ever met before?"

"No," she answered simply, the champagne cool and bubbly as it went down her throat, then fizzed up to her brain.

"Are you interested in sports?" he asked next.

She wasn't sure what to answer there. She found sports unbearably boring. But they were his whole life. "How could I be interested in *you* and *not* be interested in sports?" A neat dodge, she thought, aware that she had her work cut out for her. Tomorrow, after work at the health club, she would make a beeline for the library and studiously inhale everything to do with sports that she could get her hands on, including looking *him* up in the periodicals. She wondered what year he had played for the Green Bay Packers and what position.

"You *could* be interested in money," he replied somewhat crudely.

"Who *me*? Oh, I hate money," she declared with mock emphasis, not about to let him make her squirm. "And *you* could be interested in sex—" she noted, mimicking the kidding-on-the-square accusation.

"Who *me*? Oh, I hate sex," he rallied back with a great belly laugh. They were sitting closer together, trying to out-smartass each other, enjoying the heat.

"Hmmm, so I've heard," she shot back.

"What *have* you heard?"

An I'll-never-tell sort of smile appeared on her lips.

"So why *am* I here? Why me?" he asked, eyes narrowed again, kicking off his shoes. Waiting for her answer, he unfastened his bow tie and cast it aside.

It was a tricky question. She decided the wittiest response would be the truth. "I just moved out here from New York and I'm shopping for a husband. By all accounts you're lousy husband material, but I kind of like what I see, and I like going for the long shot."

He had just taken a mouthful of champagne and he nearly choked on it. She could imagine him hurrying to put his shoes back on, grabbing his bow tie from the chair and flying out the door before the marriage monster grabbed him.

But instead he merely picked up a cocktail napkin, dabbing at what he had spilled, while continuing to study her with even more amusement than before. She felt a happy thrill because, for some completely intangible reason, she felt her proposition wasn't wholly impossible. Maybe she felt that way because he *didn't* run, and he didn't appear mad or panicky. "Marriage, huh," he was smiling, composed again, taking another sparkling swallow of champagne.

"What the hell, it's in style again," she assured him, not missing the way he was taking in her legs.

"You want to rope me down the aisle, huh?"

"Like a bull." She winked demurely.

"I suppose I should be nervous," he said, indicating the way things had been set up with a sweep of his hand. "When you want something, you go after it, no holds barred."

"You can walk out now," she told him, slipping off her heels, drawing her legs up onto the sofa and curling in closer to him. "Now that you know how reckless and dangerous I can be."

"No. I think I'll hang around for a while," he said, clicking his glass to hers and holding her in his gaze as they both sipped to the challenge.

His lips were thin and she focused on them, pausing for effect before kissing them. She wanted to stay in command, to do the seducing.

And yet when she went to kiss him she was surprised to discover that he had stored up a mouthful of champagne that he let spill into her mouth as they joined together, creating a sensation that was at once funny and sexy as hell. He was letting her know that she could not take over completely. He was reckless and dangerous himself. He was making her skin tingle and her cheeks hot. Without breaking the kiss, he maneuvered himself on top of her on the couch, her cut-off gown rising up still higher on her thighs. The music was mellow and romantic in the background, and it all felt fabulous with the candles gleaming on the table beside the flowers, creating a lovely glow.

"What an exchange. You make the Bobbsey Twins look like a Big Mac instead of filet mignon," he said, abruptly breaking the mood as he reached for his wallet and indelicately removed a little blue capsule that contained a rubber. "So everyone feels safe," he explained tactlessly.

She was too out of breath, too stunned, to reply. Romance detonated—gone, she thought bleakly, as he hopped off of her.

Before she could even manage to lean up on her side, he had practically finished stripping off all his clothes and was tossing them casually onto the lap of the same plush wing chair where his bow tie lay. He was smiling boorishly, his extremely fit body reflecting a strong degree of vanity. "Especially nowadays, one can't be too careful," he added coarsely, before swaggering off in the direction of the bathroom.

So much for her perfect evening, Paige thought tightly, fuming. When would she ever stop dreaming? She was just another lay for this guy, not any different from the miniskirted miracles with whom she had swapped places. And why should he think any differently? Hadn't she confirmed his impression when she snipped off fifty percent of her brand-new dress and then presented it to him?

Worse, she was a decade older than the twosome had been.

Refusing to blur into his interchangeable parade of one-night stands, even at the risk of never seeing him again, Paige pushed up from the couch and grabbed a lipstick pencil from her purse.

He thought he had it made in there, the smug son of a bitch, about to slip his little protective seal over his precious cock, ready to screw. Well, tonight, guess who was going to be the screwee?

He wanted safety. She'd give him safety. But as for his sexual release, he was on his own.

Looking for something upon which to write, she snatched up his tuxedo shirt, hastily scrawling onto the back of it her second note to him this evening, simply reiterating her first: *less is more.* If he had done less talking and more kissing, he'd have most likely gotten laid.

Burning mad, Paige scooped up the balance of his evening clothes, leaving his inscribed tuxedo shirt laid out for him on the chair to ponder, his wallet, and money clip. Grabbing her overnight case from the closet, her glitzy Judith Leiber evening bag, her overpriced Maud Frizon high heels, she walked out on him. Damn Nicky Loomis. And damn Stan Parker, too. Damn them all.

Hurrying dispiritedly down the stairs, one shoe on, one shoe off, feeling embarrassingly conspicuous with his heap of evening clothes and her own cut-off Valentino gown, she caught her plight reflected, mimicked, in the mirrored wall that wrapped along the staircase. The picture she saw of herself chasing down the flight of stairs like that was more funny than sad, she told herself as she felt some of her anger beginning to fall away. Erratic, crazy, and funny. What was she so depressed about?

Her goal this evening had gained a face, a name, a persona. And that was progress. She had definitely set herself apart, she thought with a grim, nervous laugh. This was one little screwing session Nicky Loomis wouldn't be so likely to forget.

It was *lucky* she had been jarred into her senses. Joining the scores of fun-time lays would have only sabotaged her case, which she had, by chance, stated flat out for him. Feeling more and more hopeful, Paige reviewed her position, concluding that, in the end, the evening may have just turned out to be a smashing success.

Her objective had been to make him intrigued enough to set her apart from the multitudinous others, and to make him want her. She thought she may have accomplished both.

On the other hand, she hoped she hadn't overdone it. She didn't want to leave him so stripped of his pride that he wouldn't want to see her again.

Not to mention stripped *literally,* she thought, looking down at the load in her arms.

Passing the antique vitrine displaying a neat stack of the Château Marmont T-shirts alongside a stack of flowered jams like the pair she had seen the pianist wearing earlier, she abruptly backtracked, deciding her dilemma was solved.

The picture that had appeared in her head of *the* Nicky Loomis, Mr. Sports King himself, slipping out of the Château Marmont thus dressed struck her as one for the records.

"Can I help you?" asked the desk clerk, looking dully up at her from the paperback he was reading.

Experiencing the same rush of excitement she had felt earlier because the challenge, in some way, was still on, Paige took him up on his offer, pressing a couple of bills into his palm and sending him off to execute another fragment of her still-evolving plan. She instructed him to knock on the door of the penthouse and, if nobody answered, to slip inside, deposit a set of the jams and a T-shirt onto the blue wing chair, and then slip back out. As an afterthought, she handed the desk clerk Nicky's shoes and socks.

One round for me, she thought, climbing into the Aston-Martin Lagonda and ripping out the driveway, feeling a great gush of exhilaration and pride.

Chapter 17

It had all happened so fast. But then she presumed that's what life with Richard Bennetton was like, and the way things were going she had better get *used* to it fast.

Fast, like the shocking velocity at which Richard's private Gulfstream jet was now traveling, ripping through the heavens high above the Amazon, just bounding Bolivia, after stopping for fuel in Panama, en route to Argentina.

Overnight, Tori's life had changed. It was exciting and she relished the speed, which kept her lost in the stratosphere, zooming, gaining altitude, defying gravity. She was a kite, and Richard was directing her course higher and higher, clear of the chronic tug of Travis, until her hard-to-shake Georgia love was a mere nostalgic speck on the red-clay horizon of another life. It was wonderful and completely unreal.

Work wasn't work at all. As opposed to working her tail off in Atlanta, twelve-hour days, pushing to meet project deadlines, responsible for an entire division, plus a significant hike in pay, Tori's job, so far, appeared to be merely to amuse the senior vice president of Bennetton Enterprises—namely, Richard Bennetton. That could have sounded boring, trivial, unrewarding, or unworthwhile compared to the high-powered position she was used to. But at the moment it was just plain fun.

Besides, boring meant doing the same thing day in and day out, and life with Richard contained not even the suggestion of sameness. It was an adjective he avoided like the plague.

At the moment, all his attentions were being lavished on Tori and she was reveling in it for however long it lasted, though he kept assuring her it was going to last forever. What he felt for her was different, he claimed; *she* was different. He was totally flipped out over his little Georgia Peach. He loved her accent, her perspective on the world, her straightforwardness, and the way her skin smelled after making love. He loved the brand-newness that his world held for her and her intelligent appreciation of it. She wasn't indiscriminately "gaga" over everything, and yet she wasn't in the least bit jaded. Instead, she treated everything as a curiosity, something to try out, to regard, to taste, to like or dislike, simply depending on how it struck her own selective palate. He was thoroughly unconcerned about her apprehension that he would grow tired of her as he seemed to do with everything else—once conquered moving on to meet the next more interesting challenge—insisting that he wanted to meet new challenges *with* her. For the first time, he felt secure, happy, as if he had someone on his team, someone spectacular, whom he could genuinely admire and respect, whom he wouldn't be embarrassed to take to dinner at his father's house.

That's when he had caught Tori's attention and she had let herself begin to believe him. Elliott Bennetton, the senior Bennetton whose picture inspired fear among his legion of employees, Richard being no exception, was off sailing on the *Royal Viking* near India right now with Richard's stepmother. Tori hadn't yet had the opportunity to meet the legend face to face.

Dreaming of what her Latin adventure was going to be like, she relaxed, sinking deeper into the softness of the luxurious suede seat of the private aircraft, staring out the window at the cloudless sky, trying to make out the utterly foreign continent that awaited her below. In preparation for the trip she had already read Isabelle Allende's stunning book *House of the Spirits,* seen *The Official Story,* and rented a videotape of the old Argentine classic *Camila.* With her imagination thus fueled, she felt primed and eager, already envisioning the great *estancia* where they were to be staying as special guests of one of Argentina's premier horse breeders, Alejandro Carballo.

Richard's latest extravagance was sponsoring a polo team for the upcoming season in Santa Barbara, and he had wanted to go to South America to procure not just the finest and most expensive polo ponies bred in the world but the most sought-after riders as well. Alejandro himself was included in that exclusive inner circle, his presence alone on a team insuring a sponsor immense status. Richard had already decided he was prepared to pay an astounding quarter of a million dollars to get Alejandro to ride with him, a coup that he said would have him the most envied sponsor in the tournament. Beginning the sport practically before they had even learned to walk, Argentine polo players were known to be in a class of their own. The experience, Richard promised Tori, would be unforgettable, with every imaginable courtesy being extended to the rich American guests, since the sky was obviously the limit on what a prospective buyer could spend on such a venture.

After their stay on the *estancia,* Tori and Richard were jetting off to Buenos Aires for a few days, then Rio, where they were meeting up with an old friend of Richard's who was taking them island-hopping on his yacht. From there they would hit Peru, picking up the intrepid Death Train, given its name because of the precarious path through which it traveled, following the more adventurous route through to Machu Pichu where they would get to wander among the historic Inca ruins.

And for this Tori was getting paid. *Take notes,* Richard had told her, playfully justifying the expense. She couldn't help but wonder how he was going to justify it to his father, however. Or maybe they were just so rich that his father wouldn't care. Whatever, Tori was way beyond her ken.

The Carballo *estancia* was indeed like something out of an old Argentine movie. It felt as though time had stood still here, no traffic, skyscrapers, or urban litter to connect her to the present. The ranch house was a rambling pink stucco structure with a dark green tiled roof and dark green shutters, built all on one level on rolling green acreage that stretched as far as the eye could see. It had been built by Alejandro's grandfather, also a polo pony breeder, in the early nineteen twenties and all the original details had been painstakingly preserved. In addition to breeding horses, his family also raised cattle on the *estancia,* and there were tall, billowy fields of wheat and corn harvested for export. The stables were huge and neatly kept up. There was also a polo field on the property, an amenity Richard told Tori that was as common as tennis courts in the backyards of the houses in Beverly Hills. There was also a tennis court.

The interior of the old house was elegant but extremely masculine, with dark tiled floors, dark wood around the fireplace, dark green leather furniture, dark massive wood tables, everything oversized and heavy. The kitchen served exclusively as a workplace for the servants, big and functional-looking, with huge slabs of meat, all blood-red and incredibly fresh, laid out on the dark green tiled counters, eerie to Tori because they comprised the limbs and flesh of animals that had been raised right here on the ranch. *All grain fed, with no hormones,* boasted their host.

After their tour of the *estancia* and a light lunch, Tori and Richard were shown out to the lovely guest house where they were to be staying, and left alone to relax and rest up until evening. Horse business would begin the following day, with an exciting and probably exhausting agenda, they were assured. But after their hosts had departed, tempted by the crisp fresh air that smelled of clover and lush lolling pastures, Tori and Richard set out by themselves on a leisurely walk, taking along some of the fruit that had been left for them in the cottage.

Tori was anxious to know what to watch for when viewing the horses the next day, and she asked Richard dozens of questions, curious as to how the animals would be shown and for exactly what characteristics he would be looking.

He explained that they would be working the horses first in figure-eight formations, to demonstrate how they handled, and after that in a straight line.

The trainer would ask them for speed, then bring them back very quickly into a halt to show how nimble they were. How they moved was critical for polo, where they were required to stop and turn, stop and turn erratically, at a wild pace.

He told her to pay extra attention to the horses' hind legs, which had to be strong for stopping; they had to be very strong behind but nimble for quick turning.

If the animal was fast, could stop quickly, and be able to turn on virtually no notice, it was a perfect horse, he asserted, as they strayed farther and farther from the cottage, passing the stables, training areas, the garages housing farming equipment, and on out into the wider open spaces, where various crops were growing and livestock were grazing in the fields, until it was just them and great stretches of silky green pasture beckoning them for a nap.

"Also the size and shape of the horse's neck is important," Richard added, stooping down to rip a yellow wild flower from its roots and tickle her with it until she grabbed it from him, tucking it behind her ear and smiling at him as he went on with his explanation.

"*Why* should the horse's neck be flat?"

"So that it doesn't obstruct the polo player's view. You want a short, flat neck, also a soft sensitive mouth for turning and handling well," he stressed, guiding her over toward a big oak tree that looked to be a thousand years old, pausing to put his arms around her. "Let's see how soft and sensitive this mouth is," he suggested, kissing her and murmuring accolades, going back for more.

"But not so easy to handle," she warned him.

"Good," he answered, approving.

"What about the size . . . the height, the weight—" she asked conscientiously, while kissing the tip of his nose.

Running his hands all over her in desirous assessment, he declared, "Perfect—"

"The horses," she reminded, backing only momentarily away.

He sighed, giving in, but reluctantly. "Not too big—there's a height limit for good polo ponies. They should be only fifteen hands high. Big horses are difficult to turn. And they must turn with both sides—" Then with a growl of frustration, he wrestled her down onto the grass below the tree, concluding that she now knew *everything* that he knew about what to look for in buying polo ponies.

She told him that she seriously doubted it, as they stretched out close to one another, finally feeling the seventeen-hour flight catching up with them, happily expired from their walk. Lying on their sides, snacking on juicy pears and kissing between bites, they fell lazily asleep in each other's arms, hidden from view by the tall, grassy fields. They slept like that for over an hour until a ruddy brown-and-white-streaked calf, who had apparently strayed from its mother, startled them awake, contentedly licking their faces.

After returning to the guest house to continue their *siesta,* then bathe and dress, it was time to join the ensuing barbecue party their host was holding in their honor out in the courtyard.

Standing around on the bricked-in patio, laughing, talking, drinking red wine from short, sturdy-looking glasses, was a crowd of about twenty guests, all around Richard and Tori's age, the women tan and fashionable-looking and, as was the custom on the old *estancias,* the men wearing the traditional gaucho outfits called *bombachas.* It looked like a lively South American costume party.

Although Richard himself had opted for jeans, he had already predicted to Tori what the other men would be wearing, explaining how Argentine men loved to dress up, that they were like peacocks who liked to strut and show their stuff. The effect, she had to admit, was debonair and rather sexy, with the baggy-style pants tucked into sharp-looking riding boots, white shirts showing off their dark, healthy-looking complexions, and *rastras,* which were wide, interestingly-fashioned belts weighted down with silver coins, slung low on their hips, handsome silver knives wedged into the back. It was part of the old country pride, the celebration of customs they still held dear.

Over to the side of the courtyard, were a dozen or so gaucho-outfitted servants, only less flamboyantly so, attending to the cooking for what was going to be an elaborate, traditional feast. Skewered on a spit in the center of a huge pit was a whole baby goat, a *chivito,* and surrounding the pit were ranch hands continuously shoveling fire around the animal to cook it and char it to perfection. Another group of workers attended the bricked-in barbecue, cooking other parts of various animals, sweetbreads called *mollejas;* small intestines, *chinchulines;* veal kidneys, *riñones;* and blood sausages, *morcilla.* There were also skirt steaks and beef ribs. The smoky aroma was rich, kicking up Tori's appetite.

It was a chilly September night, spring in the southern hemisphere, and Alejandro's wife had piled high up onto a table a selection of brightly colored shawls for all the women to use in case they got cold. Tori, wearing tight white jeans and only a thin cotton sweater, happily accepted the one Alejandro held out for her as they stepped into the group and he went about introducing the two of them, making sure they were each given a glass of wine as he did so. Richard, with his arm linked through hers, gave her an amorous squeeze.

"Tori Mitchell and Richard Bennetton, please meet our good friends," Alejandro said warmly in that melodic Spanish accent of his. He was tall and dark-complected, with jet-black hair and flirtatious eyes the color of Tori's. The guests were introduced far too quickly for her to catch all the names, so Tori just smiled politely, glancing from one to the next, shaking hands. It was a blur of Spanish anyway, lilting names like *Mariana, Clara, Lita, Esmerelda,* and, for the men, *Aldo, Clemente, Maximo, Angel, Ignasio,* and *Hector.*

The name that both stood out and shocked her, was the name *Dustin Brent.* He was the last to be introduced, and they remained engaged in their handshake for a prolonged period of time, both equally astonished, and yet unsure as they appraised one another, both thinking that it couldn't possibly be.

"Not mountain-climber-adventurer Dustin Brent who lives at 13288 North Summit Drive?" she asked, laughing as he began to laugh.

"Not Tori Mitchell who lives at 13288 North Summit Drive?" he said in response.

"My English may not be so hot, Ricardo, but something strange is going on here," Alejandro chided Richard, enjoying whatever coincidence was transpiring.

Tori laughed again, feeling her cheeks flush. Like Richard, Dustin was also in jeans, wearing the *American* costume. Only she noticed that he was on crutches, with a clumsy plaster-of-paris cast on his left foot.

"I can't believe this," he exclaimed, catching her off guard with an exuberant embrace, crutches and all. It was great to see a familiar face and she hugged him back, delighted, wondering what had happened to him and what he was doing here. After living in his house, among his personal possessions for the last couple months, she felt a strange and satisfying bond with him.

"I can't believe it either," Tori cried, turning quickly to Richard to explain and repeat the introduction, but he had already caught on. After all, he too had been in Dustin Brent's house, heard the story, or a modified version of it anyway, on how the girls had come to house-sit for him.

The two men shook hands, Dustin friendly, Richard less so.

"So who's looking after my house, with you off playing in South America?" Dustin queried lightly, when the introductions were all finished and Alejandro had led Richard off in another direction to talk polo.

The warm brown eyes fixed onto her own, causing her to recall the various photographs of him she had been seeing daily throughout his house, lived with. It was weird to be with him suddenly in person again, the three-dimensional Dustin Brent, laughing, talking, as vibrant as she remembered him. "Paige and Susan," she answered.

"Wait a minute, weren't you the one who *wasn't* going to be coming out, who got engaged?"

It was a touchy question and Tori didn't quite know how to field it. "It was a twenty-four-hour engagement, or something like that. A long, boring story," she assured him, careful to disguise the wound.

"Oh, I'm sorry," he said kindly.

"No, look, those things happen. It was for the best."

There was an awkward pause in which they busied themselves with their wineglasses. Her eyes were level with his cream-colored cashmere sweater, which he had pushed up at the arms, and she flashed on what his secretary Evonne had referred to as his "pounds of cashmere" sweater collection, wondering lightly how Paige had managed to restrain herself from digging into it all this time. "So, it looks like you got over him pretty fast anyway—" Dustin posed after a moment or so, with a sly gesture over to where her handsome date was standing.

Tori smiled in response, looking over at Richard. Richard caught her eye as she did so and winked affectionately, mouthing an I love you.

Tori winked back at him, slightly embarrassed, then returned her attention to Dustin. "It's been an eventful summer," she explained, grinning self-consciously. "Thanks to you. Your house is wonderful. We really appreciate—"

"Hey, I appreciate that you're all looking after it for me," he interrupted graciously.

"No, but you've been incredibly generous—"

He smiled, shrugging off any further thanks. "So catch me up on all the gossip. What's going on with all of you? Did you all get jobs?"

"Yes. Susan got a terrific job working at a big downtown law firm. Paige is teaching exercise at a health club, Sports Club/ LA."

Dustin grinned as though revisiting a picture of Tori's bombshell roommate in his head. "I like Paige. She's got guts. Great guts, great energy, and a great sense of humor," he said, both with amusement and admiration. "So, has she found herself her rich catch yet?"

Tori blushed, unable to recall exactly how much they had told Dustin. Knowing Paige, Tori figured she had told Dustin everything, unabashed and unabridged. Tori wondered if Dustin didn't have a slight thing for Paige. She remembered thinking so at the time.

"Not yet," she answered, thinking of Nicky Loomis, sure that Dustin would know who he was. "She's still dropping her bait."

"She'll probably draw up five at once," he kidded.

"Probably. But, meanwhile, the guy she's seeing every day is an economics professor at UCLA, who knows all about her rich-man agenda and is amused by it. Obviously he doesn't qualify, but he's hanging in there."

"Who knows, maybe love will triumph over money. What about you? I've heard this Bennetton character you're with is plenty loaded, here to purchase a couple hundred G's worth of polo ponies. Flew in on his own private jet—"

"I'm looking for love *and* money," Tori cut in, thinking she would be a whole lot better off if she were only kidding.

"And have you found it?" he persisted.

That was the million-dollar question—or billion-dollar, if she were to keep up with inflation. Who knew? She smiled, considering, glancing over toward Richard again. Was she in love? Could she be in love with him? Could he *stay* in love with her? He looked like the quintessential Marlboro man tonight, hard to resist in his faded jeans, work shirt, and cowboy boots. Tori definitely wanted to be in love with Richard, to be able to toss fate to the winds and let the pieces of her life fall wherever they were meant to fall. But it wasn't her nature. Her nature told her it was just too early to tell.

"Actually, I'm working for Richard. Bennetton Enterprises. They're in the building business—" she said, sidestepping his question, then smiling because she could see he was not going to let her off the hook so easily.

"Interesting job—" he observed. "Handsome young boss. Trips to South America. Y'all doing a housing project here?" he asked, plainly joking.

Tori just smiled again, raising an eyebrow. "Looks like you got put out of commission from your mountain climbing trek. What happened?" she asked, wisely rerouting their conversation.

"I shot myself in the foot," he said, frowning down at the injury.

"You *what*?" Tori broke up laughing, then felt bad and put her hand to her mouth to try to stop. "I'm sorry. That just sounds so—"

He shot her a mock dirty look as she continued to laugh, helping her out with the balance of her sentence. "Klutzy. Clumsy. Totally unmacho."

"Hmmm. *Totally,*" she agreed, still chuckling, sipping her wine while looking down at his cast. "It does sound pretty absurd, you know. Here you are off on this macho expedition, climbing the highest peaks across seven continents, and how do you get injured? You shoot yourself in the foot—"

"Well, I'm glad you find it so amusing. But it hurt like hell."

Tori winced. "I know. I'm sorry. I'm sure it did."

"Uh-huh—"

She watched as he took a thoughtful swallow of wine.

"You were climbing the Andes, I take it?" she said.

"About to. We had just flown in from Santiago a couple weeks ahead of schedule, and there was this raging blizzard going on. Everything was covered in snow.

"One of the guys suggested we wait out the brunt of the blizzard, hunting for guanacos in Mendoza—that's the wine country at the bottom of the Andes—and hold off on the climb for a day or so."

Tori wrapped her shawl more tightly around her shoulders. "Bad idea?" she asked, trying to imagine.

"Terrible idea. You couldn't see a thing through that blizzard. I was scared to death I'd end up shooting one of the guys instead of a goddamn guanaco. So I aimed a lot, just to amuse myself, but I never fired. Except once, accidentally, when I heard a gun shot that sounded too close for comfort, and I threw myself onto the ground to avoid getting hit and, in the process, managed to send a bullet from my own rifle whizzing past my ankle, fracturing the bone."

Tori apologized, grimacing. "God, I'm sorry I laughed," she said. "Poor you."

But Dustin was laughing right along with her. "Served me right," he said. "I'm a mountain climber, not a hunter. I should have stuck to mountain climbing."

"So are you going to have to go back to the States?"

"Hmmm, and move in with the three of you?" he considered with a lingering grin. "It's tempting, but I think I'm here for the duration. Another couple of days and this thing comes off."

"The doctor said you could continue climbing?" Tori was surprised.

"No, but Alejandro's *vet* said to go for it. I figured if he's good enough for Carballo's twenty-thousand-dollar polo ponies, he's good enough for me."

Tori thought he was a little crazy, but she liked his spirit. "How do you know Elena and Alejandro? You a polo player too?"

"No. We met years ago in Egypt—"

A loud *gong* resonated through the air from where a ranch hand sounded it, signaling them all to dinner, creating a hungry stir.

Dustin, inhaling the rich barbecue aroma that pervaded the air, put his arm around Tori again and escorted her, hobbling, toward the table. "California definitely agrees with you. That, or I'd just forgotten what a knockout you are. Maybe I *should* give my poor little ankle a rest and head straight back for the States. If it weren't for Bennetton, I'd be booking my flight home right now."

Tori flashed him a dubious look. He was funny, cute, down-to-earth, and she liked him.

"So you haven't told me, how're my good friends Kit and George?" he wondered.

"Great. Kit's pregnant," she informed him excitedly.

He smiled broadly, looking genuinely pleased. "That was fast work."

"What did I tell you about keeping an eye on these two?" Alejandro mischievously reminded Richard, as the four of them came together, awaiting seating assignments by their hostess.

Richard, only feigning concern, put his arm around Tori's waist, displacing Dustin, and kissed her proprietarily on the lips.

Dinner was served out on the courtyard, around one long table, with the cooked meats arranged on huge platters, being passed around by the ranch hands. There were also big plates of crusty bread for them to make their own sandwiches, big rustic bowls filled with colorful medleys of salads—tomatoes and onions, green salad, celery salad, shredded carrot salad, everything served vinaigrette. Perfect-tasting ears of corn, handpicked that day from the fields, were also brought out to the table, along with a big basket of fruit with bowls of water to wash it.

Everyone was very friendly, and the general table discussions were all spoken in English for the benefit of the Americans present. Tori was seated next to her host, Alejandro, while Richard and Dustin flanked Alejandro's wife, Elena, down at the other end of the table. The conversations were lively and spirited, heated at times. Especially on the subject of inflation, which Alejandro leaned over to inform Tori was a subject that was never absent from a single meal.

"Doesn't it give you indigestion?" Tori wondered, biting into a delicious-tasting *chinchulines,* the size of a finger, curled.

"Always. There's no excuse for it. We have the best natural resources here, you know. The best. Cattle, wheat, corn, minerals. Our country should be wealthy, our economy flourishing. And instead, the whole thing's a disaster.

"The budget is perpetually out of balance and to correct it the government just keeps printing more money, devaluating it, giving it new names. They took the peso, and changed it to something called a *peso ley,* took the *peso ley* and changed it to *peso nuevo,* on and on until it got so completely out of control that a million-peso bill became worth only two American dollars. After that, the geniuses decided to chop about four zeros from the peso and change the name of the currency altogether, calling it an *austral* instead of a *peso.* For a while we felt like we were making a comeback. A great economic recovery. The *austral* was at eighty cents to a dollar, and everyone felt optimistic. But that was only temporary. The *austral* is sliding back down, and God only knows what it will be worth next week. The government is trying to do something about it, but—"

Alejandro threw up his hands, as though to say, what could he do. "The military flunked the test, so now these fellows are trying to strengthen the economy, but it's an uphill battle."

"And take a wild guess at who's going to get squashed in the battle. Lousy leftists—" Alejandro's cousin Clemente complained, referring to Argentina's present constitutional government and its civilian president. "Alfonsin went to school with Mitterrand. He's a socialist. We were better off with the military in control."

"Never better off with the military," someone else put in

"If only we could have a civilian president . . . if only we could go back to the military," Elena mimicked. "I'm so bored with this. We vote a government in and then about three weeks

later everyone is already turned around and against them. As soon as they try to tighten belts, *poof,* then nobody likes them."

"Do *you* like them, Elena?" Alejandro teased his wife from across the table. "They're raising our local and export taxes on meat again. That cuts directly into your shopping budget you know—"

"No, darling, anything but that. Quick bring back the junta," Elena sparred playfully with her husband, her hazel eyes flashing in a bewitching contrast to her ginger-tan skin. Like all the other Argentine women at the table, she was an ardent sun worshiper, tan for them being almost as significant as money. "And speaking of shopping, Tori, when you get to Buenos Aires, don't bother with Florida Street. It's way too touristy now. Richard, darling, take her into the *La Recoleta* district—"

"Oh, are *you* in trouble!" Alejandro empathized. A few of the men at the table snickered their sentiments.

Elena gestured to her husband to mind his own business. "It's expensive, but they have great things. Also some great antique shops—"

Tori caught Dustin Brent looking at her, raising his eyebrows in a knowing way.

"Thanks a million, Elena," Richard joked, hitting his palm to his forehead in mock concern.

From shopping tips they moved to travel tips, talking about the mystical and daring Death Train excursion Tori and Richard were planning on taking. About Brazil. What was happening in real estate there now, in São Paulo. Back to complaining about the government, and finally into the most sobering topic, about the *desaparecidos,* the missing people. A couple of days ago there had been a bombing in one of the banks in Buenos Aires, and there was fear that terrorism was starting up again.

One of the guests at the table had lost a sister and an infant niece a couple of years ago, during the last military regime, and the family was still looking for the baby, believing that, like many of the other children whose parents had disappeared, their niece had been taken and given up for adoption. It wasn't an uncommon story, unfortunately. Apparently, the sister had worked at the university, associated with a lot of radicals, and it had been no surprise when she had suddenly vanished. But of course that had been under the military regime. The same regime so many of the wealthy Argentines now wanted back in power.

After dinner, during dessert and coffee, the tone changed and became partylike again. Alejandro brought out a few guitars, and everyone sat around in the courtyard, away from the table, singing regional folkloric songs, swaying to the music, laughing, and joining in. It was a spectacular night, full of music, stirring Latin love songs and more stars in the sky than Tori had ever seen before. The moon was an awesome round ball. Sharing a hammock beneath its soft light, propped up by pillows, Tori and Richard lay together with their arms around each other, drinking and feeling happily swept into the mood. Although neither of them spoke Spanish, they were at least able to join in on some of the more redundant refrains, singing gaily along and probably butchering the piece. Dustin's Spanish seemed to be flawless as he sang right along with the others, even accepting a guitar at one point and playing as well.

"Alejandro thinks you're *la máxima*," Richard whispered into her ear. He had the faint scent of whiskey on his breath. It filled her nostrils, smelled sexy, nice.

"Yeah. He's got good taste." Tori felt contentment wash over her as Richard squeezed her hand.

"Marry me," he murmured softly, nuzzling her neck with the tip of his wonderful nose. "They've got their own private chapel right here on the ranch, a service tomorrow morning. We'll borrow the priest and have him marry us."

"We're not Catholic," Tori reminded him, shimmying involuntarily as he kissed her behind the ear.

"So, we'll convert."

"I don't want to convert."

"So, I'll offer him some *pesos*."

"You can't buy off a priest."

"Watch me."

"Richard, you're crazy."

"Hummm. I know. But marry me anyway."

"We don't even know each other."

"That's part of the excitement. And I know I'm going to love every new phase of you that I unravel."

Tori laughed, high again, her head in a cloud. Speeding faster and faster, too full of wine and good food. Too full of steamy Latin music and fantasies, when she was a die-hard realist at heart. While she didn't trust his impetuousness, the offer was powerfully heady.

"Okay. What do you need to know about me first?" Richard asked cooperatively, shifting up over onto his side so he could see her face.

"I don't know," she said.

"Ask me anything. It can be as personal as you want. *But marry me.*" His deep marine eyes flickered and made her smile, evoking paradise, a hidden cove of water somewhere in the Caribbean, warm, safe, and full of unimaginable pleasures. *I want to love this man,* she thought. *I want to trust him.*

"How many other women have you proposed to?" she asked.

"Before my sixth birthday, or *after*? Between four and five I was really into marriage," he admitted.

She played with his hair that was growing long and sexy at the nape of his neck. "Then what happened?"

"I got into dinosaurs."

"And then?"

"Space."

"And then?"

"Model cars."

"And then?"

"The Beatles."

"And now?"

"You," he said kissing her sensuously on the lips. "Will you marry me?"

"If this still feels this good in Machu Pichu I might have to," Tori answered, scaring herself half to death at the recklessness of her words. She felt Dustin Brent's eyes on her as Richard whispered in her ear that he couldn't wait to get back to their room and make love to her. God, what if she came home from this trip married? Mrs. Richard Bennetton. Tori Bennetton. Or would she keep her own last name? Babies? Did he want more kids? What was she even thinking? She honestly didn't know him, other than what he wanted her to know about himself. She still wasn't over Travis. And she hadn't discouraged Dustin Brent from sending a raft of flirtatious glances her way all throughout the evening. She was plainly screwed up.

"You think too much," Richard told her, and she couldn't help but wonder if he didn't know her better than she thought.

"Anyone up for a midnight ride?" Alejandro asked, setting down his guitar and rising up to his feet to take a count. "My horses are in their glory at night during a full moon—"

There were a few incurable romantics who couldn't pass up the offer, Richard among them. Tori was surprised when he slipped out of the hammock and whisked her up into his arms, volunteering the two of them. It was a wildly romantic notion and she felt charged with excitement, renewed as she watched the ranch hands armed with jackets and flashlights, distributing them. She looked to see who else was going. Ignasio and his wife, Lita. Mariana, Clemente, Alejandro. And, she had to give him credit, Dustin Brent, cast and all.

The more energetic guests mounted the gorgeous animals, which the ranch hands brought round for them, and they all took off, equipped with flashlights and silver flasks provided by their host, riding off into the wondrous moonlit Argentine night.

Chapter 18

Susan had been working such grueling hours that she had fallen asleep in the library at her law firm, her head supported by a thick stack of computer printouts, her glasses lopsided at the tip of her nose. There were legal volumes, pulled from the rich walnut bookshelves, spread in every direction across the immense conference table, her clients' files, her own notes, her dictaphone, and about a dozen pencils, all of them worn down because she had been too lazy to keep having to sharpen them.

A hand on her shoulder jarred her awake, and she had to squint at the early morning sunlight disorienting her as it imposed itself into the plush, oval-shaped room.

"Susan?" It was Mr. Kreegle, one of the letterhead partners, a short, funny man without much hair but with the warmest smile. "Good God, what are you doing here? You've only been with the firm a few months—you bucking for a raise, an early partnership —or did you get into a fight with a boyfriend?" he asked sweetly.

Susan looked up at him, pushing her glasses back into place, feeling herself turning crimson. "First I have to *find* the boyfriend," she lamented. "No, I just wanted to get through this Mutual Cable case and I knew I wouldn't be able to sleep until I'd finished."

"I guess you were wrong. You were sleeping like a baby."

Susan looked down at the mess in front of her, just to be sure she hadn't only dreamed that she had finished it. "As a matter of fact," she said with a sleepy smile, indicating the work in front of her. "Mutual Cable contracts—done!" Feeling groggy but content with accomplishment, she looked at her watch and winced. "Seven-thirty. Time to run home for a quick shower." Then as an afterthought she added, "Hey, what are *you* doing here so early, Kreegle? Bucking for a raise?" she teased the senior partner.

He smirked and announced that his gorgeous wife, who was leaning against the door behind Susan, looking radiant, untired, unharassed, wearing chic chamois western-styled jeans and shirt, was on her way to rest up at the Golden Door health spa. "Susan, you've met Liz," he said, as Liz breezed in toward them.

"Sure. Hi," Susan said self-consciously, feeling like a mess, imagining circles under her eyes, wishing she could at least sneak on some lipstick, swallow some mouthwash. *Oh, the hell with it.*

"Teddy needed me to sign some papers," Liz explained. "We just bought a place in Aspen. You'll have to come skiing with us sometime. Maybe *I* can work on finding that boyfriend for you." She had on a pretty shade of glossy melon lipstick that matched her earrings. Her teeth were perfect, as if she had them buffed at the dentist every couple of months.

"Matchmaking is Liz's specialty," Kreegle said.

Susan smiled politely, feeling exhaustion creep in as the obviously happy-together couple began to walk out of the library arm in arm. Kreegle paused to put his hand on Susan's shoulder one last time and gave her a warm squeeze. "I'd tell you to go home and take a nap, not come in until eleven or so, but I need you out on a strike problem that's suddenly escalated at one of our clients' factories out in Commerce. Dickson was handling it, but his wife just had a baby about an hour ago, and I'm afraid we're going to need you out there today. I'll brief you as soon as you get back," he said. "Oh, and it's best you don't take your own car. Leave your secretary a note to get you a rental. I hear it's gotten pretty rough—"

Susan was used to field-rough, but not factory-rough. His warning made her wonder. But on the other hand, after all the boring paperwork she had been doing, she realized she would welcome the change of pace.

"Teddy, honey, I hate to rush you, but I'm going to miss my ride," Liz said apologetically. It was her turn to look at her watch.

"Sorry, sweetheart. Susan, I'll have to catch up with you after—"

"Sure. No problem." Susan stifled a yawn as she watched the two of them disappear through the doorway and down the hall. She could hear the clicking of Liz's palomino-colored suede boots on the firm's hardwood floors, the melodic sound of her carefree laugh. Liz and Susan were about the same age, and Susan was surprised to find herself feeling envious. Having a profession had been so critical to Susan, so essential. She had sacrificed her marriage for it; she had sacrificed her twenties. But suddenly, sitting here too dead tired to move, considering the life of her contemporary, she had to wonder about who had chosen the smarter path, whose life was richer and more fulfilling. At the moment, Susan believed there was no contest.

What was so wonderful and satisfying about working her ass off as an attorney, falling asleep over dull and lengthy documents? As usual, Paige was right. How clever to let someone else do all the work and just get to enjoy life, to play, and to be supported. Kreegle's wife could hardly be accused of being dull or a parasite. She was active in the contemporary art museum, bringing into the fore budding artists. She was a talented potter herself. She always looked perfect, was able to fly off to Europe to buy the latest designer collections, had time to master the various languages of the countries to which she traveled. She had *time* to read newspapers cover to cover, *The Los Angeles Times, The New York Times,* to be informed and well read. She had time to maintain an impressive seventeen handicap on the golf course, ski, play tennis. Participate in worthwhile causes. And raise her two adorable little kids.

So Susan had her career. That was clearly all she had. That and a case of bloodshot eyes from straining over small print all night long.

* * *

In the short time it had taken Susan to drive home, shower, get dressed, and wolf down breakfast, the sun had vanished behind thick, fast-moving clouds the color of coal, which looked ready to burst with a downpour at any second.

Flying out the door, she bumped into Mark just arriving on his motorcycle, a beat-up helmet on his wonderful head, golden curls still visible beneath it. He kissed her a quick hello as she hurried past him, seemingly oblivious of the fact that he had broken her heart.

"You look fantastic," he said, grabbing her hand and detaining her a moment longer, breaking down the defenses she kept thinking she had constructed so immutably in his absence.

Then why are you mooning over my roommate instead of me, she wanted to snap. Instead, she smiled and produced a breezy thank you, inwardly thanking God for the invention of makeup that had blessedly concealed last night's all-nighter. She was wearing a lightweight winter-white suit, a knockoff of this year's Chanel, or so the woman who had sold it to her had claimed. Her briefcase added just the right touch. It made her feel secure.

"Paige and I are catching a movie tonight. Want to join us?" he asked, following her to her car and opening the door for her.

"Thanks. But I may have to work late tonight," she answered, scooting inside.

"Never going to snare that eligible multimillionaire if you keep working these hours," he was quick to tease her, his blue eyes connecting with hers, both from behind pairs of glasses, making her think of the beautifully blue-eyed but farsighted kids they could have together.

"I may just be on my way to *snare* one now," she replied too sharply, regretting the remark immediately after she had said it.

As sweet as ever, Mark closed her door for her, tucking her skirt inside so that it wouldn't get caught. All day long she knew she would be remembering the feel of his hand passing along her thigh, touching her knee.

And yet he was probably going upstairs right now to screw his brains out with Paige. Damn it all. Mostly damn Paige.

Only an hour later, driving toward the City of Commerce in

her rented Toyota, with her windshield wipers swiping at the torrent of rain, having been briefed by Kreegle on her assignment, Susan found herself part nervous, part excited, part amused. As it turned out, she *was* on her way to meet with one of those eligible multimillionaires Mark had been ribbing her about, though *snaring* him appeared unlikely.

Her destination was a factory that manufactured fiberglass hot tubs, catamarans, Windsurfers, surfboards, and dinghies. The *client,* and owner of the company, it turned out, was none other than Kit and George's friend, Susan's dinner partner of the other night, the "Rat" who had never bothered to ask her for her phone number or call. She wondered what his response would be when he saw her. God, L.A. was turning out to be as small a town as small-town Stockton.

According to Kreegle, Jack Wells' factory was in a state of severe upheaval. Only a couple of months ago Jack's workers had voted to bring in the Teamsters' union, claiming unsafe working conditions, inequitable treatment, no health insurance, low pay: and now management was in the throes of heated union negotiations, with the workers out on strike because of management and union's inability to come to terms.

The unruliness was increasing daily as the truckloads of replacements continued crossing the picket lines, inciting a mounting rage and uproar among the strikers that was apparently getting out of control.

No wonder Jack's stance on unions had been so adamant. Probably *that* was why he had neglected to pursue her, she tried to rationalize, though weakly. He had sensed where her real sympathies lay . . .

All personal thoughts of Jack Wells and Mark flew out of Susan's head the moment she actually drove up to the plant. She found she had entered a near war zone. There was virtual pandemonium, with yelling and screaming and egg throwing. A truck was being torn apart as a horde of enraged strikers broke a shipload of surfboards in half, while others smashed bottles in the driveway that was already ankle-deep in the sharp debris so that the armored trucks bringing in the replacements would be obstructed from driving through.

Susan was just considering turning around and getting the hell out of there, thinking she would never get through this bedlam and into the building in one piece, when suddenly one of the big armored trucks full of replacements came barreling up from behind her, going maybe forty miles an hour and causing her to have to swerve out of the way, nearly running down a throng of picketers and finally crashing into one of the garbage cans that had the traditional strike fire blazing within it.

The fire had her terrified, and she tried to get out of the car but could not. First of all, the door was locked and she couldn't figure out how to unlock it. Where was the button or the latch on this damn rental? There were people pounding at her windows; someone had smashed open the one on the passenger's side; there was a hose spraying water; and, for the life of her, she couldn't work the contraption that released the seat-belt harness. The noise was almost as upsetting as the flames beginning to lap at the front of her car, and she was having trouble breathing, although she couldn't tell if it was because of the smoke or her own suffocating panic, the thought of the car blowing up, premonitions of further disaster reeling in her head.

She remembered thinking she needed a white flag in order to emerge safely. She remembered worrying about the papers in her briefcase, the letter in there from her mother that she had not yet gotten to read, which she had only just picked up this morning from the house. And then she remembered nothing.

"Feel any better?"

Susan was sitting in a plain, industrial-looking office, not much bigger than her own, that looked carelessly thrown together with an old, commercial-type desk and drab walls that had pictures and ad campaigns of the various products Jack Wells' company manufactured. The windows looked down into the plant itself instead of outside, with the noise, she presumed to be deafening because of the workers' protective ear coverings, sealed out.

Jack Wells himself was sitting close to Susan, administering a towel with ice to her forehead, which felt more frozen than bruised. She kept trying to keep her hands from shaking as she held unsteadily onto a Styrofoam cup filled with water.

She nodded, and then smiled self-consciously. "I'm fine. Embarrassed, but fine."

He removed the improvised ice pack and set it onto the desk. "Embarrassed? Why should you be embarrassed? Those guys are maniacs out there. I can't believe your firm even sent you over here, with what's been going on this week—"

Susan was about to argue. This was, after all, her job and the incident had nothing to do with her being female, which was what he was getting at; it had to do with her driving a dinky Toyota instead of a monstrous armored machine. The same thing would have happened to Joe Dickson, her colleague who had been in on the bulk of the union negotiations, but Jack cut her off, reapplying the ice and smiling as he read her thoughts.

"Okay, Dickson probably wouldn't have fared any better. He just wouldn't have looked as pretty or as vulnerable, and so we wouldn't have made such a fuss over him. I'd have let him hold his own damn ice pack." Jack grinned again. He was dressed like one of the workers in a plaid lumberjack-type shirt, grubby jeans, and a Budweiser cap crooked on his head, the look definitely more his style than the put-together dinner clothes she had seen him in at Kit's. With his shirt sleeves rolled up she was able to get a good look at the tattoo on his forearm, though she still couldn't decipher what the design was intended to be, other than that it was clearly Oriental and strangely exotic.

"It looks like you're going to be stuck with me for a while anyway, *female* or not," she informed him. "Joe will be here tomorrow and the rest of the week to smooth the transition of my replacing him, but he's taking off a month for maternity leave starting next week."

"Maternity leave? What is this?" he asked, as though she were joking, unconsciously rubbing at the persistent growth along his jaw, which she remembered as being heavy from last time.

"It's a new world," she reminded him, taking a sip of her water, feeling herself beginning to relax. "His wife is a gynecologist, and it's tougher for her to take time off than it is for him. She had only two hours of labor, no episiotomy, feels fine, and is ready to go back to work. The law firm gives *two* months maternity leave to all its female lawyers, so this morning Joe requested half of the same privilege."

"What about all those fancy nurses or nannies?"

"Joe thinks the first month or two is critical for bonding. He doesn't want the baby bonded with a stranger. Actually, we're all having a lot of fun with it." Susan winced because the ice pack was getting too cold again and she took it from his hands, setting it back onto the desk.

"You're going to have a nice bump," he diagnosed, examining her forehead with his fingers.

She helped herself to a metal letter opener from his desk and by angling the blade was able to assess the damage through the reflection. Unsurprisingly, her forehead was swollen and gaining in color, but with a quick adjustment of her bangs she had it nearly hidden. "What bump?" she asked with a cavalier shrug, and they both smiled.

"So here we are talking babies again," he said.

The reference to the night when he had neglected to ask her for her phone number caught her up short, but she laughed in spite of her bruised ego.

"Honestly, Susan, with all this violence and uproar, I still don't get why your firm didn't replace Dickson with a man," Jack said as diplomatically as possible. "I'm serious. It's really gotten rough. You saw what's going on here."

Susan glanced evasively over at a framed newspaper clipping of Jack sitting on a stretch of untamed beach in the midst of a bunch of eager Chinese, all wearing straw hats and broad grins, a couple of surfboards wedged into the sand, accenting the photo. The caption read Surfing Diplomacy Goes to China.

He followed her gaze, waiting for her to respond.

"Believe it or not, I'm an ace labor lawyer," she said smiling to soften the cockiness of her reply. But the fact was she wanted this assignment. She didn't want to remain in the law firm, pencil pushing; she wanted an opportunity to prove herself. "Why don't you wait a few days before you start complaining," she suggested in a firm but friendly challenge.

"I wasn't complaining, and I'm sure you *are* an ace labor lawyer. I'd just hate to see you a mauled labor lawyer. One egg on your head ought to be enough," he added, touching the throbbing memento she already sported.

"Just think of me as one of those five seven, wiry, and supremely courageous Tunnel Rats," she joked, watching carefully for his reaction.

He threw up his hands and slouched back in his chair, resigned but not displeased. "Tunnel Rat, eh? I guess that means I'll have to lend you my TR badge and bush hat."

"Sounds good to me. What color is the hat?" she wondered, glad because she could see by the amused curve of his thin lips that she was finally winning him over.

"It'll look great on you. And I must say, counselor, I like your spunk."

Susan only wished she were as spunky as she sounded now. This was going to be a tough act to keep up. She was just plain, shy Susan, wired now because of all that had happened. "What's this—Surfing Diplomacy Goes to China?" she asked, curious about the clipping on his wall, his fixation with the Far East.

"A little over a year ago I organized an expedition to introduce surfing to China, the first surfin' safari to hit the People's Republic—" Jack glanced over at the photo, readjusting his Budweiser cap. "This was shot on Hainan Island."

"Where's that?"

"Off the coast of North Vietnam. Between the Gulf of Tonkin and the South China Sea. They've got a lot of great virgin coastline."

"A slump in American sales?" Susan teased.

"Not funny," Jack joked back, pointing a finger at her.

A loud beep coming from the telephone interrupted them, and they both turned toward it. "Jack, Malcolm Lear just called from his car phone. He's been stuck in traffic, but he said they're only about twenty minutes away." It was the husky, smoker's voice of his secretary.

"Union agents," Jack explained to Susan.

She nodded, already having been briefed on the cast of players to expect at the negotiating meeting. There would be the Teamsters' agents, Malcolm Lear, a beefy guy with a bad temper, and his shadow, Buddy Clayton, a beefy guy with no temper, who had the soul of a social worker trapped inside the body of a thug. Also present would be a committee of four employees who Joe Dickson had said weren't long for their jobs anyway, because they were the ones who were holding up the works, voting everything down, imposing the stalemate. Jack was apparently champing at the bit to get them all canned, which was tricky to do legally. And of course there was the company committee, Jack himself, his general manager, Carlos Urizer, and his attorney, formerly Joe Dickson, now, at least for the time being, Susan.

"The meeting won't start for another thirty minutes or so. You up for a quick tour before we get started?" Jack asked, rising up from his chair.

Susan checked her watch. One of the things Kreegle had stressed was that she be sure to get statements from the witnesses about the violence of the strikers on the picket lines, some additional statements from the replacements inside, and from the union officials too. They were trying to get as many strikers fired as possible to finally tip the voting ratio, since they all knew the Teamsters could exercise some muscle over the replacements' vote. The incriminating statements were crucial since, legally, a worker couldn't be fired for striking, but he *could* be fired for causing violence on the picket line, and Jack made no bones about it: he wanted the worst of the troublemakers caught in the act and axed. The negotiations had been going on so long that, at this point, all union and management both wanted was to get a contract agreed upon and signed.

Guessing what she was thinking, Jack told her she could get the statements tomorrow. Nothing was going to change, he assured her. "You've seen the strikers in action. Come see what it is they're *supposed* to be doing."

Susan had to smile as she followed him out of his office because she could see how eager he was to show off the huge and clearly productive plant that he had built entirely on his own.

In the forty-five minutes it took to tour the factory, with Jack carrying around a cordless phone and accepting dozens of brief, to-the-point phone calls along the way, Susan felt as if she were learning everything there was to know about the production of hot tubs, catamarans, dinghies, Windsurfers and surfboards, viewing the procedure through glass-lined corridors. The plant was noisy, colorful, and exciting, with everyone working at a pace that seemed almost frantic.

For the hot tubs, the process began with ceramic-and-metal molds of varying shapes. The molds were sprayed with hot liquid fiberglass, which shot out of thick, unwieldy-looking hoses. In that division, everyone wore masks. The smell was apparently awful and the fumes dangerous. The procedure demanded working quickly because the fiberglass would harden almost immediately, leaving a lot of chance for error, something the workers were up in arms about because they were held personally accountable, getting docked in pay for any imperfections, though *they* blamed the cause of the imperfections on imperfect materials, cheap resin, and flawed molds. The tubs, after being sprayed, were moved into either heated rooms or ovens to dry. Then to separate the fiberglass from the molds, workers would force air through heavy hoses between the mold and the tub, causing the dried fiberglass to pop free.

The procedure for manufacturing Windsurfers and surfboards Susan found to be equally fascinating to watch. They would begin with huge old blocks of Styrofoam, which would be skillfully sanded with an electrical sander into the appropriate and familiar shapes. Thin sheets of fiberglass were then stretched onto the shaped foam and, after that, the fiberglass was painted with vibrant colors. The workers' grievances in this area were that the Styrofoam used in making the Windsurfers and surfboards was a by-product of gasoline, and the dust created by the electric sanders was dangerous since the body is incapable of breaking down any form of gasoline. Another dispute was that production people on the Windsurfers and surfboards were sometimes given bad gloves, or no gloves at all when they ran out, and ended up with glass particles embedded in their skin from stretching the fiberglass sheets over the forms.

Watching the buzz of activity and the staggering output, it was difficult to even remember that there was a strike going on outside. Jack Wells was hardly being put out of business.

The factory was substantially larger than it appeared to be from the outside, and Susan presumed that Jack had to be making an extraordinary living from the water sports industry of America, hot tubs included as sport. She couldn't help but feel the spirit of Paige trailing behind her, performing an extensive mental inventory, calculating copious profits. Worse still, Susan had already spent so much time with Paige that she could even hear her brazen roommate's words, clear as day, as though she were watching from some invisible post, her advice reverberating plainly in Susan's head. *Think of the easy life your boss's wife has, Kreegle's well-rested, gorgeously outfitted, well-traveled wife . . . shouldering none of the financial responsibility. Free to do what she wants. Free from the monotony and pressure of work. Think of Kreegle's well-rested, gorgeously outfitted, well-traveled wife . . .*" Paige's telepathic message came through unrelenting, unambiguous.

"Here, have a sailboat," Jack said when they were all through with their tour. Susan couldn't believe the size of the souvenir he was thrusting on her. "Do you know how to sail?"

"Yes. But, I can't accept this," she objected, as he hollered instructions to one of his men to crate up the sabot-type sailboat for her and have it sent.

"You do?" he asked, looking surprised, and continuing to ignore her protests. "Where'd you learn how to sail, hailing from inland and coming from a trailer park? I was hoping to toss in private lessons as part of the package."

Susan felt a tingle of pleasure at his recall, and was definitely flattered by his offer. "San Francisco Bay," she answered. "It was my weekend escape during law school. But honestly, Jack, I really can't accept this kind of gift."

"Why not?"

"I don't know. It's unprofessional—" she tried, but they both started to laugh.

"No, unprofessional is being late to our meeting," he argued, pointing to the clock on the wall that indicated they were already fifteen minutes late. "Oh, and tell the firm that as far as I'm concerned they ought to give the new father *two* months maternity leave," he added. "As long as we're all keeping the kinds of hours we're keeping—these meetings can go on until midnight—

I'd sure as hell rather be working around the clock with you.
. . . No offense to Joe," he joked.

Susan laughed, finding his smile hard to resist, *unable* to resist
a quick glance back at her new sailboat.

Chapter 19 ~

From the moment Nicky Loomis had seen her on the dance floor, he had known not only that they would meet but that it would be more than just an ordinary encounter. She reminded him of himself twenty years ago, when he had been known as "lightning legs Loomis," the great wide receiver of the Green Bay Packers, out to conquer, out to play, to win and to love, so that it was always one for the records.

That thick mane of russet-colored hair that she would unconsciously sweep up off of her face, her sassy smile, those wild green eyes, the color of new money, continued to haunt him with ever-increasing clarity.

He couldn't get the feel of her out of his mind, the smooth, sensual quality of her skin, her shapely curves and the way she knew how to use them, sweeping against him, making him aware of every square inch of his body, of her body, so that only kissing, with which he ordinarily tried to dispense, had taken him back to the days when he had to worry about his passion exploding in his pants.

He hadn't been long in the bathroom, fussing over his hair, swishing some of the hotel's complimentary mouthwash in his mouth, taking a leak, then manipulating his cock back into an erection so that he could put on the rubber. With his penis erect and shielded, breath freshened, and ready to fuck her brains out, he had emerged from the bathroom in sweet anticipation of finding her already nude in bed waiting for him, hot, wet, and wanting.

When he found the bed undisturbed, vacant, flowers intact across the pillows, he had simply presumed she was in the bathroom off the living room, that she would be joining him momentarily.

He remembered lying there alone beneath the cool sheets, stroking himself as he waited for her, envisioning her rapturous bare form, thinking about her on top, riding him, his hands overflowing with those ripe breasts. Then he had imagined her there, *along with* the Bobbsey Twins, their three sumptuous bodies entangled all around him, devoted to pleasing him, the redhead's mouth on his cock, the blonde's mouth on his thighs, Paige's mouth on his mouth, creating a great panoply of legs, breasts, and taut rear ends—an enviable collection of perfect but varied female forms.

Beyond paradise.

Still stirred, he recalled how his thoughts had then jumped to business, to their upcoming hockey-season blackboard, where they were in the midst of making some final decisions, to the storm reportedly moving up from Mexico, threatening death at the box office for the following night's tennis matches.

Rain and peak news events pouring in all in one day insured instant indigestion.

After awhile, growing curious at Paige's failure to materialize, Nicky had finally gotten out of bed and gone into the living room to look for her.

He remembered thinking it would be just like her to have something wild and wanton planned for him in there, to keep him on his toes. Another game, another surprise.

He had pictured her nude on a fur spread in front of a lit fireplace, or even lying below the great span of window, illuminated by moonlight, drinking champagne straight from the bottle, ready to pour it all over him and lick it off. He expected to discover her with an impish look on her ravishing face, primed to play and tease him into blissful exhaustion.

What a shock he had had when he found her gone, himself stranded, without his tuxedo, his underwear, without anything except his lipstick-graffitied tux shirt bearing a message obviously meant to put him in his place.

And that it had. With a towel wrapped around his waist, he had relaxed down onto the couch to polish off the rest of the champagne and enjoy a good laugh. He had always been a good sport, and he took in Paige's ploy with surprise and hearty appreciation, wanting her even more than before.

This broad was going to be a real challenge, for a change, he had noted, eyeing the comical outfit she had sent up for him. This had been her show and he had mistakenly tried to take over. He had treated her like all the other little groupies he was accustomed to having just lie back on the bed with their legs spread, and she was letting him know that she was not one of them.

He was the kind of man that even if he were robbed, if the crook did it well, he'd have to be impressed. He was impressed by Paige, by her style and ingenuity, by her guts.

Nothing near to this had ever happened to him before. The way in which she had orchestrated this whole thing in the first place, getting herself invited to his home, cutting off her dress and sending it to him the way she had, exchanging their respective dates, and then succeeding in luring him up here to a scene that had been admirably set.

On *her* terms she had taken him to *her* room to lay *him*.

Which was where he was sure he had gone wrong. He had tried to commandeer the controls. He had moved into automatic pilot once on top of her on the couch, dispensing with the requisite foreplay too abruptly, making a premature dive for one of his trusty rubbers, and then hitting her with those smug, admittedly insensitive remarks, especially the one about the Bobbsey Twins.

However, while he was a man who enjoyed being taught a lesson, he hadn't banked on not being able to track her down afterward.

He had tried everything. First, the desk clerk at the Château

Marmont, only to learn with a mix of frustration and fascination that her suite had been registered under the name of *Joe Smith.*

There was no phone number, no address, no credit card by which to trace her, something he found surprising since he was sure she would *want* to be found.

The Aston-Martin Lagonda she had been said to be driving, the parking lot attendant claimed had no plates. Nicky couldn't help but wonder about the two-hundred-thousand-dollar English car. Who was this gal?

Amused and intrigued, he had plodded on, trying the telephone book, where there was no listing, pulling strings with contacts at the Department of Motor Vehicles, which had no record of a California driver's license ever being issued to any Paige Williams. He even had his secretary locate this Stan Parker, with whom Paige had supposedly gone to his party. But when they had gotten him on the phone in Philadelphia, where he lived, he claimed to know nobody by the name Paige Williams.

Later, Nicky learned that Stan Parker was married and attributed his plea of ignorance to the fact that his wife's family owned the company of which he was president.

It did occur to him that Paige Williams might not be her real name, but his instinct told him that it was. She responded too naturally when addressed. The name suited her.

He found it curious to realize that they had talked only about him; they hadn't talked about her at all. He had no idea where or if she worked. Where she lived. Or who her friends were.

"Your Cinderella obsession again? I can't wait to meet her," exclaimed Nicky Loomis's attractive daughter, Marni.

They were in his office at the StarDome, where she had dropped in to visit him, and she snatched the photograph of her father's mysterious obsession from out of his hands, softening her gesture with a kiss on the cheek.

The StarDome, built by Nicky Loomis only ten years ago, was located in the San Fernando Valley, near the Burbank Studios. His office, housed within the large domed sports arena complex, was cluttered and buzzing with commotion. There were people wandering in and out to consult the blackboard of events slated for the StarDome, a separate blackboard of events slated for other stadiums, plus a network- and cable-ratings readout featured on a large-screen terminal. Leaning up against a dated-looking hunter green plaid couch was the final mock-up for the hockey billboard about to go up on the Strip, to be seen as well riding along the sides of nearly twenty-five hundred buses across the Los Angeles metropolitan area.

Familiar faces dominated the room; large color photographs of sporting events in dark wood frames eclipsed the walls, paying homage to Nicky's illustrious career and his unique life-style. There were photographs featuring McEnroe playing tennis, Nicky surrounded by Olympic gold medalists from the U.S. team, Nicky with his L.A. Stars hockey team, the Harlem Globetrotters, a shot of him with Pete Rose from the Cincinnati Reds. And there were a couple more weathered photographs of Nicky in his youth—one with him in a semihuddle formation with his teammates from the Green Bay Packers, another showing him with his arm around the man who had been like a father to him, the General Patton of sports, coach Vince Lombardi. Even idols had idols, and Vince Lombardi had been his.

Attesting to Nicky Loomis's obsession about staying fit was a framed spread from *Los Angeles Magazine,* with a glossy photo of Nicky in only a pair of gym shorts, flexing with a set of weights, featured in a special issue on celebrities and their private trainers.

Nicky leaned back in his chair, swiveling toward his daughter, who was curiously examining the photograph of Paige. He had found it in the pile of proofs that had been taken on Carnival Night at his house.

The two females, while close in age, both beautiful, bright, and savvy, weren't anything alike. While he sensed that Paige had street smarts, was as tough and unconventional as he was, a risk-taker, highly competitive, and choosing to live on the edge, his daughter, Marni, was the protected, soft, and extremely conventional product of all his money, her speech and carriage marking her privileged, moneyed, Ivy League background.

Father and daughter were mutually fascinated with each other. Marni put up with her father's often embarrassing antics, his endless stream of women half his age, his abandonment of her mother; and Nicky put up with his daughter's straitlaced snobbishness. Though different, the two were the best of friends. He had told her all about Paige and, while untrusting, his sleek, auburn-haired daughter was as caught up in the suspense of it all as he was.

"Maybe she simply didn't like you, Daddy," Marni teased him now, fiddling with the waistband of the leather pantsuit they had recently bought together in Italy. It was the color of Paige's almost iridescent green eyes. "Maybe you didn't work out to be the stud you're reputed to be—" she chided with a cruel wink.

Nicky gave his daughter a swat on the behind and laughed. "No. *That* was the problem. My being such a stud—"

"Yeah, you keep saying that, but y'know, you're getting up there. Pushing sixty . . . Or maybe she didn't like the way you kissed—"

"She loved the way I kissed, you little smartass," he teased back, patting his thinning head of hair into place.

"I think she's moved on to bigger and better—"

"You're such a little bitch. How'd I raise such a bitch?"

"Really, I'm just jealous, Daddy. Usually you don't give them even a passing thought. Now you've got a picture of her on your desk. There aren't even any pictures of *me* around here—"

"Bring one in for me. I'll put it on my desk."

Marni regarded the clutter. "Yeah, where?"

Nicky smiled, and slid some of the mess over to one side, freeing up a spot on his desk and patting it with his hand.

"Maybe it was just a joke—" Marni considered, back on the subject of Paige Williams again. "Played by one of the millions of teenyboppers you never called back. Like the one whose mother kept calling and pleading with you to see her precious Mary Jane again—"

"Her name was Mary Jane? I thought it was Sue Ellen—"

"Mary Jane. Sue Ellen—" Marni tossed Paige's picture back down onto Nicky's desk.

He picked it up, smiling because he loved looking at Paige. "A *joke*, huh? If it was all a joke, what's the punchline?"

Marni thought for a moment, looking away. Then curiously she seemed to change her mind.

Nicky, following her gaze, turned toward the door to his office, where his secretary was carrying in his shanghaied tuxedo, draped neatly with a plastic cleaners' bag. Stapled to it was a sack, presumably containing everything else he had on that night.

"This girl has nice timing. She probably has your office bugged—" Marni remarked drolly, catching his eye.

"And a messenger stationed at reception—" Nicky added, noting the royal blue writing printed across the clear plastic sheath. There was a receipt stapled onto it, and he tore it off, disappointed but not surprised to find that it bore his own name and address, not Paige's.

"Well, now we know she wasn't just out to steal your tux, Dad," Marni said, taking the dry-cleaned tux from his hand and moving primly over to hang it up in the closet.

Intrigued and relishing the game, Nicky balled up the receipt and tossed it into the trash, slouching back down thoughtfully into his chair, doodling on an unfinished crossword puzzle from his desk.

"Hold on a minute. Let me give this a try," Marni said, returning to retrieve the crumpled receipt, then picking up the phone from the opposite side of his desk and punching out the number.

"No way," Nicky said to her, more amused than frustrated, as she smiled at him. "There won't be any record . . . they won't have a clue who she is."

Marni put her finger to her lips. "Shhh," she ordered, but with her pretty face displaying a waning confidence.

Nicky leaned back in his chair and watched her, only half listening to his daughter's interrogation of the cleaners, who as he had guessed, knew nothing. It only confirmed how well he had this one pegged. Paige Williams remained, for now anyway, untraceable.

She was playing with him, and it would have been too simple if he could have tracked her down this way. She was going for more punch. The returning of his tux was probably simply so he wouldn't forget about her. She may not have even figured out yet how she was going to engineer their next meeting, but he had no doubt that when she did, it would be more dramatic than the cleaners.

"Whatever woman catches him will have to be a cheerleader, a prostitute, and a hell of a cook," Paige had determined, after three weeks' worth of extensive research on Nicky Loomis.

Following along with a Julia Childs videotape on the compact TV in the kitchen, whipping egg whites for the "no-fail" soufflé she was learning to master and, at the same time, trying to memorize football basics from one of the sports books she had checked out from the library, Paige let out an exasperated sigh.

Not only were the egg whites failing to form light, fluffy peaks and amass volume, but in one month's time, which was the timeframe she had allotted herself for research, she wondered if she would ever be able to absorb enough sports material to have anything worthwhile stick.

The day after her encounter with Nicky, Paige had headed straight for the library, culling a stack of sports-related titles, thinking that if she wanted to snare "Mr. Sports King" then she had better at least learn the vernacular.

She had already been through a series on basketball and hockey, undertaking them first because they were the two kinds of teams Nicky owned.

Current information, sports industry gossip, such as who was being traded to whom and why, salaries, drug problems, personality problems, Paige had been garnering from television broadcasts, magazines, and newspaper articles.

The book on football she was reading now, about Vince Lombardi, she had been especially interested in since she knew that Nicky not only used to play for the late, great coach, but that Vince Lombardi had helped shape his life. There hadn't been a single interview in which Nicky hadn't deified his old coach, crediting him with the success he had gone on to achieve in his later years, away from the football field.

But unfortunately the book was a whole lot drier than the man.

Chapter One: "Defensive Line Play . . . Linebackers and Defensive Backs. . . ."

A long, boring definition caused Paige to go on to Chapter Two, then Chapter Three, then back to Chapter One again, where she was intent on absorbing the fundamentals and techniques of the sport, the responsibilities of each player, the subtleties that were purported to make champions.

Tackles, defensive ends, linebackers, receivers. Passing, pass receiving, pass blocking, the kicking game, special teams.

She pored over a couple of the illustrations, trying to make sense of the diagrams, reading the same captions over and over again until something penetrated.

Good God, couldn't she have found Mr. Fashion King or Mr. Music Industry King or Mr. Movie King, or anything other than Mr. Sports King?

"And now . . ." Julia Childs' grating voice in the background, recaptured Paige's attention. "When your egg whites are all nice and white and frothy . . . *like this* . . ." she instructed.

Paige looked apprehensively away from Julia Childs' snowy concoction to regard the white slush in her own copper bowl and frowned. Disheartened, she switched off the electric beaters and pushed the bowl aside, attentive to the next series of directions. She and Julia both had a chocolate mixture cooling on their respective countertops, and she went to get hers, waiting for the next step, wondering why her sauce had gotten grainy-looking, when Julia's was as smooth as pudding, wondering why she was bothering with soufflés altogether.

Just because she had read how much Nicky liked to eat? Maybe he was a meat-and-potatoes man. Maybe he hated the sweet, airy stuff, preferring something into which he could sink his teeth. The man was a jock, not a gay gourmand. He probably liked plain old chocolate cake, cheesecake, and pie à la mode.

Besides, her arm was getting sore from having to hold it in that position over the bowl for so long, elbow up, wrist suspended over the bowl and moving in a circular motion.

It had been almost two weeks since Paige had returned Nicky's tuxedo to him, and she was beginning to grow uneasy about not having figured out what her next move should be. Daily, she racked her brain, devising different schemes, then discarding them.

She wanted to come up with something original, something that would make him laugh, perhaps something connected to sports.

If only she knew how to play hockey and could show up on his team, she mused, dumping the chocolate sauce and the gross-looking egg whites into the sink, also giving up on Vince Lombardi's football tips.

"So much for your unsinkable soufflé, Julia," she sneered aloud, snapping off the video, the oven, and then retreating into the den to watch the news. "Now all I'm left with is a mess on the maid's day off."

Allowing herself a handful of nuts, she rested back against the soft down pillows, watching Jerry Dunphy but not really listening. Once she got caught in the groove of trying to figure this thing out with Nicky, she could stay on it for hours, appearing to function on the outside but actually in a trance on the inside, fixated on her dilemma.

Nicky. When, where, and how. She had considered applying for a job at his office, imagined letting him discover her working there—his vanished Cinderella reappearing miraculously behind a Selectric or behind the wheel of one of his collection of limos as his chauffeur, her mass of hair swept up into the cap. But then she decided she didn't want to be one of a series of gold-digging female employees trying to lay her boss.

Thoroughly obsessed, she had even driven by his house numerous times, seen his daughter and son, both of whom she recognized from an article on his family, hoping through osmosis to gain a clue, any clue. Laughingly, she had pictured them having to address her as "Mom." *Hardly.*

She had also gone to some of the restaurants which she had read he frequented, The Palm, Morton's, and Jimmy's, hoping to see him there, though not yet ready to let him see her.

The doorbell rang and Paige, startled, looked at her watch, surprised to see how late it had gotten. Jerry Dunphy was long gone, replaced by Lucy, Ricky, Ethel, and Fred all shouting at one another on a rerun of *I Love Lucy.*

The doorbell chimed a second time and she sprang up from the couch to get it. It would be Mark arriving for dinner, and she decided it was a good thing he had offered to bring in a pizza. The way things were going in the kitchen she would have probably burned a frozen Celeste.

Knowing Mark, he had also had the foresight to stop by Robin Rose's Ice Cream and pick up a pint of their fabulous chocolate-raspberry chambord for dessert. Just in case . . .

"Well, did it *rise*?" he teased, when she opened the door for him, an impish grin on his face, the predicted Robin Rose ice cream bag balanced on top of the pizza box.

"Not as well as this," she teased back, as he rubbed playfully against her, hoisting dinner up over her head and out of the way. The wonderful aroma of the pizza clung temptingly in the air.

"No? That's too bad. I was kind of looking forward to being your test case."

Paige grinned, framing his great baby face with her hands. "I'm sure you were."

"It's probably significant—" he murmured, pausing to kiss the tip of her nose, then moving over to her neck. "You know, one thing rising and one thing . . . not."

"Yeah?"

"Seriously." His blue eyes sparkled at her from behind his glasses.

She ran her pinkie finger along the crease of his dimple, deciding to shift the subject away from Nicky. "How were your classes today?" she asked.

"You ought to sit in sometime. Learn what to do with all that *money* you want to have one day—"

"Well, we both know I don't need an economics class for that—" Paige touched her tennis shoe to his, trying to get the bow of his shoelaces to flip the other way, not missing his sarcasm, but not acknowledging it either. "I'll know exactly what to do with it," she promised.

"My courses focus on making it multiply, not disappear."

"So, why don't you do it then. Instead of just *professing*—"

"Why? Would you marry me if I did?" he challenged, maneuvering the toes of his shoes to pin down hers while kissing her on the lips. Then, turning away from her, he headed toward the kitchen.

"It depends on how long you thought making it would take—" she answered lightly, catching up with him. "I haven't got all the time in the world, you know."

"God, you're a superficial bitch," he replied, careful to match his tone to hers.

"Why? Because of the money? Or the time?"

"Maybe both."

"I'm honest," she rallied in her own defense, scooting around him to open the kitchen door and let him in.

"To a fault," he pointed out, glancing at a Johnny Cat cat litter commercial playing on the TV set, then sticking the ice cream sack into the freezer. She watched, feeling more guilty than she thought she should feel, as he pried the pizza from the cardboard carton, dropped it onto a cookie sheet, and then rammed it noisily into one of the ovens, squinting through his glasses to set the dial. It was a gesture that she knew had more to do with anger than poor sight.

"Would you rather I lie?" she asked, frustrated.

"I'd rather you *lie down*," he snarled, shoving her roughly against the granite island, then tenderly fondling her breasts.

She looked at him leerily, then running her hands along the taut muscles of his back, she sighed. This was getting to be more and more difficult. They weren't supposed to get involved. And yet they were.

Mark was becoming increasingly possessive, though he kept insisting he was not, that their relationship was just as Paige had set it up, for fun, for friendship, great sex, and lots of laughs.

The truth was, it wasn't easy for her, either. If she didn't keep a careful guard on her emotions she could easily let herself get too deeply involved with him as well. She was crazy about his looks, his brains, the way he made love, everything, *except* his financial status and his patent lack of drive. There wasn't anyone else with whom she could talk the way she could to Mark. She could be herself around him. He was nonjudgmental.

It took all her willpower, all her collective years of lousy, hurtful, go-nowhere romances and the cynical outlook she had cultivated through them, to keep herself from letting down and falling for him.

She kept asking herself—was that the way she wanted to live the rest of her life? Scrimping on a professor's salary, in a tiny rented apartment, a life like Kit's down the tubes.

No. Emphatically no.

The romance would wear off. The fantastic sex would wear off. He'd probably be off fooling around with his cute little co-eds. At least if Nicky fooled around on her, she would be taken care of; there would be some compensation; there would be *great* compensation.

"Paige, listen, I'm sorry," Mark apologized, his hands gently caressing her breasts again, arousing her. "I'm glad you're honest to a fault," he said, taking off his glasses and rubbing his eyes as if they ached. "Maybe it's what I like best about you."

"No, it's me who should apologize," Paige whispered. "I don't know, Mark, maybe this is unrealistic. Maybe I'm not being fair." She shivered, tingling all over from his touch. "Maybe we shouldn't see each other anymore," she forced herself to say, hoping that he would counter, not sure that she could handle it if he didn't.

She didn't know what to think when he didn't answer, pressing his lips against hers again, harder this time, their tongues colliding, their kiss gaining momentum, lips grazing, brushing, then driving against each other's until the world seemed to swerve upside down. She felt a thrill of relief when he began tearing her shirt out of her jeans, seemingly possessed, unhooking her bra almost in the same motion, until his hands closed on the silky fullness of her breasts.

With equal longing she was tugging his shirt up and out of his jeans, languishing in the feel of his skin, the heat behind it, his scent.

Her nipples rose like hard little rocks beneath his fingertips while his cock pressed urgently against the front of her jeans.

Supporting her by the waist he lifted her up and onto the countertop, undoing her jeans and wrestling them, along with her panties, down below her knees. The granite was like ice against her bare behind, but it felt tantalizingly sexy, with his hands eagerly massaging her thighs and then between her thighs, while she unfastened *his* jeans and then struggled from her awkward position to get them and his Jockey shorts down. When she had succeeded, his penis sprang free, released from the stretchy white cotton, and she caught it lovingly between her palms, growing more and more excited from his excitement.

The expression on his face jarred her, evoking the still-vivid memory of Nicky standing in the buff like that at the Château Marmont, having stripped down to nothing in a moment's time, so proud of himself, so sure of himself, strutting his swollen cock like a medal, a prize he was going to share with her. Here was Mark, worlds apart from Nicky in every way imaginable, and yet here he was with that exact same look in his eye.

Mark's *prize,* she noticed with a touch of irony, was bigger than Nicky's prize—as though to balance out the purse.

"This is so fucking cold," Mark cried out, when he heaved himself up onto the slippery countertop, on top of her, sliding them both backward so that there was enough room.

"But it feels so fucking fantastic!" they both bellowed at the same time, laughing and enjoying the shock of it as he entered her with a delicious moan and wild-man's thrust, moving deep inside her.

Paige was responding to the awkwardness of their clothes half on, half off, their bawdy, frenzied reflections mirrored in the stainless-steel fixture above her, the brazen, off-color image of the two of them screwing frantically on top of the freezing island in the kitchen.

There were some reprehensible thoughts rushing through her head, fueling her approaching orgasm, arousing her still further. Bad, teasing thoughts pledging Mark as just a playtoy, *her* toy, a silent pact with herself that they were fucking just for the fun of it. No entanglements. Just great sordid screwing. Mark couldn't possess her; nobody could possess her. His moaning heightened her pleasure until she could barely stand it anymore.

Then on the brink of a climax, she happened to glance over at the TV set where she noticed a news teaser highlighting the World Championship boxing match slated for next week at the StarDome, promoting the station's preshow interviews.

Nicky Loomis's StarDome.

The idea struck Paige with luscious force, a force that nearly put her over the edge. *The World Championship Boxing Match at the StarDome.* It was a stroke of genius. It was a stroke of luck.

Of course Nicky would be there, in the private box she had been reading about.

She would flash him their private password across the big advertising message board. *Less Is More.* He would understand immediately.

Less Is More. It was *their* phrase. *Go to concession stand at aisle number . . . whatever.*

Nothing could be more perfect. She would meet him there.

He would want to screw her on the spot.

But she would make him wait, insist that he had to understand. After their last episode, if he wanted her he was going to have to get to know her first, of course with the unsaid promise that she would make it well worth the wait when he did.

She could see it clear as day. They would embark upon a relationship that would be totally novel for Mr. Fast-Fuck Sports King. He would bring her up to his box, introducing her to his daughter, son, groupies, and assorted friends.

Probably none of them would trust her. Probably none of them should.

Paige imagined herself making love with Nicky now.

She conjured up the look of him, the feel of him, drawing on sensations still intact from the Château. But the image wasn't as satisfying as the reality, as opening her eyes and seeing her gorgeous lover going out of his mind on top of her, listening to him moan and cry out.

His lovely eyes opened, as though he had sensed that she was watching him. His mouth formed an exalted O.

And like that they came together, in unison, holding each other tightly, letting the glorious release take over.

Paige felt like crying afterward, pleasure producing guilt, producing tears.

Maybe it was guilt. Maybe it was nerves. Maybe she was just premenstrual.

*   *   *

She drove up to the StarDome a nervous wreck, having changed clothes thirteen times, trying to decide on the image she wanted to portray.

Miniskirt—yes or no? Jeans? Maybe better. Leather pants? Suede skirt? The long flowing one or the short, tight Alaia knock-off? Innocent or sexy, or both?

She had to remember that his kids would probably be there with him, his friends. Some of them might remember her from her last stunt at his party. They would be watching her carefully. Judging her.

Still torn, she had finally put back on her stone-washed jeans, faded blue workshirt with big shoulder pads, a tan snakeskin belt, which matched her cowboy boots, and a bold tan Stetson hat.

Stealing a last glance in the rearview mirror and adjusting the angle on her Stetson, she took a deep breath and got out of her car, heading toward the modern-looking structure of the StarDome. The parking lot was jam-packed with every imaginable mix of car and fight fan. There was a potent, aggressive, very male-type anticipation in the air, the sense of rowdy aggression about to be vented, lots of lusty whooping and drinking and big bets.

Paige's first hurdle was going to be getting in without a ticket. She had made every effort to buy one, calling scalpers, offering to pay far more than she would have ever dreamed of paying, but for the first World Championship boxing match ever to have been fought in L.A., there simply were no seats to be had. Or bought, anyway.

The sell-out event was yet another major coup for sports entrepreneur Nicky Loomis, another bold feather in his cap.

Paige pressed anxiously through the crowd.

Usually there were people hawking tickets at the door. But now all she saw were people trying to buy. The tickets, if there were any to be had, would be up to about nine hundred dollars now, she figured.

She was getting closer to the entrance, fretting over still not having come up with a solution. She was barely even moving at this point, finding it unnecessary, thrust forward by the movement of the crowd.

She noticed a number of tickets held precariously in unsuspecting hands. If only she could snatch one of them away, one lone ticket that would surely mean more to her. She saw a woman in very dark chic-looking sunglasses who appeared bored to tears, the type who would hate fights, would find them barbaric, was only there to appease her husband. Paige was longing to grab *her* ticket. The woman would undoubtedly be relieved to be spared having to go inside and endure all that sweat, blood, and brutality. The woman would be grateful.

"Ticket please." Paige looked up, startled. The man accepting the tickets at the admission gate shot her a dirty look. He waved his hand impatiently at her, annoyed. The crowd was growing annoyed behind her. They were all in a hurry to get inside. Pushing. Crowding up behind her.

"Here," Paige said, winging it, handing him air.

"Very funny, lady. Try again." His yellowed teeth were bared in a snarl.

Paige glanced innocently down at her empty hand, then cried out, pretending confusion, her heart pounding for real. "It was just here. I had it a second ago," she stammered. "Somebody must have taken it!" Acting for all she was worth, she broke into a panic, an easy emotion to summon up at this point, with the chance of not getting in looming closer, not to mention all these angry people shouting and shoving behind her, the line swelling out of proportion. Producing an appropriate welling up of tears in her eyes, she continued her performance. "Honestly. I . . . I just had it. I don't know what happened . . ." She let her voice trail off as she bent down onto the ground, searching desperately, not sure where to go from there.

"Yeah. Sure, lady." When she spied the ticket taker cocking his head at Security, her pulse sped up even faster. She had to hold to her story. Maybe somebody would feel sorry for her and let her in.

The crowd behind her was demonstrating split sympathies. Some of them were yelling at Paige. Some of them were yelling at the ticket taker to just let her in. Paige played it on the brink of tears, exclaiming how important this fight was to her. *They had no idea. She had to see it. They had to let her in.*

Then in the midst of the commotion, a white stretch limousine pulled up to the curb directly outside the entrance. Nicky Loomis, bulky and bursting with energy, along with a raucous entourage came barreling toward them, with Nicky asserting his position as owner of the sports arena, wanting to know what all the ruckus was about. When he discovered Paige in the center of it, he broke out laughing.

Paige, ready to shrivel up and die of embarrassment, recognized his daughter standing coolly behind him, regarding her with an unreadable smirk.

"We meet again, Miss Williams," Nicky said expansively, running his large hands along the thighs of his jeans, beginning to get the picture from all the shouting in the background. "Or *is* it Miss Williams?" he questioned, the look in his small, lively eyes charging her with hope, making her believe that he had been doing her homework as well.

Encouraged but ever-vigilant, she held her breath as he guided her artfully away and out of the path of his paying customers, astonished by the crowd's rowdy support. They were rooting for her now, cheering, shouting, "Oh, c'mon, let her in, *Nicky*. The gal's a looker." It amused Paige that he was so recognizable, that these people were fans of *his*. A few of them asked for his autograph.

She felt herself loosening up as she waited, watching him distribute signatures. Her plan was now definitely down the tubes, but thankfully a *new* plan had been born out of luck.

When he was finished signing his last autograph and had doled out his last public smile, he turned expectantly back to her, warning her in a look that she was playing with fire.

Undeterred, conscious of the attention they were continuing to draw, the various looks his family and friends were communicating, she slyly met his gaze. Many men she knew had the kind of presence that filled a room. But Nicky Loomis, she noticed with a flush of pleasure, had the kind of presence that filled a stadium. *His* stadium.

"You're a hard gal to find," the still powerfully built sports mogul observed.

She felt a flood of relief at the confirmation that he had tried.

She smiled, saying nothing, not missing the signal he gave his daughter, who then ushered their group away and into the building.

"So where do we go from here?" he asked shrewdly after they had all left, his thin lips drawn thoughtfully together as he appraised her. "To bed, I hope—"

"Still not pulling any punches, are you?" she replied, continuing to be winded by his style, or lack of it, watching him grin as if he had her at last. "Didn't you get the picture last time? I'm dying to go to bed with you, Nicky Loomis," she pronounced carefully, with a green-eyed glare and a smile that could always turn heads. "But first I'm going to get to know you. And you're going to get to know me." While she felt herself blush at the tight delivery of the words, she had rehearsed a variation of it and rationalized that it had to be said.

Saying nothing, giving nothing, feeling like she was playing poker with big stakes and an only so-so hand, she watched as he broke up laughing again, that great belly laugh that she remembered, his penetrating eyes reading her with amusement. "You didn't strike me as being that traditional," he charged.

There was a brief contest of wills as they stood, each waiting for the other to give ground.

Then he laughed again, a what-the-hell kind of laugh. "Are you really that good?" he dared her.

"Are *you* really that curious?" she shot back, feigning absolute confidence.

"Yeah, I guess I am," he acquiesced, raising a smoky gray eyebrow as he took her hand.

Paige felt herself glowing as he escorted her into the StarDome, past the agitated ticket taker, through the crowd that was *his* crowd, up a special elevator, and into the famous private box.

A burst of applause shook the stands, and even though it was for defending champion Tommy Sykes, Paige felt like it was all for her.

Chapter 20

Paige and Susan were sitting out by the pool drinking coffee and eating breakfast as Paige read aloud from the letter Tori had sent to them.

"Dear Paige and Susan," she began. "I'm so full of the native drink they invented here called *batida de cocos* that I hope I'm coherent enough to write you this letter. (Note: This marvelous and *very* potent brew prepared by the children on the island warrants a quick description. The adorable native kids climb up the coco trees like monkeys, bringing down bunches of green coconuts, which they chill in ice chests. Once the coconuts are cold, the kids use machetes to whack off the tips, then spill out enough of the coco water to make room for a sugar cane brandy called *pinga*. Slip in a straw and, *voilà,* the sweetest concoction I've ever sampled. Hmmm . . .)

"Even if I'm *not* coherent enough to write you this letter, I'm going to proceed anyway, so bear with me because I have stupendous news.

"On top of being smashed from *batida de cocos* on the private totally deserted beach here, I'm also madly in love.

"At long last, we can nail down the lid on Travis Walton's

coffin. Dead and buried, girls. No regrets. Richard Bennetton, it turns out, was the perfect antidote to my former Georgia love.

"I'm not only in love, but I'm also *engaged*.

"Paige, you'll just love this one—my engagement ring is an eight-carat Colombian emerald, which we bought in Buenos Aires. It's absolutely the most dazzling, mesmerizing thing I've ever laid eyes on.

"Richard said that when I present him with a son, I'll receive earrings to match. When I present him with a daughter—a necklace. Optimistic and crazy as he is, he already has the jeweler looking for three similar stones for us, which, thank goodness, are not easy to find, or he would be finding himself in even greater debt than I'm sure he's already gone into so far on this trip.

"Truly, the kind of money he's been spending makes my head spin. You should see the polo ponies he bought from Alejandro. These horses are magnificent—*riding* them was magnificent. Susan, you would go out of your mind; I can't wait for you to come out to Santa Barbara with us when we get back (the horses will probably beat us there), so we can all go riding together. Paige, you'll come too; we'll 'un-urbanize' you a little.

"I feel like I'm living this dream fantasy—traveling in a stratosphere that's totally foreign to me. Richard has friends everywhere, each of them more interesting than the last. We've been switching back and forth from English to Spanish to French, with a little Italian sprinkled in—*so* cosmopolitan.

"Everywhere we go, we're extended a brand of hospitality that makes even my own homegrown southern-style hospitality look inadequate.

"It's as though there's a global clique, the super-rich from every continent, all of them connected in one way or another, relating on the same level, sharing the same elevated culture, the same elevated tastes, the same elevated obsession with fun.

"Like Dustin Brent being there at the Carballos' *estancia*. Wasn't that too much? (I trust you did get my postcard from Alejandro and Elena's *estancia*.) I still can't get over it. Whoever might happen to still be unattached when he returns to the States has cause to remain optimistic. Just in case you've forgotten,

Dustin Brent is Michael Douglas, Mikhail Baryshnikov, Armand Assante, and William Hurt all rolled up into one. And speaking of machetes, you should have seen our handsome benefactor splitting open his cast with a machete, mounting a big strong spirited horse directly afterward and galloping off to his next adventure—our hero!

"Anyway, it's a new dizzying world for me. And yet every now and then, when I feel the effects of it wearing off—like the tail end of a champagne buzz—I feel guilty. We could feed nations, as they say, on the extravagant whims of our country's rich. The poverty we've seen all over South America is so acute and so upsetting that you either need to block it out entirely or roll up your shirt sleeves and do something about it.

"That's the kind of mood I was in when we happened to stop for gas in this one particular town. Seemingly from out of nowhere, we were suddenly surrounded by all these pathetic-looking children, with those big hungry eyes staring out of gaunt faces, their bellies distended from want of food, their hands extended to beg for pesos. It wasn't an unusual sight, but at that moment it struck me as such an unjust contrast to life at home, their listlessness and their utter lack of hope. We've all had the privilege of growing up with a sense of control over our destinies, the sense that we could dream and work hard to achieve those dreams, but these kids—it's hard to even imagine what kinds of dreams they've got.

"On an impulse, Richard had money wired from the States and presented the obscure little town with a hundred thousand dollars to improve their hospital. He *seems* spoiled and even callous at times but, underneath it all, he has the biggest heart.

"He's terrifically thoughtful. Romantic. Everywhere we go, he writes me these wonderful little notes on napkins or matchbooks or whatever, numbering them, telling me to save them for my scrapbook, which of course I have.

"I just wish I could fly you all out here to be with us—it's been so interesting, and so much fun.

"From Rio we met up with another friend of Richard's who sailed us on his yacht down to a group of islands known as Angra dos Reis and we've been island-hopping ever since. It's a rare experience because there are no hotels on the islands, only sprawling private homes, nestled away in this unforgettable landscape, surrounded by wild palm and coco trees.

"Today we had lunch in the small village of Buzios, on the coast—supposedly Brigitte Bardot's favorite spot. There was one main street with shops where the most popular item to buy was their daring 'string bikinis.'

"Of course I bought us each a couple. The Brazilian girls *known* for their perfect bodies wear them well, but we will too . . .

"The island we're staying on now is privately owned by a world-renowned plastic surgeon (Paige, you may have heard of him), Ivo Pitanguy, and we've been invited here as his guests. It's paradise, with nothing else on the island *except* Pitanguy's house, and nothing to do except laze around, water-ski and scuba dive in water that is nearly transparent as it washes up onto a spectacular stretch of crystallike white sand.

"I'm so tan and healthy-looking that, I swear, y'all wouldn't even recognize me. Richard says that my body looks like perfectly molded milk chocolate, so what do y'all think of that? From Caspar the Ghost to molded milk chocolate! I'm also getting rounder and rounder with all the wonderful food they have here. Bowls full of rich black beans. Lobsters either grilled or steamed, caught fresh right off the island for dinner every night. *Farofa,* a typical Brazilian dish referred to as 'slave food,' which they make by melting butter in a pan, stirring in eggs, then stirring in *mandioca,* a coarse native flour, and a dash of salt. It comes out all warm and crusty and loaded with butter. Mmmm. Am I making you hungry? I'll be sure to try to re-create it when I get back.

"The weather is sublime—warm, with the barest whisper of a breeze. I'm not sure how I'll ever come back down to earth.

"Anyway, I gotta run. One of the kids on the island is going to teach us how to boogie board. It's the big thing here. Like string bikinis. As a gal who can barely swim, I sure hope I don't drown and miss the heavenly life Richard's been promising me. I'd hate to hit heaven quite so literally right now.

"Can't wait to see y'all. I miss you lots. Love, Tori."

"Well. That's one down," Susan said, grinning and toasting her coffee cup to her absentee roommate. Paige raised her cup as well, incredulous.

Chapter 21

A ray of light danced vividly in Tori's emerald engagement ring as Richard held on tightly to her hand, causing the two of them to smile as they glanced down at it.

"It's really exquisite," Richard shouted over the wind. *"You're* really exquisite." They were racing along the freeway in his jet-black Ferrari, the gentle evening air rushing through their hair as they sped away from LAX, having just returned home from South America, on their way to Richard's parents' house to announce their engagement.

It seemed like an appropriate forum; Richard's father and stepmother were having a big black-tie bash there now, celebrating their ten-year wedding anniversary.

Tori and Richard were already dressed for the party, having showered and changed into their formal evening wear on board Richard's plane. The dress Tori was wearing was emerald green to match her ring. It was a very simple, short silk strapless—the color and contoured fit of the design making just the right statement; a matching green silk cape was worn over it as a wrap. Richard had bought it for her in Buenos Aires expressly to wear to the party, just before catching their flight home. With her Brazilian-born tan and the happy sparkle in her eyes, she looked as dazzling as the gem on her finger. Richard was in a smartly tailored tux.

He squeezed her hand even more tightly, knowing she was a bundle of nerves at the prospect of meeting his parents. "Relax," he said, winking at her.

"Maybe we shouldn't tell them tonight. Maybe we should wait until tomorrow—" she began again.

"Tori, they're going to love you. How could anyone not love you?"

But she was already smarting from the reception she expected to receive. She knew what they would think. She knew what *she* would think if she were in their position. "That's not the point. The point is that we hardly know each other—"

"Oh, but I can prove how well we *do* know each other . . ."

Tori looked into his eyes and melted.

"What's my favorite color?" he demanded, making her laugh.

"The color of your eyes, blue."

"And . . . what's my favorite song?"

"Richard!"

"C'mon—"

" 'Satisfaction'—"

Scrunching up his face in formidable Mick Jagger fashion, he belted out the rock refrain, abandoning the steering wheel in favor of a mock guitar. "Do I like *ice* in my diet Coke?"

"No—"

"What kind of *underwear* do I prefer?"

Tori felt her cheeks color and a happy laugh bubbling up in her throat. "Plain white boxers for you," she replied, "the short ones. Pink lace panties for me, cut high on the thigh."

"Sounds like you know me pretty well," he warranted, as he maneuvered his hand beneath her dress, beginning at her knee, then working his way up to get at the pink lace panties she was wearing for his benefit now. "Okay, here's a tougher one." His perfect teeth flashed at her. "If I were to order a cheeseburger and the waitress gave me a choice of three cheeses, Jack, Swiss, and Cheddar, which one would I choose?"

She looked at him, caught, trying to think back to the omelets or cheeseburgers she had seen him order, debating. He smiled a good strong smile that sparked her memory: *the first day in Bue-nos Aires, at the hotel, at breakfast.* "First you'd ask for Muen-ster, and then if they didn't have it you'd choose Cheddar."

Richard began flashing the lights of his car, like a game-show signal for *win,* cheering along with the display.

Tori turned to look nervously behind her. If there were any cops, they would have gotten stopped for sure. "You're crazy," she hissed.

"Crazy about you, Georgia Peach. Say 'panties' again, sounds so sexy with your li'l ol' *drawl*—" he drawled himself, his long, stick-straight saffron-colored hair whipped back by the wind.

The senior Bennetton's condominium was in one of the loftier high rises on Wilshire Boulevard. Tori and Richard rode up the all-brass and mirrored elevator in silence, each of them preparing in his or her own way, gearing up.

Richard had insisted that he wasn't in the least bit nervous, but Tori could tell that he was. There was a tenseness in his face she had never seen before. His eyes seemed more complicated, dis-tracted. His jaw was tight, almost clenched. When she reached for his hand it was clammy.

A butler opened the door for them before they even had a chance to ring the bell. He greeted Richard formally, taking Tori's wrap, and escorting them in. "Hello, Mr. Bennetton. It's nice to see you."

"Nice to see you, Raymond. Meet Tori Mitchell . . ." Tori felt her heartbeat speed up and her face flood with color again as Richard smiled in charming hesitation, his words hovering pre-cariously. "My . . . uh—"

"Hi. It's nice to meet you," she jumped in nervously, pumping the butler's hand, slipping Richard a look at the same time. They had deliberated about her wearing her engagement ring, with Tori uncomfortable that everyone would notice it. Now touching her vacant wedding-ring finger with her thumb she felt relieved that she had finally convinced Richard to carry it in his pocket until the correct moment.

A waiter passed by with a tray of empty champagne glasses

and a bottle of Taittinger's Compte de Champagne, pausing obsequiously to pour out a glass for each of them.

Tori's glass teetered as she brought it up to her lips, her taste buds totally nonfunctioning at this point, but her brain in acute need of its medicinal effects. She was in a dumb state of oblivion as Richard introduced her to a whirl of guests, smiling, accepting handshakes and compliments, beginning to feel nauseated.

Nobody's name registered. Nobody's face registered.

She was stealing glances around the starkly furnished penthouse, awed by the panorama of galvanizing views, the glow of city lights rippling in the mirrored walls, producing an almost dizzying effect, she thought.

Or maybe she was just overwhelmed, her nerves and energy shot from the seventeen-hour flight. Her body felt taut, on alert as she waited for the *key* introduction, trying to be ready for it.

Pretend you're Paige, she urged herself in response to a mounting panic. *Be cool and collected. Sassy and lighthearted like Paige. In charge. Pretend it's a game. Snow them with your southern charm.*

Tori, they're going to love you. How could they not love you? Richard's reassuring words, already repeated to her dozens of times, floated back into her head, helping to steady her some, as her reflection bounced out at her from one of the mirrors across the room. Her image appeared superimposed onto the sparkle of city lights as though to buoy her confidence, proof of how dazzling she looked, with her deep, glowing tan setting off the fiery green of her dress, creating an aura that was both exotic and radiant at once.

She tried to convince herself that it didn't matter if his parents liked her or not. Their son did. Their son wanted to marry her.

"Richard! You made it." Tori turned to see an older version of Richard striding purposefully over to embrace the younger version, a small but befitting proportion of extra bulk to his tall frame, his hair a steely gray next to Richard's ash blond and his keen blue eyes aglow with fatherly affection as he held his son close for an extra moment.

Tori held her breath as the debonair senior turned politely toward her, his hand outstretched in greeting. "And *you* must be the illustrious Tori Mitchell I've been hearing so much about," Elliot Bennetton said with friendly caution. *"Not* from my son, he never tells me anything, but through the grapevine at the office. Though I understand they haven't had the opportunity to see too much of you, my dear."

Tori smiled woodenly at the not-unwarranted dig. It was true —she had been hired by Bennetton Enterprises, at a significant salary, but she had been absent more than she had been present, getting paid while gallivanting across the globe with his jet-set, playboy son. "Hello, Mr. Bennetton. I'm so glad to finally meet you," she responded, measuring each syllable. "And I'm afraid that's true, about my being off the job more than on it," she apologized guiltily, venturing her best smile. "But hopefully you'll approve of my contribution to your company in the months to come."

She felt her confidence returning as he smiled approvingly back at her, enveloping her hand warmly between both of his, those keen Bennetton eyes taking her in. "I'm sure I will," he remarked generously. "Your résumé was impressive. And I happen to know your former employer quite well. We did a project together once in Kentucky."

Tori felt him measuring her surprise as he touched his index finger to his temple, rubbing it there for a moment, seeming to grow lost in the calculation, or maybe the memory, as though sent back in time for an instant.

"Really? Jake Shavelson—?"

"Years ago," he acknowledged. "Around 1952, I think. Long before you were born. When I saw his name and telephone number on your résumé right there in front of me, I couldn't resist giving him a call."

Elliot Bennetton smiled, responding to her look. His smile was so remarkably like Richard's that it disarmed her. She had expected suspicion, but not a private-eye routine, requisitioning her résumé, checking her out. His son was hardly that vulnerable.

She made an effort to contain her surprise. Not that the call could have possibly hurt her. She knew Jake would only have had flattering things to say on her behalf. Then she wondered if Elliot Bennetton had mentioned that she was off in South America with his son. She wondered if news of that had leaked back to Travis. Hopeful that it had, she felt a more genuine smile taking form on her lips. "Well, did I pass muster?"

"Jake couldn't have praised you more highly. Sounds like I'm lucky to have you. Every which way," he added meaningfully, his expression growing more complex as he turned to appraise his son. The senior Bennetton looked suddenly at a loss for words, circumspect. Yet he didn't appear the sort of man who would be at a loss very often.

"Isn't she a find?" Richard exclaimed, attempting to cut through the cloud of tension that had abruptly moved in, putting his arm around Tori and drawing her in close to his side.

"She's gorgeous," Elliot Bennetton concurred, smiling kindly, yet that tense, complicated look on his face, remained. "According to Jake, she's gorgeous inside and out." He seemed to have something to say, but no comfortable way of saying it. It made Tori wonder about the relationship between father and son. It was difficult to ascertain who was afraid of whom. She suspected it was mutual. Richard had said so little about his father. Tori thought it was a sad fact of so many parental relationships, parent and child *wanting* to communicate, but neither party really knowing how.

"So, how was that part of the world? Did you have a nice time?" Elliot Bennetton finally broke the silence.

Tori replied with guarded enthusiasm, looking to Richard.

He smiled as one would for a photograph, responding to his father's mood. It was as though there were some sort of contest beginning, as the two men resumed their quiet study of one another. Maybe an old contest that had never ended. Tori wanted to find a way to excuse herself. She was just about to ask where the powder room was, when she lost her chance.

"So, I heard about your six-figure horse acquisition," the senior Bennetton announced thinly in a controlled voice. It became less controlled as he went on. "I see you're really going through with that sponsorship business—"

Richard's younger blue eyes narrowed combatively. "That was the purpose of my trip—"

"Two hundred thousand dollars on polo ponies?" Elliot Bennetton forced a laugh, then glanced uneasily at Tori, clearly wishing he had his son alone, but unable to stop himself.

"Jones reporting to you now?" Richard asked tersely.

"He *is* my accountant."

"It was a good investment."

"Don't bullshit me, Richard."

Tori was so taken aback by the confrontation that she didn't know what to think.

Elliot Bennetton smiled again—so much emotion contained beneath that smile. Tori felt a compounding urgency to disappear, a sense of foreboding, without understanding anything. Their smiles had *all* borne so many different meanings. This particular smile revealed a man of immense power—losing it.

Richard snorted. "Never bullshit a bullshitter?"

"I think we should talk about this later," his father said, getting a grip on himself at last, his eyes losing their anger, looking old.

Richard's eyes were still blazing. "Suit yourself," he yielded. Then, rather childishly, after a pregnant pause, he held up his glass in the gesture of a toast. "Happy anniversary, Dad," he declared levelly.

"Richard!" A statuesque woman in a glistening amber gown, which matched her very chic, bronze-schemed apartment, rustled toward them.

"Here we go again," Richard projected under his breath, taking a deep swallow of his champagne before she got there.

"Richard, I'm so glad," his stepmother effused, breathless from crossing the room. "With your flying in today, we didn't expect you here until late, if at all." Smiling warmly at them both, she looped her arm through her husband's.

"I never break a promise, Phyllis. And I promised to be here. Happy anniversary." He kissed her dutifully on the cheek, eyeing his father, who took a deep breath, then looked down at his shoes.

They were all waiting for Richard to introduce Tori, who held her breath, wishing for a way to preempt Richard from saying anything about their engagement just yet. The timing was clearly all wrong, and she was embarrassed at the size of the ring he would be sliding defiantly onto her finger.

But the look on his face told her that it was too late.

"Phyllis, I'd like you to meet my fiancée, Tori Mitchell," Richard announced indelicately, undisguisedly relishing the impact of the jolt as he dealt it.

Phyllis, plainly caught off guard, turned to face Tori, who was so tense she didn't know what to say. The older woman's umber-pencil-lined orange lips were parted in surprise, her intelligent-looking gray eyes blinked as she managed a polite congratulations.

"Thank you," Tori replied dully, shattered by the whole turn of events. Her mood had come plummeting down from cloud nine; the little bit of paradise she had glimpsed evaporated like a mirage. She felt used and was tempted to storm off. If her ring hadn't been in Richard's pocket she thought she might have thrown it at him.

Instead, she avoided looking at him altogether, afraid that if she did she would dissolve into tears. She felt Elliot Bennetton watching her, taking in her response.

"Well, this is a surprise! Is it official?" Phyllis Bennetton wondered, directing an uneasy glance over at her husband.

Richard dropped his hand ceremoniously down into his pocket, withdrawing Tori's engagement ring and then placing it onto her finger.

It had looked so magnificent only a little while ago in the car. Now it looked ostentatious. Blanching, she realized it was actually larger than the diamond belonging to her prospective stepmother-in-law.

What she didn't know was that Phyllis Bennetton could have bought *herself* that kind of ring without the help of Richard's father, that she was a very wealthy woman in her own right, having founded a chain of contemporary young women's clothing stores long before she met him. She was a brilliant merchandiser, enormously successful, and far too low-key to engage in the kind of flash Richard favored. It was no secret that she disapproved of his excesses.

"I guess it is," Phyllis acknowledged, an undecipherable expression on her face as she eyed the ring.

This time Richard's father spoke up, unrestrained. "All right, Richard. We have to talk."

"I thought you said we should talk later," Richard remarked, looking him squarely in the eye.

"I changed my mind—"

Phyllis put her hand on her husband's shoulder to calm him. "Elliot. Please, darling. Later—"

"Phyllis, I'm sorry. I just can't—"

"*No,* Phyllis," Richard interrupted. "I'm a big boy. I can take whatever it is he wants to say."

Tori felt like the incredible shrinking woman, growing smaller and smaller, the world around her looming more and more out of proportion. Nobody seemed to give a damn what she thought or felt, and yet she was being thrust into the vortex of this family feud.

"Darling, please," Phyllis reiterated, indicating the festivities going on just beyond where they were standing in the entry, the party they had only joined peripherally.

"What are you all doing hiding out here!" demanded a big-gutted man with a loud laugh and a pungent cigar. "Having a little family meeting? Richard, who's the pretty girl? He always finds the prettiest girls," he confided to Tori, by way of a backhanded compliment, folding his hands onto his belly. "Did you import her from South America?"

"Only her tan. Lawrence Keeler, meet Tori Mitchell, my fiancée," Richard reported cheerfully, shaking hands with his father's old friend.

"*Congratulations,* you sly dog, you. That's some news," Lawrence Keeler replied heartily, signaling for his wife, who was standing with a group of friends across the room. Tori noticed Richard and his father exchanging a look.

"Betty, Richard here is engaged. And this is his lovely young fiancée—what's your name, dear?"

Tori spied his wife and the three friends she had brought along with her, all gaping at her ring. In a kind of fluttery chorus they exclaimed their congratulations.

In no time, the party had converged around them, forcing the four of them toward the center of the room, with all of the Bennettons' guests rushing up to extend their best wishes, to dispense congratulatory hugs, to take Tori's hand and gawk at the eight-carat emerald Richard had bought for her.

It was as terrible a moment for Tori as when Travis had stood her up at Tiffany's, maybe worse, if that were possible. She was obviously jinxed when it came to rings and engagements. Instead of bringing her joy, as she had always imagined, all the occasion ever brought her was humiliation. And she had a sense that the worst was yet to come.

For the remainder of the party, she, Phyllis, and Elliot Bennetton all stood around smiling hollowly, enduring the gush of congratulations. Only Richard remained animated—looking like the cat who had swallowed the canary.

After all the guests had left, he looked more like a cat who had swallowed rat poisoning.

"All right. The party's over. *Literally over,*" Elliot Bennetton issued quietly, walking wearily over to pour himself a shot of whiskey before retiring onto the couch. Phyllis Bennetton sat down supportively beside him, saying nothing as he loosened the bow tie at his throat, releasing the neck of his shirt after that, and dropping the Cartier studs into a crystal ashtray.

Tori didn't know what to do with herself. With a stab of reluctance at staying altogether, she settled tentatively into a suede tub chair, facing an Andy Warhol portrait of Mao printed on Chinese silk. Richard, who had been holding her hand, crossed over to the travertine fireplace, leaning smugly up against it, ready to do battle. He had hardly spoken two words to Tori since they had arrived, although he had squeezed her hand, and delivered an occasional it'll-be-okay kind of wink, and she found she was more confused than angry with him.

"Tori, I'm sorry to be having this out with my son in front of you, but if you're planning on marrying him, this concerns you as well," Elliot Bennetton said, catching her by surprise, going on to surprise her further. "Richard, I don't know how to say this except to say it flat out. I'm cutting you off."

Richard's cocky, controlled expression vanished. Tori

watched, stunned, as he stood rooted in shock, unable to reply,
his expression registering astonishment, fear, and then rage as he
digested his father's curt decision. He never once looked over at
her or at his stepmother. "What do you mean you're cutting me
off," he demanded finally, his voice tight. "You can't just cut me
off at will. I have a trust, from Mom. You can't touch that—"

"I can't touch it, Richard. But wait until you see what you
have left after all this. You'll find it's all been frittered away."

"No fucking way."

"Give the bank a call in the morning."

"I thought you didn't believe in strings," Richard mocked bitterly.

"This has nothing to do with strings. It has to do with *abuse.
That's* what I don't believe in—*abuse.* Talk to Ted Jones tomorrow. He'll lay out your financial situation for you. You'll be receiving your exact same salary, provided you don't go off on any
more four-week jaunts for a while. You'll be treated like all of
Bennetton's other employees. Three weeks' vacation time—and
you've already had more than your share. Medical insurance.
Plus the perks specified in your contract."

"Contract? What *contract*?"

"Jones will go over it with you."

"Well, just maybe I won't sign along the dotted line—"

"Then don't."

Richard glared hard at his father, making Tori wonder at the
depth of bitterness, the malice that had sprung up in him tonight.
She was torn, conscious of the obvious degree of truth in his
father's accusation, having been a recipient of that excess herself.
But the undercurrent of hurt she sensed in Richard, hidden directly beneath that malice, that bitterness, made her want to protect him, to rush over and hold him, to soothe him and tell him
that it was all going to be all right.

"Richard, this is long overdue, and you know it," Elliot Bennetton said, with a surprising calm, sipping resignedly at his
whiskey, looking down into the unlit fireplace beside his son,
then looking him straight in the eye. "You can't go around piss-
ing away money the way you do. Excuse my language, Tori, but
that's the way it is. Your multi-carat emerald engagement ring

probably didn't even seem all that extravagant as you listened to the numbers being tallied up on my son's other commitments there, the polo ponies, the sponsorship commitments, the *hospital* in that little village. I'm surprised he didn't buy himself an island. Richard, you've gone through two separate trusts already. Four million on your house. God only knows how many hundreds of thousands you have in cars, in your *subterranean parking lot* there.

"You appear to be competing with Norton Simon on your art collection. Your traveling gets more and more extravagant. Your lousy movie investments. And now this polo business—I've had it. You make it on your own and, fine, you can blow it any way you like—"

"*She* put you up to this, didn't she?" Richard raged, turning on his stepmother, whose lily-white complexion flushed with red.

"*She* has nothing to do with this—"

"My ass!"

Beginning to lose his temper now, Elliot Bennetton pointed a shaky finger at his son. "You just watch yourself—"

"She did, didn't she? What's the matter, Phyllis? Trying to steal a little more for yourself and your daughters?"

"I *told* you, she had nothing to do with this," Elliot Bennetton shouted.

But he was intercepted by his wife who left her place beside him and stormed over to slap Richard hard across the face. "Your father has given you *everything*," she hissed. "*Everything!* And you've given him nothing in return. You're self-centered, spoiled rotten, and this just might teach you some humility. This was unequivocally my idea, and I'm *happy* to take credit for it. I've been pleading with your father to do this for years. But he wouldn't listen to me. He felt too guilty over your mother dying. Over his being happy, and your *inability* to be happy. It's high time for him to stop taking the blame and for *you* to begin to bear some responsibility for your own life."

Richard's hand was still holding his cheek where his stepmother had slapped him. The two of them looked at one another, a store of old resentment bursting to the surface.

"If you want my opinion, which I'm sure you don't," Phyllis

went on more calmly, smoothing her already perfect bubble of hair, a stately expression on her face, "I think you should go to work somewhere other than at Bennetton. I think you should learn what it's like to really earn a living on your own, to feel the sense of pride and accomplishment that goes with that. I don't think you'll ever be happy, Richard, until you've learned that you're smart enough and capable enough to do that. I know what you think of me, and I really don't care because I feel so sorry for you."

Tori was astonished when Phyllis Bennetton's eyes welled up with tears, and she went from staunch and in control to awkward and self-conscious.

"I happen to love you, Richard. I know you'll probably never believe that. But I do. And I honestly believe, in my heart of hearts, that this is the right thing to do. I'll be pulling for you more than anyone you know. And so will my daughters, who incidentally, don't need one red cent of your money or your father's. I made it on my own, and they're making it on their own, and that's the way I believe it should be."

Everyone was silent after Phyllis's speech. Tori felt as though she had come into the middle of a movie, without the benefit of really knowing the players or their backgrounds, but was moved to tears anyway, rooting for a conclusion that would give everyone what he or she wanted.

Blinking, and forcing back the stirred emotion, she looked at Richard, finding him clearly more enraged than moved.

With a hard-boiled look on his face, he broke into a kind of mock applause. "Bravo, Phyllis—you and your great puritan work ethic. Except that I don't need to *work* to feel worth something. Going into an office eight hours a day every day doesn't make me feel any more of a man than having fun and doing whatever the fuck I want to do. I'm more interesting *because* I travel, *because* I meet interesting people and do interesting things. You're just jealous, and your values are hopelessly middle class."

Tori was mortified when he stalked over to grab her up by the wrist onto her feet, shoving her bejeweled hand in Phyllis's face. "Is this too *ostentatious* for you, Phyllis? Is it *too* breathtaking?

Too bedazzling? You work your butt off—but what's it all for if it's not to have a good time?

"You know, Phyllis, you really take life much too seriously. And, Dad, you're letting her take you down with her. Fuck you both. I'll do fine on my own. I won't gain any sick pleasure out of slaving away to get the bucks, but once I'm there, and I have no doubt that I'll get there, contrary to your dime-store psychoanalysis, I'm certain that I'll do just fine. So just fuck you both. And, Phyllis, I suggest you pass up the psychology bit and stick to young women's apparel—at least you're in the ballpark there."

The look of anguish on Elliot Bennetton's face made Tori turn around, hoping impossibly for a reconciliation as Richard stormed out of the room, still holding on to her hand, tugging her along with him.

The short stretch from the Bennettons' penthouse to Dustin Brent's home felt like an eternity, the stormy speed with which Richard attacked the distance only intensifying the interminability of the ride. Tori was afraid to utter even a single word.

When at last they approached the electronic iron gates sealing off the large Mediterranean-style house that reminded her now of a mini *estancia,* gingerly she handed Richard the key that would gain them admission.

As the gates hummed open, he impatiently threw his gears into a rough first and then sped up the grand palm-lined circular drive, only barely missing the fish pond as he killed the engine with a loud sigh. It was the first sound Tori had heard from him since they had left.

They sat there like that for as long as ten minutes, until she finally mustered up the courage to speak.

Slipping her engagement ring off her finger, she held it out to him. "Richard, I think you should get your money back for this," she began tentatively, trying to read what was behind his eyes, wishing some of the tension would break so that they could talk. "I don't need it—" she shrugged, taking his hand to place the ring in his palm. *I need you* was what she was about to say when he cut her off.

"Oh, that's very good. Fast work, Tori. I lose my inheritance, and you're gone with the wind—"

"I'm not *breaking off* our engagement," Tori argued, stung. "I'm just giving you back the ring. It's ridiculous, Richard. You're going to need the money; *we're* going to need the money. And I certainly don't need an eight-carat rock on my finger. If it's so important to you, you can buy me another one when you've gotten back on your feet."

Full of hostility, Richard shoved the emerald right back at her. "That's not the way I do things. You don't want it; then the engagement is off."

Tori looked at him, uncomprehending. "But Richard, I don't want it."

"Do you *not* want to marry me?" he insisted sullenly.

"Why are you doing this?" she asked.

"A test of faith."

"I don't like these *games* anymore, Richard."

"No games. A simple test of faith. Do you trust me? I need to know whether or not you trust me."

Trust him? He looked completely crazed, the object of a betrayal, plotting his revenge, his eyes dark with that brooding intensity that puts normal people over the edge. Tori felt backed up against the wall. "Yes. Of course I do," she said warily, not sure at all if she did.

He leaned across the car to kiss her coldly on the mouth. "Why would you want to marry me now, anyway?" he speculated edgily, toying with the delicate silk rose at her waist, then suddenly, as though asserting his wounded masculinity, ripping it off, arcing it up and out of the open top of the car. *"Now that I'm in hock up to my ears?"* he emphasized, watching the wisp of silk land in the gutter and then looking at her hard for a reaction.

"Because I love you," she answered trembling. "Because your money was not the reason I was marrying you."

Dustin's sprawling estate, lit up against the blackness of the night, rose up in silent contradiction, a symbol for the real purpose of the move out to Beverly Hills. Who was she kidding? That *was* why she had gone out with him; that *was* why she had fallen for him. She and her friends had moved out to California to meet and marry rich men, to obtain for themselves a life like Kit's.

"Would you have married me if I were a struggling artist?" Richard persisted huskily, "A ditch digger or a telephone repairman—" Then interrupting his own interrogation, blocking her protests, he began kissing her so roughly that he was actually hurting her.

"Richard, stop it," she cried, wrestling away from him, unable to shift her position even a fraction of an inch. The car was small and cramped, and she couldn't move.

"Why? Do I turn you off now?"

"You're hurting me—"

"So hurt me back," he dared, his breathing heavy and erratic as he cut her off, forcing his mouth over hers so that she could barely catch her breath.

He had her pinned against the seat, and he climbed completely over to her side, attacking the silk bodice of her dress, attempting to rip it right off her, growing more and more frenzied at his own violence. She couldn't hold back the tears any longer, and she finally began to cry and fight back in earnest.

Who was this person who was trying to hurt her, who had gone stark raving mad and was taking out all of his fury on her? "Richard, dammit, get a hold of yourself. Stop it!" she cried, wincing as the silk made a terrible ripping noise and a fresh spill of tears washed down her cheeks.

"Why should I! I'll buy you another one. It's just a dress. I'll fucking buy you another one! I'll fucking buy you anything you want," he shouted hotly, unzipping his pants and pulling out the swollen proof of his manhood, of his authority.

"I'll fucking buy you . . . ." he ranted repeatedly.

"And I'm fucking getting out of this car," Tori shouted back at him, shaking as she tried to wrench away from him.

She felt the tears on his cheeks as well, hot, wet, mingling with her own, all that pent-up anger and hurt as his hard-on fizzled and he began to hold her close, apologizing and pleading with her not to leave him.

She gave up any further struggle and, maintaining a low whisper in his ear, insisted that it was okay, that it would all be all right, that she would help him, that she loved him for *him* and not for his damn money.

She wasn't that kind of person.

But even as she said it and she listened to her own words, she wasn't sure.

This had all shaken her to her roots, and she realized she wasn't sure of anything.

The Richard who swept her off her feet was lost to her. There was a different man in his place, who was icy, deeply troubled, shutting her out, but at the same time sending signals for help.

Or maybe before, she had been seeing only what she wanted to see.

The familiar sense of despair that she felt inside, of dreams cruelly shattered, the crushing ache of her heart, caused her to slip into thoughts of Travis again, a habit she had hoped she had finally kicked.

In doing so, she found herself hating him more than ever. And for a change she was blaming Travis more than ever.

Otherwise she had to blame herself.

Chapter 22

Tori and Richard were sound asleep in his bed when the telephone woke them up. Through a fog of sleep, Tori watched him reach over to fumble with the receiver, then grab it anxiously up to his ear, the trim clock radio beside the phone registering the predawn hour. Careful to keep her eyes closed, feigning a continued slumber, she found herself hanging on to every word of his end of the conversation, tensely conscious of him watching her.

It was the same tense state that had pervaded every aspect of their lives for the last two weeks, since their return home from Argentina and the freezing of Richard's trust.

In the beginning, after the initial shock, he had been fairly certain that he could get a bank loan, that he could sell enough stock and liquidate enough assets to insure that his life-style remain relatively unaffected.

But when he discovered that he had already sold most of his stock, except for a few certificates still registered in his father's name, that all the real estate he owned, he owned in family partnerships, with his share being nontransferable, *and* that his financial situation was dire enough so that even his closest banking relationships had stopped returning his calls, he panicked.

And yet stubbornly he refused to give up anything, refused to

back down on any of his South American commitments, such as
the polo ponies or Tori's emerald or even the polo matches themselves. The horses had already cost thousands of dollars each,
just to fly them over to this country and transport them up to
Santa Barbara, where they were being stabled, for God only
knew how much a month.

Tori was immensely frustrated because she couldn't talk to
him. He was distancing himself from everything and everybody,
becoming impossible to connect with, possessed with finding a
solution to his out-of-hand debts. Tori knew she would have had
to be blind not to see that he was in way out of his depth, as she
watched him stoically pursuing alternative resources, and blind
not to guess that the bulk of the most recent ones fell on the
wrong side of the law.

From his end of the conversation, Richard's terse responses
gave away nothing, and Tori opened her eyes to find him still
watching her. She gave him a small, sleepy smile, her eyes beginning to adjust to the dark, able to make out the purplish circles
that were becoming more pronounced beneath his eyes.

"What time tomorrow night?" he asked into the phone, not
happy at her sparked attention. After a couple more blandly delivered responses, he hung up the receiver and bounded out of
bed, offering no explanation, looking unapproachable as he
rushed around the room beginning to pack.

His bedroom, on the second floor of his architecturally celebrated home built on one of the better-view lots of Bennetton
Hills Estates, was designed with a rectangular glass panel framed
into the wall, positioned to look down into the living room and
out through the room's sweeping expanse of windows, making a
veritable theater of the city. His lacquered bedroom walls were
painted the same color as the night, with voluptuous sand-
colored ottomans, gently curved sofas and chairs all grouped
around a modern stainless-steel fireplace. Through the panoply of
gleaming surfaces, the beveled mirrors, the welded steel sculpture
in the corner, Tori was able to observe Richard's reflection as he
threw his belongings together with swift economy.

Dressed in a pair of jeans, an old Columbia sweat shirt and

Reeboks, he slung his packed duffel bag over his shoulder and started toward the door.

Tori, feeling completely rejected, looked at him for an explanation.

"I have to go to Santa Barbara for a couple of days. I'll call you," he said, softening and retreating back toward the bed where she sat on her knees, the sheet wrapped around her body, feeling miserably vulnerable.

She wanted to ask him why he had to go, what was so urgent at three o'clock in the morning. She wanted to ask if she could go with him. She wanted to talk.

But after a distant kiss, he drew away, his mind occupied with something else, leaving her alone and worried, wishing she could turn back the clock.

Weary but awake, she watched him through the window-lined wall of his bedroom, his long-legged stride minimizing the distance as he passed through the living room snatching up his briefcase and then turning to look tensely back at her.

She hadn't been able to sleep all night after that and drove to the office when the streetlights were still sending off a diffused yellow light.

It reminded her of her early ambitious days at Jake Shavelson's company, when she had often been the first to arrive and the last to leave. The empty hallways and vacant offices always gave her a special kind of feeling. She cherished the absolute quiet those hours insured, the rare chance to operate in peace, with the phones at rest, offering stolen time to catch up, to work twice as fast and be twice as productive, with the sheer luxury of no distractions.

After depositing her purse, jacket, and briefcase in her own office, and then making herself a quick cup of coffee in the coffee room, Tori slipped self-consciously into the private sanctuary of Richard's office. She didn't believe in spying, but her curiosity and a sense of heightened foreboding had led her there anyway.

Leaning back in his glove leather chair behind his sweeping black granite desk, she sat there for a while, drinking her coffee and thinking.

Why was Richard running off to Santa Barbara in the middle of the night? Receiving disturbing phone calls at that hour? If only she knew what the conversation had been about. If only she knew what was going on.

Her relationship with him was rapidly deteriorating, and she felt absolutely powerless to do anything about it. She was in a helpless state of limbo, not breaking up with him because she felt too guilty.

She didn't want to desert him; she didn't want to confirm his assertion that the only attraction had been the money. Besides, in between shutting her out, there were those other times when he broke down and needed her.

Richard's father had shifted critical job responsibilities away from Richard and had assigned Pete Sharbut, one of Bennetton's experienced vice presidents, overlapping responsibilities to cover when Richard was not present, as though his son's disappearances were not unusual. Tori was assigned to answer to Pete and she found it almost a relief to be back in the swing of things, working normal hours, back under the gun, feeling productive.

Tori was also enjoying the opportunity of getting to know Richard's father. She could see that this was all just as hard on him. It had cost him nothing to let Richard run through money the way he had in the past because he had plenty of it. What had cost him was having to withhold it, having to endure his son's anger and the estrangement. Richard was his only son and he clearly wanted to give him every advantage. But by the same token, he also didn't want to ruin him.

Tori surmised that without Phyllis's influence, Elliot Bennetton would never have had the strength to go through with this. Though she would never have admitted it to Richard, Tori was inclined to believe that Richard would be better off for having made it through the impending ordeal—*if* he could make it through.

He was always running fast in too many directions, lacking some basic fulfillment inside. He was insecure and resentful. She just hoped it wasn't too late. No doubt Elliot Bennetton hoped the same thing.

Tori looked up at the photograph of Richard with his father.

They were so alike physically and so unalike in every other way. Or maybe it was only their backgrounds; maybe it was an interesting study in growing up hungry versus growing up "fat," their perspectives of the world, of themselves, and their needs being entirely different.

Needs. What were Richard's needs? Why did he seem to need so much? What was he trying to prove? Tori was growing increasingly worried about how mercurial he was. How could she ever hope to make a man like that happy? She wondered if he was capable of being married for the long haul, kids, station wagon, enduring the inevitable marital problems and crises, growing old together and not minding so much.

He had accused Phyllis of having middle-class values. Well, Tori had them as well. Middle-class values were solid values. What was Richard talking about, anyway?

Leaning forward in his chair, beginning to scan the various papers and files across his desk, looking for something, but having no clue as to what, she passed over big color brochures and materials on their various projects—Bennetton Estates, Bel Air Highlands, Sienna Heights, files on property just acquired downtown, a project in Irvine. Another in Seattle.

There were stacks of bills and they had been left all askew, as though Richard had been in the middle of paying them, or trying to pay them anyway, when he had left work the day before. His MasterCard bill was among the ones left open, and Tori uncurled the sheet of paper, glancing down at it.

The forty-five-thousand-dollar total she saw reflected in the little box at the bottom of the statement didn't seem possible and she picked the bill up off the desk, sure she had misread it. When she saw she had not, she was flabbergasted, finding it hard to imagine that MasterCard would even run such a limit.

Growing concerned about the time, she began to rush, looking through his other bills, rationalizing that if she were going to marry him, his debts and his problems were hers as well.

MasterCard.

American Express.

Visa.

Tiffany.

Neiman-Marcus.

Claud Montana.

Neon.

Jimmy's Restaurant.

There were additional overdue statements from his landscape architect, his pool engineer, the company that had put in his tennis court. The total picture was beyond her comprehension and, when she picked up his checkbook, which had also been left out, opening the register portion and leafing through the first month, it became too clear not to acknowledge that Richard's father was probably justified in cutting off his son, after all. The monthly payments on his four-million-dollar house alone were a sobering twenty-two thousand dollars.

Tori threw the statement she was holding back down onto the desk, amazed that, with his life collapsing down around him, he refused to back down, refused to sell anything or give up anything, refused to even talk about it.

It was beyond her understanding why he wouldn't just take his medicine and adjust his life-style until he could afford it on his own. Why he didn't at least have the sense to return the horses he bought from Alejandro in Argentina, or arrange a resale, and call off his polo sponsorship. The Chubb Insurance binder covering the horses, which she had seen on his desk, made it apparent that he had no intention of giving ground there.

He was too damn proud. That was his problem. He was spoiled and proud and hurt, and his ego had him fired up to do battle at any cost. Which was precisely what had her so concerned.

She jumped when the phone rang, feeling caught, alarmed because of last night's unsettling call *and* because it was Richard's private line. Tempted to pick it up, she listened to it ring over and over again. What if it were Richard trying to find her?

But why would he call her there? she realized. He wouldn't.

After the ringing had stopped, the metallic black phone began to seem ominous, as though it contained a secret, a missing piece of the puzzle. When it began ringing again, as though in direct response to her anxiety, she made a deal with herself. Seven rings and she would pick it up.

One. Two. Three . . . At the seventh ring, she snatched up the receiver, waiting for the party on the other end to say hello first.

"Hi, handsome. I miss you *desperately* . . ."

Tori was caught up short by the breathy female voice on the other end of the line. It was the kind of voice that went with a *Vogue* face.

"Richard—?" the voice sulked.

Tori debated. "No. This is his *secretary,*" she lied, strained. "I happened to be walking by and heard his phone ringing. May I take a message?"

The voice lost its seductive tone. "Is he in town?"

"Yes. I mean, no . . . not today. Who's calling?" she stammered, wanting to hang up.

"Jo-Jo. Listen, honey, tell him that I heard that he's engaged, that I send my congratulations. And that . . ." Jo-Jo laughed breezily. "And that I'll *miss* him."

Doing her best to sound secretarial, Tori assured Jo-Jo that she would pass on her message and then hung up. Served her right for answering his private line, she told herself, chagrined.

When the line rang again, she picked it up without thinking, only remembering after she had already said hello that it was his private line again.

"Richard Bennetton, please."

She thought about hanging up, but then, instead, curious about the thick Spanish accent, asked, "Who's calling?"

"Rio Grande Trucking Company."

"May I tell him what it's in regard to?" Tori found herself asking.

"I have the bid for him on transporting his horses from Santa Barbara to Nogales."

The Rio Grande Trucking Company? Transporting horses across the border . . . Tori felt her heart stop and she hesitated over the long-distance crackle. "Oh, good," she managed, stalling, the implications beginning to connect in her head. "Uh . . . I can take that information down for him." Her eyes shot warily over to the Chubb Insurance binder as she reached for a pencil and

unsteadily wrote down the information he was giving her, trying
to think, write, and understand his heavy accent all at once.

After she hung up the phone she sat dazed for a while, staring
down at what she had written, trying to guess the full picture.
She had come into Richard's office convinced she would find
something, and now that she actually had she was shaking.

Frustrated, she began opening his drawers, rummaging
through his benign-looking belongings, finding only pencils, pens,
loose rubber bands, business cards, matchbooks, gum.

In another drawer she noticed an unlabeled file folder and
brought it out, scanning the loose slips of paper it contained, then
the top several sheets of a legal pad. When she saw Lloyds of
London and then Chubb Insurance written down, along with fees
and policy notations, she arranged the material in front of her on
the desk and began examining it more carefully. His notes were
messy and abbreviated, but clearly what she was looking for.

On another sheet of paper she found a list of border towns,
specifying Tijuana, Mexicali, Calexico, and Nogales, with
Nogales underlined. Beneath that he had compiled a series of
trucking companies, both here in the States and in Mexico, all
listed with phone numbers. There was Ace Trucking Company,
Allied Trucking Company, Rio Grande Trucking Company,
Pronto Trucking Company, plus a couple additional Mexican-
sounding names, one of which was starred.

Carlos Aguilar's Camiones de Servicios.

Deliberating, Tori picked up the phone, about to dial their
number, then hung up again, debating about calling Paige or
Susan instead, but then not doing that either, since she hadn't
even told them yet that Richard had been cut off. He had insisted
that she not.

Beginning to feel sick to her stomach, she dumped the now
cold remains of her coffee into his wastebasket, then picked up
the phone and forced herself to dial *Carlos Aguilar's Camiones de
Servicios,* having no idea what she was going to say.

After a series of rings, someone answered in rapid-fire Spanish.

"Habla Ingles?" she tried, afraid that she would get nowhere
with her pidgin Spanish.

"Yes, but not too much," came the heavily accented reply.

Tori took a deep breath, then plunged blindly in. "My husband spoke to someone at your company about transporting some horses for us. He asked me to call to confirm the arrangements. Only I've forgotten exactly to whom it was I was supposed to speak," she said stumbling. It was a shot in the dark, but she had to go for it.

"*Sí, señora,*" the voice answered, not indicating the slightest bit of confusion. "Your horses are being transported from where?"

"Santa Barbara," Tori replied cautiously. Then, reading from Richard's list, she added, "To Nogales, I think."

Something seemed to register on the other end of the line. "*Sí, señora,*" he said again, this time with recognition. "I believe our driver should be on his way there now. If you want, I could find out for you—"

"No, never mind," she interrupted hurriedly, wondering why she had even called, dreading the possibility that Richard might find out she had.

As she hung up and glanced anxiously back over at the notes in front of her, she knew Richard's scheme could mean only one thing.

Richard was planning on defrauding his insurance company, on having his horses transported across the border so he could claim theft and collect on his policy. She wondered if he had already arranged a resale on the other side.

When his private line began to ring again, Tori nearly flew out of his chair. As it continued ringing, she restored his file to the condition in which she had found it and replaced it in his drawer.

Then she looked around for any other signs of her having been there, retrieving her coffee cup from his wastebasket, the file folder she had initially brought in with her from his desk, and slipping out just as the main line joined in the chorus of sound, marking that the day had begun.

Fortunately, nobody had seen her at Bennetton and she crept out, calling in sick from a pay phone in the parking lot.

"Yeah, there's a lot of flu going around," the receptionist sympathized in response, then asked her to hold as another line began to ring.

Tori held impatiently, feeling nervous, trying to collect her thoughts. She was staring down gloomily at her engagement ring, turning it to catch the light, all the complicated ramifications of the ring weighing on her, when she was suddenly hit with what she needed to do.

Sell the damn ring . . .

"Sorry Tori, but that was for you. A Travis Walton from Atlanta," the receptionist said, imitating Travis's drawl. "He said it was personal."

Travis. Tori was too taken aback to even respond as she took down the number, which was *their* number, and in a stupor hung up the phone.

Damn him for still having this effect on her, she thought, wanting nothing more than to be over him, to stop caring. She was engaged. Their relationship was history. And yet her heart was soaring at the mere mention of his name, rising with reckless velocity, paying no heed to the fall that was never very far behind.

The worst of it was that she needed to be sharp right now, and she couldn't begin to think straight, wondering and trying to anticipate what he wanted.

She guessed he had heard about her engagement, but *why* was he calling? To congratulate her? To plead with her not to marry Richard—to marry him instead?

Unquestionably, to throw her all off again.

Resolved not to let him, she reached for the bulky telephone directory, which was chained to the shelf beneath the pay phone. The pawnbroker listings were numerous, occupying nearly a full page, and she scanned the small text, barely able to concentrate, but trying.

Distrustful but desperate, she finally settled on one of the more established-looking boxed-in ads and dialed.

The first few calls got her nowhere; then she was referred to a jeweler in the 607 building downtown by the name of John Logan, whose primary business was dealing in colored stones.

In a nervous monotone, Tori repeated her inquiry to him.

"I can't tell you anything over the phone, if that's what you're looking for," John Logan interrupted her straight off the bat. "I'd need to see the stone—"

"If you could just give me an idea," Tori pleaded with him, trying to keep her voice even. "I don't have a lot of time, and I'm only asking for a ballpark figure. I also wanted to know if you have that kind of cash on hand—"

"The cash is not a problem, dear, but I'd still need to see the stone," he reiterated. Then, after a thoughtful pause he added, "I don't suppose you'd like to tell me how much you paid for the ring."

Tori frowned and decided, why not? "I don't mind," she replied. "We paid three hundred thousand. I don't have the receipt, but you can check with Ricardi Jewelers in the Plaza Hotel in Buenos Aires to verify the origin if you want—"

"That's a lot of money," he remarked, implying that she had been ripped off.

"It's an unusual stone," Tori argued. "My husband's not new to buying jewelry—"

"Well, you have to understand, dear, you paid retail and I buy wholesale—"

"How soon would you be able to get the money if you were to buy it from me?" Tori cut him off, getting the picture loud and clear.

"Right away," he answered coolly. "Do you have any other jewelry to sell, or is that it?"

She had to restrain herself from hanging up on him; his greed and pomposity were insulting. "No, that's it," she stated curtly. Then after asking for directions and how late he'd be open she wound up the call, bearing no false hope that this man would even begin to be fair with her.

When she saw a couple of people from the office walk by on their way to the elevator, she ducked dispiritedly around and out of sight.

Now what? Sell her three-hundred-thousand-dollar ring for ten cents on the dollar to bail out Richard, who might or might not even want to be bailed out, who might just throw the money at her and tell her she was a fool—which is exactly what she would be for making such an exchange. He had made it clear enough that he didn't want her help. But she couldn't just sit back and do nothing.

Trying to stay inconspicuous in the little alcove, she continued to fight back tears. She couldn't think straight. She needed to talk to someone. Damn it, why didn't Travis call when she was feeling great, up. She wasn't even close to capable of carrying on a coherent conversation with him now. And she was so miserably vulnerable.

Damn Richard, He didn't want her to tell anyone about this; well, that was just too bad. She was going to find Paige. Paige would know what to do.

Tori arrived at Sports Club/LA just as Paige was winding up an exercise class, and she stood at the back of the room observing, as her sexy roommate, clad in a scintillating leopard-patterned bodysuit led her frazzled group in a final round of stretches.

As usual, Paige looked like a million bucks. Svelte and radiating energy. No wonder she had Nicky Loomis eating out of the palm of her hand, waiting with boyish exuberance for her to finally decide to gift him with her body, unaware of Mark, who was getting it all the while for free—but not for keeps.

"Reach! Higher, *higher,*" Paige called out as though climbing an imaginary ladder. "Now let it go!" she ordered, folding her upper torso forward so that her honey-colored ponytail swept against the carpet. "Let all the tension drain out of your body— because all it does is make wrinkles and ulcers, anyway. And what's a good body with wrinkles and ulcers, huh, kids? Now let it *go* . . .

"Think about rejuvenating, making that deal you've been dying to make or the project you've been dying to start or get into . . . Or that man or woman you've been dying to . . ." she let her voice trail off insinuatingly. "Think energy! Think productivity! Think sex!" she teased.

The class laughed, used to Paige's playful repartee, pitching in with their own comments.

Then they all shook out their toilworn limbs, blew twenty-five times up toward the ceiling along with Paige, and applauded their instructor for a class well led.

Tori didn't think Paige had noticed her, but she realized she was wrong when Paige made a beeline across the room in her direction.

"Hey, what's wrong? You okay?" she asked, wiping the sweat off her face with a towel from around her neck, her green eyes full of concern.

Tori, conscious of the attention they had drawn, afraid that she couldn't even respond without breaking down crying again, could only shake her head. *No. She was not okay.*

Paige, reading her wish for privacy, took her arm and directed her out of the exercise room, giving another instructor a signal that she was taking off, then veering off down a series of hallways.

"Do you want some carrot juice or something? We can spike it with vodka," Paige kidded, pushing open the white lacquer door of the club's snack shop and holding it open for Tori. "Actually the celery-apple juice tastes better with vodka . . ."

Tori made a face, looking distractedly around the all-white-and-chrome snack shop while Paige selected a quiet table off in the corner, mouthing to the busboy for coffee for each of them. "You hungry? Want anything to eat? Toast?"

Tori shook her head no, inhaling the aroma of the rich blend as the busboy slid a pastel-colored mug in front of each of them.

Unsure where to begin, she looked at the soft recessed lighting above her head and took a deep breath. "Richard's been cut off," she said after a moment, turning to watch Paige's intense green eyes narrow with the news, gauging her reaction.

"When? What happened?"

"The night we got back from South America," she confessed, relieved to finally be talking about it. "At his folks' anniversary party."

Paige looked surprised but said nothing, so Tori went on, getting it all off her chest, backtracking to the unfathomable high of their trip, which she had felt awkward talking about before, in light of how it had ended, catching Paige up to the present.

Her attention kept tearing back down to the ring sparkling on her finger, the vibrant green gem that could have been cut glass. It was a souvenir of a fantasy that had died.

Paige, slouched down in her chair, was digesting the information with a tough expression on her face, interrupting every now and then to cut through to what she considered the hard-line essentials, wanting to know exactly what kind of shape he was in. Did he have anything of his own? Was he bust? When she heard about the insurance fraud and Tori's decision to pawn her ring, she frowned and threw up her hands. "You don't want this guy. *No way,*" she asserted, worried. "Even if his father has a change of heart and reinstates him. Forget about him—"

"Oh? You're the one who's so into money," Tori argued with a weak attempt at lightheartedness, nervously rotating her mug again, taking a sip.

"Not like that, I'm not."

"I can't just run out on him—"

"He's bad news," Paige insisted.

Tori sat back in her chair and smiled ironically. "Speaking of bad news, guess who called this morning?"

She didn't take her eyes off Paige, who looked at her blankly, then buried her face in her hands. "Oh, God, don't tell me! You've had a helluva morning," she observed with a groan as Tori nodded. "He heard from your old boss?"

Tori shrugged uncertainly. "I didn't talk to him. He called just as I was calling in sick."

"You want my advice?"

"Probably not. But that's why I'm here."

"Forget them both."

Tori laughed futilely and rolled her eyes. *Easy to say,* she thought dryly, as Paige went on with advice she knew she could never follow.

"Don't call Travis back. Let this play out naturally with Richard. Don't even let him know that you know. In the meantime we'll think of what you should do, and *I'll* think of who we should replace Richard with. Honestly, Tori, he's bad news."

"It's been nothing *but* bad news since I got back from South America," Tori reflected. When she noticed a very built-looking guy in Sports Club/LA sweats giving her the eye, she leaned in across the table toward Paige. "I just hate this scene," she charged under her breath. "Getting *checked* out. The kinds of inane conversations you have to have meeting someone. I've always hated it—"

"Well it's not the smartest solution in the world to get yourself tied up in the wrong relationship to the first guy that comes around to avoid it—"

"Look, *you* have fun dating. You can take it lightly, not care. And men go nuts over you. I'm too serious. I don't think it's fun at all. I'm too old for this—"

"You were probably too old for it when you were sixteen. Why can't you just look at it like you're meeting a new friend? Having a good time? Going someplace fun? Meeting other people through them?"

"Because I can't. It's not me." Tori drank the rest of her coffee in silence, dreading the muscled menace still gawking at her, dreading her life.

"So what do you want to do?" Paige prodded gently, her clear green eyes moving down to her watch.

"I don't know. I'm sorry. Go back to work," Tori told her with a wave of guilt and indecision.

"You want to hock the ring, huh?"

They both looked grimly down at it as Tori nodded her head yes.

"You would," Paige mocked. Then with a resigned sigh she pushed up from her chair. "Okay. C'mon with me," she directed, taking charge. "But we're sure as hell not going to get picked off by some shark, or you might as well not bother. This is going to take some astute finessing."

Paige's specialty, Tori thought, relieved and grateful as she allowed herself to be tugged up to her feet and steered out the door, Paige's leopard-simulated spandex-covered form drawing envy and attention as they hustled toward the ladies' locker room.

She should have known to come to Paige in the beginning.

Execution of Paige's plan began at Van Cleef and Arpels on Rodeo Drive, where they were to do some groundwork and establish price.

Inside of the swank jewelry shop, she let Paige take over,

watching her attractive friend with keen admiration. Book smart, no, but Paige still had it all over anyone she knew.

She was unquestionably in her element now, wearing Tori's emerald, letting it flash as she canvassed the glass display cases, admiring pieces, turning to Tori to ask her what she thought of this and that.

"Would you like to see something?" one of the salesmen asked.

Paige turned breezily around to respond, replying that she was looking for a necklace to match her ring. She told him she was interested in getting a stone of a similar size and quality, and that she wanted to know about how much something like that would run.

Tori watched tensely as Paige wriggled the ring off her finger, handing it to the gentleman to appraise. The two women had decided that a realistic price for the ring would fall somewhere between Van Cleef's inflated price tag and what John Logan would think he could steal it for.

He took out a loupe and meticulously studied the stone, prolonging Tori's anxiety. "It's a nice stone," he commented, looking up to regard Paige curiously for a moment, then glancing at Tori. "A very nice stone. Good color. Clear. Very few inclusions. How long have you had it?"

Paige smiled professionally. "Only a few weeks. My husband bought it for me in Argentina."

"Hmmm." The man took a final inspection of the ring, clearly impressed, then handed it back to Paige. "We don't have anything in as large as yours; generally nobody does, but we can check around and get back to you. Or we do have several loose stones in the back, from about four to four and a half carats. One that's almost five—"

"What are you asking for the five carat?" Paige asked, giving Tori a sidelong glance.

"A hundred and seventy-five thousand. It's a spectacular stone. One of the best I've seen in a long time—"

"So for an eight carat of that quality—?" Paige probed.

Tori held her breath while she waited for him to respond. *Please let it be enough to make hocking it pay off.*

He toyed with the loupe, figuring. "It's hard to say. Between four and five hundred thousand. The price doesn't go up proportionately; it jumps because of the rarity of a good stone that size."

Exchanging an encouraged look with Paige, Tori masked her relief while Paige gracefully wrapped up their encounter, saying that she would talk to her husband and, hopefully, return with him.

"*Now* we go and see your Mr. Logan," she told Tori once outside, taking her hand and ushering her toward the car, ready to do business.

The jewelry mart was located in a bustling section of downtown and Tori stood outside of the large, congested complex waiting for Paige, who had gone in to see John Logan on her own.

Paige's scheme was to make Logan think she was interested in buying a stone of the same basic size and quality as Tori's, to set him up so that when Tori went in to see him afterward, she would be in a position to negotiate a fair price. A proponent of props, Paige had torn a Bulgari necklace ad from out of an issue of *Town & Country* and brought it in along with her, planning on saying that she had just recently been in the South of France and had seen a woman in a restaurant wearing one like it, that she wanted to know if he could make one up for her, and for how much.

She had rehearsed a series of little finishing touches to make it all look more credible, how she wanted to make sure the stone fit into the hollow of her neck, how maybe he could design the piece to double as a necklace *and* a pin. She would confess she had just been to Van Cleef, where the largest stone there was a five carat, which would do, but she would rather have a bigger one. She would add that she didn't have a lot of time to look around, that her husband had just closed a big deal and was in the buying mood *now*.

Leaning against the old art deco building while waiting for Paige, her stomach a vat of butterflies, Tori tried to busy herself people-watching. There was an energy and a pace to downtown Los Angeles that made her think of New York. The urban resurgence was exhilarating, and the new crop of buildings sprouting high into the skyline glistened beneath the strong afternoon sun.

Tori was just wondering which modern glass and steel tower housed Susan's law firm, when Paige sidled up beside her, her tight topaz T-shirt suggestively outlining her bust, her long linen skirt blowing in the breeze. "He's all yours, dearie," she announced grinning.

Tori closed her eyes in relief, wishing Paige could perform the next step for her as well.

Allowing a couple of hours for Logan to sweat over whether or not Tori was even coming in, and to keep it all from appearing too suspicious, the two of them headed up the street, attempting to kill time, looking disinterestedly into the windows of the various wholesale shops, on the lookout for someplace to eat.

Tori was in a fog throughout it all, going over with Paige what she should say, for what price she should settle, as well as what to say to Richard.

As for Travis, Paige made her promise not to call him back.

When it was time, they returned to the mart and Tori went inside alone, her ring back on her finger, sparkling above her clenched fist, feeling as though she were participating in some bizarre and terrible charade.

As Paige had predicted, Logan was ready to deal when Tori walked through the door. There were thick beads of perspiration clinging to his brow and over his lip, which he kept mopping away with the back of his hand as they addressed her precious green gem.

She hadn't expected to get so emotional, but as she worked the ring off of her finger, and watched him appraising it, she began to feel as though her heart were breaking all over again.

She was back in time at Tiffany's waiting for Travis to show up, the significant black velvet trays arranged across the countertop, her mother waiting without any faith in a chair just a few feet away.

Then it was a different stone with a different man, emeralds instead of diamonds, but the same cut of disappointment. She remembered the sheer intoxication she had felt shopping with Richard, the unreal thrill as he had slid ring after ring onto her finger, insisting that emeralds, unlike both their experiences with diamonds, would be forever.

Wrong. Wrong. Wrong.

Tori found herself also beginning to sweat, something a well-bred southern belle never did, as she haggled with the unctuous jeweler, neither of them budging. They went at it for well over an hour, John Logan growing more and more agitated, a sore loser and apparently unaccustomed to such stony resistance.

"Don't back down! The stone is magnificent, great quality, and exactly what he knows I want to buy." Clinging fiercely to Paige's words, replaying them over and over again in her mind, Tori held her ground, intent on not settling for a penny less than Richard had paid for the ring in Argentina.

But she wondered if it were not a Pyrrhic victory when she emerged at last from the bank on the first floor of the building, the cashier's check in hand. Looking down at it and then down at her now vacant wedding-ring finger she found herself missing the dazzling shock of green that had lit up her hand for the last couple of weeks.

She found herself having doubts over what she had done—or rather *undone*.

Chapter 23

It was just after eight o'clock when Tori arrived in Santa Barbara, still in her work clothes from that morning, a lightweight teal suit that was crumpled by now. Richard owned a condominium within the Polo Club complex, and she parked her car, hoping she was not too late.

It seemed that she and Paige had gone over virtually every scenario, *except* the "too late" scenario.

Projecting a courage she didn't feel, she climbed down from Dustin Brent's Bronco, keeping her eyes alert for any sign of Richard, his car, or a truck or trailer emblazoned with *Carlos Aguilar's Camiones de Servicios,* as she descended into the brisk night.

Ordinarily the faint scent spiking the air would have calmed her, the odor of horses, the ocean nearby, under the brilliant black sky above looking like an open treasure chest of stars pitched for wishing. But in this instance she knew nothing could calm her.

Nothing short of Richard rushing toward her, promising that the nightmare was over, that it was all okay now.

But Tori was beyond fantasizing at this point and she reached gloomily over for her purse, uncomfortable as hell about walking around with a three-hundred-thousand-dollar cashier's check. It was as though the soft pouch-fashioned leather bag contained something lethal. Maybe it did, she considered, as she slipped it over her shoulder and began walking toward the brightly lit condominium complex, feeling the crunch of gravel beneath her heels.

Richard's condo was up on the first level, overlooking the sprawling stretch of polo field, and Tori knocked tentatively on his door, unsure what to expect, if he would even be there.

When she heard his voice, she felt more nervous than relieved, even thought about turning and running off. But then the door was suddenly opened and he was standing facing her, surprised, but not unfriendly.

"Tori. What are you doing here? Something wrong?" he asked guardedly.

She swallowed hard, trying to find her voice. "I need to talk to you," she murmured uncertainly, feeling like an intruder as she peered beyond him and into the room he seemed to be screening off from her, wondering if there was somebody inside.

His jaw tightened, and he ran his hand over his unshaven face. "I guess I should have called," he apologized quickly, mistaking the reason for her being there. "But I had something up here that I had to take care of, right away, and I just didn't get a chance to get back to you. It's been kind of crazy. I'm sorry." He looked awful and Tori felt sorry for him. His eyes were bloodshot and the circles beneath them more pronounced.

"It's okay," she said, slipping her unadorned wedding-ring finger out of sight and into the back pocket of her skirt, undergoing a rash of second thoughts. What if this were all innocent? she considered guiltily. What if she were completely off base? This had all happened in such a compressed timeframe that she began to wonder if she hadn't jumped to false conclusions.

"You cold?" he asked, surprised because it was a warm night and, even though she was wearing a jacket, she was shivering.

"No, just nervous," she answered truthfully, trembling from a prickly, anxiety-induced chill that had nothing to do with the climate. She was wound up so tightly inside that she could barely respond, could barely think. Her conversation with the Mexican trucking company hovered like a black cloud.

He eyed her curiously, as though sensing something. "Nervous? That's not like you. Why?"

She felt as if she were being *Gaslight*ed. He had to know why. Unable to hold it in any longer, and lacking the presence of mind for tact, Tori blurted it all out, everything, how she had gone into his office in the morning, the phone calls, the file she had found, weakly justifying her actions, but shrinking under his mood.

He dropped all pretense of friendliness and went stone-cold as he listened, turning darkly away from her and stalking off into his condo.

She followed timidly, closing the door for privacy, relieved to see that there wasn't anyone else there.

"What kind of fucking game do you think you're playing?" he shouted, as she told him about selling the ring. His face had gone beet-red with rage and when she reached into her purse for the cashier's check she had gotten from John Logan, Richard seized her purse from her grasp and sent it flying across the room.

"This is just fucking great," he ranted, looking betrayed, violated. "First my father, then my *fiancée*—"

"Richard, I was *concerned*—"

"*Concerned?*"

"Yes—"

"That doesn't give you license to—"

"I knew you were in trouble and I was only trying to help—" Tori argued, stunned at the depth of his anger, his bitterness.

"I don't need your help. I don't need anyone's fucking help—"

"Everybody needs help. Why can't you just admit that you're human. Okay, so you have to change some things in your life for a while, until you get back on your feet and get everything squared away—"

"You don't get the picture. I *am* changing things. And this is none of your fucking business. Don't you *ever* fucking *spy* on me—"

He had his finger pointed in her face and she recoiled, pushing it angrily out of the way. "It *is* my business. I'm you're fiancée. Or have we called all that off?"

"Hey, *you* called it off when you sold your ring," he sneered vindictively. "I told you how I felt about that ring. About your trusting me. Now *I* don't trust *you*—"

"Richard, you can't go around defrauding insurance companies—"

"So instead of the insurance companies getting to fuck me, this time I'm getting to fuck them," he scoffed. "After a lifetime's worth of paying their damn premiums, I assure you they'll still come out on top."

"That's not the point—"

"No? What is the point?"

"That you can't go around making dirty deals and getting away with it. This is stupid. It's shortsighted. I just got three hundred thousand dollars for you. Take it and call this damn thing off, if it's not already too late."

"It's not too late," he replied treacherously. His contemptuous look shot right through her. "But I have no intention of calling it off. *God,* are you naive! While it's none of your fucking business, Tori, just to set the record straight—do you want to know about all the *dirty deals* my pious father made in order to get to where he is today, in order to earn his pillar-of-the-community status? The payoffs? The agreements he reneged on? The guys he picked off or cheated along the way? All so sanctimoniously in the name of *business* . . .

"Don't delude yourself, princess. There isn't anybody who's made a lot of money who hasn't stepped outside the law, worn blinders. Look at all the robber barons, like Joe Kennedy or John D. Rockefeller. You think they didn't bend the rules to suit their purposes? You think they didn't walk all over people, engage in *questionable* business practices, joint ventures with guys they knew were on the take? Only their descendants had the *luxury* to go straight. After the family had made it. Now *I* need to make it."

Richard was so overwrought that Tori thought it pointless to even go any further. While she wanted to help him, this was all so far over her head she didn't know what to do or say. He was obviously messed up, cracking under all the pressure. And she half wondered, Who wouldn't? There were partially consumed bottles of Scotch and cognac out, grass and coke paraphernalia, greasy pizza cartons, Chinese take-out. Quite a binge for only one day.

She had no idea if it were true or not, what he was saying about his father, and she didn't even know if it mattered. What mattered was that this was a different time, and Richard was a different person, with different opportunities—opportunities that he was about to blow. She didn't want to see him doing something foolish, something for which he would find himself paying for the rest of his life, just because he was hurt and angry. Tori knew it had to be difficult growing up in the shadow of a man like Elliot Bennetton. She could see after working there these last couple of weeks that while Richard's father was a generous man, fun, with a keen intellect, and deeply loved his son, his ego could easily be emasculating. He would want Richard right up there beside him, but then, unable to control himself, he would *compete* with him. The powerful elder sparring with his younger, greener seedling, out to prove to himself that his excessive virility was still intact, that he was still on top.

Hoping to break the ice, to turn things around, Tori crossed over to Richard, standing very close.

He drew her left hand up quietly, fondling where the large emerald rock had occupied her finger, looking wounded by its absence.

"I'm sorry," she whispered, wishing she had listened to Paige. Even if Richard were wrong for her, even with what she had learned about him after his disinheritance, she hadn't been prepared for what she had provoked. She ran her hand gently across his beard, grazing the blond-hued stubble. "It was *only* a ring, Richard," she ventured timorously.

"No. It was *more* than only a ring," he countered with acerbic regret, his voice so low that it was unnerving. "It was my *engagement* ring to you. *Remember?*"

Releasing her hand he walked across the room, bending down to retrieve her purse, and then flinging it over to her to catch. "Like I said once before, no ring, no engagement. You can do whatever the fuck you want with the three hundred grand, little Georgia Peach," he remarked stingingly. "I don't give a damn about it, and I don't give a damn about you. The fact is, now it *is* only *money*."

"Don't kid yourself. It was always only money—and you happen to need the cash from it right now more than I need the ring. Break off our engagement because you're not in love with me. That I can accept. But this is bullshit," Tori exploded shrilly, struggling to get the check out of her purse and throw it right back at him. "Keep your bullshit *and* your money. I don't want any part of either."

But Richard was already on his way out the door, his back to her, one of the half-empty bottles of Scotch dangling from his hand. Sneeringly he turned around, refusing to acknowledge the money falling at his heel.

Wishing she could think of something that would finally penetrate his thick skull, but unable to, she walked out without saying anything, stepping around the check, chasing out past him, through the doorway, and then moving swiftly to where the Bronco was parked.

"You got too much fuckin' pride, Georgia Peach," he shouted after her, a mocking grin on his fatigued but handsome face, taking a swig from the whiskey bottle. "You oughta at least keep the money. *You earned it!*"

Tears stung her cheeks as she sped up her pace, working hard to ignore him as he continued calling after her.

"Oh, *I* know. You want *love*. Not money. Payment in *kisses* and *reverence*. *Love* and *virtue*. You want to be *loved to distraction*."

"So do you, you bastard!" she couldn't help hollering back at him, whipping around just long enough to get the words out.

"No, I'm far more practical than that. You should be too," he urged loudly, his words dripping with sarcasm. "I want *money*, first and foremost. See where love gets you? You should have learned that li'l ol' lesson from your hunk *boyfriend* in Atlanta. Love begets pain whilst money begets *more* money—begetting power and then all the love you can handle."

"Well, it all kind of loses something in a jail cell, don't you think!" she shot fiercely back over her shoulder without turning around. "You better hurry up or you'll miss your Mexican truckers."

"Ooooh! Very good! You're so *cute* when you're mad, Tori." She could hear him beginning to run only a few feet behind her now and she tried to wrench free as he caught up with her, grabbing her by the waist. "C'mon, let me buy a little fuck in the bushes. Take the three hundred grand and let me fuck your little pussy in the moonlight," he growled, pleading, overpowering her, dragging her behind the hedge and then tackling her onto a stretch of damp grass.

"Goddamn you! Get away from me!" she screamed, fighting him off with every ounce of strength she possessed. *"Not for all the money in the world."*

"Okay. Have it your way then, *for free.*"

"Not on your life," she shrieked even more fiercely, swinging at him as he grabbed her hair and yanked her head back. She tried to catch her breath as he thrust the whiskey bottle into her mouth, pouring, so that it went sloshing all over her and him and onto the ground, causing her to gag. It was impossible not to swallow, and the rush of Scotch traumatized her throat as it went down. The fumes reeked heavily on his breath as he eclipsed her mouth with his, his tongue probing hard, running along her teeth.

If she had known how to gauge the blow so that it would only knock him out but not kill him, she would have torn the bottle away from him and cracked him over the head with it.

"Oh, don't even think about it," he taunted, seeing where her eyes were fixed, reading her mind.

Laughing lustily and pinning her down on the grass with one hand, he pulled up her skirt, then began pouring a stream of whiskey over her panties, spilling it generously, then soaking it up with his mouth.

"This is a cock*tease,* not a cock*tail,*" he crooned lewdly, his breath hot, moist, making her squirm. Intent on arousing her, he continued to pour, pulling down her panty hose and then her panties, so that the Scotch washed over her directly, stinging and yet feeling unexpectedly sensuous at the same time.

Alarmed but past struggling, confused, she lay absolutely still, every muscle taut. She was intent on making him think she felt nothing as she lay frigid, that she had given up on fighting and was merely enduring. She was too angry, too upset, to give in to the oddly erotic sensations she was beginning to feel.

He was crazy; this was lunacy. Who knew who could walk by? And she was still smarting from all the verbal assaults.

She had no idea what to think. She had never felt so mixed up in her life. Was their engagement genuinely off? *And what did she even want?* Was Richard just venting his frustration before giving in, his pride fractured, behaving like a kid at the windup of a tantrum? Maybe she had gotten through to him and he was going to call off the horse theft.

"Let go of me, you son of a bitch," she screamed, trying to wrestle free from him again, a fight he seemed to enjoy because he smiled meanly, climbing over to straddle her. "This is too much. I don't care what you're going through . . ."

"You love it," he shouted back through gritted teeth.

"You arrogant bastard! I hate it! I hate you!" she screamed, infuriated at the inequity of physical power.

Breathing heavily, he unzipped his jeans and pulled them down, his erection bold and exposed as he drained what was left from the bottle of Scotch then leaned over and in the pretense of a kiss released it into her mouth, instructing her to hold it there, then hastily moving up to crouch braced over her face.

"Take me in your mouth," he ordered coarsely, his blue eyes narrowing.

Demoralized, she shook her head, still sustaining the mouthful of Scotch, tempted to spit it in his face instead.

Without waiting for her consent or compliance, he thrust his cock into her mouth, in doing so releasing another cascade of the alcohol. *"Oh, God! Yes, darling, darling . . ."* he bellowed, moaning with what seemed like a culmination of pleasure and pain, calling out her name, continuing to deify the experience, thrusting into her mouth until she began to gag and he had to pull out.

Before she could even react, he had lowered himself and was screwing her in an almost cruel pursuit, his hips slapping hard against hers, thrashing into her with an emotional vengeance, his pace harsh and demanding.

As he drew her legs up and around his waist, he began telling her how much he loved her, breathing heavily into her ear. She didn't know where to concentrate first, with all the mixed messages, receiving sensations from all directions, still conscious of the damp grass beneath them and the faint breeze stirring the air as he began kissing her passionately on the lips.

And then in the distant background of this ghastly experience, she heard him crying out as he climaxed.

They lay together quietly for a moment. She was afraid to even breathe, feeling used, mortified, and at the same time torn because she could see the kind of pain Richard was in. She was wondering if this were some kind of bizarre reconciliation, wondering if that's what she wanted it to be. She was half expecting Richard to break down and apologize, to reveal to her all the things he was feeling inside, the turmoil, the conflict, the crushing emotional anguish.

But then instead, his abruptness seeming intentionally ruthless, he sprung off her, zipping his jeans closed with a curt motion, and then, taking a moment to glance at his watch, he strode off.

"Time for the *big* score," he clarified mockingly over his shoulder, heading into the darkness, presumably toward the stables to meet with the Mexican truckers.

Feeling like a hole had been blown into her heart, Tori couldn't do anything other than lie there and watch, pledging, never, as long as she lived, to allow herself to be so humiliated again.

She cried the whole way home from Santa Barbara. One of those long, deep-in-the-chest cries that begins triggered by one thing and then, by the time you're really into it, snowballs so that finally you're crying about everything, feeling as though your world is completely collapsing, with no way out, nothing salvageable, no solution.

She kept envisioning driving into the center divider of the freeway and just getting it over with simply, the coward's way. She could barely see where she was going anyway, needing a windshield wiper for her tears.

She thought about driving into the ocean, submerging her misery beneath its great mysterious depths, or walking along the beach, unresistant and perverse prey for a prowling derelict, who unsuspectingly would be doing her a favor by adding her to the murdered-while-walking-along-the-beach-alone-at-night mortality statistics. But, God, what if *he* raped her too?

She needed to be cleansed. Purged.

It was a case of melancholy unleashing melodrama—the Pandora's box sprung. Dominoes.

Richard. Travis. Her mother. God! even work. Bravo, Tori. She had even managed to screw up her career, formerly the only safe and secure area of her life.

Was this all her fault? she wondered miserably. Was she so self-destructive that she made these things happen?

Bleakly, she went on with self-recriminations, hearing her mother's voice, adopting her tone, expanding perfectly, poignantly, so aptly and so realistically that it was as if she had her mother sitting in the car beside her or plugged into her thoughts. She thought if she called her at home in Atlanta right this very moment, she wouldn't even wake her because she was already up, busy sending extrasensory communications to her daughter anyway. She thought that her mother would be relieved to know that her communications were being received.

When Tori drove back home through the electronic wrought-iron gates of Dustin Brent's home and up the driveway, it wasn't her *own* voice in her head caustically and, yes, enviously, noting Mark Arent's motorcycle in the driveway.

Nor was it her own voice that predicted that Paige and her prize-sap boyfriend were upstairs screwing in Paige's bedroom, when Tori let herself into the big old Spanish house.

Nor was it her own voice snidely commenting after each message left on the answering machine as she played them all back, listening through two from Nicky calling from New York, where he was away for a couple days on business, a couple more for Paige from other men, one for Susan from an associate at her law firm, calling to fix her up again *but warning* that she was about to give up since Susan refused to ever come up from work for air.

It was indubitably her *mother's* voice, continuing to point out, again and again, what a failure Tori was and would always be.

The cutting edge of her voice faded only after it tore apart the last two messages, which were both from *Travis,* and after a last nasty commentary on how Paige and Mark were *definitely* upstairs screwing, must have been for quite some time, since there was such a pile-up of messages left on the machine.

As Tori wrote down the last one, trying to eradicate her mother's domineering presence from her mind, the phone rang and she picked it up, thinking *Travis, Richard,* praying *not Mother,* then deciding it was *probably just another call for Paige.*

The familiar, honeyed drawl of Travis's voice coming in uncertainly over the line permeated every aspect of her being. If she had been a high-risk heart patient, she would have gone into cardiac arrest and died, but *ah, so contentedly.*

Was it Travis to the rescue, just when she needed him more than ever? Had he come through for her this time?

She couldn't concentrate on a single word he was saying or decide how to respond, knowing only that, after a seeming eternity, she was hearing his voice again.

He rambled on about how much he had missed her, telling her everything she wanted to hear, wreaking havoc on all her stored-up resolve. It was a dot-to-dot conversation composed of so many only previously fantasized ones, connecting smoothly and in all the right places, spelling out sentiments that were so sweet and dear to hear that they seemed fresh and almost as though she hadn't heard them all a million times before.

Travis had learned about her engagement through Jake Shavelson and then through her mother who had seen his mother at the market. He told her how he had been going crazy these last couple of months, pining away, unable to believe that she had really meant business this time.

He said he found it impossible living in their place without her, every inch of space reminding him of her. The art on the walls that they had collected together. The all-knowing living room couch on which they had made love and war, and sometimes a little of each within the course of the same battle. The selection of Laura Ashley wallpaper in the bedroom, for which she had spent weeks lobbying. The colored tissue in the bathrooms. The stereo that was always on when she was around, that was now never on. All the empty spots where their photographs used to be.

It was a better speech than usual because their separation had been longer than ever before and because the stakes had soared, with her now living in L.A. and having become engaged.

Thank God, she was composed enough to not let him know that her engagement was off, she thought, feeling otherwise out of control.

"Tori. Would you at least say something?" Travis insisted. "Go ahead and let me have it. Tell me to drop dead, to go to hell if you want, but at least *say* something."

He was telling her exactly what she wanted to hear, what she had been waiting a lifetime to hear, and yet she was powerless to react.

She had worked so hard all these weeks at *not* caring, applied all that self-hypnosis on how to get over her lover, spent so much precious energy trying to quell the fire that had burned her repeatedly, that now she was caught between relieved, giddy excitement and, on another level, feeling nothing.

It was so tough to discern if the emotional block producing the "nothing" was for real or not.

Trying to cut through the emotional thicket to read her heart accurately, she glanced out through the large, arched window of the den where she was sitting at the bar, out through to the softly lit garden where he was supposedly laid to rest, pronounced "dead, buried, and forgotten" beneath a patch of purple and yellow petunias now in full bloom, a profusion of macabre celebration.

"Tori?" Travis repeated, exasperated, very much alive.

What was he asking her to say, she wondered in a trance. *All's forgiven? I'm coming home?* His voice felt farther away than Atlanta. More like an echo from a dream, and she was so tired that she had to wonder for a moment if it weren't.

She felt herself melting as she pictured him as clearly as if she had seen him yesterday, wanting to throw her arms around the image and yield.

If they were on the "all-knowing" couch now, they would simply be making love, and she wouldn't have to answer him with words, only with her soul, which said *yes* always to anything he asked.

But her words were governed, at least partially, by another force. Not only her heart, but her brain, her mind, logic, and some small grain of self-preservation, which told her emphatically that she was *not* out to self-destruct, in spite of what had happened only a couple hours ago with Richard.

The message *resist* unfurled from the same part of her brain that issued pride, dignity, and reason, by way of past experience and memory.

And it was this part of her brain that generated the words that reminded Travis how she had heard so many versions of all this before, that made her stop and ask if he had gotten any farther on in obtaining his divorce, and that sorted through the bullshit of his response to see that, for all practical purposes, he had not.

In the middle of a slightly updated alibi she hung up the phone, resisting only a weak, dull urge this time to pick up the phone and call him back.

Her temptation was equally great to call Richard in Santa Barbara. And yet she knew that would only result in a downward spiral.

She kept thinking about all the abusive things Richard had said to her, feeling dirty, used, and even ashamed.

A door closed upstairs and Tori tensed, wondering if Paige had heard her. The last thing she wanted to have to do right now was talk to anyone, even to Paige. She didn't want to have to talk or explain.

When nobody appeared, Tori, relieved, looked over in the direction of the bottle of Armagnac, whose contents were steadily disappearing. Longing for a drink, longing to drink herself into oblivion, she stepped to the bar to pour herself a glass then lifted it up to toast her reflection in the mirror.

What a sobering sight she was, with makeup smeared all around her bloodshot eyes from crying, streaked down her cheeks.

A grim view of a young woman's sorrowful state—a young woman who kept messing up when it came to men.

Tori raised her glass up higher, following the angle with her chin. "To the new life I moved out here to find. To putting old things behind me and going forward. To staying on track," she proposed sincerely.

As she brought the glass to her lips, tasting a residue of salt from so many spilled tears, a picture of Dustin Brent that she hadn't noticed before caught her eye.

Wryly she redirected her glass up toward him instead, drawn by his smile that was so genuine and so comforting she found it hard not to smile back at him.

The truth was she had *him* to thank, to toast, for her new life, for the possibilities and opportunities opened up to her, waiting to be experienced if she only possessed the nerve. Looking at him now she felt inspired to try.

His kind of nerve, she thought, tipping her glass to him, thinking about the kind of fortitude that drove and sustained him in building a multimillion-dollar company from scratch. Then the kind of grit and spirit to sell it as he had, turning to meet new challenges.

Maybe it was that his ego seemed so healthy and buoyant, freeing him to be honest, straightforward, and unshrinkingly sure of himself in a way that Travis or Richard could never be. She thought of the postcard she had received from him when she had returned to L.A., congratulating her on her engagement to Richard and telling her that if she changed her mind he'd catch a flight right back to the States to claim his rightful place, if only he'd had his eyes open at Kit and George's wedding when he'd met her. The tone of his note had obviously been joking, but she considered the irony, thinking of him clear across the world, where he said he'd now be keeping tabs on her.

It was the sense of Dustin watching her from afar, like a wise and caring old friend that kept her from picking up the phone now and calling either Travis or Richard.

She could handle Dustin Brent watching her drink herself silly, as she sat there consuming shot after shot of Armagnac, growing woozy but failing to feel its full numbing effect. But she couldn't handle him watching her swallow her pride and play the fool.

Dustin's presence, growing as real as her mother's earlier, fused with the Armagnac, finally lulled Tori to sleep, right there at the bar, feeling distantly surprised that she could still smell the fresh scent of her soap from this morning's shower as her nose nestled into the crook of her arm, which was the best she could do for a pillow right now.

Just before she lost consciousness she thought fleetingly of Paige and what her reaction to all this would be—Paige who was upstairs gamely enjoying the best of both worlds.

Chapter 24

Seated at his corner booth in the steak house near his plant, Jack Wells had his ear to the phone and was speaking dogmatically to the party on the other end of the line. His brow was furrowed. His wide, hooded eyes appeared even moodier than usual. The small, white-clothed table in front of them was littered with paperwork, files, and newspaper clippings about the strike, all crammed around his unfinished plate of plain broiled sole and rice without butter. It looked as cluttered as his desk in his office, Susan thought.

As usual, it was a working lunch. Just as dinners with Jack Wells were always working dinners. As far as Susan could see, her client did little else.

Of course he would probably say the same of her. They were a perfect pair. All work and no play. Except that as a pair they had never yet gotten beyond work.

It was a very strange relationship. Jack Wells was a very strange man.

Susan vacillated in her feelings for him, finding him appealing but tough, difficult to connect with for any length of time. Just as they would start to relax and have fun, talk about themselves, laugh a little, he would tighten and retreat, giving her mixed signals, making it so that she never knew where she stood.

The strike negotiations at his plant had escalated to such a degree that they were all working around the clock, with Susan now working exclusively on Jack's case, breaking her neck to work out a resolution between her thick-headed client and his equally unyielding workers, in what had become an unbridgeable stalemate. Every session, their arguments went round and round in the same vicious circles, the union leaders ready to give way, and the rank and file members refusing to compromise.

"Goddamn," Jack said, hanging up the telephone.

"What's happened?" Susan asked, dragging a French fry though a mound of catsup on her plate, then eating it.

Her client was stewing. "Some joker got that incident this morning on video, and ran it for the police and the networks. It'll make more great copy," he remarked, slapping a pile of newspaper clippings with the back of his hand. "A Mercedes hauls ass through the picket line and winds up with a Teamster decorating its polished German hood. As it lurches to a stop, the striker reels off and onto his feet, cocks his arm, and discharges his fist through the driver's window, redefining the glass into a spider-weblike mass and wrecking his hand. The driver of the Mercedes is unimpaired. But he gets the message: 'The poor angry strikers.' I'm so tired of all this publicity crap. Why doesn't everybody just go back to work and do their job?"

Susan smiled over her glass of Pepsi, the top of her glass knocking into her eyeglass frames as she polished off the balance.

"Hey, Kendell Brown, you represent *me,* counselor, not *them,* this time. So knock off the smirk and keep your sympathies in line with the source of your paycheck."

"They are," Susan insisted, even though they were not. "You have a problem with my representation?" she teased.

"Your representation is perfect. But I can read your mind, and I don't necessarily like what I read all the time," Jack frowned and stabbed at his fish with his fork. "Hey, so go represent the workers again. You know how it goes: you represent management, you eat steak; you represent the workers, you eat pre-wrapped sandwiches and tacos."

Susan smiled again, and he allowed himself a brief laugh, running his finger absently over the slashlike scar across his face.

"I know, you *like* tacos," he said.

Going for her last French fry, she shrugged in accord. Then conscious of maintaining the appropriate level of professionalism because she knew that was important to him, she shifted gears, launching into a strategy that had occurred to her this morning on her way over to the plant.

He interrupted her midstream, looking down at his watch, and beginning to grab up his files. "We'd better start back, huh?"

"I take it you're not too keen on my strategy," Susan observed, dabbing at her mouth with the cloth napkin from her lap, then discarding it onto the table.

"Actually, I am," he said, leading the way out, looking down at his watch again. "We'll just be more comfortable discussing it in my office. Your lunch all right?"

"Fine—"

"Listen, what are you doing tonight? How about a nonworking night together, for a change," he asked, surprising her by putting his free hand around her waist. "No business discussions permitted." It was the first clear-cut romantic overture Jack had made to Susan and, caught off guard, she looked at him.

"What did you have in mind?" she asked, skeptical but pleased. They'd gone this long maintaining perfect professionalism, she couldn't help wonder how this might affect their working relationship.

He smiled mischievously, continuing to lead the way out. "Have you ever had a shiatsu massage?"

Surprised and still dubious, Susan laughed. "No."

"Hmmm. You can't imagine what you're missing . . ."

"Oh, really?"

"Trust me."

She eyed him again and then they both laughed.

"I thought I'd take you to my Korean hideaway in Koreatown."

"What's that?"

"It's built over a natural hot springs, very therapeutic, and very exotic. They have spectacular private baths, all done in marble and sparkling clean. Private hot and cold mineral baths, steam, sauna, massage, where they really do walk on your back, and a wonderful Korean dinner."

"Your average first-date kind of place," Susan joked. "Let me guess the attire . . ."

He grinned, looking her up and down in a way he never had before and making her blush.

"Can't we work our way into something like this? I hate to sound like a prude, but—"

". . . you're a small-town girl from Stockton, I know," he finished for her. "Listen, you and I have had more dates and spent more time together than I've spent with any woman in a long time."

Susan looked at him curiously, wondering if that was true. Given the amount of time he seemed to spend away from work, she believed him.

"They have towels and kimonos. The Koreans are very modest. I'll close my eyes and behave like a perfect gentleman," he promised, deadpan.

Susan wanted to ask him why the sudden change? What had caused him to want to shift gears? Then she decided she was taking this all too seriously. Why not just let everything play out? Wasn't this the kind of overture she had been waiting for? Why was she thinking so much? Why couldn't she just go with it?

"Mr. Wells," the maître d' called after him, just as they were about to step outside. "Telephone for you, sir. Would you like to pick it up at the front desk?"

When Jack asked the waiter to forward the call to his office, stuffing a fiver in his hand without slowing down his pace, Susan looked at him surprised. It was completely uncharacteristic of Jack Wells to not take a phone call, any place, any time, to not even ask who it was. He missed her perplexity because he was already preoccupied, looking down at his watch.

They returned to the plant to find the truckloads of plant replacements just leaving, lined up and waiting to exit behind the gate, which was routinely opened at this hour by a guard.

It was a typical scene, unruly but usual, with strikers hurling eggs at the trucks, both sides shouting at each other, actively venting their anger and frustration. Susan, in her heels, had to step over the broken shards of glass, alert and ducking eggs. She nearly bumped into a dummy, which had a placard strung down around its neck, forewarning Death of a Scab.

Here was *exactly* the kind of tension that put fists through car windows, she thought, recalling this morning's incident and taking in the chaos around her, watching the picketers taunt and curse the truckloads of temporary workers, accusing them of stealing their jobs.

The substitute workers replied by waving their paychecks in the air.

And this strike was tame compared to some of the strike lock-outs involving the bigger chain operations, like the big chain markets or meat packers unions where trucks were being towed to the warehouses, with radiators and tires shot out, having been ambushed with gunfire, substitute drivers wounded.

Susan remembered the time a driver was treated for burns after a large firecracker had alighted in his lap and exploded. Then another time when four substitute workers driving out of one of the big chain supermarket warehouses were rammed from behind by a pickup truck, reeled around, and rammed twice more. One person had been only slightly injured, but the supermarket chain, distraught over all the bad publicity, had offered a ten-thousand-dollar reward for the arrest of the driver of the pickup. After that, they had felt compelled to hire a horde of additional security guards, many with permits to carry guns, to follow the trucks.

Thankfully, the strike at Jack Wells' plant hadn't risen to that degree of warfare.

It was a more common-looking strike zone, full of aggression but no flying bullets. On one side of the front there was the Teamsters' bivouac, where portable toilets were lined up. Nearby, lazy flames were lapping from inside a rusty fifty-five-gallon drum (they had cut back on the fires since Susan's accident), and across the way was an old camper belonging to a retired trucker and his wife who were there daily, sustaining the strikers with homemade chili, chicken soup, hot coffee, and moral support. Susan couldn't help her deep-rooted feelings of sympathy as she passed through troops of picketers, thinking of her father and his friends, trying not to look anyone in the eye.

With the aggression mounting, it suddenly occurred to her that there was no guard on duty to open the gate for the departing trucks. Instead, a burly-looking replacement had finally taken it upon himself to jump down off his truck and open it himself, muscling his way through the throng of jeering strikers.

As he approached the gate, amidst the usual shouting and commotion, he passed close by the group of workers Susan knew from the strike negotiations; then, for no apparent reason, he shoved the pregnant wife of one of the men down to the ground. She was also a worker in the plant, and as she hit the pavement, falling back spread-eagle, her picket sign went reeling through the air.

Without thinking, Susan started to run off to see if she was all right, then was surprised to feel Jack's grip on her arms holding her back, insisting under his breath what a pain in the ass the woman and her clan were, that they had been asking for this.

Restrained from interceding, Susan was forced to watch, baffled and helpless, as the husband, in response to the incident, went berserk and threw himself onto the replacement, pummeling him until four more scabs climbed down out of the truck and jumped *him*, setting off a full-fledged riot as packs of strikers rushed to the aid of their coworkers, bloodying the replacements who, by now outnumbered, were wisely retreating, fighting their way back into the truck for safety.

What struck Susan was that just as the violence had begun to grow out of hand, at least two dozen security guards had appeared, as though on cue, some armed with billy clubs, others armed with cameras. Since photographs were not permitted in peaceful picket lines, Susan was dubious of the seemingly induced outbreak that had conveniently legitimized their admissibility. She wasn't buying the sudden timely appearance of all these cameras, produced just at the right moment by suddenly double the ratio of security guards than had previously been in Jack Wells's employ, all ready to converge at this instant to document the uproar.

It seemed staged to her.

Jack's anxiousness to rush back to the plant. The camera-armed guards exchanging silent communications with Jack, as though they were carrying out his orders.

And the key subjects whose pictures had been taken, by no coincidence, Susan feared, just happened to be the workers who were refusing to go along with the union leaders and yield in the strike settlement. They were the one group holding up the works.

She could already guess Jack's scheme; the set-up seemed so blatant. Everyone in the pictures would get fired, creating an unscrupulous but efficient way for management and union to finally come to terms, maneuvering a legitimate axing of those impeding the process. Susan couldn't help but wonder if she wasn't one of the pawns in his plan as well—if his sudden romantic interest wasn't a calculated maneuver meant to manipulate her or distract her from the unjust method he was using to settle his strike.

Susan felt a renewal of pressure on her arm, as Jack, apparently having seen enough, began to direct her away from the commotion and over toward the building.

He looked almost satisfied, she thought, turning back around to see if the pregnant woman was all right, expecting to find her collapsed in a friend's protective embrace, crying.

Instead, she found herself looking at a woman who knew how to hold her own against bullies of her employer's sort. The pregnant female striker stood glaring, unintimidated, in Jack's direction, punctuating her rage with a proudly arced spit toward his back, looking as if she could have just as easily have aimed it squarely in his face, if proximity had permitted her to do so.

Unsurprisingly, Susan and Jack's Korean adventure had been postponed at the last moment, with Jack getting called off to an urgent meeting, one in which Susan had not been included.

The part Susan *had* found surprising, as well as extremely confusing, was that Jack had seemed genuinely disappointed. If he had planned all this anarchy at the plant he would have known that he wouldn't be free to *play* that night. Unless that was part of the strategy.

Maintaining the new personal dimension he had added to their relationship, he had made her promise him a rain check. And not knowing what to believe or think, Susan had kept her thoughts and suspicions to herself and accepted. If he was using her and trying to throw her off, he was a convincing actor and for the most part succeeding.

It was past midnight when Susan returned home from another one of her late-night work marathons at the office, tired, still puzzling over the day's turn of events.

As much as she wanted to believe otherwise, Susan couldn't help but feel that something unethical was going on, and as Jack's lawyer, she especially didn't like being kept in the dark.

Like it or not, she smelled a rat, a decorated sort of Viet Nam Tunnel Rat, with special training to move swiftly and devastatingly through to any specific end, viewing himself as above the law and duty-bound to eradicate interferences when they got out of hand.

Clearly he would see the dissenting workers as an interference.

Tentatively, she had suggested her suspicions to Kreegle when she returned to the firm, but he had only made light of them. "It's the union's job to look after the workers," he had reminded her.

Jack had called her at the office later to check on a legal matter involving something else, completely ignoring what had happened earlier. He had such an intimidating way about him that she found she was unable to bring it up herself, either.

Their relationship was so unsettling. They hovered on romantic involvement without ever crossing the line, working intense hours, on the verge of being physical and then not. Not that Susan knew whether or not she wanted to be; his moods seemed to conduct her feelings, making them rise and then deflate on a moment-to-moment basis. She thought her vulnerability was a function of not having anyone else.

The fact that Jack had never made a pass at her, other than his perplexing invitation for tonight, hadn't helped to buoy her confidence. She had kept wondering, was it *her,* or was it *him*?

The question had plagued her for weeks.

Was she so undesirable that her former boyfriend in Stockton had felt compelled to cheat on her? That made her invisible to

Mark—so that he had eyes only for Paige? That had enabled Jack to maintain perfect professionalism—even though they had been working halfway through the night together, often fortified by brandy or a bottle of fine red wine from his cellar?

Or was Jack gay? Or asexual? Or did he have a sexual problem and not want to put himself in an uncomfortable position? Maybe his work was enough for him, she had speculated. Maybe he was one of those men who didn't need a woman. He was certainly self-sufficient.

Feeling half asleep, and only more baffled than ever by Jack's curious and long overdue proposition, she punched the house alarm code into the security box outside the front door and then let herself inside, nearly tripping over a pile of UPS boxes addressed to Paige, which tempted her to kick them across the gleaming terra cotta floor.

Paige somehow always ended up with it all. Clever, sex kitten Paige, who underneath that soft facade was just a wily barracuda.

First, all the gifts arriving from Philadelphia. Now, a steady flow from Nicky Loomis.

Susan felt strangled with envy and resentment. *She* hadn't even received as much as flowers—nothing—from anybody. Except the painting from Mark, which she refused to count since in nearly the same breath he had offered *himself* to Paige.

It drove Susan nuts to see her provocative roommate with her hands all over Mark all the time. Prompting the kind of public displays of affection that should be reserved for behind closed doors.

Susan would be having a conversation with the two of them and then, midsentence, Paige would give Mark that doe-eyed God-I-can't-keep-my-hands-off-you look and start making out with him right on the spot, so that Susan would be left standing there, feeling like a jerk, as if she were a videotape on pause.

It was obscene and highly inconsiderate.

It made Mark look like the first-rate jerk that he was, putting up with Paige's craziness. She was using him. Just as she used everybody. Mark had been an interim plaything for her. And with her relationship growing more serious now with Nicky Loomis, she was treating Mark worse and worse, canceling on him at the last moment because *Nicky* wanted to see her, or meet her somewhere, *anywhere.*

God, didn't he have any pride? Was Paige really that good in the sack that he could justify putting up with her!

Susan's own relationship with both of them had become so strained that she avoided being around them.

Happily, nobody was here at the house now. She had it all to herself. Relishing the silence and the privacy for a change, Susan dropped her briefcase in the hallway by the stairs, then hiked up yawning toward her bedroom, thinking how even Maria, Dustin's housekeeper, was out for the evening, her boyfriend having bought tickets to a Miami Sound Machine concert.

Tori and Paige were out with Nicky Loomis and some friend of Nicky's with whom they were fixing Tori up.

God, how Susan dreaded all these blind dates. She couldn't bear thinking of how many she had endured since she had been in L.A., well-meaning fix-ups arranged by Kit and George, by her law firm colleagues who generously included her in their plans for football games or dinners or the symphony, or urged her to meet available clients, if *only for a drink.*

Susan called it "lottery dating" and wasn't particularly optimistic about coming up lucky. The truth was, she found dating in Beverly Hills not much different from dating anywhere else. The men here were just richer and more spoiled, with eccentricities that appeared more pronounced. Like Jack, or even Richard Bennetton. Like Nicky Loomis. They seemed to feel they could buy anything, do anything, that their money made them omnipotent, providing them with the passkey for any obstacle.

Susan preferred to stay sequestered behind the safe shelter of her work, content with a quiet night of writing, researching, thinking, analyzing, or even working with Jack. It saved her from having to be "on" with people who didn't make her *feel* "on" naturally. It was such an effort to have to rush home after work and get all showered and dressed to kill, then have to smile and be entertaining for the duration of the date.

Movies were the best dates because they afforded two hours of not having to manufacture conversation—a time-out period. It was a way of being with someone without having to be with him.

Then after the movie they had a guaranteed common ground to tide them over through the quick cup of coffee that was the obligatory follow-up on that kind of date.

Longing to soak in the tub and say nothing, think of nothing, Susan, in the mood to treat herself, ran an extremely hot bath, pouring a blend of fragrant oils and powders beneath the faucet and watching as the foamy turquoise-tinted water rose to the desired height, in the mood to treat herself.

Ordinarily, she was meticulous about hanging up her clothes, but she was so tired and so anxious to get into the bath that she simply dropped her linen suit into a pile on the floor, jacket, blouse, skirt, panty hose, bra, and panties, expending effort instead on picking out a mellow Steve Wyndham compact disc from her collection and switching on the player. She didn't even bother to tie up her hair; she just let it fan out in the water, drenched in bubbles and oils, smelling and feeling wonderful. As she had hoped, the steamy temperature of the water penetrated her tension, drawing it out, melting it away. Therapy.

Funny how the relief of tension dulled grudges, lifting them, she thought guiltily, removing her steamed-up glasses and parking them on the side of the bath, filled with forgiveness toward Paige, Mark, Jack, even Kreegle. Even Billy Donahue. Even her father.

They were all just being themselves. People couldn't be more than they were.

Susan's head was resting against an inflated plastic pillow and she felt herself pleasantly drifting off, little nerve endings untying, leaving her loose and free.

She made a mental note to remember to call her parents tomorrow and see how they were.

To call Lisa too, to do a little fishing to find out what *was* going on with Billy Donahue.

She made a pledge to herself to try to be more patient with Paige.

Then she thought of Mark, and her thoughts held there, filling her up with a multitude of emotions and sensations, soothing and so deliciously real as she let herself fantasize about him. She imagined that he had a change of heart. That he wanted *her* now instead of Paige.

She imagined him telling her that he couldn't hold it inside any longer. Paige was only a fling. But with Susan he envisioned a serious relationship. Susan was everything he had always dreamed of. *And more.* Smart. Beautiful. Sensitive. She imagined his big blue eyes full of frustration and longing, *longing for her now, not for Paige.*

She imagined herself resisting, then caving in.

She saw herself sailing with him, the two of them alone and working in concert with the wind, riding the crystal-white crests of the Pacific on her boat.

Or hiking, camping out near Santa Barbara, listening to the quiet, roasting marshmallows by campfire, making love by the glowing embers.

All these magical things that she would love to do with him that didn't cost a dime.

Paige and Tori could have their extravagant gala parties, expensive trips and restaurants, all the costly clothes that lost something anyway the second and third time you put them on. Susan wanted a man with whom she could be happy doing the more mundane things—who made the mundane things *feel* extravagant. She was tired of pretending just to be polite that the hundred-dollar bottle of wine tasted any different from the seven-dollar bottle of wine.

Instead, she conjured up the lazy, vivid sensation of Mark there in the bathtub with her, climbing into the big tub and luxuriating in the silky texture of her richly oiled skin, massaging her breasts with the precious oil, her stomach, her thighs, kissing her, making love to her.

She felt her nipples taut beneath her fingertips as she imagined Mark's fingertips, his hands enveloping the slippery fullness of her breasts, the slinky sensation of the path that led down toward her hips and beyond.

If only she could have reached out to him through her mind, made him want her as she wanted him now, this instant, made him want to possess her as she wanted to be possessed.

She set her body and soul to the task, *focusing,* trying to master the air waves to his mind, to the essence of his being, wishing herself into his psyche, wanting to control it. Anything to have him there with her, touching her, loving her as she felt she could only love him.

Climbing toward an orgasm, she heard a knock at the door and Mark's voice, calling out her name. Mortified, she sank down into the water.

"Susan? Are you there?"

She thought about not answering, pretending she was not. *Good God, had* he read her thoughts?

It was about time!

"Yes . . . yes." She had to clear her throat and shout over the music.

"What?"

"I said, *yes. I'm here.*"

"I can't hear you. Can I come in?"

"*No.* I'm in the bathtub. Can you wait a min—"

"What? I can't hear you."

"I said, *not yet,*" Susan hollered, flushed, sighing and deciding she had better get up and answer the door. She wondered what he was doing here? How had he gotten in?

"Yes?" he verified uncertainly.

"*No.* One sec."

But as she stood up to reach for a towel, the fragrant, airy white bubbles of her bath clinging to her skin and glistening from all the oil, he walked in, their eyes meeting head-on before she could grab a towel.

It was like an amusing addendum to her fantasy, only it was real.

Laughing, embarrassed beyond words, Susan lunged for a towel and wrapped it modestly around herself, dripping wet as she stepped out of the bath, automatically reaching for her glasses. "Hi," she said, still laughing, warmed by the blush that went clear down to her toes.

"Hi," Mark replied, equally awkward, putting his hands to his eyes, then looking at her. "Sorry. I couldn't hear you over all the—"

"S'okay," she assured him, the fantasy he had interrupted still stirring her thoughts. "What are you doing here?" She was smiling the kind of smile that started deep inside of her soul and radiated out. She wondered what Paige would think if she were to come home now and find the two of them here like this in her bathroom.

Undeterred by any feelings of guilt, the thought amused her. Mark belonged to her first. It would be a case of stealing back what was rightfully hers to begin with.

He smiled. Still embarrassed. Looking additionally embarrassed by the reply he was about to give. "I was supposed to meet your roommate here, but it looks like I've been stood up. Maria let me in before she left, and then I fell asleep rereading *War and Peace* on the couch. When I woke up and saw your briefcase and shoes by the stairs . . . I just wanted to say hi—" he trailed off self-consciously.

Susan couldn't help the impulse to let him squirm a little longer before replying. She was enjoying the moment and wanted it to last. She imagined she was Paige, taking full advantage of her soapy, wet state of undress. She let her eyes roam over his pale, angelic face, then travel down to his work shirt and jeans, thinking how he looked so right in them. Nicky had picked Paige up here numerous times in his work shirt and jeans, but it hadn't been the same. Nicky looked like a middle-aged man trying to dress cool. Mark looked genuinely cool.

And now Susan needed to *act cool*. "You want a cup of coffee or something?" she asked, enjoying how uneasy he appeared watching her as she tucked the top right corner of her towel into place to secure it around her torso before reaching for another towel for her hair.

"Sure. Thanks," he answered agreeably. "Why don't you let me make it," he offered, recovering with a smile that made her heart lurch forward.

"That'd be great. Thanks."

"God, we're polite," he laughed, not yet moving to leave.

"All things considered," she observed, resecuring her towel, then smiling ironically as she went to sit in front of the dressing table to blow-dry her hair. She had to raise her voice over the noise of the dryer as she switched it on. "How's your art going?"

"Painting or selling?" he asked, picking up a perfume bottle from the table in front of her, smelling it briefly, then smiling as he returned it to the table. "Hmmm. That's nice."

"Thanks. I like it."

"It reminds me of you. Fresh, innocent, but not too sweet. Straightforward—"

"A straightforward scent?" Susan mused skeptically, aiming the dryer at her roots as she ran her fingers rapidly though her hair, sifting through layers for fullness and then scrunching it for curl.

"Nothing contrived or *trying* to be complicated about it," he explained thoughtfully, "more like the wild outdoors on a clear spring day just after a good torrent of rain."

"Hmmm. Sounds heavenly," Susan replied, easily conjuring up the picture, watching him through the mirror watching *her*. She was surprised when he took the blow-dryer from her hand and began blowing her hair himself, stirring his fingers through her hair as he directed the dryer.

"An artist, an economics professor, *and* a good blow-dryer, all in one package. You could be too much to resist," she chided, nervously responding to the feel of his hands in her hair, amazed at how sensual the ordinary task had become, performed by him.

She held on to her towel as he motioned for her to bend and flip her hair upside down. She was overly conscious of being naked beneath it so close beside him, the feel of his hands massaging her scalp. She felt her glasses slip down her nose and pushed them back up, trying to think of something witty to say.

"I love the feel of your hair; it's baby-fine, like silk."

"I hate to tell you this, but that's considered lousy hair."

"Not in my book," he countered suggestively, his fingers working at the nape of her neck, confusing her more than relaxing her, making her wonder what was going on.

What was this new-found intimacy? Why was he flirting with her, playing with her this way? Was he mad at Paige and trying to get back at her through Susan? Or was he just lonely? Or was this a belated revelation?

Not sure what to think, she sat subdued, saying nothing as he shut off the blow-dryer and then picked up a brush from the dressing table, brushing her hair with smooth, competent strokes, sending a trail of goose bumps all down her spine and down her legs.

"What are you trying to do? Seduce me?" she asked with a lightness she didn't feel, leaning her head back and succumbing to *whatever* it was that was going on.

When he didn't reply their eyes met in the mirror, where he continued to study her, looking torn, still playing with her hair, which fell soft and blond around her shoulders, full and radiating out. She looked pretty and surprisingly relaxed, her blue eyes clear and connecting with his. She felt a restrained, anxious surge of pleasure as he continued brushing her hair, his movements slow and leisurely, then becoming tentative. The moment seemed to link them back to square one, pre-Paige.

"I was asking you about your art," she reminded him distractedly, jumping back to the presumed safety of her initial, unanswered inquiry.

"I'll have to show you what I'm doing. I've started a new technique. I'm still working with plastic and acrylics, but this has a smoother, glassy look. It's more—"

"I'd like that . . ."

There was a hesitant pause by both of them. Susan surmised that they were both thinking about Paige.

"I've really enjoyed my 'Mark Arent.' I get comments on it all the time," she said truthfully.

"Do you?" He looked so pleased with the compliment that she had to laugh. It was the first time they had referred to the painting since he had hung it for her. She hadn't been able to before. In fact, she had been tempted over and over again to take it down. Its presence had been like a pressed corsage delivered in advance of a date who had stood her up.

The phone rang before she got a chance to say anything else, startling them both, and she reached for it, wondering who would be calling at a quarter past one in the morning, then wondering if it was Jack. "Hello?" she said, still looking at Mark.

"Susan Kendell Brown, please."

"Yes. Hello. This is Susan."

"Hi. Sorry to bother you at this hour, but you've got several urgent messages from a Juan Jimenez—" It was the law firm's answering service, and Susan realized that, with her upset over Jack and the pregnant striker, she had neglected to check her messages when she left the office. After seven, calls went directly to the service. "We just received another call from him and he said it was an emergency—"

"Juan Jimenez?" Susan repeated, interrupting, trying to place the name, then remembering him as one of the rabble rousers. She took down his phone number from the answering service and then, hesitating, called him back.

The anxious-sounding Mexican answered immediately, his tone clandestine, expecting Susan's call.

He explained briefly and without ceremony how he had sought her out in the belief that he had found a sympathetic ear. His situation and that of his peers was dire and they needed her counsel. Somehow he had discovered that prior to her present job, she had represented unions and not management, and he was sure that she would want to know the truth of what was going on. He implored her to meet with him right away, insisting that it couldn't wait until tomorrow, nor could it be done over the telephone.

"I'm not letting you go out there on your own in the middle of the night. Are you crazy?" Mark said.

"Mark, I'm used to this kind of thing." Susan assured him, though she wasn't really. The intensity of the strike was escalating and she was leery of going on her own, worried that she was merely being used.

"I'm going with you," he maintained.

"No, it's okay. I'll be fine," she countered, leaving him an out if he wanted one, but hoping he would argue as she rushed over to find a pair of jeans and a sweater.

"I know you're brave and self-sufficient. But I also know you have better judgment than to go out there on your own at this hour."

"What is it you think they're going to do to me?" Susan laughed. "And what do you think *you're* going to be able to do to protect me?"

Mark was sitting on one of the twin beds, juggling three small pillows up into the air, watching her. *"Run,"* he teased, trying to capture her off guard and tossing one of the pillows at her.

As she dove to catch it, her towel came unfastened and dropped to the ground, embarrassing them both again.

"God, would you get dressed already," Mark pleaded as she tried to cover herself with the jeans and sweater she was holding, retreating, bare-assed and blushing again, backward into the bathroom to change. "Before I wind up unfaithful to your already unfaithful roommate."

"Spare me," Susan stressed, refusing to feel even an iota of guilt or sympathy for Paige, kicking the door closed this time to insure some privacy, smiling at him as she did so, and, for the first time in a long time, feeling alluring.

Chapter 25

The factory was dark and silent as Susan and Mark rode up to the entrance gate on Mark's motorcycle. Susan's car didn't have enough gas, and they didn't know where to go for a refill at this hour, so they had taken his bike. They were both wearing heavy leather jackets, oversized goggles covering their glasses, and around her head Susan had tied a scarf, which she undid now, shaking her hair free.

"Well?" Mark asked, turning around to her, producing a flashlight and shining it just under her chin. "You nervous?" he asked, squeezing her arm before releasing it.

The excitement of her arms still clinging tightly around his waist, his leather jacket scrunched up just beneath her nose, the wind-whipping ride on his bike, and the dangerous sensation of being here with him now like this in the middle of the night to meet surreptitiously with the *other* side, the sympathetic side, had Susan barely thinking straight. "A little," she admitted, snatching the flashlight from him and swinging her right leg around and off the bike. "I'm only *L.A. Law,* you know, not Nancy Drew."

"What does that make me?" he asked, getting down also to catch up with her.

"I don't know—*Lassie*?" She chuckled, feeling giddy and nervous at once. If she had been alone it would have been a straight case of nerves.

"Make me a hero, but not a canine one, okay? How about Superman?" he suggested, joining his arm through hers.

"I don't know—can you fly?"

"Effortlessly."

"You *want* to be Superman?"

"Only if you're . . . what's her name?"

"Lois Lane."

"Yeah."

"Shhh. There they are," Susan whispered, sobered by the sight of the three figures walking toward them. The plant itself was surrounded with barbed wire. There were very few lights. She switched the flashlight back on and aimed it at them. They waved in acknowledgment and began to step up their pace.

Their introductions were awkward. Susan was acquainted with both men from the strike meetings, but she hadn't met Carmen Jimenez, Juan's pregnant wife, whom Susan suspected to be at the vortex of the crisis, given the incident that had erupted earlier on the strike line.

As bold as the pregnant woman had seemed then, that's how shy she seemed now, looking down at her flowered maternity dress, her hands stuffed into the pockets of the parka she had over it, every minute or so removing them from the pockets to rub them protectively over the new life she carried in her belly. She was wearing heavy dark hose and pumps the same pink as the background of her dress.

"This is my friend, Mark Arent," Susan said, continuing with the pleasantries as they all shook hands.

Juan Jimenez and his small group were proud but still deferential as they exchanged cautious hellos. Then without any pretense of small talk, Juan took up his lead as spokesman for his peers and began an explanation for having called her, not bothering with an apology this time.

"Today on the strike line, with Carmen getting pushed down and everything, man, we *know* it was a set-up," he reported hostilely, grabbing one thick finger, then the next, as he ticked off his suspicions. "Like, when I took a swing and four scabs got out of the truck and got all four of us. The guard just *happened* not to be there at the gate. The security guards just *happened* to be there taking pictures for documentation. And those scabs, we hear, all just *happened* to get jobs somewhere else in union shops."

Susan stood absolutely still, thinking that it was a mistake to have come out here. But what had she expected? To be confronted with something that *wouldn't* put her in a position of conflict? What the worker was saying mirrored her own feelings, and she was torn, wanting to right the situation, but on the other hand conscious of her professional obligation to her client, not to mention her *own* position at the firm.

It wasn't her duty to save the world, or these people, she thought, looking away as they looked at her for answers. If there were an easy way, perhaps she might have been swayed. But there were dirty dealings on both sides of the fence. And as Kreegle had said, it was the union's job to look after the workers. Not hers. Not the firm's.

The squat swarthy striker construed Susan's silence as sympathetic interest and went on, nervously rubbing his hands along the sides of his jeans, insisting that the union leaders were trying to cut a deal with management and, in the process, were selling out their workers.

"Everyone knows that the union brass are only interested in getting their dues," he asserted bitterly. "They got us to go out on strike to get *rid* of us because they know management'll never go for what we're asking. Man, they had this planned all along, as soon as they realized they weren't gonna get us to go along with their bullshit contract. All of us out on strike, we're all gonna lose our jobs."

Again, Susan couldn't argue. The strikers probably *would* all end up losing their jobs. She felt Mark watching her, waiting for a response. But there was nothing safe to say. She was trying to keep a professional distance, something she recognized she had already sacrificed by being there in the first place.

"Man, what we're asking for is fair," he contended, his face tight. "Your client, he's got serious health violations. You know that. *Enséñele sus manos, Carmen,*" he ordered his wife, prying her hands from her stomach to hold them out for Susan and Mark to see. They were chalky and rough, with dozens of tiny little scars. "You see these marks? They come from fiberglass splinters because your son-of-a-bitch client is too cheap to get enough gloves for everybody. Look at my hands. Look at Carlos' hands. Happens to all of us.

"And we're sick and tired of paying for the rejects that come from *his* using cheap materials. Man, he's buying cheap resin, cheap materials and using molds that should be junked and *we're* getting blamed; we're paying for it outa our paychecks—"

Carmen Jimenez placed her hand lightly on her husband's back as though to get him to settle down. He took a deep obliging breath before going on. His cohort continued standing very still, saying nothing.

Susan took the moment to glance at Mark, who seemed intrigued by the whole encounter, feeling grateful he was there with her.

"Can't you get us our jobs back?" Jimenez began again, upset but controlling himself. "*They're* the ones in violation. We're just out there trying to earn an honest living. Sure, we got a lot of anger and frustration. But *you* know there hasn't been any real violence in this strike. Guys just getting their frustration out, that's all.

"They want people to think we're the bad guys. We're not the bad guys. *They're* the bad guys," he charged, gently cupping his wife's engorged belly with the palm of his hand, his face toughening again. "But let 'em start *firing* us like this. Then they're gonna see some real violence."

Carmen Jimenez enclosed both of her smaller hands over her husband's larger one, finally getting the nerve to speak up. "Ees true, Miz Susan, it get . . . *muy malo,* very bad, *rough,*" she interjected, reticent about her English, which was not as practiced as her husband's but still desperate to appeal to Susan. "*Pero* violence, *no!* No ees true. We make some tires go flat, throw some eggs," she shrugged. "Ees not such big thing. No? *'No big deal,'* like you say. *Pero,* lose jobs over this—this no ees right. These strikers, they ees good people, they ees all good people. Nobody want hurt nobody."

Juan Jimenez looked emotionally from his wife to Susan. "Can't you do something for us?" he pleaded. "Maybe negotiate for us with them? Tell them we know we were set up. All we want is our jobs back and a fair deal."

As he shook his head and directed his eyes down at the ground, Susan found it hard not to be affected by the frustration he was trying to contain, the kind of injustice she had spent all her years as a lawyer working against. She turned to Mark, needing some sign from him, some grounded confirmation that what she was about to do was the right thing.

Juan Jimenez, Carmen Jimenez, Carlos, all of them. These people had been sold out, set up, as they said. Her client had most likely initiated the double cross; he had supported it anyway.

Without committing herself, she told them that she needed some time to think about it, that she would get in touch with them the following day, dully aware that she had *already* committed herself when she had driven out there.

Her head was throbbing, pounding, as she held on to Mark's waist afterward, riding behind him on his bike through the streets of east L.A. There was a crushing pressure at her temples, behind her eyes, at the back of her head, and continuing down her neck. Mark was sensitive enough to know not to talk. To let her ingest what had just gone on, what she was involving herself in, to mull it over without distraction.

God, what a day! What a long day. It was three in the morning. The city for the most part seemed asleep.

They ripped through the seedier portion of downtown, taking in the run-down tenements, the street people who made the pavement their home arranging bags of trash to lean against and use as pillows, cardboard cartons set up as tables, wearing worn wool hats, torn gloves, and heavy jackets, even though the last days of summer hadn't yet passed.

She felt someone looking down at her, and she met his gaze uncomfortably. Hanging out of a double-hung window over a liquor store in an old brick tenement building was a man in a white tank-style undershirt drinking from a bottle of beer. He had it better than the poor bundled-up bums on the street, she thought, her thoughts shifting to Juan Jimenez, Carlos, the others, wondering what their living conditions were like.

There were so very many levels in this country. All of them cognizant of the top level, bombarded by the subliminal tease of affluence in advertisements, seeing it on TV or in the movies, reading about it in books and magazines, and striving toward it in one way or another, if not for themselves then for their children.

Except the street people, who she could see now sporadically lining the sidewalks. Somewhere along the way they had abandoned the race, given up, were existing on food stamps and charity, *barely* existing, from the looks of it.

And then there was the blue-collar working class, the Juan Jimenezes of the world, trying to better their lot, to make the world a decent place for their children, putting in an honest effort, an honest day's work—and getting shafted.

Susan was surprised when Mark veered over into a parking place and cut his engine. Looking around, she realized they were in the flower-market district.

"What are we doing here?" she asked as he turned around to her. "It's the middle of the night."

"Aha, to you and me, yes. But to them it's not," he corrected her, indicating the bustle of another world that surrounded them. Operating in full swing, accustomed to working by moonlight instead of sunlight, the flower market's world didn't begin until midnight and didn't end until most others began, around seven or eight in the morning.

The area was so well lit that it didn't feel like the middle of the night at all. There were trucks all over, people carting dollies loaded with newsprint-wrapped bunches of flowers contained in plastic buckets of water. There were people walking around eating fast food snacks from wax paper wrappers that they had most likely bought from the catering food truck just a couple of yards away. It was all action. Action and breathtaking masses of flowers, as the wholesale trade loaded up to service the retail trade.

"I wanted to buy you some flowers to cheer you up, but I wanted to be sure you had a good selection," Mark said, lifting off his helmet as he got off the motorcycle, then taking her hand to help her off the bike as well.

He removed her scarf, untying it from under her chin, then stuffing it into her pocket while she looked around, thinking it would be impossible *not* to be cheered up with all this, enchanted by the riot of colors and floral varieties that overwhelmed the district.

Why did my roommate get you, instead of me getting you? she thought, her head still pounding, feeling burnt out from the range of emotion. She wished she could say it aloud. It was blunt, true, direct, with a little bit of humor and irony splashed in. It was the *self* she rarely displayed. The self she wanted him to know.

His framed blue eyes studied her for an extra beat, looking confused, uncertain, as he removed his goggles. Maybe even uncertain as to what he wanted now, as though he were reading her mind and didn't know or understand the answer. Susan sensed the pull. At last she felt the attraction that had been waylaid, shortstopped by her sex-goddess roommate. Susan knew exactly why. And it was tough to compete.

Paige was *Penthouse.* Susan was . . . Lois Lane.

Superman or, perhaps more aptly, her curly blond-haired Clark Kent, took her hand and led her inside the flower market, where she was hit with the intoxicating blend of fragrances from all the hundreds of varieties of flowers. Bottled, it would have been a miracle scent. It was surely a miracle moment.

Mark appeared to be known and liked by many of the vendors, who said hello to him by name and shared best-buy leads, cutting prices for him out of earshot of other workers or customers, so that before Susan and Mark knew it they were weighted down with more cone-shaped wrapped bundles of flowers than they could carry.

He said he loved being surrounded by flowers, and since they were so expensive in the retail shops and not nearly as fresh, he liked to come down here a couple of times a month and load up.

"Feel any better?" he asked, catching her eye as they rounded a corner down another aisle, accepting a cart from a sympathetic bystander and releasing their bountiful score into it.

She did feel better. Her headache wasn't gone, but it was lifting. She was thinking about French tulips, French roses, lilac branches, lilies of multitudinous varieties, the showy, white bell-shaped version blooming from a thick green stalk, the more delicate-looking tiger lilies, the exquisite and yet still hearty Journey's End, which were a vivid white with speckles of hot pink. They had gathered bunches of peacock-blue hybrid delphiniums, iris, baby roses, new breeds of daisies, and, from another area, tall tropically bred stalks of ginger and birds of paradise imported from Hawaii. Their more exotic finds ranged from garlic strands to Brussels sprout stems to reindeer moss to horsetail. The world had grown small enough to be able to enjoy flowers grown and picked fresh from all over the globe—Jamaica, Africa, Australia, New Zealand, Israel, Mexico, Holland, France, the Orient, exchanging blossoms otherwise never glimpsed and enjoying flowers off-season.

Across the street from where the American vendors were set up were the Japanese vendors, the street dividing the two factions tagged the "Suez Canal."

The Japanese side, Mark explained, was especially interesting because it still embodies so much tradition. Many of the Japanese had relocated during the war, and most of them were growers selling their own product.

It was fascinating to see the way their stalls were run, with the elderly Japanese grandfathers remaining behind the scenes, still preferring to do their accounting calculations sliding beads back and forth on their archaic abacuses, while their sons and grandsons manned the front wearing Walkmen and blitzing through tallies on their micro-sized calculators.

Amazingly, Mark was able to cram their multiple flower purchases into soft leather saddle packs he kept fastened onto both sides of his bike, so that there was even enough room left over to add a sack of produce they picked up afterward at the equally bustling produce market on their way to the legendary Vickman's for a predawn breakfast.

The old cafeteria-style restaurant, located in the hub of the produce market, was always packed at any hour. It was filled with regulars from the area, the produce moguls seated beside lower-level workers or truckers at the long strips of Formica-topped tables, all of them minding their own business—which was, while they were there, most frequently a small glass beaker of coffee, a danish, and one of any of the array of newspapers sold up in front.

Walking very close to each other, charged with something different in the air, Susan and Mark took one of the booths that lined the length of the wall, waiting for the short-order portion of their breakfast to be brought to them by the waitress. Mark had their coffee and blueberry muffins on a tray, which they had already picked up cafeteria-style.

"Thanks, Mark, for everything," Susan said, feeling calm and grateful, her headache finally gone. This was a moment she never in her wildest dreams really expected to realize and she found herself nearly shaking as she tried to let the nearness of him register, flooded with relief, with gratitude and with all sorts of feelings she couldn't even fathom.

He was sitting across the table from her, watching her trying to slow her pace as she wolfed down her blueberry muffin, both of them hungry from their all-nighter.

"The only thing you and Paige seem to have in common is your appetite," he observed, breaking off a chunk of his muffin and depositing it thoughtfully into his mouth as he regarded her.

The mention of Paige's name acted like a short-circuit in Susan's brain.

Maybe it was the lack of sleep. Maybe it was all the wild emotion of the day. Maybe it was the gut feeling that Jack didn't really give a damn about her either, that he was just using her because of the strike situation and the slippery, dishonest dealings he was hoping to get away with. But she felt herself losing her grasp.

Was Paige Williams all Mark could think about? Was that why he was here with her now? To pour out his heart to her? Had she only imagined everything else? "What about *you*? I guess you could say we have *you* in common," she snapped brashly, wanting to stun him, wanting to force a reaction. Susan rarely lost her temper, but when she did there were no holds barred. The censoring mechanism that kept such a tight lid on just about everything she ever thought or said would go haywire.

Mark seemed surprised, confused by her outburst, by the flash of anger. He picked up his coffee cup and took a long contemplative swallow, clearly at a loss as to how to respond.

She was too keyed up to let him off the hook and she sat very still watching him. Inside she was quivering, wanting to run out of the restaurant, wanting to run fast and hard away from the confrontation she couldn't stop herself from bringing to a head.

"You have *me* in common?" he repeated uncomfortably.

"Don't pretend to be surprised. Please. I'm not an idiot. You know damn well how I've felt about you. Admit it. It was a shitty thing to do, coming over to see me and then falling all over yourself with my roommate the way you did."

Mark sat back against the scruffy orange-painted booth, hesitating, looking guilty. "I know," he said finally, his voice low, confessional. But she was going for the jugular. "I'm sorry," he apologized, groping, picking up his coffee cup again, then returning it to its saucer without taking a sip. The rattle of dishes being carted off by busboys seemed amplified.

What did *sorry* really mean? That he felt sorry for her? That he was sorry that he was still in love with Paige? That he couldn't force feelings for Susan he didn't have?

When she didn't reply, he went on. "I've never done anything like that in my life, coming over to see you and then leaving with her like that. But you all had dates. And she was there. I don't know, I realize that's not much of an excuse.

"But then, when she told me why you'd all moved out here, I figured it didn't make any difference. It put everything on another level. Or that was how I justified it anyway. I don't know what got into me. I couldn't help myself."

Susan knew exactly what had gotten into him. It wasn't only sex. It was Paige being persuasive, wanting Mark, and manipulating the situation. As she manipulated everything.

"What's the difference, anyway? You all moved out here to meet and marry rich men," Mark summarized bitterly. "And I'm sure you will. Paige has her prince all lined up. Tori's Bennetton prince turned into a frog, but I'm sure she'll find another royal prospect without too much ado. And you have yours—"

"Mine?" There was an edge to Mark's voice that Susan matched in her own as she cut him off. "I have mine? Who's *my* prince?" she came back dryly, knowing full well he meant Jack Wells, that he was presuming more than there was to their relationship because of all the long hours they spent together at work. His dig seemed to reach deeper, considering what he had learned about Jack tonight.

The waitress delivered their scrambled eggs to the table, rearranging cups and plates to make room for them, providing a tense lull. "The rich, but not necessarily ethical client—" Mark reminded her darkly, after the waitress had left.

"I don't *have* a prince to turn into a frog," Susan replied angrily.

"No?"

"No. And I don't believe in fairy tales," she added with a tough glare across the table. "Who do you think you are, anyway? Do you think you're better than these other guys because you *don't* have money? That your lack of wealth makes you the genuine article, the prince without the facade?"

Mark took a couple of bites of his eggs, looking as if he weren't tasting them. The directness of Susan's response seemed to throw him and he answered curtly, looking as upset as she was. "So why did you move out here with them, then?"

"The same reason that they all moved out here. Because we were all stuck in our own kinds of ruts. Because we needed to make changes in our lives. Not that it's any of your damn business. Who the hell do you think you are anyway, sitting in judgment? You don't know anything about me, really. Or Tori. And Paige is so damn complicated you probably don't even really know anything about her, either, other than how to satisfy her in bed." In a burst of anger and frustration Susan stood up, reaching into her purse for some money to throw onto the table, wanting to get out of there as fast as possible. She didn't have to sit there and justify herself to him.

"Now that's a low blow," Mark shot back, standing up also.

"I can't help it. You deserved it," she exclaimed angrily.

"What are you doing? Sit down," he argued, blocking her way.

"Just leave me alone, Mark. I'm tired. I'm leaving. I've got a lot on my mind."

"What, you're going to catch a cab at this hour?"

"Just get out of my way." She wished she had never started this. Paige could have him, for all she cared. She couldn't believe she had said as much as she had said. She had made a complete fool of herself. "Now would you just get out of my way?"

"Not until we finish this—"

"I am finished—"

"Well I'm not."

The two of them stood there staring at each other until Susan finally averted her glance down to the cheap linoleum floor, close to tears.

Gently, Mark directed her back down into her seat and then slid in beside her, backing her all the way into the corner. Her heart was pounding and she couldn't stop herself from trembling.

She was thinking about Juan Jimenez. His pregnant wife. Jack. Kreegle. The blow-up she could anticipate with them all tomorrow. How she had jeopardized her job. And then she was thinking about Mark walking in on her as she was getting out of the bathtub. The way his hands had felt in her hair. The feel of her arms around him and the wind whipping back at them as they tore through the streets on his motorcycle.

"I'm sorry," Mark began softly. "I really am—"

"For what?" she interrupted defensively, feeling dizzy from the nearness of him. She felt an electric-like current from his hand only a fraction of an inch away from hers, from his lips practically touching hers.

"For a lot of things," he murmured, not letting her look away this time. "For that first night with Paige. For hurting you. And you're right. I didn't know you at all . . . And I want to know you . . ."

She felt him about to kiss her and she was scared to death. She knew she should push her way around him and out of the booth. That she should leave. That she should not be accepting Paige's sloppy seconds so easily. That she shouldn't be so sane and forgiving. But she couldn't help herself. She had never felt anything so powerful in her life. She couldn't believe they were really talking about all this. She felt weak and vulnerable.

Before she could even come close to summoning up the willpower to resist, he had pulled her into a tight embrace and was kissing her as though nobody else in the world existed. They both took off their glasses at the exact same moment, laughed about it for half a second, and then resumed kissing, as though making up for all those months of lost time.

Without even thinking, Susan had slipped her hands inside his shirt and was feeling the chest she had only envisioned feeling before. It was warmer than the chest in her fantasy, and the curly blond hair growing wild and dense there felt silky and exciting.

She was reeling from all the sensations of him, the intense heat, the caress of his lips, which were soft and sensual, that familiar face pressing against her own, the blond stubble of his beard rough from the long night's growth. All the sensations previously only imagined, now being realized and explored.

"God, let's get out of here before I end up making love to you in the restaurant," Mark said, breaking reluctantly away for a moment and jarring them both into a hazy state of cognizance.

All at once aware of where she was, Susan looked up embarrassed and then relieved because nobody seemed to be paying any attention to them. The restaurant's diverse clientele were all minding their own business, busying themselves with their newspapers, their coffee and sweet rolls, looking half asleep themselves.

Susan and Mark's eyes met again like magnets. Susan figured they were probably both wondering the same thing. Where did they go from here?

She smiled self-consciously, about to put on her jacket as Mark touched her hair and then her cheek and then began kissing her again. "I want to start seeing you," he whispered, only barely coming up for air as he went on emphatically but almost nonsensically, unable to keep his hands off her. "I'm sorry for everything. I'm sorry for being so blind. For being such an idiot. And I know I really screwed up. And I know this is going to be unbelievably awkward. But just say yes. You can change your mind later if you have to, but say yes now. God, I had to be out of my fucking mind."

Moving her lips away from his for only an instant, Susan cautioned him as to how *awkward* could just be the understatement of the day.

Chapter 26

"What is this, Tori? You hock your engagement ring to bail out your rich fiancé—who breaks up with you over it—and then give him all the money, anyway. And, *Susan,* you're going to get us all killed, exposing some union conspiracy in order to get health insurance for a bunch of poor workers you don't even know. What kind of rich-husband manhunt is this?" Paige admonished, intent on getting on with her own.

It was like the good old days when they had first moved out here, all of them together at the house gathered around in the den and sharing crises.

Paige thought all they did was bump into one another now in passing, on their way out the door. But this morning it felt collective again, collective problems, collective help. Tori and Susan were the sisters she never had and she looked at them, unable to smile through the tight, egg-white face mask itching and restricting, but, hopefully, beautifying her face, trying to convey what she felt for them through her eyes.

She hadn't wanted to analyze a whole other aspect of this just this moment, about what appeared to be blossoming with Susan and Mark.

It was eight A.M. and her small-town Stockton roommate had

only recently come in, looking like sunshine dropped down to earth in the guise of a woman, disheveled but radiant, loaded down with enough flowers to overwhelm a shop. She was keyed up over the union situation, but clearly distracted and glowing on account of her escort.

Paige, on the other hand, looked like hell in her Bloomie's nightshirt and facial mask, her hair full of shark-oil conditioner, drawn back into a ponytail, and a trail of Kleenex separating her toes from the pedicure she had just given herself. She had gotten up early to squeeze all this beautifying in, since she had a couple of private sessions to teach at clients' homes before her first class at Matrix.

At least Mark wasn't mad at her for having stood him up the night before, she had been forced to rationalize, swallowing any jealousy she may have felt, unquestionably taken aback at the sight of her roommate and her boyfriend sailing in together after having been out all night.

Their good-bye to one another was awkward but unmistakably intimate, Paige had thought, wondering about it, reminding herself that she had basically dropped Mark like a hot potato when she had started seeing Nicky. Reminding herself that Mark was a poor, starving—by her standards—professor who was great in bed, but not cut out for the boardroom.

Wide awake for someone who hadn't slept in twenty-four hours, Susan plopped down on the couch, gratefully accepting coffee from Maria and telling them all about her dilemma with the strikers, the set-up revolving around Carmen Jimenez, their suspicions about a conspiracy, and the precarious position it put her in with her law firm, with Jack Wells. Not to mention the union thugs, who wouldn't be too pleased with any investigative efforts.

Tori, Paige thought, resembled a sleepy Persian cat, cuddled up in one of the big overstuffed chairs, wrapped in the mink-colored silk bathrobe Kit had given her for being one of her bridesmaids, also drinking from a mug of coffee and listening intently to Susan's story.

Her blind date from the night before, Nicky's friend, had flipped over her, but even Paige had to admit what a geek the man was, even *with* his millions. Not only was he so short he needed a special booster seat for his Rolls-Royce in order to see over the steering wheel, but he wore one of those foppish wigs that had you tempted all evening to yank it off.

The encouraging aspect of the evening was that Tori had finally shown a sense of humor about enduring a blind date, which they both took as a good sign, laughing their heads off about him during ladies' room runs, and afterward. Maybe the dreamy-looking brunette was getting over the rotten men in her life after all.

"We're counting on *you,* Paige, to save the day," Tori chimed in, accentuating her southern drawl. "You marry your rich husband and then take care of all of us."

"Tori, I think you personally will be able to support us, the way you're doing at Bennetton these days," Paige said, duly impressed with the accolades Tori was receiving at Bennetton. Now that she was working there without the distraction of Richard, who had disappeared off on another of his extended vacations to God only knew where. "I'm waiting for the old man to appoint you as his successor. To take you under his wing to supersede him when he retires, since we can certainly write off his son. And Susan will be *dead.* So that's no problem. We all know how the union handles their opposition. Why do you think all their presidents wind up dead themselves or in jail?"

"Not the present one," Susan corrected her. "The FBI is too entrenched with this one, so he's only been under investigation." Her blue eyes sparkled beneath her glasses, the same sky-blue tint as her jeans.

"Great. And you want to start investigating their *conspiracy*? I thought you were supposed to be the brainy one here."

"C'mon. I'd just be like a fly to them, a small irritant, buzzing around on a small deal."

"Wonderful. And what do you do to flies? Do you let them *buzz* around, or do you run for the fly swatter?"

"Spray Raid," Susan joked.

"What does Mark think about all this?" Tori interceded, curiously meeting Paige's glance for only a moment.

"Mark!" Paige answered for Susan. "Mark and Susan are a

great pair. He'll be all for this kind of escapade. He'll think he's Zorro or something."

Susan laughed, tempted to correct Paige and call him Superman.

She had been waiting for some remark from Paige. She hadn't missed the look in her eyes when she and Mark came into the house together. If Paige's face hadn't been concealed behind a mask, it would have turned colors.

"Mark doesn't have a shred of common sense. Or business sense. He lives in a romantic bubble," Paige continued, her warning not exactly unbiased as she rose to go wash off her mask, complaining that it felt like hardened fiberglass; if she didn't remove it now it would be sealed onto her skin for good. Also complaining that it was making her nauseated; it was so tight and so restrictive it made her feel claustrophobic.

"You're using so much junk, how can you tell what's working and what's not?" Tori asked, giving Susan a significant smile as they followed Paige upstairs and into her cluttered, topsy-turvy bedroom. If Dustin were to return home and find his guest room turned upside down like this, he would probably kick them all out, Susan thought, aghast at the mess as she realized how long it had been since she had been in there. She wondered what Mark thought about Paige being such a slob.

"I can't," Paige admitted freely, going into the bathroom and turning on the sink faucet, then leaning against it for a moment as though she really didn't feel well. "I'm covering all my bases using *everything*," she remarked, as though deciding not to give in to her discomfort, instead to get the mask off as soon as possible.

"I'm impressed that you can remember what to put where, when to put it there, and why," Tori commented, as Paige went about melting down her mask with a hot washcloth, removing it carefully.

Susan, leaning against the door, surveyed the confusing array of creams, oils, vials, scrubs, and masks scattered across the white marble countertop, and laughed at Tori's question.

"I *can't*," Paige quipped again, pausing to roll up the sleeves of her nightshirt, before they became soaking wet. "The ones that really get me are the preventatives. Sixty dollars for some mysterious anti-aging serum that offers no visible results but promises to speed up cellular renewal, the effects of which you can only take the manufacturer's word for, and wait. They sucker you into these because of the what-if-they-do-work? syndrome. Who can afford to take the chance?"

Paige leaned in critically toward the mirror, frowning at hairline flaws still visible beneath her eyes and around her mouth, imperfections that were supposed to have been corrected by the expensive chemist's concoction she had just washed off. It was a mask made from dried egg whites and other rejuvenating elements, which were supposed to completely correct the skin, clean it, lift it, nourish it, smooth out lines and *also* help slow down the aging process, at forty dollars a crack.

They're all such liars, she thought, looking into the mirror, opening a tube of botanical eye gel and smearing it around her eyes for a temporary plumping affect, still stubbornly hoping for magic, *needing* magic in order to keep up with the demands of a man like Nicky.

Gifts aside, they didn't cover her overhead.

It wasn't like dating Mark, where, no matter what she did to herself or wore, he always thought she looked terrific.

Terrific to Nicky meant hair and makeup done just right, dressed to kill, dressed to wow his friends and turn heads. The look that appealed to him was high heels, a lot of leg, and clothes that showed off her figure.

Paige called it "the kept-mistress look," only she was still keeping herself at this point, and it was a struggle. She always worried that if she appeared in the same outfit twice it would signal the beginning of the end, reminding Nicky of just how long and how frequently he had been seeing her, and that he would run for the hills.

She already knew from his friends and kids that she was a living, breathing record for him. And that was some record, considering that she and Nicky weren't screwing yet, that there was the added pressure to their relationship of having to talk and get to know each other.

"Why couldn't I be dating a man who didn't have such perfect vision?" she went on. "Can you believe he was giving me a hard time about these wrinkles? Saying that most of the girls he dates aren't old enough to have developed 'expression' lines. One of those only *half-kidding* remarks that sends you straight to a plastic surgeon for comfort."

"Did you tell him that most of the girls he dates aren't old enough to have any expression, period?" Tori asked.

"Don't make me laugh. It'll just make them worse." Paige steadied her expression, waiting for the eye gel to set.

Tori took the tube out of her hand and began reading the directions and claims of wonder aloud. "Here, Susan—after staying up all night, you could probably use some of this," she said, handing it over to her.

"Why? Do my eyes look that bad?" Susan asked, squeezing in to look in the mirror, thinking she looked pretty terrific for someone who had gone without any sleep and attributing her glow to Mark. *Nothing a little Visine and Moon Drops won't cure,* she decided, unconcerned, tossing the tube of eye gel back to Paige.

"Suit yourself," Paige said, thinking *lucky Susan;* Mark wouldn't mind soft, natural aging. He would find it becoming. But let's see how Susan looked next to Paige when they were both forty, and what Mark thought then.

She maneuvered around Tori and Susan, out of the bathroom and over to her closet to get her work-out clothes. Feeling a sudden rush of impatience at seeing the two of them not any farther along with their personal lives when her *own* mind was made up as to exactly what she wanted, she decided tonight was the night for her big move.

Sure, Tori and Susan had changed cities, but they were back in their old patterns, still channeling all their brain power and energy into their careers, feeling thwarted because the rewards were not the rewards for which they were looking right now.

Paige believed in taking little steps, but all in one direction, and all of them exceedingly well thought out. She believed in linear focus. So she would put her career aside for now. Later, if she felt the urge, she could pick it up again or go for a new one. She knew she could go only for one thing at a time, if she wanted to reach.

And swinging a marriage proposal from Nicky Loomis was unquestionably reaching.

Tonight she was going to sleep with him, using all of her resources to drive their relationship up to the final level, the level that would have him hooked on her for good. She hoped.

Nicky's world was an exciting one, and so far she had managed to jump right into the swing of things, fitting in with an ease that continued to catch him by surprise, proving that she was sharp, funny, gutsy, not at all intimidated by his celebrity friends or life-style, showing him that he might have met his match in this younger female counterpart.

What made it easy for her was that she wasn't in love with him, so she wasn't worrying about getting hurt. She didn't feel vulnerable.

Or did she? she asked herself, still feeling queasy and beginning to have doubts. Maybe her system was upset from having seen Mark and Susan together, looking at each other the way they did. Paige had been able to feel her hold over Mark evaporating, like a sorceress's fading power. It was like a sappy ending to an old tale, with the sweet, innocent heroine stepping in during the final act to reclaim what was rightfully hers, power to the benevolent restored.

Maybe the queasiness had to do with taking the simple step she had inadvertently turned into a quantum leap, making love with Nicky. Why did she keep putting it off, if she were so sure of herself?

The answer suddenly appeared obvious; because making love *would* make her vulnerable, vulnerable to rejection. Vulnerable to the heightened possibility of a collapsed goal that would put her back at square one again, if he were to lose interest immediately afterward, the challenge she had posed suddenly met, his conquest complete.

She reminded herself that she had felt ready to sleep with him the last few times they had been together, ready, even eager for the consummation, but there was a small part of her that wouldn't yield, that was reluctant, even afraid.

After this big build-up, she wondered what it would take to not have it all feel like a lot of hot air. It was a pressure she hadn't anticipated and she was surprisingly shy now about initiating the next step. *He* had finally stopped trying, once she had started taking care of him. He was playing it her way now, waiting for her.

And so it was up to her.

And it was time.

Holding on to a lavender bodysuit and a pair of leg warmers, she turned reticently to her friends, who were both stretched out and talking to each other on the bed.

She wanted to tell them about her concerns, to air them and ask for support. She wanted to let them know just how momentous this evening might be for her and how nervous about it she was. She wanted to tell them how she felt it in the pit of her stomach, about the weakness in her limbs.

But she found she simply wasn't able to.

That wasn't the Paige Williams they knew and loved.

Susan arrived at her law firm by ten o'clock, showered, dressed in a new fall suit that was a lightweight linen but bronze and beige to accommodate the nearing shift in seasons, feeling surprisingly refreshed for having missed a full night's sleep.

She walked down the corridor to her office, busy volleying options in her head as to how to handle her suspicions about union and management's off-the-record cooperation, anticipating calls from Jimenez, from Jack, from Hank Piedmont, one of the union lawyers, reports of workers being fired, of retaliation, hoping there was a call from Mark.

"Hi."

"Good morning."

"Yo, Susan."

"How ya doin'?"

"Hey, sexy."

"Have to talk to you later."

Susan responded to the various greetings as she rounded a corner near her office.

The final greeting came from her secretary, followed by an offer of coffee.

Promising to cut back soon on so much caffeine, she accepted.

"Thanks, Linda. God, who didn't call?" she remarked to her secretary, hanging her jacket on the hook behind her door, then riffling through the small stack of messages.

Linda chuckled. "Been one of those mornings. Nice suit."

Susan smiled. "Thanks."

"Is Mark Arent the artist who did your painting?" Linda asked, pointing to the colorful collage of chicken wire overwhelming the wall behind Susan.

"Yep," she answered, happily coming upon his message and thinking that no matter what happened with this incident with the strikers, even if she got fired today, nothing could burst her bubble. The message gave his number and read "Dinner tonight at eight, chez Superman. Regrets only."

"Cute," Linda noted, chuckling. "He paints. He cooks. What else can he do?"

"Hair," Susan answered, more to herself.

"What?"

"Economics. He's an economics professor. Where's my coffee?"

"Coming right up."

"Good."

Susan sat down at her desk, her brain humming with thoughts. She stole a last glance down at the message from Mark, rereading it with a wave of pleasure, tucking it into her top drawer to save, then looking up at the painting he had given her.

Jimenez, she reminded herself, *think Jimenez, think strike, think of all these calls you have to return, think of how you're going to handle your unenviable position of possessing evidence that your client may be in violation of the law.*

A mug of steamy black coffee was placed in front of Susan. "Who do you want me to get on the phone for you first?"

"What time is my first appointment?"

"You've got a ten-thirty here with a prospective client. And I have you blocked out from noon on to be over at the surfboard plant. Maybe you should return Jack Wells' call first. He said it was important."

"Get Kreegle for me first. I need to talk to him. Never mind, I'll just walk down there," Susan decided on second thought, getting out of her chair again and heading down the hall toward the senior partner's large corner office at the end of the corridor.

She knew what Kreegle was going to say. The same thing he had said yesterday—to turn her head, that it was the union's job to look after the workers, not hers. But she simply couldn't look the other way. She might attempt to do so, but it was an ability she knew she didn't possess. One pathetic pleading call from Jimenez or his wife and she would be right back where she was now, feeling compelled to investigate the situation, to right what she knew in her gut was clearly wrong. Her background and all her true sympathies, were with the workers. They weighed too heavily on her conscience for her to turn the other cheek.

"Susan, I don't understand you." Kreegle responded as predicted. "You've been working around the clock for us since you started. You're certain to set a record for speed on associates made partners. We think your work is outstanding. Don't let yourself get distracted." Kreegle gave her a fatherly smile. But she could see he thought she was being a pain in the ass.

"Distracted?" What kind of response was that?

"You've got a lot of promise. You're smart. You're pretty. You're a hard worker. You've got the potential to be working on some of the biggest labor cases in this country. Don't blow it over trivialities. Over small-potato inequities."

"You misunderstand my ambition, sir," Susan replied hotly, sick of this.

"How's that?" Kreegle made an unsuccessful stab at masking his surprise.

"Not all ambition is aimed at money and prominence," she replied bitingly, looking around at his expensive wood paneling, the antique furniture, the blue-chip art on the walls, the massive photo-on-canvas portrait of his family in a field of grass, leaning against Kreegle's Bentley. "Some ambition is still aimed at integrity and excellence first."

"Don't give me this holier-than-thou crap, Susan," Kreegle charged, rising, whipping off his glasses and tossing them angrily down onto his desk. "I marched in peace lines, did my share of drugs, and swore off materialism too. If you want to get stuck in the time warp of the sixties, enmeshed in causes that only take you around in circles, be my guest. Go ahead and blow your whole career on health insurance for a bunch of poor workers you don't even know. But don't plan on doing it here."

Susan couldn't believe he had hit upon the same remark as Paige. *Getting health insurance for a bunch of poor workers who she didn't even know.* Maybe she was wrong. Maybe she was being incredibly naive. For all she knew, *she* was set up. These were the rabble rousers who had been causing trouble all along. Why was she just accepting their suspicions at face value?

Because they went along with her own, that's why.

"What kind of evidence do you have, Susan? Huh? Some pissed-off striker's assumptions? Grow up!" Kreegle snapped, sitting back down in his chair, his anger fading. Susan continued to stand rooted, but wilting. "Listen, I like you. Otherwise I'd have sent you packing for this kind of indiscretion. You don't owe those strikers anything. The union owes them. Let them carry their own responsibilities. Be smart about this and don't return Jimenez's phone calls. Just go on with your work as though nothing ever happened."

"They're going to retaliate if they're fired," Susan pointed out softly.

Kreegle threw up his arms. "If they retaliate, they retaliate. Jack Wells is a big boy. If he made some kind of deal axing these guys out of their jobs, he didn't expect to get off scot-free. Just do your job and mind your own business."

Susan took in the better part of downtown Los Angeles through Kreegle's expanse of window, weighing her position, sizing up her chances if she were to go against the firm and go to the mat for Jimenez and his group.

Her prospects for battle were depressing. The obvious alternative was for her to go to the National Labor Relations Board, but she would have to have enough of a case to prove that this was a conspiracy to violate the workers' rights, that the union did not represent the workers fairly, and that part of the conspiracy was the employer. All the laws were against her and she knew it would be almost impossible to prove. Not to mention that she could wind up disbarred. She didn't know anyone who had ever prevailed in any similar case. Another route would be going to the Teamsters for a Democratic Union, which was an organization within the Teamsters attempting to right what they saw as wrong. But from all she had heard, they were just as rough a group as the Teamsters' leaders themselves.

Even if Jack were to admit the truth to her, he would be protected by attorney-client privilege, so she was powerless there as well.

"I'm taking a group of people to L'Orangerie tonight for dinner. Would you like to come? One of Liz's friends is recently divorced and a real terrific guy." Susan knew it was Kreegle's way of bridging and burying this whole episode. He knew he had her. Or at least he thought he had her, anyway.

Susan wasn't sure where she stood. "Thanks. That's really nice, but I've got a date," she replied pleasantly. As she said it she couldn't help but smile in spite of everything else. The date was with *Mark*. A real, honest-to-goodness date and she couldn't wait.

Kreegle mistook the smile as a surrender, but she didn't think it mattered one way or the other. "Yeah? Who's the lucky guy?" He swept his hand unconsciously over his head, smoothing what little hair was left to smooth. His grin was cute and warm.

She smiled again, relaxing a little. "A friend," she replied shyly.

"A rain check then?" He wagged his finger at her waiting to elicit a yes. "Soon?"

"Sure," she replied, frustrated, wishing they could discuss the strike situation as colleagues, not as employer-employee, where his only concern was simply not to alienate their client. "Listen, uh, I've got an appointment in my office with a prospective client," she said, awkwardly dismissing herself, looking down at her watch.

"Raymond West?" Kreegle asked.

"Yes," Susan replied, incredulous that Kreegle managed to know everything that was going on at the firm. It meant always watching her step.

Jack called just as she returned to her office, before her client got there.

She picked up the receiver nervously, wondering if he knew

that she knew about the set-up, if he had heard, somehow, that she had met with the strikers last night, unsure what to say to him if he confronted her.

"There's been a bomb threat. We've all been evacuated," he stated.

This was the last thing she expected to hear. She was too stunned to even reply.

"We had to shut down the plant and get everyone out of there."

"My God! When? What happened? Where are you calling from?" Susan reached for her coffee cup, but it was empty. Then, worried, she searched through her messages looking for the ones from Jimenez to read them more carefully. Obviously he had interpreted her not returning his phone calls to mean that she wasn't going to help. She couldn't really blame him. He had reason to be wary.

"We're at my apartment. I've got a bunch of guys over here discussing how we're going to handle this. We're sure it was the group of picketers we axed yesterday."

Susan swallowed deeply. "What's the union's reaction?"

"They're trying to find them, talk some sense into them. They think the bomb threat is bogus. But we don't want this going any further—"

"How many people did you let go?"

"Ten, I think—"

"All of Jimenez's group?"

"Damn right."

"Why don't you just give them their jobs back?" Susan asked flatly, sorry as soon as she had said it.

"I'm not going to give those bastards their jobs back. Are you crazy? We're finally going to reach a resolution without them there holding up the works, and you know it."

She was shaking but she couldn't stop herself from going on. She kept seeing Carmen Jimenez's face, her swollen belly, those hands. It was a stupid thing for them to have done, but her heart bled for them. Her father would have never agreed to those tactics, but her father was meek. She could imagine plenty of the guys she had known growing up doing exactly this. "Then give them some settlement so they won't be flat broke while they're looking for new jobs. Give them something. Jack, these guys have been backed up against a wall. You haven't given them any choice."

"Choice?"

"Yes, choice."

"What are you talking about? If I'm not happy with someone's work, all of a sudden I can't *can* 'em?"

"This had nothing to do with their work, and you know it."

"Watch it, Susan."

"I represent *you* . . . I *know*. But dammit, why can't I be honest with anyone? What if *you* had a whole house full of little kids and couldn't support them, and you were being shafted at work?"

"C'mon Susan. Give me a break here—"

"What if *your* wife were carrying your baby and your baby's life was being threatened by unhealthful working conditions?"

"That's all environmental bullshit. They haven't proven anything. Those statistics are incomplete, they're—"

"Yeah, but what if those studies do bear out? The kid gets cancer and you say, Oops, sorry. The statistics didn't really *sound* so bad—"

"They've got too many damn kids, anyway," Jack joked.

Susan tried to contain her temper. "What if *you* were being fired unfairly and didn't have a dime to put food in your family's mouths?"

"Why don't they save their damn money? Why don't they stop having so many kids if they can't afford them?"

"That's none of your business—"

"And *this* is none of your business. You're out of line, counselor—"

"We're all out of line at this point. But I'm telling you, as your lawyer, that you're better off settling with them. If you don't, you're going to have a war on your hands and it'll only cost you *more* time and money."

Susan could hear some commotion coming from Jack's end of the line, a few guys talking to him at once.

He lowered his voice when he came back on the line. It was his more personal voice. The voice he used every time she thought they were getting close to breaking the barrier of their strictly-business relationship.

"Susan, knock it off," he said quietly, like one would to a good friend. "I know how you feel personally about all this, but stick it in the back somewhere. We can argue philosophy later. But right now I, *me,* your client, have a crisis on my hands. Are you going to help me or aren't you? I need a lawyer. I already have a conscience."

Susan wondered if he really did. "Just tell me this, Jack, and then I'll lay off. If you were Jimenez, what would you do? Would you just stand by and take it? Credible grievances and all?"

"I guess I really do need a new lawyer," Jack replied, sighing. "I didn't want to have to do this but *you're* pushing *me* against the wall."

"Thanks, Wells. You just answered my question. You *wouldn't* sit back and take it. Go right ahead and can me, too. Why not, you're on a roll."

They both slammed down the phone at the same time. Susan's hand flew up to her mouth. She couldn't believe what she had just done, what she had just said. What had gotten into her? How could she speak to her client that way? she chastised herself, wondering if she should grab up the phone and call Jack back to apologize, trying to imagine what he would even say to her.

She guessed she was trying to appeal to a different side of him, the compassionate side that she was sure existed buried somewhere deep inside the armor he wore on the outside. Perpetual jerk that she was, she still believed that to be true. In the midst of her anxiety she was half expecting the telephone to ring and for it to be Jack calling back, apologizing. She couldn't comprehend that she couldn't—if she really applied herself or pressed the right buttons—get through to him.

Kreegle was passing by Susan's office and he paused to stand in the door. "You all right?" he asked, sounding concerned.

She looked up at him, certain that she didn't look all right at all, sure that most of the blood had drained from her face and that she had turned a ghastly white. "Fine. Thanks," she said, also sure that he was going to receive a scathing telephone call from Jack any minute and that when he did all hell would break loose.

"Sure you're okay?"

"Mmmm. Thanks."

He put his hands in the pockets of his trousers and rocked back and forth on his heels. "Raymond West still not here? I thought I'd stop by and say hello."

"No. Uh—"

Susan's secretary, Linda, appeared in the doorway. Kreegle let her pass. "Mr. West called. He said he'll be another fifteen minutes. He got held up."

"Thanks," Susan said, turning back to Kreegle, glad for the answer so that she didn't appear uninterested.

The phone rang again and, since her secretary was standing there and it was easier for Susan to catch it herself, she picked up the receiver.

"Should we add you to the list of fired casualties yet?" Mark's voice came in soothingly over the line. Her eyes must have lit up because Kreegle gave her a look, then mouthed: "the date?"

She smiled mysteriously as he turned to leave, then she looked at Linda as though for commiseration, since she knew Linda would have heard at least a portion of her conversation with Jack. The door was open and she hadn't been speaking softly.

"I'm in the about-to-be-fired category. And inching precariously close," she said to Mark.

"With your Wells character? Or the firm?"

"I really got into it. With both."

"Don't worry about it. If you get the ax, I'll take care of you," Mark joked sweetly. "I offered my services in the beginning and I have every intention of seeing it all the way through to the end with you."

"Promise?"

"I'm not sure I can take care of you in the manner to which you've become accustomed," he continued joking. "But you won't go hungry and I'll make you laugh a lot."

"Sounds wonderful. Now I'm really going to be aggressive about this thing, in the hopes of getting fired as soon as possible."

"Dinner at eight?"

"Unless they fire me earlier."

"Do you miss me?"

She had to laugh. She had been missing him for months.

Paige's day had been manic.

First the blow of seeing Susan and Mark together, looking at one another in that ridiculous moon-glow way, as though they were on the brink of discovering something that every idiot falling in love hadn't already discovered a thousand times over.

Didn't they know the condition is called "*falling* in love" for a reason?

The verb preceding the noun is a dead give-away, an obvious reference to the casualty. When you *fall* you get hurt.

Fall.

Drop.

Ouch.

That rude awakening at the end of the fall, to which people still in motion believe themselves impervious.

The high, heady sensation merely comes from being off-balance.

Paige wasn't off-balance. She was just nervous. Nervous about beating out all the fantasies she had planted in Nicky's head about how memorable she was going to be in bed.

And she was run ragged from rushing from one place to the next.

This morning she had taught two back-to-back private sessions at clients' homes, pulling in some extra cash to pay for the present she was going to buy for Nicky.

Then one of the instructors had called in sick at Sports Club/LA, so she had had to teach a double shift there, pushing well past her endurance, having to keep up with her bionic students. She had been so fatigued after the last class that during the cooldown, she had thought she was going to faint. Then overcome with nausea she had finally had to run into the ladies' room to throw up.

After that, she had squeezed in two more privates, then gone driving around the city collecting extravagant foodstuffs for the surprise picnic she was planning on setting up in Nicky's bed this evening, all of which had her back at home considerably later than planned.

Fortunately, she had gotten bathing and getting ready for him down to a forty-five-minute science.

Nicky's daughter, Marni, was pulling out of the driveway as Paige pulled in and they waved to one another. She had gotten her hair cut kind of punk, and Paige was surprised to see her looking so hip. She figured the change had come about on account of the rock promoter Nicky kept complaining about. Marni had met him at an after-concert party in the StarDome's green room and Paige knew Nicky was having the guy checked out, looking for skeletons in the closet, maybe even hoping for them. His persistence made her wonder if he weren't the type of father who found something critically wrong with all his daughter's suitors. The old Freudian complex squashing his perspective.

Although it was only twilight, the lights of the twenty-two room mansion were already glowing as Paige got out of her car and approached the entrance. She drew a quick breath before ringing the bell this time, her mind busy planning. What if he was already downstairs and ready to leave? What then? What was she going to say when he asked what was in her shopping bags?

Inside one was the present she had bought for him, a gorgeous Bijan robe, which she had really bought for herself to wear because the color of his was all wrong for her and she didn't like the cut. Inside the other shopping bag was the dinner that was going to replace their dinner at Chasens.

The door was answered by Sammy, Nicky's Filipino houseman. "Hi, Miss Williams. You look great!"

She had on a clingy white knit dinner dress, which she had thought was appropriate for the occasion, sexy but sophisticated, perfect for the girl he would want to whisk off to bed, still in good taste for a wife.

"Thanks. He upstairs?" she asked, hoping he were to simplify the logistics of her seduction.

"Yes. I'll let him know you're here," Sammy said, about to move to do so when Paige put her hand on his arm.

"It's okay," she said, stopping him, then heading toward the stairs on her own and giving him a little wink.

Nicky was just putting on his tie in front of a mirror over his dresser when she tapped lightly on his open door and walked into his room, slyly leaning back against the door to close it behind her. Naturally there was a sporting event on TV.

"Hi. Don't you look ravishing!" he exclaimed, turning to appraise her with a wicked leer. He looked exceptionally dapper in a dark suit and tie. If they had kids together, Paige thought they would be great-looking, tall, nicely built. If they had a girl, and she had his nose instead of Paige's she might need a little plastic surgery, but the glint in his eyes, if she got that, would make her a winner.

She walked over to help him with his tie, even though she had no intention of letting him leave to go anywhere. Their dinner date at Chasens with his friends was about to be intercepted.

While she measured and looped the dotted Italian silk at his throat, he circled his fingertips around her nipples, making them grow hard so that they stood out through her dress.

Leaving one hand on her breast, he dropped his other hand down around to her behind, murmuring over the perfection of the shape. She wasn't wearing any panties and when he realized that, he lifted up the skirt of her dress and cupped the bareness of her ass with a look of eager surprise.

"God, how am I ever going to concentrate at dinner," he complained, running his hands down the sides of her thighs, pressing his swollen excitement against her. "You're such a tease. One of these days I'm going to just jump you, you little bitch," he threatened huskily.

Paige perfected the knot on his tie, then moved in closer to trace her tongue along his large athlete's neck, inhaling the familiar scent of the soap from his shower, tasting the freshness. "Promises, promises."

"Oh, yeah?"

"Yeah."

"How are *you* going to concentrate?" he asked bringing his hands around to where her panties would ordinarily have been, reacting to the wetness there.

She enveloped his hard-on with both of her hands and massaged lightly, moving down to encompass his balls and then up slowly again along his shaft, applying more pressure while biting gently at the tip of his earlobe.

"You make me so crazy. I can't even talk to you on the phone without getting a stiff prick."

Her thighs drew in tight around his hands as they played there, inducing a pleasurable weakness that she hadn't let herself feel with him before. At last she felt free to let go, released, because tonight there would be no need for restraint.

"Oh, shit. I can't go like this, Paige," he groaned, starting to unbuckle his pants and tug at the zipper. "I want to feel your sassy little mouth around me. C'mon baby, suck me off before we go."

Paige stepped back and laughed, enjoying the anguish on his face, unzipping the back of her dress and letting it drop to the floor. "I'll do better than that," she offered, with a wily smirk, standing in only a pair of high-heeled lizard pumps, her long legs accentuated as she stepped out of the puddle of fabric and saun-tered over toward his ornate bed. She took her time while undo-ing the bed covers, then climbed up and stretched out on her side to bid him to come closer. The mirror over his bed demonstrated that the effect was a good one.

But so did the expression on his face, which she thought was priceless, along with the massive bulge distorting the line of his custom-tailored pants.

"We're supposed to be meeting everyone at Chasens in fifteen minutes—" he began, torn, having to clear his throat.

She laughed and rolled over onto her back, sensuously cupping one of her breasts, stroking the ripe mound of flesh there, then looking up into the mirror as she continued drawing her fingers luxuriously down her belly. "Where would you *really* rather be in fifteen minutes? Eating chili at Chasens, or here in bed with me."

An executive decision. While shedding his clothes, Nicky picked up the phone by the side of the bed and began dialing.

By the time he finished getting his party on the line and giving them the message that he wouldn't be able to make it, she had his pants down and her tongue maneuvering up the inside of his thighs, moving stealthily up toward the engorged target of his private parts. As he was about to say good-bye she laughed again, savoring her power, *relieved* because she felt confident again. Looking up playfully into his adoring eyes, she snatched the phone out of his hands and dropped it down onto its cradle.

"I'm going to fuck your brains out, Nicky Loomis," she warned, boldly snapping off the damn remote control of his TV set as they slid together to the center of the bed, the rest of his clothes discarded in all directions. "Mr. Sports King," she chided lovingly, nibbling at his love handles, then kissing his cock. "I'm going to make you *lose consciousness.*"

"You little bitch. You still trying to rope me down the aisle?" he asked, closing his eyes and exclaiming in pleasure as she enveloped his enormous erection entirely in her mouth, drawing in cool breath to react against the heat, and sucking at the same time.

"Did you think I was kidding?" she asked, pausing for a moment to read his eyes, which were glazed with longing.

He laughed and shook his head. "No—" But before he could comment further he lost his train of thought and let out a loud, long moan instead that seemed to travel all the way up his barrel of a chest and then out his mouth.

Paige had never been very musical, but when she was making love, she felt musical. He was the musical instrument she had never before played, and her natural rhythm from dance took over until they were both carried away in a song in their minds.

She was playing him her way, making him lose consciousness, as she had said. She was feeling close to losing it right along with him, seduced by the silkiness of his skin, his body hair which she found even softer than silk so that she couldn't stop running her fingers through its dense growth.

Intent on maintaining control, she drew herself up over him so that she was on top, kicking away the sheets and straddling him. His thick arms she pinned back behind his head so that she could watch the intensity of expression on his face.

His eyes were squeezed closed, tense, his mouth open, almost wincing, wanting, reaching, his thin lips nearly disappearing in the grimace as she rode him, instinctively attuned to his pace.

As she arched back and felt him thrusting still deeper inside of her, she caught his face again in the mirror overhead. It was filled with something primeval, something so raw and passionate that a massive thrill shimmied down her spine. She could see that he was about to explode, that he was riding the crest of his nearing climax as long as he could, while she continued taking him higher and higher, wanting to shatter all known limits. They were both drenched in hot sweat, hers mingling with his. She could see that he was going to come any second and she couldn't take her eyes off him. She was on an odyssey of total control, feeling riveted by the sense of power.

His face had gone from completely relaxed to this amazing, almost savage ruthlessness giving way to a total abandon, a take-over of the senses.

It all felt so incredibly private and intimate, a rare, otherwise forbidden, glance into his very being.

She felt as though she were glimpsing a secret part of him that you had to screw him in order to know, only she wanted to stay linked into that view for a longer fragment of time, to draw it out, maybe forever.

When he started to come, she was actually disappointed be-cause their moment was going to be over. She found herself actu-ally fighting back tears, when she *never* cried. *Never!* She believed fiercely that crying only made people more vulnerable. Paige hadn't cried since the day her mother died.

But then the power of his orgasm ripped through her, sweep-ing her into a climax of like force toward the last wave of his, creating an overlapping of private sounds and feelings so intense it made her head spin.

"Oh, God, Paige! I can't even believe what you do to me!" he cried, holding her close afterward, maintaining himself inside her as he turned them both over so that now he was on top, his cheek pressed against hers, until his spent erection slipped out anyway, followed by a warm sensation that felt sweetly significant.

It was the quiet after the storm and Paige was taken aback because he didn't roll impatiently off her immediately afterward, as she had anticipated. Instead he arranged one of the soft, down-filled pillows beneath her head.

His unexpected tenderness had her overwhelmed. *God, could I really have it all?* she wondered, scared to hope, fighting tears again because there was this broken but pasted-back-together part of her that didn't believe she could.

Money, great sex, *and* tenderness, she thought to herself with her usual edge, knowing that her anxiety would be crushing while she waited for the fall.

The inevitable drop.

The ouch.

Chapter 27

Fans were already pouring into the StarDome, keyed up in anticipation of this evening's game that had all basketball aficionados in suspense. A rookie from Arizona State with "can't miss" written all over him was playing with the L.A. Stars and everyone was abuzz with his pro debut.

Nicky and Paige climbed out of the backseat of his white stretch limousine and hustled toward the entrance, besieged by autograph hounds. She felt a sense of importance, being ushered through the boisterous crowd by the tall, bawdy sports mogul, his arm wrapped proprietarily around her waist, both of them pausing every few seconds so he could dash off a signature while making their way toward the awesome round structure he had erected.

When they reached the entrance they were met by guards who then shielded them the rest of the way, seeing to it that they were able to get into the elevator alone.

After a quick interview spot for a local television station, where he delivered the obligatory two-sentence answer to the question he had been asked twenty times in the last two weeks. "What do you think the prospects for your team are now, with the addition of the rookie, Roberts?" Nicky and Paige then joined Nicky's guests in the private dining room of his StarDome Club, where he routinely hosted a large horseshoe-shaped table filled with friends and acquaintances, many of them celebrities.

Tonight she knew Joe Namath was going to be there with his little boy. Jimmy Connors and his son. O.J. Simpson. Astronaut Scott Carpenter was supposed to be there. Mayor Tom Bradley. Kirk Douglas. His son Michael Douglas. And crazy-as-a-loon Jack Nicholson.

The established protocol of Nicky's pre-show entertaining was for the guests to order and eat whenever they got there. Usually steak and lobsters. It was all very casual. Nicky was generally one of the last to arrive.

Threading their way through the narrow aisle, Paige followed Nicky to the place always reserved for him at the head table, where she could see tonight she would also be sitting next to his son, Tip Loomis.

On their way to their seats she noticed Nicky nodding to an attractive redhead at the other side of the table, who was laughing with a group of friends. "She's going to be the new Revlon girl," he explained quietly to Paige, who had followed his glance. "Her fiancé, the guy with the leather jacket, claims to be Jimi Hendrix's illegitimate son or something. And that young lady with them is about to be the hottest new sex symbol since Raquel Welch. I used to date her."

Date being synonymous with *screw,* Paige thought, giving him a frosty smile as she sat down in the chair he had pulled out for her, taking in the dozens of young pretty women with whom she knew she would always have to contend if she did manage to permanently snare Nicky.

"Who, *her,* or Raquel?" she remarked.

He smiled so that she could have killed him. "Both."

It served her right for asking. She had been set up for that one. *Of course both.*

A waiter appeared, ready to take their order.

"I know, you're *starving,"* he kidded Paige, because it was her usual greeting to him. She was perpetually starved.

She shook her head no and ordered only a bowl of soup instead of her usual lobster. The word alone triggered a fishy odor in her brain that made her feel instantly sick to her stomach, a feeling she had been experiencing all too often lately.

"*Not* starving? You feeling okay?" The waiter looked at her askance, his pencil still poised over his small pad of paper.

"I feel fine. Just not *ravenous* tonight," she replied, glad that Nicky had turned the other way and had all his attention focused on a joke one of Hollywood's old-time comedians was telling.

She was beginning to have this low, gnawing anxiety about the queasiness that never seemed to go away, about the aching fullness in her breasts. It wasn't so much that she had missed a period and was now late for this one that had her wary, since her menstrual cycle had rarely been reliable. But it was the constant nausea.

"What about you, Mr. Loomis? New York rare—?"

The comedian had just finished delivering the punch line of his joke and had everyone seated around him laughing loudly. Nicky, naturally laughing the most raucously of them all, turned around briefly to confirm his dinner order, then turned back to the guys to deliver his own joke.

When a four-letter word appeared in the first sentence of the joke, one of Nicky's guests kiddingly protected his son's ears with his hands, as though shielding him from his host's profanities.

"I've heard the word *fuck* before," his kid argued, loudly draining the balance of his Shirley Temple drink while pushing away his father's hands.

"Yeah?" someone asked him. "What does it mean?"

"I forgot," he said, his small cheeks filling with color.

"But you *did* know?"

He shrugged shyly and went back to draining his already empty glass.

Everyone laughed as his father also shrugged and Nicky went on with his joke.

"So how's business?" Paige asked, turning toward Nicky's thirty-two-year-old son. He was extremely good-looking, with his long hair drawn back into a ponytail, but moody as hell. "Doing well. Thanks," he replied vaguely.

The *business* she was referring to was a small computer business, which his father had happily funded after Tip had returned to Los Angeles, lost, floundering, and stripped of his inheritance.

Tip Loomis had been one of the thousands of lost souls seduced and brainwashed by the Rajneesh up in Oregon where, in order to be members of the secret cult, they had to surrender all their earthly belongings to him.

It was a great racket the leader had going for himself, inculcating his wishes into the heads of these groping kids. They all wound up penniless and trusting, supposedly happier for their lack of material baggage, while the great and pure Rajneesh greedily stockpiled his own.

Until one day, out of the blue, the infamous leader suddenly ceased talking.

His sea of followers, lost without their voice—*his* voice, would come out daily and just sit, waiting for him to begin to speak again or do something. Finally, to the great relief of the parents who had lost their kids to the cult, there was nothing left to do but give up and return home.

The great charismatic Rajneesh had apparently done his last bit of prophecy. Maybe he had screwed too many women in too short a timespan and his brain had short-circuited.

Nicky had been so grateful to have his son back and doing something halfway normal that he had completely backed Tip's computer venture and updated all the StarDome's systems through his new company. Nicky said Tip was bright, just weird.

Paige half wondered if he weren't dealing drugs as well as dealing Apples. She had never seen him when he didn't look like he was on something.

God, how hard it had to be, raising kids, she thought, pressing the palm of her hand to her own flat belly.

Whose kid would it even be if she *were* pregnant, she worried, growing even more squeamish at the thought. Would it have curly blond hair, dimples, and intense blue eyes? Or would it be big and burly, with small, impish brown eyes like Nicky?

She might have wanted to *pretend* it was Nicky's, but the timing, she knew, had to be off by at least a month.

Nauseated by the potential glut of complications and tired of calculating, she directed her attention back to Tip, who hadn't noticed that he'd lost her attention in the first place.

"Do you do much advertising for your company?" she asked him, hoping to draw him out.

She caught Nicky looking over at her as though he were pleased that she and Tip were talking to each other. She slipped Nicky a quick private look, thinking no wonder he was such a magnet for his friends and the press. It wasn't just his money and his position because even in this power-stacked group he managed to stand out. He had a special aura about him. The way he looked so relaxed, so in control, so powerful, and yet still so exuberant.

But could she put up with his stadium-sized ego or the grabby groupies always lurking around?

"We do some advertising," Tip answered.

"Like where?"

He took several stabs at his salad, collecting as many leaves of lettuce onto his fork as possible, while appearing to consider her question. "Oh, the usual."

He wasn't the easiest dinner partner she had ever had. "Newspapers? TV?"

He looked at her as if she were an idiot. "TV's way too expensive. You don't advertise for a store like ours on TV."

So she'd asked a dumb question. "You should have your dad flash it on the electronic board out in the stadium. Mass exposure for free."

Giving her no reaction whatsoever, Tip went back to his salad and Paige felt relieved when the waiter finally brought her soup to the table.

Not that she could manage to eat it. She couldn't even stand the smell of it.

She felt as if she were going to throw up, between the mingling of food odors wafting her way and her futile attempt at connecting with Nicky's moody son.

She had had much better luck with Marni. Marni at least was from this planet.

* * *

After a triumphant basketball game a group of them went out to celebrate at one of the new underground clubs downtown, pumped up from the exciting finale of the game where, with only two minutes left to go, the L.A. Stars had retrieved the lead and snatched victory from the jaws of defeat.

The club was smoky and packed. Paige, barely able to stand still, with the music blasting inside, held on tightly to Nicky's hand as they were admitted in front of the mile-long line, their coterie in tow. Dancing never failed to recharge her battery. She couldn't wait to get out there onto the dance floor and lose herself in the beat. Her nausea had finally vanished, quelled by bread and later by popcorn, and she felt relieved, spirited even.

The music shocking the sound waves inside the tight, frenetic quarters was more New Wave than disco, and she worried Nicky would find it loud and grating. Be too old for it.

She was surprised when he instead seized her hand and swung her out onto the dance floor, moving so that he was a match for any of the twenty-year-olds.

Everyone was staring at them, excited by the celebrities who were in the mood to take the club by storm.

The sea of young, hip kids parted to make room for them on the dance floor.

Nicky must have known at least half a dozen of the girls there, or at least they knew him. They materialized in a dependable stream, coming up to kiss him hello—to flirt with the famous party laureate.

It was irritating, but Paige could take it. These blossoming females *looked* like women, until they opened their mouths and were revealed as the innocuous teenagers they were.

Dancing and drinking went on until about two in the morning, when they all piled back into Nicky's limousine and were driven home.

After the chauffeur had dropped off the last of their bunch and returned to Nicky's house, Paige started to climb out of the car in front of Nicky, but he held her back. There was something serious about the way he maintained his grip on her arm and kept looking at her.

"What?" she asked with a giddy, self-conscious chuckle.

"You're gorgeous. You take my breath away."

She leaned in and gave him a tender, lingering kiss on the lips. "Honestly. And you were great tonight."

She didn't really know what he meant, but she said thanks anyway.

"With my friends, my kid—" he trailed off, his long legs stretched out over the jump seat in front of him. He hadn't said more than a couple of words to her after they had dropped off the last of their group and she looked at him curiously, wondering what was on his mind.

She smiled, trying to look understanding, hoping to encourage him to go on. The driver was standing a few feet off from the car, smoking a cigarette and looking out at the bushes.

"He's a tough cookie, that kid of mine."

That kid was only a year or so older than Paige, and it felt odd to hear Nicky keep referring to him that way.

"He's all right," she replied, thinking it couldn't have been easy growing up as *Nicky Loomis's son.* Failure seemed inherent in the typical rich-kid syndrome. Tip, Richard Bennetton. There was too much expected of them.

And most likely too much competition while they plodded after their goals.

Perhaps it was easier for a daughter, she considered—unless the mother was the superstar.

Paige wondered how she would have turned out, raised in the shadow of a spotlight. Some kids were strong enough to jump into the spotlight themselves. Some kids were strong enough to not have it affect them, period.

Most kids, it seemed, got squashed.

Up in his bedroom, she waited stretched across his bed and drinking champagne, wearing only a skimpy jade satin bra and panties she had bought to bring out her eyes, and a pair of bronze high-heeled pumps. She was busy singing along with an old Frank Sinatra album she had put on the stereo, drinking in the rich sound of his voice while trying to mimic that unique Sinatra phrasing.

"Close your eyes, gorgeous," Nicky ordered her from outside of the room.

"What?" she asked, turning to look for him.

"I said close your eyes."

"Why?" she asked, though obliging without waiting for an answer.

"*You're* always playing games. This is *my* game. Now shut your gorgeous mouth . . ."

It felt weird, eerie, lying there in the darkness, just waiting and having to wonder what was going on.

The shade of darkness seemed to deepen, as though he had turned out the lights.

She kept thinking she felt him nearing the bed, but then nothing would happen. There were several seconds of silence between songs on the stereo, and the absence of sound felt amplified. She started to giggle out of nervousness, excitement, and anticipation, dubious as to what he had in store for her. She kept wanting to ask him questions, but she was afraid that he would get mad, that she would break the mood.

Finally she felt one side of the bed begin to sink beneath his weight, and she knew he was there beside her. She kept waiting for him to touch her or to say something. What kind of charade was this? Why all the mystery? She couldn't help but feel a tinge of apprehension, wondering if he were going to do something kinky or depraved.

Then, before she knew it, she was reacting to something light and ticklish being drawn up between her legs, over her panties, her belly, circling her breasts, trailing up the line of her neck, then passing over her lips to pause beneath her nose.

It was silky and fragrant. There were different sections to it.

It was a rose.

She smiled at the recognition, and it was suddenly whisked away, as though she had guessed right and he was moving on to part two of the quiz.

Next came something plump and cold. Heavier.

It was taken up the same path, only he rocked it back and forth.

It was a ball of some sort, only not completely round. Firm and *so* cool on her skin. When it reached her mouth she instinctively licked it but tasted nothing. The smell didn't get her the answer, either.

"Take a bite," he suggested, putting it over her mouth again.

"What is it?"

"Just bite it; bite into it."

She laughed, feeling nervous. "What if I don't like it?"

"Then spit it out."

Warily, she took a bite. The skin was tough. She had to really sink her teeth into it, and as she did the juices came streaming down her face.

It took a moment before she was able to identify it as a *tomato*. The delayed ability to recognize the taste mystified her, and she found herself eager for his next diversion, the next sensory illusion.

Clearly not food this time, she thought, as he dabbed at the mess trickling down her cheeks, down the side of her neck, and onto the pillow. He used something soft and fleecy-feeling.

As he dangled it over her arms, swinging it provocatively across her stomach and thighs, it felt like cashmere or a baby blanket or a diaper.

But what would he be doing with a baby blanket or a diaper?

A rush of queasiness came over her again as she began worrying about the real significance of his game. What if he somehow suspected she was pregnant?

But that was ridiculous.

She was just psyching herself out, and she vowed to go out and buy a home pregnancy test to resolve her anxiety once and for all. The moment the test results read negative she knew her nausea would vanish, and her belated menstrual flow would be released.

This wouldn't be the first time she had sweated over a late period.

"You give up on this one?" he asked.

"You know me better than that."

"Don't open your eyes!"

It was so hard keeping them closed. Letting her mind wander, she concentrated on the sensation, the texture of what she was sure was some kind of fabric, wanting to give it another shot. "A sweater or scarf. Cashmere—"

Whatever it was, it disappeared. The next sensation felt arctic-cold, slender, and fairly lightweight as it tickled her toes, then traveled all the way up from her ankle, around her calf, her thigh, stopping at her crotch where he began drawing small deliberate circles over and around her panties.

It felt like a tool or utensil of some sort.

The icy metal sensation was arousing. Arching up her hips, she decided it was definitely metal but nothing as crude as a tool; it was too sleek-feeling, the surface too smooth.

Maybe it was a watch, she guessed uncertainly, growing more and more relaxed, enjoying herself as he drew the mystery object up along her shoulder, her neck, and then stuck it in her mouth.

Her teeth clinked on the hard metal and, as he let her lick the form of it, its shape gave it away as a *spoon*. She was three for four. Not bad.

Now he's getting dirty, she thought smiling, wanting to open her eyes but not wanting to ruin his game. Down at her ankles again was a small bulbous form that was either his tongue or the tip of his penis. It was slippery and it felt great. And she tried to stop smiling as it slinked up along her hips, velvety and hard, curving in with her waist until she decided it was too large and spherical to be his tongue. "I would know that anywhere," she said, as he held his nasty little treat just beneath her lips.

"You would, huh?"

Reaching with her tongue, she began to lick the tip teasingly, demure flicks meant to alter the balance of power, but then as she went to take a tender, ladylike bite, her teeth sank into something elusive and bland, surprising her as it crumbled in her mouth.

It was a hard-boiled egg, that rat!

"That's what I love about you, Paige. You have such a dirty mind," he said, abandoning the egg to drag something of an entirely different composition across her stomach. "You'll like this one."

It was long and cordlike, with an almost sticky, rubbery texture. In fact, it felt like a utility cord or a whip of some sort, and Paige conjured up images of what he planned on doing with it.

"Just so there isn't any confusion, I don't like pain," she enlightened him, wishing she could open her eyes just a sliver to see.

"No pain, no gain," he teased in a sinister voice, starting to tie her wrists together. "I'll Never Smile Again" began to play nostalgically in the background.

"Help . . . help . . ." she called out in a small voice, the heroine tied to the tracks.

He cackled like the villain, then brought her bound wrists down toward her mouth. She decided it smelled too sweet to be a cord. The scent was more like clay, Play-Doh, or even a candle.

"Edible restraints," he told her, as she bit tentatively into the hard rubbery cord, thinking it didn't taste terribly edible. It tasted like cherry cough drops, but by the shape she realized it was a *licorice whip*.

Funny, she always thought she loved licorice whips! What a surprise to find out how awful they tasted with her eyes closed.

Securing her bound wrists above her head, and barking at her to keep her eyes closed, he brought out his next prop.

Smiling, she thought it felt like a slab of marble, but not quite cold enough. Maybe a candle or a brick of clay.

It was luxuriously smooth and probably additionally stirring because now she had lost not only the control of being able to see, but the command of her hands as well.

She was vulnerable and at his mercy.

The velvety slab of whatever it was had curves; it was oval she discovered, as he began moving it up over her stomach, which shrank involuntarily from the contact.

The fragrance hit her as soon as the object reached her chin. "Hmmm, smells so good," she murmured, sniffing at the fresh scent of *soap* that smelled like Nicky after a shower.

Sticking out her tongue to complete the experiment, she found the taste foreign, a little bitter, but she wanted a few extra moments to take in the pleasure of the clean, memorable herbal scent.

Next came something light and airy. It felt weightless like a silk scarf dancing over her skin and giving her goose bumps as he drew it over her crotch.

It had edges to it, she realized with surprise as he swept it up higher, making her think it could be paper of some sort. Or gauze.

When it reached her throat, she thought it could be a fan, a greeting card, or even a playing card. Except it seemed too flimsy, not stiff or thick enough.

Sniffing hard as he held it beneath her nose, recognizing the distinct odors of paper and ink, the answer came to her.

How could she miss the smell of crisp new *money*!

"Okay, now open your eyes because part of this is in the visuals," Nicky insisted.

It took Paige a moment to have her eyes readjust. Before she knew what was happening, she found herself being showered with bills.

Hundred-dollar bills.

A seemingly endless downpour of that same crisp, new money she had just been feeling all over her body, feeling, smelling, and trying to place.

Nicky was sitting beside her on the bed, wearing the new robe she had given him, his pile of props on the nightstand beside him while he continued to pour from a bucket that must have been overflowing.

He was right, the visuals made it unforgettable.

As sensuous as everything had been that had preceded the bills, this broke the bank on erotic.

They were languishing in the cool bills, which felt fresh off the press, crisp and vivid, throwing them up in the air and watching them float back down again.

It even beat the sacred pleasure of romping in the first fall of leaves, bountiful autumn piles that in her childhood had felt profoundly sensual.

"Hmmm. Do I get to keep all this?" Paige joked, biting into the licorice whips securing her wrists, literally eating her way to freedom, then laughing as she got up onto her knees to study the effect in the mirror above them, playfully stuffing her bra with the bills.

"Not for that," he said, releasing a cascade of cash as he unhooked her bra and tossed it across the room. "They're perfect without embellishment. Firm and softer than satin," he pronounced, closing his eyes as he continued caressing them, "round and just the right size. I know," he teased, as though playing his game again, only this time playing the subject's role. "They're tits —nice, big, American breasts!"

"You're good at this," Paige teased him, swiping the sash from his robe and then tying it over his eyes while she crawled on top of him inside the robe, enjoying the warm contact of their skin and letting her long mane of hair drag over him. He groped for her panties and pulled them off.

"Did I ever tell you that green makes me sexy?" she confessed, arranging herself on her knees just behind his straining erection, which she took possessively in her hands. She plucked a bill off the bed with her teeth and flicked it lightly across his chest. "Green makes me dangerously sexy. *Beware,*" she emphasized, with the cash gripped between her teeth.

"You didn't *need* to tell me. I saw it in your eyes," he assured her, arching up to maneuver his mouth around one of her breasts, doing pretty well for a guy wearing a blindfold. "There are *sea-green* eyes, *jade-green, apple-green*. You, my love, have *money-green eyes.*"

Smirking, she let the *money-green* bill drop out of her mouth and bent down to gnaw gently at his lower lip. "So after we make love, *inspired* by its glorious *money-green* value, how are we going to spend all this lovely loot?" she demanded, unhurried, as she mounted him, her hands grasping his thick, athletic thighs, her lips pressing against his.

He untied the sash from his eyes and looked up into the mirror, cupping her bottom with his hands and letting out a deep groan of pleasure as she continued riding him.

She rolled her head back and met his gaze in the mirror, feeling her hair dangling low near her waist.

"You sure you can handle it?" he asked, bringing in an element of suspense, flipping them both over so that he was on top riding her, thrusting harder and faster with a mounting speed, his weight heavy and pounding against her.

There were bills sprayed in every direction, beneath her, on top of her, and on both sides as she looked up in the mirror again. Nicky's ass was tight, the muscles constricting and growing more defined as he pushed for satisfaction. "Hmmm. I can handle it," she promised, moving her hips to meet his as he controlled the pace.

"I don't know why I'm doing this," he hedged.

"Because you can't help yourself," she suggested, growing intrigued, both of them growing more turned on by the second.

"God help me for this decision."

"What decision?"

Nicky looked as if he couldn't stand it anymore.

He was going to burst inside her any second. She felt herself climbing with him, being elevated higher and higher until she could barely concentrate, but she couldn't *not* concentrate.

What decision? She was waiting.

"Oh, God, Paige!" he bellowed so loud that she was sure he could be heard throughout the house.

"Tell me," she insisted, stopping to hold up his orgasm, to tease him past his limits. *"Tell me!"*

His face was filled with tension; she was sure he had been thinking about changing his mind, of backing out of what he had admitted he might regret, and she was pressing him.

"I want you to go out and buy yourself the most ostentatious diamond rock you can find," he managed in a choked voice that still held the appropriate tone of irony.

Then the second she started moving again, he started to come. "Marry me, you gorgeous little bitch, you," he finished, grasping her closer still.

Marry me.

Marry me.

Marry me.

Marry me.

It was an implausible echo. The words rolled off her like honey over oil; the sweetness of the message eluding her. She couldn't manage to get it to stick.

"Yes," she rejoiced, exalted, relieved, soaring straight toward heaven, higher than she had ever been before.

Chapter 28

Paige left Nicky's house the next morning in shock.

She had anticipated a prenuptial contract. A man in his position would be foolish, she realized, not to insist on one. But for him to stipulate no children, specifying if she got pregnant and had a baby while she was married to him, she would lose everything—that she found unconscionable.

She had never, by any stretch of the imagination, been obsessed with having babies. But it was an option she didn't like having revoked in writing, especially with the penalty for noncompliance so drastic, she thought, gunning the gas pedal of Dustin Brent's Aston-Martin as she wound down around the canyon, driving away from Nicky's pristine pink mansion, her hands clutching the steering wheel.

"There's just one detail we have to get out of the way" was how he had broached the prenuptial, walking nude across the room to his briefcase, putting on his reading glasses, and bringing the contract back to the bed.

Paige had presumed the very legal-looking document would spell out a series of details she would find less than pleasing. And the very concept of a prenuptial stung. But, on the contrary, as she began to read she had been pleasantly surprised.

"I think you'll find this all more than fair," he had insisted, scrutinizing her as she scanned the pages.

She had been relieved, even excited at first because the terms all seemed favorable; she was about to become a very wealthy woman. If something were to happen to Nicky, if he were to die, she was going to inherit a fortune. Even if they were to wind up divorced, she was going to find herself exceedingly wealthy.

But just as her excitement at the generous terms of the contract began to build inside her, it was dashed when she came to the fateful provision.

If she got pregnant and chose to have the baby, he had provided that she would receive only minimal support for the child, and nothing for herself.

"God! What have you got against kids?" she had asked him, flabbergasted and yet struggling for lightness, sliding over and wrapping her long legs around his waist.

The king-sized bed was still strewn with hundred-dollar bills and they appeared to mock her as she picked one up, reading uncomfortably into Benjamin Franklin's enigmatic expression, as though he were judging her, waiting to hear how she would resolve her dilemma. "What—you're going to abandon me if you knock me up by accident?"

It was hard for her to believe, but the look on Nicky's face had left her cold. Seeming uncomfortable, he replied, "Look, I'm selfish at this point in my life. I just want you. No kids. No job for me to have to compete with. Just *you.*"

His look had softened as he'd drawn her up close beside his chest, stroking her hair. "Look, Paige, I'm wild about you. I don't want to have to *share* you. I want to be able to travel with you. I want the freedom to be able to say *C'mon, let's go to Italy tomorrow.* I want to be able to pick up and do it with a free conscience. Without feeling guilty about having left a baby behind."

As he sat there struggling to make her understand, she wanted to argue, but there was nothing she could think of to say.

And it was so strange to find herself in the position of arguing for something she wasn't even sure she wanted herself. She would be resisting only to keep the option open, and the stipulation out of the contract.

Of course Paige had consented.

He had offered to let her have a lawyer look over the terms, Susan or someone at Susan's law firm. Whoever she wanted. But Paige had merely reached over, taken the pen from his hand, and then signed over her fate on the dotted line.

Waiting for the light to change at the corner of Sunset and Whittier Drive, Paige felt all at once so sick to her stomach she threw the car into Park, clambered out the door, and then rushed over to the curb to throw up.

She stayed there for what seemed like a long time, crouched on her knees on the grass and hugging herself, feeling scared and vulnerable. She couldn't understand her reaction at all.

Sure, *Tori* and *Susan* wouldn't be able to handle the idea of not having any kids, but not *Paige*.

Paige who had never cared that much one way or the other.

She hadn't been the kind of girly-female whose *lifeblood* was to have babies.

She hadn't even been that big on dolls. And when she *had* played with dolls, it was only to live out the fantasy of being a teenager, playing with Barbie or Barbie prototypes in the context of how they related to Ken, their wardrobes, and what kinds of exciting things they were going to do with their lives.

It certainly hadn't been to satisfy any overpowering mothering instincts. She hadn't ever been *into* mothering.

And yet, suddenly, she missed her own mother. She wished she could communicate with her, wherever she was, up in heaven, playing cards, probably, with her girlfriends. Mah-jongg or pan.

She wanted to ask her mother what she should do. She wanted to be *held* by her mother, comforted, reassured, and given strength.

But her mother would only have been baffled. She wouldn't have understood Paige any more than she had understood Paige's father. She had had no patience or compassion for dreamers, for people who felt compelled to reach beyond comfortable— *jeopardizing* comfortable in the wake of their reach.

She was convinced her mother would think she was a terrible person.

She certainly felt like a terrible person.

Marrying for money instead of for love. Not even believing in love anymore.

Why should she? Had her parents stayed in love? No, they had only stayed "in guilt," resenting each other.

Why couldn't she think of anyone who had truly stayed in love, who could give her something to aim for, a reason to go for something bigger or more real or more spiritual.

A reason to tear that prenuptial contract to shreds and throw it in Nicky's famous face.

If she had believed, even a little, in perfect packages, she would never have signed. In fact, she wasn't sure she could live with herself for having done so.

What a betrayal of the baby she suspected to be growing inside her. And what a betrayal of Mark.

Dissolving into tears and crying as she hadn't cried since she was a kid, that profound sobbing that results in breathless, stuttering gasps afterward, she returned to the car and, instead of driving to work, drove straight to Mark's apartment.

Scared, vulnerable, desperately in need of some tender loving care, she sat down in the hallway outside his door, praying he would return home from his classes early.

"Paige?"

She felt like hell, hung over, even, when she heard her name being called out. It was the soothing sound of Mark's familiar voice at last and she woke with a start, looking up to see him walking toward her, his key in one hand, his satchellike briefcase swinging from his other. He looked so refreshing, his curly blond hair forming a wild halo. Those wire-rimmed glasses and their cockeyed fit. As usual, he was in jeans and he was wearing a blue plaid cardigan sweater she had never seen on him before.

Her vision was muddled instantly, tears spilling over as she tried to talk.

Concerned, Mark helped her up from the floor, putting his

arm around her while leading her into his apartment and then
sitting her down on the couch.

She'd had no idea that she had been sitting outside his door so
long. She was surprised to see that the sky outside was a bright
orange. Mark's window looked out onto another apartment complex similar to his, and the balcony directly across the way had
laundry hanging from an improvised clothesline. With rent control, the landlords did little to maintain the buildings; they all
looked sorely in need of paint.

It had been about a month since Paige had been there, and his
apartment seemed smaller, more dingy than romantic, which it
had seemed to her before. The fabrics on the antique furniture he
had picked up here and there were worn and probably cheap to
begin with. From where she was sitting on the couch she could
see just about every inch of every room. Nicky was so much of a
Goliath; picturing him there was like picturing him in a cabin of
a ship, where he would practically fill the whole room, having to
move sideways and duck a lot.

"It's okay," he assured her, while she tried to pull herself together to explain.

"Shhh.

"Don't talk yet.

"Just calm down.

"Nothing can be that awful; we'll fix it."

He had sat down beside her and was holding her close. She had
her head on his shoulder, and his shirt was becoming soaking wet
with her tears.

It felt so comforting to be in his arms again, relaxed, not having to work at being *on,* but feeling free to be herself. He kissed
her head and made soft soothing sounds, encouraging her to just
let it all out.

"You want something to drink?" he asked, pulling away for a
second to look at her.

She nodded.

"Some juice? Milk? 7-Up? Something harder?"

She nodded for something harder. He disappeared and then
returned a moment later carrying a bottle of red wine, an opener,
and two glasses. She knew it was one of his more cherished bot-

tles, a gift from another professor, and she was touched that he was opening it for her.

Under his arm, he braced a Kleenex box, which he let drop into her lap. "You want something to eat? You hungry?" he asked while removing the wine cork.

Though it was nearly dinnertime and she hadn't eaten since breakfast, she felt another swell of nausea and shook her head no, covering her mouth with a sheaf of Kleenex.

Then after a couple of calming sips of the wine she turned to him, afraid of what his reaction was going to be. Unsure what she *wanted* his reaction to be. Keeping her voice just above a whisper, she said, "Mark, I think I'm pregnant."

She flinched at the abrupt shift in his body language as he got up and walked across the small room, his hands thrust down so low in the pockets of his sweater it looked as if they would tear through. "So, is it mine? Is it *his*? How late are you?" he asked guardedly, without commitment.

"I've been sleeping with Nicky only a little over a month. If I'm pregnant, then I'm at least two months pregnant."

The realization registered quietly in Mark's face. But he seemed too hurt to give in to it.

Trying not to cry again, she took a deep swig of wine, hoping to swallow back the painful lump in her throat.

She watched him guzzling his wine as well, leaning uncomfortably against the bookshelf, at a loss as to what to say to her.

Dammit, she hadn't cried in years and now she couldn't stop herself. The attacks came in waves and her eyes burned as she fought against the determined flow. Mark's suppressed response was killing her and she kept wondering what Nicky's reaction would have been if she had told him the baby had been his, if he would have had second thoughts on the prenuptial and ripped it up.

"Last I heard, there are methods of finding out if you're pregnant or not," he snapped at last. "Why don't you go and take a damn test?"

Paige slammed her wineglass onto the table and glared at him, sorry she had come over in the first place.

He glared right back at her, his tone fierce. "What do you want from me, Paige? I'm just your *toy*, remember? What kind of reaction am I supposed to have? Dammit, you can't play with people the way you do—"

"I know. Forget it. I'm sorry," she interrupted, too conflicted to continue. "Mark, I'm sorry. I'm leaving—"

"The hell you are. I'm entitled to some answers! Like why are you even telling me this? Are you going to have the baby? Or are you going to have an abortion? What—?" he ranted.

"I don't know what I'm going to do. I'm just all mixed up and I don't know anything anymore. Okay! I probably shouldn't even have come over here in the first place. I just needed to—" She had to stop for a second, grappling with another rush of tears.

"You needed to *what*?" he pushed angrily.

"I needed to talk to you. I needed . . . I don't know what I needed." She put her hands over her face because she couldn't bear to look at him as she delivered the next blow, thinking she would give anything if she could only soften it. "Last night Nicky asked me to marry him."

She felt Mark's rage mounting to an even higher pitch. "Congratulations," he hissed, wrenching away her hands and forcing her to face the pain he was in. "What did you tell him? Did you tell him you were pregnant?"

Paige shook her head no.

There was another long pause while Mark tried to sort out his thoughts. She tried to read his expression, but this time it was blank.

"I can't imagine you said no when he asked you to marry him. That would be too much for you to pass up."

Paige's silence confirmed his charge.

"What are you going to do?" he asked, his voice tight, the verdict out of his hands, divided somewhere between her belly and her brain.

She shrugged uncertainly, wondering about her *heart*, feeling worn down. She was sitting on the couch again and she leaned over to fidget with a primitive art book he had on the coffee table. "Why did you have Susan get on the phone and talk to your mother?" she asked impulsively, suddenly crying again.

"*What?*"

"Susan told me about how she had this cozy conversation with your mother. You never had me talk to your mother—"

"Did you *want* to talk to my mother?"

"Maybe."

"Paige. You wanted us to be something that had nothing to do with real life. Remember?" He charged, exasperated. "Just fun. Play. Make-believe. How was I supposed to explain that to my mother? *Here, Mom, say hello to the girl I'm sleeping with, but who doesn't want to get involved with me because I'm not upwardly mobile enough for her, not rich enough to fit into the bigger scheme of her dreams.*"

Mark went on acting out the whole conversation, elevating the pitch of his voice when he spoke for his mother, which was, Paige realized, really speaking for himself, releasing an anger and resentment he'd had trouble containing toward the end, anyway.

HER: The bigger scheme of her dreams?

HIM: She wants to be rich. Filthy rich. She wants to be so rich she doesn't have to feel or think—just glide—on a kind of gilded automatic cruise control—insulated.

HER: No! What about love? What's the matter with this girl? What's she hiding from?

The truth smarted like a slap in the face.

"She's not hiding from anything," Paige defended herself. "She's tired. She wants to be taken care of." Then after a moment of neither of them saying anything, she asked, "Are you falling in love with Susan?"

"Why? Are you jealous?"

It was more of a revelation for her than a confession. "Yes, I am," she admitted tentatively.

"Paige . . . I don't know," he answered, his anger appearing to drain as he downed what was left of his wine and then sloshed out another full glass for each of them.

"Are you sleeping with her?" she pressed, knowing she shouldn't.

"It's none of your business."

"If I'm carrying your baby, then it is my business."

"You're *acting* like a baby. You don't even know if you *are* pregnant. So what's this all about? Huh? I think you're just jealous. And greedy. And scared about marrying a guy who's old enough to be your father, that's what I think. You're not sure if the money's worth it, after all. It's called buyer's remorse, Paige. Don't worry. It's kind of like a twenty-four-hour bug. It goes away. Does the old bastard even want to have any more kids?"

Paige started to lie and say she didn't really know, but she had always been completely honest with Mark about everything, and she found herself telling him the truth.

His reaction was thoughtful and sympathetic as he listened. "Do you really want to marry him? Can you live with that?"

"I don't know." Paige gulped back more tears, looking at Mark through the compelling veil that continued to obscure her vision. "I'm scared. I don't know what I want. I don't know what I'm doing with my life. *I miss you.* If I *am* pregnant, there's this part of me that wants never to see Nicky again, that wants to say the hell with the money; I'd rather have you and love." The insecurity she heard in her voice sounded so alien to her.

Mark returned to the couch and sat down beside her, enveloping her in his arms again. "You don't have a clue what you want really, do you?"

"I *do* know what I want," she heard herself insisting. "I want you. I *miss* you." And she really did. She missed being in his arms like this, being coddled and indulged. She wished she could just freeze time and let the moment be her eternity. She wished life were less complicated than it was. She wished her needs were less complicated.

"You know what I think?" he asked, holding up the Kleenex box for her to take a fresh one.

Reluctantly she shook her head. "No. What?"

"First of all, I think we should walk to the drugstore and pick up one of those home pregnancy tests and you should take it. And then I think you need to honestly sort out what it is you want from you life, what it is that's going to make you happy."

"Oh, that's a simple prescription," Paige said sarcastically, aware that the latter half could take her a lifetime to figure out.

"C'mon." He kissed her softly on the lips, then looked into her eyes for a moment before tugging her up to her feet. She wanted to keep kissing him, but it hadn't been that kind of kiss.

They held hands walking through the narrow streets of the Venice neighborhood, looking out over the street-lit canal, having to dodge bikers and roller skaters as they headed over toward Main Street where the local pharmacy had been in business for years, before the area had become chic again. There was an ice cream shop on the way and he bought them each a double scoop of peppermint.

The pharmacist gave them a knowing sort of look when they purchased the home pregnancy test. "Good luck," he offered, seeming to mean it which ever way good luck applied.

Doing this alone, Paige knew she would have been a wreck, seeing only the bleakest side of everything, agonizing over the outcome and what to do about it.

Instead, back at the apartment with Mark, opening up a second bottle of wine, none of it seemed so grave.

The alcoholic haze helped to diminish the reality.

While they waited for the results, they sat getting looped from the wine and crying their hearts out over *An Affair to Remember* with Cary Grant and Deborah Kerr. Mark had made up a batch of popcorn the purists' way, in an old iron pot, and the old-fashioned taste felt comforting.

"Are you a gambler? Do you believe in fate?" she dared him during a commercial, feeling dizzy from all the wine as she snaked over to the easy chair he was sitting on and popped a fat white kernel into his mouth, her anxiety intensifying because in ten more minutes the results of the pregnancy test would be ready to read. She couldn't get rid of the image in her mind of a rabbit lying dead on the bathroom countertop where they had left the simple test-tube kit that should have seemed more humane.

"Why?" he replied, looking wary.

She knew he felt funny about being alone with her like this. She had been sensing it all evening, whenever they seemed to get too close. She wondered what he would have done if Susan hadn't had a staff meeting that evening at the law firm. "Just *are you* or *are you not* a gambler?"

"It depends—" he said, his eyes bloodshot from all the wine.

"If you have to think about it, then you're not—"

"Actually, I think I am, but I'm not a stupid gambler. I like to gamble from an informed perspective, and with a chance to analyze the odds—"

"Oh, don't be so intellectual about this. Are you a gambler? Yes or no? No qualifying allowed."

"Okay, yes," he yielded, tensing as she dumped a kernel of popcorn down his shirt and then slipped her hand down inside to retrieve it. One of his buttons came unfastened as she reached in and let her hand linger. "Really, I'm too drunk to follow any of this. Or to be held to any wager. You'd be taking advantage of me in one of my weaker moments."

Weaker moments, my ass. Men are just the weaker sex. Or that's how he would justify his being unfaithful to Susan, anyway. She felt him getting aroused, looking at her the way he used to look at her only a month ago, and yet still fighting it. His jaw was tight and his breathing heavier. It was obvious he was trying to make excuses in case he did get carried away, his libido overpowering his willpower, leading him astray.

So much for Susan's true blue love, she thought, recognizing how men are all alike, resenting his ready erection and that glazed look in his blue eyes.

How many times had she seen that look in Nicky's eyes? She could imagine him in this situation, with another woman endeavoring to put him under her spell as Paige was, and she couldn't picture him doing anything other than giving in.

Mark, misreading her tears, held her close again and as she started to kiss him, he began kissing her back.

She found herself clinging to him, aching to blot out all reality. There was so much riding on the results nearly ready to be read and she didn't want to think about it. She wanted to keep kissing him instead. She wanted to make love with him more than she had ever wanted to make love with anyone in her life.

"So, what's the wager?" he asked huskily, giving in to the sensuality of the moment.

"The wager is," she proposed, breathing into his mouth, keeping her lips lightly in place over his. "If I *am* pregnant, you and I run off and get married. If I'm not, I let you off the hook and I marry Nicky. We'll read the test like an order of fate."

"You're crazy."

"I am," she confessed, trying to keep the desperation out of her voice as she gnawed at his lip, kissing him with such force that she felt him submitting completely, roving his hands all up and down her, and cursing because he hadn't wanted to give in. It was the kind of recklessness that made Paige feel free and daring, mean, but invincible, reducing things to a state of insignificance so that she couldn't be hurt.

They both stripped off all their clothes and stood touching one another. Mark ran his hands over her belly as though trying to glean the truth through his fingertips. He bent down onto his knees and put his ear to her navel, listening for some suggestion of life inside her womb.

She waited, sharing the suspense, as though he possessed some kind of rare mystical power, thinking he was the most sensuous man she had ever known.

As he began kissing her waist and her stomach, scattering light, tender kisses, she found herself wondering for whom they were meant, for her or for the baby conceivably blooming within her. She sensed an attachment already forming, and it undid her.

As though thinking along the same lines, Mark suddenly straightened back up and took her hand. "I have to know," he said with such urgency that she was taken aback. "The damn results should be ready."

"Make love to me first," she said, scared.

"No. C'mon—"

She grabbed his arm as he started to turn away from her. "I want you to make love to me. *Now.*"

"I said no—"

"Why?"

As he looked at her she saw how confused he was. It was because of Susan. She knew it. His guilt had overtaken his libido at the critical moment. Redeeming him? Maybe. But not completely.

"Make love with me now, or I'm leaving and I never want to see you again," she challenged rashly, feeling monstrous but out of control. His mind was clearly telling him one thing, his hard-on, which was still intact, another.

Wouldn't anyone ever love her enough to take a risk for her? To do something he shouldn't do? Apparently not.

Instead of getting mad, Mark wrapped his arms around her again, the proof of his desire still hard against her thigh. "Paige, you're going to have to sort out your life first. I *can't* make love with you now. I obviously want to. But I just can't. *God, you're so selfish.* How do you think I feel? If you're pregnant, then that's my baby, too. *You* at least have control. Try and imagine how frustrated *I* am. *I* have no control. If I were carrying the baby, I would have it."

Paige had no doubt in her mind that he would. With or without her.

Like two children themselves, they walked hand in hand toward the bathroom, unselfconscious about their state of undress and Mark's still-prominent erection, bracing themselves.

They both seemed to know before they got there. Call it parental instinct—they simply knew.

The vivid red ring that had materialized on the test tube was irrefutable.

It read positive and was clear as could be.

Unfortunately the decision as to what to do about it couldn't have been more *unclear.*

Paige felt overwhelmed by what she had already known inside, as if she were standing alone atop a giant precipice, the drop so great she could not see what lay below or on either side. And yet she was going to have to jump one way or the other, make a choice. Only she was paralyzed by the gravity of either commitment.

"I really don't want to be by myself tonight," she said to Mark in a small voice, turning to him, wanting to put the decision off until morning.

His blond head bobbed as he nodded in understanding.

"I promise. No more seducing. I just want to sleep next to you in bed. I think I'll go crazy otherwise."

He nodded, looking as if he were fighting tears himself. "Okay. But don't let me seduce you, either."

"You're really losing your head over my roommate, aren't you?" she said, smiling but hurting inside.

The expression on his face confirmed her answer. Saying nothing further, he took her hand again and led her toward the bedroom where they climbed into his creaky but comfortable old bed, his grandmother's bed, which Paige would miss.

On the pretense of getting something to drink she disappeared into the kitchen for a moment and took the phone off the hook. It was her last night with him, and she didn't want to be disturbed. *Sorry Susan. He's all yours. But not until tomorrow.*

He fell asleep with his hands resting protectively on her belly.

She fell asleep with her cheek in a puddle of tears, in the midst of thinking she would never be able to fall asleep.

Torn about what to do.

What a marvelous day!

What a load off her mind.

Susan's thoughts were spinning so fast and she was so elated that she could hardly sit still at the staff meeting.

Concentrating on what her colleagues were saying was out of the question. Their legal jargon floated right over her head while she sat there at the long conference-room table doodling with her pencil and feigning quiet interest in what was being debated.

First of all, she was amazed that she hadn't been fired.

Ever since the incident with the strikers, she had been waiting in dread suspense for the moment when she would be called into Kreegle's office to receive his grand termination speech.

And though she had been on pins and needles waiting for the bomb to drop, it hadn't happened.

He had been pleasant to her in all their dealings.

He hadn't uttered a word about Jack Wells, other than to say he was putting Joe Dickson back on the case and taking her off it to work on some of the many entertainment contracts the firm handled.

She had been conspicuously shifted into an area where she would be less likely to get herself into trouble, negotiating contracts that would hardly incite her passions.

The stars' contracts were a little hard to take. For instance, negotiating into soap-star Zelda Cooper's contract a white limousine, and *white only,* or she would have grounds to not show up on the set. Her own dressing room trailer, which she refused to share with her costar (and it had to be *larger* than the one assigned to her costar). Plus her own private yoga instructor to keep her calm between takes.

It was definitely an area in which Susan was not going to get riled up. Or inspired.

With all this circumspect shifting around, she couldn't help but feel as though she were on probation, being scrutinized, with a chance for redemption before getting dropped.

Her worries were finally quelled this afternoon when, returning to her office after lunch, she spotted an envelope marked "Susan Kendell Brown" lying on top of her desk. Anxiously she had opened the envelope, half expecting a dismissal notice. What a relief when she found instead a pair of round-trip tickets to Europe along with a note from the law firm's senior partner informing her she had just become a partner in the firm. Moments later, Kreegle stepped into her office to tell her that while her actions with regard to Jack had not been well advised she was too damn good a lawyer for the firm to lose, and that making her a junior partner in the firm was their way of telling her she had a bright future and they expected big things from her.

She was jubilant at having preserved her integrity and her job at the same time. Notwithstanding the fact that she might never see Jack Wells again, she was satisfied that she'd had some impact on him, that the workers who had been fired had been reinstated, and that many of their terms had actually been met in a contract that, according to Joe Dickson, was close to being put to bed. She had asserted her opinion, made a stand for fairness, and, in her mind anyway, won.

God, she was so excited she couldn't wait to call her folks in Stockton and tell them of her new status as junior partner. To call Lisa and Buzz. Her brothers. They would all go out of their minds.

She considered calling her old law firm in Stockton and casually letting the news drop while in conversation with her old philandering boyfriend, Billy Donahue. What a thrill it would be to hear his reaction to the *new* Susan Kendell Brown. Assured. Happy. More sophisticated. Her name on the letterhead of one of L.A.'s most prestigious law firms. But then she thought, *who cares about Billy? Not me. Not anymore.*

The person she wanted to share her excitement with most of all was Mark. She couldn't wait to drive over and tell him the news tonight, the second this interminable meeting was adjourned. She also couldn't wait to see his reaction when she produced the pair of round-trip tickets to Europe. They could plan to take off and go together during his Christmas break.

The truth was, making her most happy was this growing sense of excitement inside that she could barely contain, the feeling that she just might have found her Mr. Right, after all.

Screw Paige for thinking she should "step up her goals" and the nerve of her for pointing out how much more money Susan made than Mark. As though Susan gave a damn. She was so tired of hearing that.

Mark was smart. And sincere. And talented. Good-hearted. *Not* twice her age, like Nicky Loomis. And not all screwed up like most of the rich jerks they had all endured. Mark had his feet on the ground. She could count on him.

The staff meeting had finally come to an end. Everyone was joking around, shuffling papers back and forth, closing up briefcases, closing up shop.

Congratulations were forthcoming from all parts of the room. Kreegle regarded her from across the table; his smile hadn't lost its measured edge.

Smiling back at all of them, Susan rose up from her seat, briefcase in one hand, airline tickets in the other, anxious to get to Mark.

She hurried down the hallway into her office to give him a quick call. It was eleven o'clock. He had said he was going to spend the evening painting.

His number was in her automatic memory dial; all she had to do was push 4, which she did with sparked expectation.

Hi, Mark—

Hi, handsome—

Hey, sexy—you in the mood to celebrate?

I can't hold it in any longer. Even if this scares you away—I love you!

She blitzed through the greetings in her head, dismissing one for another when, in the end, all she would say would be hi.

Busy. Damn.

She pushed the code for redial.

Still busy.

She pushed it again.

Then she set it for automatic redial and sat down at her desk to go over some papers. Realizing that all she was doing was pushing papers back and forth, that she was so excited to see him she couldn't possibly concentrate on anything else, she decided to skip the phone call and just drive over there.

Her excitement shriveled at the sight of Dustin Brent's Aston-Martin parked out in front of his apartment, and she wasn't sure what to think.

Was her sexy roommate there as an ex-lover seducing Mark—or just there as a friend?

Trying to ward off panic, she told herself that maybe his motorcycle had gone on the fritz, so Paige had lent the car to him, that Paige wasn't there at all. But his motorcycle was parked right beside the car, and it appeared perfectly fine.

Glancing up, she found herself growing more and more agitated. The windows of his apartment were all dark. What she couldn't see seemed worse than what she could see. If he were asleep, why was his telephone busy?

Too uncomfortable to go inside and uneasy about what she might find if she were to do so, Susan drove around killing time and returning every twenty minutes or so.

Her worst suspicions were confirmed when she finally gave up and drove home, finding Paige not there, and a number of messages from Nicky looking for her.

Chapter 29

Susan couldn't get the scream of sirens out of her mind.

The rage of sound overpowered her own scream of warning and Paige's of powerless dread.

It replayed mercilessly in her head, the tense, shrill blare of alarm unaided by the tranquilizer they had insisted she take in the ambulance on the interminable drive to the hospital.

The little yellow pill muted the volume but failed to make the picture any less ominous. When she closed her eyes there was *red*. The color of alarm. The blood-red lights of the ambulance. The blood-red of the water enveloping Paige. The blood-red deluge from her scalp . . . The blood-red sailboat. The blood-red screams that had filled the thick sea air.

And then the blood-red silence of her friend lying unconscious. Vacant. Looking like a different person, without that mind of hers flying a million miles an hour.

Still in her jeans and tennis shoes from sailing, Susan was roaming helplessly back and forth in the dreary emergency waiting room of the hospital in Santa Monica, going over in her mind for the thousandth time what had happened, trying to understand it, desperate to recapture the moment and turn back the clock.

The gloomy-looking room was mobbed. There were kids running around, some injured, some fine and only along for the ride. One kid had a deep gouge below his eyebrow and was waiting for the doctor to stitch him up. Another one had lost a tooth. There was a man stretched out on a bench and moaning from a kidney stone.

It had all happened so fast. That's what Susan couldn't get over.

A surge of murderous thoughts on her part, the kind of horrid ones only Paige could inspire, and then, suddenly, as though she had wished it so, this monstrous accident.

An accident she had helped set in motion, which she had inadvertently activated, provoked.

Susan felt shaken to her roots from all that had transpired in the last forty-eight hours.

Thursday night seemed like an eternity ago, when she had driven over to Mark's and found Paige's car parked out in front of his apartment.

After a sleepless night, remaining alert for any sound of Paige returning home, unable to think about anything else, Susan had fled Dustin's house before sunrise, intent on avoiding a premature confrontation with Paige, who would undoubtedly return to shower and change for work. Feeling too shattered to even run into Tori.

The plan that had evolved, as she'd sat there seething at the office, kidding herself into thinking she was working, was to go ahead and go sailing with Paige the following day, as previously planned, pretending nothing had happened, as though she knew nothing and then, once out alone in the water, just the two of them, with no distractions, nowhere for Paige to run and hide, she would have it out with her.

Mark, whose calls she had been dodging all day and whom she still couldn't face talking to, she decided to call back when she knew he'd be in class. She'd leave a message with the department secretary at UCLA, saying she had to break their dinner date on account of work, that she would be incommunicado all day, but would talk to him late Saturday.

That evening, Paige went to a game at the StarDome with

Nicky. Tori went to dinner with George and Kit and a man she had been out with a couple of times.

And Susan stayed sequestered in her office—hiding from everybody, refining her plan of attack, ready to pounce.

Then that morning, when the three women were all having breakfast together in the kitchen, Paige had attempted to back out of their sailing date, feigning fatigue and an upset stomach.

Guilt. She can't stand facing me, Susan remembered thinking, bristling, loathing her attractive roommate and how easily things always came for her.

She probably planned on marrying Nicky and keeping Mark on the side. It would be just like her to want *everything* and find a way to have it all.

She wondered how long Paige and Mark had been seeing each other on the sly. At the beginning, when Susan first started going out with him, she was sure he and Paige weren't seeing each other. But when had they started up again? Was Thursday night a first? A first and last? Or one of many?

God, how Susan hated Mark for leading her on. For making her feel like a first-rate fool.

What had ever possessed her to think she could compete with Paige, live up to her sex-goddess image, when Susan was so blatantly only mortal.

Paige probably knew all these exotic, sensual maneuvers.

She was soft and feminine and flirtatious.

A man's woman. A rich man's toy—out on loan to her not-nearly-rich-enough but irresistible artist-professor boyfriend. *Susan's* boyfriend, *dammit.*

It wasn't fair. Susan embodied wholesomeness, while Paige embodied sex.

And what wholesome American male wouldn't prefer sex?

It was driving Susan mad, agonizing over all the comparisons Mark must have made.

Like all of Paige's scintillating lingerie, when Susan felt contrived in anything other than sensible cottons. Susan's big move in that direction had been to buy *sexy* sensible cottons but, honestly, how sexy can sensible cotton underwear really ever get? Compared to Paige's array of lacy little nothings.

Things like black lacy stockings with lacy built-in garters that held them up at the thigh. Scanty, sheer black lace teddies in lieu of a bra and underpants, which snapped at the crotch for convenient access.

Susan would feel like a French whore in the kind of underflash Paige wore. And ridiculous because she didn't approach suiting the part. While Paige would savor playing it to the hilt, getting *into* the role and driving him crazy.

How could he ever get over her?

Tori had checked Paige's pulse to see if she had a fever, swallowing her act about not feeling well. Sweet, guileless, Tori who would never suspect a thing. Susan knew Tori couldn't understand why she had kept pressing, when Paige clearly didn't want to go.

Well, now she would know. Now everyone would know everything.

Susan had called Mark and left a message for him indicating briefly what had happened and that they were at the hospital. She had also put a call in to Nicky, who she was told was unreachable, out flying in a small plane somewhere, scouting property for a real estate deal.

Tori was the only one she had succeeded in getting on the line, and she was on her way to the hospital now.

A kid threw a paper cup at Susan's head and she jumped, on edge anyway. "Noah, knock it off now. Just sit down next to your brother or I'm taking you home," his mother snapped at him.

There was some tittering as the two brothers sat down on the vinyl-cushioned bench next to one another, endeavoring to contain their restless energy.

Their father was the man on the bench with the kidney stone, and he glared at them between groans.

"Excuse me," Susan pleaded, barreling over to the woman at the admittance desk, feeling as though she were falling apart. "I've been here over an hour. Can't someone please give me some information on how my friend's doing?"

"Now, who's your friend again?"

Susan could have strangled her. She had only told the woman twenty times. "Paige Williams," she repeated painstakingly.

"Paige Williams . . ." It was taking her forever to locate Paige's name on her clipboard. Finally, Susan reached over and jabbed at where *Paige Williams* was clearly written. "Oh, yes. The boating accident."

"I just want to know if she's regained consciousness, or what's going on, how she's doing. Nobody's told me anything—" Susan was drumming her fingers impatiently on the desk.

"If you'll have a seat, I'll get back to you."

"What seat?" Susan demanded, indicating the overcrowded waiting room. "Look, you keep saying that and nobody is telling me anything—"

"I'm sorry, but it's a weekend and we're very busy."

"Can't I just go back there?" Susan pleaded.

"I'm sorry, but you'll just have to take a seat like . . ." Catching herself, she eyed Susan, then coolly completed her sentence. "You'll just have to wait in the waiting room like everyone else."

Telephone call for Susan Kendell Brown. Susan whirled around as the announcement blared over the loudspeaker.

"Where do I catch that?" she asked, turning back to the half-wit at admittance.

The woman pointed to a phone off to the side.

Taking a deep breath, Susan picked up the receiver, feeling guilty and nervous at once. It had to be either Mark or Nicky, and she didn't know what to say to either of them.

Hi. I pushed your girlfriend out of the boat and into the water, shouting at her that I hoped she drowned, and she almost did.

Susan had confronted Paige as planned.

They had both been especially quiet as they headed out the channel in Susan's sailboat, seeming to lose themselves in the rhythm of tacking and trying to catch the wind while Susan directed them just outside the breakwater, where there was not quite so much traffic.

Fuming, without any preamble, Susan had let her have it, launching into a full-blown inquisition.

She was there, Thursday night, at Mark's apartment, wasn't she? Susan had seen her car. Dustin's car—

"Yes," Paige had replied somberly, without resistance.

She was there alone with him. Trying to seduce him. Going after what was no longer hers. By her choice—

"Yes."

She had spent the night with him. Taken the phone off the hook so Susan couldn't get through—

"Yes."

She couldn't stand not having Mark at her beck and call anymore, could she? There whenever she wanted him.

She was all messed up. Not so sure she could go through with marrying a man nearly twice her age.

Just because he was rich and powerful.

The sacrifices were starting to get to her, weren't they—

"Yes."

Like the thinning hair he had to swirl way over from one side of his head to cover up the vacant patches.

The old skin that there was no disguising. No matter what kind of shape he was in.

Paige was forfeiting youth for money.

Selling herself.

Being Nicky Loomis's wife had nothing to do with sharing her life for love, building a future together, becoming a partnership greater than any other partnership.

Marrying Nicky was more like accepting a job.

Title—Mrs. Nicky Loomis.

Job description—hostess-slash-whore.

Salary—high.

"Yes."

Maybe she was panicking about all of his vintage friends?

The kids she would be inheriting. Who would never accept her. Who would always think of her as their father's whore.

Just another fortune hunter. And wasn't she?

"Yes."

She couldn't stand it that Susan and Mark were so happy, without money, starting to fall in love, with a shot at the kind of life with which Paige wished she could be satisfied, but could not. She had to go and prove to herself that she could still have Mark if she wanted him. She had been jealous since the morning Susan and

Mark had walked in together, hadn't she? Caring only about her-self. Not caring that she was screwing things up for Mark and for Susan. Supposedly her friends. Maybe her best friends. Was there anyone on this earth to whom Paige was capable of being loyal? Whom she cared enough about not to run roughshod over or use them?

"Stop just saying *yes!*" Susan had finally screamed at her. "Give me reasons. Make me understand. Make me understand how you could be so selfish. How you could do this to me. How you could do this to Mark. You're going to go off and marry Nicky anyway, so why do you have to go and screw up our lives? What kind of monster are you?"

The small sailboat had suddenly become so confining that Su-san had felt as though she were crawling out of her skin. Paige wouldn't fight back. She wouldn't deny a thing. Susan could have been talking to a wall, except that the wall looked ready to crum-ble.

"Goddamn it, Paige, you owe me an explanation. Now give me one. What happened to your big mouth and all your famous courage? Say something, or I'm going to explode."

Finally, enraged, desperate for a response, Susan had broken into a flood of tears and shoved Paige out of the boat into the water, shouting at her that she hoped she drowned.

For a second, it had been a release of tension for both of them. They had connected. Something in Paige's immutable surface had broken, and she had begun to cry also. Susan had never thought she would see the day when Paige would cry.

But then before they knew what had happened, it had been sheer panic for both of them. A boat pulling a water-skier had seemed to appear from out of nowhere and was ripping across the water in their direction. The driver of the boat attempted to veer away but it was too late, and the quick motion of the detour had sent the skier flying across the wake, crashing into a terror-stricken Paige.

It was all one big blur after that. A patrolling coast guard was radioed onto the scene and Paige, unconscious and badly injured, was rushed to the hospital, accompanied by a shell-shocked Su-san.

"Susan? It's Mark. What's going on?"

Susan's mind went blank at the sound of his voice, confused and urgent over the line.

"Are you okay? What's happened? Is Paige all right?" he asked.

She found herself gripping the telephone cord, twisting it, trying to get her brain to work. She was submerged in guilt. Yet his frank, vital concern over Paige smarted so; she found herself wanting to lash out at him.

She spoke rapidly, trying to conceal the hurt. "I was out in the boat with Paige. We got into an argument and I got so furious I shoved her out. She had on a life jacket. We both did. It shouldn't have been any big deal. But then all of a sudden there was this boat careening in our direction, pulling a water-skier. The boat tried to cut away but it was too late, and the skier came flying across the wake and into her."

There was an awful silence on Mark's end. Susan cradled the phone and wrapped her arms across her stomach. She felt weak and ill. Frightened beyond measure. But still, a small ravaged part of her remained angry. A small but deep pit of anger and resentment. Of jealousy. Mark didn't dare ask what the argument had been about.

"I'll be there in five minutes," he stressed, pushing some hidden button inside her heart that released another flood of tears.

Her poor brain felt waterlogged. She was too choked up to manage much more than a clipped "Okay. Thanks."

"And Susan—" he said as she was about to hang up.

"What?"

She felt him hesitating, torn. What did he want to say? To confess and get it off his conscience that he was sorry? That he loved Paige and couldn't help himself? That he would rather have part of her than all of Susan? The last thing Susan wanted was pity from him.

"I miss you," he whispered, sounding grief-stricken. "I don't know what your argument was about, but I have an idea. You shouldn't feel so guilty about this. It was an accident. I know you, and you wouldn't ever deliberately hurt anyone."

"You don't know me at all. I wanted to hurt her. I wanted to hurt her so badly it was killing me," Susan shouted, crying. "But I didn't see the boat, obviously. I would never—"

"Shhh. It's going to be okay. Paige is tough."

"She's *unconscious*. And she was hit in probably the only instant in her life when she wasn't tough. It was Paige like she must have been when she was young, *pre-hurt,* or whatever it was that made her this way, *pre-bravado*. She didn't even look like herself. If I'd seen her being wheeled down the aisle here on a stretcher, I'd have barely known her. *Mark, I'm so scared.* She was really cut up badly, too. I'm sure they had to take a ton of stitches."

"Anything broken?"

"I don't know. They won't tell me anything. I'm going crazy. Please hurry," she urged him in a small, unsteady voice, still crying.

"I can't stand it that I'm not there with you now," he replied, quietly hanging up the phone.

"Susan!" Tori walked through the doorway of the emergency room, eliciting stares as she hurried over to Susan. The stylishly cut skirt of her smart cherry-red suit hugged just above her knees, causing her to have to take twice as many steps to maintain her pace. "What's happening? Is Paige all right? Has she regained consciousness?" she asked all at once, throwing her arms around Susan. "Have they let you in to see her yet? Are *you* all right?"

"I can't get anyone to give me any information," Susan said, sniffling and wiping away tears with the back of her hand.

Tori took a packet of Kleenex from out of her purse and handed it to her.

"Thanks," Susan said, blowing her nose and then stopping to catch her breath before going on. "I tried to go back there, but a couple of nurses pounced on me and sent me back to the waiting room. I don't even have any idea where she is."

It was such a relief to have someone there with her, Susan thought as she watched Tori weighing what to do.

"God, what was the name of that surgeon I went out with? George's friend—" Tori said, trying to jog her memory. "Maybe I should call him. You know how it is with doctors. If *he* inquires, we'll at least get somewhere."

"I didn't even think to call Kit," Susan realized, feeling remiss.

"*Ed Littner* . . . wasn't that his name?"

"I'm not sure—"

"C'mon. Where's the phone? There it is," she said, heading over toward the hospital extension Susan had just used.

"There are pay phones near the rest rooms—"

"Pay phones? *Fuck 'em,*" Tori drawled defiantly. "This is Dr. Mitchell," she asserted into the line, taking Susan's hand. "We have an emergency here. Would you please get me Dr. Ed Littner."

"He's not with this hospital, Doctor—"

"Yes, I know that," Tori bluffed. Then within four minutes Dr. Littner was on the line, anyway. "This is a Paige maneuver," Tori said under her breath to Susan.

Of course she didn't realize that it was the wrong thing to say just then.

Susan stood by quietly while Tori very briefly explained the situation to the surgeon she had snubbed.

"He's actually very nice," she whispered to Susan at one point, covering the receiver with her hand. "Ed, thank you. I really appreciate this. We're all worried out of our minds."

Ed told Tori he would call her right back, to sit tight until he could get some information for her.

Susan looked over to the entrance just as Mark was walking through the doorway. He jogged over to them. There was an awkward moment as he and Susan looked at one another, but then it was broken by the white-clad nurse hurrying toward them.

"Excuse me, Miss Kendell . . ."

The nurse's face was a mask—a study in the withholding of expression, but her hesitation made Susan sure something had gone wrong.

"Uhmm . . . your friend has regained consciousness," the nurse began deliberately, as though there were a hitch. They all braced themselves as she went on. "She's alert. She'll have to be watched closely for the next twenty-four hours or so. She shouldn't be alone or get out of bed. The doctor had to take quite a few stitches, but there appears to be no internal injury and miraculously there are no broken bones. However—"

Nobody wanted to hear the however.

"However, I'm sorry, the accident caused quite a trauma, and I'm afraid she did lose her baby."

Her baby!

Susan was dumbfounded. Her complicated and overwrought emotions ran all the way from guilt over having caused the accident and the loss of the baby she knew nothing about to jealousy and reignited rage about Thursday night.

She wanted to wheel around and look at Mark, but she was afraid to. Whose baby was it? His or Nicky's?

Feeling all eyes on her, Susan wanted to run and hide. She couldn't look at anyone and instead kept her eyes focused down on the ugly, speckled, vinyl floor.

The nurse, misreading Susan's reaction, reached for her hand. "Your friend's okay about it—she really is. It was the first thing she asked when she came to, and of course we told her. Then she closed her eyes and got a kind of sad, funny smile on her face and said something about how it was just meant to be. *She* told all of *us* not to worry. That maybe life would work out perfectly and she would have one in a later passage of hers. She wanted to know how old the fetus was, and we told her. It was about nine weeks old. And then she asked me to explain this to all of you. And afterward to have Susan come in to see her."

Blinking away tears, still not looking at anyone, Susan followed the nurse back toward Paige's room.

Bewildered, shocked, guilty, and greatly despairing, Susan ventured inside the antiseptic-looking recovery room where Paige lay on a small white bed, her eyes closed, her head swathed in bandages that were soiled where some blood and yellow ointment had seeped through. She was in a white hospital gown and Susan could see where some of the stitches had been taken on her arms and chest. In spite of her condition, she still looked beautiful.

Feeling Susan's presence, she opened her eyes and looked at her, indicating for her to come closer, to come over to the bed.

Susan was surprised to see tears in Paige's eyes again; they seemed so incongruous with the cat-like glimmer ordinarily lighting them up. Now they were mesmerizing green pools, brimming over with what looked like genuine regret.

And yet there was an ease to her expression.

Probably she is doped up, Susan thought, trying to distance herself, wondering what Paige planned on saying to her.

"C'mere, dammit," Paige said, weakly reaching for Susan with her arm and then grabbing her in closer when Susan finally did approach. "You have a right to despise me," she admitted falteringly. The green pools overflowed and Paige didn't bother to block the tears or even to wipe them away. *"That's* why I was over at Mark's Thursday night," she said softly. "I had been worried about being pregnant for at least a month, but I kept not wanting to believe it, wanting to block it out. I don't know how I felt, really. It was complicated. But then Wednesday night, Nicky asked me to marry him," she announced, surprisingly coherent for someone who was only just recovering from being unconscious. But that was Paige, Susan thought, far too anxious to hear what Paige was leading up to, to comment or interrupt.

"I may not be in love with Nicky the way you think you're in love with Mark," Paige said, "but I'm crazy about him. I don't see him as old. I see him as fascinating and full of energy, younger in many ways even than Mark, younger than his kids, who have all kinds of things repressed inside them. Nicky's not repressed at all. The kid in him, the kid that's in everyone, is right there at the surface. Never been buried. He's full of life and fun. And challenge."

This time Susan did try to interrupt, but Paige blocked her attempt with her hand, indicating for her to let her finish.

"Sure, if he didn't have any money I wouldn't feel this way about him," Paige went on honestly and with the same surprising display of clarity. "But taking his money away from the picture is like taking my looks away from my picture. We fall for the package. Not isolated areas of someone. Nicky's exactly what I want. I know what I'm giving up. But it's a conscious choice.

"The reason I didn't shout the news or tell anyone except Mark was because right after he asked me to marry him, he handed me a prenuptial contract his lawyers had drawn up, stipulating no babies. If I were to get pregnant and have the child, I was on my own, and without a red cent from him. Minimal support for the kid, but basically bust. Maybe the impact of it wouldn't have been so dramatic if I hadn't thought I was pregnant. But the stipulation of no kids when there was life growing inside me right at that very moment was too much for me."

The tears had stopped and they started up again. "Susan, you should know that I did not sleep with Mark. I wanted to. And I tried. But he wouldn't sleep with me. As nuts as he's been over me, when he had to make a choice he chose you. He let me spend the night in his bed because I was scared to death to be alone. But he didn't touch me."

Susan closed her eyes, overcome with relief and, oddly, grateful.

"Dammit, now it's *you* who won't say anything. Only there's nowhere to push you. Do you forgive me or not?" Paige demanded in spite of having insisted on Susan's silence.

"If *you* forgive *me, I* forgive *you,*" Susan responded, looking at her lunatic roommate through a haze of tears as they embraced.

She was being careful holding her, worried about all the bandages. "Does that hurt a lot?"

"Shit, yes, it hurts. But if you forgive me, I can bear it."

"I do. I really do," Susan said, realizing how deeply relieved she was that Paige was all right. "As long as you promise to keep your goddamn hands off my boyfriend, I forgive you," she added, somehow trusting she would.

"Hey, he chose you."

"Yes, but he may not always."

"He will," Paige said with quiet confidence. Then tensing, growing visibly anxious, she asked if Nicky was there. Had he been there when the nurse came out and told them about her losing the baby?

"No. I left a message for him with his secretary. But he hadn't—"

"Oh, thank God," Paige moaned with relief, sinking lower in the bed and looking more like her old self again. "I don't know what got into me. Hormones, probably. I had decided to take a chance and leave it to fate. If he were there and heard about my losing the baby, which clearly, by the age of the fetus, wasn't his, then I figured that would be the way it was meant to be, and however he reacted, he reacted. But by the same token, if he *weren't* there and didn't know, it would mean he wasn't meant to know. I don't know what I'd have done if he'd been there."

Susan was about to smile at Paige's logic when Nicky burst into the room, all out of breath, his face tight with concern, Tori and Mark hurrying to keep pace just behind him.

"Babe, I've been worried sick. I got the message from Dee and I didn't know *what* to think." Susan stepped out of the way as Nicky bounded toward the bed to envelop Paige in his big strapping embrace. "Are you all right? What did they say? Is anything broken?" He couldn't get it all out fast enough.

Susan felt touched by his concern, and she glanced at Mark, remembering with some guilt how she had felt at *his* concern. She found him looking at *her,* not at Nicky and Paige.

He was probably wondering what Paige had told her. If he had been exonerated or not.

She bit her lip, and felt her eyes well up again as she went to stand close by his side, wondering what he was thinking about Paige having lost the baby. She wanted to never let go when he seized her hand and continued to hold on so tightly it hurt.

"Are you okay?" he asked in a low murmur.

She shook her head yes, then asked him the same question.

"Now I am," he whispered in her ear.

Tori slipped Susan a little half-smile and Susan smiled back at her, her smile broadening when holding hands didn't seem to be enough for Mark and he pulled her into his arms.

"I've been going out of my mind," Nicky was saying to Paige as though they were the only ones in the room. The thought of losing her had obviously thrown him into a frenzy. "I was imagining the worst and kicking myself for not having run off and eloped with you Thursday night. Then we'd have been off in France or Italy or Spain, or someplace, celebrating our honeymoon and this would never have happened. Look at you," he insisted, examining the bandages on her head, all the bruises and areas that had been stitched. And yet Susan thought Paige looked unjustly radiant for someone who had nearly lost her life that day.

"I'm okay," Paige assured him. "Really, Nicky, I am."

"I don't want to wait. We're getting married a week from Saturday night," he said, making it clear he would not take no for an answer. As though Paige actually might protest. "At my place, *our* place." He grinned. "I could barely afford to pay a minister the first time I got married. I want this wedding to be the event of the season. It's going to make my Carnival Night affair look like it never woke up in the morning. I want to celebrate!

"And we want all of you standing up there with us," he said, turning for the first time to Susan and Mark and Tori. "We're going to put on a wedding like nobody's ever seen before. Decadence like F. Scott Fitzgerald only wished he had dreamed up. What do I work my ass off for if it's not to have a hell of a good time?"

Nicky sprang up from the bed where he was sitting beside Paige, and started hollering at the nurses down the hall to bring him a grapefruit or an orange or any damn piece of fruit, as long as it was round. When a lanky male nurse returned shortly with a grapefruit, Nicky asked him for a marker.

Within moments the burly ex-wide receiver had turned the ordinary piece of fruit into a small yellow globe, drawing out all the continents and starring a couple of cities. "Here, gorgeous," he said, presenting it to Paige. "You pick out any damn place you want to go for our honeymoon. The sky is the limit. Hell, if we could go to space, I'd buy us a rocket ship."

Paige, glowing, closed her eyes tightly, rotating the small makeshift globe in her hands and then stopping. Holding it in one hand, her eyes still closed, she aimed her index finger and pointed. "Here. I want to go here."

They all hovered in to see where *here* was.

"Egypt it is," her fiancé confirmed, peeling the grapefruit and then distributing the sections to all of them.

Chapter 30

As promised, Paige and Nicky's wedding became the affair of the season, the event everyone in town was talking about. All the more so because of its two weeks' planning fuse.

But that was typical of Nicky and typical of Paige, too The more splash and the more attention they could elicit, the better.

There was no time for invitations so he had sent out a bundle of bright white Casablanca lilies to everyone, accompanied by a note spelling out the specifics.

All the guests were requested to dress in white formal attire, and the effect it produced was as spectacular as Nicky had planned, with this mass of people, all in white, flowing inside the house and outside into the gardens, being seated for the ceremony.

It was all white and wondrous. The flowers. The candles. The linens. The people. Everything sparkled. Paige was probably the only person Tori had ever met who would be confident enough to know she would still stand out. And Tori had no doubt she would.

Everybody was there. Kit and George, with Kit now extremely pregnant. Susan and Mark. Nicky's son, Tip. His daughter,

Marni, and her rock promoter boyfriend. Nicky's StarDome circle, of whom Tori had now met many. Surgeon Ed Littner, whom they had called to thank for his efforts at the hospital. *Miami Vice* stockbroker Dan Sullivan, who was as dull as Susan had originally perceived him to be, but who, it turned out, was one of Nicky's stockbrokers. Evonne, Dustin Brent's secretary.

With a guest list of four hundred, Tori thought it would be easier to keep track of those *not* present.

There were so many high-profile celebrities and politicians that there were guards posted on the roof with guns. They were the only ones not in white.

Standing misty-eyed under the lavish umbrella of a magnolia tree reminiscent of home, in position for the processional, Tori watched the last of the guests being ushered into the rows of seats, feeling nostalgic.

She was thinking of Kit's wedding. How she had felt then, standing and waiting for her cue to walk down the aisle, feeling as if she were doomed to be the bridesmaid forever and never the bride.

And blaming it all on Travis at the time as if he were the only man in the world who could alter her fate.

What a fool she had been to bank all her hopes on him and be so afraid to venture beyond the false cloak of security he offered.

More than anything else, moving to California had accomplished that for Tori and she was grateful. She felt free for the first time in her adult life, free and whole on her own.

It took distance to realize she should have left Atlanta *and* Travis a long time ago. That she would never grow up under her mother's vast and dominant wing, which there seemed to be no escaping as long as she stayed within a thousand miles of Georgia. That Travis was only a temporary refuge for her and, regardless of how hard she tried, she could never convert him into the man who would be right for her.

The fact was, Travis was already living with someone again. Tori had been replaced in her own condominium.

Her first reaction when she had heard was to feel violated. This girl was sleeping in *her* bed, looking at *her* Laura Ashley wallpaper, sleeping and screwing on *her* sheets, using *her* bathtub, eating cereal from *her* bowls, reading the newspaper that was from *her* subscription, going to dinner with *her* friends. The woman's picture was probably now even in *her* frames, smiling beside *her* man.

But then she realized it would be the same story all over again, only with a different woman playing the dolt.

He wouldn't marry her, either, if that's what his new live-in had in mind. As his friends had said bluntly enough from the start, Travis didn't want to get married again. He didn't want to get a divorce. And he would not. Tori just hadn't listened.

And while she would have gone to the ends of the earth for him all those years, the truth was she didn't even miss him anymore. Nor did she miss Richard Bennetton. It was strictly the *concept* of them she missed. The boyfriend. And yet she was handling it fine.

For the first time in her life she was not *with* someone, and she was *okay.*

She had a history that went back to the sixth grade of always healing her heart by falling in love with someone else, soothing the wounds and pasting the heartbreak of her last affair back together with another affair patched over it.

Finally, for the first time ever, she was beginning to feel genuinely healed.

Sure, she wished *she* were walking down the aisle. But she no longer had that sense of panic or desperation about it. Instead she felt a kind of peaceful patience, a confidence that in time she would. And that waiting for her at the altar would be someone well worth the wait.

Tori felt someone's hands at her waist and she jumped, startled. She tried to turn around, but the hands were strong and wouldn't allow her to turn or maneuver.

"What? Who is that?" she asked, struggling to see. Each time she turned her head, the angle of her body was propelled in the other direction.

Kit and Susan, who were standing in front of her, both turned around, their sumptuous white gowns swishing behind them, looking surprised but guarded, not giving anything away.

"Who is that? George? Mark?" she asked the joker behind her. The ushers for the wedding party were out of view in another area of the garden. When she continued to receive no reply, she twisted around and found herself looking into the arrogant peacock-blue eyes of her former phantom fiancé, Richard Bennetton.

As far as she knew Richard hadn't been invited, and a million thoughts rushed through her head as she tried to regain her composure.

She wondered if Paige had arranged this.

Then thought not. Or if he had wangled an invitation from Nicky.

Or if he had just heard about the wedding and decided to crash it. She wouldn't put it past him. He had the nerve to do that.

"When did you get back into town?" she asked numbly, conscious of her friends' polite efforts to appear as though they weren't listening.

"Yesterday," he said, looking at her as though his look held some special significance. Of what, she had no idea and she tried to ignore it. She hadn't seen or heard from him since their blowup in Santa Barbara. She had heard from the office that he had been on one of his extended European excursions, but that was all. There had been an updated photograph of his twin daughters, who lived in France with their mother, in Elliott Bennetton's office so she had presumed Richard had gone there for a while as well and mailed it to him.

"Welcome home," she said icily.

"Thanks. You look beautiful as always."

"Thanks."

"I hear you're taking Bennetton by storm. They say you could be promoted over me if I don't watch my step."

Tori didn't reply. She wished the wedding procession would start. She felt like she was talking to a stranger. But, really, wasn't she?

Whom had she been kidding to think she and Richard were anything other than strangers to each other? The man she had fallen for seemed to have vanished the minute the wheels of the Bennetton jet touched down in Los Angeles. He was an apparition left behind in Buenos Aires. A spirit lost to her.

"Tori, I have to talk to you," he said, looking suddenly vulnerable.

"Why?" She vowed not to be duped.

His voice was so low she could barely hear him. He had steered her off, apart from the others. "I've made amends with my father. I've been reinstated. *I miss you—*"

"Why?" she asked again.

"Look, I'm sorry about Santa Barbara. I don't know how to make you understand, but I did what I had to do."

"Forget it. I've forgotten it."

"No, you haven't."

"Why don't you quit while you're ahead?"

"Because I'm not ahead."

"What do you want from me, Richard?"

"I was half expecting you to run back to Travis."

Tori smiled coldly, happy she'd had the strength not to. "Maybe I did," she hissed, finding herself wanting to hurt him as he had hurt her. "Maybe I'm moving back to Atlanta."

He smiled, relaxing. "I have my sources. You thought about it. Didn't do it. And he's got a replacement living with him now."

"Sounds like your father's kind of tactics," Tori replied galled. "How much did you have to pay for that kind of information? I could have saved you some money if you'd only asked." Richard was more like his father than he liked to think. She remembered how she'd felt when *he* had gone around checking her out. She wondered if they had used the same source.

"It's more fun to get the other way. It affords me a two-dimensional perspective—"

"You hypocrite! I thought you didn't like that kind of snooping around. That kind of lack of faith—"

"Hey, don't get so riled up. I'm here to make peace, not war." Richard raised both of his palms up in the air, gesturing his surrender. In accordance with the requested dress, he was all in white. His razor-straight blond hair looked as though it had just

been cut. He was tan and looked as though Europe agreed with
him.

"I don't want to make anything with you, Richard."

"Not even love?" he joked, with a smug glint in his eyes.
"Sorry. I couldn't resist that one. Tori, this is going all wrong.
Would you just relax? Don't you get the picture? I want to buy
back your fucking ring and give it to you. I want to *marry* you."

"Why? You're not in love with me."

"How do you know what I am or am not," he asked, angry
now.

"Because you don't talk to people the way you talk to me when
you're in love with them."

"Oh, are you some kind of expert on love now? Where do you
get these ideas?"

"God, why are they so late in starting weddings," Tori said,
wanting to get away from him.

"Look, I said I was sorry. What do you want? Do I have to get
on my hands and knees and grovel? I made a mistake. You want
me to go use the minister's mike and shout it to the world. Hell,
the whole world's here, isn't it? *Do you, Tori Mitchell, accept the
apology of this man, Richard Bennetton? Will you be joined in
fucking matrimony or not—"*

Tori felt as though she'd had the breath knocked out of her.

Richard was mean. And cunning. She wouldn't put it past him
to be using her to get back in his father's good graces. Telling his
father that he had been off in Europe, thinking seriously about
his life. That he'd come to the conclusion he wanted to mend his
ways.

Richard knew Elliot Bennetton would think Tori would be the
ideal wife. She was smart. Strait-laced. He liked her and was
under the impression that she had her head screwed on right.

If Richard returned to work at Bennetton, contrite, becoming
engaged to Tori, heading in the direction of a more orthodox life
—orthodox for Richard anyway—Elliot Bennetton would melt
in three minutes and reinstate him.

Tori didn't even believe that he had already been reinstated.
Maybe Richard was planning on going to his father *after* he had

talked to her. On the other hand, Richard was cocky enough to have been certain she would say yes, so maybe he already had.

Sure she was right, or at least close to being right, and not feeling even tempted by Richard—on the contrary, feeling cold as ice, Tori told him he could take his proposal and shove it.

She had a vivid picture in her mind of their confrontation in Santa Barbara. She had tried to block it out but it had been rekindled, and all she felt was rage.

"You'll regret this," Richard promised her. But then the music started and the wedding coordinator signaled her back over to the line.

"No, I won't," she replied confidently, feeling as though her dignity had been preserved.

"Yeah? Well, don't forget whose signature's on your paycheck!"

"As long as it's your father's and not yours, I figure I'm safe," she shot back, feeling liberated as she returned to her place in line behind Susan and Kit, in front of Nicky's daughter, Marni, who looked intrigued.

There was a slow dissolve of commotion as the wedding music started up and the processional began.

Each of the bridesmaids' dresses was different. They had all been commissioned by a young designer Paige had flown in from Milan. For the couple of weeks the designer was there, she and her assistants worked day and night, turning out one creation after another, each one more sensational than the next. Huge silk balloon sleeves worn off the shoulder on one. Fortuny-type pleats on another. Paige's was the only gown nobody had seen.

Tori watched, feeling half in a dream, mesmerized by the tall white candles flickering brightly from lavish, flower-festooned candelabra, drinking in the potent perfume of the flowers, which hung heavy in the air.

Competing flashes of light popped sporadically from the half a dozen photographers strolling around, angling for shots.

The violin strings seemed to be tearing at Tori's heartstrings as she watched Kit proceeding down the aisle first, a vision of loveliness, the all-white wedding serenely effective. The music was soft and old-fashioned, the kind you would have to be made of steel to not become emotional over.

She thought of Travis. And then of Richard.

Dreams gone up in smoke. Like the smoke rising from the candles, fading eerily into the atmosphere.

Susan walked down the aisle next, looking as glorious as a bride herself as she was joined by Mark, who looped his arm through hers, both of them taking slow, cautious steps as though they were on a test run. Tori was filled with warmth seeing the two of them looking so radiant together.

Susan had on the seed-pearl choker her old boyfriend from Stockton, Billy Donahue, had given her last year for Christmas, and it gleamed under the lights. Part present, part peace offering was how she described it, given to her after she had caught him sleeping with her secretary. She had almost not worn it. Putting it on and then taking it off again. And then she had decided the hell with Billy Donahue. The necklace was *white*.

It was Tori's turn next, and she smiled self-consciously as she stepped gracefully into view, met by Nicky's closest friend. Familiar faces smiled at her and she smiled back, all the way to the altar, where she and her escort parted to anchor opposite posts.

Following her came Marni and Tip.

Then a knee-high pair, resembling a pint-size version of the bridesmaids and ushers, stepping shyly down the aisle, eliciting *ahhhs* and laughter as the little girl sprinkled rose petals from a basket while the little boy balanced a velvet pillow bearing the rings. They were Nicky's niece and nephew.

The tension in the music mounted, then came to a complete halt, commanding everyone's rapt attention in anticipation of the bride and groom.

Paige had been so secretive about the details of the wedding and what she was going to wear that Tori was half expecting something like Madonna's "Material Girl" instead of "Here Comes the Bride" to come blasting forth from the orchestra for her long-awaited march down the aisle.

When the familiar conventional bridal march pounded forth instead, it came as far more of a surprise than anything else possibly could have, seeming to reveal another dimension of Paige, whose intriguing beauty took everyone's breath away.

This nostalgic, traditional side of her was evident in her awesome white train that seemed to go on and on, the illusory white veil draped over her composed, porcelain-perfect face, the lacy Victorian high band collar of her gown, and her father, flown in from New York for the happy event, there by her side to give her away.

But then, as she continued her demure walk down the aisle, Tori soon realized the gasps drawn from the audience were not solely for this breathtaking vision in white but because the back of the irrepressible Paige's gown was designed open and cut all the way down to her ass.

Now *that* was the sassy, venturesome Paige they all knew and loved, Tori thought. The Paige who had managed to captivate and snare Nicky Loomis. No wonder she wouldn't let anyone see her dress.

Leave it to Paige to make an entrance.

Tori noticed the minister standing there, smiling and waiting for the bride. *Wait till he gets a load of the back of her,* Tori thought, suppressing a laugh as she exchanged tickled glances with Susan and Kit.

The minister had no idea what all the hushed snickering was about as he delivered the words of the ceremony. He was just pleased that everyone was so alert and interested.

Nicky seemed to be enjoying Paige's show most of all. He kept peeking around behind her, amused, fascinated, looking as though the dress were a complete surprise to him, and a surprise he found wildly arousing.

As soon as the pair had pronounced their I do's, a gleaming white helicopter circled low above the property and then landed on the lawn. Nicky swept Paige up in his arms, dipped her down for a long, unvirginal-looking kiss, and then leaned over to borrow the minister's mike. "The rest of this party is for you!" he bellowed lustily to all his guests. "Have a helluva good time because it's costing me a helluva lot of bucks!"

The ethereal bride, laughing and holding on to her veil so that it wouldn't slip off, blew a kiss to them all.

First pausing for a moment of drama, she flung her hand-wired bouquet of white roses and imported Dutch white lilies high into the air toward the girls. But then a gust of wind from the helicopter intercepted its course and carried it off the other way, landing it in the arms of an innocent male bystander who would have had a hard time trying to catch it if he had tried, since both his arms were out of commission, encased in cumbersome fiberglass casts and then further restrained in a double sling. Sitting next to him was his secretary, Evonne.

"My God, I don't believe it! Dustin Brent!" Paige, Susan, and Tori all realized at once, exclaiming in unison.

"Did you know about this?" Paige demanded of Nicky, astonished as he carried her through the crowd over to the noisy aircraft, waving jovially to all their guests.

He smiled at her wickedly. "I wasn't chancing you changing your mind. I figured if he came back you'd need someplace else to live," he hollered over the whirr of the chopper.

"I'm serious."

"So am I."

"You tracked him down and invited him?"

"I asked his secretary to wire him an invitation."

"What about those broken arms of his?"

"Made his return make even more sense. Besides, he said he had additional incentive," Nicky replied jocularly.

"What was that?"

Nicky's eyes gleamed suggestively as he ducked into the helicopter, depositing Paige and all the yards of fabric from her gown onto the seat.

She turned to look out the window and saw Dustin and Tori sending each other silent but momentous messages through the highly charged air. Awkwardly, Dustin maneuvered the bouquet up to his nose and took an exaggerated sniff, his gaze remaining fixed on Tori, his smile seeming to promise her a brighter future.

As the helicopter spun off into the air, the rest of the bridal party still in their places at the altar, Paige leaned in to kiss her husband. She didn't buy for a moment that Nicky had really been responsible for getting Dustin back to the States. More likely, Dustin had injured himself again, and Evonne had phoned to tell Nicky that he would be back in town and wished to attend the wedding. After all, if it hadn't have been for Dustin, none of this would ever have come to pass. Dustin Brent had been their sponsor, the man responsible for all this magic.

But Paige preferred to nurture and let her new husband enjoy his fantasy that she believed every word he told him.

He could retain his fantasies.

And she would retain hers.

From rags to riches—it was a modern-day Cinderella story. Only she didn't slave by the hearth, she slaved over . . . . , and her rags were not really rags, but knockoffs of designer labels. And, finally, her prince was not really a prince, but a very rich . . . . . . who fell madly in love with his lovely young female . . . . . . And the pair was to live happily ever after in Beverly Hills . . . .

Lynda La Plante
The Legacy   £3.99

At a Welsh pithead at the turn of the century, a gypsy girl, a romany
princess driven out by her people, waited for the pitman father of the
bastard son in her arms.

When he emerged from the black coal seam, he turned away and
walked off with his pals to the pub, while her curse echoed after him
down the hillside . . .

A vast and panoramic novel . . . possessed of a splendid narrative
sweep . . . its pages teeming with compelling characters . . .
its richness stemming from the age-old traditions of the romany
people . .

The Legacy is the first part of Lynda La Plante's splendid saga of
four generations of a bloodline tainted by a romany curse . . .

After the death of Freedom, his sons are despatched by fate in very
different directions. While Edward goes up to Cambridge . . Alex
goes into a remand home . . . and on to prison . . . serving his time
for a killing he did not commit.

It was not until twelve years after the end of *The Legacy* that the
brothers met again . . . standing at their mother's graveside.

Lynda La Plante continues her magnificent saga in *The Talisman* . . .
following the curse down through the third and fourth generations.

Lynda La Plante
The Talisman £3.99

The long dark skein of the romany curse runs down to the fourth generation . . .

The sons of Freedom Stubbs meet again at their mother's graveside, twelve long years on.

Edward . . . the first born son, brutally born of his prizefighter father's trade and his razor-sharp wits honed by a Cambridge education. He inherits not only the dark romany looks, but the powers and dangers of second sight – *the curse of Midas* . . .

Alex . . . the second son, his colleges the prison cells where he paid for a crime he didn't commit, his talent the ability to manipulate and shape his brother's Midas touch into a powerful empire . . .

Evelyn and Juliana . . . the fourth generation, born to wealth beyond dreams, heirs to a legacy in the long shadow of a romany curse . . .

The Talisman completes the vast and compelling saga that began with *The Legacy* The story that originated in the pit villages and prize rings of years ago, moves on through the mineral mines of South Africa and the fashion houses of Paris to the boardrooms and brothels of modern London, tracing a dark curse down a bloodline tainted by darker secrets . .

This Pan edition contains Books 6–14 of *The Legacy*, first published in hardback by Sidgwick & Jackson Ltd Books 1–5 are published as *The Legacy* in Pan Books.

Frances Patton Statham
The Roswell Women   £3.99

The Civil War took their men, their land and their way of life – but it would never capture their hearts and minds

In 1864 the violent Civil War which threatened to destroy the young nation of America reached south to engulf the women of Roswell, Georgia. Left without their men, they kept the Roswell mill running to provide the flagging Confederate army with proud grey uniforms. But their courage and defiance branded them as traitors in the eyes of the North. In an act of historic brutality the women were mercilessly transported to the Yankee strongholds . . .

Allison Forsyth – Beautiful widow and regal plantation mistress, she survives the ravages of imprisonment – only to find a ghost from the past threatening to destroy her love.

Madrigal O'Laney – The fiery redhead lures men from both sides of the war with the promise of her love. But the promise has a price.

Rebecca Smiley – A faithful servant to Allison, she had groomed her mistress for the life of an aristocrat. A war would not stop her quest.

Flood Tompkins – Disguised as a man, she survives the war to stake her claim to a fortune . . . and to make a choice that will change Allison's life for ever.

Bound by courage and united in tragedy, *The Roswell Women* gives voice to women caught in the explosive corridors of war.